PRAISE FOR
THE FLIGHT OF THE SILVERS

"This first volume in a planned trilogy is fascinating.... Price's strong, engaging characters and fast-moving plot will keep readers on their toes. Highly recommended for fans of apocalyptic and dystopian fiction."

—*Library Journal* (starred review)

"Both the innovative and the enjoyably familiar mark this hefty, intriguing introduction to a multivolume, multiversal saga . . . an absorbing adventure with a fresh take on both the parallel-universe and the paranormal subgenres. You'll get pulled in."

—*Kirkus Reviews* (starred review)

"The cast is engaging . . . and the author has created an alternate-reality world that is both bewilderingly different and reassuringly familiar . . . a highly imaginative exercise in world building that also features characters it's very easy to care about."

—*Booklist*

"Daniel Price has given readers the first installment of what promises to be a well-wrought sci-fi saga, colored by intriguing ideas and complex characters adrift in a wonderfully weird world. *The Flight of the Silvers* is thought-provoking, cinematic in scope . . . and very, very good."

—TheMaineEdge.com

"I could list the wonders of this new world for a while, but I'd rather let you discover them for yourself.... The story is really different and imaginative. The characters are distinct.... I loved *The Flight of the Silvers*.... It really is an amazing book."

—SF Crowsnest

continued . . .

"Price deserves credit for creating immediately relatable characters whose motivations are understandable even when not so commendable. But he deserves out-and-out praise for doing so while constantly upping the temporal ante. The reader's uncertainty concerning the rules of this new world may well mirror that felt by the protagonists, but the shared confusion never ruins the immersion. As a result, any hours spent reading *The Flight of the Silvers* will be time well spent."
— *BookPage*

"In *The Flight of the Silvers*, Daniel Price's time-bending X-Men travel through an alternative America that is both alien and disturbingly familiar. Fast-paced, poignant, and absorbing."
—Emily Croy Barker, author of *The Thinking Woman's Guide to Real Magic*

"This is an intricately plotted novel, and it is also a beautifully written one. Enjoyable wordplay—including the creation of new words and the clever use of phrases—makes *The Flight of the Silvers* as intellectually engaging as it is fun . . . an extraordinary work of science fiction and fantasy."
—For Winter Nights

ALSO BY DANIEL PRICE

SLICK

DANIEL PRICE

NAL NEW AMERICAN LIBRARY

THE
FLIGHT
OF THE
SILVERS

THE SILVERS SERIES

New American Library
Published by the Penguin Group
Penguin Group (USA) LLC, 375 Hudson Street,
New York, New York 10014

USA | Canada | UK | Ireland | Australia | New Zealand | India | South Africa | China
penguin.com
A Penguin Random House Company

Published by New American Library, a division of Penguin Group (USA) LLC. Previously published
in a Blue Rider Press edition.

First New American Library Printing, January 2015

REGISTERED TRADEMARK—MARCA REGISTRADA

NEW AMERICAN LIBRARY TRADE PAPERBACK ISBN: 978-0-451-47276-2

THE LIBRARY OF CONGRESS HAS CATALOGUED THE DUTTON HARDCOVER EDITION AS FOLLOWS:
Price, Daniel
The flight of the silvers/Daniel Price.
p. cm.
ISBN 978-0-399-16498-9
I. Title.
PS3616.R526F55   2014   2013030273
813'.6—dc23

Printed in the United States of America
10   9   8   7   6   5   4   3   2   1

Designed by Gretchen Achilles

THE
FLIGHT
OF THE
SILVERS

PART ONE

SISTERS

PROLOGUE

Time rolled to a stop on the Massachusetts Turnpike. Construction and wet weather clogged the westbound lanes at Chicopee, turning a breezy Sunday flow into a snake of angry brake lights.

Robert Given puffed a surly breath as his Voyager merged with the congestion. Two long hours had passed since he hugged the last of his grieving siblings and herded his family into the minivan. The rain had followed them the whole way from Boston, coming down in buckets and thimbles by turns. Now the sky dribbled just enough to make the windshield wipers squeal at the slowest setting.

After five squeals and ten feet of progress, he pushed up his glasses and studied the speedy trucks on the overpass. He had no idea which highway he was looking at, aside from a better one.

"Don't," said Melanie, from the passenger seat.

"Don't what?"

"I see you putting on your explorer's hat. I'm saying don't. I'd rather be stuck than lost."

His wife had spoken the words gently, and with a small twinge of irony. Melanie was typically the flighty one of the duo, the titsy-ditzy actress who rarely reached noon without making some heedless blunder. Today's reigning gaffe was her choice of funeral dress, a clingy black number that was a little too little for the comfort of some. Worse than the sneers and leers of her stodgy in-laws was the scorn of her ten-year-old daughter, who chided her for disrespecting Grandpa with her "showy boobs." That hurt like hell. It wasn't so long ago that Amanda needed help buttoning her blouses. Now the girl had become the family's stern voice of propriety, the arbiter of right and wrong.

Melanie straightened her hem, then turned around to check on her other brown-haired progeny, the sweeter fruit of her womb.

"You all right, angel?"

Hannah warily chewed her hair, unsure if it was safe to be honest. At five years old, she was too young to understand the grim rituals she'd witnessed today. All she knew was that she had to be on her best behavior. No whining. No showboating. No wriggling out of her itchy black dress. She'd spent the morning on cold metal folding chairs, staring glumly at her feet while all the grown-ups sniffled. It was a strange and ugly day and she couldn't wait for it to be over.

"I want to go home."

"We'll be there soon," Melanie said, prompting a cynical snort from her husband. "You want to sing something?"

Hannah's chubby face lit up. "Can I?"

"Sure."

"No," said Amanda, her stringy arms crossed in austerity. "We said no songs today."

Her mother forced a clenched smile. "Sweetie, that was just for the funeral and wake."

"Daddy said it was for the day. Out of respect for Grandpa. Isn't that what you said, Daddy?"

Melanie winced at the buckling to come. She knew Robert would eat his own salted fingers before disappointing Amanda.

Right on cue, he bounced a sorry brow at Hannah in the rearview mirror. "Honey, when we get home, you can sing all you want. Just not now, okay?"

Friends often joked that Robert and Melanie Given didn't have two children, they each had one clone. Nearly all of Amanda's genetic coin flips had landed on her father's side. She bore his finely chiseled features, his willowy build, his keen green eyes and ferocious intelligence. The two of them doted on each other like an old married couple. Rarely an evening passed when they weren't found curled up on the sofa, devouring one heady book after another.

Hannah was Melanie's daughter through and through. While Robert and Amanda were made of sharp angles, the actress and her youngest were drawn in soft curves. They shared the same round face, the same brown doe eyes, the same scattered airs and theatrical temperament. Hannah had also been born with a gilded throat, a gift that came from neither parent. The child crooned like an angel and never missed a note. She could perform any song flawlessly just by hearing it twice. Her mother worked with her day and night, honing her talent like a fine iron blade. Hannah Given would carve her name in the world one day. Of this, Melanie had no doubt.

Sadly, the skews in parental attention—the balanced imbalance—were starting to bear bitter fruit. With each passing day, Amanda treated her mother more and more like a rival while Hannah increasingly saw her father as a stranger.

And the girls themselves weren't the tightest of sisters.

Magnanimous in victory, Amanda rummaged through her neatly packed bag of backseat boredom busters. "Look, why don't we do a puzzle out of my book?"

"Why don't you shut up?"

Both parents turned around. "Hannah . . ."

Amanda fell back into her seat, matching her sister's pouty scowl. "I was trying to be nice."

"You're not nice. You're bossy. And you don't want me singing, 'cause I'm better than you."

"That's enough," Melanie snapped. She rubbed her brow and blew a dismal sigh at the windshield. "This is our fault."

"No kidding." Robert rolled the Voyager another ten inches, tapping the wheel in busy thought. "Maybe next weekend, Hannah and I—"

The piercing screech of tires filled the air, far too close for anyone's comfort. The Givens spun their gazes all around but no one could see movement. Every vehicle was stuck on the flytrap of I-90.

The noise gave way to a thundering crunch. A long and twisted piece of metal rained down on the Camry in front of them, shattering the rear window.

Melanie covered her mouth. "Oh my God!"

Robert raised his wide stare at the overpass, where all the trouble was happening. A speeding tanker truck had flipped onto its side and skidded through the guardrail. Now the curved metal trailer teetered precariously over the edge. Robert barely had a chance to formulate his hot new worry before the Shell Oil logo bloomed into view like a mushroom cloud.

No . . .

The truck toppled over, plummeting toward the turnpike in a messy twirl. The parents froze, breathless, as their minds fell into an accelerated state of alarm. While Melanie voiced a hundred regrets, Robert hissed a thousand curses at the invisible forces that brought them here, all the cruel odds and gods behind their senseless demise.

After an eternity of wincing dread, they heard the dry squawk of the wiper blades, the rustling scrapes of Amanda's black taffeta.

"Daddy?"

Robert and Melanie opened a leery eye, then stared at the fresh new madness in front of them.

The fuel truck hung immobile in the air, a scant nine feet from impact. Floating bits of debris twinkled all around it like stars in the night. In every other vehicle, silhouetted figures remained flash-frozen in terrified poses. Only the thin wisps of smoke from the cab's engine seemed to move in any fashion. They rippled in place with the lazy torpor of sea plants.

Amanda leaned forward, her face slack with bewilderment. At ten years old, her universe had settled into a firm and tidy construct. Everything fit together with mechanical precision, even the squeaky gears of her little sister. But now something had gone horribly wrong with the clockwork. Amanda was old enough to know that things like this simply didn't happen. Not to the living. Not to the sane.

"Daddy, what . . . what is this?"

Robert turned around as best he could, struggling to rediscover his voice. "I don't know. I don't know. Just stay where you are. Don't do anything."

Melanie unclasped her seat belt and reached a trembling hand for Hannah. "Sweetie, you okay?"

The child shook her head in misery. "I'm cold."

Now that Hannah mentioned it, the others noticed the sharp drop in temperature, enough to turn their breath visible. They glanced outside and saw a strange blue tint to the world, as if someone had wrapped their van in cellophane.

Amanda flinched at the new life outside the window.

"M-Mom. Dad . . ."

The others followed her gaze to the center of the freeway, where three tall and reedy strangers watched them with calm interest. The man on the left wore a thin gray windbreaker over jeans, his handsome face half-obscured by a low-slung Yankees cap. The woman on the right sported a stylish white longcoat and kinky brown hair that flowed in improbable directions, like Botticelli's Venus. Her deep black eyes locked on Amanda, holding the girl like tar.

Hannah and her parents kept their saucer stares on the man in the middle.

He was the tallest of the group, at least six and a half feet, with a trim Caesar haircut that lay as white as a snowcap. He wore a sharp charcoal business suit, eschewing a tie for a more casual open collar. Melanie found him beautiful to the point of unease. His skin was flawless, ageless, and preternaturally pale. His only color seemed to come from his irises, a fierce diamond-blue that cut through glass and Givens alike.

The trio stood with the formal poise of butlers, though Robert found nothing helpful or kind in their stony expressions. Melanie gripped his shoulder when he reached for the door.

"Don't. Don't go out there."

The white-haired man blew a curt puff of mist, then spoke in a cool honey bass that might have been soothing if it wasn't so testy.

"Calm yourselves. We just saved your lives. If you wish to keep living, then do as I say. Come out of the vehicle. All of you. Quickly."

He spoke with a slight foreign accent, a quasi-European twang that didn't register anywhere in Robert and Melanie's database. Despite all floating evidence in support of the man's good intentions, the elder Givens had a difficult time working their door handles.

The stranger shot an impatient glower through the driver's window. "I took you for a man of reasonable intelligence, Robert. Must I explain the danger of staying here?"

Robert once again eyed the fuel truck at the base of the bridge, now six feet from collision. Suddenly he understood why the smoke rippled slightly, why the hovering bits of metal sporadically twinkled. The clock hadn't stopped, just slowed. Their fate was still coming at the speed of a sunset.

Robert pushed his door open. "What's happening? How—"

"We're not here to educate," snarled the female of the trio, through the same odd inflections as her companion. "We came to save your pretty rose and songbird. Would you rather see them perish?"

"Of course not! But—"

"Then gather your daughters and come. Bring the cow if you must."

While Melanie and Robert scrambled outside, the white-haired man kept his sharp blue gaze on Hannah. She'd never seen anyone more beautiful or frightening in her life. He was a Siberian tiger on hind legs, a snowstorm in a suit.

Robert opened the side hatch and pulled her into his quivering arms. "Come on, hon."

"I don't like it here."

"I know."

"It's cold in the bubble and I want to go home."

Robert didn't know what she meant by "bubble." He didn't care. He clutched her against his chest, just as Amanda climbed out the door and wrapped herself around Melanie.

"Mom . . ."

Thick tears warmed Melanie's cheeks. "Stay with me, sweetie. Don't let go."

Soon the family stood gathered outside the minivan. Robert held his wary gaze on the strangers. "Can you please tell me what—"

They ignored him and split up. The man in the baseball cap turned around and moved a few yards ahead. The woman took a shepherding flank behind the Givens. The white-haired man stayed in place, bouncing his harsh blue stare between Robert and Melanie.

"We walk now," he said. "Tread carefully and stay within the field. If even a finger escapes, you won't enjoy the consequences."

They began traveling. Robert noticed that everything within thirty feet of them existed at normal speed and color, a pocket of sanity in the sluggish blue yonder. The field seemed to move at the whim of the man in the Yankees cap. He walked with strain, fingers extended, as if pushing an invisible boulder.

Battling his panic, Robert retreated into his head and imagined the analytical discussion he and Amanda might have in a calmer state of mind.

"Daddy, what did he mean about the finger and the field?"

"Not sure, hon. I'm guessing it's not healthy for a body to move at two different speeds."

"Did they slow down the world or did they speed us up?"

"Good question. I don't know. In either case, I figure we're just a blur to the people in the other cars."

"How is this happening?"

"I don't know, sweetie. It's entirely possible that I've lost my mind."

He looked up and saw exactly where the drizzling rain stopped, a perfect dome that extended all around them. A bubble.

Suddenly his inner Amanda posed a dark new stumper.

"Daddy, how did Hannah know the shape of the field?"

Robert's heart pounded with new dread, enough for Hannah to feel it through his blazer. She wrapped her shivering arms around his neck and buried her face in his shoulder. The air outside the dome carried a thick and smoky taste in her thoughts, like a million trees burning. She just wanted it to go away, along with the freezing cold and the scary white tiger-man.

Her mother and sister trailed five feet behind them, their arms locked together. Melanie's stomach lurched every time Amanda threw a backward glance at the fuel truck. For all she knew, one more peek would turn the girl into a pillar of salt.

"Honey, don't look. Just keep moving."

"But there are still people back there."

"Amanda . . ."

"We can't just leave them!"

Melanie bit her lip and winced new tears. Though her daughter often wielded her morality like a cudgel, there was no denying the depth of her virtue. The girl was good to the core.

Five feet behind them, the female stranger shined a soft smile at Amanda. "You're a noble one to worry, child, but little can be done. Even those who survive have short years ahead. I see the strings. I know the death that comes."

Amanda had been nervously avoiding eye contact with the woman, but now drew a second look. She was a shade over six feet tall, with an immaculate face that put her anywhere between a weathered thirty and a blessed sixty. Whatever her age, she was jarringly beautiful, at least on the outside. Her dark eyes twinkled with instability, like matches over oil.

"W-what do you mean?" Amanda asked.

Melanie tugged her forward. "Don't talk to her."

"It's no matter," the woman replied. "Just take comfort that you have a future, my pretty rose. I've seen you, tall and red."

"Leave her alone," Melanie hissed.

The stranger's smile vanished. Her stare turned cold and brutal.

"Be careful how you speak to me, cow. We spare you and your husband as a courtesy. Perhaps we should slay you both and rear the little ones ourselves."

"NO!" Amanda screamed.

The white-haired man sighed patiently at his companion. *"Sehmeer . . ."*

"Nu'a purtua shi'i kien Esis," said the other man, without turning around.

The madwoman pursed her lips in a childish pout, then narrowed her eyes at Melanie.

"My wealth and heart oppose the idea. Pity. Your flawed little gems would thrive in our care." She tossed Amanda another crooked smile. "We'd make them shine."

The Givens moved in tight-knuckled silence for the rest of their journey—past the turnpike, over the guardrail, and up a steep embankment.

The tall ones stopped at the peak and surveyed the falling truck in the distance. The fuel tank had just touched the concrete and was starting to come apart.

"Brace yourself," said the white-haired man, for all the good it did.

In the span of a gasp, the bubble of time vanished and a thunderous explosion rattled the Givens. Robert covered Hannah as a fireball rose sixty feet above the overpass. A searing blast of heat drove Melanie and Amanda screaming to the ground.

The strangers studied the swirling pillar of smoke with casual interest, as if it were art. Soon the madwoman swept her slender arm in a loop, summoning an eight-foot disc of fluorescent white light.

The family glanced up from the grass, eyeing the anomaly through cracked red stares. The circle hovered above the ground, as thin as a blanket and as round as a coin. Despite its perfect verticality, the surface shimmied like pond water.

Before any Given could form a thought, the quiet man in the windbreaker pulled down the lip of his baseball cap and brushed past the family with self-conscious haste. He plunged into the portal, the radiant white liquid rippling all around him. Robert watched his exit with mad rejection. It was the stuff of cartoons, a Roger Rabbit hole in the middle of nothing.

The dark-eyed woman gave Amanda a sly wink, then followed her companion into the breach. The surface swallowed her like thick white paint.

Alone among his rescuees, the white-haired man took a final glance at the Givens. Melanie saw his sharp blue eyes linger on Hannah.

"Just go," the mother implored him. "Please. We won't tell anyone."

The stranger squinted in cool umbrage, clearly displeased to be treated like a common mugger.

"Tell whoever you want."

Robert stammered chaotically, his throat clogged with a hundred burning questions. He thought of his minivan, which no doubt stood a charred and empty husk on the road. Suddenly the father who'd cursed the gods for his horrible fortune knew exactly what to ask.

"Why us?"

The stranger stopped at the portal. Robert threw a quick, nervous look at Amanda and Hannah.

"Why them?"

The white-haired man turned around now, his face an inscrutable wall of ice.

"Your daughters may one day learn. You will not. Accept that and embrace the rest of your time."

He stepped through the gateway, vanishing in liquid. Soon the circle shrank to a dime-size dot and then blinked out of existence.

One by one, the survivors on the freeway emerged from their vehicles—the injured and the lucky, the screaming and the stunned. In the smoky bedlam, no one noticed the family of mourners on the distant embankment.

The Givens huddled together on the grass, their brown and green gazes held firmly away from the turnpike. Only Hannah had the strength to stand. She was five years old and still new to the universe. She had no idea how many of its laws had been broken in front of her. All she knew was that today was a strange and ugly day and her sister was wrong.

Hannah moved behind her weeping mother and threw her arms around her shoulders. She took a deep breath. And she sang.

ONE

On a Friday night in dry July, in the Gaslamp Quarter of downtown San Diego, the Indian-dancers-who-weren't-quite-Indian twirled across the stage of the ninety-nine-seat playhouse. Five lily-white women in yellow sarees flowed arcs of georgette as they spun in measure to the musical intro. The orchestra, which had finished its job on Monday and was now represented by a six-ounce iPod, served a curious fusion of bouncy trumpets and sensual *shehnais*—Broadway bombast with a Bombay contrast. The music director was an insurance adjuster by day. He'd dreamed up his euphonious Frankenstein three years ago, and tonight, by the grace of God and regional theater, it was alive.

The curtain parted and a new performer prowled her way onto the stage. She was a raven-haired temptress in a fiery red *lehenga*. Her curvy figure—ably flaunted by a low-cut, belly-baring choli—brought half the jaded audience to full attention.

The spotlights converged. The dancers dispersed. All eyes were now fixed upon the brown-eyed leading lady: the young, the lovely, the up-and-coming Hannah Given.

With a well-rehearsed look of sexy self-assurance, she swayed her hips to the rhythm and sang.

> *"Whatever Lola wants, Lola gets.*
> *And little man, little Lola wants you . . ."*

She shot a sultry gaze at the actor sitting downstage right, a handsome young man in a cricket player's uniform. He was theatrically bewitched by her. In reality, he was mostly bothered. Her neurotic questioning of all creative decisions made rehearsals twice as long as they needed to be. Still, he was casually determined to sleep with her sometime before the production closed. He wouldn't.

"Make up your mind to have no regrets.
Recline yourself, resign yourself, you're through."

A sharp cough from the audience made her inner needle skip, throwing her Lola and dropping her into a sinkhole of Hannah concerns. She fished herself out on a gilded string of affirmations. *Your stomach looks fine. Your voice sounds great. Gwen Verdon isn't screaming from Heaven. And odds are only one in ninety-nine that the angry cough came from the* CityBeat *critic.*

You know damn well who it was, a harsher voice insisted.

She narrowed her eyes at the dark sea of heads, then fell back into character. The rest of the song proceeded without a hitch. At final-curtain applause, Hannah convinced herself that the whole premiere went swimmingly aside from that half-second skip. She figured the misstep would haunt her for days. It wouldn't.

She wriggled back into her halter top and jeans and then joined the congregation in the lobby, where half the audience lingered to heap praise on the performers they knew. Hannah had given out five comp tickets, including two to her roommates and one to the day job colleague she was kinda sorta a little involved with. None of them showed up. Lovely. That only left the great Amanda Ambridge, plus spouse.

Hannah had little trouble finding her sister in the crowd. Amanda was a stiletto pump away from being six feet tall, with an Irish red mane that made her stand out like a stop sign. She stood alone by the ticket booth, a stately figure even in her bargain blouse and skinny jeans. At twenty-seven, Amanda's sharp features had settled into hard elegance, a brand of uptight beauty that was catnip to so many artists. Hannah felt like a tavern wench in the presence of a queen.

Amanda spotted her and shined a taut smile. "Hey, there you are!"

"Here I am," Hannah said. "Thanks for coming."

After a clumsy half-start, the two women hugged. Hannah stood five inches shorter and twenty pounds heavier than her sister, though she'd squeezed it all into a buxom frame that drove numerous men to idiocy. Amanda felt hopelessly unsexy in her company, the Olive Oyl to her Betty

Boop. Her husband did a fine job fortifying her complex tonight. The only time Derek didn't writhe in agony during the awful show was when Hannah graced the stage with her grand and bouncy blessings. Amanda had hacked a sharp cough at him, just to throw sand in his bulging eyes.

Hannah scanned the lobby for her brother-in-law, a man she'd met six times at best. "Where's the doc?"

"He's getting the car. He's tired and we both have to be up early tomorrow."

"Okay. Hope he didn't suffer too much."

"Not too much." Her smile tightened. "He really enjoyed your performance."

"Oh good. Glad to hear it. And you?"

"I thought you were terrific. Better than . . ."

Amanda stopped herself. Hannah's brow rose in cynical query. "Better than what? Usual?"

"That's not what I was going to say."

"Then just say it."

"I thought you were better than the show deserved."

A frosty scowl bloomed across Hannah's face. Amanda glanced around, then leaned in for a furtive half whisper.

"Look, you know I like *Damn Yankees*, but this whole idea of turning it into a Bollywood pastiche was just . . . It was painful, like watching someone try to shove a Saint Bernard through a cat door. But despite that—"

Hannah cut her off with a jagged laugh. Amanda crossed her arms in umbrage.

"You asked me my opinion. Would you rather I lie?"

"I'd rather you say it instead of coughing it!"

A dozen glances turned their way. Amanda blinked at her sister. "I . . . don't know what you're talking about."

"Now you're lying."

"Hannah—"

"You just couldn't hold in your criticism. You had to let it out in the middle of my big number."

"That's not what happened."

"Bullshit. You know what you did."

"Hannah, I don't want to fight with you."

"Oh my God." The actress covered her face with both hands. "You do this every time."

"Well, I'm—"

"'—sorry you're upset,'" Hannah finished, in near-perfect synch with her sister. "Yeah. I'm well acquainted with your noble act by now. You might want to change it up a little. You know, for variety."

Amanda closed her eyes and pressed the dangling gold crucifix on her collarbone. This, Hannah knew all too well, was the standard Amanda retreat whenever her mothersome bother and sisterical hyster became too much for her. *Give me strength, O Lord. Give me strength.*

The lights in the lobby suddenly faltered for three seconds, an erratic flicker that stopped all chatter. Hannah furrowed her brow at the sputtering laptop in the ticket booth.

Amanda checked her watch and vented a somber breath at the exit. "He should be out front by now. I better go."

"Fine. Say hi for me."

"Yup."

The sisters spent a long, hot moment avoiding each other's gazes before Amanda turned around and pushed through the swinging glass doors.

Hannah leaned against the wall, muttering soft curses as she gently thumped her skull. Between all her regrets and frustrations, she found the space to wonder why a battery-powered laptop would flicker with the overhead lights. She pushed the concern to the back of her mind, in the dark little vault where strange things went.

Seventeen years had passed since the madness on the Massachusetts Turnpike. The Givens never spoke a public word about the bizarre circumstances of their rescue. With each passing year, a welcome fog grew over their collective memories, until the family embraced the cover story as the one true account. They saw the truck teetering. They fled before it fell. That was just how it happened. End of subject.

Eight years after the incident, death came for Robert a second time and won. His cancer and passing had shattered Amanda in ways even her mother couldn't divine. She spent her final summer at home like an apparition and then disappeared to college, coming home once a year with thoughtful gifts, a practiced smile, and at least one major change to her state of being. First she found God. Then Hippocrates. Then a credible shade of red. And finally, during her brief stint at medical school, she found Dr. Derek Ambridge, who was eleven years her senior. From there, the arc of her life went into gentle downgrade.

Hannah, meanwhile, had cratered early. A spectacular nervous breakdown at age thirteen ended both her and her mother's resolve to turn her into a child star. After a year of therapy, she landed comfortably on the civilian teenage track, where she became lost in a routine tsunami of highs and lows, LOLs and whoas, breakups, makeups, and adolescent shake-ups. Upon graduation, she went west to San Diego State, where she dyed her hair black and experimented with all-new mistakes. On the upside, she rediscovered her theatrical ambitions. She stayed in town after college, found an office job, and began the slow process of rebuilding her résumé.

Six months ago, fate reunited the sisters when Derek accepted a partnership at a private oncology practice in Chula Vista, California, nine miles south of San Diego. For Melanie, the move was a golden opportunity for her daughters to finally connect.

"I want you to see Amanda as often as you can," she ordered Hannah. "Because she's going to leave that guy sooner or later and she'll be the one who moves away."

Though Hannah promised to try, she'd only met with Amanda three times in the last half year. Their first two encounters had been brisk and cordial and as tender as a tax form. No doubt their mother would be even less pleased with how the Great Sisters Given fared tonight.

With a thorny glower, Amanda emerged from the theater onto J Street, where her hybrid chariot awaited. Cigarette smoke rose from the driver's side.

Amanda slung herself into the passenger seat. Her husband tensely tapped ashes out his window.

"In case you're keeping score, I lost five IQ points tonight. Plus my faith in man."

"I know," Amanda sighed. "I'm sorry."

Derek was two years shy of forty. Though nature stayed kind to his boyish good looks, he regarded his impending middle age like a Stage 3 carcinoma. He worked out every day, ate raw vegetables for lunch, and overstocked the medicine cabinet with pricey creams and cleansers. Nicotine was his last remaining vice. He was never happier to have it.

"If you love me, hon, you won't make me go to her next musical."

"I don't even know if I'll go," Amanda admitted with a hot blush of shame.

"What's the matter? You two have a fight?"

"Yeah. I tried to tell her she was good tonight and somehow she took it as a personal attack."

"Well, you always said she was a minefield."

"I know, but there's something else behind it. I think she resents me for moving out here. Like I'm crashing the nice little world she built for herself."

Derek jerked a weary shrug. "I'm sure you gals will work it out."

He propped the cigarette in his mouth and merged into traffic. Two blocks passed in dreary silence.

"I'll say this for your sister, she's got quite a set of pipes on her. Quite a set of everything. Jesus."

"That was classy, Derek."

"I know. I'm a real charmer after ten. If it's any consolation, you have the better face."

Amanda snatched his cigarette and took a deep drag. She spat smoke out her window, at an illuminated bank sign. The digital clock had become hopelessly scrambled, forever stuck in crazy eights.

"Just drive."

The electricity continued to surge and dip throughout the night. Citywide power fluctuations were spotted in various pockets of the globe, from Guadalajara to Rotterdam. The night owls screeched and the utility workers scrambled, but most of the West slept through the muddle. In London, the morning commute was hamstrung by a chain of mini-blackouts. In central Osaka, the sun set on a flickering skyline.

And then at 4:41 A.M., Pacific Time, the entire world shut down for nine and a half minutes. Every light and every outlet. Every battery. Every generator. Even the lightning storms that had been swirling in 1,652 different parts of the world were extinguished by invisible hands. For nine and a half minutes, the Earth experienced a mechanical quiet that hadn't been felt in centuries.

At 4:50, the switch flipped again, and the modern world returned with confusion and damage.

The American power network was as complex and temperamental as the human psyche. In some areas, the electricity came back immediately. In other regions, the circuits stayed dead forever. On some streets, people struggled to help their neighbors out of stalled elevators and plane-wrecked buildings. In others, there was panic and violence. Accusations. Tribulation.

Throughout all the chaos, the sisters slept.

Amanda woke up an hour after sunrise, her alarm clock blinking confusedly at 12:00. She made a sleepy lurch to the shower and heard Derek's off-key crooning over the running water. She used the other bathroom.

"Power failure last night," he said twenty minutes later, as they both dressed.

"Yeah. I noticed."

"I'm not getting a signal on my phone either."

Her shirt still undone, Amanda turned on her smartphone and patiently waited for the little image of a radar dish to stop spinning. She gave up after a minute.

Derek crossed into the kitchen and nearly slipped on a pair of magnets. Yawning, he stuck them back on the refrigerator. Amanda flipped on the living room TV. Channel after channel of "No Signal" alert boxes. She peered out the front window and relaxed at the normal procession of cars and joggers, the comforting lack of screams and sirens. Aside from the all-encompassing power burp, life seemed fine in Chula Vista.

Soon her mind drifted back to the mundane—chores and cancer, Derek and Hannah. Her bleary thoughts kept her busy all the way to the medical office. She didn't notice the two separate plumes of black smoke in the distance, spreading like stains across the flat gray sky.

Two of the nurses failed to show up for their Saturday shift. From the moment she threw on her peach-colored coat, Amanda became a whirlwind of activity, spinning between the office's endless rooms and needs. Along the way, she picked up morsels of chatter about the blackout. Her fingers curled with tension when one of the patients mentioned something about a crashed Navy jet.

Tommy Berber eyed Amanda balefully from the far end of the hall. He was a barrel-chested biker with a bandana skullcap and a bushy gray beard that hung in knotted vines. Mechanical beeps emanated from inside the chamber.

"Yeah, hi. Remember us?"

She held up a bag of clear liquid. "I'm here. I have it."

Berber followed her into the treatment room, where his son Henry lounged in a plush recliner. The sweet and skinny twelve-year-old had already lost his left arm to osteosarcoma. Soon he'd lose his hair, his lunches, and any last semblance of a normal adolescence. But his long-term chances of survival were mercifully good. Out of all today's patients, Henry was the luckiest of the unlucky.

Amanda shined him a sunny smile, then adjusted his chemo dispenser until it stopped beeping.

Henry grinned weakly. "Thanks. That was getting old."

"Twenty minutes!" Berber yelled. "We've been waiting twenty minutes!"

Amanda nodded. "I know. I'm sorry. We're short staffed today and our computers are down."

"Is that supposed to make me feel better about this place?"

"Dad . . ."

Amanda replaced the empty bag of doxorubicin with a fresh dose of cisplatin. She reprogrammed the machine, then tapped the plastic tube until the liquid started to drip.

"You're going to feel a hot sensation," she warned Henry.

"Right. I remember."

She watched the liquid flow into his arm. "All right, my darling. You're all set. Anything you need?"

"Yeah, a sedative. For Dad."

"Oh, he's just mad because you and I are eloping. We're still on for that, right?"

Henry laughed. "Absolutely. Did you tell Dr. Ambridge yet?"

"Nah. I'll call him from the road."

The moment she left the room, she heard Berber's heavy footsteps trail her down the hall. He had to wait for a shrieking emergency vehicle to pass the building before he could speak.

"That can't happen again, nurse. You hear me?"

Amanda turned around to face him. "Mr. Berber—"

"I don't want his chances going down just 'cause you people don't have your shit together. You get him his doses on time. You understand?"

She understood all too well. In her two years as a cancer nurse, Amanda had seen every breed of desolate parent—the weepers, the shouters, the sputtering deniers. The tough dads were always the worst. They wore their helplessness like a coat of flames, scorching everything around them.

"I'm sorry, Mr. Berber. I'll do better next time."

"You're just giving me lip service now."

"I am," she admitted. "Ask me why."

"Why?"

"Because I can't fix computers and I can't conjure nurses out of thin air. All I can do is apologize and remind you that your beautiful son has a seventy-eight percent chance of outliving the both of us. Being twenty minutes late with the cisplatin won't affect those odds. Not one bit."

"You don't know that for—"

"Not one bit," she repeated. "You understand me?"

Berber recoiled like she'd just sprouted horns. Amanda had seen that look countless times before on others. *You can be a little intense,* Derek had told her. *You may not see it, but it's there.*

Soon the biker's heavy brow unfurled. He vented a sigh. "Got any kids of your own?"

Amanda's face remained impassive as a cold gust of grief blew through her. She once had a son for seventeen minutes. Those memories stayed locked in the cellar, along with her father's last days and the incident on the Massachusetts Turnpike.

"No," she said.

Berber eyed her golden cross necklace. "But you do have faith."

"Yes."

"How do you reconcile? How do you spend all day with sick, dying kids and then thank the God who lets it happen?"

Still fumbling in dark memories, Amanda lost hold of her usual response. *I thank Him for the ones who live. I thank Him for the ones who have loving parents like you.*

All she could do now was roll her shoulders in a feeble shrug. "I don't know, Mr. Berber. I guess I'd rather live in a world where bad things happen for some reason than no reason."

Her answer clearly didn't comfort him. He scratched his hairy cheek and threw a tense glare over his shoulder.

"I should get back to him."

"Okay."

Amanda heard a high young giggle. She turned her gaze to the reception desk, where Derek charmed the fetching young office clerk with his witty repartee. The moment he caught Amanda's gaze, his smile went flat. His eyes narrowed in a momentary flinch that filled her with unbearable dread and loathing.

Her fingers twitched in panic as the chorus in her head told her to run. Run. Run from the husband. Run from the house. Run from the sister and the sick little children. Don't even pack. Just pick a direction. Run.

The overhead lights flickered. A second, then a third chemo dispenser began to beep. Another wave of emergency vehicles screamed their way down the street. Things were falling apart at record speed. To Amanda, this seemed a perfect time to go outside for a smoke.

Three hours after her sister rolled out of bed, a half-dazed Hannah finally joined the world in egress. Her Salvador Dalí wall clock—now warped in more ways than one—told her it was 9:41. In actuality, it was nine and a half minutes short. But to Hannah and millions of other battery-powered-clock owners, 9:41 was the new 9:50. There was little reason to think otherwise.

She woke up in a foul mood carried over from last night. An hour after her spat with Amanda, she came home to an unscheduled hootenanny in the apartment. Her two flighty roommates had ditched her premiere in favor of barhopping and eventually stumbled back with a trio of frat boys from the alma mater.

Knowing she'd never sleep in this racket, the actress stayed up with them, brandishing a forced grin as she nursed a Sprite and suffered their drunken prattle. Sometime after the group blacked out, and shortly before the world did, Hannah retreated into her room and drifted off into uneasy sleep.

Now the apartment smelled like stale beer, and every device seemed non-functional. Hannah showered, dressed, and gathered her belongings. She had no intention of going back there before tonight's show. She'd just go to the office and enjoy the Saturday solitude. Maybe she'd update her acting résumé. Maybe she'd send some e-mails. Maybe she'd scan the local apartment listings. Or maybe not so local. In her mind, all the recent annoyances gathered into a clump, like tea leaves. They predicted a bleak future unless she made changes. Maybe it was finally time to consider Los Angeles.

By the time Hannah stepped outside, the sky had turned from misty gray to fluorescent white, a disturbingly uniform glaze that looked less like a mist sheet and more like an absence. To Hannah, it seemed as if God, Buddha, Xenu, whoever, simply forgot to load the next slide in the great heavenly projector. It didn't help her nerves that the temperature was ten degrees cooler than it should have been for Southern California in July.

She wasn't alone in her anxiety. As she walked down Commercial Street, an old man urgently fiddled with his radio, testing its many squeals and crackles. A teenage girl shook her cell phone as if it had overdosed on downers. A middle-aged woman tried to control her German shepherd, which hysterically barked at everything and nothing. A young jogger launched a futile cry at a fast-moving police car. "Hey. HEY! What's going on?"

Nearly three dozen people congregated at the train stop. Hannah opted to walk to work. Two lithe young women broke away from the crowd and nervously followed her.

"Excuse me," said one. "Can you help us? We're not from around here."

That much was obvious. One of the pair was dressed as Catwoman, whip and all. The other was decked out in a blond wig and white-leather corset ensemble, clearly some other super-antiheroine that Hannah didn't recognize. She did, however, know exactly where both women were going. All veteran San Diegans were familiar with Comic-Con, the annual gathering of sci-fi, fantasy, and funny-book enthusiasts that occurred downtown for four days in July. No doubt these gals were shooting for an easy surplus of leers from the geek contingent.

Hannah smirked at them. "Let me guess. You're trying to get to the convention center."

Catwoman snickered. "Yeah. Bingo."

"I don't know what's going on with the train. If you think your heels will hold up, you're probably better off walking. I'm going that way. You can come with me."

"Oh thank you," said the fake blonde, rubbing her arms for warmth. "The power went out at the place we're staying. Our phones don't work. We're totally screwed up right now."

After twelve blocks and twenty minutes, Hannah regretted her decision to serve as vanguard for the vixens. The women were maddeningly slow in their clacking heels, and their worried chatter made her increasingly tense. Not that they lacked cause for concern. As they moved closer downtown, they could see thick plumes of smoke rising up above the buildings. Soon Hannah spotted the edge of a vast rubbernecker pool, hundreds of people gathered at the base of some tumult.

They rounded the corner, turning north onto 13th Street. Just one block away, beyond all the cordons and emergency lights, stood the broken tail cone of a jumbo jet. The buildings around it were devastated with ash and debris. One apartment complex had crumbled to rubble.

Hannah covered her mouth. "Oh my God."

More than a hundred thousand planes, jets, and helicopters had been up in the air seven hours ago, when all the world's engines fell still. A third of them plummeted into water. Another third hit the hard empty spaces between human life. The final third just hit hard. San Diego had suffered twenty-two crashes within its borders.

Hannah gaped at the tall gray clock tower of the 12th & Imperial Transit Center, just a hundred yards away. It was a local landmark, one she'd passed a thousand times on her way to work. Now it had been de-clocked, decapitated. Every window on the south side of the building was shattered, with burn marks all over the frame.

All around her, people fretfully chattered. A stringy blond teenager brandished a transistor radio, declaring to anyone willing to listen that he'd heard voices through the static. People in other cities were talking about the same things.

"This is happening all over," he insisted. "Everywhere!"

Agitated bystanders shouted at him. Hannah took an anxious step back. Perhaps it was time to stop playing Sherpa for the Comic-Con chicks and move on to a much nicer elsewhere.

"Keep your head," said a cool voice from behind.

She turned around and lost her breath at the sight of the pale and handsome stranger, as tall as any she'd ever seen. He wore a sharp gray business suit without a tie and sported deep blue eyes that nearly blinded her with their intensity. Most striking of all was his neatly trimmed hair, which was chalk-white and achingly familiar. Hannah blinked at him in stupor.

"You remember me, child?" he calmly inquired.

She shook her head, even as old recollections came flooding back. She was just a little girl when she first laid eyes on the white-haired man. Seventeen years and the guy hadn't aged a day. Hannah was almost certain he was wearing the same suit.

"I don't . . . know you."

"Deny it if you will," he replied. "It doesn't matter. We saved your life once. Now I come to do it again."

Seeing the man through adult eyes triggered a disturbing new reaction in Hannah. She found him eerily scintillating now, like a housewife's vampire fantasy. God only knew what he could get her to do without saying a nice word. Fortunately, she couldn't sense a trace of desire in him. For all she knew, she stood as the same chubby-faced toddler in his eyes.

"W-what do you want with me?" she asked.

He spoke with a slight accent that she couldn't recognize. She spun her Wheel of Uninformed Guessing. The needle stopped at "Dutch."

"The answer would require more time than we have. All that matters now is that you—"

A sudden stillness gripped the area. All the car engines stopped. All the lights on the emergency vehicles went dark and still. All electrics great and small, all over the world, once again fell dead. This time, the power wasn't coming back.

Panicked voices rose all around her. Bystanders scurried and stumbled in all directions. A shoving match broke out between two teenage boys.

As Hannah watched the chaos, she felt cool fingers on her skin. Something smooth and hard snapped together on her forearm with a loud *clack*. She jerked her hand away. Her right wrist now sported a shiny metal bracelet, a half inch wide and utterly featureless. It felt cheap and dainty like plastic, but it gleamed in the light like silver.

"What did you do?" she said. "What is this thing?"

The white-haired man grabbed her other wrist, scowling at her with frigid disdain. There was nothing appealing about him now.

"This is the end. For them, not for you. Now listen—"

"Get away from me!"

He squeezed her wrist with cool, strong fingers. Pain shot up her arm like current.

"Don't test me, child. I've had a trying day. It pains me to see all my plans hinge on weak and simple creatures like yourself, but it seems we both have little choice in the matter. If you wish to endure, you'll keep your head. Stay where you arrive. Help will come."

"What are you talking about?"

"You'll be joined with your sister soon enough."

"Wait, what—"

The white-haired man pressed two fingers to her mouth. "I've saved your life twice now. Don't make me regret my decision. The strings favor you, but there are others who could just as easily serve our purpose."

He walked away, leaving Hannah shell-shocked, speechless. A shrill scream in the distance briefly turned her around. By the time she looked back, the stranger was gone.

Hannah scrambled to process all the new and urgent developments around her. Her left wrist throbbed. Her right wrist glimmered. The temperature had dropped low enough to turn all breath to mist. The crowd fell into chaotic distress. They screamed and shouted and scrambled into one another like bumper cars.

This is the end. For them, not for you.

A booming gunshot emerged from the police cordon. More screams. A large man grabbed at the girl dressed like Catwoman, and an even larger man knocked him down. Another gunshot.

Hannah felt a strong vibration at the base of her hand. She gaped with insanity at her new silver bracelet. Mere seconds ago, it was a fat and dangly bauble, wide enough for a bicep. Now it rested snugly on the thinnest part of her wrist. Whereas once it appeared featureless, now it was split down the middle by a bright blue band of light.

She glanced up to discover the biggest adjustment of all. A curved plane of silky white light loomed all around her, closing two feet above her head. The outside world took on a yellow gossamer haze.

Hannah tried to relocate but ended up walking into the wall of her new surroundings. The light was warm, steel hard, and utterly immobile. She was stuck here, just a hair north of Commercial Street, in an eight-foot egg of light. That was enough to send her mind into blue-screen failure. She was in full rejection of the events onstage. Suspension of suspension of disbelief.

Nearby strangers caught sight of Hannah's odd new enclosure. A befuddled young man rapped his knuckles against her light shell.

"What is this?" he asked, much louder than necessary. She could hear him just fine.

"I don't know . . ."

"How are you doing this?"

"I'm not."

"What's happening?!"

Not this, she thought. *This isn't happening at all.*

The Great Hannah Given: mental ward alumnus, habitual wrong person, and unreliable narrator. Ergo, no eggo. No crowd. No crash. No white-haired man.

Everyone froze as a thunderous noise seized the area—a great icy crackle, like a glacier breaking in half. Bystanders threw their frantic gazes left and right in search of the clamor until, one by one, they looked up. The eerie sound was coming from above. It was getting louder.

More screams from afar. More gunshots. As the crackling din grew to deafening levels, the sky above turned cold and bright.

A teary young redhead scratched at the wall of Hannah's light cage. The actress could see lines of frost on the tip of the woman's nose, though the air inside the enclosure was as warm as July.

"Please!" the stranger screeched. "Help me!"

"I can't! I don't know how!"

Suddenly the tallest buildings in the skyline began to splinter at the highest levels, as if they were being crushed from above. Metal curled. Stone cracked. Windows exploded. With a grinding howl, an ailing structure gave out at the middle, causing all floors above to topple and fall in one great piece. Hannah pressed her hands against the light as she watched the other buildings crumble. The sky wasn't just getting brighter and louder. It was getting closer. The sky was coming down.

Shrieks and cries rose from every throat in the mob. There wasn't an empty square inch around her egg now. More than a dozen people pounded at the wall, weeping and begging.

The skyline was gone. Now the great white sheet descended on the clockless clock tower, cracking the jagged neck of the structure and sending huge chunks of stone flying everywhere. One of them demolished a police car, along with everyone near it.

Hannah fell to the pavement—wincing, crying, desperately trying to shut out the horrible noises. In the final few seconds, the cruelest part of her mind forced her to open up and see the world one last time.

Everyone around her was at long last quiet. Frozen dead.

Then, with a shattering crunch that would haunt her for the rest of her life, the ceiling came down and smashed all the corpses into shards. It devoured the ground and just kept going.

The actress had no idea how long she existed there in the blank white void of existence, kneeling on a floating disc of concrete and sobbing at the nothingness all around her.

Soon the void swirled with smoky wisps of blue and the nothing became something. By the time Hannah's eyes adjusted, the glow of her bracelet had faded and the eggshell of light was gone. Beneath her feet and her fallen handbag lay the same round patch of 13th Street, but it was now fused into concrete of a lighter color.

She craned her neck and saw blue sky and white clouds, the distant gleam of several tall buildings. She didn't recognize a single one.

Her hands quaking wildly, Hannah smeared her eyes and sniffed the warm summer air. Her last few working neurons struggled to process her new state of existence but all they could tell her with any degree of confidence was that right now at this very moment, she was alive. And she was elsewhere.

PART TWO

Amanda noticed a little black sticker at the base of Hannah's neck. She peeled it off.

"What is this?" She sniffed the sticky side. It had a faint medicinal scent. "It's a drug. They drugged you. No wonder you're acting so . . . Let me look at your pupils."

"I'm fine! It's just a baby spot. A mood-lifter. It works great. It did wonders for me and Theo."

"Who's Theo?"

Hannah stared with fresh discomfort at the scruffy green baseball cap in her hand. Amanda quickly connected the dots.

"Wait, is he the guy they carried in here? The one who was unconscious and bleeding from every orifice? Are you kidding me, Hannah? Are those the wonders you're talking about?"

"You don't know it was the drug that did that."

"Then what happened to him?"

Sighing, Hannah crunched the cap in her grip. In truth, she had no idea what happened. Even in a lucid state, she'd have a hell of a time explaining the curious case of Theo Maranan.

Thirty-two minutes ago, she'd discovered the ultimate recipe for joy: a baby spot and a comfortable seat in a fast-moving vehicle. The view outside the window was poetry in motion, an ever-changing canvas of color and light. Every time the van stopped at a traffic signal, she'd snap out of her euphoric daze and launch chirpy, childlike questions at her two Salgado escorts. *What makes ambulances fly? Are we getting Zack next? Do you know the white-haired man? Why isn't everyone in the world addicted to baby spots?*

With dwindling patience, Martin fielded her queries (*"Aeris," "Maybe," "Who?" "Because the more you use them, the less they work"*). His son raced through yellow lights just to keep her quiet.

Soon the van pulled into an alley behind a supermarket. Hannah peered through the front grate and studied Martin's handheld computer. The screen contained a grayscale city map, peppered with four blinking red dots.

"What are the dots? Are those the people you're looking for? And how are you finding us anyway? Our bracelets?"

The Salgados opened their doors and hurried outside.

"We'll be back in a couple," said Martin. "Just sit back and stay easy, okay?"

Hannah let out a cynical snort. "You sound like my last date."

She spent the next few minutes in cushy silence, pinching her lip with growing fluster as the awful sounds of apocalypse came trickling back into memory. The booming crackle of the hardening sky. The horrible crunching noise of the frozen corpses . . .

The back doors of the van suddenly sprung open. Hannah saw Gerry Salgado struggling with a thrashing young Asian. He wore a dirty gray hoodie over khaki shorts and sandals. Sun-bleached letters on his chest advertised Stanford University. An Oakland A's baseball cap lay askew on his head.

Martin affixed a small black sticker to the stranger's neck, then joined his son in the tussle. The captive helplessly writhed in their grip.

"Let me go! Please! I'm not ready for this!"

The Salgados forced him into the seat opposite Hannah, then held him in place until he sat still. Hannah noticed a pair of foreign script symbols tattooed on the inside of his left wrist. The silver bracelet on his other arm was all too familiar.

"There we go," said Martin. "You feeling better now?"

The man nodded at Martin. Hannah could see he was in dire need of a shave and a haircut. He couldn't have become this disheveled just from one morning.

"I'm not ready," he repeated.

"Not ready for what?" Hannah asked him, eliciting glares from both Salgados.

The stranger finally noticed her. His twitchy gaze stopped at her bracelet.

"You're kidding, right?" He glanced at the Salgados. "Is she kidding me?"

Martin rubbed his arm impatiently. "Okay, listen, we need to get moving again. I'll trust you two to get along back here. You're both in the same fix and you're both gonna be okay."

Soon they were traveling again. Hannah wasn't pleased that her window view was now obscured by 160 pounds of discombobulated Asian, but she didn't want to offend him by moving away.

Screw it, she thought. *Might as well mingle.*

"Hi. I'm Hannah. What's your name?"

He took off his cap and fluffed his messy hair.

"Theo," he replied hoarsely. "Theo Maranan."

"Hi, Theo. How you feeling now?"

He smeared his bleary eyes. "Fluffy and awkward. Like rabbits are screwing in my head."

Hannah grinned. "Yeah. That's the baby spot. It gets better."

"What's a baby spot?"

"The little patch on your neck. It's a drug. A mood-lifter."

His face crunched with confusion. "They have drugs here?"

"Yeah. Sure. Why wouldn't they?"

"I don't know. I just assumed."

For all his wear and tear, Hannah found Theo to be somewhat easy on the eyes. He wasn't especially burly but he had broad shoulders and finely chiseled features. On a better day, in a better state, she might have even flirted with him.

He raised a loose finger at her arm sling. "You mind if I ask how, uh . . . ?"

"Oh, this? I had some kind of weird mental seizure. Then I hit a bus."

"Wow. Damn. That would do it."

She looked again at the script symbols on his arm. "Maranan. That's Filipino, right?"

He nodded, impressed. "Yeah. Very good. Most folks guess wrong."

"Well, I dated one of your people."

"Fair enough. I dated one of yours."

The two of them plunged into giddy chuckles, prompting Martin to turn around and check on them.

"Okay, I see what you mean about the baby spot," Theo said. "I shouldn't be laughing at all, given what's coming."

Hannah's smile died away. "What's coming?"

"Are you kidding?"

"That's the second time you . . . No, I'm not kidding. I have no idea what's going on."

"You're better off. Trust me."

They both fell quiet for a few blocks. Theo studied her cautiously.

"Can I ask you something personal, Hannah? You don't have to answer."

She shrugged. "Try me."

"What's the worst thing you've ever done?"

The question didn't bother her as much as she expected. She chewed her lip in contemplation.

"I had a big emotional breakdown when I was thirteen. I cut myself pretty badly."

"Your wrists, you mean."

"Yes."

"Across the vein or up and down?"

She eyed him strangely. "What does that matter?"

"Well, to me it's the difference between a cry for help and a serious attempt at suicide."

Her pleasant buzz began to falter. "I guess it was a cry for help then. Still a horrible thing to put my mother and sister through."

"What about your dad?"

She looked away. "He died the year before."

Theo nodded with clinical intrigue. "I see. Suicide?"

"Cancer. Can we please change the subject?"

"Sorry. Didn't mean to upset you."

The van sailed through three green lights before Theo spoke again. "I hope you don't think I was judging you. Believe me, I'm in no position to wag the finger at anyone. I'm a law school dropout, a rehab washout, and an all-around blight on the family tree. If I told you the worst thing I ever did, you'd get the strong and rightful urge to push me out of this van."

Hannah pulled her gaze from the moving scenery and back onto him.

"I also tried suicide," Theo added. "Five years ago. It wasn't a cry for help. It was a full-fledged attempt to end it. The only reason it didn't work is because apparently, among my many faults, I'm also bad with knots."

Hannah let out a churlish giggle. She covered her mouth, mortified.

"Oh my God. I'm sorry. I didn't mean to laugh."

Theo smirked with good humor. "It's okay. You're picturing me falling through a half-ass noose, right onto my full ass. That's pretty much what happened."

They both fell into dizzy laughter again. Theo moaned and wiped his eyes. "You know what's even crazier? For all my attempts to kill myself, both quickly and slowly, I don't even know what did it in the end. I have no idea how I died."

Hannah's humor vanished in an instant. She stared at her new companion in deep bother.

"Theo, do you . . . Jesus, I don't even know how to approach this."

"Just ask."

"Do you really think you're dead right now?"

He stared at her, expressionless, for a full city block. "Okay. This is tricky. I don't want to upset you again."

"What do you mean?"

"Well, let's take this step by step. You told me you got hit by a bus . . ."

"No, I said I hit a bus. It was parked. I only dislocated my shoulder."

Theo sat forward now, his eyes darting back and forth in busy thought. Hannah blinked at him in fresh bewilderment.

"Oh my God. You think this is the afterlife for both of us."

He held up a hand. "Okay, wait now. Before you mock me—"

"I'm not mocking you, Theo. I just—"

"I was enveloped in a ball of hard, glowing . . . something. And then everything went white. When it stopped, I found myself in this place with glimmering walls and flying trucks. I mean, what am I supposed to think?"

"I don't know," Hannah confessed. "I still don't know."

"Then how do you know I'm not right?"

In a more sober state, it might have occurred to Hannah to ask the Salgados to settle the matter. Instead she found herself considering the notion that she was in fact riding the jitney to her own eternal judgment. She imagined the panel would deliberate for ten seconds before sending her to the hazy gray place where mediocre people went.

"I'm sorry, Theo. I don't think you're right. I'm alive. I'm screwed up right now, but I'm alive. It's the only thing I know for sure."

To Hannah's surprise, the idea only seemed to unnerve him more. He furiously tapped his bracelet.

"I talked to someone," he said. "I'm not religious at all, so please don't mistake me for the kind of person who sees angels everywhere."

"Go on."

"He found me at the bus station this morning. He was fierce-looking and—I say this heterosexually—very pretty. He said his name was Azral and that he'd never seen so much wasted potential in a person. He wasn't the first to tell me that, by the way, and he certainly wasn't telling me anything I didn't already know. But then he said I was moving on to a new world. That I'd finally make myself useful there. Then he gave me this bracelet . . ."

Hannah listened and nodded. She already had her next question lined up.

Theo shook his head at himself. "God. You must think I'm an idiot."

"I don't. Really. When I first got here, I thought this was Canada."

After scanning her for ridicule and finding none, Theo leaned his head back and laughed. His face twitched briefly, like he was shaking off a fly.

"I'd been riding all night from San Francisco," he told her. "So I was already at diminished capacity when I met the guy. I'll also admit that I wasn't entirely sober."

"Theo . . ."

"My point is that I wasn't thinking straight."

"Theo, did this guy have white hair?"

He stared ahead serenely. At this point, he'd lost all capacity for surprise.

"Yeah. I guess you met him too."

The van pulled to a stop along the curb. Hannah looked out the window. They were still downtown, in a decidedly less ritzy area than the one she'd arrived in.

"We'll be back," said Martin. "We got two signals, so you'll be in good company soon."

The Salgados disappeared down an alley, between a dilapidated post office and a grungy diner. Hannah and Theo fell into an awkward silence. Suddenly the actress felt an eerie chill on the back of her neck, as if someone was watching her. She turned around and scanned the street. No one.

Soon Theo's head dipped and his eyelids fluttered erratically. Hannah left him to his twitchy nap.

"Azral," she muttered, in a vacant daze. It was strange to learn the name of the white-haired man after all this time. He was no angel. As sure as Hannah knew she was alive, she knew he was no force of goodness.

Four minutes after leaving, the Salgados returned without company.

"What happened?" Hannah asked. "I thought we were getting more people."

Martin hurriedly texted his daughter. "False alarm."

Hannah could practically feel his tension. His son looked downright disturbed. She opted not to inquire further. She'd had enough agitation for one ride.

The vehicle started up again. Soon Hannah drifted off into uneasy thoughts. A floundering actress, a droll cartoonist, and a law school dropout who got plastered at bus stops. *Why us, Azral? What could you possibly want from—*

"He's right," Theo murmured.

Hannah looked at him again. His eyes were still closed. She couldn't tell if he was addressing her or merely talking in his sleep.

"I'm sorry. Who?"

"Zack. He's right. It's not enough money to get to Brooklyn."

She sat forward. "Wait, what?"

A few drops of blood trickled onto his sweatshirt. Then a few more. Then his nose became a faucet. It didn't take a nurse to see that something very wrong was happening inside Theo Maranan.

While the first two floors of the Pelletier building had been converted to office space, the top flight stayed true to its hotel origins. Thirty suites remained fully furnished with beds, chairs, and dressers. Only the locks and lumivisions had been removed, by order of the new owner, Dr. Sterling Quint.

Amanda emerged from her shower to discover that one of the physicists had taken her clothes for study. All she owned now were her gold cross necklace and diamond wedding ring. She was willing to let science have the ring, if science asked.

She fastened her robe and crossed the hall into Hannah's suite, listening to the running shower through the bathroom door. She pushed it open a crack.

"Hannah? You okay?"

Amanda could see her silhouette through the gauzy white curtain, the buxom shape that Derek had ogled fourteen hours ago. Hannah leaned against the tile in somber repose. The mood-lifters were wearing off, turning her thoughts to stucco.

"I'll be out soon," she said in a dismal voice.

"There's no hurry, Hannah. I just wanted to check on you."

"What's her name?"

"Who?"

"The quiet girl in the lobby."

"Mia."

"Yeah. Mia. She didn't look very happy."

"She just lost her whole family."

"That's what I figured," Hannah said. "It's got to hurt a little. I mean to see that we didn't."

Amanda sat on the edge of the sink and closed her eyes. "I don't know."

"You know Mom's dead, right?"

The spider-leg tingles came back to Amanda's right arm. Her fingers twitched uncontrollably. "Hannah . . ."

"This wasn't just San Diego. It was everywhere. A kid with a radio said so. The whole goddamn world."

Amanda could hear her sister's choking sobs over the water. "Hannah, you're coming down off a very strong drug . . ."

"No, I'm coming down off everything! I'm crying about our mother! How come you're not?"

A powerful chill seized Amanda's hand. She pulled back her sleeve and gasped at the mad new blight on her arm. Her skin was covered in tiny white dots from her fingertips to her bracelet. The beads looked as hard and shiny as plastic, but they moved with a life all their own. Amanda watched with frozen horror as three flea-size spots shimmied up her thumb.

Oblivious to the crisis, Hannah rested her head against the wall. "I didn't . . . Look, I don't know what I'm saying right now, okay? Don't listen to me."

Amanda shook her hand with hummingbird zeal until the dots disappeared. She searched every inch of her skin for remnants.

"Amanda?"

She threw her saucer gaze at the shower curtain. "W-what?"

"I didn't mean to say that. I'm sorry."

"It's all right. I'm not . . ." She flashed back to her alley encounter with Esis, the strange white tendril that had burst from her hand. *What did she do? What did she do to me?*

Amanda jumped to her feet. "I should . . . I should check on the kids."

"Let me know if you find out anything about Theo."

"Yeah. I'll ask."

"He said he was a blight."

Amanda stopped at the door. "What?"

"Theo. He made himself out to be some god-awful person, but he didn't seem so bad."

Hannah smeared hot water against her eyes. "I don't want him to die."

Amanda kept staring at her flushed pink arm, lost in dark imaginings. God only knew what the scientists would do if they found out about her white affliction. They'd probably have her vivisected by sundown.

"He'll be okay," the widow said, without remotely meaning it. "We're all going to be okay."

Amanda returned to the game parlor, her arm still tingling from her outbreak. She noticed David and Mia keeping a curious vigil at the window.

"What's going on?"

Mia turned to her. "Erin's back. She found another one of us."

"Looks healthier than the last guy," David added. "Though he doesn't seem pleased."

Before Amanda could peek for herself, the procession moved inside. Loud voices echoed from the lobby.

"—not until you tell me what the hell's going on! I mean, why so cryptic? Are they paying you to generate suspense? Because trust me, I'm all stocked up."

David smirked at his companions. "He's certainly spirited."

Mia noticed Amanda's tense expression. "Are you okay?"

She forced a thin and shaky smile, even as her thoughts churned with hot new worries. She'd held Mia's hand earlier. What if she infected her? What if they both had the alien blight now?

Amanda studied Mia's fingers as casually as she could. "I'm okay. How . . . how are you feeling?"

"Numb," the girl replied. "Tired. I'm happy for you, though."

"What do you mean?"

"Your sister."

"Oh." Amanda blinked in confusion, then reeled with guilt. "Yeah. I still can't believe she's alive."

"Are you two close?"

"Uh, well—"

The argument in the lobby got louder, closer. Now they could hear Beatrice's chipmunk voice.

"Sir, if you would just give me your name . . ."

"My name is Up Yours until I get some answers. What is this place? Who are you working for? What the hell do you want with me?"

"Sterling Quint will answer everything—"

"Sterling Quint? Sounds like a Bond villain. I'm not appeased. But if you can get him here and talking in five minutes, I'll become a lot nicer."

The group appeared in the doorway. Between Beatrice and Erin stood a lanky young man with wavy brown hair. His rumpled black oxford was torn at the left shoulder. He clutched a spiral-bound pad against his chest. A sketchbook.

Zack examined the three refugees in bathrobes, then chucked a hand in hopeless dither.

"Okay. Now I'm at a spa."

Czerny stopped at the end of the second-floor hallway. He squeezed a drop of clear liquid into each eye and shot a blast of eucalyptus spray up his nostrils. After several blinks and sniffs, he was finally ready. He knocked on the door to the Primary Executive's office, and then once again stepped into Rat Heaven.

Scattered among the Persian rugs and sculptures stood ten huge glass aquariums, each filled with scampering mice of the brown and white varieties. Despite the apartheid arrangement, both breeds enjoyed a life of murine opulence, filled with fresh mulch and lettuce, frequent mating opportunities, and the greatest luxury of all: time. As physicists, the Pelletier Group experimented with math, not mammals. None of these creatures would see the business end of a scalpel. Not for a few generations, anyway. Their caretaker was breeding a special strain for his wife, a university neurobiologist. Czerny could tell from the devoted pampering that these creatures were more than a pet project to Sterling Quint. They were pets.

A fat white mouse roamed free on his great mahogany desk. Quint stroked her back as she chomped a piece of radicchio.

"I'm not encouraged by the blood on your shirt."

Czerny breathed through a scented tissue. "I'm afraid the Oriental has fallen into coma, sir."

Quint scowled in pique. "Idiots."

"I'm sorry?"

"The Salgados. They should have smelled the alcohol on him. They had no business drugging him in the first place."

"As it stands, I agree. Shall I dismiss them?"

Quint pondered the matter a moment, then slowly shook his head. "No. The last thing we need are disgruntled ex-contractors spilling our secrets. Raise their wages, but give them less responsibility. Have them guard the property or something."

"Of course, sir. Clever thinking."

It had been remarked by people crueler than Czerny that Sterling Quint kept mice to make himself feel larger. A quirk from his father's genes had left him with achondroplasia, which stopped his growth at four-foot-five. While he struggled with his stature as a child, he'd made peace with it in his adult years. Now, at the distinguished age of fifty-five, he took comfort in the fact that "little" languished at the bottom of his list of pertinent adjectives.

"That doesn't solve the problem of our unfortunate guest," said Czerny. "I fear his condition exceeds my expertise."

"Maranan won't die," Quint assured him. "I have a specialist coming tonight."

Czerny knew better than to press his boss for details, or to inquire how he knew the Filipino's name. He glanced at the three-by-three bank of monitors on the wall. Seven of the screens showed empty rooms. He saw Amanda, Zack, and the teenagers on one. On another, he caught Hannah running a towel over her wet, naked skin.

Blushing, he forced his gaze back onto Quint. "Uh, I suppose you already know that our sixth guest has arrived."

"Sixth and last," Quint responded. "That's all of them."

This was news to Czerny, especially since there had been nine signals from the start. One led to a corpse. He was eager to learn what Quint knew about the other two.

"Okay. I'll inform the team. I take it you'll be introducing yourself soon?"

"Yes. I'll be down in a few minutes."

Czerny sniffed his tissue again. "Excellent. I'll let you prepare."

"Constantin . . ."

He turned around at the door. Quint leaned back in his leather chair, shining flawless white teeth.

"It's okay to smile. This is exciting stuff."

Czerny laughed. "You have a gift for understatement, sir."

Alone again, Quint held the free-roaming mouse and petted her with euphoria. There were six new people in his building today, six people who didn't exist on this world yesterday. As far as science was concerned, this was a game changer. A game *winner*. Now all he had to do was follow the wisdom that Azral had texted him twenty minutes ago.

Keep them safe. Keep them content.

Quint wasn't worried. It was easy to keep them safe when no one else knew they existed. Keeping them content was harder, given their state of mind. It was also less important. When these six people lost their world, they lost their options. In the end, they had nowhere else to go.

PART THREE

TEMPORIS

EIGHT

Zack Trillinger had earned enough screaming condemnation in his life to know that his wisecracks weren't always appreciated. His mother had called it a "cheek problem." He couldn't help himself. Serious people brought out the Bugs Bunny in him, and no amount of blowback could get him to temper his snark. On a day like today, when taxis flew through the air and actresses moved at the speed of missiles, it seemed especially important to embrace the scathing absurdity of the universe, no matter who it bothered.

Unfortunately, he wasn't prepared for the wrath of Amanda Given, a woman who was uptight even on good days, and who was still reeling from the white-specked lunacy on her skin. It took only twenty-nine seconds of mutual acquaintance for her hand problem to meet his cheek problem. She slapped him hard enough to turn his whole body.

"You shut your mouth," she hissed, her voice wavering between fury and tears. "I don't need that from you. You hear me?"

Shell-shocked, Zack held his red and stinging face. "Okay."

"I don't need that."

"I understand."

"Not today."

"I know," he said. "It was a bad joke. It was in poor taste. I'm sorry."

The moment Erin and Beatrice left him alone with his three fellow refugees, Zack had finally revealed his name. He'd introduced himself to them one by one, signing each handshake with an appropriately stupid gag, a half witticism. Upon hearing David's accent, he said. "G'day, mate." To Mia, he proposed that OMGWTF?! should be their new default greeting.

With Amanda, his first impulse was to offer some wordplay bouquet about how she looked pretty intense and intensely pretty, but then bashfully nixed the idea. The moment he spotted her golden cross necklace, his comedy writers jumped to plan B.

"Where's your messiah now?" he'd brayed, in a passable Edward G. Robinson impression.

Before either of them knew what was happening, her right hand sprung like a cobra and struck him. Amanda didn't need to see the gaping horror on Mia's face to know that she'd overreacted. Worse, she realized she might have infected Zack with whatever disease she now carried.

David rose from his chair and raised his palms in nervous diplomacy. "Okay, look, we're all in a state of disarray right now . . ."

"South California," Zack uttered.

"What?"

Zack resumed his stance in the doorway, hugging his sketchbook with vacant anguish. "We're in the state of South California. It split in 1940 when the population got too big for Senate representation. They cut the line right below San Jose. I learned this downtown, in a bookstore called Scribbles."

When Erin Salgado had traced the final signal to Zack, he'd been standing in the reference section, eliciting curious stares from his fellow browsers. It was odd enough to see a grown man gawk in stupor at the pages of a children's atlas, but this man wore a gaping tear on his left shoulder and a woman's handbag on his right. Both the bag and the tear were the personal effects of one Hannah Given.

"Zack!"

The shout came from the hallway. Zack turned around just in time to feel wet hair, soft flesh, and terry cloth pressed against him.

He awkwardly returned Hannah's hug. "Hey, there you are. Speedy McLeave-a-Guy. You know, I'm used to women running away from me, but not at ninety miles an hour."

She pulled away from him. "What are you talking about?"

Amanda blinked at them in bafflement. "Wait. How do you two know each other?"

"This is the guy I was telling you about. We met at the marina." Hannah turned back to Zack. "What do you mean ninety miles an hour?"

"You don't remember what happened?"

"I remember everything going all blue and super-slow."

"No, you went all red and super-fast. You buzzed around the bench like a hornet on crack, talking so quickly I couldn't understand you. You ripped my sleeve, then ran away. And I don't mean Benny Hill speed. I mean you were a freaking blur." He eyed her sling. "What happened? Did you break your arm?"

"No." Hannah shook her head, dumbfounded. "That can't be right. That's not possible."

"Yeah, that was the consensus at the marina."

David matched Hannah's befuddled look. "Forgive me, Zack, but even after everything that's happened today, I have a hard time accepting what you're saying."

Zack shut the parlor door, then addressed the others in a furtive half whisper.

"I don't want to upset anyone more than I already have, but I think there's more than one kind of weirdness going on here. Beyond the flying cars and new state lines, I think something might be . . . different with us. Hannah's not the only one doing strange stuff. Look."

He opened his drawing pad, flipping through a series of crisp white pages. "Last night, I only had three blank sheets left in this thing. Now I have eight. My last five drawings disappeared like I never did them. And then there's this one . . ."

He turned to a rough sketch of a nerdy couple, the two lead characters of his comic strip.

"This used to be finished. Now it's not. I lost about a half hour of pencil work. That's the kind of glitch that happens on computers, not paper."

"What makes you think you caused it?" David asked.

"Because I watched it happen," Zack said, with a delirious chuckle. "The drawing changed right in front of my eyes."

Hannah shook her head in turmoil. Amanda nervously tugged her sleeve over her hand. "Look, I don't think this is the best time to—"

"I'm hearing voices," David blurted. "I'm sorry, Amanda. I didn't mean to cut you off. I just had to get that out. Since this morning, I've been sporadi-cally hearing people that I can't see. People talking to each other, laughing, whatever. I only hope it's related to this phenomenon you're discussing, be-cause otherwise I've lost my mind."

"You're not crazy," Hannah assured him. "At least not more than the rest of us."

Zack studied Mia's dark and busy expression. "Got your own weirdness to share?"

She looked up at him. "Me?"

"Yeah. You're a quiet one, but I noticed you got even quieter when we started talking about this. Is it something you can tell us?"

For a man who'd just been slapped, Zack was awfully perceptive. Mia had been thinking about her own incident—the glowing tube with the candles and the note, a special delivery that somehow managed to find her eight feet underground. She didn't know how to bring it up without sounding insane.

"Not really."

Zack eyed her skeptically. "You sure?"

"Leave her alone," Amanda growled. "She's been through enough."

"We've all been through enough. But we're all old enough and smart enough to speak for ourselves."

Mia nodded at Amanda. "It's all right."

"It's *not* all right. We're still traumatized. Still grieving over the people we lost. The last thing we need right now is to fill our heads with supernatural nonsense."

Zack peered down at Amanda's crucifix and swallowed his next slap-worthy zinger. "Look, I'm just trying to make sense of this."

"And I'm telling you it's too soon to try."

"Too soon for *you*."

"Too soon for all of us!"

Zack chuckled darkly. "Really? How interesting that you already know me better than I know myself. Is this a new psychic power or just an old trick you learned at Judgment Camp?"

As Amanda stood up, Hannah took a reflexive step back. Over the course of her life, she'd seen every dark facet of her older sister. Shoutmanda, Nagmanda, Reprimanda. Hannah knew, as both a summoner and a witness, that few things were less desirable than a visit from Madmanda.

"You unbelievable piece of shit. Are you such a sociopath that you need to mock people just hours after they've lost everything? Is that how you were raised?"

Now it was Zack's turn to step back. His wide eyes froze on Amanda's hand. "Uh . . ."

"I don't judge! I don't preach! I don't condemn the people who don't share my faith!"

Hannah leaned forward, blanching at the bewildering new change in her sister. "Amanda . . ."

"What I *do* condemn are people who disrespect my beliefs, especially when I've done nothing to provoke you but wear a tiny little symbol!"

"Amanda!"

She spun toward Hannah. "What?"

"Your hand!"

The widow peered down at her fingers and got a fresh new look at her weirdness.

The blight had returned in full force, coating her right arm in a sleek and shiny whiteness. Though the substance looked like plastic, it fit her as snugly as nylon.

David and Mia jumped up from their chairs. Hannah covered her gaping mouth.

"What the hell is that?!"

Bug-eyed, gasping, Amanda dropped to the recliner. The glistening sheath felt cool on her skin, like milk fresh out of the fridge. She could feel every bump and fold of the armrest as if she were still bare-handed.

"I don't know. I don't—"

The sisters both screamed as Amanda's long white glove erupted in rocky protrusions. Her silver bracelet creaked in strain, then snapped into pieces.

By the time the jagged fragments fell to the floor, Amanda's arm looked like it was covered in rock candy. The crags rose and fell in erratic rhythms, an ever-shifting terrain.

David looked to the door. "Uh, maybe I should get one of the—"

"No!" Zack and Amanda yelled in synch. "Just watch the hall," Zack said. "If someone comes by, keep them out."

Amanda flinched at Mia's approach. "No, stay back! I don't want to hurt you."

Zack inched toward her, fingers extended. "Look, you just need to calm down."

"Calm down?"

Mia nodded tensely. "He's right. This whole thing started when he got you angry." She moved behind Amanda's chair and stroked her shoulders. "You're going to be okay. Just breathe, Amanda. Breathe."

Hannah cringed with guilt as she watched Mia soothe her sister. *I should be doing that. Why didn't I think to do that?*

David peeked through a crack in the door. "Someone's coming."

A four-inch spike erupted from the back of Amanda's hand. Her other arm erupted in a rash of tiny white dots. Zack jumped back.

"Jesus. All right. It's definitely stress related. If you just relax—"

"How do you expect me to relax right now?!"

"It's Dr. Czerny," David announced. "And an extremely well-dressed midget."

Amanda squinted her eyes shut. *Oh God. Please. Please . . .*

"Hannah, maybe you should run distraction," Zack said.

"What should I say?"

"Anything. I don't know. You're the actress. Improvise."

Amanda forced her mind into calming memories—the nature hikes she took with her father, her honeymoon cabin on the French Riviera, all the young patients who cried happy tears when they learned they were in remission.

Soon the milky crags and dots began to melt away. Mia squeezed her shoulder. "It's working. You're doing it."

Amanda opened her eyes and peered down, just as the last of the whiteness retracted into her skin.

"They're almost here . . ." David cautioned.

"It's all right," said Mia. "It's gone."

Zack wasn't relieved. He scooped up the remnants of Amanda's bracelet, then threw a quick glance around the room.

"Look, I don't know who these people are, but I don't trust them. Until we learn more, we need to keep this to ourselves. We'll talk about the big weirdness. We won't talk about the other stuff. Agreed?"

Hannah, David, and Mia accepted his premise with shaky nods. Amanda had the least trouble with Zack's proposal. On this matter, she couldn't have agreed with him more.

Two hazy shapes appeared in the smoky glass. David opened the door to

Czerny and a diminutive companion. They studied their five skittish guests with leery caution.

"Is everything all right in here?" Czerny asked. "We heard noises."

Zack hurried across the room to greet him. "The strangest thing just happened, actually. Amanda bumped her arm against the pool table and her bracelet broke apart."

Czerny furrowed his brow at the warped silver fragments in Zack's hand. "Huh. That is strange." He looked to Amanda. "Are you all right?"

"She'll be fine. I'm Zack, by the way. You Sterling Quint?"

"That would be me," said the other man, in a stately baritone.

The guests all took a moment to study him. He was indeed a little person, as David implied, but he carried himself with the regal airs of a maharaja. He wore a lavish three-piece suit with a red silk ascot, and his feathered gray coif was flawless to a hair. Zack figured his jeweled rings alone could fund a man's food, clothing, and shelter habit for nearly a year.

"So you're the answer man."

Quint nodded. "As it stands."

"Good," Zack replied, with an anxious breath. "Because as it stands, we have questions."

The conference room was a perfect oval of hardwood and gray marble. In lieu of overhead lightbulbs, the entire ceiling glowed with milky iridescence. Mia noticed a pair of multitiered switches on the wall—one to control the ceiling's brightness, the other to change its color.

Quint sat at the head of a long oak table, shining a sunny smile at each guest as Czerny introduced them. For five people who'd made such a remarkable journey, none of them seemed particularly remarkable themselves. *Why them, Azral? Of all the souls to sweep across existence, why these?*

"Thank you for being patient with us," Czerny began. "I know we haven't revealed a lot—"

Hannah waved a shaky palm. "Wait. Hold it. Sorry."

Mia's eyes narrowed to frigid slits. She didn't want to dislike anyone, especially on a day like today, but from the moment Hannah stumbled into the lobby with her tight clothes and ditzy airs, she struck a sour chord. She was every living Barbie doll who'd broken her brothers' hearts, every gum-chewing mallrat who'd mocked Mia mercilessly.

"Before we get to the big stuff, I just want to know how Theo's doing."

Czerny had to wait for Quint's nod of approval before answering Hannah's question.

"Fortunately, he's okay. Still unconscious, but stable. We expect he'll pull through just fine."

Amanda sat rigidly in her seat, her hands hidden deep inside her sleeves. "What happened?"

"I regret to say it's our fault," Czerny admitted. "Our security men gave him apacistene, a dermal sedative more commonly known as a baby spot."

Hannah averted her gaze from the giant neon TOLD YOU SO that sat in place of her sister.

"It's not a harmful drug by itself," Czerny explained, "but it can be particularly strong on first-time users. The problem in this case is that Mr. Maranan had a high amount of alcohol in his bloodstream. The combination caused a toxic reaction and . . . well, you saw the results."

"When can we see him?" Hannah asked.

"Not for a while," Quint replied. "Once he's sufficiently detoxified, he'll be sure to join you."

Zack glanced around uneasily. "I'm late to the party. I take it Theo's another one of us."

Hannah nodded. "Yeah. I met him right after you."

"Wow. You do move fast."

No one appreciated the joke, least of all the sisters. As he cooked in the heat of their smoldering glares, his inner Libby shook her head at him. *You never learn.*

David wound his finger impatiently. "I'm glad Theo's okay, but can we please get to the main topic at hand?"

Once again, Czerny deferred to his superior. Quint took an expansive breath.

"I know Dr. Czerny has told some of you about our organization, but for those who came in late, let me explain again. The Pelletier Group is a privately funded collective of physicists, all specialized in the study of temporal phenomena. We're not beholden to any college or corporation. Our only mission is to follow the science, no matter where it takes us. It was through keen observation and a little dumb luck that science took us right to you.

"There's a unique subatomic entity called a wavion that's been fascinating physicists for decades. It moves differently, spins differently, clusters differently than any particle known to man. Though we still have much to learn about it, we know for a fact that wavions, when positively charged, move backward in time."

David opened his mouth to speak. Quint cut him off with a curt finger.

"Thanks to their atypical nature, wavion clusters are easy to detect with the right technology. In fact, one of our first discoveries, four years back, was a fist-size concentration in a San Diego parking lot. Soon we discovered a handful of others, all scattered within a ten-mile radius. They were all the same size, all expanding at the same slow rate. After thirty months, the clusters had each grown into the same specific form."

"An egg," David mused.

Quint grinned at him. "Yes. Each eighty-one inches tall and fifty-five inches wide, all invisible to the human eye but very perceptible to our scanners. The images became even more interesting, one year ago, when we began to notice a distinct hollowness inside each formation. To our amazement, every gap took the frozen shape of a human being. Although we're seeing you today for the first time, we've been familiar with your silhouettes for nearly a year."

The room fell into addled silence. David shook his head. "That's insane. You're saying you've been observing us for months when it all just happened a few hours ago."

"Like I said, charged wavions move backward in—"

"He gets the concept," Zack said. "We all do. We're just having a hard time stapling it to reality."

David nodded at Zack. "Exactly. Yes. Just the notion of anything traveling back in time. I mean the logistics, the paradoxes . . ."

The physicists exchanged a brief glance, filled with quizzical interest and—in Czerny's case—deep astonishment. *They're surprised,* Mia noted. *Surprised at our surprise.*

Quint stroked his chin in careful contemplation. "If there's one thing we've learned in the past five decades, it's that time is more . . . flexible than we ever imagined. That's the gentlest explanation I can offer at the moment. You seem like a smart young man, Mr. Dormer, and I'll be happy to discuss it more in the days to come. But for now, in the interests of keeping things manageable—"

Zack cut him off with a bleak chuckle. "Oh, I think that ship has sailed and sunk, Doctor. But here's something you can answer. You say you spent four years watching us from a distance, waiting for our eggs to hatch. I wasn't anywhere near mine when your security goons got me."

"Me neither," Amanda added. "I was at least two miles away. How did you find us?"

"You're still teeming in wavions," Czerny replied. "They're emanating from the silver bracelets you share. It's nothing to fear. The particles are harmless. But they did make you easy to track."

Zack curtly shrugged. "Okay, fine. But none of this explains how we got here."

"Or where 'here' is," Hannah added.

"Or what these things are," said David, brandishing his bracelet.

Quint nodded at them with forced patience. "Yes. These are all pertinent questions. Mr. Trillinger, we don't have an answer for you. Not yet. We can't even offer a working theory until we speak with all of you in detail and get a better sense of the events leading up to your arrival. Mr. Dormer, we don't have an answer for you either. Not yet. Now that we have the broken pieces of Ms. Given's bracelet, we're very eager to study them."

Hannah didn't learn until Czerny's introductions that Amanda had dropped her married name. She'd thrown her sister a baffled look, only to get a vague and heavy expression in reply.

Now Quint turned to Hannah. "In answer to your question, I can only tell you what you already suspected. You're on Earth, but a far different version from the one you knew."

Hearing it out loud, delivered so bluntly, was enough to make several stomachs churn with stress.

"We've made tremendous advances in the field of temporal science," Quint continued. "But for all our progress, our understanding of alternate timelines has never advanced beyond hypotheticals. I've devoted my career to these theories, but it's not until today that I've been graced with proof. Actual living proof. Trust me when I say that your arrival is unprecedented. There's nothing on record that's even remotely similar to what we're seeing now."

Zack threw his hands up in frustration. Quint pursed his lips.

"You still seem to have a problem, Mr. Trillinger."

"As a matter of fact, I do. Look, don't get me wrong. You're excited and I'm happy for you. But at the moment, you have five people—sorry, six—who couldn't give a crap about the advancement of temporal science. We're confused and scared as hell. If you don't have answers to the big questions, then at least tell us what you plan to do with us. And before you say we're not prisoners here, you can drop the whole Mister/Miss thing. It's not helping my tummy ache."

Quint leaned back in his chair and eyed the cartoonist for a long, cool moment. "As you correctly guessed, Zack, we're not holding you here. You can leave anytime you want. But you seem like a clever man, so I probably don't need to tell you that you're not equipped to venture out on your own. You have no contacts, no valid identity, no legal currency, and little to no information about your new environment. You're not just foreigners here. You're aliens. It would be in your best interest to stay with us, at least in the short term."

"As it stands, I agree with you, Sterling. But I'm thinking ahead. And I believe I speak for the others when I say we don't want to spend the rest of our lives as specimens."

"Understandable, but—"

"Good. Now surely a smart man such as yourself realizes that without options, we *are* prisoners here. So I suggest a deal, a *Quint pro quo* if it tickles you. We tell you everything we know about our world, you tell us everything you know about yours. We give you our time, our testimony, our spit samples, whatever. In exchange, you give us money. A thousand dollars a week for each of us. You can keep it all in a safe until we choose to leave. I don't care. The important thing is that when we do leave, we won't be as helpless as you so eloquently described."

All eyes turned back to Quint. He studied Zack through a face of stone.

"That all sounds perfectly reasonable."

"Good. See? We're connecting now. But before we shake on it, I'm adding a rider. No invasive medical tests without our consent. You tell us what you're doing before you do it, and if we don't like it, you stop. That's a deal breaker."

Quint narrowed his eyes in umbrage. "You seem to have a sinister notion about our methods."

"I don't know crap about your methods. I'm just covering all bases. As you said, we're aliens here. Should we happen to do alien things, like sprout a third eye or levitate, I just want to make sure there are limits to your scientific curiosity. If you were in our shoes, you'd want the same comfort."

Amanda suddenly realized, with dizzying inertia, what a good thing it was to have Zack around.

"That's easy to agree to," said Quint, "as we're not in the habit of vivisection. Anything else?"

"Actually, yes. Not a rider. A question." Zack launched a cursory glance around the room, studying every corner of the ceiling. "Got any hidden cameras in the building?"

In the all-too-telling silence, Mia felt a hot rush of blood behind her face. *Oh God . . .*

"It's not a big deal," Zack said. "You've known for a year that those eggs would hatch people. I assume you prepared for us. You know, cameras, beds, a medical lab. Makes sense. I just want to know."

David saw Czerny's knuckles curl tightly around his pen. Quint remained stoic.

"Yes. We have cameras."

The sisters cracked the same frosty scowl.

"I wish someone had told me that before I showered," Hannah griped.

"I wish someone had told us in general," Amanda said. "This isn't the way to get our trust."

Quint shook his head. "I apologize. It wasn't our intent to deceive you. Ever since the six of you appeared, we've been scrambling to catch up. Rest assured you're only being monitored for your own well-being. Furthermore, in the privacy of your rooms, you're only being watched by someone of your own gender. This I swear."

"And of course you swear not to release any footage of us without our consent," Zack said.

"Yes," Quint replied, with all the warmth of a glacier. "Of course."

Sensing the end of his employer's affability, Czerny stood up.

"Look, you've all been through an unprecedented trauma, and you're all coping with remarkable bravery. It won't seem like it now, but you're very fortunate. Fortunate to be alive. Fortunate to be together. And fortunate to be here with us. No one knows more about parallel world theory than Dr. Quint. If anyone can solve this puzzle, he can. In the meantime, have patience and have faith. You're going to be okay."

The guests sat in anxious silence, their muddled thoughts bubbling with a thousand and one concerns. Despite all of Quint's rosy promises, Zack knew there was no way on Earth—*any* Earth—these scientists would let such prize discoveries walk away. To truly leave, they'd have to run. It wasn't a plan right now—it was an option. Zack needed one, as much as the fair and fiery redhead needed a benevolent God.

As his head throbbed and his inner self screamed with childlike hysterics, the cartoonist leaned back in his seat and forced a cheery grin.

"Well, that was a fine presentation, gentlemen. I'm sold. When's lunch?"

They spent the afternoon in an aggregate daze, more like ghosts than guests. They gazed out windows without truly looking, flipped through books without really reading, and wandered the hallways with no clear purpose or direction.

As the sky turned to dusk, a pair of scientists arrived with bags of store-bought clothing—a generic assortment of T-shirts and sweatpants, plus the most basic cotton socks and undies. Soon the refugees stopped looking like day spa clients and now resembled an intramural volleyball team. Mia noticed, with silent distaste, that Hannah had seized the snuggest tank top in the collection. *Yes. We get it. You're blessed.*

An hour later, their evening meal arrived by physicist. Whereas lunch had been a casual buffet set on the pool table, Czerny had opened up the dining room for supper. In its hotel days, it was known as Chancer's, an upscale bar and bistro that hosted gospel brunches on Sundays. The scientists had briefly used it as a cafeteria before shyly settling back to desk dining.

The guests served themselves from steaming tins. Amanda and Zack were the first to sit down, each with a grilled chicken breast and a scoop of pasta salad.

"They're sure leaving us to ourselves a lot," Amanda observed.

"They're probably giving us a day or two to adjust. I figure come Monday . . ."

Zack trailed off as Amanda lowered her head and closed her eyes in prayer. Hannah wasn't sure if the blessing was real or just a showy middle finger to Zack. She didn't know how anyone could thank God after everything that happened today.

The actress sat down with a plate full of greens, the only thing her ailing stomach could handle. "Okay, here's a stupid question. If we're on an alternate Earth, does that mean there are alternate versions of us walking around somewhere?"

"No," said David, from the serving table.

"Doubtful," Zack added.

"Why not?"

Zack lazily motioned to David. The boy sighed and turned around to Hannah. "Okay, obviously our two worlds have a shared timeline. If they didn't, people wouldn't be speaking English here. They might not even be humans as we know them. So clearly our histories split at some point. From what Dr. Czerny told me, they still have Abraham Lincoln on their pennies. But from what Zack discovered, they separated California in 1940. That suggests the point of divergence occurred sometime between the American Civil War and the start of World War Two."

Mia stood behind David, eyeing him with rapt fascination as he expounded.

"Now, even if it's the latter end of that spectrum, the butterfly effect can change a lot in seven or eight decades. Our grandparents may have still existed as children, but the odds of them meeting and breeding as adults, then the odds of their own children meeting and breeding as adults . . . it's just astronomically small. And that's not even factoring the biology. The same sperm, the same gestational factors, the same hereditary toss-ups. At the most, you'd have a genetic relative walking around. But as you and Amanda prove, even genetic siblings can look quite different from each other. So, long answer short, no. Don't expect to find a twin out there."

In the resulting silence, David surveyed his stunned audience. He raised a cautious brow at Zack. "Was that, uh . . . was my answer somewhat in line with yours?"

The cartoonist chuckled grimly. "I was just going to say it's cliché. Jesus. I'm glad you went first."

"How the hell did you put that all together?" Hannah asked David.

"The only thing my dad loved as much as science was science fiction. We read a lot of books together. Guess I picked up a thing or two."

Amanda bit her lip as she thought back to her own reading nights with her father. "I bet he was so proud of you."

David rolled his shoulders in a dismal shrug. "I guess so. He wasn't the type to say."

As Mia sat down, Zack shined a contemplative gaze at Amanda and Hannah. "David has a point. You two don't look a thing alike. You're not half sisters or adopted, right?"

"Full sisters," Hannah replied. "It's a little more obvious without our dye jobs."

"And you both got bracelets," Zack pondered. "That can't be coincidence."

David nodded. "That's what I said."

Amanda kept silent as she sliced into her chicken. Zack could see she was agitated by the subject. He didn't care. He was just a stiff breeze away from a fierce and unseemly breakdown. He needed this distraction.

"Yeah, that's a hint right there. The question is why would, uh . . ."

His attention was seized by David, who sat down at the table with a teeming plate of green peas. The boy sprinkled heaping dashes of salt onto his pile, then looked up at his four confounded friends.

"Quite an interesting diet there," Zack said.

"Just fussy," David replied. "She did mention something about our potential."

"Who?"

"The woman who gave me my bracelet. Esis."

"*Ee*-sis?" asked Hannah.

"Yeah. Tall and lovely woman. She told us—me and my dad—that I was very important. She said that I was part of something larger now, and that I had the potential to help bring about a great and wonderful change to all humanity. That's not verbatim, of course, but—"

"She's insane."

The others looked to Amanda. She aimed her dark gaze down at her plate.

"I'm sorry, David. If we're talking about the same person, then I wouldn't trust a single thing she said. She was completely out of her mind."

From his frigid expression, David clearly didn't enjoy her analysis. "I had a hunch you met her too. What did she say to you?"

"I don't remember the specifics. I just know her behavior was completely erratic. One second she was complimenting me, the next she was grabbing my hair. She . . ."

Thinking about her sister, Amanda decided to censor the part where Esis launched across the alley with blurring speed. That part struck a little too close to home now.

"She was just crazy."

David shrugged. "Well, the Esis I met seemed intelligent and kind. Not even remotely crazy. In either case, you and I would be dead without her intervention."

"Am I supposed to be grateful? For all we know, they're the ones behind all this."

"Oh, come on. You have no evidence to support that."

Zack raised his palms. "Okay, hold it. Wait. David, I agree we're getting ahead of ourselves—"

"I don't even know why we're talking about this at all," Amanda snapped. "Can't we have *one* night to recover?"

"Hey, I was about to throw you a bone. As it stands, I'm deep on your side of the crazy issue. I didn't meet this Esis, but I have nothing nice to say about the guy who gave me my bracelet."

David raised an eyebrow at Zack. "Do tell."

"There's not much to tell. He wore a mask. All I could see were his eyes. But he looked like he was having the time of his life while people were burning to death all around us. That alone makes him someone I'd very much like to unmeet and hopefully never come across again."

"That's how I feel about Azral," Hannah added. "The white-haired man. I mean I know he saved my life twice, but he still scares the living—"

"What do you mean twice?" Zack asked.

Hannah could see her sister tense up across the table. She figured any mention of their childhood incident would send Amanda to tears.

She lowered her head. "It doesn't matter."

Frustrated, Zack glanced over to Mia, the lone holdout in the conversation. She stabbed at her food with a dismal expression.

"She didn't see anyone," David replied on her behalf. "She was asleep when she got her bracelet."

Zack scratched his neck in edgy thought. "So from the looks of it, we're dealing with two, possibly three different people."

Three, the sisters thought in synch.

David scooped another forkful of peas. "We don't have enough information about them to form any theories."

"I think we do," Zack replied. "The fact that Amanda and Hannah are here right now is a big fat clue that these people chose us for genetic reasons. Why else would they give bracelets to two biological—"

With a choked sob, Mia pushed her chair back from the table and fled the room. Amanda rose from her seat, shooting a harsh green glare at Zack before trailing out the door.

The cartoonist sighed at Hannah. "Your sister's not the most relaxed of women."

"She just lost her husband."

"I know. I just . . ." Zack frowned with self-rebuke, then flicked a somber hand. David listlessly poked a fork at his peas.

"We lost people too," he told Hannah. "We're just trying to figure out why they died. And why we didn't."

Hannah could finally see a hint of strain behind the boy's handsome face. She figured she could live to be a hundred and still not understand the way men handled their emotions.

Amanda and Mia returned eight minutes later, their faces raw from crying. Mia brushed her bangs over her puffy eyes and stared down at her half-eaten dinner.

"I have four brothers," she announced, with matter-of-fact aloofness. "I know for a fact that they're my biological siblings and I'm all but sure they didn't get bracelets."

The room fell into bleak silence. Zack placed a hand on Mia's wrist.

"I have an older brother back in New York. Josh. We're about as different as two siblings can be, but we get along." He gestured at Amanda and Hannah. "When I found out these two were sisters, my heart nearly jumped out of my chest because it made me think that maybe he got a bracelet too. Who knows? With all the crazy things that happened today, maybe we both have a brother out there."

Mia raised her head to look at him. "I don't know. I hope you're right."

By the time Czerny came back to check on them, the clock on the wall had reached 8 P.M. The food had grown cold and the conversation had settled back to mundane mutterings, increasingly hindered by gaping yawns.

Czerny suggested, with droll understatement, that perhaps it was time to call it a day.

In a sleepy drove, the group—which Zack took great pleasure in calling the Sterling Quintet—climbed the stairs to the third floor. Zack and David disappeared into their chosen suites without so much as a good-night. Never had a sentiment seemed so pointless.

Amanda urged Mia to share a room with her and Hannah, just for warmth and company. Though tempted, Mia politely declined. She expected to do a lot more crying between now and dawn. She didn't want to muffle herself out of some misguided sense of courtesy.

After three restless hours, she regretted her decision. No matter what she did, she couldn't get comfortable in her room. When the lights were off, the darkness pulled her straight back to her morning grave. She could feel the dirt in her hair again, the creepy-crawly bugs on her skin. When the lamp was on, she couldn't stop thinking about the scientists who watched her every move.

Just as her eyelids finally fluttered on the cusp of sleep, a soft and tiny glow seized her attention. It hovered directly above her, like a distant moon or a penlight. The radiant circle spit a small object onto her nose, then disappeared in a blink.

Baffled, Mia sat up in bed and retrieved the item from her pillow. It was a small scrap of paper, tightly rolled into a stick. She turned on the lamp and unfurled the note.

> *You just survived the worst day of your life. I won't say it's all candy and roses from here, but it does get better. Hang in there. Put your faith in Amanda, Zack, and the others. They're your family now.*

The note was punctuated with a U-shaped arrow, a symbol Mia herself often used to indicate more content. She flipped the note over.

> *Yeah, that includes Hannah. Cut her some slack. She's a really good person. She even saves your life.*

Mia read the words over and over, her heart thumping with agitation. She remembered the curvy feminine letters of her first note, the one that had encouraged her to keep digging for air. Not only did the penmanship on this message match her memory of the original, it triggered a new and disturbing sense of familiarity.

She climbed out of bed and flipped on the desk lamp, transcribing a snippet of her note onto a blank sheet of stationery.

After comparing the two handwriting samples side by side, Mia choked back a gasp. She wasn't sure if she should laugh or cry at the true scope of her weirdness. She wasn't speeding or blanching. She wasn't hearing voices or losing artwork. She was simply getting notes. Notes of prescient knowledge. Notes in her very own pen.

Mia lay awake for hours in furious bother. By the time her eyes finally closed, the darkness had given way to pink morning light. Her second day on Earth had already begun.

NINE

There were nine Silvers at the start.

Though Sterling Quint's physicists had monitored all nine arrivals in progress, only six of the refugees made it to the Pelletier compound in Terra Vista. The remaining three signals led the Salgados to a dead woman, a dead man, and a cracked and empty bracelet.

Quint was upset to learn that he'd lost a third of his future case studies, but his benefactor strangely didn't seem to mind. Azral assured Quint that the three fallen subjects were expendable in the grand scheme.

But what of the missing one? Quint had texted. **I assume the owner of the empty bracelet is still at large.**

An hour later, while Quint sat in the conference room with his new guests, the handphone on his desk lit up with a curt new message.

You're better without him.

Before his cosmic migration and universal upgrade, Evan Rander wasn't a fan of his native Earth. His favorite things in the world, in fact, were the ones that helped him escape it. Sci-fi movies. Video games. Internet smut. He was—by sight, sound, and self-acknowledgment—a geek. Even in his rare bouts of style and swagger, he resembled a meerkat with his narrow frame, sloping shoulders, and hopelessly juvenile features. At twenty-eight, he was continually mistaken for a ginger-haired boy of seventeen. He'd given up correcting people.

With each lonely year, Evan became increasingly convinced that Earth wasn't a fan of him either. Most of his frustrations came from the pretty young women of his world, who continually rejected his awkward attempts to engage them, his creepy leers. It had been theorized in more than one ladies' room that Evan Rander had a stack of restraining orders at home. Or worse, a stack of bodies.

If his lovely detractors could have seen inside his mind, they would have learned that his fantasies, while hardly chaste, were actually quite romantic. But after a lifetime of cold shoulders, Evan feared he didn't have the looks to attract a suitable girlfriend. He certainly didn't have the money. His lean existence as a part-time computer specialist had left him in a sinkhole of debt, enough to force him out of his apartment and into his father's house in City Heights West.

No baron himself, Luke Rander was far from happy to share his meager abode. For years, his best hope for Evan was that the boy's baffling nerd proclivities would one day lead to some profitable nerd venture. Soon his furtive disappointment began leaking out of him like sweat. *No work again today, huh? You should be pounding the pavement instead of playing computer games. At least get some exercise. How do you expect to find a woman if you're all pasty and scrawny? Guess the family name's dying with you. No work again today, huh?*

Round and round the record spun, until the stress caused Evan to wake up with ginger hairs on his pillow. The only ray of sunshine in his dismal life was Shannon Baer, a young account executive at his main worksite. Though she'd failed to make his A-squad of office lusts, she was an indisputable cutie, and she bucked the trend of her peers by treating Evan with smiles and banter. He even detected flirting when she teased him about his LEGO coffee mug.

Eager to learn her feelings without the risk of asking, Evan used his administrative access to log into her e-mail archives. She'd only invoked his name three times. The first two mentions were work related. The last one, in response to her teasing boss, was a knife in the eye.

> Oh shut up. It's not like that at all. I just feel sorry for him. Anyway, Evan's not as creepy as everyone thinks. Of course if I ever go missing, be sure to check his basement first. :)

The next day, he returned to the office in his nicest clothes and warmest grin. After engaging Shannon in friendly chitchat, he told her he needed to install a new antivirus program on her PC. He joked that she was getting the special package, despite her misguided hatred for LEGOs. She laughed and let him do his thing.

Unfortunately for Shannon, his "thing" was a custom malware script that, at the stroke of midnight, erased her project files from her computer and every backup server. Thirteen months of work, irrevocably destroyed. For Evan Rander 1.0, it was the cruelest punishment he was capable of inflicting, though he'd spent the night imagining far worse.

His vengeance quickly backfired on him. Once his handiwork was discovered, the president of Shannon's company had him blackballed from all his freelance agencies. With a simple series of phone calls, Evan had become a toxic commodity, unemployable.

Luke Rander gritted his lantern jaw when he learned of his son's comeuppance. "You know, for all your flaws, I never thought you were stupid until now. But you did it. You screwed up your life, all because you couldn't handle a little rejection."

For the last three weeks of his endemic existence, Evan moved through the house in a grim and listless state, his thoughts frequently dancing around the handgun under his father's bed. Maybe it was time. Maybe it was high past time to put the world out of his misery.

On the third Saturday of July, he woke up in freezing cold, his gadgets blinking in confusion. He barely had a chance to process the new peculiarities before a large, round pool of radiant white liquid bloomed on his wall like an oil slick.

Evan watched in bug-eyed wonder as a towering stranger stepped through the surface, a white-haired being of crystalline perfection. Despite his splashing entrance, there wasn't a hint of wetness on his skin, his hair, his tieless gray business suit.

Expressionless, the man approached the bed and addressed Evan. His voice was honey smooth, peppered with an anomalous accent.

"Listen up, boy. Time is short and I have much to do. In five minutes, everything around you will cease to be. If you wish to continue living, extend your wrist quickly."

Evan raised his arm with meek and dreamy deference. Azral's thin lips curled in a smirk.

"Your cooperation is a welcome change. I won't forget that."

He procured a featureless silver bracelet from his pocket. Evan's thoughts screamed as he watched it break into four floating elbows. They glided over Evan's fingers, reconnecting at the thinnest part of his wrist with a *clack*.

"What is this?" Evan asked in a tiny voice. "Am I dreaming?"

"I don't have the time or mind to explain your situation, child. Just keep your head. Stay where you arrive. Help will come for you shortly."

Azral squinted with revulsion at the unwashed garments on Evan's floor. "You'll wish to find proper clothes, if you have them. Then say good-bye to your father. You won't be seeing him again."

Amidst all the daft and scattered notions in Evan's head, it occurred to him that he'd rather eat his own arm than suffer one more look of disapproval from the bearish old man.

Suddenly Azral's white brow crunched in wrathful scorn. He lurched forward and grabbed Evan by the collar.

"Only a weak man fails to honor his parents. You should be grateful. It was your father's unique genes that saved your life today. Clearly I didn't choose you for strength of character."

As the fearsome stranger walked back to his white liquid portal, Evan suddenly found himself in a small pool of yellow.

"Pathetic," said Azral, before disappearing into the breach.

Over the course of his long and lawless existence on Earth's wild sibling, Evan would find many reasons to hate Azral Pelletier. Near the top of the list was the ridiculously short amount of time he'd given Evan to prepare for his great upheaval. He'd only just zipped his jeans over fresh boxers when the silver bracelet buzzed with life. Shirtless and barefoot in his father's moldy bathroom, he was sealed in light, safely preserved as the house and sky collapsed around him.

It was in that final moment that he forgot his fear. In the space between worlds, the space between lives, he was briefly at peace with himself. The old Earth faded away to an empty white void, and Evan Rander felt nothing at all but gratitude.

As the proprietor of a dreary midtown mini-market, Nico Mundis was used to seeing odd behavior in his store. Aside from the typical assortment of ne'er-do-wells who would rob him at gunpoint or speedlift his wares, he'd suffered his fair share of rants, raves, threats, and propositions. The sexual come-ons always baffled Nico the most, as he was sixty-eight and quite obese.

His favorite strange incident occurred three years ago, when a group of egghead scientists traced an invisible signal to his canned goods aisle. The group leader, a spiky-haired Poler named Constantin Czerny, offered Nico three thousand dollars to let them affix a small device to his wall. Some kind of particle scanner enhancer thingy. Sure, why not? Money was money. At the end of the transaction, Czerny gave Nico his phone number and advised him to call should anything unique happen. Nico had no idea what Czerny meant by that and wasn't sure if Czerny knew either.

Now, just minutes before opening for Saturday business, something unique happened.

As Nico filled the register, the overhead lights died. The table fan came to a stop. Even his electronic watch went blank. Only the white tempic barrier continued to function. It coated the windows from the outside, giving the shop a hazy, snowed-in look.

A flash of light filled the back of his store. Nico grabbed his shotgun and aimed it at the disturbance. He blinked through the dancing brown spots in his eyes and reeled to see a shirtless young man where previously there'd been no one.

Evan blinked twice at the gun, then raised his scrawny arms in terror. "Don't shoot! Don't shoot!"

Nico moved closer to survey the damage. The blast had taken a curved bite out of his store, leaving a concave groove in the wall and slicing half the cans and shelves around the intruder. Tiny wet vegetable morsels dripped onto the floor, covering broken pieces of bathroom tile that had come from God knows where.

"Who are you?" Nico shouted. "What are you doing here?"

"Look, just don't shoot, okay? I have no idea! The last thing I—"

His eyes rolled back into his head and he launched into violent convulsions. Nico took an anxious step back. He couldn't tell if the boy was suffering an epileptic seizure or an otherworldly possession. He wasn't entirely wrong on either count, but what he was truly witnessing at the moment was nothing less than the death of the original Evan Rander.

As Evan stood and stirred, a tidal wave of cerebral data flooded into him. Millions of vivid new facts and memories. They filled his brain node by node, reshaping his psyche. On the outside, he was still a twenty-eight-year-old man with a seventeen-year-old face. In his altered consciousness, he was older now. Many years older and exponentially sharper.

His upgrade had arrived.

Evan breathed a weary moan, as if he'd just given birth. For a moment Nico feared the intruder would fall into tears, but Evan soon let out a delirious laugh.

"Oh man. Man oh man oh man."

He swept his blinking gaze around the store. Nico was amazed at how differently the stranger carried himself. He looked fiercely confident now. Not even a tad confused.

With a hammy grin, Evan spread his arms out wide. "Nico! Nico-Nico Mundis! *Ti kanis?*"

The shopkeeper took another step back. "How do you know my name?"

"Ah, Nico-Nico. You and I go way back. You're my Square One Buddy, buddy. Always here at the beginning to greet me with a friendly smile. And since we're such good buddies, hey, why don't you put down the boom-stick?"

Evan was unsurprised to see the gun remain fixed on him. As he sighed and stretched, his hidden hand seized a can of string beans.

"Well, I figured it was a shot in the dark, no pun intended. Guess I can't blame you for being sore. For years you've been praying for some young and topless beauty to pop into your *Efta-Edeka*, and here I am. You should've been more specific."

He swung his gaze to the cloudy white doorway. "Oh, hello, bishop."

As Nico reflexively turned his head, Evan hurled the can—a perfect throw that connected squarely with the shopkeeper's temple, driving him down. Evan rushed around the counter and grabbed the shotgun off the floor. He jammed the barrel into Nico's stomach, then his nose.

"Why must we do this dance every time, Nico? You know I don't like hurting you."

Evan launched a swift kick into his ribs.

"Well, I like it a little. So do us both a favor. Waddle your ass over to that wall and stay there. I'll be gone soon enough. I just need to do a little convenience shopping."

Snorting through bloody nostrils, Nico crawled to his checkout stand and sat up as best he could.

Evan unwrapped an epallay and stuck it to his chest. "Oof. Mama. These reboots never tickle. My head's all fourped. But who am I to complain? I'm alive, right?"

Nico eyed the silent alarm button at the floor of his station. It was so easy when he could just step on it. Now it was five feet away—a mile in his condition.

Evan sauntered over to Nico's sparse selection of clothing. He threw on a black *Viva San Diego* T-shirt and cheap bresin sandals.

"Since I last saw you, Nico-Nico . . . well, I'll be honest. This last round sucked. Everyone was extra annoying. The Pelletiers. The Gothams. The Deps. And don't even get me started on You-Know-Who. Hannah had her tits in such a wringer, I had to kill her to keep her from killing me. And then her sister came looking for blood. Nearly killed me with her goddamn tempis."

Evan grabbed a handbasket and filled it with items: a quart of rubbing alcohol, a pint of orange juice, a hammer, a hunting knife. He stopped at the soda/vim dispenser and grabbed a large drinking cup.

"Between you, me, and the green beans, Nico, I'm still kinda pissed about it. So now I have two Givens at the top of my shit list."

Evan retrieved a near-empty tube of Crest from the floor. It had traveled with him from his father's bathroom and was now a one-of-a-kind relic. He stashed it in his basket.

"I don't know, Nico. Part of me's tempted to sit this one out. Maybe find an island somewhere and sip margaritas while the idiots do their idiot dance. I haven't written myself out of the story since . . . God, what round was it? Twenty-five? Twenty-six? Oh, hey. That reminds me."

Evan unwrapped a magic marker and drew a large "55" on the back of his right hand. It was a mnemonic device, a way to help organize his multiple sets of memories. He'd eventually hit the laser-brand parlor and get a more lasting reminder. For now, this would do.

"Aw, who am I kidding? I can't stay away from the fun and games. You didn't believe it for a second. You know me too well."

Nico had managed to halve the distance between himself and the alarm trigger. He shuffled another inch to the right, then froze when he spotted Evan's smirking face above the dog food bags.

"Pathetic, man. You're usually within slapping distance of the button by now. Are you even trying?"

"Please. I have children . . ."

"No you don't. Stop it. You're embarrassing yourself."

Evan doubled back to the checkout stand and emptied his goods into a knapsack. He popped open the cash register, then arranged the crisp blue bills into a folded pile. There was no need to count it. It was $212, just like always.

"All righty. The power's coming back and I have a date with a sweet Georgia peach. So this is where we . . . wait! The synchron! May I have your watch, *parakalo*? I need it more than you do."

Nico hurriedly removed his timepiece and held it out to Evan. He snatched it away and wrapped it around his wrist.

"Thanks. Now we're ready."

He checked the ammo in the shotgun, then blew dust off the barrel. Nico crawled backward.

"No! Please!"

Evan aimed the gun at his face. "You know, I remember a time, long ago, when I was the one crying and begging for my life. You didn't kill me but you still weren't nice. I'm just saying."

"Please, sir! Please!"

Evan lowered the weapon. "'Sir'? Did you just call me sir?" He laughed in amazement. "Wow. Fifty-four times and you never called me sir. I'm not sure how to feel. I mean I like it, obviously. I love it. But how much?"

Staring ahead in whimsical thought, he opened the shotgun. Two fat shells dropped to the floor.

"That much, it seems. Good job, Nico, you silver-tongued devil. You just charmed your way to a minor life extension."

Just as he tossed the gun over his shoulder, the overhead lights flickered back to life.

"Hey, look at that. Right on cue."

Evan turned the keylock next to the register, causing the tempic barrier to vanish. Cars and pedestrians became visible on the other side of the glass.

He grabbed his bag and patted Nico's cheek. "Always a pleasure, my friend. Until next time."

Evan ventured outside to a City Heights West that—unlike its shabby, old-world counterpart—actually resembled a city. Split-level houses had become replaced with sprawling office complexes. Trees had given way to animated lumic billboards. He chuckled at how he noted the difference every single time.

Soon his smile disappeared and he stopped cold. Evan didn't let Nico Mundis live very often, and he just remembered why. The fat man's testimony to the local police would enter the national law enforcement database, where certain key phrases would ring bells among the eagle-eyed *federales* in DP-9. Most of the Deps were easy enough to evade, but some, like the exotic Melissa Masaad, were annoyingly sharp. She could make Evan's life that much harder.

He closed his eyes in concentration until his head went light and he felt a full-body tingle, as if swimming in seltzer. Wild colors streaked all around him as the clock of his life reversed ninety-two seconds. Soon Evan found himself back inside the store, back behind the barrier, back with a loaded shotgun aimed at Nico Mundis.

With no memory at all of Evan's prior clemency, the shopkeeper raised a thick hand, crying. "No! Please!"

"Sorry, buddy. I forgot I had my reasons for doing this."

"Please, sir! Please!"

Unfortunately for Nico, Evan was no longer surprised or charmed by the honorific. He fired the shotgun. A cracking boom. A spray of blood. A good portion of Nico spattered onto Evan.

"Oh great. Lovely."

Evan rewound ten seconds, this time killing Nico from a slightly safer distance. He left the store clean.

As a hopeless perfectionist with a very unique talent, Evan Rander was no stranger to repetition. The act of undoing and redoing had become as natural to him as breathing. Sometimes the tedium was enough to drive him crazy. But it sure as hell beat living the one-take life, with all its indelible gaffes and consequences. Regret was something Evan had abandoned a long time ago. It died on his native Earth, with his father, his debt, and his crippling insecurities.

He returned to the street and hailed the first cab he saw. Evan knew the driver's name before the car even stopped, but chose to play dumb.

"Take me downtown, my good man. Childress Park. I'm on a squeeze, so 10× and aer it."

Before the driver could question him, Evan pressed two blue twenties against the glass. Proof that he could afford the speed and flight surcharges.

With a steamy hiss, the vehicle ascended forty feet to the taxi level, then folded its tires inward. The doors and windows locked shut, the classic winged-foot icon lit up on the fare meter, and the cab shot off like a bullet.

It took sixty-three seconds to cross five miles of urban scenery. Inside the taxi, eleven minutes passed. Evan stared out the window at his slowed surroundings. He spotted a puffy plume of chimney smoke that, in the sluggish blue tint of the world, reminded him of Marge Simpson's hair. He sighed with lament. They had nothing like *The Simpsons* here in Altamerica. Satire escaped these fools.

The taxi landed at the edge of an enormous green park, a lush oasis in a field of modern glass office towers. Like the rest of the business district, the place was sparse of life on Saturday.

Evan tossed sixty dollars at the driver. "Don't go away. I'll be back in five."

As he exited the cab, the synchron on his wrist beeped, informing him that it had readjusted to local time. By external clocks, it had only been seven minutes since he and his fellow Silvers crash-landed into this part of existence.

Some crashed harder than others.

In the middle of the park, on a flat patch of grass between picnic tables, a fetching young blonde lay sprawled on her back. Unlike the scattered homeless dozers who malingered here on weekends, the woman was barefoot in a lacy pink nightgown. The silk was marred with dirt and gashes. Only her silver bracelet remained spotless.

She fixed her cracked red eyes on Evan, speaking through wheezes and bloody gurgles.

"I can't move. I can't feel anything. I don't know what's happening. Please help me."

Evan kneeled by her side, clucking his tongue with sarcastic pity. She must have been ten stories up when the whole world changed on her.

"Oh, Peaches," he said, in a mock Savannah drawl. "I do declare this is not your day."

Evan made a habit of visiting Natalie Tipton in her dying moments. By his twentieth encounter, he'd pieced together her life in fragments. She was born Natalie Elder in Buford, Georgia, the only child of a waitress and a rail worker. She'd overcome dyslexia to earn a full scholarship to Emory University, where she studied to become a veterinarian until a well-placed kick from an ailing mare shattered her knee and ambitions.

But life had a way of working out for the terminally pretty. She soon met Donald Tipton, a campus football legend. They fell in love, got married, then moved out west when Donald scored a place with the San Diego Chargers.

If there was any drama during her time as a footballer's wife, Natalie didn't say. In the face of her demise, her only regret was not finishing college and becoming a veterinarian. She'd confessed this to Evan, back when he bothered to feign sympathy.

Having no recollection of their previous encounters, Natalie stared in terror at this creepy, grinning stranger.

"W-what happened to me?"

"You've taken a dreadful fall, sugah. And now you're bone soup, ah say, bone soup from the neck down."

"Please. Call an ambulance. I'm begging you."

"Oh, I've tried that, darling. But it's a big park. The paramedics never find you in time. Shame too, because they have a machine that could fix you right up. Reverse those injuries like they never happened."

"Why are you doing this to me?"

"I'm not the pilot of this plane wreck, sweetie. Just a passenger with a better seat. If you're looking to file a grievance, the people you want are the Pelletiers. Though in their defense, I'm pretty sure they warned you to stay on the ground floor."

He was right. Natalie had woken up in the utility room of her building, twenty floors down from her penthouse suite. A hand-scrawled note on the floor strongly advised her to stay where she was. She didn't listen. When the power died, she was stuck in the elevator between the eighth and ninth floors. Then her bracelet shook, the scenery changed, and Natalie Tipton had nowhere to go but down.

"I don't understand why this happened," she cried.

"Oh, honey bear. You don't even have time for the short answer. Trust me. You're not long for this world either."

Natalie closed her eyes and wept. "Why are you so cruel? What did I ever do to you?"

For once, her dialogue crossed into new territory. Evan's smile dissolved.

"Huh. Weird. I usually get that question from Hannah, not you. For her, I have a long list of grievances. For you?" He gave it some thought. "I don't know. Maybe you remind me of her. You both go wet for dumb muscle. You both seem to confuse lust with love. Now, granted, I never met your husband. But somehow I doubt you would have fallen for him if he was a professional chess player."

Natalie turned her head, wincing. "Oh God. I just want this to stop."

"Well, you're about to get your wish." Evan checked his watch. "It's curtain time."

While her shallow breaths settled and her consciousness slipped away, Evan stroked her arm and stared pensively at the trees.

"You know, I chat with the Pelletiers on occasion. I once asked them why they didn't stop you from falling. I mean they can see the futures better than anyone. They could have tied you down, broken your foot, done a hundred other things to keep you on the ground floor. Hell, they could still go back and save you. I'm not the only one with a rewind button.

"So when I asked, that crazy bitch Esis just gave me a shrug and said, 'Natalie's but one of many.' Can you believe that? They destroy a whole damn world to bring us here and we're still nothing to them. Just rats in their maze."

He checked her pulse, then breathed a wistful sigh. Natalie Tipton was gone.

"Ah, Peaches. You're better off. I've seen the way this story ends, again and again. It never changes."

Evan reached behind her and unhooked her necklace. The chain ended at a dime-size silver disc, engraved with the electric bolt logo of the San Diego

Chargers. Despite his utter disdain for football and the people who watched it, the trinket had become a cherished piece of old-Earth memorabilia. Worth the trip every time.

With a creaky groan, Evan clambered to his feet and clasped the charm around his neck.

"I'd stick around for the wake, darlin', but I've got a meeting with my old platoon commander and he's a real bear about punctuality. Sorry to say your whole life was pointless, and your death even more so. But what can you do? That's just the way the peach crumbles."

He walked away whistling, quietly resolving to be nicer to Natalie next time. In the grand scheme, she never did him wrong. She was the only Silver he could say that about.

While the cab soared to its next destination, Evan dumped the contents of his knapsack onto the seat. He stashed the drinking cup between his thighs, then poured himself a cocktail of rubbing alcohol and orange juice.

The noise of glooping liquids caused the cabbie to peer through the mirror. Evan smirked at him.

"Ease it, flyman. I won't spill a drop."

He stirred the concoction with his new hunting knife, then plunged his fist into the cup. The moment his silver bracelet became submerged, the liquid churned with hissing bubbles.

Soon the taxi landed in a run-down patch of the Gaslamp Quarter. Evan tossed another pair of twenties to the driver, then made his way down a dingy alley. As he crossed into the dark shadow of an elevated highway, he could hear a man's heavy breaths.

Evan bloomed a devilish grin. "Hello, hello, hello? Is there anybody in there?"

He stepped on a circle of concrete that was darker than the rest—a patch of the old San Diego, fused into the new. The upper half of a guitar case, complete with upper half of guitar, lay nearby. It had been sliced in a smooth curve. As always, the Great Cuban Leader hadn't ventured far from his landing spot.

"Just nod if you can hear me," Evan teased. "Is there anyone home?"

In the darkest corner of the alley, between two metal trash cans, a thirty-year-old man huddled against the wall. Black-haired, olive-skinned, and powerfully built, he wore a silk blue button-down over jeans. Even in his rattled state, the man was disgustingly handsome. Evan had lost count of the number of women who'd made complete fools of themselves to get his attention. Unlike Nico and Natalie, people he'd only encountered a few minutes at a time, Evan had years of experience with Ernesto "Jury" Curado. There were few folks on Earth he knew better, and few he hated more.

Evan watched with great amusement as Jury pressed his fingers against his temples, trying to will the universe back into order.

"¿Qué bola, asere? Welcome to beautiful downtown Other San Diego. Don't forget to try our Other Krullers. They're out of this world."

"Shut up," Jury said.

"Hey. Ouch. Hostility. What seems to be the problem, officer? Are we having a bad trip?"

Jury rose to his full six-foot-two height, grumbling at Evan through a sleek Cuban accent.

"Look, I don't know if you're a hallucination or a street nut. All I know is that someone drugged me and I'm freaking out. So go away."

Two years ago, upon receiving a Certificate of Commendation for exceptional performance, Officer Jury Curado had been called a "man of absolute conviction" by the Deputy Commissioner of the California Highway Patrol.

Yesterday morning, his twin sister had a different way of phrasing it.

"You're a stubborn ass!" she screamed, from behind her locked bedroom door.

Ofelia Curado knew better than anyone that when Jury got an idea in his head, there was no force in the heavens that could get it out. When they were fourteen, he was convinced that leaving Cuba was the only way to save Ofelia from their monstrous father. He was right. In Miami, he was convinced it would be better to fight for citizenship than to buy fake papers. He was right. He was right about better opportunities in California. He was right about his sister's hideous boyfriends. He was right about her drug problems and her eating disorder. He was right. He was right. He was right.

"I can't take it anymore!" she yelled. "You make my life a living hell! Just leave me alone!"

Like Jury, his sister was a raven-haired stunner, even on bad days. Sadly, the lingering traumas of childhood had made every day a bad one for Ofelia. She was, as Jury sang, a beautiful mess, and he had frequent cause to rescue her from some not-so-beautiful men. Whether they were lowlifes who exploited her for fun and profit or Lawrence Nightingales who sought to become her savior-with-benefits, they'd all left Ofelia worse for the wear. Some of them had nearly killed her. At Jury's hands, some of them were nearly killed.

Six months ago, his sister had found solace in the arms of a good woman. Martina Amador was a social worker, a squat and ugly matron who was a full twenty years older than Ofelia. Jury could only imagine their coupling was just another form of self-punishment for his sister, another way to lash out at the universe. And yet under Martina's care, she actually improved. First she got clean. Then she got hungry. And finally she found employment as a receptionist. She *worked* now.

Despite all improvements, Jury remained wary of his sister's lover. When Ofelia declared her intention to move out and live with Martina, the twins fell into strife. They screamed Spanish at each other through her bedroom door twenty-six hours ago.

"How long before she moves on to another fixer-upper?" Jury asked. "How long before she leaves you for a woman even younger, prettier, and more screwed up than you?"

"That's what you want, isn't it? You want me to fall back into my old ways so you can be my protector again!"

"You're wrong!"

"No, *you're* the one who's wrong this time! *You're* the one who needs a screwed-up woman to take care of. So just go out and find one already. I can't be that person anymore!"

Friday was a bad day for Jury Curado, which made it an awful day for the moving violators of Interstate 5. Over the course of his final workday, he reduced three different speeders to sobs and nearly broke the arm of a belligerent drunk driver.

Every Friday night, he played guitar at a tiny downtown coffeehouse. Most of his songs were mellow instrumental numbers, though he'd occasionally sing in Spanish when there was a fetching young woman in the audience. On the eve of his final performance, melancholy and desperation pushed him to snare his chords around a middle-aged bottle-blonde with a screeching, high laugh. He followed her home for drinks and debauchery, then woke up in her bed at 7 A.M. with the scent of bad sex in his nostrils and a thundering drum in his skull.

On the long walk back to his apartment, the oddities of the world began to stack up and unnerve him—the white sky, the chilled air, the blinking traffic lights. He turned a blind corner and was shoved against a building by an unseen aggressor. The guitar case fell to the ground.

"What the hell are you doing? Are you crazy?"

With cold hands and shocking strength, the attacker bent Jury's arm behind his back.

"You don't want to do this," Jury said. "I'm a cop."

"Shhhh," a silky smooth voice whispered in his ear. "You hush now, *hermano*."

Jury could feel something cool and metallic clasp around his right wrist. He was sure he was being handcuffed, but the second loop never clicked.

"What are you—"

With a warm blast of air, he was suddenly freed from his armlock. He launched from the wall and scanned the area. The only other soul within eyeshot was a tall man in a black T-shirt and slacks, watching him from two blocks away. He tipped his baseball cap at Jury in mock courtesy, then dashed away at a speed normally reserved for cheetahs.

His thoughts in free fall, Jury grabbed on to the nearest logical explanation. That batty woman he slept with must have laced his drinks with something. PCP. Mescaline. There was no other explanation.

Soon he reached his neighborhood, and the end of all doubt.

The debris of a crashed commercial airliner had turned 13th Street into a hellish horror. A battered nose cone lay in front of his local bodega. A smoldering pile of wreckage stood where his apartment building used to be. Jury covered his gaping mouth, stifling a delirious cackle. No. This was just a psychedelic nightmare. A jet plane never crashed into his home, his sister.

Thus Jury Curado, the man of absolute conviction, rode his fervent denial through the end of the world and into the next one. He kept crouched and still in a quiet corner, waiting for the hallucinations to go away.

Unfortunately, the new stranger—this smirking little imp—made the situation more difficult.

"Who the hell are you?" Jury asked.

Evan stood upright and rigid, his lip curled in sharp ridicule. "Sir! Evan Rander reporting for duty, sir!"

"Why is your hand in that cup?"

"Sir! I'm trying to start a trend, sir!"

"Why are you *talking* like that?"

Evan relaxed his stance. "Can't help myself. You're our great leader. Our stalwart commander. You whipped our sorry maggot asses into shape and turned us into a crack fighting unit. Well, except for Mia. Poor little thing."

Jury clenched his fists, trembling with frustration. Evan exhaled in sympathy. "I know. It's all very confusing. You want to know why my hand's in a cup? The answer's right there on your wrist."

Now Jury examined his new silver bracelet, the most innocuous of all the recent anomalies. "What is this?"

"You know, I asked Azral once. I mean I know what the bracelet does, but I wanted to know how it does it. He gave me a haughty little grin and told me that any answer would be futile, like explaining a handphone to an ancient Egyptian." Evan laughed. "Asshole, right? Well, what Mr. Snooty McFuture doesn't realize is that even an ancient Egyptian can figure out how to break a handphone. Look."

Evan removed his hand from the liquid. The band on his wrist was now cracked and white, as if frozen solid. He pulled the hammer from his knapsack and tapped the surface until a small section shattered. The remainder slid easily over his hand.

"Ta-da! See? If you want to ditch your own, feel free to use my mixture. It's a special cocktail I invented. I call it the Unscrewdriver."

Jury resumed his huddle. Evan shrugged nonchalantly.

"Suit yourself, Sarge. But you should know that there are people tracking us through these things. The Salgados will be here in two minutes to take you to their fancy building in Terra Vista. You don't want to go there. Trust me. In six weeks, that place will be a bloodbath."

Jury sprang to his feet, red-faced. *"Shut up! For God's sake, just shut up.*

I'm freaking out right now and the last thing I need is some creepy little geek who makes no sense!"

Evan's glib smile vanished. Now Jury could see the hatred on his face. Though the policeman had fifty pounds of muscle on his new acquaintance, he raised his palms in contrition.

"Look, I'm not myself this morning. I took a drugged drink and . . . God, you wouldn't believe the stuff I'm seeing."

Evan fished through his knapsack with fresh cheer. "Well, why the hell didn't you say so? Just so happens I have something that can help you."

He carefully approached Jury, his hand still buried in the bag.

"Now, I want you to keep an open mind, okay? The thing about this—"

He plunged the hunting knife deep into Jury's chest.

"—is that it really hurts."

Gasping, Jury fell back against the wall, feebly clutching the hilt of the knife as he sank back to the ground.

Evan furiously stood over him, pinching a thumb and finger. "You know, I came this close, *this* close, to letting you live this time. I was ready to find a whole new way to screw with you, just for variety. If you were living the same five years over and over again, you'd know how crucial it is to mix things up."

In Jury's final moments, Evan no longer existed. The whole world bled away. All he had left were thoughts of Ofelia. He realized she may have been right after all.

"But no," Evan continued, "you had to remind me why the world's a better place without you. So now once again, you've reduced yourself to a bit role. You don't get to play the hero. You don't get to lead the Silvers. You certainly don't get the big-titted love interest. Nope. So sorry. No Hannah for you."

By the time Evan finished ranting, the last spark of life had left Jury Curado. His eyes fell shut and his head dropped back against the brick.

Evan crouched down and hissed a gritty whisper in his ear. "Rot in hell, *pendejo.*"

A long green van rolled to a stop at the mouth of the alley. Evan plucked the wallet from Jury's pocket, then climbed the fire escape ladder. He smiled down from the roof as Martin Salgado and his square-headed son traced their wave signal down the alley. They squawked in fluster at the sight of Jury's corpse.

"A little too late there, fellas," Evan murmured.

He scurried to the front of the roof and looked down at the van. From his high angle, he couldn't get a glimpse of Theo Maranan, the great Asian prophet. But Evan had a perfect view of Hannah.

"Come on, baby. Turn around and show me those big browns."

Hannah twisted in the cushions and aimed a nervous glance out the window. Evan chuckled. For all her twitchy instincts, the actress had no idea what she just lost in that alley, the great and awful edit that Evan just made to her story. When left to their untampered fates, Hannah Given and Jury Curado would meet in Terra Vista and smack together like magnets—the man of absolute conviction and the woman of no conviction at all, locked in a vapid dance of physical worship and wall-piercing orgasms. It was an excruciatingly painful spectacle that Evan had suffered a long time ago, back in the days when he tried to be a good little Silver.

Fighting bitter memories, he plucked the twenty-dollar bill from Jury's wallet and sniffed it deeply. Ah, the green, green cash of home. Funny how he'd hated his Earth so much when he lived there and now he missed it terribly. Sadly, his rewind talent stopped at the canned goods section of Nico's store. He couldn't jump back any further. Home was forever just a few seconds out of reach.

Now here at the start of his fifty-fifth play-through, his fifty-fifth trip through the same half decade, Evan Rander was not a fan of his adopted Earth. He knew there was only one escape from his carousel hell, and yet he couldn't find the nerve to end himself. What else could he do then but keep on spinning? What better way to fill his endless days than by punishing the sisters and Silvers who'd wronged him?

As the Salgado van pulled away from the curb, Evan stood up and straightened his shirt. He whistled a happy tune on the way back to the fire ladder. He didn't know where he'd heard the song before. He wasn't even sure which Earth it came from.

TEN

Sunday was a day of rest for the Silvers. Though the physicists attended to their needs like conscientious butlers, the guests were left to wallow and mingle amongst themselves. Amanda learned that Mia harbored authorly ambitions, and had earned an academic award for the fifty-page biography she wrote about her grandmother. Hannah learned that David was a fellow stage performer, one who'd danced and crooned at high schools all around the world. His bare rendition of "Johanna" from *Sweeney Todd* was gorgeous enough to melt her. She spent the rest of the day uncomfortably aroused.

Zack, meanwhile, discovered that plastic was called *bresin* in this neck of the multiverse. He also learned that he could bend time.

He remained tensely withdrawn in the wake of his revelation, sketching tiny shapes in the corner of his pad and then erasing them with the sheer act of thought. By his thirtieth undoodling, he finally saw the prudence of Amanda's argument. It was too much to deal with, too soon.

On Monday, the work began. The group was ushered through an eight-hour gauntlet of medical tests. To Quint's surprise, Zack remained perfectly docile through all the pokings and proddings. This time it was David who caused the trouble. The boy refused to submit to a single examination until the scientists gave him back his heirloom wristwatch. The moment they complied, his cordial smile returned and he became fully cooperative.

On Tuesday, the guests were ushered to individual rooms and asked to recount the awful events of Saturday morning. They relayed their tales with varying degrees of detail and tears, Hannah winning readily on both counts. She was also the only one brave enough to divulge her weirdness, her strange attack of acceleration at the downtown marina. The news triggered an avalanche of chatter among the physicists, forcing Quint to send a staff bitmail.

People, let's not get ahead of ourselves. We need to understand the basics before we get to the unusuals.

The interviews continued throughout the week, question after question about the Earth that no longer was. The Silvers were asked to name the U.S. presidents in reverse order, a task that four of them botched after Franklin Roosevelt. Only Mia, six weeks fresh from her eighth-grade history final, was able to rattle off names without pause. Her interviewers stopped her at William McKinley.

By Friday, the queries had turned from vague to specific to suspiciously pointed. One in particular had the group talking at dinner.

"'Do you know of any historical event that occurred on October 5, 1912?'"

"Yeah, they asked me that one."

"Me too."

"What did you say?"

"*Titanic.*"

"I said *Titanic.*"

"That happened in April."

"Really? Damn. I was so sure I got that."

"Don't feel bad," David told Hannah. "I think they got the answer they were looking for."

"What do you mean?"

"They're cataloging the differences between their history and ours. Trying to pinpoint the first major event that happened on one world but not the other. Given the fact that none of us know the significance of October 5, 1912, I'd say they found it."

While the table fell silent in heady dither, Zack scribbled furiously into his sketchbook. "This is bullshit. Quint promised us a two-way exchange of information. He hasn't told us a thing."

He pressed the pad to his cheek and aimed it at the ceiling camera. A large and angry word balloon pointed to his mouth. *WE WANT INFO!*

One floor up, Quint leveled an icy stare at his monitor. He dialed Czerny from his desk phone.

"I think our guests are in need of entertainment."

The next day, physicists installed a sleek device in the lounge: a dark gray console the size of a pizza box. Above it, a five-foot pane of smoky black glass rested on metal stands.

The group watched Czerny with puppy-headed interest as he inserted a small cartridge into the machine. For the next two hours, the Silvers sat wide-eyed, mesmerized by their first taste of lumivision. Crystal-clear sounds filled the room from every corner. The colors popped off the screen like oil paint. Mia couldn't spot the image pixels, even when pressing her eyes to the glass.

They were soon given a teeming box of blockbuster movies, enough to keep them busy for months. It didn't escape anyone's notice that the films were all space operas and fantasy sagas, nothing that would shed light on the world outside their window. Once Mia figured out the console controls, she confirmed Zack's suspicion that the physicists blocked their access to live broadcast channels.

"It's nothing sinister," Quint later assured them. "We're merely trying to limit your culture shock. Have patience. When the time is right, we'll tell you everything we know."

None of them was convinced, but at least now they were distracted. The Silvers gradually settled into their routine like office drones, cooperating with the scientists by day and retreating into escapist entertainments at night. By the end of July, even Zack had grown lazy in limbo. The shock of apocalypse had settled into a more enduring malaise. He wasn't in a hurry to have his mind jostled again.

On August 6, a million angry pathogens invaded the property on the skin of a sniffling physicist, clobbering the foreign immune systems of every guest. Only David got off lightly with a runny nose. The rest were thrown deep into flu.

For Beatrice Caudell, part-time biologist and full-time germaphobe, this was Armageddon. She squeaked a litany of worst-case scenarios to Czerny—tales of viral mutation and global decimation. None of her fears came to pass. But when Hannah sneezed her way into a whole new velocity, when a fever dream caused Amanda to pulverize the ceiling, when Mia received a get-well note from her future self, and when everyone started hearing the voices in David's head, there was no more hiding from the issue. For Sterling Quint, his physicists, and the poor beleaguered Silvers, it was finally time to address the weirdness.

———

Zack was the first to get a handle on his new peculiarity.

From the moment he grasped the temporal nature of his talent, he embarked on a cautious secret mission to study it. He retreated under his blanket with a penlight, squinting at the pencil strokes on his sketch pad until they disappeared at will. Zack found it a basic but slippery trick of concentration, like spelling words backward.

After a mere day's practice, he was able to banish all sorts of paper-related maladies to a state of never-happenedness—crumples and smudges, rips and spittle. Anything doable was suddenly undoable, a prospect that terrified him as much as it thrilled him. He began smuggling fruits into his room to unslice and de-ripen.

On the day the flu virus invaded his body, he tried to send an orange on an accelerated journey back to its infancy. Instead he accidentally aged it rotten. To Zack's astonishment, he could spin the clock in both directions, though it would be weeks before he gained control of his fast-forward feature.

On August 9, he warily revealed his weirdness to his hosts. Quint, Czerny, and a trio of associates eyed him from the far end of the conference table as he blew his nose into a tissue.

"Okay, this cold's knocking the crap out of me, so I'll keep it short. I seem to have acquired the ability to affect time. I can reverse or advance the chronology of small objects, like a sheet of paper or a piece of bread. I don't know how or why this is happening. I just know that I'm too freaked out to keep it to myself anymore. I'll also stab the first one of you who tries to dissect me. Questions?"

They had questions, enough for Quint to assign a dedicated team to study Zack's new talent. The physicists observed him in a laboratory, recording and measuring as he worked his way through an endless gauntlet of test materials. Glass, metal, bresin, stone—there was seemingly nothing he couldn't de-age. He even restored the missing leg on a wooden horse figurine, though the new limb looked bleached by comparison.

When Zack described his feat to David at their next dinner, the boy became vexed.

"That's insane. I assume the original horse leg still exists somewhere. Did it magically teleport from its location when you restored the figurine? Or did you somehow create a duplicate?"

"The eggheads seem to think it's a duplicate."

David shook his head in agitation. "I can't tell you how much that violates the basic laws of science."

Zack had expected to see the same amount of hair-pulling from the scientists themselves, but they remained oddly placid. If anything, they seemed more interested in the biology behind Zack's power than the physics.

Soon Zack felt daring enough to test his magic on his silver bracelet, with surprising results. Just a small bit of reversing caused the band to break apart into four even quarters, all perfectly polished at the edges.

After showing his accomplishment to Hannah, Mia, and David, he indulged their request to undo their own adornments. Mia hugged Zack with gushing relief. The bracelet had been a wasp on her wrist for days now. She thought it would never go away.

When Amanda learned about Zack's stunt, she pulled him aside in the hallway.

"That was reckless. You could have overshot and hurt someone. You don't know what your time stuff does to living creatures."

The next morning, he found out. Quint interrupted Zack's lab session to release a tiny brown mouse on the table. It had glassy white eyes, a chestnut-size lump on his left side, and several battle scratches.

"This poor fellow's at the end of his road," Quint told Zack. "See if you can fix that."

All throughout dinner that night, the cartoonist remained uncharacteristically quiet. While the others conversed, he stared ahead in vacant consternation.

Mia touched his arm. "You okay?"

"Yeah. I . . ." He stammered a moment, then let out an incredulous chuckle. "I reversed a mouse today. The thing was old and dying. And then suddenly it wasn't. Quint says I sent it all the way back to adolescence."

The others eyed him through deadpan faces, waiting for a smirk or some other indicator he was kidding. He stared in wide-eyed wonder at his hands.

"Jesus Christ."

While David and Zack discussed the philosophical implications of his ability, Mia envisioned his next bombshell announcement. Today Zack rejuvenated a live rodent. Tomorrow he could be resurrecting a dead one. Hannah couldn't help but wonder if his skill worked the other way. Could he turn a young mouse into an old one? Could he do it to a human? *Would* he?

It was Amanda's thoughts that concerned Zack the most. She remained silent for the rest of the meal, and stone-faced throughout the evening movie.

At bedtime, she approached her room and noticed Zack watching her from his doorway.

"What?"

"You've been quiet since I mentioned my mouse trick. Did it upset you?"

"A little," she admitted.

"You want to talk about it?"

She crossed her arms, bathing him in the same inscrutable look that had bugged him for hours.

"No. I'll work it out." She opened her door, then eyed him one last time. "Good night."

Amanda skipped her hygiene and prayers and went straight to bed, her jade eyes dancing in restless bother. She'd devoted half her life to God and medicine and now suddenly this mordant atheist could heal with a flick of a finger. And what came out of her hands?

She rolled on her back and cast a contemptuous glare at her creator. Apparently, among His other faults, the Lord had Zack's sense of humor.

The sisters weren't eager to face their paranormal afflictions.

For their first two weeks in Terra Vista, Hannah and Amanda lived in quiet hope that the churning forces inside them would simply go away—a one-time outbreak, like chicken pox.

Fearing that anger was the catalyst of her unholy white weirdness, Amanda kept an iron lid on her temper. She sat calmly through her daily scientist interviews, answering all questions with clenched-jaw amenity. She held her tongue when Hannah voiced her growing attraction to David, and held her scream when David spoke glowingly of Esis. She ignored all the puns, cracks, and antics of Zack Trillinger, a man who irked her even when he was being nice.

Though the restraint nearly burned her an ulcer, Amanda's perseverance paid off in exactly the way she hoped. For fourteen days, her hands remained blessedly pink and normal.

On August 7, illness and sibling disharmony eroded the walls of her composure. The sisters were the first and worst victims of the invading virus. They spent the afternoon laid up in their room. By nightfall, their foul moods turned on each other.

"I'm just saying he's sixteen, Hannah. It's not healthy."

"Would you shut up about that? I told you we're not doing anything. We're just taking walks together. Jesus."

"Well, you need to be careful. You don't always make the best decisions when you're grieving."

Hannah covered her face. "Oh my God."

"What? Am I wrong? Do you not remember—"

"No, Amanda, you're absolutely right. I make cruel and awful decisions. Like, you remember how I dropped my married name an hour after my husband died? Oh wait. That was you."

Amanda raised her head from the pillow. "I can't believe you said that. I honestly can't believe you just said that."

"Yeah, well, here's a cross and some nails. Have fun up there."

After an hour of livid silence, Amanda fell into fevered dreams. She replayed her final moments with Derek in the waiting room—the frost on his nose, the bitter rage in his voice. *I'm actually glad we're going to different places. What does that say about you?*

A thunderous crash jerked her awake. Coughing in dust, Amanda turned on the lamp and found half the room covered in broken plaster. The outer shell of the ceiling had rained down on them, leaving a rug-size patch of dangling wires and cracked wooden beams.

Hannah had gotten the worst of the downfall. Her face and hair were white with dust. Thin trickles of blood oozed from her forehead, her shoulders.

Amanda rushed to her side. "Hannah! Are you okay?"

"No! What happened?"

"I don't know. I think maybe it was an earthquake. I . . ."

Amanda suddenly registered the jarring nakedness on her arms. Her shirtsleeves were shredded. The fiber cast on her wrist had mysteriously vanished. Even her wedding ring was gone.

Oh no . . .

Three hours later, she sat in the medical lab, staring darkly at her lap while Czerny made a replacement cast for her.

"Your sister's fine," he assured Amanda. "She's already sleeping. The damage—"

"I want to see the surveillance footage."

Czerny paused his work. "I'm not sure that's wise, Amanda."

"I have to see it. Please."

Soon she sat in his office, watching a bird's-eye recording of the sisters in slumber. As Amanda writhed in bed, a thick and craggy whiteness expanded from the skin of her arms—snapping her ring, rending her cast. She threw her palms upward in somnolent fury. They exploded like fire hoses, shooting flowing cones of force at the ceiling camera. The video turned to snowy static.

The shock of the incident sent Amanda into self-imposed exile. She retreated to her new single, accepting no visitors, opening her door only for food trays and sedatives.

"I don't care what it takes," she told Quint over the phone. "I'll consent to any test. Any procedure. Just find out what's in me and *get it out.*"

At noon, Hannah shambled out of bed and joined the others for lunch in the bistro. She poked a feeble spoon at her chicken soup, her body wallowing under its many new aches and bandages.

"Has anyone spoken to my sister?"

"I did," Mia replied, through a sickly rasp. "She'd only talk to me through the door. She won't let anyone come near her until she's cured of her thing."

Zack shook his head. "There's no cure. She just has to learn how to control it."

"Tall order," David griped. By all accounts, the boy was having his own weirdness issues—strange, ghostly sounds that plagued him day and night. Just five minutes before Hannah came downstairs, an invisible baby cried right in his ear. Zack and Mia heard it too.

"Maybe you can talk her out," Zack said to Hannah.

She snorted cynically. "I was never able to convince her of anything. And after the awful thing I said to her last night, I'm better off . . . just . . ."

Hannah turned away for a soul-rattling sneeze. The moment it passed, she felt a deep chill on her skin. She saw her own spray fluttering lazily in the air, like tiny bumblebees. Her vision turned a deep shade of blue.

"Okay, this is strange. I . . ."

She noticed others staring at her in motionless silence, their eyes widening at a creakingly slow pace. The steam from David's tea dawdled in fat, languid puffs.

Hannah launched from her chair. "Oh no. It's happening again. Oh God. Someone get Dr. Czerny!"

She realized that none of them could understand her in her accelerated state. Her words were probably coming out as fast as shoe squeaks.

She made a stumbling exit from the bistro, praying to any available god to please, please, please let this madness be temporary. She couldn't think of a worse hell than spending the rest of her life in prestissimo, an incomprehensible blur to the people around her.

Determined not to dislocate another shoulder, Hannah proceeded up the stairwell with tightrope caution. She knocked on the door to Czerny's office, then pulled her hand back in agony. Her knuckles throbbed like she'd just punched a mailbox from the window of a speeding car.

By the time Czerny stepped outside, Hannah's velocity spell had ended. He found her crouched against the wall, crying and holding her injured hand.

"What's happening to me?"

After a baby spot, a hand splint, and a long night of rest, Hannah met with the physicists for her first controlled attempt at triggering her anomaly. She concentrated, meditated, ruminated for hours. Nothing. The next day, a stray thought accidentally brushed the ignition switch in her mind, triggering seventeen seconds of blue acceleration. Czerny patted her back and offered lyrical promises of a better day tomorrow.

He was right. At 8 P.M. the next night, Hannah excitedly knocked on her sister's door.

"Amanda? It's me. Open up."

Amanda stumbled out of bed, her eyes drooped and bleary from opiates. "Hannah?"

"Yeah. I have good news but you have to open up."

Amanda cracked the door three inches and peeked at her. By now all Hannah's cuts had healed into faint red lines. A new wire splint kept her sprained knuckles flat.

"Did I do that to you?"

"No. I did it. I had another attack but I'm okay. Dr. Czerny helped me find the trigger. I can control it now!"

"I have no idea what you're—"

"My weirdness," Hannah explained. "I can turn it on and off. Once I found the mental switch, it was so easy. Like going from talking to singing. If I can do it, so can you."

Amanda eyed her jadedly. Hannah's smile faded away. "Look, you're going to have to do something. You can't stay in there the rest of your life."

"I almost killed you, Hannah."

"Well, you didn't. I'm fine now. And I'm not the only thing that got fixed up. Look."

Hannah passed her a small item from her pocket, Amanda's diamond and gold wedding ring. Despite its violent expulsion from the widow's finger, the band seemed good as new.

"I found it in the wreckage," Hannah told her. "The thing was so messed up, it looked like a half-melted horseshoe."

"It looks great now. How did you fix it?"

"Zack. He says, 'You're welcome.' And I'm saying come out and join us again. Please? We miss you. *I* miss you."

The next morning, Amanda sat alone in a second-floor lab, surrounded by towers of elaborate monitoring equipment. A team of physicists watched her from the next room, assuring her through the intercom that it was safe to conjure the whiteness. Though Amanda tried for three hours, the creature wouldn't come out. She was mostly relieved.

Hannah, meanwhile, continued to work with the scientists to gauge the limits of her velocity. On Monday, she crossed the lawn at an external clock speed of ninety-two miles an hour. On Tuesday, she topped out at ninety-nine. On Wednesday, she broke the three-digit barrier, then nearly snapped her leg when she tripped on a sprinkler nozzle.

"You need to be careful," Czerny reminded her. "Though it doesn't feel like it, you're moving with ten, twenty times your usual momentum. In that mode, you're all but made of glass."

On Thursday, Hannah reached a running speed of 128 miles per hour. She fought a giddy cackle at the readout. Time had consistently gotten away from her in her old life, leaving her in a perpetual state of scrambling lateness. Now suddenly the clock bent to her will like a love-struck suitor. This world would be rushing to catch up to her.

"It is amazing," David admitted. "You've been given a true gift."

The two of them had made an evening custom of strolling the property together. They walked arm in arm inside the fenced perimeter, trading feather-light chatter and crooning soft duets of pop classics. Normally they refrained from discussing their burgeoning paranormalities, but things had been going uncommonly well for one of them.

"Well, let's not go nuts," Hannah said. "I'm just zipping around."

"It's not the speed I'm marveling at. It's the way you experience more time than the rest of us. You could live a full hour in the span of a minute, or a day in the span of an hour. Now that we're aware of how fragile the universe is, our time seems more precious than ever. And now you have the power to make more of it. That's pretty incredible to me. But what do I know?"

Hannah studied David with uneasy regard. For all her protests, she knew she'd become a little infatuated with the boy. He was a world-class genius, a vegan, a thespian, a sweetheart. All that and gorgeous too. She was almost grateful that he was sixteen, and quite possibly gay. The actress had enough drama to handle.

She squeezed David's arm and breathed a wistful sigh.

"You know plenty. For a kid."

While Hannah continued to conquer her talents, Amanda languished in hopeless stagnation. Frustrated, she tracked Zack to the kitchenette. The cartoonist had grown tired of catered food tins and insisted on making his own meals. His culinary prowess didn't extend far beyond cold cuts.

Amanda watched in bother as he reversed a burnt sandwich roll to a healthy golden brown.

"How do you do it, Zack?"

"If you're asking about the science, you're talking to the wrong nerd."

"I'm asking how you got control," she said. "You seem to have a perfect handle on your condition. I feel like I have a big white beast living inside of me."

"Well, that's your problem right there."

"What is?"

"The way you're looking at it. Whatever's going on with us, it's not a disease. It's not a beast. It's just a new muscle. You're never going to control it if you're too afraid to flex it."

She narrowed her eyes at him. "That's easy for you to say. You heal things with your hands. I hurt things with mine. One wrong move and I could kill someone."

"So?"

Amanda blinked at him. "What do you mean 'so?'"

"I mean 'so what?' You think this is the first time you've been at risk of killing someone? You're a nurse. The wrong injection and *boom*, dead patient. That never stopped you from working. You could run over three people on the way to the office. That never stopped you from driving. You did these things, despite the risks, because you knew they were necessary to living. Well, guess what? Controlling this thing of yours is now a necessity. It's your new day job. So if you're as strong as I think you are—and I think you are—you'll stop worrying about the maybes and do your job."

On August 13, Amanda successfully summoned the beast. The whiteness neatly emerged from her hands and only mildly spiked when a physicist approached her. The next day, she formed solid blocks around her arms, then just as quickly dispatched them. Contrary to Zack's assumption, Amanda found her talent worked less like a muscle and more like a language. Each construct was a sentence, one she could make long or short, crude or elegant. The choice was hers, as long as she kept calm.

Two days later, she indulged Zack's request for a demonstration by forming little shapes around the tips of her fingers. Cubes, spheres, pyramids, cylinders. She coated an arm in a sleek sheet of whiteness, an opera glove that moved perfectly with her wiggling fingers.

Zack gawked in bright marvel. "Holy crap. That is . . . wow, you're like Green Lantern without the green. I'm officially jealous."

"I'd trade you if I could," she told him. "I'd rather heal mice."

"Come on. You have to like it a little now."

She didn't, but she hated it less. Though Amanda now wore her wedding ring on a cheap string necklace, she no longer worried about fatal outbursts. She'd acquired enough control to move forward, into the larger issues.

"I still don't know what this stuff is," she told Czerny, at the end of a long practice session.

He promised her the answer was coming. Dr. Quint was preparing a presentation that would soon explain many things.

The following week, Amanda dazzled her fellow Silvers with an eight-inch snowflake, beautifully complex and symmetrical. It balanced on the tip of her finger, slowly rotating like a store display. She took a satirical bow to the applause of her friends.

Though Hannah had joined in on the clapping, her cheer was half performance. She didn't know the name of Amanda's aberrant energy. She just knew that it was the same white death that had rained down on their world, toppling buildings and crushing bodies. Since the eve of her sister's sleeping attack, Hannah had suffered a few nightmares of her own. In her cruel visions, Amanda didn't just bring down the ceiling. She brought down the sky.

While the other Silvers wrestled with their formidable new talents, Mia Farisi became a growing enigma to the Pelletier physicists. Unlike her companions, who brazenly broke the laws of time and nature, the girl had yet to display a single hint of chronokinetic ability.

In truth, Mia had been struggling with her weirdness from the day she arrived. Her temporal quirk was too subtle for the cameras to register, too insane to share with others. She figured even Zack wouldn't believe her when she showed him her precognitive paper scraps. He'd probably assume her mind had cracked into split personalities. She wasn't ready to rule out the possibility herself.

On her third night in Terra Vista, Mia returned to her bed and found a tiny new roll of paper on her pillow. Unfurling it revealed a fresh missive, once again scribbled in her handwriting.

I know you're freaking out right now. So was I. I know you're skeptical about these notes. So was I. But trust me when I say that our power's a blessing, not a curse. I'm loving it now. And I'm only six months older than you.

She continued to manage her problem in secret, receiving at least one new dispatch each night. The messages ranged from the obscure to the inane.

Took my first ride in a flying cab today. Holy @$#%!

Commemoration has to be worst holiday ever. Learn to dread October 5th.

If you see a small and creepy guy with a 55 on his hand, run. That's Evan Rander. He's bad news.

There are no words to describe what they did with New York. So beautiful, it brings me to tears.

On her fifth night, Mia finally saw a portal up close. A shimmering disc, as small as a button and as bright as a penlight, hovered a foot above her pillow. Its tiny surface rippled like a thimble of milk. Before Mia could get a closer look, the portal spit a new note and then shrank out of existence. She unrolled the paper.

Don't trust Peter. He's not who he says he is.

Ten minutes later, she was awoken by another tiny breach just inches above her face. A new piece of paper dropped onto her nose.

Disregard that first note. I was just testing something. Peter's good. He's great, actually.

Daunted by all the baffling new intel, Mia asked Czerny for a journal. "Just to collect my thoughts," she told him, with loaded candor.

The next day, he indulged and insulted her with a ferociously girlish pocket diary—neon-pink, and covered in cartoon hearts. She tepidly thanked him, then transcribed every note she'd received. The original papers were flushed into the sea.

Soon it became routine for the others to find Mia scrutinizing her journal, tapping her pen in deep contemplation.

"What are you writing in there?" David asked her one night. He playfully peeked over her shoulder. "Anything about me?"

She slammed the book shut. "No. Go away."

Despite his blistering intelligence, David often displayed the social tact of an eight-year-old. He openly guessed that the scar on Hannah's wrist was self-inflicted. He idly observed that Amanda and Zack had nearly identical builds. He informed Mia that she would suffer fewer stomachaches if she ate more sensible portions. After each thoughtless gaffe, he turned sheepish in the heat of his victim's stare.

"I was raised by a brilliant scientist with atrocious personal skills," he explained to Mia. "From an early age, I was dragged through a gauntlet of foreign nations, each one with different rules of etiquette. Suffice it to say I'm a little bit strange. I might as well be from a third Earth entirely."

Once Mia caught David canoodling with Hannah, walking arm in arm around the property like old Victorian lovers, she lost her fluttering crush on him. For all his alleged nonconformity, his fondness for large-breasted dingbats made him tragically typical. On the upside, Mia could finally relax around him. Her stomachaches gradually stopped.

On the second night of August, she received a tear-stained message on a scrap of motel stationery.

> God, it makes me sick to look at you. The fat, clueless idiot I used to be. You think you're adjusting? You think you're getting a handle on your new life here? Trust me, hon. Your problems haven't even started.

Beatrice Caudell watched on the monitor as Mia crumpled the note into an angry ball. An hour later, while the Silvers dined, Beatrice searched Mia's room and found the paper under the bed. Soon it lay flat and wrinkled on the desk of Sterling Quint.

He suddenly became very interested in his youngest guest.

Brace yourself, an older Mia warned her. *Things are about to get hairy.*

On August 7, twelve hours after Amanda brought the ceiling down on her sister, Mia stood outside her door with Czerny, hoping to coax her out of exile. While the good doctor expounded with flowery optimism, Mia teetered miserably with flu. She would have killed for some of her grandmother's minestrone, or at least a good long nap. But Amanda needed her support.

Don't ever take her for granted, her future self insisted. *She's the best person you'll ever know on this world.*

Suddenly Mia noticed a shimmering disc of light in front of her. She assumed it was another spot in her vision until it spit out a roll of pink paper.

Czerny furrowed his brow at the tiny object. "What is that?"

She scrambled to pick it up. "Nothing. I dropped something."

Unconvinced, the good doctor harangued her until she finally confessed her predicament. The news spread like current through the building. Quint was exuberant to the point of giddiness. The Holy Grail of temporal physics was now resting under his roof, nestled inside a meek little girl.

It wasn't until the hullabaloo of the day finally ended that Mia remembered to read her latest message.

Sorry you're sick. Feel better soon.

She rolled her eyes. "Thanks."

Two days later, Mia lunched in the bistro with Zack and David, chortling with laughter as they tried to one-up each other with tales of past social blunders. A small glow suddenly materialized above the table like a firefly. David and Zack jumped back in alarm.

"It's okay," Mia told them. "It's mine. A note should come out any second."

The men leaned closer to look, but nothing emerged. As she moved toward the portal, Mia was stunned to discover that, for the first time, she could glimpse through the keyhole. She saw her own face, red-nosed and puffy-eyed. Her future self was sick with flu. *Again?*

No. The more she saw through the portal, the more she *felt* through it. She could feel herself standing outside Amanda's door, nodding off to Czerny's blather.

"Oh my God . . ."

"What?"

"What are you talking about?"

He let out a feeble sigh. "Look, we're obviously going back to the police station. There's not much we can do about that. But if we coordinate our story, only one of us will be put in a holding cell. All you have to do is tell them I kidnapped you—"

"No!"

"No way!"

"It's the only chance we have of escaping!" Zack insisted.

"For us," Amanda shot back. "Not for you."

"There has to be a way through the barrier!" Mia exclaimed. "Why would I write it to myself if it wasn't true?"

Amanda winced in frustration. She could feel the tempic wall in her mind. She could even touch it, in ways she couldn't explain. But as sure as she knew anything, she knew she couldn't do more than make a few ripples in the surface.

Twenty feet from the passenger side, a policeman shouted through the ghosted window. "Turn off the engine and step outside with your hands up. It's the only way you're getting out of this in one piece."

Theo lifted Rebel's gun by the edge of the handle, then carefully placed it under his seat. "I hate to say it, but I think we're out of options."

"Let's just do what they tell us," Hannah said, her eyes welling with tears. "I don't want to die. I don't want to see any of you die."

"But what'll they do to us?" Mia asked.

"I don't know, sweetie, but is it any worse than getting shot to death?"

David shook his head in bother. "I can't believe what I'm hearing. We just survived six murderous people who had talents like ours. They attacked us without warning and we still beat them. Now after all that, you're looking to surrender to four mere coppers?"

"It's not that simple," Amanda said.

"Of course it is. They have weapons. So do we. We know theirs. They don't know ours. If we work intelligently, we could disarm them before they even know what hit them."

Once again, everyone stared at David in dark wonder. He was getting used to the look.

"That's crazy," Hannah griped. "You're going to get us all killed."

Theo nodded. "She's right. We only got out of that building through dumb luck. We push it again and someone's going to die."

Mia bit her thumb in tense deliberation. She fell well on the side of the cautious majority, and yet she knew that without David's reckless gallantry, she'd be a frozen corpse in the security room.

Zack kept his tense gaze fixed on the windshield. He could see hints of the tempic barrier through the clouds and cracks, an urgent puzzle that taunted him. If only Quint hadn't been so damn stingy with his information.

His brow suddenly rose. His mouth fell open. "Oh. Wait a second."

While David continued to argue with Theo and the sisters, Zack turned around in his seat.

"Wait a second! Guys!"

He got their attention. Between his wide eyes and hanging jaw, his friends saw a glimmer of hope.

"I know how to get through it."

Zack's good news wasn't good at all to the Great Sisters Given.

"No!" Amanda yelled. "Absolutely not!"

It took him just nineteen seconds to explain his idea. While he filled in the others, he removed the Salgados' nightstick from the door holster and passed it to an incredulous Hannah.

"One of those two posts has the generator. It could be on the outside. It could be on the inside. In any case, you break it and the wall goes away."

Two weeks ago, when Quint demonstrated a tempic barrier in action, Zack had noticed a thermos-size power pack on the frame. According to Quint, tempis didn't run on electricity. It was fueled by something called solis. But power was power. Lack of power, in this case, was freedom.

There was, however, one significant drawback to the plan.

"You're risking my sister's life!" Amanda snapped.

"It is a risk," Zack acknowledged. "I'd do it myself if I could. But Hannah's the only one who can smash it. She's the only one fast enough to get away."

"It could work," David said. "If she attacks from the woods, as Zack suggested, they won't even notice her until the barrier's down."

Mia peeked out the ghosted window as stealthily as she could. "But the motorcycle cops are wearing speedsuits . . ."

"Yes, but they're not wearing shifters," Zack replied. "The shifters are in the bikes. They can't speed on foot."

"How the hell do you know that?"

He looked back to Amanda, suddenly sheepish. "I saw it on lumivision."

"Oh my God . . ."

"I'm right about this. I'm telling you."

"No. I'm not letting you do this. You're not throwing my sister's life away on some stupid—"

"I'll do it."

"—half-assed plan that doesn't even make sense."

"I'll do it," Hannah repeated, in a tiny voice. She held the nightstick with white-knuckled fear. Rubber and wood, against two metal posts and four men with guns.

"Hannah, you can't!"

"If there's a choice besides dying and getting arrested, I'll take it," she said. "I don't want us getting separated. I don't want to end up in some government facility or wherever they put people like us. I just want to live in a nice apartment and do musical theater. I'm sick of all the weirdness."

Theo looked to the semblant rear doors. Gloved fingers briefly popped through the surface, testing the nonmaterial before hastily retreating. His mind fell into a jackhammer refrain. *Tear gas tear gas tear gas tear gas . . .*

"Tear gas," he said. "They know the back door's fake and they're going to throw in tear gas."

"What?"

"How do you know?"

"I think I just overheard it."

He didn't, but he was right all the same.

"We have about a minute before—"

The van was suddenly filled with a blast of heat, accelerated air molecules spreading in all directions. The Silvers winced. By the time they opened their eyes, Hannah was gone.

———

She ran into the woods at 155 miles an hour. Pebbles flew like buckshot from beneath her sneakers. The air around her was icy cold and her vision had turned almost uniformly blue. There was a fresh new ringing in her ears that, when she focused on it, sounded a little bit like music.

The actress slipped between the trees, then surveyed the road from a hidden distance. In her accelerated vision, the tempic barrier swirled with smoky gray wisps. She studied the thick metal posts of the blockade. She wasn't sure she could break them, even at top speed.

"God, Zack. What were you think—"

"Quit squirming!"

Hannah scanned the area in a startled twirl. The words had come through a woman's harsh whisper, but there was no one else around. She shouldn't have been able to hear anyone in her shifted state.

She figured her nerves were playing tricks on her, with good reason. The motorcycle cops had caught her blurry dash to the trees and were now beginning a slow turn in her direction. Hannah watched their speedsuits in breathless anticipation. They didn't light up. *Oh thank God. At least Zack got that part ri—*

"I mean it, Jury! Quit moving! I don't want to rift you!"

Hannah glanced to her left and now saw a young, dark-haired couple hiding behind a nearby tree. The man was olive skinned, muscular, and exquisitely handsome. He wore a black T-shirt over jeans and grasped his companion tightly from behind. Though the woman's face was obscured, she was built and dressed like Hannah. Her shoulder-length hair was even beginning to show its brown roots, just like Hannah's.

The pair kept an anxious vigil on an empty patch of highway, twenty yards north of the tempic barrier. Despite their edgy posture, Hannah saw the tender way the man and woman touched each other. They were clearly intimate.

Before Hannah could speak, the brunette brushed her hair behind her ear. Now Hannah had a clear view of her face. *Her* face. Her own side profile, as seen in countless photos.

With a high scream, Hannah fell out of velocity and toppled to the dirt.

The illusive couple disappeared in a blink. Hannah reeled in mad perplexity. She couldn't shift. She couldn't move. She couldn't stop looking at the empty space where her ghostly self and lover once stood.

Four seconds after her sister left the van, Amanda heard her fragmented shriek from the woods. Her mind stammered in panic. *Something, something, something went—*

"Wrong. Something went wrong. She's in trouble."

Zack launched a nervous stare through the clouded glass. "She just left. Give her time."

"No. This was a bad idea, Zack. You're going to get her killed."

Theo flinched in worry as Amanda moved in front of a clear window. "You shouldn't stand there."

David nodded. "He's right. Please sit down."

Amanda ignored them. Her green eyes bulged as the highway patrolmen proceeded, guns drawn, to the edge of the woods.

"No. No. No no no no . . ."

Mia kept her wary gaze on Amanda. She had one warning left from her future self, the worst one by far. Now all the alarms in her head were ringing.

"Amanda . . ."

With frantic eyes, Amanda looked to the intangible rear doors. Mia slid down the seat, speaking in a low and maternal tone. "Amanda, you can't go out there . . ."

"She's my sister."

"You promised me you'd stay in the van."

"They're going to shoot her."

"They'll shoot *you*! If you leave this van right now, they will shoot you and you will die! It already happened! I got the note!"

The men eyed Mia with fresh apprehension. This was news to them.

"I really think you should listen to her," Zack implored Amanda.

"Please! Please listen to me!"

Amanda's shallow breaths slowed down to gulps. "Okay. Okay."

Mia closed her eyes and exhaled. *Thank God.*

"I'm sorry, Mia . . ."

"It's all right. You listened. It's not—"

"I'm sorry."

Amanda turned to the window. "I'M COMING OUT! DON'T SHOOT!"

"No!"

With a final look of remorse, Amanda brushed past Mia. She hurried through the ghosted doors, out into the open air.

"Amanda!"

In another string of time, another elsewhile, Amanda might have burst through the illusory hatch without a hint of announcement. Her sudden emergence might have startled a policeman into firing a fatal shot. But Mia's warning prompted Amanda to issue one of her own. With five shouted words, she eased the pressure on the policemen's triggers just enough to exit the van unharmed.

The cruiser cops raised their guns at her. Amanda kept her bloody fingers pointed at the ground.

"Show me your hands!" a cop shouted.

Amanda eyed them with savage defiance. "Call your other men back here."

"Show me your goddamn hands!"

"You call your other men back here *right now*!"

Blood rushed to Mia's face. She scrambled to the exit, only to be caught by her shirtsleeve.

"Let me go!"

"No," said Theo, grimacing in pain. "No more bad ideas."

It was Theo's bad idea to grab her with his wounded arm. She broke free and sprinted toward the doors. David rushed after her.

"Mia, don't!"

It never occurred to Mia that she already saved Amanda's life, or that she was making the very same mistake she helped Amanda avoid. The moment she burst through the ghosted doors without warning, the policemen aimed their pistols at her head.

One of them fired.

Mia Farisi never considered herself a lucky girl, any more than she considered herself tall or svelte. And yet there were a few scattered nights on this

world when she marveled at the miraculous circumstances behind her continued existence. She'd been spared from apocalypse by mysterious forces,
saved from asphyxiation with the help of a future self. And then just twelve
minutes ago, she was rescued from death by a brave and beautiful boy who,
for reasons she'd love to hear one day, preferred a world with her in it.

She was lucky, never more so than now.

The bullet flew past Mia's face, brushing her cheek with warm air before
passing through the van and piercing a hole in the windshield.

The moment the shot rang out, Amanda stopped thinking about her sister. Her skin turned hot. Her mind went blank.

She showed the policemen her hands.

The tempis exploded from both palms, launching up the highway in two
jagged cones. In the half-second journey between Amanda and her targets, a
giant white hand had bloomed at the end of each projectile. They grabbed the
policemen like rag dolls, pinning them down to the concrete. Amanda could
feel every button on their shirts, each newly broken rib in their chests. She
idly began counting the fractures as if she were merely having a strange
dream.

"Amanda, stop!"

The tempic arms vanished at the sound of David's voice. Amanda cast a
stunned gaze at the cops, then David, then her own twitching palms.

"What . . . what did I . . . ?"

"Come on!"

David seized Mia and Amanda by the wrists, pulling them back inside.
Zack hit the gas pedal. The van traveled a hundred feet before the fog of Mia's
shock cleared away.

"Wait. What happened to the barrier?"

"It's down," said Zack. "Hannah did it."

Amanda looked through the grate, at the empty passenger seat.

"Where is she?"

Hannah heard the loud standoff between the cruiser cops and Amanda.
Even in her muddled state, she could tell her sister had once again become
Madmanda—unyielding, unforgiving, impervious to fear or reason.

When the gunshot was fired, Hannah finally broke her paralysis. She jumped to her feet and scanned the area. Amanda was still standing, thank God, but the cruiser cops weren't. The sight of her sister's giant tempic arms was enough to rattle the two motorcycle patrolmen. They retreated from the edge of the woods and raised their pistols at Amanda.

"NO!"

Hannah shifted back into high speed and rushed toward them, thumping the barrel of each gun with her nightstick. As the weapons fell to the earth in a slow-motion twirl, Hannah noticed the twisted bouquet of broken fingers she'd left behind on each patrolman. Their faces were already beginning to contort in pain.

"Oh my God! I'm so sorry!" she yelled, hopelessly incoherent.

She ran to the tempic barrier, smacking the metal post with her baton. The reverberation shot all the way up her arm, rattling her bones. The barrier seemed no worse for the wear.

"Damn it! Come on!"

Hannah ran to the other post and noticed a metal protrusion on the outer edge. It was the size of a salt shaker, and sported three tiny green lights. Maybe Zack was right after all.

"Come on. Please."

She struck the protrusion. The barrier flickered for a moment, then recovered.

"COME ON!"

A final desperate swing, and the generator exploded in a ball of sparks. The nightstick broke in half. Hannah de-shifted and clutched her throbbing hand, then scanned the results of her last strike.

The tempis was gone.

Zack didn't waste a breath hitting the gas pedal. Hannah watched the clouds disappear from the driver's-side window as the van screeched past her. Zack caught her gaze and pointed straight ahead. Hannah threw her arms out, flummoxed.

"Wait. What does that mean? Where are you going?"

The vehicle moved on without her, a fact that hadn't gone unnoticed by the others.

"What the hell are you doing?!"

Zack threw a quick glance back at Amanda. "We need to get off the high-way before those other cops get back on their motorcycles. It's the only chance we have."

"You left her back there!"

"She'll catch up."

"Not if she's hurt!"

"She's not hurt. I saw her."

"Zack, turn around and get her! Now!"

"Listen to me. Your sister can run at over a hundred miles an hour. This van can't even crack fifty. She'll catch up. Trust me."

"After all your stupid decisions, I don't trust you at all!"

"You're criticizing *me* for stupid decisions? What you just did—"

"Zack, I'm telling you for the last time . . ."

A small hand grabbed Amanda's shoulder, turning her around. She barely had time to process Mia before the girl slapped her across the cheek. Heavy tears ran down her face.

"You didn't listen! You didn't listen to me and you almost got killed!"

Stunned and hurt, Amanda took a step back. "Mia . . ."

"Don't you *ever* do that again! You *listen* to me!"

"I'm sorry."

"I can't lose anyone else!"

"Mia . . ."

"I can't lose anyone else!"

Amanda pulled her into her arms, holding her tight with aching grief. The two of them had met right here, in the back of this very van. Six weeks had never felt like such an eternity to Amanda. Time never felt so broken.

Theo scanned the empty road behind them, then turned grim. "Zack . . ."

For the twentieth time in the last ten seconds, Zack checked the rearview mirror. The exit was approaching fast, and Hannah wasn't. His stomach seared with acid.

"She'll catch up," he uttered. "She knows what she's doing."

Amanda took a deep wet sniff over Mia's head. "Zack, I'm begging you . . ."

She didn't have to. He slowed to a stop at the off-ramp. He hated making mistakes, even on small things. This was not a small thing.

"All right. I'm turning around."

A dark blur crossed the windshield. Another blast of heat filled the front of the van. By the time Zack turned to look, Hannah glared at him from the passenger seat.

"Go!"

With a hot breath, Zack stomped the pedal. The van hugged the winding exit from Highway V, then disappeared into the tree-lined suburbs of South California.

FIFTEEN

Quint didn't like what he saw in the mirror. At every stop on his morning commute, he examined the dark new bags under his eyes, the jaundiced hue of his skin. He'd spent a long and sleepless weekend devising a scheme to kill Zack Trillinger, for reasons he convinced himself were absolutely vital to science.

By the time he reached the garage, at 7:25, he'd smothered the last of his doubts. This could work. This *would* work. The plan would go off without a hitch and everything would be okay again.

At 7:26, the universe sharply corrected him.

Quint's knees buckled with strain as he eyed the bloodbath in the lobby— four dead strangers in multiple pieces, plus a frozen body that Quint could only guess was once a Salgado. He sidestepped the blood on the landing, only to find another spatter on the wall of the second floor hallway.

Having spotted Czerny's car in the garage, Quint unlocked the door to his office and found Beatrice Caudell splayed dead on the rug. Her small blue eyes were bloodshot and frozen open in shock.

Quint held the wall for support and staggered down the hall. His office was the last room in the building to contain life—ninety-eight rodents, plus two surprise visitors he only loosely deemed to be human.

"Hello, Sterling."

Azral sat on the edge of Quint's desk, his face a calm and genial mask. Esis stood among the mouse cages, petting the fur of a small white youngling. Quint noticed that all the other rodents were engaged in rampant copulation. The madwoman had redistributed his creatures, mixing browns with whites, males with females. Five years of meticulous breeding, ruined.

"What in God's name happened here?"

"The facility was attacked," Azral informed him.

"Attacked? By who? Who are those people downstairs?"

"Brown mice," said Esis, with a look of wry mischief.

Though Azral smirked with humor, the joke flew several feet over Quint's head. He wanted to wring both their necks.

"They're natives like yourself," Azral told him. "Though a more unique strain."

"I don't understand. How could this have happened?"

"How indeed?" Esis asked, with a pointed glare at Azral. He sighed with soft contrition.

"The error is mine. I underestimated these people, despite the warnings of my ever-wise mother."

Esis crossed her arms in a showy pout. Quint studied her in daft surprise. The woman looked ten years younger than the man who called her Mother.

"Where's everyone else? What happened to the subjects?"

"The Silvers are alive," said Azral. "But they won't be returning. The plan has changed."

"Changed how?"

"That's no longer your concern. Though I hold you blameless in this latest trouble, I'm afraid this is the end of your involvement in our project."

Dumbfounded, Quint studied Azral in the vain hope that this was just another peculiar gag.

"No. You can't cut me loose after all this time, without any explanation."

"You'll find I can indeed do such a thing."

"You owe me answers, goddamn it! One of my employees is dead!"

"All of your employees are dead," Esis casually informed him.

The nausea came back full force. Quint leaned against a bookshelf. "What? Why?"

"A necessary evil," Azral sighed. "I seek to prevent future complications. If it's any comfort, none of your people suffered much. Most of them died in their sleep."

Quint took no comfort in that at all. "Then why . . . why am I . . . ?"

"I wanted to thank you for all your hard work, Sterling. You did everything I asked of you. And aside from that early issue with Maranan, you handled your tasks superbly. Know that we'll always value your contribution."

Quint's eyes darted back and forth in busy thought. "Look . . . look, why don't we compromise, okay? Just give me the girl. Give me Farisi and we'll go our separate ways."

"Sterling . . ."

"You said she was expendable!"

"To us," Azral said. "Not to them. The Silvers will be traveling now. They'll need her unique insight."

"But—"

"Furthermore, you misunderstand your situation. I said I wanted to thank you. I never said you were spared."

The walls of Quint's mind suddenly constricted into a narrow tunnel, as a million floating concerns melted away to just one. White-faced, he fumbled the knot of his tie until it came loose. He knew that pleading for his life would be futile, like begging the mercy of a great white shark or a snowy avalanche.

Suddenly the esteemed physicist erupted in a low and untimely chuckle. The Pelletiers watched him with furrowed bother.

"Did you not understand what—"

"Oh, I got it," Quint said, still chortling. "I may be many things, Azral, but I'm not stupid."

Esis eyed him warily. "And yet you laugh in the face of your own demise."

No one was more surprised than Quint, a man whose whole life had been an upward climb, filled with endless battle. Now after fifty-five years, there was nothing left to do. No one left to fight. The revelation was . . . liberating.

"I'd explain it," he said, through dwindling snickers. "But I doubt you'd understand. If the two of you represent the future of mankind, then this is an excellent time to stop progressing."

Azral and Esis exchanged a stony glance, then bloomed a matching set of grins.

"Oh, the pride of the ancients," said the son.

"Truly a sight to behold," said the mother.

Their condescension cracked the walls of Quint's serenity. He shot a wrathful glare at Azral.

"Just get it over with already, you stretched stain. You chalk-faced bowel.

If I have one regret, it's that I won't get to see all your plans crumble right on top of you. Don't think it won't happen. You're clearly not as smart as you think you are."

Expressionless, Azral rose from the desk and approached Quint. The physicist smiled.

"It'll be even more amusing if your grand design gets foiled by the very people you brought here. The great Azral Pelletier, brought low by an actress, a cartoonist, and all their little friends. It's a shame I'll miss that. Talk about a sight to behold."

With a soft and solemn expression, Azral rested a gentle hand on Quint's scalp.

"I thank you again for your help, Sterling. Your work here is done."

Quint closed his eyes in anticipation of pain, but he felt nothing more than a faint and bubbly tickle under his skin. He peeked an eye open.

"What—"

He dropped through the rug as if it were nothing more than mist. Down he fell, through the floorboards and wires, the lobby chandelier. He passed through all objects like an apparition but he plummeted like a stone.

When he reached the underground parking lot, Quint finally screamed. He disappeared through the concrete and then continued in darkness. By the time he succumbed to suffocation, he'd already descended an eighth of the way into the Earth's crust. His body kept on falling, all the way to magma.

Grim-faced and silent, the Pelletiers exited the complex. The moment they reached the front yard, Azral turned around and closed his eyes in concentration.

A dome of piercing white light suddenly enveloped the building—a bubble of backward time moving at accelerated speed. Inside the field, corpses vanished, plants shrank, mice perished as zygotes. The hint of past life appeared in split-second intervals, like aberrations in a flip-book.

By the time the dome disappeared, the entire structure had been reversed fifty-two months, reverted to the failed hotel that Quint had yet to purchase. Every file, every photo, every mention of the Silvers was now erased from existence.

Esis peevishly crossed her arms and addressed Azral in a foreign tongue, a byzantine blend of European and Asian languages that was still over two millennia away from being invented.

"I warned you not to overlook our ancestors, *sehgee*. You should have listened to me."

"I know."

"You and your father both."

Azral held her hands, his sharp eyes tender with affection. "Just forgive us, *sehmeer*, and embrace the new course."

Esis heaved a wistful breath and fixed her dark stare at the blooming sun.

"I can't help but worry for those children. There are so many futures open to them now. So many strings."

"There's only one outcome that matters," Azral insisted. "They go east. To Pendergen."

"Assuming they don't fall on the way."

Azral wrapped his arms around Esis and cast a soulful gaze down the driveway.

"They will not fall," he assured her. "Not the important ones, at least."

Nobody knew where they were going, least of all Zack. His only goal now was to avoid looping back into police search paths. Every chance he got, he drove east into the rising sun.

Twelve miles from the site of their standoff, the engine fell to sickly whirrs. Zack veered onto a narrow forest road and pulled over to the dirt. He felt relatively good about ditching the van here in a desolate area, under the thick canopy of trees. He could only assume that the police hunt had extended to helicopters or whatever they used here to make pigs fly.

He gave everyone five minutes to gather their wits and scant belongings, but Amanda insisted on ten. She'd discovered a sterilized pack of sutures at the bottom of Czerny's med kit and was determined to close Theo's wound before they all proceeded on foot.

While the others exited, she remained with Theo in the back of the van. She saw him wincing with every stroke of the needle.

"Sorry," she said. "I'm an oncology nurse. I don't do this very often."

it was only professional pride that kept the bakers from selling rejuvenated bread.

"I hurt that guy back in the building. Rebel. I panicked and I aged his hand. If Dr. Czerny—rest his soul—was right about what that does to a body, then I probably shot a bunch of fatal air bubbles into his heart."

"You were defending yourself," Amanda said. "That man was trying to kill you."

"Yeah, and you didn't attack those cops until one of them fired a bullet at Mia. It's also worth noting that Rebel would have killed me and Theo if you hadn't stopped him. I'm sorry I never thought to thank you until now. I just hope the next time you think about the two men you hurt today, you also remember the two you saved."

Amanda looked up at him with red eyes. Though she was loath to praise him in their tense early days together, she'd noticed from the start that Zack was humble to the point of self-deprecation. There wasn't a vain bone in his body.

She took a deep wet sniff and gazed across at the bread boxes.

"They'd have to be big bubbles."

"What?"

"Rebel. You'd have to make big bubbles in his bloodstream in order to kill him. A few centimeters at least. Even then, he could still survive if he got treated in time. You don't need a reviver. Just a hyperbaric chamber. Most hospitals have one, at least where we come from."

Zack almost laughed at his conflicting reactions to her information. He was relieved to be that much less a murderer, and worried that Rebel would be that much more alive to murder Zack someday.

"Thank you. It's been bugging me all morning. I needed that perspective."

"No problem," she replied, with black humor. "I'm here to help."

What began as a snicker soon escalated into a series of near-maniacal giggles. She caught Zack's puzzled grin.

"I was just thinking about that pawnbroker. The expression on his face when I got all pissy on him. I can't tell you how many times I've gotten that look from people, Zack. Complete strangers. My husband always said I made a strong first impression on people. It wasn't a compliment."

The cartoonist smirked sardonically. "That's all right. I once had a woman slap me just thirty seconds after meeting me."

Amanda laughed. "Yeah. I remember. Guess I made a strong first impression on you too."

"Well, part of me."

She wiped her eyes and brushed back her hair. She realized now that she'd have to dye it a different color. *God. I'm already thinking like a fugitive.*

"Zack, why does that trash bread look so good to me?"

"Because we haven't eaten all day. Come on."

He rose to his feet and extended a hand. As he helped her up, she wrapped herself around him.

"Oh. Hey. Huggage."

"Thankful huggage," said Amanda. "I'm glad you were still with us when all this stuff happened. I'm glad you're still with us now. You're a good man, Zack. Sometimes, on rare occasions, you're even funny."

He grinned along to her surprisingly droll humor, his hands falling awkwardly on her back. As a jaded New Yorker from an aloof and broken family, he was severely unskilled in the art of physical contact. But there was something jarringly beautiful about this embrace. They were both the same height, with the same limber frame. Her warmth and symmetry were a little too nice to handle right now.

At the end of their hug, Amanda suffered a sudden flashback to Esis Pelletier. The madwoman had approached her in an alley much like this one, uttering words so bizarre and cryptic that Amanda quickly forgot them in the chaos that followed. Except now a tiny fragment came back to her, an angry warning to not entwine with something. Or someone.

She crumpled the thought into an angry little ball and buried it in the back of her mind, along with the policemen, the pawnbroker, and Derek's harsh words. No more of that business. It was time to be strong again.

They returned to the park with nourishing goodies, their first meal on Earth that wasn't provided by physicists. For a gratifying twenty minutes, the Silvers sat around the picnic table, devouring their bounty like a pack of wild predators.

Amanda returned David's T-shirt after the meal. She watched with puzzlement as he sniffed the fabric. She wasn't sure if he was checking for sweat stink, cooties, or something worse.

While the others waged a run on the nearby department store, Amanda stayed in the park with Theo. Their clothes were too bloody for close public mingling. Theo was in no condition to go shopping anyway. Once Amanda finished changing his bandage, she led him to the shade of the pine tree and ordered him to take a nap. Though he insisted he was fine, he quickly drifted away on a bed of grass.

Amanda rested against the tree, mindless in the wake of her meltdown. She occasionally heard Theo mumble in his sleep. He called out to a woman named Melissa, then mumbled something about a girl with two watches. Amanda hoped he was at least having a good dream.

An hour and a half later, the others came back with fresh supplies. New clothes for all. Better shoes for some. A map. A compass. Two flashlights. Six knapsacks to carry it all.

Amanda wasn't encouraged by Zack's crabby expression. "How much do we have left?"

"Don't ask."

"Tell me."

He sighed defeatedly. "About a hundred and fifty."

"What?"

"We bought the cheapest stuff they had. But even bargain basement clothes add up when there are six of us."

"So what are we going to do about money?"

"I don't know," he said. "You think you can write the Harry Potter books from memory?"

Amanda fought a grin. "No."

"*Twilight*?"

"Zack . . ."

"I have some ideas. We can talk about it later. In the meantime, you may want to have a chat with your sister. Or Mia. Or both."

"Why? What—"

Hannah dropped her bags on the picnic table, then brusquely walked away. Her face was grim. Her eyes were red from crying. Mia soon slapped her own purchases on the table and shuffled off in the other direction. She looked even worse.

When Amanda turned to Zack, he chucked his hands in hopeless quandary. He had no idea what had happened between Hannah and Mia. Neither one of them was talking.

They'd split up four ways inside the Harvey Mark, with a plan to reassemble in an hour. Mia wandered the aisles in a moony daze, marveling at the daft embellishments to this otherwise familiar environment. A stock boy pushed giant boxes on a hovering aeric platform. A two-dimensional ghost woman hawked the benefits of a Harvey Mark purchase account. A young boy hobbled after his mother on legs of pure tempis.

More alarming were the fashions, a mix of 1950s and 1980s clothing styles, flavored with a twist of madness. Mia saw two teenage girls dressed in sleeveless turtlenecks with cleavage holes cut in the fabric. One wore a bob of orange-red hair that was teased to looked like flames. The other sported blond bangs that were long enough to obscure her eyes. Mia couldn't tell if the girls were cookie-cutter trend slaves or bold fashion rebels. All she knew was that she'd never be anything more than an alien here.

Soon Mia and Hannah spotted each other in the women's clothing section. Their overwhelmed expressions were identical, enough to evoke a mutually nervous giggle.

"This place is like Wal-Mart on acid," Hannah said. "It's freaking me out."

Despite Mia's resolve to think nicer of Hannah, she found herself squinting with reproach at the box of black hair dye in her handcart. *Your sister sold her wedding ring so we could eat and live, not touch up our roots.*

It was actually Amanda who'd requested the product for herself. Though Mia had misjudged again, Hannah wasn't entirely innocent this time. She'd convinced her sister to go black over blond just so she could use the leftover dye on her roots.

Peering into Mia's cart, Hannah winced at the pair of dark, long-sleeved shirts she'd chosen for purchase. *Oh sweetie. You're going to bake like a muffin in those things. Is it worth getting heatstroke just to look slimmer for David?*

Loath as she was to jeopardize Mia's fresh goodwill, Hannah plotted a course of delicate pestering. "Uh, hey, listen—"

"Oh, you've got to be kidding me."

Mia spun a quick circle, urgently scanning all shoppers within eyeshot. From her panicked expression, Hannah feared the girl was on the verge of a gastric catastrophe.

"Are you okay?"

"No. She couldn't have picked a worse time. What the hell is she thinking?"

"What? Who are you—"

A bead of light suddenly appeared ten inches in front of Mia's chest. Hannah took a step back.

"Whoa. Jesus. Is that . . . is that the thing your notes come from?"

"Yeah."

Mia raised her handcart until it obscured the glowing breach. Hannah skittishly peeked inside.

"Wow. I've never seen one of these before. It's like a tiny sun. How long before a note pops out?"

"It varies," said Mia, increasingly tense. Something wasn't right about this delivery.

"And does it usually—"

"Hannah, I can't talk right now. I need to focus on this."

"Okay," she said, dejectedly. "I didn't know. I'm sorry."

Wincing with guilt, Mia bent her knees until she was eye level with the portal. She could see another Mia through the tiny circle, anxiously pacing the carpet of her Terra Vista suite. She was dressed in the same clothes Mia wore now, and radiated a sense of worry that was painfully easy to recognize. It was her just fourteen hours ago.

Mia's skin blanched as she grasped the scope of her new problem. "Oh God. Oh my God."

"What? What's the matter?"

"This is a past portal. I'm not receiving, I'm sending. I know exactly what I need to write but I don't have the right pen. You need to find me a red pen, Hannah. It has to be ballpoint and it has to be red."

"Uh, okay. Why—"

"I'll explain the rest when you get back! I promise! Just please go! Hurry!"

Hannah rushed toward the school supplies, wondering just how scared she should be. She vaguely recalled David mentioning something about Mia's newfound fear of paradoxes, the devastating consequences of changing the past. He didn't seem to share her concern.

"I don't believe it works the way she thinks it does," he'd told Hannah. "I certainly can't imagine that some minor inconsistency in her notes will somehow bring the universe to collapse. Then again, what do I know?"

David knew plenty, enough to alleviate Hannah's fears. Still, after everything that happened to their world, she could understand why Mia would be deathly afraid to screw with time.

Hannah quickly returned with an assortment of red pens. Thin trails of sweat rolled down Mia's temples.

"Oh thank God. I don't know how much longer it'll stay open."

"I'm here. I have it."

Hannah shielded the portal from all prying eyes while Mia tore a pen from its packaging. She ripped a careful swatch from the back of her journal and then double-checked the archive of her original message. She didn't know why she bothered. The words had been laser-burned onto her psyche.

They hit you all at sunrise. Sleep with your shoes on. Get ready to run.

During the eighty-two long seconds of Hannah's absence, Mia had considered all the things she wished she could write in place of that vague warning. With the right words, she could have ensured that the building was evacuated hours in advance. Nobody would have died.

Conversely, she pictured what would happen if the portal closed without any warning sent at all—a revised chain of events in which Rebel and his people killed everyone in their sleep. It was too terrible to think about. It was worse to think that it could still occur retroactively, just because Mia didn't have the right pen.

Mia rolled up the note and deposited it into the breach. As the portal vanished silently into the ether, she wrapped Hannah in a delirious hug of relief.

"Oh God. Thank you so much. I'm sorry I made you go running like that. And I'm sorry if I was ever cold or mean to you. It's just stupid jealousy. You're so pretty and you have this amazing body. But I know you're a good person too. And I promise from now on . . ."

She suddenly realized that Hannah wasn't returning the embrace. Mia pulled back to find her white-faced with horror, stammering as if Mia had stabbed her.

"You knew."

"What?"

"Your note. I saw it. You knew we were going to be attacked today and you didn't say anything."

Mia tensely shook her head. "No. Hannah. I didn't know. I mean not for sure."

"'They hit you all at sunrise'? 'Get ready to run'? What did you think it meant?"

"You don't understand. I've gotten bad notes before. Conflicting notes. I wasn't sure what was happening and I didn't want to worry people without—"

"You didn't want to *worry people*?"

In hindsight, it sounded pretty bad to Mia too. "Hannah, I'm so sorry."

The actress didn't care about Mia's remorse. She didn't care how this whole scene looked to the bystanders who were watching. Her mind was trapped six hours in the past, lost in battle with the Motorcycle Man.

"I went out jogging at sunrise," she cried to Mia. "Do you think I would have done that if . . . do you know how close I came to dying?"

"I'm sorry!"

"Sorry doesn't fix it, Mia! People died! Czerny died! Erin got cut in half, all because *you* didn't want to worry people!"

The tears flowed wildly on both of them now. Hannah held up a trembling hand.

"I can't even look at you."

She retreated down the aisle, crashing into a fellow shopper as she brusquely turned the corner. Both their handcarts fell to the floor.

"Oh God. I'm so sorry."

"My fault," the man assured her.

He wasn't wrong. It took five rewinds for Evan Rander to stand in just the right place for a spilling collision. Now he shined a cordial grin as he stooped to gather Hannah's belongings.

"Oh, you don't have to—"

"No, no, no. I insist. What kind of gentleman would I be?"

Even in a better state of mind, Hannah wouldn't have recognized him from their first encounter. Evan had swapped his ostentatious cowboy getup for a simple gray business suit. His hair had been respectfully parted to one side, and he wore soulful blue contact lenses behind rimless glasses. He was the humble good Samaritan now. He was Clark Kent.

Soon he presented Hannah with a refilled handcart. She sniffed and wiped her nose. "Thank you."

"No worries. I sense you're not having the best of days."

"Yeah. That's putting it mildly."

"I saw you arguing with your sister back there. Listen, I have siblings myself. These things always blow over."

Hannah rubbed her eyes. "She's not my sister."

"Oh."

"Look, I'm sorry. I really need to go."

"Of course. Of course. I understand. You take it easy now, all right?"

There was very little for Hannah to find creepy or suspicious about this incarnation of Evan. And yet as she made her brisk journey to the restroom, a dark voice in her head urged her to not look back. She couldn't shake the feeling that the man was still standing at the scene of their accident. Still watching her. Still smiling.

David studied the map on the picnic table. The nearest cradle of civilization was ten miles to the north. Their abandoned van lay a scant eight miles to the southwest. It wouldn't be long before the police search made its way to Ramona, if it hadn't happened already.

"We can't do ten more miles today," Amanda insisted. "We can't even do two miles. Look at us, David."

Over the boy's grumbling objections, the Silvers bought two rooms in a cheap motel off the main drag. The accommodations were pitiful compared to their suites in Terra Vista, but each room had two beds and each bed was soft. By three o'clock, they were all out cold.

Mia woke up four hours later, groggy and alone. Purple clouds peeked in through the curtain gaps. She could hear the shower running.

As she sat up, her hand brushed a small object on the blanket, an eight-inch cigar tube. Future Mia must have sent another delivery in her sleep.

She unscrewed the lid and shook out a roll of blue currency. Her jaw went slack as she counted fifteen hundred-dollar bills.

Mia used her finger to fish out the other two pieces of the parcel: a small white scrap containing a Brooklyn address and an eight-by-ten sheet of note-book paper densely crammed with text. The lettering was blocky and angular. A man's handwriting.

Hello, Mia,

You don't know me yet, but I'm a friend of your future. In fact, you're sitting next to me as I write this. The Mia I know is fourteen, just like you. But this one traveled across the country to get to me. She made it here with flying colors, along with all her friends.

Mia spotted her own scribble in the margin. Hey girl! See you on the other side!

The author continued:

It's of great importance that I earn your trust, which makes this next part all the more difficult. I'm sorry to say that the people who attacked you in Terra Vista are my people. My clan. There's a group of us who live in the outskirts of New York: forty-four families, all natives of this world, all gifted like you and your friends. We even have a few folks who can fly on wings of aeris, though they can't do it as often as they'd like. Through discipline and the occasional use of misdirection, we've managed to keep our talents hidden from the public at large. We don't want to be lab rats any more than you do. For us, the price of living free is living quietly.

Recent developments, however, have put us all in a bad state. In the weeks since your arrival, several of our own have gone missing. Worse, the augurs of our clan—the ones who can see the future, live the future, and hear from their future selves—have all gotten wind of a terrible event coming. A second Cataclysm, of sorts.

Shortly after our troubles began, a man named Richard Rosen (you know him as Rebel) determined that the disaster ahead can be averted by destroying all the new people who arrived in this world. He believes you're all living ruptures in the fabric of time, breaches that need to be plugged. Though his theory isn't entirely based in fiction, it's deeply flawed. Unfortunately, fear won out over reason and Rebel got the clan to see things his way. For your sakes, I wish I'd fought better. All I managed to do was get myself banished from the councils.

But I'm not out of the game yet. I've got my own plan to stop what's coming, one that doesn't involve murder. Unlike Rebel, I don't think you and your friends are part of the problem. In fact, I believe you're part of the solution. One of you in particular.

So I'm writing you now, Mia. I'm asking you to come find me at the enclosed address. I can provide you all with shelter, safety, and crucial information. For those of you looking for a purpose on this world, I can sure as hell give you that too.

Come to Brooklyn. You won't have to worry about Rebel for a while, but there are other people on your trail. I'll let your older half tell you about those folks, on the other side of this note.

I'd say I look forward to meeting you, but I already have and I'm already glad. I'll just say I look forward to you meeting me.

All the best,
Peter Pendergen

Beleaguered by all the new information, Mia turned the letter over. The other side was written in Mia's hand, an assortment of quick thoughts scrawled at various angles. A passage at the top caught her attention. It was circled twice and garnished with a smiley face.

Apology from Hannah in 3 . . . 2 . . . 1 . . .

Mia jumped when the door opened. Hannah stepped out of the steamy bathroom. She adjusted her towel wrap and aimed a soft expression at Mia.

"Hi."

"Hey. Where's, uh . . . ?"

"She's checking on Theo. How are you doing?"

Still reeling from the letter, Mia could only shrug. Hannah fixed a somber gaze at her feet.

"Listen, I talked to Amanda. She told me you spent all night in the security room with Erin, looking out for intruders. She also said you're the one who pulled the fire alarm and warned Zack about Rebel. I'm . . . I don't know what came over me. When I learned about your note, I just flipped out and assumed you didn't do anything with the information. But it turns out you did a lot. So, I'm sorry. And I'm so sorry for saying you were responsible for Erin and Dr. Czerny. Can you forgive me?"

Mia bit her lip, nodding in warm accord. Hannah leaned against the doorframe and crossed her arms.

"Okay. Now that I got that out, I have a favor to ask. In the future, should you get another—"

"Evan Rander."

Hannah blinked at her. "What?"

"A note I got. A warning. If you see a small and creepy guy with a '55' on his hand, run. That's Evan Rander. He's bad news."

Though Hannah had failed to notice any numbers on anyone's hands, she could think of two different men who'd set off her creep alarms today.

"Okay. Wow. I don't know what to make of that yet. But I'm glad you told me. Thank you."

Hannah glanced at Mia's journal on the end table, then nervously scratched her neck.

"Is there, uh . . . is there anything else from the future I should know?"

With a flustered sigh, Mia looked down at the fresh new dispatch in her hand. Yeah. There was something else.

EIGHTEEN

Nobody knew what to make of Peter Pendergen. The Silvers convened in one motel room, debating all the revelations and implications of his letter. When they didn't talk over each other, they fell into a pensive silence, one so deep they could hear the slow drip from the showerhead.

Hannah dumped the empty plates and wrappers of their takeout dinner into the trash, then reclaimed her spot on Zack's bed. She peeked over his shoulder as he sketched a man's face on motel stationery.

"I don't trust him," she uttered.

"Me neither," Amanda said from the desk chair. She kept an eye on the muted lumivision. The nine o'clock news would begin in five minutes. She fully expected to be the top story.

"I don't think any of us are ready to marry the guy," Zack replied, "but are you both suggesting we avoid him completely?"

Zack had made it clear that he was very much in favor of meeting Peter. He admitted that his vote was influenced by his desire to go to New York and search for his brother. It also didn't hurt that Brooklyn was 2,500 miles away from the site of their police standoff.

Amanda flicked her hand. "I don't know. It just feels like a trap to me."

"What are you basing that on?" David asked.

"Azral let us go. Maybe this is the reason why. After everything we learned about Dr. Quint today, is it really such a stretch to believe that Peter's also working for the Pelletiers?"

David shook his head. "I think you're being overly paranoid."

"I think she makes a damn good point," Hannah said. "I also find it weird that he didn't include a way for us to contact him. No phone number. No e-mail."

"Well, keep in mind this letter's from Future Peter," Zack said, aware of how silly he sounded. "Maybe the current Peter isn't in a position to hear from us. It might put him at risk somehow. Or put us at risk."

The sisters crossed their arms in synch, wearing the same dubious frown.

"I don't buy it," said Hannah.

"Me neither," said Amanda.

"And what about the fact that Mia got a warning flat-out telling her not to trust him?"

Mia sighed from the foot of David's bed. She'd spent an uncomfortable amount of time in the hot seat tonight, answering numerous questions on behalf of her future selves. She knew she couldn't talk about Peter without mentioning the two conflicting messages she'd received about him five weeks ago:

Don't trust Peter. He's not who he says he is.

Disregard that first note. I was just testing something. Peter's good.
He's great, actually.

After reading the messages aloud, Mia had glanced up to five dim and bewildered faces. "Yeah. Now you know what I've been dealing with."

Sadly, there was nothing in this latest parcel to clarify the confusion. On the flip side of Peter's letter, Future Mia addressed the matter with a virtual shrug.

I wish I could explain those notes, but I still don't know why we got them. All I can tell you is that I've known Peter for six months now and I trust him with my life. He's a good man. He's not half as funny as he thinks he is, but he's a good man.

Below her passage, Peter scribbled a brief retort. *I am very funny.*

"I'm honestly not sure what to think about him," Mia said. "But if he is who he says he is, if he really does have shelter and safety to offer us, then I'd hate for us to blow our chance because I got a bad message."

David nodded vigorously. "Exactly. This is an opportunity. I can't speak for the rest of you, but I still want the answers that Quint and Czerny promised us. Maybe Peter can provide them. On top of that, there's also the matter of that second Cataclysm. If Peter's right—"

"—then we'll be walking right into it," Hannah griped.

"He didn't say it was happening in New York," David replied. "He just said it was happening. He also said we're potentially part of the solution. Don't you think that's worth investigating? Isn't that a better way to spend our days than aimless wandering?"

Once again, the discussion hit a weary lull. Theo sat cross-legged on the desk, staring out the window at a municipal impound lot.

"Theo?"

He glanced up at Zack. "Huh?"

"You've been Johnny Tightlips over there. What are you thinking?"

There was no safe way to answer truthfully. From the moment Mia revealed her surprise cash endowment, Theo's dark inner demon had snapped awake in its cage. It eyed the money hungrily, calculating the sheer amount of liquid solace that $1,500 could purchase. It would carry Theo for miles, all the way to the next world.

"I don't know. I mean I understand what David's saying. I respect it."

"But?"

"But this is our first day out in the world. We're still flailing around like newborns. And now you're talking about crossing the country to help some stranger stop a Cataclysm? That's not just ambitious. It's nuts."

Theo saw David's eyes narrow to a cool squint. The dark demon smiled. *The boy doesn't like you. He sees you for the burden you are. You think he's the only one?*

"Looks like we're split down the middle on this," Amanda said.

David chucked a hand in frustration. "You guys can do what you want. If I have to go to New York alone, I will."

"Hey, come on . . ."

"David!"

Zack raised his palms. "Okay. Stop. We've had enough drama for one day. Can we just agree in the short term that we need to get the hell away from California?" His posit was greeted with soft nods. "Good. Then we can all keep going northeast. Maybe Mia will get more info along the way. Maybe we'll dig up our own. The point is that we have days to decide."

Everyone tensed up as the sound of police sirens filtered in from the street. The Silvers sat motionless, fingers extended, until the noise faded away.

Zack sighed exhaustedly. "We also have more pressing concerns."

Mia's older self had succinctly explained the scope of their legal problems.

It's not the cops you need to worry about. It's the Deps. DP-9 is the federal agency that handles temporic crimes, and they're very good. They already know what we look like and what some of us can do. They're extremely eager to meet us, especially Amanda.

The news had caused five stomachs to drop, and sent Amanda to the bathroom with dry heaves. But the warning came bundled with advice, three simple rules for avoiding detection:

1. Stay away from civic cameras. That means no hospitals, no bank machines, and no public transportation of any kind. They're all heavily monitored. You will get spotted.

2. Don't get friendly with the locals. The more you talk, the more you expose yourself as foreigners. They do not like foreigners here.

3. No public displays of weirdness, ever. Keep your talents hidden. Even if you think no one's looking, assume they are. It's the only way you'll make it to New York.

David lurched forward in bed, matching Mia's prone position. He playfully brushed her shoulder.

"Thanks to our invaluable messenger here, we have nearly everything we need to keep ahead of the federal agents. The one thing we're missing is transport. If we can't take buses or trains, then we'll have to acquire a car."

Amanda eyed him sharply. "I hope you're not talking about stealing one."

"I am, actually. Is your objection moral or practical?"

"Both," she said.

"For the moral objection, I assume they have auto insurance on this world. Anyone we steal from will be reimbursed."

"Yes, and I assume they have LoJack on this world, or some other high-tech system that makes it easy to track stolen cars. Are you really that eager for another police chase?"

"Well, that's the practical objection, but—"

David stopped at the sound of Theo's dark chuckle. For a moment, the boy's expression turned so cold that Mia felt the unprecedented urge to move away from him.

"I was about to say that we could target an older vehicle, one less likely to have a tracking device. But by all means, Theo, go ahead and mock me. At least I'm offering options."

"I'm not mocking you, David."

"Then why were you laughing?"

Theo couldn't safely answer that question either. He remembered what it was like to be sixteen and fearless. He remembered the false security his own brilliance afforded him. Now, at twenty-three, it was far too soon to play the role of the hardened old crank. And yet here he was, chuckling at David's impertinence, fighting the urge to say, "Boy, it ain't that easy."

"I was mocking myself. But for what it's worth, you're right that we need wheels. We're going to hit desert soon. That won't be fun to walk."

Zack continued his memory sketch of Evan Rander. "As long as we bring enough water and don't pray to any golden calves, we'll make it through the desert. I'm more concerned about the financials. Fifteen hundred isn't enough to get us across the country."

"You don't think so?" Amanda asked. "I mean we're stocked up on supplies now. If we're careful—"

"If there's one thing I learned today, it's that 'cheap' times six equals 'expensive.' Unless Future Mia fronts us another loan, we'll have to come up with more."

"I'm not so sure."

Theo shook his head. "No, Zack's right. It's not enough money to get to Brooklyn."

Hannah looked at him with sudden puzzlement. He caught her hot stare. "What?"

"You said that before."

"Excuse me?"

"That thing you just said. You used those exact words back in the van."

Now it was Theo's turn to become baffled. "I don't recall saying that."

"I don't recall him saying that either," David attested. "I was there the whole time."

"No. I don't mean the van today. I mean six weeks ago. When I first met you."

In the wake of everyone's dumbfounded looks, Hannah bared her palms. "I'm not making this up! We were on our way to Terra Vista. You'd fallen asleep. And then suddenly you mumbled, 'He's right.' I said, 'Who's right?' and you said, 'Zack. He's right. It's not enough money to get to Brooklyn.' Then your nose got all bloody and you fell into your coma."

The showerhead dripped ten more times before Zack broke the muddled silence.

"Uh, normally I'd write that off as a strange coincidence. But after everything we've seen, Theo, I'm going to go out on a limb and suggest you might not be entirely weirdness-free."

Theo felt a hot rush of blood in his face. He stammered for a response.

"I really don't see how—"

"Oh my God!"

The others followed Mia's gaze to the lumivision, where the nine o'clock news had just begun.

Contrary to Amanda's expectations, the broadcast didn't open with her police sketch. In fact, the standoff on Highway V would merit just forty seconds of airtime. In the absence of any fatalities, and the coordinated silence of all law enforcers on scene, the incident was treated as just another police chase. Another irksome traffic jam.

The top story of the day was much juicier. The star of the tale was Sterling Quint.

At 6:34 this morning, operators at Triple-5 Emergency received eleven distress calls of the exact same nature—eleven spouses, lovers, and siblings who'd all succumbed to the same fatal stroke. When record checks revealed that the deceased were all employees at the same organization, authorities suddenly became quite interested in the goings-on at the Pelletier Group.

By sunset, the last of the bodies had been discovered. Four names on the payroll had yet to be accounted for: Erin and Eric Salgado, Beatrice Caudell, and the head honcho himself, Sterling Quint. The world-renowned theorist had left for work at 7 A.M. and was never heard from again.

The story quickly caught fire at newsrooms across the nation. Some broadcasts filled their screens with juxtaposed photos of a dour Quint and a nervous Beatrice—a saucy suggestion that the pair had perpetrated the massacre and were now lovers on the run.

The Silvers watched the lumivision with wide eyes and white faces, processing the deaths of everyone they knew outside the motel room. Hannah thought of poor Charlie Merchant, barely a year older than her. Her eyes welled up with tears.

"I don't get it. Why would he kill them?"

"I assume you're not referring to Quint."

"You know I'm not, David. Come on. I'm talking about Azral."

"It had to be him," Amanda said. "Him and Esis."

The widow couldn't get her mind off Czerny. His death had seemed so inconsistent with his type of injury. Now she knew why. She bit her trembling lip.

"They threw them away. They didn't need them anymore, so they just tossed them like garbage."

David shook his head. "For all we know, this was the work of Rebel's people."

"Doubtful," said Theo. "If Rebel's people had the ability to kill remotely, they wouldn't have come at us with guns and swords."

Mia couldn't bear the thought of anyone having that power. She pictured Azral standing before some necromantic circuit breaker, shutting off lives from miles away. She could only imagine he had six more buttons, all labeled with the names of people in this room.

"Do you think maybe Beatrice got away?" she asked.

The lack of response was enough to confirm her grim suspicion. She took a moment to mourn the poor woman who'd baked her a cupcake for her birthday.

Zack remained silent from his perch on the bed, stewing over the large new problem this tragedy created for them. The Salgado van and the body of Dr. Czerny were two thick chains that tied the Silvers to the Pelletier slaughter. While the media continued to chase ghosts, the federal agents would have a stronger notion of who to blame.

By ten o'clock, Melissa Masaad was angry enough to break the law. It took twenty minutes of research to uncover the location of the nearest tobacco den, hidden away beneath a Terra Vista bowling alley. Six more minutes of digging earned her the passphrase.

"Are your bathrooms clean?" she asked the cashier, just as she was told.

For once, Melissa's foreign attributes worked in her favor. The greasy old man at the counter would have never suspected she was a Dep. Even if she had been with DP-4, the illicit substances division, she wouldn't have wasted time on such a piddling sting. The Bureau didn't care about smoke-easies.

"We have a clean bathroom downstairs," the cashier replied. "They're pay toilets."

"How much?"

"Twenty dollars."

"Goodness. Do these exceptionally clean toilets come with Eaglenet access?"

For an extra ten dollars, they did. Melissa carried a handtop under her arm. She was determined to keep working, all through the night if she had to.

Two stairwells and one purchase later, she sat in an overstuffed recliner in the corner of a dim and smoky lounge. She closed her eyes as she savored the taste of the cigarette, her first in twenty-two months. She'd been hoping to enjoy her life in America without the crutch of nicotine, but today was a day of extraordinary frustrations.

"It's out of my hands," Cahill told her, five hours ago. "We hunt where they tell us to hunt."

Melissa had crafted a no-nonsense approach to tracking the fugitives—a strategic sweep of every pawnshop and panhandle park in the ten-mile radius of the abandoned van. From all appearances, these runners were low on resources. Finding them was simply a matter of anticipating their chosen method of fund-raising.

Unfortunately, the mystery of the dead physicists crashed her plans like a wayward truck, dominating the team for the rest of the day. Nine hours ago, Melissa walked through the empty corridors of the Pelletier building, marveling at the results of her wave scans. From all gauges, the entire building had been temporically reversed, a feat that was as bizarre and unlikely as broiling a high school. Soon policemen stumbled across a bloody Japanese sword, just one foot outside the property perimeter, a discovery that made even less sense. The only encouraging find was a missing door from the stolen van, direct evidence that the fugitives had been there.

Seven hours ago, Melissa had sat at the bedside of Janice Salgado, the widow of Martin and mother of the three security guards who were either missing or dead. She was a heavyset woman with a cherry-red bouffant that matched her freshly cracked eyes. A constellation of baby-spot sedatives was peppered across her neck, twisting her mouth into an unholy union of a smile and a scream.

"There were six people living in that building," Janice told Melissa. "Marty didn't know where they came from. He said they just showed up one day with bracelets on their wrists and . . . weird stuff. They could do weird stuff. Erin took a real shine to one of them. Young girl named Mia. Poor child. Erin said . . . she said the poor thing lost her whole . . . she lost her whole . . ."

Janice sobbed and clutched at Melissa's blouse. "Please. Please find my youngest. I know in my heart they're gone, but they need to be buried with the family. Please."

Five hours ago, Melissa stood at the city coroner's office, watching through a window as men in masks examined Constanin Czerny. As they finished their work, her handphone rang. Cahill didn't sound pleased.

"Just heard from the directors. Our scope has changed. For the short term, they want us to devote all our resources to finding Sterling Quint."

"What? But sir, the runners—"

"I know. I know. It's all image control. The story's gone national. They reckon we'll look like humps if we can't track one of the country's most famous dwarves."

Melissa clenched her jaw. She had a grim hunch that Quint, Caudell, and the two Salgados had all been inside the Pelletier building when it was mysteriously reversed. Dead or alive, their bodies would have been erased out of existence. The British referred to the process as "nulling." The Americans called it "zilching." In both countries, it had become the cornerstone of waste management, as well as a favored tool for criminal evidence disposal. They'd never find Quint.

"Sir, this is the most perplexing case I've ever seen. There's so much I don't understand. But one thing I know is that every trail leads back to those six people. We need to find them."

"I agree with you, hon. But look at the bigger picture. I'm still five signatures away from making you the new me. This isn't the time to kick sand."

Twenty minutes later, she received a preliminary autopsy report on Constantin Czerny. He had died of the same subarachnoid hemorrhage as the other victims. But from the unique attributes of his abdominal wound, he'd been stabbed by a projectile made of pure tempis.

Melissa was downright smarmy when she updated Cahill.

"Shame we don't know anyone who can cause such an injury, sir. Perhaps Dr. Quint will know."

That was when Cahill told her, with a hopeless sigh, that it was out of his hands. If Melissa wanted to do more digging on the tempic redhead, he wouldn't stop her. But she had to put in face time on the Quint search. Such was the price of career advancement.

After three hours of pointless legwork, Melissa escaped to the tobacco den, puffing cigarette after cigarette as she scanned through digital mug shots. The red-haired woman was, as Melissa feared, a virgin to the justice system. Odder still, there was nothing in the news archives about a girl named Mia who lost her entire family. Were these people in *any* systems?

In a desperate last effort, she accessed the Eaglenet bitboards and launched a keyword search through today's online discussions. There was much talk of tempis and even more talk of redheads, but not a lot of chatter about both. After wading through a number of false double-positives, Melissa found an interesting post in a customer support forum for a popular brand of armored safe:

> This incredibly intense redhead came into my store today and slapped her hand on my counter. Suddenly the tempis on my Shellbox started rippling. Has anyone else seen anything like that?

A profile search on the author revealed him as John Curry, a pawnbroker here in South California. His shop was just eight miles from the site of the fugitives' abandoned vehicle.

Melissa took a final drag of her cigarette, closed her handbook, and hurried outside to the company van. She steered it thirty feet into the air and then shifted to 10×. She could still taste the tobacco on her lips as she shot through the night like a missile, straight toward Ramona.

NINETEEN

Amanda didn't know how to feel about her latest transformation. She watched her reflection from the desk chair while Hannah brushed inky dye into her tresses. Stroke by stroke, lock by lock, red to black, red to black.

At midnight, the job was finished. Now Amanda stared in wonder at the dark-haired stranger in the mirror. To her surprise, she didn't hate the new color. And yet she couldn't help but lament the latest upheaval to her personal status quo. She was a widow now, an alien, a fugitive, a brunette. Mad events were slowly turning her into a parallel-universe version of herself. Bit by bit, piece by piece, she was becoming Altamanda.

Hannah removed the drip-stained towel from Amanda's shoulders, then studied her reaction. "I did the best I could."

"What? No, you did great, Hannah. It's perfect. I'm just upset about the reasons behind it."

"Well, it'll work. I doubt anyone who's looking for you will recognize you now."

"That's really all that matters. Everything else is . . . I just need to get used to it."

Amanda bounced a mirrored gaze at Mia. "So what do you think?"

Mia had peeked up from her journal many times to watch the recoloring in progress, this strikingly cozy endeavor between women. Having grown up in a house full of brothers, it was strange for her to witness the feminine rituals of siblings.

"Looks good," she listlessly replied. "You two finally look related."

Hannah tossed her rubber gloves in the sink. She was too tired to color her own hair. Too upset. She plopped herself onto her bed, sending Zack's drawing fluttering down to the floor. She was sick of thinking about the bothersome man in the picture.

On the flip side of Peter's letter, Future Mia had reserved some words for a new orbiting threat.

I'm not even sure how to explain Evan Rander. He's from our world, but he acts like he's been here forever. He knows us all disturbingly well, and yet none of us knows him. We still have no idea why he hates us so much. He always seems to find us when we're alone and at our most vulnerable. He likes to twist the knife, especially on Hannah.

Once Evan's identity was uncovered in retrospect, Zack worked with Hannah to provide a composite sketch of the smiling cowboy who'd greeted them at the side of the van.

"It makes no sense," said Hannah. "What could we have done to make him so angry? What could *I* have done?"

Mia shrugged. "I don't know. Maybe he's just crazy. If I had spent the last six weeks wandering alone out here, I might have lost my mind too. I probably would have slit my wrists."

The sisters traded a dark look in the mirror. Amanda tensely wrung her fingers.

"I don't know who this guy is. Right now, I don't care. We have bigger problems."

"Easy for you to say," Hannah growled. "He hasn't singled you out."

Amanda turned her sharp gaze on her. "Do you want to trade places? Because I'd rather have a stalker chasing me than a team of federal agents."

"Hey, fun fact: the feds are after me too."

"And this Evan guy is following all of us! Why do you..." Amanda closed her eyes and waved a tense palm. "I can't handle a fight with you right now."

"Then don't start one."

Amanda tightened her towel wrap and shot to her feet. Mia watched with puzzlement as she closed the bathroom door behind her.

"Okay, what just happened?"

Hannah threw herself back onto the mattress, throwing a dismal gaze at her scarred wrists. "It's nothing. Old wounds."

"Will she be okay?"

"She'll be fine," the actress replied, with dripping venom. "She's a rock, that one."

Mia returned to her journal, her thoughts twisting with unease. She wondered if she had dodged a bullet by not having sisters. All things considered, she preferred the way men fought.

Zack and David crossed midnight like frigid old spouses, puttering away in parallel beds. While David browsed a local paper, Zack drew an elaborate pen sketch of Bugs Bunny. There were only a handful of people who'd recognize the poor rabbit now. Zack wasn't even sure David was one of them.

The boy glanced with concern at the stack of glossy blue cash on Zack's nightstand. He checked the door to the bathroom, where Theo had been showering for forty long minutes.

"Maybe we should put that money in a safer place," David suggested.

"What, you mean a hedge fund?"

"No. I mean perhaps I should give it to Mia or one of the sisters."

"Oh, you're just hoping to catch them in their undies, you scamp."

"Zack, I think you know what my issue is."

Zack did know, and he was trying not to get angry about it. "What do you have against Theo anyway?"

David lowered his voice. "Nothing. I'm sure he's a fine person. But at this stage of his alcoholic recovery, he's a liability to all of us."

"That liability got shot trying to save me."

"I'm not asking you to expel him from the group. Just hide the cash."

"Fine. You asked. And I'm saying no. Now drop it."

They languished in icy silence for several minutes. Zack finished his sketch and let out a loud exhale.

"Look, I'm as cynical as the next guy. Normally you wouldn't have to tell me to be nervous about someone. The problem is that we have too many problems already. Rebel and his people are looking to kill us. The Deps want to lock us away. God only knows what the Pelletiers are after. And now we have some twisted little creep following us around like our own personal Gollum.

Given all that, I'm in a rather desperate need to trust the people in my tent. Do you get that?"

"I do," said David. "Just as long as you understand my concern."

"Yeah. You don't want to lose the money."

"I don't care about the money, Zack. I'm sure Mia could send herself more if she had to. But after reading Peter's letter, it seems absolutely crucial that we get to New York. Not just some of us. All of us. For all we know, Theo's the 'one in particular' who stops the second Cataclysm."

Zack lowered his pad and studied David carefully. The boy was usually logical to a fault, but now he treated Peter Pendergen's words like they'd come down from Mount Sinai. It was an odd shift for one such as David, but who knew? Maybe the kid needed to believe in Peter as much as Zack needed to believe in his friends.

"Look, I'll make you a deal. We'll leave the cash out for one night. If it's still here in the morning, we'll know we can trust him and that's one less thing to worry about."

"And if it's not?" David asked.

"Then I'll dance on the street for money till I can buy you an apology bouquet."

David eyed him with furrowed bother until he emitted a dry chuckle.

"I like you, Zack, but you can be awfully strange sometimes."

"Says the kid who eats like a six-foot rabbit."

"I just hope you're right about him."

Zack looked to the bathroom door and heaved an airy sigh. "Guess we'll find out."

Once his long shower ended, Theo wiped the steam from the mirror and stared at his chest. An angry red scar ran across his left pectoral—six inches long, five years old, and as jagged as the mouth of a demon. Theo was well acquainted with its voice by now. It had pestered him all throughout the evening, dousing him in noble reasons to break away from the group. *They'd get so much farther without your mouth to feed. They'd be so much less conspicuous without an injured Asian among them. They'd have a chance, Theo. Why must you rob them of their chance?*

By the time the steam cleared, the matter had been settled. He'd leave them tonight, after Zack and David fell asleep.

Ecstatic in victory, the demon took no time to rest. As Theo dried himself off, it broached the delicate subject of severance pay.

The squad room was a slice of Old London, a dank basement of dripping steam pipes and moldy gray brick. Melissa found it a refreshing contrast to the unrelenting modernism of South California. The whole damn state seemed obsessed with hiding its history.

Fourteen law enforcers eyed her cynically from their chairs as she paced in front of the screenboard. Half the men were uniformed officers here at the precinct. The other half were her fellow Deps, all summoned to Ramona in the middle of the night for reasons they had yet to process. Even Cahill seemed skeptical as she activated the display. The flat ghost images of all six Silvers loomed behind her. She pointed to one with her coffee-cup hand.

"Her name's Amanda Given. At least that's what she told the local pawnbroker at 11:36 this morning, when she sold him a wedding ring." Melissa motioned to Zack's picture. "She was accompanied by this man, the driver of the stolen van and quite possibly the leader of the group. Now there are several factors—"

"That was fifteen hours ago," an agent griped. "What makes you think they're still in town?"

"There are several factors that lead me to believe the fugitives are still here in Ramona. We can assume they didn't steal a vehicle. Only two cars were reported missing today. One was recovered. The other was a two-seater, far too small for this crew. We know they didn't leave by bus, train, or aership. Their facial maps were entered into the Blackguard database. Had they approached any ticket counter, the civic cameras would have recognized them. Excuse me."

Wincing, she reached up the back of her blouse. Several sleepy eyes lurched awake as she pulled a lacy black bra from her sleeve.

"Sorry. I've been wearing that thing for twenty hours."

Cahill shook his head at her in dark wonder. With a small grin, she continued.

"It seems unlikely that a group this size could hitchhike out of town. I also believe they were too fatigued to walk. Given their state and their fresh influx of money, the likeliest scenario is that they're resting in one of the twenty-one budget motels that are currently open for business in Ramona."

She distributed a series of clipped packets, each one containing a list of motels, plus a color printout image of every Silver.

"Check the numbers on your handouts. I've split you into seven pairs, with the task of covering the three circled motels on your list. If the night clerk doesn't recognize the photos, find out if any double or triple room purchases have been made with cash today. If you get a lead, call me. If you should see any of these fugitives, do not engage them. They don't look it but they're dangerous. They already hurt six policemen today and may be responsible for at least two dozen deaths."

Melissa took another sip of coffee, then checked the wall clock: 2:45 A.M.

"I can only imagine they'll be making an early start out of town. That means we have a limited window to take them by surprise. Does anyone have any questions?"

No one did. "Good. Let's move out. And please be cautious."

Despite her call to action, nobody moved. The Deps looked to Cahill, who eyed them sternly. "Did anyone have trouble hearing her?"

The men grudgingly proceeded upstairs. Cahill smirked at the bra in her hand. "You sure like to poke the hive, don't you?"

"It was mostly a comfort decision."

"I wasn't talking about the skimpies, hon. You have any idea what you're risking here?"

"A pay raise, I imagine."

"That and more. It wouldn't have killed you to wait until these people surfaced again."

"No, sir, but it might have killed someone else."

On seeing his weary face, Melissa took his arm. "Come on. You can lecture me in the car."

Cahill didn't lecture her. He finally saw the futility in trying to instill political sense in this woman. Melissa Masaad was ultimately her own creature—gifted and reckless and hopelessly strange. Cahill could see why she had an easy time getting into the heads of these six runners. Perhaps on some level they were odd birds of a feather.

Theo rose from his blanket on the floor and gauged the sleeping breaths of his roommates. After five years of drunken hookups and trespasses, he'd become quite skilled at the art of the stealthy escape. He could move through the dark like a cat, even while his head pounded, his body throbbed, and his sense of worth dangled low enough to trip him.

He tied his shoes by the light of the moon, then slung his knapsack over his shoulder. Between all his frantic inner debates over staying and leaving and robbing his friends blind, a lone voice gibbered in unrelated panic. *Run run run. People are coming. Run run run from the people who come.*

As he spied the glistening currency on the end table, Theo's demon assured him that the group would be fine without it. Mia Farisi was a temporal cash machine. Hell, her next delivery would probably include tomorrow's winning lottery numbers.

He snatched the money, moving two shaky steps toward the door before halting with a guilty wince. He counted eight hundred dollars from the top of the stack and returned it to the table. Maybe now he could slink away as a half bastard, a half wreck of a human being.

While passing the desk, he noticed Zack's skillful rendition of Bugs Bunny on a stationery pad. Theo seized it and scribbled on the lower corner of the sheet.

I'm sorry, guys. I'm just not

He struggled on the next words until he realized he didn't need any. It was perfect just like that. As he closed the door behind him, he caught a reflected gleam in David's eyes, as if the boy were looking right at him. Theo's heart lurched. He shut the door and fled.

Soon he returned to his bench at the playground park, his heavy gaze fixed on the one store that remained open. The Genie Mart was embellished with faux-Arabian minarets and sported a cartoon mascot that looked like a sneering devil in a turban. A beer poster in the window hinted at great treasures within.

Theo pulled the money from his pocket and studied it. Nestled between two twenties was a scrap of paper he'd been carrying since Sunday, the phone number of Bill Pollock. He was one of Quint's older physicists—a husky, white-haired genius who could have passed for Santa Claus were it not for his eternally dour expression.

As the only recovered alcoholic on staff, Bill had been put in charge of Theo's rehabilitation. He'd wasted no time professing his unsuitability for the task.

"I honestly don't know how to help you," he'd told Theo, as the young man thrashed and screamed in withdrawal pain. "If I were any good with people, I wouldn't have become a scientist. The only argument I can make is a mathematical one. It seems you're one-sixth of your world's remaining population. You're the living marker for a billion people. Given the numbers, I suppose it'd be especially tragic if you threw your life away now. It wouldn't just be suicide. It'd be genocide."

As the weeks passed, the two men grew into their roles as counselor and patient, improving in synch until Theo finally became clean. When Bill learned that Theo was leaving with Zack, he came to work on a Sunday just to hand off his phone number.

"Look, I think your departure's premature, but you're strong enough to make your own decisions. Just call me if you ever feel weak or tempted. I won't tell Quint a thing."

Now, forty-two hours later, Theo felt weak and Theo felt tempted, but he couldn't call Bill Pollock because Bill Pollock was dead. Good people kept dying and yet Theo kept on living. The karmic balance of the universe was fatally broken.

He squeezed the money in his hand and took a teary-eyed glance at the Genie Mart. Whether it was suicide or genocide or something else entirely, the living marker for a billion people was ready to drink enough for all of them. He rose from the bench.

"Finally."

Theo spun around in surprise. Twenty feet away, a ginger-haired man leaned against the swing set, casually examining his cuticles. He was dressed like Theo from head to toe—same jeans, same sneakers, same gray sweatshirt. It was a surreal and discomfiting vision, like staring at a true dark genie.

"Who the hell are you?"

Evan grinned. "You'll figure it out in a minute."

"How long have you been standing there?"

"As long as you've been sitting there. I saw you wrestling with your conscience and I wanted to see which way you'd go. Now, while I respect your decision to party like there's no tomorrow, I'm afraid it was all for nothing. You can't buy liquor. Not without one of these."

Theo squinted as Evan flaunted a small blue photo ID. He held it up as he approached.

"They call it a wet card. You can apply for one when you turn eighteen. Just take a one-day class, a one-hour test, and then ta-da! License to drink. You have to be careful though. You get caught in a drunken misdemeanor, the card's suspended. Get caught in a felony, the card's revoked. And if you serve alcohol to someone without a wet card, even in your home, you're in for some hefty fines, fella. The civil liquortarians shit a blue pickle when they heard about this plan. But when they saw what happened to cigarettes, they suddenly became a lot more flexible."

Now he stood close enough for Theo to read the card, which featured Evan's cheery photo next to a cryptic pseudonym.

"Gordon Freeman?"

"The card's a fake," Evan explained. "So's the name. Zack would get the reference. He's awesome that way."

The pieces finally came together in Theo's head. "You're Evan Rander."

"Ding ding ding! Told you you'd get it." Evan laughed. "Oh, that Farisi and her spoilers."

Theo tightened his grip on his book bag and took a hasty step back. "Listen—"

"Oh relax, guy. I'm not so bad. In fact, I come bearing gifts and valuable info. Just hang a bit. You won't regret it."

He hopped over the bench, then motioned for Theo to join him. After a few silent moments, Theo took a wary perch on the far end.

Evan shined a soft grin at the Farsight Professional Augury. "You know, folks here are nutty about the future. Obsessed with it. Corporations have their own augurs on staff. Politicians rely on them like pollsters. It's still a bunch of crap. All cold readers and educated guessers, spouting flowery

Hannah in Her Element. She wasn't even the rickety Hannah that Theo had known before. She was falling apart.

"We could have had weeks, you asshole. We could have healed each other."

"That wouldn't have happened."

"Oh, just get the hell out of here already. You're such a coward, I can't even look at you."

"Hannah . . ."

The tears flowed freely down her face. "Theo, I swear to God you have three seconds to get out of this room before you see the real and awful me."

He took her at her word and left. He sat motionless on the living room sofa for over an hour before stretching out for sleep.

At 1 A.M., Hannah emerged with a folded blanket and pillow, then dropped them on his stomach. Theo saw his phone in her hand. A tiny bulb flashed green in announcement of new text messages.

"Don't read that. It's—"

"I know who it is."

She stepped outside to the balcony, hurled the phone over the railing, and then raised her middle fingers high in the night. It was her own message to Evan Rander, in whatever patio he'd chosen as his spying perch.

Theo watched her cautiously as she marched back through the living room.

"Give me one night to hate you," she said.

"Okay."

He wrapped himself in the blanket, steeling himself for the return of bad dreams. On the plus side, he knew he had only one night to spend on the sofa. Their feel-good week would finally end in the morning. At long last, the Silvers were checking out.

As the sun rose on Saturday, September 18, a tiny breach of time opened above Mia and spat an urgent message. The note rose and fell with her sleeping breaths for ninety-five minutes, until a waking turn rolled it into a blanket crevasse. She yawned her way to the bathroom, unaware.

Hannah woke up five minutes later, dark eyed and unrested. She shook

Theo awake in the living room and pulled him back to bed. She didn't want the others to see him sleeping on the couch like a punished husband. The less they knew about the whole debacle, the better.

While Hannah showered, Theo lay awake on the mattress, lamenting the loss of access to her ravishing body and suffering a vague new sense of dread. There was a bad wind blowing from the future, and it was centered around the sisters. Theo relaxed when he spotted Amanda in the living room, as cheery as he'd ever seen her. A week of rest and charity had done wonders for the widow's state of mind.

By ten o'clock, everyone was dressed, packed, and waiting at the balcony table. In light of the beautiful morning weather, Amanda insisted on having a final patio brunch. Zack led a sardonic round of applause when she wheeled in the food cart. Room service had taken over an hour to deliver their order.

"They're having some kind of bellhop crisis," Amanda explained. "A hotel manager had to bring this. He gave us free mimosas as an apology."

David studied the six flute glasses. "That's strange. He didn't ask to see your wet card?"

Zack scowled in mock outrage. "Can we go one morning without your crude euphemisms?"

The boy ignored him. "They have laws against serving alcohol to people without proper ID. The manager's putting the hotel at serious risk."

Amanda shrugged. "Well, it was a young guy. He's probably new. And who cares? Is anyone here planning on reporting them?"

"I am."

"Shut up," she said to Zack. "You're having a drink with me. Who else wants?"

Amanda turned sheepish when she saw Theo's heavy expression. "There's probably an ounce of champagne in these things. Not even enough for a buzz."

"It's okay. I'll pass."

Amanda wasn't surprised when the teenagers abstained, but Hannah's refusal threw her. "Are you sure? You used to love these."

"I said I don't want any."

Raising her palms in surrender, Amanda backed away. Soon everyone took turns at the kitchen juve, reversing their food to a piping-hot state. Amanda passed Zack a glass and a whisper.

"There are at least three of us here in bad moods. Please save me before I become the fourth."

"I can do that."

The two of them quickly dominated the meal with their boisterous celebration, trading silly quips and toasts between each sip of mimosa.

"To happy fugitives," said Amanda.

"To well-rested fugitives," said Zack.

"To tall and skinny atheist fugitives who can be somewhat cute when they're not obnoxious."

Zack retracted his glass. "Sorry. Can't drink to that without correcting you."

"You're not cute?"

"I'm not an atheist. I have no idea if God exists or not."

"Then why do you make fun of the people who do?"

"Because I'm obnoxious," Zack replied. "That part of the toast was accurate."

"I see. You're an obnoxious agnostic. You're agnoxious."

"I'm antaganostic."

Amanda roared with laughter. "How could you think you're not cute?"

"I never said I wasn't!"

Though Mia giggled at their goofy banter, the other three Silvers remained grim and humorless. Halfway through Amanda's second drink, her fingers turned shiny and white. When Mia awkwardly told her that her weirdness was showing, Amanda laughed, shook her hands pink, and then raised a toast to tempis fugitives. The pun launched Zack into bellowing guffaws.

"I'm thinking those drinks are stronger than you realized," David mused.

Zack waved him off. "We're not hammered."

"We're just having fun," Amanda insisted, with a pointed glare at Hannah.

It had taken only five minutes of her sister's excruciating revelry to make Hannah swallow down the three spare mimosas. But instead of joining Zack and Amanda in tipsy exuberance, the actress felt worse than ever. Her skin burned. Her legs bounced uncontrollably. Angry notions exploded in her mind like popcorn.

Once Amanda propped her feet on Zack's thighs, Hannah stood up fast enough to wobble.

Theo grabbed her. "Whoa. You okay?"

Hannah yanked her arm away. "I'm fine."

She washed her face in the bathroom, gritting her teeth as a sneering inner voice taunted her. *Hey, Hannah Banana, Always Needs-a-Man-a. Funny how you can't keep them while your sister can't keep them away. Shame Jury's not here to balance things out. Oh well. That's just the way it goes here in Evansville.*

She returned to the balcony with forced poise, determined to ignore Theo's patronizing look of concern and the escalating flirtations between her sister and Zack.

"It's true!" Amanda insisted. "You have physical contact issues. You don't like hugging."

"That is bull-pucky of the highest order. I hug everyone. Even my enemies."

"Remember that time we hugged in Ramona? You were awkward about it."

"That's because we were in an alley. I could feel the hobos judging us."

"There were no hobos, Zachary. You have issues that need fixing. Stand up."

"No."

"Fine. We'll do it sitting down."

Amanda planted herself on Zack's lap, fastening his arms around her slender waist.

"And what is this supposed to accomplish?" he asked.

"Immersion therapy. You need to get over your resistance."

"Boy, the charity never stops with you."

She leaned back against him and blew him a frisky whisper. "This isn't charity, you clueless man. I want more hugs."

Hannah jumped to her feet, rocking the table. As drinks spilled onto plates and laps, the actress threw an empty glass to the floor. It exploded all around her shoes.

"What the hell is wrong with you?!"

Shocked into sobriety, Amanda climbed off Zack's lap. She raised her taut fingers.

"Okay, take it easy . . ."

"Do you even see how pathetic you're being right now? You've been a widow for eight weeks! Eight weeks, and this is how you act!"

David held Mia's arm. "Let's get the bags ready."

Mia gave him a shaky nod. They disappeared inside. Amanda fought to stay calm.

"Look, I don't know what's really bothering you . . ."

"You think it isn't upsetting enough to watch you disrespect Derek?"

"You barely even knew him!"

"I know he'd hate to see you give a lap dance to some other guy!"

Zack shook his head in seething pique. "Hannah, you're way off base and way out of line."

"Well then let me be the second one to call you clueless. I swear to God, there isn't a single man in this group who knows a single thing about women."

"Look, you're angry at me," Amanda said. "Don't take it out on him."

Hannah laughed bitterly. "Oh, you just love being noble. The great and noble Amanda Given. Oops. Sorry. I meant Amanda Ambridge. Hey, Zack, I hope you're not intent on having her take your name. She'll just drop it the minute you die. That's how noble she is."

Amanda gritted her teeth. Her eyes filled with tears. "You sad little child . . ."

"Yeah, the child. Your other favorite meme. You just love being better than me."

"Well, you make it so easy!"

"Oh, go to hell!"

"*You* go to hell! We did this for you! We took this whole week so you could feel better! Of course you'd do everything in your power to stay miserable! That's all you know how to do!"

"Shut up!"

Theo reached for her. "Hannah, don't—"

She turned to him, red-faced. "You do not say a word to me. You do not say a word!"

Amanda eyed the two of them with dark revelation. She burst into a caustic chuckle.

"Oh, I get it now. I see why you're so pissed."

"Shut up! You don't know a thing!"

"And you call me the pathetic one? Amazing. You never learn."

Theo and Zack both yelled as Hannah hurled a second glass. This one hit Amanda in the face.

Mia gathered her bags from her room, her stomach churning with bitter acids. For all she knew, this latest fight would plague them for months. Worse, it could split them up forever. What would happen then? Who'd go with who?

As she adjusted her bedspread, she noticed a rolled-up note. She read it with growing fear, then fled back to the living room.

The flute glass cracked in two against Amanda's forehead, leaving a pair of gashes along her brow. She touched her new wounds, then stared in trembling rage at the blood on her fingers.

Hannah covered her mouth in white-eyed horror. "Oh my God . . ."

Zack made a furious beeline for Hannah. "What the hell's wrong with you?!"

The cartoonist could suddenly feel every molecule in Hannah's body. It scared him to think that he could rift her dead with a single thought. Scarier still, a part of him wanted to.

Mia ran to the door. "Zack, stop! The drinks were drugged! You're all drugged!"

Though her future self hadn't elaborated, the chemical that affected them was called pergnesticin. It was initially developed as a mood enhancer, as it did a fine job turning good feelings into great ones. Unfortunately, it also had a tendency to turn bad moods into violence. The drug was illegal in the United States but remained wildly popular as contraband. In dermal patch form, it was appropriately known as a leopard spot.

Theo could suddenly see the shape of the problem ahead. He knew now that Evan wasn't content to return a middle-finger gesture at Hannah. He was going to give her the whole hand.

"Hannah, you need to get out of here . . ."

"I'm sorry, Amanda! I didn't mean to do that!"

The widow's world fell hot and silent as chemical rage overtook her. There was no sister, nurse, or Christian inside her anymore. There was only the tempis.

The whiteness exploded from her left palm, a spray of solid force that toppled everything in its path. A wooden chair fell while another snapped to pieces. The dining table flipped over, spilling drinks and dishes everywhere. By the time the tempis reached the other end of the balcony, it took form as a six-foot hand. It shoved away the two men who had the unfortunate luck of standing near Hannah. Theo toppled to the right, colliding painfully with the hot tub. Zack flew to the left, flipping over the side of the balcony railing. He caught a loose hold of the edge.

The tempic palm barreled into Hannah, shoving her six feet through the air. Amanda retracted her hand in time to see Hannah crack her head against the far brick wall. She spilled to the floor in a lifeless heap.

David lunged toward the railing, rushing to grab Zack before he lost his grip. Between the blood in her eyes and the many alarms in her head, Amanda processed the simple but devastating notion that the boy wouldn't make it in time.

Indeed, just inches before David could reach him, Zack's fingers lost their hold. He dropped from the side of Tower Five.

Ten days ago, as he floated over Kansas in a giant teacup, Zack wondered what it would be like to plummet to his death. He debated how much time his mind would give him to process the sad and messy end of his tale.

The answer, he now knew, was "quite a bit."

For the second time in his life, the cartoonist fell into a state of breathless suspension, an almost supernatural acuity that allowed him to register dozens of details in the span of a blink. He could count the number of balcony railings between him and the ground (*eight*). He could scan the unforgiving elements of his future impact zone (*wood and concrete*). He could envision the reactions of his surviving friends and enemies (*Oh God, Amanda . . .*).

As he passed the fifth-floor balcony, something odd happened. The shift in his momentum was so abrupt and painful that he feared he'd already hit the pavement. A cold, hard pressure immobilized Zack's body, as if he'd been packed in dense snow. When he opened his eyes, he could see the ground fifty feet below him. It wasn't getting any closer.

He turned his head and caught his reflection in a patio door. A giant tempic fist had seized him, snatching him from above like the hand of God itself.

She caught me, he thought. *Jesus Christ, she caught me.*

Zack once again gazed down at the grotto, where dozens of bystanders began to gather in a messy clump. They pointed up at him, gawking and shouting, snapping photos.

His last thought before blacking out was of Peter Pendergen, a man who'd worked so tirelessly to keep the public cynical about chronokinetics. Zack cast him a weary apology for the unwitting countereffort. All the minds they changed today. All the new believers.

TWENTY-THREE

Evan woke up in a sour mood on Saturday, haunted by the memories of his multiple pasts. They leapt at him from his cutting room floor—scenes deleted but not forgotten, words unsaid but not unheard, all the hurtful actions of a woman he'd cherished but now despised. They always hit him worst in the morning.

With a drowsy yawn, he crossed the floor of his hotel suite. He showered and shaved, dressed himself in a sleek charcoal business suit, then tucked his hair beneath a wavy brown wig. Once he applied his putty nose and chin, Evan chuckled at his reflection. He could have passed for Zack's dapper young brother.

After a hearty breakfast in the grotto café, Evan rented a room on the tenth floor of Tower Five, just a few doors down from his fellow Silvers. He ordered six mimosas from room service and then called the front desk to launch an incoherent complaint about his new accommodations.

Soon a manager knocked on his door. He was bald and barrel-chested, with a strong lantern jaw that unpleasantly reminded Evan of his father. The manager did a double take at Evan's suit, a nearly exact replica of his own.

"Good morning, Mr. Freeman. I'm Lloyd Lundrum. What seems to be the problem?"

Evan tapped the square brass pin on the man's blazer. "Lloyd Lundrum. Good name. I like it. Listen, the room's fine. I'm just hoping to play a gag on some friends down the hall. I'll give you a thousand dollars to lend me your name tag for an hour."

The manager's eyes narrowed to frosty slits. Evan laughed.

"Okay. Wow. You even glare like my dad. I guess there's no point in raising my offer."

"No, sir. There's not. And I don't appreciate you calling me here under—"

Evan's skin tingled with tiny bubbles as he reversed his life fifty-eight seconds. He straightened his sleeves, then answered the knock at the door.

"Good morning, Mr. Freeman. I'm Lloyd Lundrum. What seems to be the problem?"

"Well, Lloyd, there's an ugly red stain on the carpet and frankly, I'm not happy about it."

Sixty seconds later, the manager lay crumpled at the foot of the bed, a trickling bullet hole between his frozen white eyes.

Evan stashed his silenced .22, then stooped to remove Lloyd's ID pin. He could only imagine that Luke Rander was shaking his head from the great beyond. His father never understood him in the old world and sure as hell wouldn't get it now. In Evan's Etch A Sketch life, nothing mattered. All that was done was inevitably undone. The screen would wipe clean for Round 56, and Lloyd Lundrum would live again to scoff at wealthy pranksters.

Evan whistled a chipper tune as he stirred a vial of crushed pergnesticin into the mimosas. Soon he heard Amanda in his earpiece, placing the room service order. He waited in the hallway until a freckly young porter emerged from the elevator. Fortunately the kid was more flexible than Lloyd, and was happy to relinquish the food cart for a thousand dollars. Evan dawdled in his room for another half hour before wheeling the cart down the hall.

He stashed his hatred behind a genial grin when Amanda greeted him at the door. Evan couldn't look at her without recalling the trauma from his last life, the cold and rainy night she jammed a tempic sword through his chest. That Amanda had died before Evan could get his revenge. But this one was standing right here, just ripe for the plucking.

"Good morning, ma'am. I'm Lloyd Lundrum. I sincerely apologize for the delay."

"What happened?"

"We're short on bellhops today. It's a madhouse. I've been delivering food all morning."

Amanda looked over the cart. "Are you sure this is our order? Those drinks—"

"I threw in the complimentary mimosas as our way of saying sorry. If you don't want them—"

"No, that's fine. My sister loves those."

Evan smiled. "Well then I hope you and your sister have a wonderful brunch."

As Amanda processed him with her sharp green gaze, he fought the urge to rewind and start over. But soon she passed him a twenty-dollar tip and then pulled the cart inside. Evan grinned all the way to the elevator until he realized the bitch never once looked at his name tag.

Twelve minutes later, he sat on the balcony of his Tower Five rental, listening to Zack and Amanda's giddy banter in his earpiece. When Evan first discovered they were staying in the Baronessa Suite, he rewound two days and became its previous occupant. Tiny listening devices were concealed in various parts of the living room, the balcony, and of course Hannah's bedroom.

The hardest part of Evan's week was having to once again hear her dulcet moans of pleasure, each one a pinch of salt in a very old wound. But he knew her fling with Theo never lasted long or ended well. Evan had only seen two men pierce the formidable shell around Hannah's heart. He'd already killed one of them. The other would crash her life next year, with deliciously tragic consequences.

Evan had been wiping the makeup off the back of his hand, scrubbing his "55" tattoo back into visibility, when Hannah smashed her first flute glass. He launched forward with the binoculars, hoo-hooing and oohing as the sisters traded angry barbs. When the second glass cracked across Amanda's forehead, Evan squealed with delight. This was a thing of beauty, a moment so perfect that he had to watch it six times.

His smile vanished when Amanda's tempic hand knocked Zack off the balcony. Evan shot to his feet now, staring in alarm as Zack lost his grip and fell. Screaming, Amanda threw herself against the railing and launched a tempic arm at Zack. She caught him at the fifth floor.

Evan closed his eyes and moaned with hot relief. He didn't want to reverse such a beautiful chain of events, but he would have done it to save Zack. The cartoonist was the focus of Evan's next mission. More than that, he was a friend.

Amanda's mind howled with chaos, a fire in a crowded theater. Panicked thoughts trampled each other on the way to her mouth as her body twisted painfully over the railing. Her hands were submerged in an enormous white arm, fifty feet long and as thick as a manhole cover. She could feel Zack's body in her thoughts, resting limp and unconscious in her titan grip.

"I got him. I got him. Oh my God."

David pressed up against her backside, holding her in place. "Okay. Good. Good, Amanda. Now you have to bring him back."

"It's not working! I can't control it!"

"Yes you can," said David. "Concentrate."

Six weeks ago, Sterling Quint's physicists had attempted to gauge the limits of Amanda's tempic talent. Her creations took an increasing amount of willpower to maintain. At sixty seconds, it felt like squeezing a tight fist. At two minutes, it felt like squeezing a tight fist around thumbtacks. Czerny had stopped the endurance test at 148 seconds, when Amanda began to cry and bleed from her nose.

David laid his hands on Amanda's wrists. She could feel the giant arm contract.

"What are you doing? David, how are you doing that?"

"I'm not doing anything," he said. "It's all you. Just keep focusing."

Theo fumbled his way up the side of the hot tub, throbbing with pain. He yanked a small shard of glass from his thigh, then looked to Hannah. The actress lay motionless on the floor.

Amanda turned her head as much as she could. "Theo! Are you okay? Is Hannah okay?"

"Concentrate on Zack!" David yelled.

Theo took an anxious reading of Hannah's pulse and future, then exhaled at the presence of both.

"She's all right. She's okay."

"Don't move her. She could have a broken—"

Amanda screamed when Zack slipped in her grasp. David seethed at her.

"Goddamn it, Amanda! If you care about him . . ."

"I do! I'm sorry!"

Theo looked to the patio doorway, where Mia stood frozen in dread. Her inner voice chanted Zack's name over and over.

"Mia . . ."

The urgent note from the future still dangled from her fingertips, warning her of Evan's drugged cocktails. If only she'd seen it sooner . . .

"Mia!"

She snapped out of her daze. Theo jerked his head at the living room.

"Security's coming. We need to go fast. Gather as many bags as you can carry. Leave the stuff we don't need. Can you do that?"

She gave him a trembling nod, then disappeared inside.

Theo scooped Hannah in his arms, praying she didn't have a spinal injury. He saw a thick stream of blood trickle down her hair. *Goddamn you, Evan.*

By the time Zack reached the ninth floor, Amanda's brain felt like it was wrapped in barbed wire. David wiped sweat and blood from her forehead.

"Hold on. Just a few more seconds."

"I can't hold it . . ."

"You can, Amanda. You have to. You'll never forgive yourself if you let him drop."

With a final scream, she raised Zack to eye level. David grabbed his arms just as the tempis vanished. He pulled Zack over the railing, then checked his vitals.

"He's okay, Amanda. You did it."

Amanda fell back onto the one chair that was left standing, her face drenched and white.

Theo turned around in the doorway and looked to David. "You think you can carry him?"

"Yeah. I can get him to the van."

With a loud grunt, David hoisted Zack into his arms. Amanda cast a shaky palm.

"Be careful! He could have a broken neck! They could both . . ."

Now the images in Amanda's head turned melodramatic, a theater in a crowded fire. She pictured Zack and Hannah as paraplegics. Her fault. Her hands. Her tempis.

"Oh my God. I did this . . ."

David gritted his teeth. "Amanda, we don't have time."

"He's right," said Theo. "I know you're drugged and I know you're hurting, but you need to pull yourself together. We have to go right now."

Wincing, she struggled to her feet. "Okay. Okay."

They turned their gazes to the airy distance, at the sound of approaching sirens. Now Theo's future howled. There was no way they'd make it to the van without being spotted. There was no hope of making it out of Evansville without another chase.

Zack came to life on the way to the elevator. Hot knives of pain stabbed his chest while his body bobbled and dangled in David's arms. He raised a weak gaze.

"David . . . ?"

Amanda rushed to his side. "Zack! Are you all right? Can you feel my hand?"

He fought a cracked and addled laugh. *I think we all felt your hand, honey.*

"I'm okay. Anyone else hurt?"

"Hannah. She's unconscious. I don't know how bad it is yet."

As Mia jabbed the elevator call button, Theo checked the progress displays above all four doors. Two of the cars were on their way up, one from the first floor, the other from the fourth. His thoughts flashed with images of six security guards in the lower elevator.

He pointed to the north-side doors. "This is going to be close. We need to jump in that thing the second it opens."

"Put me down," Zack said. "I can walk."

The moment he touched the ground, he winced at another painful chest stab. Amanda held his arm. "What is it? What's wrong?"

"Nothing. I'm all right."

The elevator was two floors away. Theo shifted Hannah in his arms. "We're never going to make it through the lobby. Not like this . . ."

"We have no choice," David said. "We'll have to fight our way through."

Amanda eyed him with dark concern. "There has to be a better way."

"Here it comes . . ."

As she lifted her knapsacks, Mia felt a familiar twinge in the back of her mind. *Oh no . . .*

The doors opened to an empty elevator. "Come on!" Theo yelled. "Hurry!"

They rushed into the lift. Mia dropped her bags and propped a door.

"What the hell are you doing?" Theo asked.

"I'm getting a note!"

A small bead of light floated a foot above the carpet, an arm's length outside the elevator. Theo looked to the display across the hall. The other elevator was at Floor 7.

"Forget it! We don't have time!"

"It could be important!"

"Mia, I'm almost positive there are six security guards in that other elevator . . ."

"We wouldn't be in this mess if I'd seen my other note! I'm not making that mistake again!"

David pressed the hold button. "I got this. Move your hand."

Mia pulled her arm inside. David ghosted a pair of closed elevator doors just as a chime issued from across the hall. The Silvers stood frozen behind their illusive cover, listening to the gruff voices and heavy footsteps just ten feet away.

The clamor quickly moved down the hall. David breathed a whisper at Mia. "Be careful."

She dropped to the ground and crawled through the ghost doors. Once she plucked the note from the carpet, she glanced down the hall. Theo was right. Six armed guards now stood outside the Baronessa Suite. They didn't bother to knock before keying into the room.

With a deep exhale, she backed into the lift. The real doors closed over the ghosted ones. Mia read the note with bulging eyes, then pressed the emergency stop.

"What are you doing, Mia?"

"We can't go down. We have to go up."

David blinked at her. "Are you insane?"

"What's the message?" Theo asked.

"'You won't make it to the garage without hitting cops. Go up to Suite 1255. It's being repainted but nobody will touch it until Monday. Hide in there until things quiet down.'"

She pushed the cancel button until the lobby light went dark, then reset their course for the top floor.

David shook his head. "I don't like this. In a matter of hours, this place will be crawling with Deps. They have ghost drills. They'll track us."

tails, unable to discern the true outcome until it stared at him from his wrist.

Mia rejoined Theo at the study table, watching him read the passage with vacant consternation. She noticed that he'd become sluggish and distant over the past few days. She often found him skimming the same page over and over, or staring out the window with a glazed expression. Though he insisted he was fine, Mia feared he was coming down with an illness.

He closed Quint's book and passed it back to her. "I'm not sure what to make of that."

"Me neither. But I keep thinking back to Ramona, when I got the fifteen hundred dollars from the future. You remember that?"

Theo could hardly forget. He'd stolen off into the night with half of it. "What about it?"

"The next day we found a quarter of a million dollars in the van. That always confused me. I mean why would that Mia bother sending me cash if she knew we were about to be swimming in it?"

"So now you're thinking she didn't know."

Mia nodded. "Right. Maybe she was from a different future, one where we never found the van and money."

Theo pressed his knuckles to his lips as he fell back into his own conundrum. His foresight had gone into overdrive these past couple of days, barraging him with split-second glimpses of moments that had yet to occur. Though most of the visions were vague and benign—moving snapshots of strangers in strange places—he was particularly struck by the ones that involved Melissa Masaad. In one flash, the stalwart Dep bound Theo's wrists in handcuffs on a crisp and cool evening. In another, she shot him in the rain. In a third, she handed him a DP-9 identification card with his name and photo. And in yet another, he rested his cheek on her taut and naked belly, feeling the flutters under her skin as she stroked his hair. Even if these were premonitions and not just figments, he couldn't believe they were all from the same timeline.

"That's . . ." He pressed a taut thumb to his chin. "Huh."

"Yeah. I can barely wrap my head around it."

"If there are an infinite number of futures and we're just seeing one or two at a time, then what's the point? We're no better than guessers. We're not even educated guessers."

Mia puffed in bother. "I don't know. I just know this is exactly the way David said it was. How does he always know these things?"

"He reads a lot of sci-fi. I'm still not convinced it works that way."

"I'm thinking it does," said a third voice.

They turned to the woman who sat two tables away, a honey-skinned blonde in a flimsy white sundress. Though she carried herself with the self-assuredness of an adult, she could have passed for a teenager with her large hazel eyes, cute waifish body, and cropped pixie haircut. Theo was intrigued by her nebulous ethnicity, an incongruous blend of European and Asian features.

The girl closed her book and approached them, standing at their table like an auditioning actress. Mia noticed the pair of watches on her right wrist. One was analog with an ornate silver band. The other was digital and cheap-looking.

She flashed the pair a pleasant smile. "Sorry. I hate to be a snooping Susie, but you two are having a *very* interesting discussion."

Mia turned skittish. "We're just messing around. You shouldn't take us seriously."

"Don't worry. I'm not a psychologist. I'm probably nuttier than both of you. But I do know a thing or two about futures." She motioned to a chair. "May I?"

Theo and Mia exchanged a wary glance before indulging her with nods.

"Cool." She took a seat, then studied their research pile. "Well, no wonder you're confused. These books are crap. If I really wanted to stick my nose in your business, I'd put you in touch with an experienced augur. I mean a real one."

"Frankly, we're not sure there are any real ones," Theo said.

The girl grinned at him with enough mischief to make Mia suspect a flirty hidden motive.

"Oh ye of little faith. Are you familiar with the Gunther Gaia Test?"

Theo nodded. It had come up several times in research. In 1988, a wealthy skeptic named George Gunther publicly offered twenty million dollars to anyone who could correctly predict five natural disasters in the course of a calendar year. The test had become an annual lottery to the would-be augurs of America, with thousands entering each January. So far only a handful had managed to get even one forecast right, an endless source of swagger for the nonbelievers.

"Well, I have it on good authority that this year's challenge isn't going quite the way Gunther likes," the girl told them. "There's a man who entered a whopping seventeen predictions, and so far he's been right on the money. He has four guesses left, all for the last three months of the year. I have no doubt they'll happen too. You might want to steer clear of Tunisia this Christmas."

Mia sat forward in rapt attention. "Who is this guy?"

"He says his name's Merlin McGee, though I know for a fact it isn't. Young fella. Very shy. Very cute. I've met him twice now. He's the real deal. When I congratulated him on his impending wealth, he merely shrugged. He said he's not sure if Gunther will honor the arrangement."

"If he can truly see the future, wouldn't he know?"

The girl tapped Mia's hand. "I asked him the same question. You know what he told me? He said he only wished that people were as easy to predict as God."

Theo winced as a hot knife of pain cut through his mind. The first one had hit him three days ago. Now they seemed to come every hour.

Mia held his arm. "You okay?"

"Yeah. I'm all right. It's nothing."

From her sympathetic expression, the girl clearly disagreed. "You know, there's a health fair going on at the other side of the park. You don't need insurance. They'll take anyone."

"I appreciate it, but I'm okay."

Despite the kindness of their new acquaintance, Theo grew suspicious of her. It seemed odd that a person so friendly hadn't offered her name by now, or asked for theirs.

Mia brandished Quint's book to the girl. "This guy says a real augur wouldn't know anything because he'd see every possibility at once."

"Oh, please. There's an expression people like to give me whenever they notice my wrist. They say, 'A girl with two watches never knows what time it is.' That's bullshit." She checked her dual timepieces. "It's 3:30."

"How do you know for sure?" Theo challenged.

"Because they're synchronized. That makes me twice as sure. What Sterling Quint, God rest his missing soul, doesn't take into account are the redundancies. You look at a million possible outcomes, you start to see repeats. From repeats come patterns. From patterns come probabilities. A true augur can look at the big quilt and see which futures have the best chances of happening."

She tilted her head at Mia as if she suddenly just noticed her. "You have *amazing* hair."

Mia fought a bashful grin. Theo remained skeptical. "It's still guesswork though."

"So?"

"It wouldn't matter for coin tosses, but for life-or-death situations . . ."

The girl waved him off. "Oh, suck it up, man. You're never going to be a good augur if you live in fear of regret."

"Who said I wanted to become an augur?"

"You're already an augur, Theo. You're just not a good one."

Now both Silvers stared at her in hot alarm. She sighed at herself.

"Shit. I didn't want to make a whole thing of this. I don't even know why I came here. This isn't my battle."

"Who are you?" Mia asked.

"I'm nobody. Just a stupid girl who can't mind her own business. You both seem like nice people and you looked so lost. I just wanted to give you a push in the right direction and then flutter away."

"You won't even give us your name," Theo griped. "Why should we believe anything you say?"

The girl shrugged. "You don't have to believe a word, hon. Doesn't affect me one bit. It also doesn't change the reality of your situation. Big things are coming, whether you like it or not."

"Yeah? Like what?"

"Like you," she told Theo. "You have no idea how much power you're carrying in that stubborn brain of yours. There's a great prophet buried in there. Now he's clawing his way up through all that trauma and liquor damage. I wish I could tell you the process will tickle, but those headaches you're getting are just previews. Come tomorrow, you're really not going to like being you."

"What are you talking about?"

"What does it matter? You don't believe me anyway." The girl looked to Mia. "I'm hoping you'll be a little more receptive to what I have to say. You're a sweet and pretty girl with a sharp mind and killer hair. But one thing you're not and never will be is an augur."

Mia's heart lurched. "What . . . what do you mean?"

"You don't have the sight like me and Theo. You just have your portals, and they aren't meant to be used the way you're using them. It's not your fault. Nobody told you. It's just that there are a lot of Mias out there in the future. The stronger you get, the more of them you'll hear from. If you're not careful, every minute of your life will be a ticker-tape parade. I don't think you want that."

The thought turned Mia white. "I don't! What do I do?"

"Talk to Peter. He'll set you straight. The man can be a pigheaded fool sometimes, but he sure knows his portals."

Theo eyed her cynically. "Is that what you are? A Gotham?"

"No, but I've met a few. They hate being called that, by the way."

The girl rose to her feet and slung her purse over her shoulder.

"You know why Merlin McGee only predicts natural disasters? Because he's lazy and they're easy. They're constants across the many branching futures, well outside our influence. It doesn't matter which way we zig or zag. It's still going to rain in Nemeth tomorrow."

She fixed a heavy gaze on Theo. "Bad times are coming. First for you, then your friends. If there was a way around it, I'd tell you. You're all just going to have to stay strong and weather the storm."

The girl walked ten steps to the bookshelves, then took a final look at Mia.

"I really do love that hair."

She disappeared in the aisles, leaving her new friends in quiet turmoil. Theo aimed his dull stare out the window. Mia's gaze danced around the letters of Quint's book jacket.

"Are you okay to drive?" she asked him, a half hour later.

"I think so."

"Okay. I think I'd like to go home."

"Yeah."

They left the library in grim silence, without looking back. They didn't need foresight to know that they wouldn't return here. They'd already learned more than they wanted to know.

The grandfather clock ticked away as the Silvers sat behind the remnants of their supper. Ten elbows rested on the dining room table, ten fists propping five chins. Only Theo sat slouched in his chair. He wished Mia hadn't told the others about the girl with two watches.

"She's either a skilled augur herself or a time traveler," David surmised. "I can't see how else she'd profess to know about Theo's potential."

Amanda peered at David's plate, still half-filled with boiled peas. The sisters had initially tried to prepare more elaborate vegan dishes for him. He never took more than a few polite bites before returning to his vegetable piles.

"And we're absolutely sure this woman wasn't Esis?" Zack asked.

David squinted at Mia. "Describe her in detail."

"I don't know. She was thin. Pretty. Short."

"No," said David.

"No," said Amanda. "Esis is not short."

The cartoonist shrugged in grim surrender. After exploding a deer today, he wasn't confident in his opinion about anything.

Hannah sat back in her chair and seethed. In the four hours since the death of the fawn, her melancholy had turned into something hard and prickly. She found herself despising everyone at the table for reasons of little merit. She hated David for his stupid vegan diet. She hated Mia for her inexhaustible sweetness. She hated Zack and Amanda for not screwing like rabbits already. She hated Theo for all the usual reasons.

At the moment, she hated the fact that her companions were all brilliant in one way or another, and yet none of them considered the obvious.

"She's an actress."

The others glanced up at her with blank expressions. She met their gazes one by one.

"Evan's messing with us again, only this time by proxy. He hired that woman. Coached her through and through. And now once again we're all dancing to his tune, wondering if up is down, left is right. It'd be funny if it wasn't so tragic."

The clock ticked five more times before David broke the silence.

"That's a very solid theory."

Zack nodded. "I've been wondering why we haven't heard from him in a while."

"I don't know," said Mia, her nervous eyes fixed on Theo. "I'm hoping it's all a lie."

Hannah peered across the table and was surprised by the tender smile Theo shined at her. He didn't think she was right at all, but she killed the discussion and he loved her for it.

At five minutes to midnight, Hannah made a drowsy trip to the kitchen and poured herself a glass of water. She crossed into the darkened living room and jumped at the shadowy figure in the easy chair.

"Just me," Theo croaked.

She pressed her chest. "Jesus. You scared the hell out of me."

"Sorry."

She turned on the lamp and faced Theo from the sofa. His eyes were dark. He slumped against the cushions as if he were boneless.

"Are you okay? You don't look good."

Theo couldn't help but grin. Hannah never looked better in her snug white tank top and panties, her bed-tousled hair. While the angel on his shoulder plotted a course of emotional reconciliation, the devil in his sweatpants insisted he was a few deft moves away from couch sex.

"I'm okay," he assured her. "For now."

"So you think that girl was telling the truth."

"I know she was. I see it now, clear as day. Right after breakfast, I'm going to get a nosebleed. Then a splitting headache. By noon, I'll barely know where I am."

Hannah sat forward. "God, Theo. Are you sure this isn't some self-fulfilling, psychosomatic thing?"

"Yup."

"That's crazy. You were talking about infinite futures at dinner. How can this be so certain?"

"Well, there's some wiggle room on the nosebleed."

"This isn't funny. I'm worried about you."

"I know. I can see that. I have to say it's kind of nice, all things considered."

Hannah shot a hot breath at the floor, then matched his lazy stance.

"I've been pretty pathetic, haven't I? Taking two weeks to get over a one-week fling."

"Well, I certainly haven't helped."

"I don't know," she said. "I think I've been angry just for the sake of being angry. Hell, I got mad at you all over again today when that poor fawn died."

"How was that my fault? I wasn't even there."

"Exactly. I was upset and I needed someone to screw me numb. I'm not like my sister. I can't just draw on inner strength. I don't have any."

"That's not true."

"I don't know. Feels like it. So while I understand your reasons for the breakup, and even agree with them in retrospect, I'm still mad that you took away my crutch."

Theo struggled to stay noble, even as he ripped the clothes off her mental image.

"I'm sorry I can't handle the kind of relationship you want, Hannah. Sorry for both of us. I'm looking at you now and I'm thinking about what's coming. I wish I could screw us both numb."

The grandfather clock chimed in the midnight hour, heralding the official start of October. By the twelfth echoing ring, Hannah clenched her jaw in tense resolve.

"First thing tomorrow, I'll go to the pharmacy with Amanda. Get you a ton of painkillers."

"They won't help."

"Well, we'll try, goddamn it. Just because it's destined to happen doesn't mean we can't fight it."

Once again, she was surprised by Theo's thin and tender smile, out of place given the situation.

"Yesterday I had a snapshot premonition of you and me," he told her. "We were sitting just like this, chatting away at midnight in our sweatpants and underwear."

"Is that why you came down here?"

"No. This was somewhere else. Some house on an army base. You looked a bit older. My guess is that it's still a good four years away."

"Wow."

"Yeah. It's nice to know there's at least one future out there where you and I are still alive in four years. Still friends."

Hannah glumly stared out the window, listening to the owls.

"Friends. Strange word to use for any of us. I can barely separate you guys from Amanda anymore. It's like you're all my siblings now. Even you, as screwed up as that sounds."

The two of them sat in silence for another long moment. Hannah rubbed her eyes.

"You're a good man, Theo. You're a good man and I love you and I really hope you're wrong about tomorrow. You don't deserve it."

The augur breathed a long sigh of surrender. It seemed a cruel joke of the universe that the easiest things to predict were the ones that couldn't be prevented. The pain. The rain. The natural disasters. And yet he couldn't help but disagree with Hannah's last sentiment. The girl with two watches had attributed alcohol damage as a primary cause of his neurological crisis. That made it his fault, which strangely made it easier to accept. For once there was justice, there was balance, there was karma in the situation. Theo planned to wield it like an umbrella. Like Hannah's screwed-up love, he'd carry the blame with him, all the way through the storm.

Everything happened as foretold. At 5:02 in the morning, the sky over Nemeth offered ten seconds of warning drizzle before coming down in sheets. Dawn arrived in the form of a hundred lightning flashes.

At 9:20, Theo glanced down at his eggs and noticed a fresh drop of blood, another warning drizzle. He pressed a napkin to his nose, then looked to his troubled friends.

"Shit."

The pain hit him like a cyclone. His muscles turned to liquid and he fell out of his chair. By the time David carried him to the couch, he'd lost all sense of time and place.

Theo lay on his back, writhing on the cushions like an uneasy dreamer.

He was only marginally aware of the conversations that occurred around him, the feminine hands that comforted him in turns. While Mia stroked his fingers with sisterly affection and Amanda tended to him with clinical diligence, it was Hannah's intimate caress that brought him back to the present. He lifted the damp cloth from his brow and tossed her a bleary stare.

"What time is it . . . ?"

She checked the grandfather clock. "Quarter after one. How you holding up?"

"Worse than anything I ever felt. I wanna . . . I wanna die."

Hannah squeezed his hand. "Oh, sweetie. Just hang in there. The pain won't last."

"It's not the pain . . ."

"What do you mean?"

Amanda rushed into the room and pulled at Hannah's shoulder. "Let me look at him."

"Just a second. We're talking." She looked to Theo. "What do you mean? Are you having visions?"

"I'm not just seeing," he moaned. "I'm feeling. I keep feeling you guys . . . dying. Over and over. I feel Zack's blood all over me. God. I can smell it."

He seized Amanda's arm, his eyes red and cracked. "I can't take it. You have to knock me out. I don't care how you do it. Just knock me out. Please."

Amanda rooted through their pile of store-bought painkillers, then fed him the one with the drowsiest side effects. He gradually drifted off to sleep. Judging by his somnolent moans and cries, it seemed the future followed him there.

The next forty-eight hours passed like weeks for the sympathetic Silvers. By the morning of Sunday, October 3, they were all as pale and unrested as Theo.

They sat around the living room in a dreary daze, watching David jab the fireplace with a metal poker. Hannah cradled Theo's head in her lap as he twitched in restless half slumber. Nobody thought he was getting better.

Hannah spoke in a hoarse and weary rasp. "We need to do something. He can't take another day of this."

"I'll go to the drugstore," Zack offered. "See if there's something else."

Amanda curled up with Mia on the love seat, absently stroking her hair.

"We've been there twice. It's all the same weak stuff. He needs a prescription-strength remedy."

"We're back on this," David complained.

"Yes, we're back on this. I've made up my mind. I'm taking him to Marietta."

Yesterday, during their umpteenth discussion of Theo's plight, Mia shared the information that the girl with two watches had given her about the local health fair. Amanda confirmed by phone that it was still going on and that anyone was welcome to bring their untreated ailments.

Even as she'd broached the idea, Mia wasn't sure it was a good one. David had a stronger opinion on the matter.

"Perhaps you didn't hear me last time . . ."

Amanda sighed at him. "I heard you, David. I understand your concern. But a health fair isn't the same as a hospital. There's no reason to assume it's being monitored."

"It's a place where fugitives are likely to seek treatment. Of course it's being monitored. You might as well phone the Deps now and tell them you're coming."

"David, I've worked at these things—"

"On another world."

"They're understaffed, overcrowded, and wildly disorganized. Even you wouldn't be able to find us in that chaos."

"You're willing to bet your freedom on this?"

"I am," said Hannah.

"I am," said Amanda. She looked at her sister. "You're not going."

"Bullshit. You think you can lift him by yourself? Your arms are like pipe cleaners."

Amanda shook her head. "We can't carry him in. He'll have to walk. I can get him there."

"I'll go with you," Mia said. "I know the way."

"No."

"Hell, no," Zack uttered.

David chuckled with bleak derision. "Like lemmings off a cliff."

"What do you suggest we do instead?" Hannah asked.

"You know what I suggest. We could be there by nightfall."

She flicked a brusque hand. "Of course. I should've guessed. Peter, Peter, Peter. Your magic-bean solution for everything."

"He may know the nature of Theo's illness. He may have a cure."

"Or he could be a trap," Amanda countered. "Or a Pelletier. Or he might not be there at all. We're not ready to face the next step, David. Not with Theo like this."

David threw a pleading look at Zack. "Are you going to help me here? Or are you relishing the thought of a smaller group?"

The cartoonist exhaled from his easy chair, splitting his pity between Theo and David. The boy's rational insights were consistently drowned out by the emotional concerns of the majority. Clearly he was about to be outvoted again.

Zack looked to Amanda. "For what it's worth, I agree with him. You're taking an insane risk for a bunch of pills you might not even get. I mean without ID—"

"I'm bringing a sick man and a fat wad of cash. That'll be enough."

"And if they give you a written prescription?"

"They should have samples. I'll ask for extra. I'll pay through the nose if I have to."

Zack shrugged with hopeless uncertainty. "Well, you know that scene better than I do. I'm just telling you where I stand. That said, if I were the one in Theo's shoes, I wouldn't want this put to a group vote. It's his pain and your risk. It should be his decision and yours."

Amanda leaned back on the couch and looked to Hannah's lap. In all the hubbub, nobody had noticed until now that Theo was awake. He fixed a dull gaze at the ceiling.

"Did you hear all that?" Amanda asked.

"I heard enough."

"What do you think?"

He barely had the space for thoughts. Over the last two days, the future had been thrown in a blender and funneled into him. He'd progressed beyond fretting over individual images and now worried about the patterns. Hannah kept suffering at the cruel hands of Evan. Zack kept dying at the tempic hands of Esis. The skyline of San Francisco kept crumbling in a distant cloud of dust.

Between all the flashes and glimpses, Theo detected a hint of a much larger problem, a lingering shade of despair in the minds of his elder selves. It always stayed the same from future to future. The only merciful aspect of his ordeal was that he never stayed in one place long enough to see the true shape of it. Theo didn't consider himself a particularly strong or brave man. He was willing to take any risk, any detour to avoid the awful thing ahead of him.

"I can walk," he said, in a weak and jagged voice. "I can go."

Amanda's preconception of the health fair was generous in hindsight. The admission line was a hundred-yard backlog of impoverished treatment-seekers, all as surly and grim as the weather itself. Volunteer organizers in white rain slickers floated around them like angry ghosts, shouting incomprehensible orders. A line cutter provoked a fistfight, causing a human domino topple that ended ten feet shy of Amanda and Theo.

After snaking through the rain for sixty-eight minutes, they finally reached the admission tent. Amanda filled the reception clerk's ear with an elaborate tale of muggings and lost wallets before learning that ID was required only for those who wished to waive the hundred-dollar entry fee. She paid the money so cheerfully that the clerk wondered why she even bothered with the sob story.

Amanda led Theo to the waiting room tent and sat him down in a folding chair, rubbing his back as he rested his face in his palms. She nervously glanced around for cameras, then jumped in her seat when she spotted an elderly man reading a magazine with her own tempic fist on the cover. In the center of the shot, Zack winced in purple-faced agony while Amanda's giant fingers dangled him from a hotel balcony, cracking ribs.

And you wonder why he's been so cold to you, she thought.

They waited in silence for thirty more minutes, until a young and anxious nurse led them to a small private tent. An hour passed without anyone checking on them, then another. Every time Amanda flagged a staffer, she received a shrug and a jittery assurance that a doctor was coming.

"I don't like this," Theo moaned from the cot. "Something's wrong."

"I told you these places were disorganized."

"No. I don't like this. We need to get out of here."

She parted the curtain and peered at the waiting room tent across the way. Just five minutes ago, it had been packed with patients. Now all the chairs were empty.

Her fingers curled in tension. "God. I think you're right."

Theo struggled to a sitting position. "Shit! Shit! I didn't see it in time!"

"What are you talking about?"

"It's too late. They're here."

"Theo, what—"

"Hold your breath!"

A glass ball the size of an orange rolled through the doorway and exploded in white smoke. While Theo covered his mouth and nose, Amanda breathed a pungent gas that tasted like nail polish remover. Her senses went topsy-turvy. The tempic walls of every tent rippled like liquid for four eerie seconds, until the widow fell unconscious to the grass.

Half-blind, mindless, Theo fled the tent. He only made it a few feet before he was tackled to the ground by three men in black fiber armor. They subdued him like spiders, rolling him around and binding his limbs in sticky white string. Six arms hoisted him above the ground and strapped him to a floating gurney.

Theo looked at his captors—over a dozen armed agents, all wearing the same protective gear. Their faces were obscured by long white gas masks with dark eyeholes. They looked frighteningly surreal, hulking black panthers with possum heads.

Soon the slimmest figure approached and removed her mask. Even with rain in his eyes, Theo had no trouble recognizing the dreadlocked woman in front of him. His lips curled in a feeble smile.

"Melissa Masaad."

Though the Deps within earshot all traded baffled looks, Melissa wasn't entirely shocked to hear her quarry say her name. She'd seen the man's work in two different states. It was because of him that she now believed in augurs.

"Hello, Theo."

He muttered something under his breath before falling unconscious. Melissa looked to her team in confusion.

"Did you hear that?"

"No, ma'am. I couldn't make it out."

Neither could she. The part she heard was nonsensical. She could have sworn she heard him say "private school."

Disturbed, Melissa wiped the rain from her face. "Take him to the hospital. Call me the minute you learn what's wrong with him."

A trio of agents emerged from the tent with Amanda strapped to a stretcher. Even in her unconscious state, the other Deps kept their rifles fixed on her. No one wanted to take any chances.

Melissa approached the gurney and checked her prisoner's pulse. After four weeks of chasing ghosts, it was a marvelous thing to finally touch the real Amanda Given.

She rooted through Amanda's pockets, procuring a handphone. The tiny light flashed green in announcement of a new text message from David's phone.

<We haven't heard from you in a while. Is everything all right?>

Melissa smiled. She'd just captured two dangerous criminals without spilling a drop of blood. Now she had the tool that would lead her to the rest of the group. Everything was more than all right. It was a beautiful day.

TWENTY-SEVEN

She'd grown used to her conspicuous nature. Everywhere she went in her great adopted nation, she could feel the heat of inquisitive stares. She was a dark-skinned beauty with overpronounced cheekbones, exquisite almond eyes, and a flowing hairstyle that was far too exotic for uncultured minds to process. She spoke with an accent that few Americans had ever heard before. To top it all off, she carried a badge.

Her fellow Deps were no closer to cracking the enigma that was Melissa Masaad. Even those who saw beyond her standing as a dusker, a limer, and an occasional erection-inducer couldn't get around the fact that she was a little bit off. She talked to herself in hallways, chewed on her hair in meetings, and derailed conversations with peculiar non sequiturs. Though she scored her fair share of acrimony for her early rank advancement, it seemed rather fitting that Melissa would seize the reins on the Bureau's strangest case to date.

Now fifteen agents watched Melissa with muted puzzlement as she lay atop her guest desk in the bullpen. She'd spread herself out like a bearskin rug, her chin propped on a thick phone directory. Her handtop rested on the edge of the neighboring desk.

"Advance."

The screen displayed a new page of transcribed dialogue. Through ghost drills, the Deps had reproduced more than seventy hours of fugitive chatter, every word the Silvers had uttered in the Ramona motel and the Evansville resort. Melissa had read all twelve hundred pages. She had enough questions to keep her captives busy for weeks.

Howard Hairston stood at the hallway junction, glaring at the two local agents who peered up Melissa's skirt. She raised her head to look at him.

"Is everything ready?"

"We're all set."

The skinny young Dep had become Melissa's right-hand man in the wake of her promotion. *You can't do it all yourself,* Andy Cahill had warned her, on his last day of work. *The minute you become the new me, you need to find a new you.*

"How is she?"

"Surprisingly calm," said Howard.

"Did you find a—"

He held up a tempic screwdriver. Melissa smiled.

"Wonderful. Thank you, Howard."

She climbed off the desk and arched her back with a wince. After the day's double raids, her spine was a sore and angry beast. Now she was about to interrogate a woman who, under the worst circumstances, could snap it like a breadstick.

The Charleston outpost was a small operation—seventeen employees in an old brick building that stood alone on a tree-lined hill. The hallways were lit by antiquated filament bulbs and stacked with dusty radio equipment. The local Deps specialized in solving broadcast crimes, everything from the illegal transmission of foreign film and video ("mudding") to the hijacking of lumivision signals for the purposes of mischief ("surping").

The most wanted felon in the office was a legendary figure known only as Surpdog. At least twice a month, the mysterious assailant would preempt a random broadcast with fifty-four seconds of guerrilla video, an ever-changing montage of beautiful images from other nations. After eighteen years and 452 surpings, all the agents knew about their target was that he hated American isolationism and was extremely good at covering his tracks. Melissa liked Surpdog's message. She hoped the Deps never caught him, if he even was a he.

She stopped at the door to the makeshift interrogation room and blew a heavy breath. Howard eyed her cautiously.

"Be careful in there. We don't know those machines will work."

"I appreciate the concern, Howard. I'll be fine. Say, when's your birthday?"

"Uh, February 10. Why?"

When she was a field agent, Melissa didn't do much hobnobbing with her peers. Now that she was a supervisor, she figured she'd have to start asking people how their weekends were. She'd have to give them cards on their birthdays.

"No matter."

She cleared her throat, adjusted her skirt, then opened the door to her eminent guest.

Amanda sat on a worn brown sofa, the only conventional piece of furniture in the large room. Her wrists and ankles were fastened to the floor by thick metal chains, giving her just enough slack to sit upright. She wore a dark blue jumpsuit with the DP-9 logo emblazoned across the right breast, plus a grated metal collar that wasn't tethered to anything. A quartet of slim mechanical towers surrounded her in a perfect square formation. Each one was six feet tall and filled with humming blue bulbs. They reminded Amanda of bug zappers.

Melissa pulled a folding chair to the center of the room. The two women studied each other.

"Well, here we are," said Melissa.

"Here we are," Amanda echoed.

"You like the new color?"

"What?"

"Your hair. That was quite a change, going from red to black."

Amanda blinked distractedly. "Oh. Yeah. I don't know."

"You don't know if you like it better black?"

"I don't know why you're asking me about my hair."

"It's just an icebreaker."

"Well, congrats. You made me more nervous."

Amanda still reeled from the knockout gas. She had no idea of time or place. For all she knew, she was in some government black site in central Asia. Or maybe she'd died and gone to a strange little corner of Hell, where all the demons were beautiful and droll.

Melissa flipped through a stack of color printouts. "And your physical state?"

"Queasy. My ears are ringing like murder."

"Normal side effects of the gas. You'll recover in an hour or two."

"I feel like none of this is happening. Like this is all a dream."

"That could also be a side effect," Melissa said. "Or possibly just denial. In either case, I assure you you're not dreaming. Unless I'm the one in denial."

Amanda eyed her in leery wonder. She'd spent many nights imagining her interrogation at the hands of federal agents. This woman couldn't have been further from her expectations.

"Where are we?"

"West Virginia," Melissa replied. "Roughly eighty miles from your place of capture. Do you know my name?"

"No. How the hell would I?"

"I thought maybe Theo told you. He seemed to know it."

"Is he here? How is he?"

Melissa chewed her lip in contemplation. It was too soon to start bartering for information. Amanda could use a good faith token.

"He's on his way here. He was taken to a hospital for tests. From what I'm told, he's been given painkillers and is now sleeping like an infant."

Amanda let out a dismal chuckle. Melissa cocked her head at her. "What?"

"Nothing. That's all I wanted. I just wanted him to get some relief."

"Well, that you accomplished. I'm Melissa Masaad, the DP-9 agent in charge of this investigation. I've been eager to meet you for quite some time."

"No doubt," said Amanda. "Where are you from? I can't place the accent."

"I'm North Sudanese, formally educated in British schools."

"How long have you been here?"

"About two years," she replied, with a provocative glance. "You?"

Amanda narrowed her eyes defiantly. "Born and raised in the USA."

A storm of mad cackles brewed in Melissa's throat. Seemingly every page of the ghost drill transcripts featured one of the fugitives remarking on how much they missed their world, how different things were on this one. Chronokinesis by itself was difficult enough to process. No one in the Bureau was ready to embrace the idea of chronokinetic aliens.

Heavy chains rattled as Amanda scratched her neck. "You're lucky I'm so stupid, Melissa."

"How are you stupid?"

"I was warned there'd be civic cameras at the health fair. I didn't listen."

Melissa shook her head. "Whoever told you that was misinformed. We have no cameras there."

"You don't?"

"No. Installing a civic camera is a monstrous bureaucratic procedure.

Mia vented a heavy breath and continued to pet the purring feline in her lap. Her grandmother always told her that black cats were good luck for good people. Mia didn't even think she needed it. While her friends all suffered fractures and gunshots, concussions and amputations, she had yet to get a single scratch. The one bullet that was fired at her had missed her head by millimeters.

She peered down at the cat, her tortured mind bargaining with the forces of fate. *Give me the next one,* she implored them. *Whatever bad thing happens, you leave them alone. You give it to me.*

Hannah spooned Theo on the futon, listening to his gentle snores while she stared at the wall in restless discomfort. The musty little office reeked of old age and iodine, and her wrists still throbbed from shoving that agent. Every time she closed her eyes, she could see his body skid across the highway in slow motion, scraping bloody patches with each impact.

She gave up on sleep and sauntered out to the hallway. Through the crack of a bedroom door, she saw Mia snoozing away on Xander's queen-size bed. The fat black cat sat dejectedly at her side, mewling for his new best friend to give him more love.

The sound of whistling laughter drew Hannah to the stairwell. She crouched down and peered into the living room, where Amanda and Zack stretched side by side on a wide chaise longue. They looked like a cozy married couple in their long T-shirts and underwear. Morning light cracked through the wood blinds, striping their bare legs.

Amanda rolled onto her side and fought an indignant grin as Zack giggled deliriously.

"You just find that hilarious, don't you?"

She'd just finished explaining how she subdued Owen Nettles in the back of the truck. While the peculiar little agent paced and mumbled, Amanda summoned a burst of tempis from her toes. Owen turned around just in time to see the man-size foot coming at him. Before the whiteness could even touch him, his eyes rolled back and he fainted to the floor.

Amanda had been too stressed at the time to find it funny. Even now her humor was tempered by the fact that she owned only one shoe.

Zack wiped his eyes and moaned. "You should've seen us outside the truck. We were so scared of what that guy might do. Melissa made him sound like Joe Kickass."

"He was not Joe Kickass," Amanda said. "I'm just glad I didn't hurt him."

Disenchanted with Mia, the cat sauntered down the hall and rubbed against Hannah. She caressed his back, praying she wasn't her sister's next topic of discussion.

Amanda pursed her lips in a droll pout. "I'm so glad David called me stupid. That's just what my self-esteem needed today."

"At least he didn't call you a coward."

"Right. I lack a brain. You lack courage. All we need now is a tin man."

Zack plunged into another fit of punch-drunk giggles, until his humor gradually melted away. He smeared his bleary eyes.

"I shouldn't have gotten on his case like that. He was probably just blustering out there. It's not like he hurt any of them."

No, Hannah thought. *I'm the one who left a victim.*

"He's just in pain," Amanda told him. "He has a long recovery ahead of him. The best thing we can do is be there for him, without judgment. He needs siblings now, not parents."

Hannah suppressed a jaded laugh. It took an extraordinary lack of self-awareness for Amanda to equate siblings with nonjudgment.

Zack closed his eyes and cracked a boyish grin. Amanda eyed him flippantly. "Still tickled about the tempis?"

"No."

"Then what, pray tell, are you smiling about, Zachary?"

He folded his hands over his chest, his expression serene and contented. "Just nice to have you back."

Hannah scowled cynically in the tender silence that followed. *Shit. Here we go.*

Amanda nestled up against him, resting her hand on his. As their fingers laced together, she suffered an unwelcome flashback to her alley encounter with Esis, the madwoman's stern and cryptic warning. *Do not entwine with the* [something something]. Amanda couldn't salvage the rest from her trauma-scarred memories. She had larger concerns now anyway.

She heaved a jaded sigh across Zack's chest. "You're a schmuck."

He chuckled at her *shiksa* Yiddish. "Why am I a schmuck?"

"Because you're being all sweet and I know it won't last. You always run hot and cold with me."

"Says the woman who sat on my lap, then threw me off a balcony."

"You still blame me for that."

"No. I always blamed Evan."

"Then why did you get so distant after that?"

Zack considered pinning that on Evan too, but then he'd have to explain the teasing hint about Amanda and Peter, a romantic prophecy that still bothered him to no end.

"I'm too tired to open that box," he replied. "Let's just agree I'm a schmuck and move on."

Hannah watched the cat roll around on the carpet, purring in mindless bliss. For a moment, she thought Amanda and Zack would do the same. Now she wasn't sure if they'd kiss, fight, or fall asleep on each other. In any case, it was time to leave them alone.

Just as she rose to her feet, Amanda took Zack's advice and changed the subject.

"I'm worried about Hannah."

A sharp new panic gripped the actress, freezing her in place. Her inner self waved her on with flapping arms. *Go! Leave! You don't want to hear this!*

"She'll be all right," Zack assured Amanda.

"You've only known her ten weeks. I've known her her whole life. I know what trauma does to her."

"You're looking down from the big sister perch."

"I'm not looking down, just back. She has a history, Zack. It's right there on her wrists."

A storm of screams brewed in Hannah's throat. She clenched her fists and vanished into the bathroom. The startled cat bolted down the stairs, past the chaise longue.

Amanda raised her head at the scurrying footsteps. "What was that?"

"Bad luck," said Zack.

"Great. Like we need more."

Amanda fixed a tense gaze at the sleeping-gas collar on the coffee table, a grim souvenir of her incarceration. Forty minutes ago, she asked Zack to reverse the lock, a task he'd initially refused out of fear of rifting her. She had to remind him that he was a man of minor miracles, able to rot a swinging banana from twenty feet away, grow keys out of keyholes, and turn old mice into young ones. He'd led an actress and two teenagers into battle with armed federal agents, and won.

Ultimately he'd indulged her, concentrating on her collar with the sweaty apprehension of a bomb defuser. The moment he popped the lock on her very last shackle, Amanda's regard turned a hot new color and she fought the urge to kiss him. Now as she pressed against him, his heartbeat thumping against her breast, she wished she had her sister's skill with men. She wished she could find just the right words to express her feelings, her qualms.

Then she considered that Zack was an artist. Maybe he didn't need words.

Thin white strands of tempis slowly sprouted from her forearm, twisting around their locked hands like ivy. Zack watched with marvel as small white leaves sprouted from the vines.

"Wow. Amanda, that's beautiful. You ever do that before?"

"No."

Her ropes wrapped tighter around them, driving the point home. The cartoonist aired a loud, somber breath.

"Guess we have a bit of a problem."

"Guess we do," she said.

"I don't know what to do about it," said Zack. "I spent four years in a bad entanglement."

Amanda fixed a heavy stare at her naked ring finger. "Five and a half."

"With everything going on, I'm not sure I can handle another one. I'm not saying it's inevitable. Just possible. And after all the drama with Theo and Hannah . . ."

The tempic leaves withered. The vines retracted into Amanda's skin. Zack checked her grim expression.

"I just pissed you off again, didn't I?"

She shook her head. "No. I understand your hesitation. It's smart."

"Then why do I feel so stupid right now?"

"Because you know."

"Know what?"

"That we don't have much longer to live."

Amanda struggled to her feet. Zack watched her as she moved to the shuttered window.

"You know they're going to get us sooner or later, Zack. Whether it's the Deps or Rebel or Esis, it's just a matter of time. And yet here I am, worrying about being a proper widow. Here you are, worrying about the fights we might have a month from now. There is no month from now, Zack. Not for us. Maybe we should just . . . I don't know . . ."

Zack joined her at the window and gently turned her around. When she realized he was simply drawing her into a hug, she fell into his arms with maniacal relief. Yes, yes, yes. Hugs were good. Hugs were safe.

"I'm sorry, Zack. I'm all over the place. I don't know what I'm saying right now."

He caressed her back. "It's all right. You had a crappy day by anyone's standards."

"Make it better. Say something sweet to me."

"Can it be about your looks?"

"No."

"Because you're very, very pretty."

"I don't care," she said, though she held him tighter anyway. She cared a little.

"All right. Give me a moment to think it over." He rested his chin on her shoulder, amazed that her hair could smell so good after twenty hours of captivity.

"You remember when we were on the balcony—"

"Oh God, Zack."

"No, no. I'm not talking about that. I'm talking about the moments before, when you and I were cracking each other up with silly wordplay. I said I was antaganostic. You called yourself a tempis fugitive."

She bloomed a wobbly smile. "I remember."

"Yeah, well, that's when I started to get nervous, because there aren't a lot of people who can crack bad puns in Latin, or go joke for joke with me like you did. I knew from the start that you were strong and smart and very, very pretty, but nobody told me you were funny."

The widow's lips curled in a wavering smile. Zack pulled back to look at her.

"I have no idea what's going to happen with us, Amanda. I just know that women like you are jackpots to guys like me. You don't think short term with jackpots. You don't screw them on the couch when they're feeling vulnerable. I'll wait as long as it takes for us to get our shit together. I don't want to go the way of Hannah and Theo. We do this right or we don't do it at all."

Amanda held him so fiercely, she feared she'd break his ribs all over again. When she first met Zack, she had no idea that he was a rigid perfectionist, an uptight moralist, a minder, a mender. No wonder it felt so good to hug him. They were practically twins.

She ran a gentle hand down his cheek. "I really want to kiss you right now, but I won't."

"I wasn't saying it to—"

"I know. I'm just thinking ahead. Wherever we end up running, whether it's Brooklyn or Canada or God knows where, the six of us are going to rest and heal. And then once we get our act together, you and I are going to slip away for an evening. I don't care if it has to be the second room of our criminal hideout, we're going on a date. Some things have to be done the normal way. Even for people like us."

His responding smile was warm enough to melt her. Amanda embraced him again, speaking stern but trembling words over his shoulder.

"Just don't die on me, Zack. Don't you dare die on me."

He pressed her back and let out a glum sigh. "I can only promise to try."

"Well, if you ever need more incentive, you think about our third date. I'm not Catholic about everything."

Amanda covered his loud laugh, and then tensely bid him good night. She would have loved to rest with him down here on the couch, but the temptation to do something—

(do not entwine)

—would mess up their wonderful new plan.

She scrambled upstairs in dizzy haste, then conducted a stealthy check on the others. Theo and Mia were visible in their rooms. David and Hannah were tucked away behind closed doors. Amanda stowed her concerns, then climbed into bed with Mia.

As her eyelids fluttered with teeming fatigue, the widow's mind shot like fireworks into the many branching futures. She pondered all the obstacles between her and a happy life, counting her issues like sheep.

Just as she began to drift off, the dangling wires of her memory connected and Esis breached her thoughts once again.

Do not entwine with the funny artist.

Amanda's eyes sprang open in hot alarm. She stayed awake and disturbed for hours.

At the jagged tail end of his twenty-hour slumber, Theo fell into a dream that by now had become painfully familiar. He existed as a disembodied spirit, a formless being drifting slowly through a silent gray void. A bright white wall stretched endlessly in front of him like a vertical tundra, radiating a bitter coldness that chilled him to the core.

Theo dreaded coming here, but this was his job now. There was something he needed to find on this wall. He was the only one who could do it.

He kept moving without any idea of direction. Up, down, left, right. It all looked the same. It was only when he moved toward the wall that he could make out the infinite beads of light that comprised its surface. Each one was burning agony on his thoughts, like a magnified sunbeam. He kept his distance and never stopped moving. He had so much area to cover. Too much. Whenever he thought about it, an arch panic overtook him. *I can't do it, Peter. The wall's too big. The string's too thin. I'll never find it. I don't even think it exists.*

And yet he kept traveling, searching the wall for the one little strand that meant everything to everyone. The only thing worse than being in this cold and dreary hell was leaving it, since he knew he'd have to face his companions and tell them once again that he failed.

Though they always thanked him for trying and assured him that tomorrow would be a better day, Theo could see the heartbreak behind their expressions. They knew as well as he did that there were only so many tomorrows left. While he flittered and flailed on the other side of the wall, his friends were merely waiting. Waiting for the sky to fall again.

———

He jerked awake on the futon, his chest moist with sweat. He did a double take at the clock when it told him that it was 2:12 in the morning. Theo had slept nearly a full day in this dingy little office. Even his coma didn't last that long.

He relieved himself in the bathroom, gargled a shot of mouthwash, then lumbered down the stairs. The smell of sizzling bacon made his mouth water. He'd barely had a bite to eat since Nemeth.

The moment Hannah saw him, she dropped her spatula in the frying pan and hugged him.

"Thank God. I was starting to get worried. How you feeling?"

"Like Rip van Winkle." He saw Zack and Mia at the table. "You're having breakfast at two A.M.?"

"We did some heavy sleeping ourselves," Zack said.

The cartoonist seemed awfully chipper for a man on vampire time. Mia, by contrast, looked thoroughly morose. She aimed a dull gaze at her lap through her tangle of bangs.

Hannah pushed him to the table. "Sit. I'm making waffles too."

Theo studied her carefully as she returned to the stove. He knew her well enough to recognize the "everything's fine" voice she used when she was bottling her anger at someone. He could practically hear the creak of the crossbow string. Mercifully, the quarrel didn't seem to be aimed at him.

He took a drowsy gander at the map book in Zack's hands. "We leaving today?"

"I don't know. Depends on David."

"Well, you know what he'll say."

"I'm talking about his health, not his preferences. If Amanda says he's not ready, we're staying."

Theo gazed out the window at the lumic lamppost. "She'll be waiting for us in New York."

"Who, Melissa?"

"Yeah. She knows exactly who we're going to see."

"Peter's a dozen steps ahead of the Deps," Zack replied. "He knew just where your truck would be, how many agents were guarding you. I don't think those people are a problem for him."

"You think Peter's an augur too?" Hannah asked.

Zack shook his head. "No. I'm guessing he's more like Mia. The two of them have some kind of portal juju going on."

Mia's expression grew darker. She'd received two new messages from her future self earlier, neither of which offered any practical value. One of them was cruel enough to make her cry. If Peter shared her affliction, she pitied him.

Theo jerked a lazy shrug. "I'm still not sure what to think of the guy, to be perfectly honest. I just hope—"

A sudden stabbing jolt caused him to wince and press his temple. Hannah rushed to his side.

"Theo!"

"I'm all right," he assured her. "It's okay."

"It's not okay. If your problem's coming back—"

"It's just a headache. I'm fine."

Zack eyed him warily. "Have you had any premonitions since they drugged you?"

"Not a one," Theo said, hoping that was true. The great white wall still loomed large in his thoughts.

Mia's stomach gurgled with stress as she recalled the first vague note she'd received from her elder self today.

Don't get too comfortable. You're not out of the storm.

Amanda sat quietly on the guest bed, tending David's wound with edgy distraction. Though the widow had steeled herself with five deep breaths before knocking on David's door, she was pleasantly surprised to find him genial. His pain was just a fraction of yesterday's. The stumps of his fingers showed no signs of infection. Amanda thanked God for the double mercy. She couldn't have handled a second attack of scorn. Not in her state.

David studied Amanda warily as she unwrapped a new roll of bandages. "How's Mia?"

"She's all right. Worried about you."

He sighed with lament. "The way I acted, I don't blame her. I've never experienced pain like that before. It was . . . enlightening."

Amanda eyed him strangely. "Enlightening?"

"Ever since it happened, I've been thinking about the people of the past, the way they accepted agony as just another part of their lives. With all our advancements in technology and medicine, I'm wondering if perhaps we lost something as a species. A certain fortitude."

"No one can accuse you of weakness, David. You're one of the strongest people I've ever known."

"Well, I appreciate you saying that." He cracked a dour smirk. "If Nietzsche's right about the things that don't kill us, then Zack's really going to be afraid of me soon."

Amanda felt a hot stab of anguish at the mention of Zack. She clenched her jaw and kept working.

"He's not afraid of you," she uttered.

"Then why did he call me a psychopath?"

"For the same reason you called me stupid, okay? He was upset. If you had stayed in the kitchen ten more seconds, he would have apologized."

David eyed her with sharp surprise. He'd noticed her tension from the moment she entered the room. Now the woman who'd handled him so calmly yesterday seemed to be coming unglued.

"Amanda, I'm sorry for the way I behaved yesterday. I really am."

"That's not why I'm . . ." Her eyes darted back and forth in quandary. "Can I pick your brain about something? In absolute confidence."

"Of course. What about?"

"Esis."

His sandy eyebrows rose in intrigue. "Wow. Okay. I mean I'm not sure how much insight I can give you. I only met her once."

"Well, you're the only other person I know who's spoken to her. She . . ."

Amanda fought to explain her conundrum. All throughout her sleepless day, she'd replayed her back-alley encounter with Esis, reconstructing it word by word. By sundown, she'd pieced together the woman's full warning. *Do not entwine with the funny artist. I grow tired of telling you this. You entwine with your own, you won't be a flower. You'll just be dirt.*

David listened to the story with abject fascination, stroking his chin with the arched brow of a sleuth.

"Wow. That's . . . huh. At the risk of embarrassing you, it seems fairly obvious who she was referring to, and what she meant by 'entwine.'"

Amanda nodded brusquely. "Yes. I know that. But how did she even . . . I mean . . ."

"How did she know that you and Zack would become intimate?"

She flinched in discomfort. "We haven't. Not yet. But she gave me that warning before I even met him."

"Well, clearly Esis is an augur of some sort. It's not like we don't know any."

"But why would she care who I . . . entwine with?"

The boy gazed ahead in deep rumination. He started and stopped himself twice before speaking.

"She did say something odd to us, me and my father. He was with me when she gave me my bracelet. She just popped into our living room through a glowing white portal in the wall. Now that I think about it, I wonder if it's the same temporal mechanism that Mia uses for her notes."

Amanda wound her finger impatiently. "What did she say?"

"She told us the world was ending in minutes, that I was moving on and my father wasn't. Had the portal not lent her a certain latitude for wild assertions, we might have dismissed her as a lunatic. But my father certainly listened. The whole thing made him rather . . . Well, if you knew him, you'd know how rarely he shows emotion. But at that moment, he was overcome."

David pressed his knuckles to his lips, his face marred with twitchy grief.

"I half expected him to plead for his life, so he could continue the work that was so important to him. But to my surprise, his one pressing question to Esis was 'Will my son be all right?'"

Amanda held his arm. She could understand now how David had become so resilient. The poor boy had practically been raising himself since he was ten.

"Anyway, Esis was sympathetic," he said. "She assured my father that I'd be in good health and excellent company. I remember her exact words on this. She said, 'He'll only be alone for a short while. Then he'll be joined with his brothers and sisters.'"

The floor of Amanda's stomach dropped. The room suddenly felt three times smaller.

David shrugged pensively. "I'd always assumed Esis was being figurative. But now—"

"That's not it," Amanda stammered. "That's crazy. I know who I come from."

"And I know who I come from. I've seen the video of my birth. Doesn't rule out the possibility that our mothers were surrogates."

"How can you even say that?"

"I'm just exploring the options, Amanda. We know the Pelletiers existed on our world. We know they chose us. We just don't know when. Maybe they had an active role in our creation, forging us all from the same genetic template. If that doesn't describe siblings, what does?"

Amanda stood up on watery legs. She leaned against the dresser.

"That's insane. We can't all be related. I mean Theo's . . ."

"Asian. Yes. He might be an exception. Or perhaps their genetic engineering capabilities are more advanced than we realize."

"But no one warned Hannah about entwining with Theo." *Did they?* she suddenly wondered.

David chucked his good hand in a listless shrug. "I don't know. In any case, if the Pelletiers are indeed augurs, then perhaps they knew that Hannah and Theo were destined to fail as a couple. Maybe they foresaw a more lasting union between you and Zack."

Her throat closed tighter. "That's not . . . You're just guessing all this. None of this is proof."

"Proof? No. But Esis did warn you about entwining with your own. And there's one other thing I neglected to mention, something I've pondered every day. Maybe it's why he didn't ask more questions . . ."

"What are you talking about?"

David sighed. "When Esis appeared in our house, my father already knew her name."

Amanda closed her eyes, fighting to hold herself together. She thought back to the incident on the Massachusetts Turnpike, seventeen years ago. Her father never uttered the Pelletiers' names. But then he never asked for them either. Did he already know? Did both her parents know them?

She rushed to David's side, squeezing his biceps with rigid fingers. "Listen to me. Whether you're right or wrong about this, we have to keep it to ourselves. You hear me? Until we get absolute proof, we don't breathe a word of this to the others."

"If you wish."

"You especially don't tell Hannah and Theo. They don't need this."

"I said okay, Amanda."

David watched her cautiously as she cleaned up the bandage debris. "Guess you have strong feelings for him."

"I don't want to talk about it."

"Fair enough. But Amanda, there's something you need to consider . . ."

"No."

"Yes. This needs to be said. Whether you believe we're all siblings or not, you know for a fact that Esis doesn't want you entwining with Zack. You know she gets angry about it."

"What are you saying?"

David studied his bandaged hand with dark and heavy eyes.

"I'm saying that for your sake and his, you might want to start thinking of him as a brother."

At a quarter to three, David joined the others in the kitchen for breakfast. Mia was thrilled to see him swap warm apologies with Zack, and beamed with gushing relief when he squeezed her hand under the table. It scared her how easily David could move her to good and bad places. She wondered if that was a sign of being in love.

The bacon and waffles were nearly all gone by the time Amanda came downstairs. She met Zack's bright cheer with a nervous half grin, then avoided his gaze for the rest of the meal.

Soon Theo sucked a sharp breath in pain, grinding all conversation to a halt. He glanced around at his worried friends, then sighed with futility.

"Yeah. I think it's coming back."

Zack tapped the table in tense resolve. "All right then. That settles that."

"What settles what?"

"As soon as we're ready, we're saying good-bye to the cat and hello to Peter."

He scanned the faces of the others, lingering an extra second on Amanda. "Anyone have a problem with that?"

Hannah, Theo, and Mia slowly shook their heads, censoring their many leery doubts about Peter. Amanda merely stared at her empty plate, deeply lost in other concerns.

David was the only one who smiled. No one needed to ask him how he felt on the matter.

The bathroom mirror was nothing more than a floating lumic projection. It was impervious to fogging, and could reflect at six different viewing angles.

As Mia finished drying herself, her elbow brushed a button on the wall. Suddenly the picture changed to a rear view. Unhappy to be mooning herself, she reverted to the traditional reflection, then squinted curiously at her body. There seemed less of her now than usual. She must have shed at least ten pounds since fleeing Terra Vista.

She slipped on her clothes and ran a drying wand over her hair, examining herself with sunny awe. Between the weight loss and David's forgiveness, her mood was nearly healed from the battering it took earlier, when she received the cruelest message yet from future times.

> I hate you. I despise you with every fiber of my being. You're so hopeless, so clueless, so utterly blind to the things happening right under your nose. The Pelletiers are laughing at you, Mia. Semerjean is laughing.

> I'd spoil the joke for you if I could, but it really doesn't matter. Just take my advice and kill yourself. We should have never come to this world. We should have died in the basement with Nana.

Even now, hours later, Mia reeled from her own venom. She couldn't spend the rest of her life as the whipping girl for every Future Mia in a black mood. If the girl with two watches was right, then the problem would only get worse.

Mia suddenly heard sharp, angry voices outside the door.

"Okay! All right! I was just asking, Hannah!"

"You're not asking! You're blaming!"

Mia put down the heat wand and groaned. *God. Not this. Not now.*

The sisters stomped through the bedroom, both half-dressed and flailing in jittery rage. While Hannah stuffed unfolded garments into duffel bags, Amanda rummaged through Xander's closet.

"There's a difference between being upset and being upset at *you*," the widow snapped. "I'm upset because I only own one shoe now!"

"And you're upset at *me* because I left your other pair at the lake house!"

"Did I say that? Did I actually hear me use those words?"

"You didn't have to. It was all in your tone. Do you think we just met?"

Amanda shook her head in trembling pique, throwing shoe after shoe over her shoulder. Of course the old man had the narrow feet of a ballerina. She was destined to go barefoot to Brooklyn.

"You always do this, Hannah. Always."

"Always do what?"

"Take your bad moods out on me. I know what you're really upset about."

"Oh do you now?"

"You hurt that agent. I get it. I hurt two cops so I know exactly what you're going through. But do you come to me for help? Of course not. You decide to yell and scream at me, *just like you always do*!"

"Excuse me. Who's screaming now?"

Amanda jumped up from the floor. "I am! I'm screaming at you now because I can't take it anymore! You wear me out!"

Hannah clenched her jaw and looked away, her foot tapping maniacally.

"You think I'm weak. You think I'm so goddamn weak. Have you considered the fact that maybe I'm only weak around you? Maybe *you're* the one who—"

The bathroom door flew open. Mia barged into the room, her wet hair throwing droplets in arcs. She snatched a pair of sandals from under the bed and chucked one at the feet of each sister. She waved a quivering finger back and forth between them.

"No more. I'm not sharing a room with either of you ever again. I don't care if I have to sleep outside in a dumpster. I can't do this anymore."

Amanda and Hannah watched her in matching stupor as she stormed back to the bathroom. She spun around at the door, fighting tears.

"You think I wouldn't kill to have my brothers here? You think Zack wouldn't kill to have his brother here? You have no idea how lucky you are, and yet all you do is fight. There's something seriously wrong with both of you."

"Mia—"

She slammed the door behind her, jostling a picture from the wall.

Dead-faced, silent, Hannah made a slow trek out of the room. Amanda sat down on the bed and calmly gathered the sandals. As she slipped them over her feet, she thought once again about David's theory and realized that the DNA didn't matter. The six of them lived and screamed and hurt each other like family. They were all siblings down to the bone.

The Silvers rode the final leg of their journey in dismal silence. Xander's red Cameron Arrow was a skinny little car with two platform rows that were better suited for couples. Zack's arm brushed Mia every time he turned the steering wheel. She could feel Theo's body tense up whenever he suffered a new flash of pain. She held his hand, caressing it with worry. Her future self once told her that it was more important to get to New York in a strong state of mind than it was to get there fast. She had no illusions about anyone's current condition.

David slept soundly in the back, his head flopping in turns between each sister's shoulder. As Hannah fixed her surly gaze out the window, her dark emotions flew back and forth across the car. She faulted Amanda, then faulted herself. She hated Amanda, then hated herself.

By the time she snapped out of her doleful trance, the Arrow had shot out of a tunnel and into a great urban thoroughfare.

Hannah blinked at the sight of yellow taxis and Jewish delis. "Wait. Are we . . . ? Is this . . . ?"

Zack shined his searchlight gaze around at all the lumic signs and tempic storefronts, these alien embellishments to the city he once knew. Though he was finally back in his native Manhattan, the cartoonist never felt farther from home.

"This is it," he said, with a nervous exhale. "We're here."

PART FIVE

STRINGS

THIRTY-ONE

The traffic light was nothing but a floating disc of lumis, two feet wide and red as a sunset. Fat gray pigeons fluttered through it while a hunched old woman crossed the street between tempic guardrails. A ghosted billboard stretched the length of the intersection, hawking heart-healthy breakfast cereal to idled drivers.

Zack leaned forward and craned his view at the near and distant streams of flying cars. He'd counted seven different levels of traffic when the light turned green, the billboard vanished, and the tempic rails gave way to open road.

Mia tapped his wrist. "Zack."

He snapped out of his trance and pressed the gas pedal, marveling at the taxi in the rearview mirror. A true New York cabbie would have honked him into oblivion for dawdling at a green light. This wasn't Zack's city on any level. Calling this place New York was like calling a dog a zebra, or swapping the concepts of blue and yellow.

"This should be Soho," he uttered. "I mean we came out of the Holland Tunnel, so . . . I don't know. I don't know what they call it now."

Mia stroked his wrist with sympathy. Though she'd never set foot in the old New York, a future self had sold this world's version as a paradise beyond description, beautiful enough to evoke tears. Now she glanced through dry eyes at the windblown scraps of litter, the garish assault of animated ads. *Wrong again*, she seethed. *You just keep giving me bad information.*

Amanda writhed uncomfortably in the backseat. She could feel every tempic construct within a half-block radius, a hundred cold fingers pressing her thoughts. Barricaded storefronts stretched along both sides of the street, each one ready to ripple and dance for their visiting queen.

"What time is it?"

David checked his watch. "Half past ten."

She eyed the stores suspiciously. "Middle of a Tuesday morning. Why is everything closed?"

Hannah stroked her lip in bother. The whole city seemed eerily quiet at the moment. There were only a handful of pedestrians on each block, most of them dressed from head to toe in lily-white garments. A husky street vendor sold a wide assortment of white Venetian masks.

"Something weird is going on here."

"It's not just here," said Zack. "Everything was closed in Jersey too."

Mia's eyes bulged at a masked young couple in white bathrobes and sneakers. The man brandished a hand-painted placard that said *New York Thrives on 10-5.*

"Commemoration," she said.

"What?"

"Ten-five. Today's the anniversary of the Cataclysm."

The Silvers glanced out their windows with fresh unease. They recalled Sterling Quint's discussion of the great temporic blast that destroyed half of New York City on October 5, 1912. The day had become a major holiday in the United States and a near-religious event here in the rebuilt metropolis.

The Arrow turned north onto 6th Avenue. Mia read the scrolling lumic banner that stretched above all lanes. *This is our day, New York. The whole world is watching. Show them why this is the greatest city on Earth, now and forever.*

Zack shook his head in exasperation. "I don't know if our timing's really good or really bad."

Mia plucked Peter's day-old message from her shoulder bag and reread it. "We need to find a pay phone."

"I'm looking."

"Maybe we should look on foot," Amanda suggested. "Get out and stretch our legs. If we can."

One by one, the others checked on Theo in the front passenger seat. He'd spent the whole ride with his head against the window, twitching in restless slumber. Now his eyes were wide open and marked with deep red veins. His headaches had once again become bundled with visions, prophetic flashes too quick and obscure to make any sense. The only clear image he saw was Azral Pelletier. His harsh and handsome face popped up over and over, enough to erase all doubt. The white-haired man was coming back as sure as the moon, and probably sooner.

Theo glanced out at a distant flurry to the east. "I think I see where everyone went."

The Ghostwalk was a ritual that dated back to the first Commemoration in 1913. It began as a silent procession down 3rd Avenue—fifty thousand mourners in white robes and masks, all marching for the souls of the lost. As the years progressed and cracked hearts slowly healed, the Ghostwalk grew a fluffy tail of musicians, dancers, and other sunny revelers who sought to honor the dead by celebrating life. The cavalcade expanded each year until it became known as the March of the Spirits.

Today the twin parades were joined in bipolar harmony, the yin and the yang, the grief and the joy. The event moved to Broadway in 1942, starting at 96th Street and ending at City Hall Park.

The Silvers caught the tail end of the Ghostwalk at 14th Street, at the corner of New Union Square. They hovered at the edge of the crowd, watching the parade through their newly purchased masks. They indulged the vendor when they saw aerocycle cops scanning the crowd from twenty feet above.

Mia felt ridiculous in her butterfly eye-mask, even though half the locals around her wore sillier disguises. She stood on her tiptoes in a vain attempt to peer over the wall of spectators.

David offered her a smirk and a hand. He looked like a superhero in his white domino mask.

"Let me give you a lift."

Mia's brow curled in worry. "You're hurt."

"My spine's just fine. Come on."

She climbed onto his back with wincing dread. To her amazement, he didn't even grunt. Maybe she'd lost more weight than she realized.

"You sure this isn't hurting you?"

"You'd know," David sighed. "As you saw yesterday, I don't handle pain very well."

The procession continued past them. The majority of ghostwalkers wore plain white bathrobes. Some women sported snowy gowns. A few men were decked out in formal ivory vestments that had been passed down for three generations. The one item that never varied was the mask, an expressionless white face with black fabric eyeholes. The uniformity created an eerily powerful effect. For a moment Mia imagined she was watching the departed souls of her world, all the teachers and classmates and neighbors and cousins who didn't get silver bracelets. And to think she'd snapped at the sisters for not realizing how lucky they were. She was alive. She was alive on the back of a beautiful boy with the heart of a lion and an unflinchingly deep regard for her. Mia never stopped replaying the scene on the highway, when David threatened to kill two Deps if they harmed a hair on her head. She wasn't just lucky, she was blessed.

Mia locked her arms around David and heaved a warm sigh over his shoulder. "Don't feel bad."

"About what?"

"The way you acted yesterday. We don't care about that. You've been there for us since day one and we love you. We'll love you no matter what you do."

She breathed a soft whisper into his ear. "I'll love you no matter who you kill."

Though the mask lay still on his impassive face, David's voice carried a thin new tremor.

"You're a rare and precious jewel, Miafarisi. I dread the day our paths diverge."

Everyone turned to look as booming cheers erupted to the north. Exuberant music blared up the street. The last of the Ghostwalk was exiting the square. Now came the March of the Spirits.

Amanda crunched her brow behind her white burglar mask as confetti guns popped and the locals turned jubilant. The crowd had gone from funeral to Mardi Gras at the turn of a dime.

She sneaked an anxious peek at Zack, a parallel study in conflicting extremes. His rabbit-eared mask radiated levity while the eyes behind it screamed with bewilderment. He stood right next to her, but he might as well have been a thousand miles away.

She took his dangling hand in hers. "It has to be hard for you. Coming back to your hometown and finding it so different."

Zack threw an antsy glance at the drugstore behind him, where a public phone lay encased inside an opaque metal cylinder. A red light on the door indicated that the tube was currently occupied.

"I don't know," he said. "It seems like every big difference in this world can be traced back to the Cataclysm in one way or another. Guess I shouldn't be surprised New York changed the most."

The first of the parade platforms approached, ferrying a gorgeous young blonde in a star-spangled minidress. She crooned a bouncy tribute to New York into her microphone while a thirty-foot ghostbox displayed a giant live projection of her buxom upper half. Zack noticed the empty space beneath the platform's hanging drapes. It seemed aeris had turned all the floats literal.

Amanda stroked his hand with her thumb, then grimaced in affliction when he pulled it away.

"Zack . . ."

"It's all right. I understand."

"Understand what? We haven't had a chance to talk."

He pursed his lips in a crusty scowl. "If it's a 'let's just be friends after all' speech, I don't need to hear it. You've been wearing it on your face for the last seven hours."

Amanda threw a quick nervous glance at David, five feet away.

"It's not what you think," she said to Zack. "I've been waiting for the right time to explain it."

"You don't have to explain anything. It happens. It's not like we signed a contract."

Amanda clenched her jaw. She knew Zack well enough to see the mask behind the mask. He was determined to play the breezy teflon shrugger until one of them screamed.

"Would you listen to me? I'm not backing out. There's just . . . a new complication."

Exuberant children in brightly colored jumpsuits lined every edge of the second float. They reached into buckets and flung foil-wrapped candies at the crowd. Zack gave Amanda his full attention, even as a chocolate coin sailed between them.

"I'm all ears."

She shook her head. "Not now. When we're alone again, and when you're less angry—"

"I'm not angry."

"No. Of course not. You're just convinced I dropped my feelings for you on a fickle whim. Why would that anger you?"

"Well, what did you expect me to think? Yesterday we had a nice plan worked out. Today you can barely look at me. I've had seven hours to scratch my head over it. All I have now are a bloody scalp and a few second thoughts of my own. Maybe it wasn't such a good idea after all. Maybe it'll be easier for everyone if we just forget it."

Tiny spikes of stress tempis hatched from Amanda's feet, piercing the straps of her borrowed sandals. She banished away the whiteness, then cast a thorny glower at the parade.

"I swear to God, Zack, sometimes I think you're played by twins. I never know which one of you I'm going to get."

"Great. Maybe the four of us can go out for burgers sometime."

"Go to hell."

Amanda cut through the crowd, her jaw held rigid with forced composure. Zack tossed another glance at the pay phone before trading a desolate look with Hannah. She wished the two of them would get over their issues, whatever they were, and just screw already. She feared she and Theo were partly to blame for their hesitation. They didn't provide the best sales brochure for the carpe diem hookup.

They sat side by side on an unattended shoeshine stand, their faces both covered in weeping theater masks. Theo's head dipped and jerked erratically. Hannah couldn't tell if he was asleep or lost in premonitions. She ran gentle fingertips up and down his forearm. The caress always seemed to soothe him, no matter how far gone he was.

"Where's the happy face?"

Hannah jumped at the high voice next to her. A cute young brunette leaned against the wall. She wore a sleeveless white gown that hugged every contour of her elfin body. Her long brown tresses matched Mia's hairstyle to the strand. If it wasn't for the girl's honey skin and vaguely Eurasian features, Hannah might have wondered if a Future Mia had sent herself back in time.

"I'm sorry. What?"

"You and your fella are wearing the same theater mask," the stranger noted. "It's supposed to be one happy face and one sad face. You know, Thalia and Melpomene. The Muses of comedy and tragedy."

Hannah felt silly to be conversing through a disguise. She pulled it away. The girl studied her.

"Nope. Still sad, but prettier now. Damn, hon, you're a scorcher. I bet you drive all the boys wild."

The actress bloomed a bleak little grin. "Not enough to keep them."

"You seem to be doing all right with that one."

Hannah peered at Theo, oblivious in his torpor. "It's not like that."

"I wasn't slapping a label on it. I just see the way you're comforting him without a second thought or a 'what's in it for me?' Whatever you are to him, he's lucky to have you."

It was the sweetest notion Hannah heard in days. But for all the girl's rosiness, she wielded a sad face herself. She held a glossy mask in her hand, the plain white façade that Hannah had spotted ad nauseam five minutes ago.

"You were in that first parade."

"The Ghostwalk. Yeah. I do it every year, though I never make it the whole way without losing it. I'm probably the only one who still cries about the Cataclysm. Everyone else is thinking about their aunt Jody or that dog who ran out in the road."

"Well, you can hardly blame them. It happened a century ago."

The girl shrugged tensely. "What can I say? I'm a slow griever."

The next float ferried four lithe young women in black rubber speedsuits, prancing around the platform in slow ballet motions. Suddenly their gear glowed with patchwork strips of color and they swayed around each other in a hazy blur. Hannah watched in gaping astonishment as their streaking hues combined to form ethereal images—an ocean sunset, a city skyline, a crude American flag. The crowd cheered wildly with each new tableau.

Soon the quartet de-shifted and resumed their gentle mincing. The girl smiled at Hannah's slack-faced awe.

"Guess you've never seen lumis dancers before."

"No. That was incredible. Jesus. I don't know how they do that without breaking a bone."

Amanda gaped, thunderstruck, as Rebel's first punch drew blood from Esis's nose and sent her flying onto her back. He leapt on top of her, pummeling her with fists both flesh and synthetic.

"You threaten my wife? You threaten my *child*?"

Four blocks away, the screens of the command center flickered back to life. Gemma did a double take at the action on the center monitor. This was not the future she'd seen. Not at all.

"Oh my God. He's alive."

Ivy raised her teary face from her hands. "What?"

"He's alive! Rebel! He . . . Holy shit, he's beating her!"

Olga looked up from her table. She'd just finished tying a tourniquet around Bruce's leg and was now lowering his body temperature in preparation for reversal. Her ice pack dropped to the floor when she saw the two slaughtered kinsmen in the elevator bank. *Dear Lord. No.*

Ivy kept her rapt attention on the middle screen. "Oh God. Richard. Get the gun. Kill her."

"Kill her!" Gemma screamed.

Kill her, Amanda cried in her broken thoughts. *Kill each other.*

Rebel continued his furious assault, reducing Esis to a raw and battered wreck. The woman had been raised in a more civilized era, where only the poorest suffered the indignity of pain. Even a surgeon like her could live her whole life without seeing a drop of blood.

Now as this ancestor ape thrashed her with his brutal fists, a shrill cry escaped her bloody lips.

"SEMERJEAN!"

A nine-foot portal opened on the second floor balcony. A speeding figure burst through the surface and knocked Mercy unconscious. It continued down the stairs in a blurry streak, yanking Rebel off Esis and slamming him against a wall. Two heavy-framed paintings crashed to the ground.

Now Amanda could see this new man clearly. He stood as large and bald as Rebel, with powerful arms and a broadly muscled back. His entire body was glossy white, like a marble statue of a naked Greek god. It took two squinting glances for Amanda to see that he was covered in tempis.

Ivy stared at the screen in slack horror. "Oh Jesus, Richard. Come on. Break free."

Rebel may as well have been crucified for all the force that pinned him. When he tried to kick his aggressor, the man grew a second pair of arms from his hips. They held Rebel's thighs to the wall.

Gemma shook her trembling head. "God. What is that? Is it even human?"

Only Rebel was in a position to glimpse the man behind the tempis. Through the small round eyeholes, he could see pale skin and sandy brown eyebrows. His fierce blue eyes brimmed with savage fury, like a panther in midroar.

Rebel hocked a spiteful gob at his attacker. "Fuck you, coward. A real man shows his face when he kills someone."

Semerjean's eyes laughed with a shrewd and vicious mockery that Rebel found even more frightening than his rage. Clearly this creature wasn't just a thug on the family payroll. He was a Pelletier through and through.

Ivy cried out when the tempic man grew a third pair of arms from his rib cage. They struck at Rebel with relentless fury, cracking his jaw, breaking his teeth. Once Rebel's face matched the bloody wretchedness of Esis, Semerjean melted away his extra limbs. He leaned in toward Rebel and hissed a gritty whisper.

"You'll know when I'm killing you, boy. You'll see my true face then."

Rebel moaned in pain as Semerjean traced a finger along each cheek, rifting the skin just enough to scar him. He let his victim collapse to the floor, then gently scooped his wife into his arms.

Amanda watched in bleary-eyed anguish as Semerjean carried Esis through a new portal. The gateway shrank to a close behind them.

All was once again quiet in the lobby as the living fell as still as the dead. In the remote command room, three Gotham women stared numbly at the monitors. Gemma shuddered in her seat while she received new intel from the future.

"It's safe to get Rebel and Mercy," she told Ivy. "But you have to do it fast."

"Why? Are those monsters coming back?"

"No."

Gemma adjusted the camera displays to show a view of the street. A trio of ash-gray vans came to a halt in front of the building, with several more approaching.

The Deps had arrived in full force.

Howard Hairston parked his rental coupe at Bowling Green Park, a block away from the action. The freckly young redhead was the only member of Melissa's team to follow her here. Everyone else had been called back to Los Angeles by the regional director, who sought to sever his office from this quagmire of a case. Until Integrity seized the reins, as everyone assumed they would, the six otherworldly fugitives were officially New York's problem.

The moment Howard reached the siege site, he saw that New York was ready for them.

Seventeen government vehicles flanked the building—armored trucks, reviver vans, mobile thermal scanners. A trio of NYPD aerocruisers circled the roof like buzzards.

Howard scanned the crowd for Melissa, to no avail. He moved in on Rosie Herrera, a small and sturdy woman whose masculine features were only slightly countered by her salmon-pink ensemble. She paced the barricaded entry, commanding her men like Napoleon at Austerlitz.

"I want all exits covered before that tempis comes down. Every door. Every window. Every vent."

"Excuse me . . ."

She held up a finger to Howard, then fumed at the young agent working the gate controls. "Why am I still looking at this barrier, Jules?"

"None of the overrides are working. Someone jammed it good."

"Well, fix it already. We got thirty guys standing here with their twigs out." She turned to Howard. "Who the hell are you?"

He raised his badge. She leaned in to study it. "Huh. Another one from Sunland. You must be Melissa's boy."

"Yes, ma'am. Has she arrived yet?"

"She's here. She's changing."

"Changing?"

"You faced these perps before. How bad are they?"

"Bad." Howard sighed. "One of them broke my teammate's back. Another punched the gate off a Tug-a-Lug truck. They've got an Australian kid who's an ice-cold gangster and a Filipino who probably already knows your middle name. If they slip out this time—"

"They won't."

"—it'll be because of Maranan. That guy just knows things."

Rosie snorted. "Unless he knows how to turn into sunbeams, he's not getting out of there."

The back doors of a truck swung open with a heavy *thud*. Eight imposing agents marched down the ramp. They wore the same padded black armor, with thick-soled boots and gray metal cables that ran between their gloves and their backpack shifters.

The lone female of the group broke away from the procession and approached Howard. He smiled at the dreadlock tips that dangled from the base of her mirrored black helmet.

Melissa raised her visor and flashed him a humble grin. "Hello, Howard."

"Hi, boss. Damn. I guess I don't need to ask if you're ready."

Melissa now had the power to move at twenty times her normal speed. Her armor carried four gas bombs, three flash grenades, two sonic screamers, and a stun chaser. She kept a snub-nosed pistol in her side pouch in case Zack rusted her primary weapon. Most crucial of all were the two reviver vans parked right outside the building. In lieu of winning over her quarry's hearts and minds, she now had the freedom to shoot them everywhere else. This was Melissa's final chance to capture the fugitives alive. She wouldn't waste it on words.

She blew a hot breath, then looked to the barrier. "Let's get this thing down, shall we?"

Hannah eyed her dreary reflection in the restroom mirror. Her vision was coming back in dribs and drabs, enough to let her see the magnitude of her sister's injury. Amanda was in mortal agony and yet somehow she found the strength to fuss over Hannah's trifling burn. *You need to soak that hand,* she'd told her. *Put it in cool water, not cold.*

After forty seconds, Hannah yanked her fingers from the sink in restless anguish. There had to be something she could do for Amanda. Maybe she could make her a splint out of something, or find some painkillers. For once it was time for the dizzy actress to take care of the nurse.

She returned to the hallway and scanned the many glass doors. Though her weirdness was still smothered under a lingering sheen of solis, she figured she could smash her way into any one of these offices if she found something heavy enough.

Her search was interrupted by the sudden presence of music, a faint and tinny riff of jazz lounge trumpets. Hannah looked around and saw that the door to a nearby office—some personal injury law firm—had been opened a crack. Stranger still, she could swear she recognized the song that blared from within.

Soon her suspicions were confirmed by the unmistakable voice of the divine Sarah Vaughan.

Whatever Lola wants, Lola gets.
And little man, little Lola wants you . . .
Make up your mind to have no regrets.
Recline yourself, resign yourself, you're through.

Hannah reeled with fresh perplexity. This wasn't some Altamerican retread of her old favorite showtune. This was a haunting echo from her old dead Earth.

She pushed the door open in a dark and dreamy daze. The law firm's lobby was no larger than her old living room. Drab wood paneling covered every wall, while bubbly white chairs stood out like blisters on the red shag rug. There wasn't another soul in sight.

Through the glass wall of a conference room, she spied a clunky homemade contraption at the edge of a long table. Two large speakers were bridged at the top by a thick square battery. Clipped, split wires curled wildly in all directions.

Resting in the center of the construct, like a beating heart, was a tiny pink device that triggered another sharp flash of recognition in Hannah.

She was looking at her own iPod, the one she'd carried in her handbag on the day the world ended. Last she knew, the thing was dead and gathering dust in Terra Vista. What the hell was it doing here?

Suddenly the ground beneath her vibrated. Eight-foot poles of tempis sprang up all around her in a perfect square formation. Panicked, she shook the bars, then looked down at the metal platform below. A large engraving by her foot reminded owners to check their local laws for restrictions on using this Ellerbee-brand live animal trap.

She covered her eyes. "Oh no. No no no no . . ."

Soft footsteps approached. A high and merry whistle kept rhythm with the song. Once her captor moved close enough to pause the iPod, Hannah opened her eyes and looked at him.

Evan Rander tossed her an impish grin through the bars of her cage. He tilted his head in mock concern.

"I'm sorry. Is this a bad time?"

Rebel lay flat on the marble, a grim and battered husk. The skin of his face had become as numb as a mask while the bones beneath throbbed with jagged pain. Through the sliver of his unsealed eye, he saw a narrow figure kneel at his side.

Ivy pressed his shoulders. "Don't move, hon. Don't try to talk. Your jaw's fractured. You have four shattered teeth and that creature rifted some skin on your cheeks. But you'll live."

He could tell from her level of knowledge that Gemma had been to the future to get the doctor's prognosis. The girl had probably already spent an evening at his bedside.

"Merzee," he mumbled.

"Olga's getting her now. She's out cold, but she'll make it. So will Bruce."

Rebel couldn't give a crap about Bruce Byer. He sensed from Ivy's grim omission that all the others were dead. Ben. Colin. Nick. Freddy. *We lost four. They lost none.*

"Firdy . . ."

"Richard, don't talk."

"How?"

Ivy closed her eyes. "Gemma says he was shot in the face. She thinks the boy did it."

A guttural groan escaped his lips. Ivy held his arm. "I know. I'm angry too. But right now I'm just so glad you're okay. I can't believe you survived that creature. I just can't believe it."

Rebel knew it wasn't luck. The Pelletiers had chosen to spare him, either out of strategy or sadism. Now that he'd been rifted again, he knew he couldn't be healed through reversal. The temporal discord in his body would kill him instantly, gruesomely. He'd have to recover the slow and painful way, as Semerjean no doubt intended.

While Olga carried Mercy over her shoulder, Ivy helped Rebel back to his feet. She slung his thick arm around her and walked him to her portal on the eastern wall.

Amanda followed their progress from her hidden perch. *Just go already. Leave.*

As Olga carried Mercy through the glimmering gateway, Rebel stopped and noticed his revolver. It had spun all the way through the eastern arch, resting halfway between the lobby and the entry for Nicomedia Magazines. One more second and he would have gotten Trillinger. One more second.

Ivy tugged him along. "Come on. We have to go."

His fresh failures bubbled inside him like boiling water. All the evidence they were leaving behind. All the dead kinsmen. All the living Silvers.

Rebel broke away from Ivy and charged through the archway.

"Richard!"

He seized the gun and fired seven shots through the open door. The first round hit the leg of the reception desk. The next two shattered the white glass wall behind it. The remaining four traveled into the sea of cubicles where Zack and Mia hid. Rebel's foresight was still hobbled by solis. He shot blindly and was now blind to the results.

By the time Ivy caught up to him, he fired empty clicks at the office. She grabbed his arm.

"Richard, stop! Stop! It's over!"

"No!"

"If we're lucky, the Deps will finish them. If not, we'll have other chances. But we have to go!"

Amanda turned white at the distant sound of gunshots. She looked to the southern archway and saw David make a stealthy reentrance. He ducked behind a support column just as Rebel and Ivy returned to the lobby. Amanda's fingers dug into her thighs.

Oh God, David, don't. Just let them leave.

A half mile to the north, Gemma accessed the Nicomedia office cameras and shook her head at the image.

"Christ, Rebel. You lucky son of a bitch."

Olga looked to Gemma. "What are you talking about?"

"He did it." She chuckled in wonder at the screen. "He got one."

Zack sprawled facedown on the carpet, his fingers pressed over his head. From the moment the glass wall exploded in front of him, his body went into system crash. He couldn't move. He couldn't think. He couldn't feel anything but the thundering beat of his heart.

Two minutes after Rebel's hasty exit, Zack and Mia worked their way back toward the front of the office, darting in and out of cubicles like skittish rabbits. Once they'd reached the first row, Zack made Mia wait behind him while he scanned the reception area. He'd only made it as far as the white glass partition when the shots rang out and the world seemed to end all over again.

Now the wall lay in shards all around him. For all he knew, his body was just as broken.

"Zack?"

The sound of Mia's voice prompted him to move. He clambered to a wobbly kneel, then checked himself with trembling hands. He still couldn't feel anything. He couldn't get his mouth to work.

"I . . . I . . . God . . ."

After four more seconds of self-scrutiny, he rose to his feet and blurted a nervous laugh.

"I think . . . I think I'm all right. I'm okay. Jesus, Mia. I . . ."

He turned around and saw her now. Her skin had turned chalk-white. She pressed a weak and trembling hand to her chest. For a hopeful moment, Zack figured she was simply struggling to collect herself. Then he saw the thick blood seeping through her fingers. His delirious grin faded.

"Oh God. No. No . . ."

Mia removed her hand and stared down at the oozing hole in the center of her chest. She thought about the policeman's bullet that had narrowly missed her face a month ago, the ridiculous luck that kept her in perfect health while her friends suffered wound after wound.

She finally understood how the universe worked now. Suddenly it all made sense.

"Zack . . ."

Her legs gave out from under her. She crumpled to the floor.

Four hundred and thirty feet away, in the tiny windowless office of the building security manager, Theo screamed in synch with Zack. His scattered thoughts came together in a unified roar, a thousand voices all wailing in grief, insisting that there were no futures left with Mia Farisi in them.

He clutched his hair, throwing his elbows left and right.

"No! No! No! No!"

It was at that cruelest of moments that a final gear snapped into place inside him. His eyes rolled back, his skin glowed white, and his consciousness took him to a strange new place.

At long last, Theo Maranan was formally introduced to his weirdness.

THIRTY-THREE

Everything stopped.

The ambient hum of the building generators fell silent. The light on the desk phone froze in midblink. A fat bead of water halted its drop from a sweaty ceiling pipe. It hung in the air like a miniature planet.

All over the office, all across creation, time held its breath and waited for Theo.

The bewildered augur kept as still as his surroundings as he fought to absorb this latest insanity. What little color the room had was gone. A thin gray mist blanketed the floor and walls. He saw twinkling specks of light through the fog, like distant cities.

Vague time passed—a second, a minute, an hour—before he dared to move. He writhed in his thoughts and suddenly found himself sling-shot to the other side of the office. Dumbstruck, he turned around and reeled at the haggard young Asian in his former place. The man sat huddled behind the desk in a frozen cry of grief, wearing Theo's face and clothes, his karma tattoo. It took five rounds of furious debate for him to accept that he was somehow looking at himself. *What? How is this . . . ?*

The mist on the eastern wall suddenly darkened and swirled like thunderclouds. A tall, reedy figure emerged from the depths, trailing smoky black wisps as he moved.

Azral Pelletier shined a cordial grin at the empty space where Theo's consciousness lingered.

"Welcome, child."

He looked majestically dapper in his stone-colored business suit and tieless white oxford. His flawless skin was now as colorless as his surroundings but his eyes remained a vibrant blue. The good cheer on his face did little to quell Theo's panic.

"Ease yourself," said Azral. "Your mind is still adjusting to the transition. Soon your senses will compensate and give you form."

Though his lips moved when he talked, Azral's cold honey voice hit Theo like a second set of thoughts. He struggled to reply, unsure if his words were spoken or merely imagined.

What happened to me? Am I dead?

Azral smirked. "On the contrary. You're more alive and awake than ever before."

Awake was one of the last words Theo would use to describe himself at the moment.

You're in my head.

"Yes."

His mind flashed back to the results of the cerebral scan that Melissa had shared with him.

You put something in my brain. Some tiny metal ring.

"A harmless device," Azral assured him. "It merely allows us to communicate in this state, little more."

His "little more" struck Theo like a salesman's asterisk. He felt a nervous lurch where his stomach used to be. "And where exactly . . ."

Theo balked at the new echo in his voice. Now he looked down to see a hazy facsimile of his body.

Azral nodded approvingly. "Already you adapt."

Theo was surprised to find himself in his faded Stanford hoodie, his old khaki shorts and sandals. It was his favorite outfit, one that had comforted him through many drunken travels.

"What's happening to me?"

"You're an augur, Theo. Did you think you'd spend the rest of your life suffering random glimpses? No. You're generations ahead of your peers, the so-called prophets of this age. Their talent is a crude cudgel. Yours is a violin. This is where the futures sing at your bow, my friend. This is your true gift."

A thunderous shudder filled Theo. By the time it passed, he appeared as whole as Azral. He could feel the ground beneath his feet again, a simulation of life and breath inside him. The sensation was even more pleasurable than waking life. He felt wonderful now. Except . . .

"Mia. I saw her. She was shot in the chest. Did that really happen? Has it happened already?"

"It has occurred," Azral calmly replied. "She fades from life at this moment."

"No . . ."

"We can address the matter later. For now—"

"I have to find her!"

"Boy, look around you. What do you see?"

Theo took another wide-eyed glance around the office. The fat water droplet still dangled in the air. The clock on the wall remained rooted at 11:56 and 48 seconds, with no signs of letting go.

"So it's not just here," Theo said. "Time stopped everywhere."

Azral emitted a soft chuckle, snugly perched between fondness and ridicule.

"You can't stop time any more than you can stop a desert or a forest. Time is a landscape that stretches across all things. We're the ones who move across it."

Theo shook his head in hopeless perplexity. "I don't—"

"If it helps, think of all the people of the world as passengers on a train. You travel through time at the same speed and direction, perceiving events through your own narrow windows. The concepts of past and future are entirely human constructs. We formulated them as navigational markers, like east and west. Only now—"

"I got off the train."

Azral smiled again. "You're not the first of your kind to achieve this state, though my ancestors only seem to come here by accident. They romantically refer to this realm as the God's Eye. You'd do just as well to call it the Gray."

Theo didn't care what it was called. If he was forever stuck here at the cusp of noon, it was Hell.

"Is there . . . a way back on the train?"

"Of course. You can resume your journey at any time. I'll show you how, but not yet. Come with me. If you wish to aid your companions, there are things you should see."

Theo felt a gentle hand on his back. He'd only taken three steps out of the room when a cold force pushed him forward like a leaf in a gale. By the time his dizzy senses returned to him, he found himself outside the building.

"What . . . what just . . . ?"

"A quicker mode of transit," Azral explained. "Foot travel is a needless formality here."

Theo's next question fizzled in the urgency of his surroundings. More than twenty federal agents now flanked the building—all paused in tense and busy actions. A ghost team fixed their imaging towers around the Silvers' dusty red car while a second group wheeled a large metal device that reminded Theo of a supervillain's death ray. He shuddered to think what it would do once the clock started ticking again.

"Shit. It's worse than I thought."

"Indeed," said Azral. "In one hundred thirty-two seconds, their crude solic toy will breach the barrier."

Theo looked to the eight gun-toting Deps in armored black speedsuits. He could only assume they were all assigned to take down Hannah. "We'll never make it out of here."

"You'll escape. It's the continuing presence of these government agents that troubles me. There may yet be a remedy."

"What remedy?"

"It's my task," Azral curtly replied. "Not yours."

Theo churned with stress as he recalled Azral's remote-button slaughter of twenty-one physicists, another so-called remedy. *They worked for you and you killed them. Bill Pollock got me sober and you killed him.*

"I never wished to slay those scientists," Azral replied, to Theo's unease. "I saw the consequences of their continued existence, an elaborate chain of events that would have destroyed you and a great many others. It's the burden of foresight. Our choices often seem questionable to those around us, even cruel. You'll know this soon enough."

Theo saw the dreadlocks dangling from an armored agent's helmet and struggled to avoid all thoughts of Melissa. If the Pelletiers identified her as the face of their federal problem, she was dead.

Azral put his hand on Theo's back. "Come."

In a windy swirl, the scenery changed once more. Now they stood in the vast marble lobby, a place that had seen much violence since Theo left it.

Furniture all around the room had been smashed and singed and spattered with blood. Two wet and gory strangers lay facedown in the elevator bank while a third corpse languished on the stairwell.

Theo looked to the inanimate couple at the eastern wall, poised inches from a glowing white portal. Though the alluring Indian woman was a stranger to him, he had no trouble recognizing the bald and brawny thug who'd shot him in Terra Vista. A stagnant curl of smoke extended like coral from the barrel of Rebel's revolver.

"Goddamn it. It was him, wasn't it? He shot Mia."

Azral glared at Rebel. He'd only just now caught up on the battle in the lobby—the savage beating of his mother, the timely intervention from his father. His voice dropped a cold octave.

"You won't have to worry about him much longer."

"Why is he trying to kill us? What did we do to him?"

Azral shook his head in scorn. "Beneath all that bulk, Richard Rosen is nothing more than a frightened child. He sees a dark event coming and he can't bear the thought of it. So his weak mind conjures a theory, an enemy, a brutal solution. He's hardly the first man in history to blame his troubles on immigrants."

Theo scanned the room and caught David hiding behind a support pillar, his pistol raised high in frozen readiness.

"Oh no . . ."

Azral bloomed a small grin. "He'll be fine. The boy's remarkably capable for his age."

Theo was all too aware of that. Azral gleaned his flip-side worry.

"You believe he'll kill this pair."

"I don't know." Theo eyed the pregnant bulge in Ivy's bodysuit. "I hope not."

"Why would you show concern for those who would slaughter you without hesitation?"

"I'm mostly concerned for David. I don't want to see him go down a dark path."

"Have you?"

Theo had to think about it. He'd suffered countless premonitions over the last several days, but only just now realized how very few of them involved David. His future seemed to fall in a blind spot.

"No."

"Have faith in him then," Azral said. "Let us continue."

The next jaunt took them up to the fifth-floor walkway that overlooked the lobby. The mist was ten times thicker here. Theo had to stand next to Amanda to see her on the cushioned bench.

"God, her leg . . ."

Azral studied her broken ankle. "Yes. Strange that my mother didn't heal her. She favors this one. The child must have angered her."

"You're talking about Esis."

"Yes."

"She doesn't look old enough to be your mother."

"She would adore you for saying that."

"I've only seen her in visions." Theo scowled in hot contempt. "She keeps killing Zack."

Azral frowned. "Trillinger is a buffoon and a nuisance. I see now why Quint found him so vexing."

"He's my friend!"

"If you seek to keep him, his fate is easily prevented."

"How?"

Azral raised a long finger at Amanda. "She knows."

The white-haired man floated deeper into the fog. Theo scrambled to keep up with him, even as his screaming thoughts urged him to flee.

"Why is it so hazy here?"

"Even in this realm, none of us is omniscient. As we move farther from our own sphere of influence, our view grows weaker. Should we venture but one floor higher, I wager we'd glimpse nothing but mist."

That's why you're teaching me, Theo surmised. *You need me to see the things you can't.*

If Azral heard his thoughts, he didn't acknowledge them. He led Theo into a small office that looked like a low-grade law firm. Through the swirling mist, he spotted Hannah inside a small tempic cage. She gripped the bars, her face contorted in a silent scream.

He had to move closer to spot the source of her anguish.

"Jesus Christ! You've got to be kidding me!"

Evan Rander was dressed in the stately beige uniform of a security guard, an ensemble that looked silly on his scrawny frame. Theo could only guess the outfit was part of his personal escape plan. He'd probably put on his best Barney Fife impression for the Deps, give a few shaky statements, and then slip away while no one was looking.

The rogue Silver wore a nasty grin as he fired a bullhorn-shaped device at Hannah.

"What's he doing to her?"

"He inflicts her with a low electric charge," Azral replied. "He seeks to torment, not kill."

"Son of a bitch. Why does he hate her so much?"

"He hates both sisters. The reasons hardly matter. Rander is nothing. A pathetic fool. I only show him to you as a cautionary example."

"What, you're afraid I'll become like him?"

"In mind-set, not temperament. The boy has lived hundreds of years and yet he still fails to grasp the structure of time. He sees the past as his chalkboard, a single line to be erased and redrawn at whim. In truth, he undoes nothing. He merely jumps from train to train, forever dodging the consequences of his actions. I'm hoping you won't be so linear in your thinking."

Theo covered his face in hot distress. His friends were all suffering and Azral was giving him a primer in fiftieth-century metaphysics.

"What will it take?"

"For what?"

"For this guy to see consequences!"

Azral jerked a testy shrug. "His talents give him a unique perspective on events, which in turn provides us with helpful information. But perhaps I should reevaluate his usefulness."

"I don't want him dead. I just want him to leave us alone."

"Yes. I thought I'd dissuaded him when last we spoke. Perhaps I need to make myself clearer."

Azral studied Theo carefully as he reached for Hannah with an intangible hand. "You feel strongly for this one."

"Yeah, but not the way you think."

"You don't know what I think," Azral snapped. "If I deemed your love to be physical, we'd be having a different conversation."

Theo looked to him in wide-eyed bother. "What . . . what do you mean?"

"Just take comfort that you won't lose her. Not anytime soon."

"I know." He turned to Hannah again. "I see her all over my future. She's everywhere I look."

"You say it like it troubles you."

"It troubles me that I don't see the others as clearly. Can you *please* take me to Mia now?"

Azral nodded obligingly, though his handsome face turned grim.

"Come, then."

He'd prepared himself for the worst, but what Theo saw in the magazine office sent his proxy form to chaos. He screamed and cried with two blurry heads, punched at the air with four hazy hands. He paced the floor in all directions while five ghostly duplicates fell to their knees. He was everywhere at once—an army of Theos, all thrashing and grieving over the youngest of the Silvers.

Mia lay cradled in Zack's arms, her eyes wide with vacant horror as he pressed a bloody T-shirt to her chest wound. The cartoonist served a silent contrast to Theo's raging sorrow, a snapshot image of a man in blanket shock. His tears had paused in midjourney, lining his cheeks like scars.

Azral stood expressionless among the broken glass, calmly waiting for his protégé to collect himself.

"Theo . . ."

One by one, the doppelgängers vanished. A lone Theo crouched by Mia's side. "How long does she have?"

"Moments," Azral informed him. "She dies before the agents breach the barrier."

"Oh God. There has to be something we can do."

"I don't know, Theo. Is there?"

"Don't play games with me! I'm not in the mood!"

"It's your mood that clouds you. Your emotions prevent you from seeing."

"Seeing what?"

"The futures," Azral said, with a sweeping hand gesture. "They reveal themselves in this place. They sing to us from every corner. Have you not wondered about the lights in the mist?"

Theo looked to the northern wall, at the tiny beads that twinkled within the fog. He'd glimpsed them everywhere he turned in this dreary gray world. He didn't know why they scared him.

"What are they?"

"I said your talent was a violin, Theo. These . . ."

Azral moved behind him, plunging his fingers deep into the augur's skull. "These are the strings."

Hot white strands of light converged on Theo from every direction. His consciousness erupted in a screaming torrent of images—a million parallel futures, all as different as siblings but knotted at the ends with the same painful traumas. Every string ended with his own cold death. Every string started with Mia's.

"NO!"

Azral leaned in close, his imperious voice cutting through the chaos. "You see them now. All the branching possibilities. All the endless permutations and patterns. We've been so blind, Theo. Our species has lived for so long like moles in a tunnel. You're among the first to step into the light and see time as it was meant to be seen. This is humanity's greatest evolution. A whole new dimension of perception. It's beautiful, is it not?"

"It hurts!"

"You hinder yourself."

"She keeps dying!"

"You adopt the grief of your elder incarnations. For them, it's too late to save her. Not for you. Detach yourself and perhaps you'll find a brighter outcome hidden among the multitudes."

With a raspy shout, Theo thrust his palms and cleared a six-foot ball of space around him. The strings now ended in a curved wall of pinlights. The bedlam in his thoughts dissipated.

Azral retracted his hands. "Good. Very good."

The augur dropped to his ethereal knees, panting through imaginary lungs. "Go to hell . . ."

"I only seek to aid you. The girl can be saved."

"You're lying!"

"Look again. Search the strings more carefully. You've no reason to hurry. We don't age here. Our bodies don't clamor for food or sleep. In this realm, time is our servant. Use it."

Theo raised his head and squinted at the array of tiny lights. Glancing at it was like staring into an endless crowd of suffering children, searching for the one who smiled. And Azral expected him to do this for days, weeks, years on end. *Is this how you learned the strings, you murderous shit? Is this what turned you cold and white?*

He squinted his eyes shut. "I can't do this! I can't keep watching her die!"

"Then she is indeed lost."

"You know how to save her. Just tell me!"

"Am I indebted to you, boy? Are you the one who rescued me from a dying world, or was it perhaps the other way around?"

"I never asked you to give me a goddamn bracelet! And you wouldn't have saved us if you didn't need us for something. So just tell me! Tell me how to keep her alive!"

Azral sighed defeatedly, a reaction that nearly made Theo burst with jaded laughter. Though he was new to the Gray or the God's Eye or whatever this place was called, he was a decorated veteran in disappointing people. The familiarity soothed him like a warm shot of whiskey.

"It seems I overestimated you, Theo."

"You found me drunk at a bus stop. What did you expect?"

"I found you long before that, but no matter." Azral touched Theo's back. "Come."

Their final journey was different from the others. Instead of twirling around like a leaf, Theo shot forward at blurring speed, his vision a tableau of bright, streaking colors. Occasionally he felt a shift in direction, as if Azral steered them down a branching path. *Forks in the road,* Theo mused, though he imagined it was hardly so binary. There were likely millions of options at every juncture, millions of variations and subvariations, even a few minor miracles.

After an indeterminate period—nestled somewhere in the space between "soon" and "soon enough"—the pair emerged into a sparse but cozy living room. Venetian blinds filtered afternoon sunlight. Taped moving boxes lined the bare walls. A group of mismatched chairs and couches stood in sloppy formation around a circular glass coffee table. The cushions were occupied by five people Theo readily recognized, including himself.

His twin stretched out on a plush recliner, locking his arms around Hannah's waist as she wearily leaned against him. Zack, David, and Amanda all slouched alone in their sofas. Amanda wore a makeshift splint of broken broomsticks and duct tape. The others sported numerous bandages.

The spectral Theo peeked over David's shoulder and examined his wristwatch.

"It's a quarter after one. A little over an hour from now."

Azral cracked a patronizing grin at Theo's muddled notion of "now."

"Where is this?" Theo asked.

"Approximately five miles east of the office tower."

Theo peeked out the window at a red-leafed sycamore tree. "Brooklyn. Jesus, we really did get out."

"In this string, yes."

"But what about—"

Hannah cut him off with a melodious yawn, startling him. He thought the scene was a still frame like all the others. His friends were merely languishing in dull stupor.

Now he heard the clinking of ceramics through the kitchen door. His eyes bulged when Mia entered with a tray of steaming mugs. Though her face drooped with fatigue like all the others', she looked healthy enough to live for decades.

She placed a cup on the end table next to Amanda. "He doesn't have milk. Sorry."

The widow stared ahead in dead torpor, her voice a flimsy wisp. "Okay."

The spectral Theo continued to study Mia in slack awe. "God. It's like she was never shot. How did that happen? Was there a reviver in the building?"

"There was a reviver in that very room," Azral replied. "You simply failed to see it."

"Well, how do I find it then?"

"What do you mean?"

"When I go back. How do I make this the future that happens?"

Azral eyed him with dark disbelief, as if Theo were lost in a broom closet.

"This *is* happening, child. Every path of time exists on the landscape, one as real as the next. Did you think I merely brought you here for instruction?"

Now Theo was truly lost. "What are you telling me?"

"I said you could resume your journey at any time. You have only to concentrate to take your place in that chair. Your life will continue seamlessly from this moment. Is that not preferable?"

Theo blinked distractedly, his mind twisting in furious dilemma. As tempting as it was to be done with all the day's traumas, he couldn't shake the subtle air of incongruity that kept him detached from this scene. These friends didn't feel exactly like the people he knew. This was Zack with an asterisk, Hannah with a caveat.

Azral studied him warily. "What troubles you now?"

"I don't know. I'm just trying to wrap my head around it. I mean if I do this, what happens to the other timeline?"

"It continues."

"Without me?"

"Very much with you."

"How does that work?"

"Far beyond your understanding," Azral replied, with crusty impatience. "To explain it now would be like explaining a sphere to a circle. You're not ready. Perhaps you never will be. You're more like Rander than I feared."

Theo crossed his arms and stared at his other self sandwiched comfortably between a soft chair and a warm actress. There had to be a catch to this bow-wrapped present. This string had to have its own strings attached.

"Is this what you do, Azral? You pick and choose the futures you want?"

"As I said—"

"Right. It's beyond me. There's no denying that. But I'm not like Evan. The thought of jumping trains right now makes me queasy. It feels like I'm leaving my friends behind."

Azral shook his head in brusque bemusement. "You beg me for hints and now reject the full answer. You're a fool."

"I am a fool," Theo admitted. "I've been one as long as I can remember. But you know what? You came at me on the second-worst day of my life. You showed me everyone I care about in horrible danger and then somehow expected me to grasp the intricacies of the universe. For a master of time, you have shitty timing. You also killed Bill Pollock. So no, I don't trust this answer of yours. And I don't believe for one second that you just happened to save us from a dying Earth. I'm pretty sure it was healthy until you came along."

In the sharp and frosty silence, Theo grew convinced that Azral's next move would be lethal. Instead the white-haired man merely summoned a single strand of light from the wall. The moment it hit Theo, he felt a vague sense of familiarity, like a numb hand on his arm.

"What . . . what is this?"

"The path of return," said Azral. "This string will lead you back seventy-six minutes to the place you and your companions still suffer. If you proceed slowly enough, you'll witness events in reverse and note all the timely decisions that enabled your escape. Perhaps you'll succeed in duplicating this outcome. Perhaps you'll fail and lose more than one friend in the process. It seems a needless risk to take when you're already here, but I suppose fools will do as they do."

Long seconds passed as Theo pondered the heavy new task ahead. Azral shined his cool blue eyes on Hannah.

"*Seh tu'a mortia rehu eira kahne'e nada ehru heira.*"

Theo eyed him strangely. "What was that?"

"An old expression of my people, a rallying mantra for the soldiers and scientists who kill for the greater good. 'I shall feed Death before I starve her.'"

"Why are you telling me this?"

"You think me a monster when I'm merely a crusader. My parents and I fight for the greatest purpose of all. If we succeed in our endeavor here, we'll save countless trillions of lives. We will starve Death like none other before us."

Theo narrowed his eyes. For a cynical moment, Azral looked as silly as a biologist explaining the benefits of cancer research to his lab mice.

"Small comfort to the ones you serve to her," Theo groused. "When's it our turn?"

"We didn't bring you here to kill you. On the contrary, we've labored to keep you all alive. Do you think it was fate that rescued you from your coma? Was it the hand of God that pulled Hannah from the brink of a fatal concussion? We've provided you with comfort and aid at every turn, Theo. And yet even now as I offer a means to save the child Farisi, you see me as an enemy."

"How am I supposed to know what you are to us when you won't tell us what we are to you?"

"Crucial," said Azral. "There are those among you who are crucial to our plans. I would think that'd be obvious by now."

"But what do you *want* with us?"

Azral regarded him with a jaded leer. "I see the futures better than you, child. Telling you now serves no benefit. You'll know when it suits us."

Theo chucked his ethereal hands. "So we just go about our lives in the meantime, hoping we don't do anything to piss you off."

"If you hinder us by accident, you'll be duly warned as the elder Given was."

And if we hinder you on purpose? Theo wondered, before he could stop the thought.

The mist on the wall grew dark and stormy. Azral floated toward the swirling exit, then turned around to bathe Theo in an icy stare.

"Look to the strings, boy. See what becomes of our enemies."

He disappeared into the fog, leaving Theo alone in this quiet scene, this teasing preenactment of better times. It seemed utterly daft to throw himself back into the fray and risk Mia's life in retrospect. And yet the more he thought of Azral, the more he feared the numbing effects of this talent. If he had access to a billion Mias, how long before he stopped mourning the loss of one or two of them? How long before he shrugged off the death of one measly Earth?

He worked his hands around the lone strand of light and found it as solid as a rope. With a hearty tug, he pulled himself toward the past, determined to reverse engineer their escape from the office building. Theo didn't care how long it took him. He had all the time in the world to get it right.

THIRTY-FOUR

The seconds moved with slow-ticking fury as David watched the last two Gothams stagger toward the exit. While his maimed right hand felt light enough to float away, his other wrist was burdened with a .40 caliber pistol and a vintage silver watch. It had been forty-four ticks since Rebel's last gunshot echoed through the eastern arch, ample time for David to envision all the worst scenarios. The thought of Mia with a bullet in her eye—just one shade darker than the current reality—made his gun arm twitch with a vicious life of its own. *Tick, tick, tick.*

The hands on his watch hit 11:57 when he leapt out from behind his pillar and summoned a line of ghostly duplicates. Eight Davids aimed their pistols in synch, speaking with one firm voice.

"Stop."

Rebel and Ivy turned around at the portal, freezing at the sight of the one-man posse just forty feet away. Ivy jumped in front of her husband.

"Don't shoot us! We're leaving! We're going!"

"Try it," David hissed. "See how well that works for you."

Sixty feet above, Amanda wrung her fingers in screaming tension. *Just let them go, David. You'll get yourself killed!*

Rebel dropped his empty gun and heel-kicked it through the portal. He tried to speak but could only groan a pained garble.

The eight Davids cocked their heads. "I'm sorry. Was that English?"

"He can't talk," Ivy explained. "Look at him."

"Yes. I can see someone already had their fun with him. What's he trying to say?"

"He's asking you to let me go."

"Does he expect me to believe you're innocent in all this?"

"No. But our child is. Look at me."

David narrowed his cool blue eyes at her bulging stomach. "What's your name?"

"Krista."

He raised his gun. "Try again."

"Ivy! My name's Ivy!"

"Well, Ivy, tell me something. Why should I care about the innocent lives in your family when you clearly don't care about the innocent lives in mine?"

Rebel leaned forward in growling defense. Ivy held him back.

"You think we like doing this? We're not assassins. I'm a network engineer. My husband's a security consultant. Freddy was a college student."

"Who's Freddy?"

"The boy you shot in the face."

David balked at her knowledge before hardening again. "You sent him to kill us. I was only defending myself."

"That's just what we're doing! We're defending ourselves and everyone we know! You have no idea what's at stake here!"

"Nor do you," he said, as he peered through the arch. "See, your man just fired seven gunshots and I'm anxious to know where they went. So we're going to walk in that direction and find out together. I swear to you, if any of my people—"

A distant shriek echoed through the chamber, filtering down from the fifth floor. While the trio in the lobby looked up, Amanda turned her white gaze down the hall.

"Hannah?"

Seeing his chance, Rebel wrapped his arms around Ivy and threw them back through the portal. David aimed his pistol at the white liquid pool as it shrank closed. He muttered a curse, then waved away his mirror selves.

The door to the maintenance hall flew open with a kick. David watched Theo with blank-faced puzzlement as the augur bolted through the lobby like a champion sprinter. His urgent expression filled David with dread.

"Theo, what happened? What did you see?"

A second scream rang out from the fifth floor. David launched his troubled gaze back and forth, up and east, before forcing a hot decision.

"How far?" Hannah asked. "Amanda has a broken ankle and I can barely move my legs."

"No worries, hon. Home is just a few steps past that elevator." He unbuckled his seat belt and snatched the cane at Theo's feet. "I haven't been walking too well myself these days."

Moaning and grimacing, the Silvers extracted themselves from the van. Zack carried Amanda on his back while Mia kept her leg stabilized. Theo and David bolstered Hannah like crutches.

Peter Pendergen led the hobbling procession, moving at an impressive clip for a man with a lame left leg. He poked the call button with his cane.

"How'd you get crippled?" David asked.

Peter eyed him, stone-faced, as the doors slid open and the group boarded the elevator. He set a course for the sixth and highest floor.

"Had a cerebrovascular mishap a short while back. It's no big deal."

"You seem awfully young to be suffering strokes."

"Well, thank you. I thought the same thing. Unfortunately, these kinds of problems start early for my people. Just comes with the territory."

"Of being chronokinetic, you mean."

Peter tossed him a weak shrug. "What can I say, boy? Time always hurts the ones it loves."

The elevator fell into grim and listless silence.

"It's just temporary," Peter attested. "Few months of leg rehab and I'll be good as new." He took a bleak gander at Amanda's ankle. "Guess I won't be doing my exercises alone."

Zack kept his dark stare on the floor. Amanda rested her chin on his shoulder and studied Peter through the mirrored doors. The man was tall, well built, and ridiculously good-looking, though he carried his appeal with a preening peacock vanity that unfavorably reminded her of Derek. He'd probably charmed dozens of doe-eyed ingenues out of their tight wool sweaters. For all she knew, he was already scanning Hannah for loose threads.

And why wouldn't he? Amanda thought. *It's the end of the goddamn world. Isn't it, Peter?*

Teetering back from the edge of hysterics, she ran a soft finger near Zack's neck gash. "We'll have to disinfect that."

"We will," Peter promised. "I got everything back at the house—meds and beds, duds and suds, all an ailing body could ever hope for. You folks went through five kinds of hell to get to me. I'd say you earned some rest."

He scanned the dark reflections of his new companions, stopping at Amanda. It wasn't hard to recognize the abject despair in her lovely green eyes.

"Just wait," he told her.

Amanda looked up at him. "What?"

"Don't go losing hope just yet. Wait till you hear what I have to say."

The view from the roof was astonishing. The Silvers only had to take a few steps onto the windy lot before they saw all the way across the Hudson, to the city they'd just escaped.

From a river's distance, Manhattan was a feast for the eyes, a utopian array of artful slopes and novel curves, winding spires and colored spheres. One tower resembled a Space Needle with twenty rings. Another looked glassy to the point of translucence. Tempic tubes connected buildings at their highest levels and every street was peppered with aer traffic. For Theo, the skyline went miles beyond modernism and deep into the realm of high-budget, "holy shit," has-to-be-CGI sci-fi. Mia couldn't find the words to describe the sight. It was beautiful enough to bring her to tears.

David eyed Peter curiously as the man took a slow, wincing seat in the middle of a parking space.

"You said your home was just a few steps past the elevator."

"It is."

"Meaning we're about to take another portal."

"We are," Peter confessed, to the angry groans of Zack and Hannah. "I know. It hurts. You'll build up a tolerance. Trust me."

He tapped the ground with his cane. "Might as well sit and enjoy the fresh air, folks. I need a bit of rest before I open the next door."

While the others joined him on the concrete, Zack and Amanda stayed conjoined in their tight piggyback hug. The look of desperate solace on her sister's face prompted Hannah to lean forward and wrap her arms around

Theo, her own quasi-nonboyfriend. She traded a dismal glance with Amanda. *It's never simple for us, is it?*

Theo caressed her wrists, his vacant gaze stuck on the distant metropolis. "I can't believe we were just there a minute ago."

"I can't believe we traveled like one of Mia's notes," David said. He furrowed his brow at Peter. "Wait. We didn't jump through time, did we?"

"No. Just space. Time portals are brighter and have a strong vacuum pull. They're also quite fatal."

"Fatal?"

"A living being can't handle a trip like that," Peter explained. "I've seen folks try. It's never pretty. Me, I'm perfectly happy to stay in the present. Still plenty of places to go."

Zack eyed him sharply. "If you can jump anywhere—"

"I never said I could."

"—why did we drive twenty-five hundred miles to get to you? Why didn't you come get us?"

"There are limits to my talents, Zack. I can't leap the nation. I can't teleport someplace I've never been. If I had the power, believe me, I would've pulled you from Terra Vista before you ever met Rebel or Rander or that Dep with the funny hair."

"How do you know so much about that?" Hannah asked, in a more accusatory tone than intended. Peter smirked in good nature.

"I've had a correspondent among you all along. A pen pal, as you folks call them." He shook a stern finger at Mia. "I should've known better than to trust your self-description. I bought a whole mess of clothes for a fat girl. They're gonna hang off you like drapes."

She blinked at him in bafflement. "What? When did I write you?"

"Technically, you haven't. Not yet."

Mia caught on. "You've been getting notes from my future selves."

"Dozens of them. Nice girls. Very helpful. One of them explained how to rescue Amanda and Theo from DP-9. Another told me where you'd all be today. If it wasn't for her, I'd still be sitting at home, waiting for your call."

Theo shook his head, vexed. "I don't understand. How can you get notes from her? How can she get notes from you?"

"There are only a few dozen people on Earth who can make portals like we do. We're all linked to each other, for better or worse."

"Why worse?" Amanda asked.

Peter turned somber. "I doubt any of you had the pleasure of meeting Rebel's wife, but—"

"Ivy."

He looked up at David in dull surprise. "Okay. Guess you did meet her."

"We conversed. What about her?"

"She's a traveler too. She can't jump as far as I can, but she's much more attuned to the portal network. When I sent Mia the note with my new contact number, Ivy must have tapped the link. Snatched a copy from the ether. From there, all Rebel had to do was surp my phone line and take your call in my place." He aimed a soft glance at Zack. "That's how they got the jump on you today. I underestimated their cleverness and you guys paid the price for it. I'm truly sorry."

The cartoonist shrugged with drowsy accord. With all his friends alive and breathing, he didn't have the strength to hate anyone at the moment, even Rebel.

Peter studied Zack's spooning embrace with Amanda, then cast a pensive gaze at the eastern horizon.

"We're in the halo now."

"The what?"

He swept a slow gesture from the skyline. "The Cataclysm started in Brooklyn and blew five miles in every direction, stretching all the way out here. Over sixty thousand people were caught right outside the blast, in a ring of space we call the Halo of Gotham. Those folks were considered blessed because, aside from some blindness and emotional trauma, they survived just fine. It wasn't until the pregnant women started having their babies that . . . well, some were born healthy and some weren't. And some were just born different. Those were the first of my people."

Peter jostled a loose chunk of concrete with his cane. "There are over a thousand of us in Quarter Hill, in forty-four family lines. We've lived in quiet for four generations. Now it's all coming undone."

"I am sorry for my part," David offered. "I should have been more discreet with my lumis."

"I appreciate it, son, but that wasn't what I was talking about. And even if it was, Zack's right. You don't owe my people a damn thing. It kills me to see what Rebel's doing. I don't care if you're all from another world. You're blessed and cursed in all the same ways we are. You're kin."

A large shadow enveloped them. The group looked up to see a massive metal saucer floating 150 feet in the air, casually drifting north on bright white wedges of aeris. Luminescent letters on the hub informed everyone below that Albee's Aerstraunt never closes. Ever.

While the Silvers followed the saucer's progress, Peter clambered back to his feet.

"All right. Enough jawing. I see one lovely woman in need of an ankle brace. The rest of you could use some heavy gauze and epallays." He put a hand on Mia's back. "Hold on now."

Peter closed his eyes and concentrated until a six-foot portal swirled open on the concrete wall. Mia sucked a pained breath.

"You all right?" David asked her.

"She's fine," Peter said. "All part of our connection. It'll hurt less and less each time, just like the jaunts."

Despite his assurance, nobody lined up for a second teleport. Peter exhaled glumly.

"You folks have traveled a long, hard road. I can't say your troubles are over, but I can promise you that shelter and aid are right on the other side of that door. Just a few steps more and you can finally rest. I swear it."

His new acquaintances studied him through busy eyes, caught between their desperation and their well-paved cynicism. The urge to flee was overwhelming, but they were out of steam, out of options, out of money, out of everything. A few steps were all they had left in them.

They rose to their feet and shambled toward the light like the weary souls of the departed. Two by two, limbs locked together, the Silvers disappeared into the shimmering white depths.

Only the orphans stopped at the portal. Mia held her nervous gaze at the glowing white surface.

"I—I can't. I can't."

David wrapped his arm around her. "It's all right. We'll walk through it together."

"I can't do it. It hurts."

Peter loomed behind them like a shepherd. "Go on ahead, boy. I got this."

David eyed him suspiciously. The Irishman gripped his shoulder. "I got off on a bad foot with you, son, and I will make amends. But for now I'm asking you to trust me. Please."

After a silent consultation with Mia, he squeezed her arm, then stepped through the portal. Peter watched the ripples settle.

"You weren't kidding about him. He's a lion, that one."

She lowered her head. "I'm sorry."

"You have nothing to be sorry about."

"This whole thing could have been avoided. I should have . . . *she* should have warned us not to go in that building."

He shined a droll grin. "Right. If only she had, you'd all be alive and together now."

"It's not funny."

"No, it's not," Peter admitted. "It's tragic that a girl so lovely can be so cruel to herself. I've seen the way you talk about you. I swear, there's no worse combination than adolescence and time travel."

Mia peered up at Peter. "Do you get notes from your future selves?"

"Me? Nah. I blocked those fools out years ago. One of me's enough for everyone."

"How did you do it?"

"I'll show you, Mia. I'll teach you everything you need to know." Peter jerked a thumb at the portal. "That thing over there? That's your future. You're just making keyholes now. Soon you'll be making doors."

Mia sniffed at the great white breach. To think how easily they could have escaped all their past calamities if she'd been able to rip an exit in the nearest wall. It seemed unbelievable that anyone could do such a thing.

"I still don't know how we got these powers," she confessed to Peter. "None of us were born like this."

"I can't answer that, darlin'. But it's on the list of things to find out."

He scanned the distant city, then put a hand on Mia's shoulder. "Come on. Before the boy comes back in worry."

As they moved toward the portal, Peter stroked the back of her head, a warm and fatherly gesture that made her as conflicted as the two messages she'd received about him. All at once, she wanted to hug him and run from him. She trusted him with her life and she feared he'd be the death of her. She had no idea what lay behind any of those feelings. Apparently she wasn't immune to paradox after all.

"Where does this go?" she asked him.

"Brooklyn," Peter replied, with a cheery grin. "Home."

His brownstone lay in the middle of a chain, a slender construct of red brick and glass that stood all but invisible among its siblings. Every room in the four-story building teemed with taped cardboard boxes, bulging department store bags, and hastily placed furniture. Half the lamps still had price tags dangling from the bases.

By one o'clock, all wounds were bandaged, all faces washed, all bloody garments swapped for fresh cotton loungewear. Peter secured Amanda's ankle with broken broomsticks and duct tape before leaving the house in search of better aid.

The Silvers convalesced in the hardwood living room, slouched among the mismatched chairs and sofas. Their twelve lazy feet faced one another on the circular glass coffee table like ticks on a clock dial. Only Hannah and Theo ruined the uniformity by bundling together on a recliner. While the actress wallowed in apocalyptic grief, the augur felt downright euphoric. Azral had offered him a shortcut to this very moment and Theo stubbornly insisted on forging his own path here. Now the thrill of success was incomparable, like winning two marathons at once.

Nobody moved or spoke for fifteen minutes, until Hannah retreated to the kitchen to make tea. She returned with a tray of steaming mugs, placing one on the end table near her sister.

"He doesn't have milk. I looked. Sorry."

Amanda stared ahead blankly, her senses dulled by exhaustion and painkillers. "Okay."

Theo followed the exchange with grim interest. When he'd viewed this scene with Azral, it was Mia who served the hot drinks. The girl had looked fairly healthy in that string. But this one was listless, sweaty, and jaundiced. He feared something didn't go entirely right with her reversal.

At two o'clock, Peter returned with a cartload of gifts for Amanda—a hospital-grade ankle brace, casting tape, ice packs, crutches, even a portable tomograph to gauge the extent of her bone damage. When David asked him how he managed to score such items on a major holiday, Peter merely shrugged and said he knew people.

He sat down with Amanda and pulled her legs onto his lap, peeling away her splint with the gentle grace of a lover. Zack took a forced and sudden interest in the red-leafed sycamore outside the window.

"Where in Brooklyn are we?"

"Greenpoint."

Zack gazed outside in absent marvel. "Jesus. I grew up here. The other 'here.'"

"I can show you around tomorrow, if you want."

"You think that's wise?"

Peter flicked a breezy hand. "Some hats and sunglasses and we'll be fine. It'd be awfully cruel if you folks couldn't get out once in a while."

"Wait. Didn't you tell us the Brooklyn address was compromised?"

"I said our meeting address was compromised. This place is safe. Purchased with cash through two intermediaries. No one knows I'm here. Not even my son."

Mia snapped out of her addled daze. "Where is he?"

"With my people. He's safer there. My godmother will take care of him."

"Can you call or write to him?"

"No. Too risky. I can't even see him by portal without tipping off Ivy."

Six brows curled in sympathy as the Silvers realized the extent of Peter's sacrifice. Amanda held his wrist. "I'm so sorry."

"Oh, come on now. None of that. I'll tell you exactly what I told Liam. This is just temporary. As soon as matters are straightened out with my people, I'm going home and I'm bringing you with me. Quarter Hill is where we all belong."

"What about the Deps?" Hannah asked. "They'll be looking for us there."

"They'll be looking, but they won't see. Trust me. Our town was built for secrets."

David pursed his lips, lost in thoughts of young Freddy Ballad. "You really think the other Gothams will embrace us after everything that's happened?"

"That's not . . ." Peter chuckled with forced patience. "First of all, we don't call ourselves that, ever. Secondly, yes. This whole mess started with Rebel. It'll end with him."

"You're saying we need to kill him."

"Absolutely not. If we kill him, he'll become a martyr to the cause. The clan will forever see things his way. No, we have to do something even harder than that. We have to change his mind."

Zack's face coursed with hot blood as he rediscovered his hatred. Rebel had murdered his brother and then bragged about it. He nearly shot Mia to death. Even if the man could be persuaded to abandon his jihad, Zack couldn't imagine waving hello to him at the Quarter Hill Shop & Save.

"I still don't understand why he's trying to kill us," Zack said. "I mean he's acting like we're all walking A-bombs, or future Hitlers."

Peter shook his head. "Doesn't matter. He's wrong. None of this is your fault."

"None of *what*?" David asked. "What are your people so afraid of?"

The sisters watched Peter carefully as he stared out the window, tapping his lantern jaw. The melancholy in his deep blue eyes was enough to kill their last strand of hope that Evan had lied. They covered their mouths and wept.

Theo leaned forward and rubbed Hannah's arm. "Hey. Hey. Why are you crying?"

Zack studied Amanda in ardent concern. "What happened to you back there?"

"Someone talked to them," said Peter.

"I'm asking her."

"And I'm answering for her. The moment I saw the sisters, I recognized the look on their faces. It's the same look my people have been wearing for the last ten weeks. Someone told them the bad news. Some bastard gave them the cloud without the silver lining."

"Silver lining?" Hannah cried, in a wheezing rasp. "How is there a silver lining?"

Mia tugged tissues from a box and passed them to Amanda and Hannah. On her way back to her sofa, David gently pulled her into his easy chair and locked his arms around her like a seat belt. He threw an uneasy nod at Peter.

"All right. Tell us everything."

The Irishman leaned back into the couch with a long, sorrowful sigh. He'd hoped to wait until they were better rested.

"The future's a very peculiar thing," he began. "The best prophets in the world couldn't tell you what I'll have for breakfast tomorrow, but they know for a fact that a volcano in Hawaii will erupt in four months' time. They know a small meteor will punch the Gobi desert next April and that San Francisco will fall to an earthquake in two years. It's easy as hell to see these things because they're the same across all timelines. No one can stop them from happening.

"On July 24, the day you all arrived, the sixty-seven augurs of my clan suddenly got a peek at a whole new future. The vision hit them like acid, the single worst thing any of them had ever seen. Four of them killed themselves before the day was done. We lost a dozen more the following week. And Rebel? He used to be a reasonable guy. You'll just have to take my word for it."

The augur in the room could suddenly see where this was going. At long last, Theo understood the lingering dread that clouded the thoughts of his future selves, the same giant sword hanging over all their heads.

David reeled in bother. "I don't understand. If it's a second Cataclysm, as you implied, then why the suicidal despair? You'd have months, possibly years to evacuate."

"It's not a Cataclysm," Theo said.

The boy looked to Peter. "But when you wrote Mia—"

"I haven't written that letter yet, David. Those are the words of a future me. But I know exactly why he lied. He needed you all to get here. He didn't want you losing hope."

Zack opened and closed his mouth three times before speaking. "What . . . what . . ."

What could possibly be worse than a Cataclysm? he wanted to ask. As the words tangled in his throat, the obvious answer rolled over him like a sickness. He fell back in his chair, white-faced.

"Oh Jesus . . ."

Amanda drank him in through moist eyes. Worse than the pain of seeing Zack catch up to her was the realization that he was the only one in the room who wasn't touching or holding someone. She wanted to leap across the table and wrap herself around him, Esis be goddamned.

Peter kept his dark gaze on the two spooning teenagers, the ones who could still count their years on fingers and toes. At long last, Mia understood why a future self had urged her to come to New York in a strong state of mind, why she demanded they take a week to relax in blissful ignorance.

Now her mouth quivered in a bow, stuck on the same jagged word. "W-when?"

"No firm date," said Peter. "We know it's between four and five years, closer to five."

She fell back into David and the cruelest of math. *I'll be eighteen. He'll be twenty.*

"How?" asked the boy, in a cracked voice.

"I don't want to bog you down in the gruesome details. Just—"

"Same way," Hannah told him. That was all that needed to be said.

Peter leaned forward in fresh determination. "Okay, now that you have the bad news—"

"Why does this keep happening?"

"Mia . . ."

"Why does this keep happening?!"

All Peter could offer was a somber shrug. "I don't know the how or the why, sweetheart. My guess is that the answer's wrapped up in those Pelletiers who brought you here. I don't know any more about them than you do."

"You said there was a silver lining."

He nodded at David. "There is, but you need to bear with me while I explain it."

"Explain what, exactly?"

"Why I'm walking funny."

Their heavy brows furrowed at Peter. He blew a long breath through his knuckles, deliberating his words.

"There's a unique state of consciousness that my people occasionally achieve, a place where all the branching futures stretch out before us like a great tapestry. We call it the God's Eye, and by now one of you has become very familiar with it."

Theo nodded skittishly, unsure where Peter was going with this. "I thought it was just for augurs."

"Our blessings aren't mutually exclusive," Peter explained. "We all have a little tempis in us. A little lumis. A little foresight. We all have the chance to stumble into the God's Eye when the right or wrong wires cross in our brains. Well, on July 24, it was my turn. I'll admit my stroke wasn't the small deal I made it out to be. It actually put me in a coma for a day."

Hannah pinched her lip in twitchy rumination. It seemed mighty odd that Theo and Peter suffered a coma at the same time, for the same duration.

"Anyway, Theo can tell you that time passes differently in the God's Eye, if it even passes at all. I don't know how long I spent there. Weeks. Months. Most of the details are lost to me now, like an old dream. All I remember is following the trail to the end of the world. I saw exactly what the augurs saw. I know why so many of them committed suicide."

Mia curled against David, fighting her tears. He held her close and stroked her hair. For a moment Amanda saw the same heavy look of rue he'd worn at the Sunday mass in Evansville.

"I also remember going beyond the end," Peter told them. "Somehow I punched through the curtain and entered this . . . I don't even know how to describe it without sounding daft. I was floating in a cold gray void. I could see the end of every timeline—a trillion trillion points of light, all lined up flat as far as the eye can see. It was a cruel and beautiful thing, like a snowdrift or a desert, or—"

"A wall," said Theo, through a dead-white face. Hannah could feel the new tension in his grip.

"You saw it?" she asked.

"Only in dreams," he replied, though he knew that would change soon. He and Peter traded a dark look of understanding before the Irishman continued.

"Now I need you all to listen to me because this is the crucial part. I saw something on that wall. And I swear to you on the life of my son that I didn't imagine it. It was truly there."

Peter's eyes grew moist. His lips quivered. He held up a single finger.

"One string. I saw one string of light that extended from the wall and just kept going. One single timeline where life continued. The moment I laid eyes on it, I knew in my heart that the end of the world wasn't like an earthquake or a meteor or an erupting volcano. It's not a fixed event. There's one string of time where someone manages to stop what's coming."

The Silvers wore the same incredulous expression for five quiet seconds.

"One string out of trillions," Hannah said.

"One is all you need, hon. I saw it. It exists. Now, I didn't have a chance to reach it before I fell out of my coma, but I know it's still there waiting for us. All someone needs to do is find it and study it. See what went right. Once we know, we'll make damn sure to repeat the process, step by step."

"Uh, when you say someone—"

"I mean one of you in particular. You know who I'm talking about."

All eyes turned to Theo. He fell inside his head, struggling to wrap his thoughts around the giant task Peter was placing on him. He'd already reverse engineered one favorable outcome, but that was just for a single hour and five friends. Now he was being asked to do the same thing on a global scale over a half decade. Assuming he could even find the string. Assuming it existed.

"Why him?" Amanda asked. "He's not the only one who can see the future."

"As of now, there are only forty augurs left in the world," Peter replied, "and Theo blows them all out of the water. He's the only one who has the power to enter the God's Eye willingly."

"I didn't."

"You will."

"I can't."

"You *will*," Peter insisted. "If you don't trust me, trust Future Mia. She's the one who told me."

Hannah wanted to cry again. Theo was only ten weeks sober. He'd just overcome a painful neurological malady. Now he'd been given a burden that no one should ever have to carry.

She glared at Peter. "You can't just dump this on him. It's not fair."

"I have a son who's fixing to die at seventeen. There's very little about this that's fair."

"I'm not worried about the fairness," said Theo. "I'm just worried you're wrong."

"I'm not."

"I'm sure Rebel feels the same way about his theory," Zack cautioned.

"Rebel's seen the string too. He knows there's a solution. He just made some terrible assumptions about the nature of it. Correcting him is our next priority, one of many. The rest of us will have plenty to do while Theo's busy."

The group sat in muddled silence for nearly a full minute. Peter leaned back and flicked a weak hand in the air.

"I don't blame you at all for your skepticism. Nobody's suffered more at the hands of the universe than you six. And yet here you are, still together, still breathing. An augur, an actress, a widow, a cartoonist, a boy, and a girl. You're the most extraordinary group of people I've ever met and I will never bet against you. Ever."

The others stayed rigidly quiet, biting their lips in tight suppression. None of them felt even a fraction as formidable as Peter made them out to be. They could only see his point when they looked around the table. There didn't seem to be a single companion without a string of miracles under their belt, even just from today.

Peter finished securing Amanda's boot, then gently swung her legs to the coffee table. He stood up and let out a stretching groan.

"I think it's well past time you folks got some rest. Should your troubled minds keep you from sleeping, as troubled minds do, remember the silver lining. We'll find the string. We'll stop what's coming. What happened to your world won't happen here."

The Silvers absently gazed ahead as Peter gathered the empty tea mugs and disappeared into the kitchen. They listened to the running faucet, the gentle clinks of spoons and ceramics.

Soon Zack rose to his feet and circled the table, extending both hands to Amanda.

"Come on. I'll take you upstairs."

While he ported her onto his back, Amanda scanned the two entwined couples on the easy chairs. Judging by their dark and dreary faces, she figured none of them would be detaching anytime soon.

Halfway up the stairs, she leaned forward and breathed a soft whisper in Zack's ear.

"Stay with me."

Though his expression remained impassive, Zack assured her in no uncertain terms that he had every intention of doing so. Every damn reason in the world.

They slumbered for hours, six weary travelers on three bare mattresses. Scant words were exchanged before their bodies succumbed to fatigue. David confessed to Mia that he killed a man today, and she held him. Zack told Amanda that he healed a friend today, and she held him.

Hannah had the most to say. As she clutched Theo from behind, she swore in a tender whisper that she would be there for him in any way he needed her. If she couldn't be the messiah, she could at least be the one who kept him sane. It seemed a better use of her life than singing showtunes for scale.

As the sun set on Commemoration, the Silvers woke up feeling ten years older and no more relaxed. They dissolved their sleepy unions with little fanfare and retreated to their designated bedrooms. David and Mia set up their separate little sanctums on the second floor. Zack and Theo established their dormlike den in the basement. Hannah wearily toiled through the clutter of boxes in the master bedroom, a huge and gorgeous chamber with a cathedral ceiling and a narrow balcony overlooking the backyard.

She caught a strange flash of light in the corner of her eye. Through the top-floor window of the neighboring brownstone, a petite young brunette pranced about in a radiant speedsuit, trailing incandescent streaks of color with every rapid gesture. The sight was both surreal and mesmerizing to Hannah, enough to knock her off her axis. Suddenly the universe seemed a dreamlike place where nothing was too far-fetched. Cartoon sparrows could fly through the window and help her make the bed. The furniture could come to life and sing a song about prudence.

"What are you looking at?"

Hannah jumped and spun around. For all the world's new possibilities, she didn't expect Amanda to be standing right behind her. Her sister had been downstairs getting her leg x-rayed, or tomographed, whatever it was called. Now she was here on the balcony, propping herself on tempic crutches, holding two paperback novels under her arm.

"Sorry," said Amanda. "Didn't mean to scare you."

"No. I'm okay. I was just . . ." Hannah took a moment to register Amanda's crude white supports. "Wow. You made your own crutches."

"Yeah. The ones Peter got me are a little too short. These will be fine."

"I thought you couldn't hold the tempis for more than a few seconds at a time."

"I thought so too. Who knows? Maybe I'm getting stronger."

Amanda briefly scanned the room, then tossed a worried look at Hannah. "Listen, I hope you're not sharing a room for my benefit. I mean if you wanted to, you know, be with Theo . . ."

"No. We're actually good the way we are, as strange as that sounds."

"That's not strange."

"Well, it's strange for me. You know how stress makes me slutty."

Amanda laughed. "I think you're working off an old image of you."

Now it was Hannah's turn to grow concerned. "What about Zack? I mean . . ."

"Oh no. We didn't. We're not—"

"I didn't think you did. I just . . ." Hannah desperately tried to find a way to express her issue without mentioning their new ticking calendar. "I just don't know why you two aren't together. Especially now."

Amanda knew, though she didn't have the strength to discuss it. At some point soon, she'd have to have a long talk with Zack about siblings and Esis. She wasn't expecting a brave response.

"It's complicated."

She dropped her books onto an end table. Hannah glimpsed armored knights on the covers. They clashed swords right above Peter Pendergen's name.

"Wow. I forgot he was an author."

"Yeah. He went out of his way to remind me."

"You don't like him?"

Amanda shrugged uncomfortably. "I don't know what to think yet."

"He seems nice, all things considered."

"He does."

"He's certainly nice to look at."

"Yes. He is that."

"You're just afraid he's wrong."

Amanda's face darkened. Hannah turned around and cast an airy sigh over the railing. "Yeah. Me too."

The crutches vanished. Amanda leaned on her sister now, resting her chin on her shoulder. They stared out at the vibrant dusk.

"I don't think we're going to die of old age," Hannah mused. "Not even in the best case."

Amanda closed her eyes. "I don't think so either."

"Mia was right, though. You and I are lucky."

"We're all lucky," Amanda insisted. "We all have family here."

"Well, they may be my siblings at heart, but you're my flesh and blood and I love you."

"I love you too, Hannah. So much. You saved my life today. You carried me."

They held each other tight, sniffling in unison. Amanda eyed her sister strangely when she broke out in a high giggle.

"What?"

"Just thinking about Mom. If she could see us right now, she'd crap a kitten."

Amanda burst with laughter. "Oh my God. She's probably running around Heaven right now, looking for a camcorder."

Hannah wiped her eyes. Amanda gave her a squeeze, then re-created her crutches.

"These painkillers are making me loopy. I need to lie down again."

"Okay. I'll come inside in a bit."

Hannah spent another ten minutes watching the young lumis dancer perform in her bedroom, twirling her array of colored lines and spirals. The actress flinched with surprise when the girl suddenly moved to the window and waved a rainbow. Hannah didn't know if she was waving at her or just continuing her routine. If the dancer wasn't so far away, Hannah might have squinted at her wrist and counted the number of watches.

With that sudden reminder, Hannah dashed inside and rooted through her jeans until she found the purple note that Ioni had slipped her at the parade. Unfolding it revealed a flyer for some rock band called the Quadrants. They were playing at a Greenwich Village bar for one night only . . . in April of next year.

She flipped the sheet over and saw a few lines of blue-ink scribble:

Hannah,

Evan Rander took a good man out of your path. I'm putting one in. Go to this event. Look around. You'll know him when you see him. He's still wearing his bracelet.

Don't lose hope, my dear Given. Don't count the hours. Whether it's four and a half years or four and a half decades, you still have a lifetime ahead of you. Enjoy as many moments as you can. Find your happy face.

Hannah leaned back against the dresser, her lips and hands trembling as she reread the note. By the third pass through, her cheeks were wet with tears and she found herself hating Ioni. The girl surely knew of the hell that awaited the Silvers in that office building, and yet she failed to warn them away. *Why the hell should I trust you?* Hannah seethed.

She dimmed the lights and then joined her sister in bed, spooning her from behind while Amanda gently snored.

After a dark and restless hour, Hannah stumbled back onto a charitable thought. Maybe Ioni had a reason for not warning Hannah. Maybe she thought the only way the six of them would survive the day was if all their enemies attacked them at once, and attacked each other in the process.

Who the hell could say? Hannah lived in a strange new world now, with temporis and speedsuits and parallel strings. It was almost too much for a poor actress to handle. All she knew was that she'd go and see the Quadrants play next April. Whether the mystery man was a Silver, a Gold, or some other glimmering color, he was one of her people. He had to be found.

As she drifted off to sleep, it occurred to her that she should probably find something nice to wear for the encounter. Maybe a sleek top over jeans. Or maybe something a little more respectable. Hannah supposed there was no rush to decide. The event was six months away. She had time.

ACKNOWLEDGMENTS

Writing this book was a three-year endeavor, one I couldn't have finished without the help and encouragement of some very fine people. They include Avi Bar-Zeev, Sara Glickstein Bar-Zeev, Mike Tunison, Craig Mertens, Mary Dalton-Hoffman, Mick Soth, Huan Nghiem, Jason Cole, D'Anna Sharon, Dustin Shaffer, Dave Bledsoe, Bill McDermott, Scott Clinkscales, and Ysabelle Pelletier. Yeah, there's a Pelletier on the list.

Extra special gratitude to my alpha testers, those patient, generous souls who guided me one rough chapter at a time—Mark Harvey, Leni Fleming, Jen Gennaco, and Gretchen Walker.

Huge thanks to David Rosenthal and his team at Blue Rider Press for taking a chance on me and helping me get the Silvers ready for prime time. All readers should be grateful to my terrific editor, Vanessa Kehren. If you think this book's fat now, you should have seen it before she got her hands on it.

No acknowledgment would be complete without mentioning the great Stuart M. Miller, my longtime agent and friend who's supported every nutty decision I've made, including the one to write a multi-part, character-driven, supernatural suspense epic.

Last but not least is Ricki Bar-Zeev, my biggest fan and toughest critic. None of this—and none of me—would have been possible without her. Thank you, Mom.

Read on for a sneak peek of the next exciting book
in Daniel Price's Silvers Series,

THE SONG OF THE ORPHANS

Available in hardcover from Blue Rider Press.

All the way from the USA, dude-ranch hands demonstrate rodeo-style showmanship at Chabysh *festival near Barskoon on the southern shore of Lake Issyk Kul*
(insets) Oodarysh wrestling on horseback and waiting to wrestle!

(following page) Riders wait their turn to wrestle one another from their mounts

Horse and hunter at the annual festival (At Chabysh)
organised by the admirable Kyrgyz Ate Foundation

REVIVING THE KYRGYZ HORSE

The horses are the wings of the Kyrgyz.   Kyrgyz proverb

Mention the Kyrgyz horse to shepherds and you'll almost see their eyes mist over as they recall its magnificence. There's a mystique about this ancient breed of horse, dating back thousands of years, which still evokes enormous emotion in the Kyrgyz people today. Poems have been written about it and numerous sayings, such as the one above, record how closely intertwined the horse was with traditional nomadic life.

Despite being small, it was superbly adapted to life at high altitudes and was renowned over centuries for its strength and endurance (see pg 262). But in just a few decades of Soviet rule, it was crossbred and destroyed almost out of existence. Now a French/Kyrgyz venture, led by French horse lover, Jacqueline Ripart, has launched a campaign to revive the Kyrgyz horse before it is lost forever.

It's a campaign that has won the passionate support of people all over Kyrgyzstan. "The Kyrgyz know what they have lost," says Jacqueline Ripart.

An author of several books on horses, she initially came to Kyrgyzstan out of curiosity. "In Mongolia I'd heard of the Chinese horses so I began to read and I discovered that the Kyrgyz horse was already known back then, although we didn't know about it in the West. I was reading Russian books from the 19th century. I decided I must go there," she says.

Jacqueline Ripart has travelled all over Kyrgyzstan and into neighbouring Tajikistan, in search of the horse whose characteristics and measurements were recorded with Soviet efficiency in the early 20th century. Disturbed to find so little evidence of its survival, she founded the Kyrgyz Ate Foundation with 22 Kyrgyz partners; its twin aims are to preserve the Kyrgyz horse before it is completely lost and to revive the equestrian traditions that were almost destroyed at the same time.

For centuries the horse was vital to nomadic life. So, in order to force the Kyrgyz to settle in the early 20th century, the Soviets knew they had to remove them. First they declared horses to be "relics of agonising feudalism" and then they confiscated them, offering five chickens in return for one horse. "The shepherds were in tears," says Jacqueline Ripart.

Some of the horses went into giant Soviet stud farms but most were killed for their meat. "They banned all the festivals which were most important for horse traditions, and then killed the horses by electrocuting them. So the horses were dead and the horse traditions were dead," she says.

The Soviets also sought to 'improve' the breed by crossing Kyrgyz mares with Russian and European stallions to create a 'novokyrgyz' ('new Kyrgyz')—a bigger horse that would prove more profitable in the meat industry and be better suited to European-style racing.

Very few pure-bred Kyrgyz horses exist today but, to some extent, the breed's main characteristics have been safeguarded by the rigorous conditions of life at high altitude. Kyrgyz Ate is encouraging the use of selective breeding: "We will use nature to revive the breed," says Jacqueline Ripart.

Just as important, however, is preserving the horse traditions which were so central to Kyrgyz life. In 2005 the foundation organised the first At Chabysh horse festival, a mix of culture and sport. It was a huge success and now takes place in late October/earlyNovember each year, attended by thousands of people of whom around 80 per cent are Kyrgyz (see page 301).

Jacqueline Ripart says: "Kyrgyz people are true horse people—horses are in their blood. They don't ask for your name; they ask for your horse's name first, because you are known by your horse." For more on the foundation and the *At Chabysh* festival, visit atchabysh.com.

MANAS—THE HERO AND THE LEGEND

Let the shepherds come and hear me. Their sheep and horses will go home by themselves. Nobody—neither wolf, nor panther, nor thief—will carry off a single lamb while I sing about Manas.

The 18th century *manaschi*, Keldybek

Although virtually unknown in the West, the Manas epic is one of the world's greatest oral poems and the pinnacle of the Central Asian oral tradition. It depicts the history of the Kyrgyz people and all their myths, tales and legends, and is their greatest cultural treasure, offering moral and spiritual guidance throughout the ages. Kyrgyz look to the epic in their search for a national identity and for assistance as they navigate their uncertain entry into the 21st century.

The epic has three key figures, Manas, Semetei (his son) and Seitek (his grandson). The hero is Manas, a Kyrgyz leader who embodies bravery, strength, justice, great skill in horsemanship and martial arts. The epic tells of his adventures and search to find a homeland for his people. With the help of his advisers and trusty knights, he goes to war with bigger more fearsome foes, finally winning victory at a battle in which he is mortally wounded. It tells also of his marriage to the wise Kanykei, daughter of a Samarkand khan, as well as her expulsion with baby Semetei after Manas' death and their ensuing adventures. It describes the great traditional festivities of the day and Manas also finds time to provide philosophy and guidance on moral and everyday problems.

The epic was recited in snatches at festivities and passed orally from generation to generation for centuries, with bards (*manaschi*) weaving in topical themes and characters to comment on their times. The stories probably derived from the exploits of a range of regional military leaders, which were gradually assigned to the superhero, Manas.

Manaschi are born, not made. A child is said to receive the calling to be a *manaschi* when visited in his or her dreams by the Manas spirits. One man tells how, as a child, he started to learn the Manas text when his sister fell seriously ill. In the end a shaman was called who said that the Manas spirits invoked during the brother's recitals were too strong for his sister. As soon as the boy gave up his recitals, his sister's health returned.

(preceding pages) Changing of the Guard in Ala Too square in Bishkek [Saffia Farr]

Ulukhabar Atabek was nine when he first dreamed that he was Almambet, one of the characters in the epic. 'I saw all of them in my dream. When I woke up I began to write down my dreams.' Now aged 75 and living in Toktogul village, near Bokonbaeva, on the southern side of Lake Issyk Kul, he is a highly respected *manaschi*, and has performed all over Kyrgyzstan as well as in France, Switzerland and Turkey.

Listening to him is a thrilling experience, even if you cannot understand the actual words. He dons the *chapan*, the heavy blue-black velvet, gold-embroidered coat traditionally worn by *manaschi*, and sits cross-legged in the dappled shade of the apple and peach trees of his orchard, his moustache curling around his cheeks.

Looking down quietly for a moment, he gathers himself and then begins, slowly at first but with increasing emotion. He tells the epic with passion and commitment in a chanting, sing-song voice, rolling his r's, gesturing with anger, wiping tears of emotion from his eyes. Neighbours hear him and creep silently into the orchard to listen. Afterwards he says simply: 'When I say the epics, it leaves my heart feeling very light. You can't teach it, either you know it or you don't. It comes from God.'

Ulukhabar is one of the few *manaschi* raised in the old oral tradition, which was developed by mostly illiterate bards who relied as much on visionary inspiration as memory. That oral tradition has now died out, but fortunately attempts to document fragments of the epic were first made in the 1850s by the Kazakh anthropologist, Chokan Valikhanov. During Soviet times the oral tradition was recorded by folklorists and has since been translated into many languages, reflecting the wide range of nationalities in Kyrgyzstan. It has made an impressive revival since independence and the story is now even more accessible, in the form of novels, TV shows and poems.

There are now special *manaschi* schools, where apart from the national syllabus, children also learn the text, tempo and the prescribed gestures which accompany the epic. In their late teens they are judged by an unofficial board of *manaschi* according to whether they have infused their performance with sufficient feeling and sensitivity for the different nuances of the epic. Those who are approved by the board can begin to improvise.

During the 1995 '1000 years of Manas' celebrations, then President Akaev, attempting to sail on Manas' strength, identified the 'seven principles of Manas': patriotism, national unity, humanism, co-operation among nations, hard work and education and, in Akaev's words, 'strengthening and defence of the Kyrgyz state system'. Their source cannot be specifically located within the text but the principles have become signposts to successful nationhood.

ALAMAN-BAIGA

*T*he carcass, held firm by the rider's leg, hung there. Gyulsary was now abreast of him. Tanabai leaned over the saddle to grab one of the goat's legs, but the Kazakh quickly shifted his prize to the left side. The horses were still galloping towards the sun. Now Tanabai had to fall behind to get around to the left and overtake his rival once again. It was hard to pull the pacer away from the bay, but he finally succeeded. Once again the Kazakh in the ripped army shirt managed to shift the carcass to the off side.

"Good for you!" Tanabai shouted excitedly.

And the horses raced on into the sun.

Tanabai could not risk the manoeuvre again. He pressed Gyulsary close to the bay stallion and threw himself across his neighbour's saddle. The rider tried to break away, but Tanabai would not let him. Gyulsary's speed and litheness made it possible for Tanabai to practically lie across the bay stallion's neck. Finally, he got his hands on the carcass and began pulling it towards himself. It was easier for him to reach the right, besides, both his hands were free. He had practically got half of it over to his side.

"Watch out, brother Kazakh!" Tanabai shouted.

"No you don't neighbour! You won't get it!" the other shouted back.

And so the struggle began at a dead gallop. They were locked together like eagles fighting over prey, shouting at the tops of their voices, grunting and snarling like animals, bullying each other, their arms like steel bands, their nails bleeding. And the horses, united in their riders' struggle, carried them onward angrily, speeding to catch up with the flaming sun. Blessed be our ancestors who handed down these fierce games of courage to us!

The goat's carcass now hung suspended between the racing horses. The end of the contest was in sight. Silently, their teeth clenched, straining every muscle, the men tugged at it, each trying to get a leg over it in order to suddenly pull away and break free. The Kazakh was strong. He had large sinewy arms, and he was much younger than Tanabai. But experience means a lot. Tanabai suddenly kicked off his right stirrup and pressed his foot against the bay stallion's loins. While pulling the carcass towards himself he was also pushing his rival's horse away, and the other man's fingers finally uncurled. "Hang on!" the vanquished foe managed to shout in warning.

Chinghiz Aitmatov, Tales of the Mountains and Steppes:
Farewell Gyulsary!, *1969*

*Battling over a headless goat carcass during a game of Kok-boru,
this young man risks being unseated and trampled in the melee [J. Bjelousov]*

Introduction

A wise man isn't he who has lived the longest, but he who has travelled the most.

Kyrgyz saying

Travellers from the seventh to the 21st century have spoken eloquently of the beauty and hospitality of Kyrgyzstan, the 'jewel of Turkestan'. When the Chinese traveller-monk, Xuan Zang (Hsuan Tsang), visited Kyrgyzstan in the seventh century, he reported 'tall peaks which reach to the very sky', and warned that travellers were 'molested by dragons'. Modern visitors will find plenty of tall peaks but should be reassured that they will encounter no dragons. Instead, they will find not only a stunning natural beauty but also an intriguing semi-nomadic culture to which the visitor is a welcome and honoured guest.

Kyrgyzstan is still beset by dragons, however, though not of the kind that Zang would recognise. As the country charts its way through the unknown waters of independence, the Kyrgyz people face stiff challenges. Cornered in their mountain sanctuary, they have to deal not only with their new nationhood but must also find a way of living with some troublesome neighbours.

Kyrgyzstan's geographical position has always dictated its history. For centuries it was the gateway to the west for invading warrior tribes and Silk Route traders alike. More recently, it endured 70 years of isolation as a military research centre under the Soviets. Independent Kyrgyzstan's metamorphosis from a dependent Soviet state to a brand new player on the world stage, and the resulting collapse in its economy, has been a painful process, which is still unfolding.

What is remarkable about Kyrgyzstan, however, is that despite the difficulties, its people have retained a sense of confidence about the future. They are grappling with the challenge of 'transition' with good humour, dignity and optimism. The resilience demanded by their erstwhile nomadic lifestyle sustains them today, along with a strong family tradition, which remains at the heart of modern Kyrgyz culture.

Travel in Kyrgyzstan can be a challenge. A modern tourist industry has risen from the ruined Soviet infrastructure but visitors need to approach the country with a spirit of adventure. Those who do will be amply rewarded: Kyrgyzstan offers some of the most dramatic scenery anywhere in the world, from vast sweeping steppes to mighty citadels of ice, from jagged peaks to flower-strewn valleys, from pristine mountain lakes to lush pastures, home each summer to shepherds and their yurts.

Little visible evidence of Kyrgyzstan's long history has survived. What wasn't destroyed by the armies of Jenghis (Genghis) Khan (refer page 15 for comment about spelling of his name) in the 13th century was whisked away to the museums of Leningrad/St Petersburg by Soviet archaeologists. The fascination of modern Kyrgyzstan lies in its unique culture, the core values of which somehow survived the enforced Soviet transition from nomadic to settled life. As old and new find their places, you might see a BMW parked outside a yurt or livestock loaded onto a bus. In spite of its traumas, the Soviet period seems to sit more lightly on Kyrgyzstan than on other Central Asian states. There is an enduring sense of pride in the achievements of the Soviet period.

This is an exciting time to visit Kyrgyzstan: proud to be an independent state, it offers visitors a ringside seat at the drama of a nation in the making.

History

The seventy-year Soviet period was a mere blip in the long history of what is today Kyrgyzstan but its impact was unimaginably profound, resulting in the settlement of a people who had been largely nomadic for at least 2,500 years.

The story of how the peoples who inhabited the vast tracts of land between the Caspian Sea and China made their way to the modern age is complex and poorly documented. Amid the fierce heat and cold of desert and mountain, swathes of humanity migrated through Central Asia, replacing one another like weather fronts. Sir Olaf Caroe, historian, likened the process to:

> ... the movement of a crowd gathered on some great occasion. Groups meet and coalesce, groups melt and dissolve; a sudden interest draws a mass in one direction, only to split up again.

Central Asia is important in world history as the birthplace of the great warrior tribes who invaded Eurasia: the Huns, Jenghis Khan, Timur. It was a land unknown, which glowed in the European imagination in images of camel trains laden with silk, the rich smell of spices and in the poetic vision of Marlowe, Milton, Keats and Shelley.

The recent division of Central Asia into modern states is wholly unnatural, conjured up by Stalin for political reasons and only partly founded in the civilizations which rose and fell there until the dawn of the 20th century. Historically and geographically Central Asia was always seen as one land; distinctions were made only between steppe and mountain, desert and oasis. The mountain nomads within the borders of what is now Kyrgyzstan played little or no part in the cyclical establishment and sacking of the great empires of Central Asia, but the Fergana valley, Issyk Kul and the Chui steppes fell naturally under the dictate of settled rulers based in the great centres of Samarkand, Bukhara and Merv (present-day Uzbekistan and Turkmenistan).

ANCIENT HISTORY

The earliest Central Asian peoples probably lived 25,000–35,000 years ago but the first identifiable groups—the Scythians (also known as Sakas)—emerged in the eighth century BC. They created the first in a long line of great Central Asian nomadic empires.

They combined agriculture with their herder lifestyle and were skilled at metallurgy, creating sophisticated art. They gradually moved eastwards following a number of defeats at the hands of Persians, to occupy the Chui and Fergana valleys in present-day Kyrgyzstan. The Scythians were gradually absorbed into the vast Kushan Empire, which was initiated by an Iranian-speaking people who were ousted from their homeland in western China. In its heyday in the first century AD, their empire spread from India to the Aral Sea, giving them significant control over the early Silk Routes.

Petroglyph at Cholpon Ata

BIRTH OF THE SILK ROUTE

In 138 BC the Chinese general, Zhang Qian (Chang Chien), desperate to find a steed capable of out-riding the constantly invading nomads of present-day Mongolia, travelled westwards to the Fergana valley following rumours of the legendary speed of the Heavenly Horses of Fergana. On finding that the horse sweated blood due to a skin parasite rather than speed, the emissary nevertheless remained astute to trading possibilities and discovered the Sogdian yearning for silk.

The Silk Route was born and its many trails became arteries bearing goods, religion and learning, to connect the great civilisations of the age. The image of the Fergana horse became an artistic motif that travelled up and down the Silk Routes.

EARLY TURKIC EMPIRES

Between the fifth and 13th centuries AD the Altai Mountains, between present-day Mongolia and China's Xinjiang province, provided three great swathes of mounted warrior tribes. The first were the Huns, who by 400 AD had swept across the plains and mountains of Central Asia to the Volga River in Russia. In the fifth century they rallied around Attila the Hun and marched on Rome. Terrifying the Chinese at one end of Central Asia and the Romans at the other they endured until 560 when they were defeated at Talas and disappeared into anonymity. Their victors were the Turks, also from the Altai, descended from the mythical union of a she-wolf and a youth.

During the sixth century the nomadic empire of the Turks held sway over much of Central Asia. Split in two, the western Turkic khanate was probably based at Suyab on the river Chui, straddling a flourishing branch of the silk route. This region, stretching from the Chui river, in modern Kyrgyzstan, to southern Kazakhstan was known as Yeti Su, Turkic for 'seven rivers', and centuries later would be more commonly referred to in

Russian as Semirechye. The Chinese traveller Xuan Zang (Hsuan Tsang) came across a military encampment here in the seventh century:

> *The Khan dwelt in a vast tent ornamented with flowers of gold, so bright they dazzled the eyes of the beholder ... His officers ... were all clad in glittering habits of brocade ... the remainder of his forces was made up of cavalry mounted on camels or on horses, dressed in furs or fine wool and bearing long lances, banners and tall bows. So vast was their multitude, they stretched far out of sight*

> Ella Maillart, *Turkestan Solo*

The Turkic khanate pursued a wise policy of cultivating political and economic links with the Sogdians, who were settled and successful farmer traders centred at Samarkand. The first written record of Sogdian presence in Semirechye dates to 568. Their influence stimulated, and to a large extent determined, the character of a string of vigorous towns that flourished in Semirechye, amongst them Navekat (now Krasnaya Rechka) and, it is thought, Jul ('steppeland' in ancient Turkic) whose ruins lie under the streets of Bishkek.

In spite of the enormous differences in language, origin and culture between the settled Sogdians, of Iranian origin, and the nomadic Turks, colonisation by the former in the seventh century led to a gradual and peaceable blend of cultures, lending strength and stability to both. It was in large partthis successful co-existence that bolstered their autonomy until well into the eighth century and made them the last of the Central Asian groups to succumb to Islam.

Though short-lived, this Turkic empire was historically significant because it left the first written records of any Central Asian people in engraved standing stones found along the Orkhon river in Mongolia. These offer a rare insight into the pastoral nomadic world and are the first known source to mention the Kyrgyz tribes, then living in Siberia. The khanate also gave its name to the groups of people inhabiting the region, thus providing a unifying force that still remains today.

In this pre-Islamic period several different religions co-existed peacefully. The remains of Buddhist temples and Christian Nestorian churches have been found around Issyk Kul and Zoroastrian tombs and evidence of Manichean communities have been discovered elsewhere in the region.

Statue of Lenin

ISLAM IN CENTRAL ASIA

It was the Arab armies, invading from Baghdad, who brought Islam to Central Asia, capturing Merv (now in Turkmenistan) in 651 and advancing to Bukhara, Samarkand, Tashkent and Fergana between 712 and 715. The Sogdians and Turks showed stubborn resistance, and soon expelled the Arabs from the Fergana valley. Taking advantage of the disarray, China stormed Fergana. Choosing the lesser of two evils, the Sogdians and Turks joined with their enemies the Arabs to thrash the Chinese at the battle of the Talas river in 751. The historian V Barthold declares that 'the Arabs themselves looked upon Turkestan as a province wrested from the Chinese Emperors.' The Talas defeat put a decisive end to westward Chinese expansion, assuring the supremacy of Islam in the region.

In the wake of the battle, the rivers of the Silk Route carried the prisoners' expertise in paper- and silk-making to Europe and Persia, where its impact was immense. The secrets were out and the commerce along the Silk Road suffered in consequence.

By the mid-eighth century, the Arabs were ousted by the Samanid dynasty, founded by four Muslim brothers, which reclaimed the Fergana valley and promoted Bukhara as a great centre of learning and of Islam.

THE KARAKHANIDS AND THE SELJUKS

The Karakhanids, a Turkic people closely related to the Uighurs, finally brought Islam to Semirechye and the Tien Shan. By the end of the tenth century, having dislodged the Samanids from power, the Karakhanids had firm control over Central Asia. Sharing the Samanid enthusiasm for learning and settled life, the new rulers continued to allow Bukhara to blossom as an Islamic scholastic centre. They ruled their western realms from three cultured Silk Route capitals: Belasagun (now Burana in Kyrgyzstan), Mavarannahr (now Ozgon) in the Fergana valley and Kashgar.

During this period settlements on current Kyrgyz and Kazakh lands, previously half-hearted attempts at sedentarism, flourished as commercial and cultural centres. Mavarannarh, the elegant city on the eastern edge of the Fergana valley, was completed in the 12th century, its mausoleums the earliest example of the fine ornamental brick-work and stone relief work, which would become commonplace in the oasis cities of Samarkand, Bukhara and Khiva. This marked the beginning of a period of Muslim Turkic rule in Semirechye, which would last until 1862, with two brief interludes under the Buddhist Karakitay and Shamanist Mongols.

Halfway through the 11th century, the Karakhanids, while warmongering with their main rivals, the Ghaznavids (who were converting northern India to Islam), were taken unawares by another Turkic group, the Seljuks of the lower Syr Darya who established their own vast empire from the Mediterranean to the China border. They moved their capital to Merv (Turkmenistan), which became the biggest and richest oasis in Asia, and ruled there until 1210.

ARRIVAL OF THE KYRGYZ

Into this melee of sedentary and nomadic cultures came the fair-skinned, green-eyed and red-haired Kyrgyz tribes. The date of their arrival remains a mystery. They were living on the upper reaches of the Yenisei river, in southern Siberia, between the sixth and ninth centuries. It is generally agreed that their move south, largely complete by the 12th century, was gradual; absorbing and inter-marrying with other tribes as they went.

Well before Jenghis Khan's arrival the nomadic Kyrgyz tribes were established in the region and were a force to be reckoned with, famous for their stamina, horsemanship and their prowess as warriors. By the 15th century their epic poems, records of their struggles to carve out a land for themselves, began to appear along with fine pottery and superb gold and silver vessels. According to Dan Prior, they 'reserved the most scornful abuse for sedentary people, who were considered vermin'.

JENGHIS KHAN

In the early 1200s, nobody could have guessed the scale of destruction about to shake Eurasia. Jenghis Khan (known as Genghis Khan in the West and Chinggis Khaan in Mongolia) 'slaughtered and destroyed on a scale the 20th century alone has emulated' declares the historian, J M Roberts.

Jenghis Khan was born with the name Temujin in the latter half of the 12th century and was left fatherless at the age of nine. Temujin displayed remarkable ingenuity and personal charisma in his search for allies within the tribal society of the Mongol steppes. He deftly eliminated all rivals and weakened tribe loyalties in his determined unification of the Mongol tribes. By 1206, many clans had sworn their allegiance to him and, at a large gathering, he was proclaimed Jenghis Khan, head of the Mongol clans and a well-equipped and highly trained army.

Jenghis Khan launched his attack on Central Asia in 1219. By 1220 the glorious Silk Route oases of Samarkand, Bukhara, Khiva and, the following year, Merv, were being razed to the ground, disappearing back into the silence and secrecy of the desert.

Massacre wasn't necessarily part of the Mongol game plan—only where they met with resistance was the destruction complete. Unfortunately, resistance was the norm in Central Asia, with the result that today barely a building remains in the region from the pre-Mongol period. However, the armies wisely spared the skilled artisans and technical staff required to build and run an empire.

The Kyrgyz initially offered stiff resistance but were soon overwhelmed and almost wiped out. Most of the surviving groups joined the Mongol armies as mercenaries in their advance westward. The pax Mongolica descended over the region, stretching to China and India. According to V Barthold, 'the Mongols took measures to restore the welfare of the conquered regions'. The empire was run efficiently, trade was encouraged and, in order to keep a check on his vast empire, Jenghis Khan set up a swift postal service in the form of a relay of super-fast riders, a system not improved on until telegraph poles began to appear across the steppe, courtesy of the Russians. Law and order had never been better.

After Jenghis Khan's death in 1227, the lands were divided between his two sons, most of current Kyrgyzstan falling under the auspices of the second son, Chaghatai. While some parts of the Mongol empire adopted the habits of settled society, including Islam, the peoples of the lands in modern-day Kyrgyzstan successfully maintained their nomadic traditions.

The popular Western image of the Mongols as no more than philistine thugs, ascribing their extraordinary military success purely to strength of numbers is quite inaccurate. It is typified by such demeaning terms as 'marauding' and 'bestial' and fails to recognise the cunning excellence of their tactics. Never attacking until they were almost certain of success and drawing the enemy into the great pincer grasp of their armies, theirs was a strategy almost impossible to fathom. Western records, it seems, were unwilling to accept that Europe had been so utterly outwitted by Asian nomads.

By 1360 the Mongol empire was already in trouble.

TIMUR 'THE LAME'

On the banks of the Zeravshan River near Samarkand in Uzbekistan, Eurasia's next conqueror was born. Timur the lame—hence Tamerlane—took Jenghis Khan as his role model and aimed to rule the world. It was a poor emulation: his style was to plunder and massacre on the scale of Jenghis Khan but with less purpose and vision (although he is said to have been more appreciative of culture and art). Timur's chief rampage

The Karakhanid mausoleum at Ozgon

THE SILK ROUTE

When the Chinese emissary, Zhang Qian, set out westwards in 138 BC in search of military allies, he could not have envisaged that his discoveries would launch possibly the greatest trade route in world history. The Chinese had heard vague rumours of the world beyond their western borders; the exciting news that Zhang Qian brought back, of the 'heavenly horses' of Fergana, of Persia, the Mediterranean and the 'western barbarians', led to further expeditions. The great moving bazaar had begun, a complex labyrinth of trails over some of the most inhospitable land known to man. Trade would link the eastern and western ends of the Eurasian landmass: camels headed west from Xi'an laden with jade, porcelain, silk, rhubarb, gunpowder, the wheel barrow, furs, paper and printing. The eastward flow carried the much-admired ostrich, wine, linen, ivory, wool, cucumbers, gold and precious metals.

Central Asians were the middle-men, carrying goods west to the cities of Persian and Syrian merchants. The traditional gateway from China to the West, present-day Kyrgyzstan hosted three main routes. From Kashgar paths led over the formidable Tien Sham mountains: one crossed at the Torugart pass or Kok Art and headed for Osh in the Fergana valley (which has retained its function as a commercial highway ever since), then on to Samarkand, from where routes led east to the Caspian Sea and north to Russia. A more southerly route climbed to the Irkeshtam pass and ran through the Alay Valley to Osh. A less frequented road crossed the Torugart pass and swung round the At-Bashy mountains north to the Boom canyon, then along the Chui river past Belasagun (modern Tokmak) and into Kazakhstan.

Throughout the Talas and Chui valleys, the Silk Route promoted settled agricultural towns alongside the nomadic livestock-raising peoples, who sold horses and camels to the traders. But the unseen trade of this mammoth international exchange was perhaps its greatest glory: the interaction of religions, ideas, cultures, arts and technologies enriched and enlightened civilisations from Beijing to Rome. Like the silt left by a passing river, art and religion from far away were washed up in Silk Route oases: Nestorian Christianity and Buddhism made their way to China, visiting Belasagun and Issyk Kul on the way.

The early Silk Route began to die away with the weakening of China's Han Dynasty in the third century. Sea routes proved cost-effective and by the ninth century the Persians were skilled silk producers. For Central Asia, the Silk Road forged trade relations and established routes that waxed and waned until the area was abruptly cut off from the outside world by Soviet borders in 1924.

ended in 1395, his influence stretching from northern India to the Caucasus. Only in Samarkand did he establish a capital, putting Central Asia on the map by forcibly recruiting Asia's finest craftsmen and architects to fashion the minarets, mosques and domes which still grace the streets today.

Timur died in 1405 en route to an abortive conquest of China. His empire lived on until the death of his grandson, the astronomer and scholar, Ulug Bek in 1449.

His great-great-great-grandson was Babur who ruled for a while at Osh from the age of 12 and in 1526 founded the Mogul empire in India, having been driven from his home by the Uzbeks.

FROM UZBEKS TO OYRATS

From this period the Kyrgyz tribes were weakened. In the 16th century the oasis towns of Turkestan fell to Shaibani Khan, a descendent of a Siberian Turko-Mongol tribe, which had been founded by a man called Uzbek. As a result of the conquest the term Uzbek came to be applied to the people of the oases. Shaibani Khan ruled from Bukhara until 1655, his empire constantly plundered by a powerful confederation of Kazakh tribes. The Kazakhs were regarded favourably by the Russians whose trading operations were being interfered with by Bukhara; this formed the seeds of a relationship which eased Russia's gradual move into Central Asia. In the mid-18th century the Kazakhs accepted Russian 'protection', which swiftly became annexation.

As the Shaibanids squabbled, the Zhungars or Oyrats, Tibetan Buddhists of western Mongolia, became the last of a long line of nomadic invaders of Semirechye. They proved to be cruel and tyrannical rulers, invaded parts of China and demanded high taxes of Russia. Kyrgyz tribes beautifully evoked the anxiety of the Oyrat period in their epic poem, Manas.

As with many empires, Oyrat rule came to an end with a dispute over who was to rule after the death of Emperor Galdan Tseren. The Chinese Manchu emperor took advantage of the Oyrats' momentary weakness and invaded, ruthlessly slaying the Oyrat people. China then withdrew, realising that they were too overstretched to rule effectively in the region. The Kyrgyz were nominally vassals of the Chinese but in reality enjoyed a brief period of freedom.

THE KHANATE OF KOKAND

The last pre-Russian dynasties to rule in Central Asia were a trio of khanates at Khiva, Bukhara and Kokand. Established in 1747, the three were inward-looking and occupied with constantly brawling over their mutual and international borders and fending off raids by their nomadic neighbours. Barthold dismisses the 18th century as, 'a period of political, economic and cultural decadence'. Under the influence of corrupt mullahs, the moral and spiritual side of Islam was debased, superstition was rife and the khans and emirs of Kokand, Khiva and Bukhara ruled as feudal despots. Central Asia became isolated and entered an economic slump, partly due to the demise of the Silk Road in the wake of the discovery by western European countries of sea routes to the east. The camel trains still plodded through the region but in ever-decreasing numbers.

By the 1820s the tentacles of the Kokand khanate began to reach into the Tien Shan, the Chui and Talas valleys, Issyk Kul and the Alay and Pamir mountains; indeed most of modern Kyrgyzstan. The Kyrgyz found themselves cornered in their mountain sanctuary. To enforce their control and protect the caravan routes passing from China to the Caucasus and Russia, the Kokand khanate built a string of fortresses, one of which was Pishpek, site of the future capital of Kyrgyzstan.

Between military conscription and excessive, arbitrary taxes, life for the Kyrgyz under the Kokand khanate became almost untenable. A story well demonstrates the ferocity of the khan's rule. A drover bought a whip at the bazaar and refused to pay the tax on it. The court sentenced him to be impaled but the khan's men, warned against the danger of frightening off the rare drovers, instead took one of the more numerous herders and executed him in public and spread word of the deed around the land 'so that the khan's subjects would see his wisdom and fairness and, what was more important, would tremble with fear at the mention of his name'. The Kokand khanate was finally liquidated in 1877 but the Russians were already in Kyrgyzstan.

THE RUSSIAN CONQUEST

Soviet accounts of the Tsar's acquisition of Central Asia vary according to propagandists' needs and the political climate of the day. But the claim that the Kyrgyz tribes requested inclusion in the Russian empire and that the alternative was colonisation by another foreign power (Britain) are perennial themes.

The motives for Russia's conquest of Central Asia are complex and remain a subject of lively controversy. There appears to be a general consensus about its inevitability, however, once Russia's expansion into Siberia was complete, given the fragmented and vulnerable state in which centuries of invasions had left Central Asia. In Lord Curzon's words, 'Russia was as much compelled to go forward as the earth is to go around the sun'.

A more tangible factor in their advance southwards was Russia's need to find a secure southern border and a foothold in this strategic corner of the globe, abutting as it did against areas of British expansion and perceived British designs on the area. Russia was also driven by the notion of 'Manifest Destiny', that it was somehow their right and duty, by the lure of trade, especially once the American source of cotton had dried up as a result of the American Civil War (1861–65) and, perhaps above all, an irresistible urge to exploit the rich economic potential of the huge region.

Indeed this picture is further complicated by the debate over whether the complete annexation of Turkestan was the design of the St Petersburg Government or an ad hoc affair promoted more by the decisions of the daring Russian commanders on the spot. The ambiguous and contradictory position of the government was displayed in a series of memos from the Ministry of Foreign Affairs to the Tsar in October 1864, which denied the government's desire 'to extend the limits of its influence by conquest' while at once acknowledging that the Russian empire 'influenced by the insistent demands of our trade, and some mysterious but irresistible urge towards the East, was steadily moving into the heart of the Steppe'.

The Russian acquisition was insidious; by controlling navigable rivers, dominating mountain passes and building railways, they assured themselves political and economic ownership of incalculable natural resources of enormous strategic importance.

Interestingly, by the 19th century the Central Asian peoples, nomadic groups in particular, had not developed a concept of belonging to a particular nation state; their main focus of loyalty and responsibility being to clan and family. Political self-determination, therefore, was not an issue at this stage.

It appears to have been the behaviour and policies of the immigrant Russians rather than their presence per se which gradually generated such resentment amongst the local population. The first settlers arrived in the 1860s to establish a Russian presence on the Chinese border. By 1867 there were 14 Cossack settlements, mostly on appropriated nomads' lands. The Kyrgyz tribes, struggling under the arbitrary and cruel rule of the Kokand khanate, were ready to swear allegiance to the advancing Russian state.

Pishpek fortress was for Kokand an important military post and trading centre on the camel caravan route. The population, mostly of Sarts (sedentary Uzbeks), grew throughout the 19th century, its population boosted by yurt encampments of Kyrgyz nomads on the fringes of the town. The Russians were already firmly established along the southern edge of the Kazakh steppe, with a strong military base at Verniy (Almaty), and eyed Kokand with suspicion. In 1860, taking advantage of Kokand's distraction with internal disputes, the Russians launched an attack on Pishpek fortress. It took seven days and several tons of gunpowder to destroy the structure. Extraordinarily, the Russians then retreated and Kokand rebuilt the fort.

By 1862, however, the Kyrgyz took matters into their own hands; exhausted by the demands of the Kokand rulers they plotted its downfall. The Solto and Sarybagsh tribes joined forces under the leadership of Baitik of Solto. The Kyrgyz were particularly desperate, already weakened by the freezing winter of 1859–60 in which 80 per cent of their stock was lost. They invited Kokand's commandant to a feast and murdered him and his entourage on their way home, then attacked the fort, but lacking the appropriate weaponry, called on the Russians at Verniy for help. Colonel Kolpakovsky, the commander, was eager to oblige and in October 1862 the fortress fell and Kokand was ousted from the Chui valley for good. The Russians once again disappeared over the Zaliiskiy Alatau for the winter but returned in spring to complete the destruction of the fort. This episode has been used by Soviet historians as proof of the 'voluntary entry of the people of Kirghizia into the body of Russia'.

In 1864 Tashkent tumbled into Russian hands. Pishpek (present-day Bishkek) became a staging post on the Tashkent to Verniy trade route. Samarkand and Bukhara fell soon after. In the meantime, the dwindling Kokand khanate was finally annexed by

Russia in order to secure south-eastern Kyrgyzstan against possible incursions by Yaqub Beg, a Kokandi ruler of Kashgar. A Russian Consul was set up in Kashgar in 1882, a significant development in the Great Game rivalry with Great Britain. Russian advance into modern Kyrgyzstan had been relatively easy. In the 1850s a Kyrgyz bandit, Kutebov, carried out a series of raids from eastern Kyrgyzstan to the Aral Sea but the Kyrgyz possessed insufficient modern weaponry and, furthermore, were too preoccupied with internecine quarrels and cattle raids to pay much heed to the new presence on their lands. Clan by clan they allied themselves to Russia: accustomed to frequent invasions, how little could they have guessed at the enormity of the Russian takeover.

TSARIST RULE

From the late 1860s Pishpek grew in size and importance. In 1878 it became the regional administrative centre. Trade was vigorous and camel caravans still plodded mountain and steppe between Kashgar and Semipalatinsk, Tashkent and Verniy.

Most important of all, the Muslim educational movement began to open schools with a liberal curriculum in Kyrgyz. Many of these pupils would later become enthusiastic supporters of the Bolshevik revolution.

By 1881, 30,000 Russians, Ukrainians and Germans had settled in Semirechye, tempted by grants and tax breaks, free land and building materials. Many were landless peasants who had been freed from serfdom in 1861. There was a policy of settling Russians on so-called 'unoccupied' lands (actually seasonal grazing), which, by the nature of the Kyrgyz's nomadic lifestyle, were left vacant for months at a time.

The Russians were clear about their aims: to exploit the economic and military potential of the area and build a land for Russians to live in, without regard to the locals other than as a source of cheap labour. They built cities next to native ones, which in their provision of modern amenities—shops, parks, schools, hospitals, theatres, water supplies—were often ahead of cities in Russia, but made no improvements to local towns. They made some plans for improved irrigation but failed to implement these. Under the relative peace of the Russian occupation, the locals rebuilt their own primitive but ingenious irrigation systems that had been destroyed by Jenghis Khan.

By the early 20th century, the Russians had laid the foundations for the material improvements that would be ushered in by the Soviets. They had also sown anger in the hearts of the locals; ousted from the Chui valley, denied grazing rights in the remotest mountains, robbed of land and livestock, the Kyrgyz population began to dwindle.

The great rebellion of 1916, which rushed through Central Asia, gave expression to widespread resentment against Russian injustices. Facts are scanty and reports biased towards the Russians, but it is known that smouldering anger was set alight by an Imperial Decree of 25 June 1916 calling up non-Russians for service in World War I as road builders, herders and food producers. They had already contributed to Russia's desperate war, with land and livestock requisitions. They were affronted at being

THE LAST MANAP

While my face roasts and my back in comparison freezes painfully, I listen to the story of the Manap Kendeur, the last of the Patriarchs.

This sage, whom nowadays the people revere as a saint, was elected chief of all the Kirghiz, and before the great insurrection of 1916 ... was visited by a delegation anxious to hear his opinion in the matter.

"Bring me a bucketful of sand!" he said.

When the bucket was in front of him he took a handful up, and then, letting it fall immediately, said:

"Now find the grains that were in my hand."

The plain significance of which was: "The Russians completely submerge us, and we can do nothing against them or without them."

Then, before the revolt broke out, gathering his people, a total of many families—for under his protection were all his poor and weaker relations—the Manap made his way into China. Sarabaguich, for instance, the richest of all the Manaps, numbered seven hundred yurts in his tribe.

Later Kandeur returned again to Aksu, his region, but no attempt was made to visit his defection upon him. When he died in 1927, untold multitudes flocked to the funeral, among them five thousand Russians come to render a last homage.

Ella K Maillart, *Turkestan Solo*, 1934

required only to dig and not to fight and outraged that they should be forced to leave their lands at harvest time. The rebellion reached Kyrgyzstan in August 1916 and it was here that the worst excesses of violence were played out on both sides. Mounted Kyrgyz attacked the Russian militia, as well as sympathisers and settlers, burning villages and killing many innocent people. Russian reprisals, with more power and better arms at their disposal, were even fiercer and just as arbitrary. The rebellion was put down in October and many Kyrgyz fled for their lives over the treacherous passes of the Tien Shan to China, where the survivors were either turned back or relieved of their remaining livestock by border guards. Descendants of Kyrgyz survivors of the revolt are still living in Xinjiang province. Tens of thousands of Kyrgyz people died, either at the hands of the Russians, in the Tien Shan snows or at the hands of the Chinese border guards.

In spite of Soviet attempts to interpret these events as a class war and a popular movement against tyranny, historian R Pearce writes that, 'they indicate clearly the failure not only of the Imperial Government but of the Russian people to win the friendship and trust of the peoples of Central Asia'. Clearly the Russians made a bad start. Sadly, today, some Kyrgyz nationalists have represented the Russian retribution equally simplistically as genocide.

THE RUSSIAN REVOLUTION AND CIVIL WAR 1917–20

The facts of the Bolshevik takeover of Kyrgyzstan are scanty. The Soviet claim that the oppressed masses welcomed the revolution with open arms is not quite the full story. The revolution that shook Moscow and St Petersburg in November 1917 was generally ignored by some of the nomadic and largely illiterate Kyrgyz. Even if they seriously intended to resist the revolution, they possessed no modern weapons to do so. The resistance that did exist remained uncoordinated and the Kyrgyz were used to operating in much smaller units than would be required to take on the Red Army. Another factor that ranged against a successful local resistance was the total pre-occupation of surrounding nations with their own dissolution—Afghanistan, Persia, China, and the Turkish empire were all experiencing political collapse. Moreover, the presence in Central Asia of 40,000 prisoners of war from Austria, Germany and Hungary, as well as resident Russian settlers, provided a ready-made European group receptive to a new political system that expounded a fairer distribution of resources.

Furthermore, conditions were perfect for a change of government: in 1917, heartily sick of being robbed and exploited by the Tsarist system, local people optimistically understood the revolution to mean the return of their land and water rights and possibly an end to Russian rule. They were to feel sorely cheated.

Indeed there was some justification for Kyrgyz high hopes at this time; the Communist revolution was very clear about its duty to grant self-determination to subject peoples. But Russia was deeply reluctant to relinquish its Asian states. Regardless of how it might be represented by Soviet historians, the wholesale and violent suppression of indigenous attempts at self-rule (even within the context of a Soviet Union) between 1917 and 1920 was surely a betrayal of all declared Communist principles.

Tashkent was the pivotal point during the Bolshevik acquisition of Turkestan and Semirechye. As early as November 1917 the Tashkent Soviet had taken power and was courting the Russian military, making no attempt to appeal to the local population. Throughout it acted without the authority of the Russian Government.

A perfect audience for revolutionary rhetoric was the workforce of the Chui valley irrigation system, amongst them hundreds of Russians and thousands of Kyrgyz and Kazaks, many of whom had been displaced by the 1916 war labour decree. Who could be more ripe to embrace the stirring revolutionary diatribes of Aleksei Ivanitsyn? On January 1 1918, following a demonstration in Bishkek's Dubovy Park, the Bolsheviks seized power and ousted the provisional government. Within three months Ivanitsyn was elected chief of the city executive committee, effectively making him leader of the whole district, and a newspaper and bank had been established.

The end of 1918 saw a counter-revolutionary offensive from Tashkent, believed to have been inspired by the anti-Bolshevik Paul Nazarov, who was in Tashkent jail at the time. The force marched towards Pishpek from Belovodsk, a village 30 kilometres to the west. According to Dan Prior, the junta membership list 'reads like a yellow pages of anti-Bolshevists: ... underground counter-revolutionaries from Tashkent, White Guards of Semirechye, British Indian forces, the Tsar's former diplomatic representatives to Xinjiang, leftist socialist-revolutionaries and the Turkish Alash-Orda movement.' They called for the return of free trade. After eight days fighting in Pishpek, the Bolsheviks were victorious. By January 1919 it was all over.

In the shadow of these events, the first stirrings of national (as opposed to tribal) consciousness began to emerge throughout Central Asia. In late 1917 an all-Muslim Conference in Tashkent demanded autonomy for Turkestan within a Russian federation. Not only did the Tashkent Soviet ignore these demands but in November the Third Congress of Soviets passed a special resolution which entirely excluded Muslims from government posts.

THE KOKAND GOVERNMENT

A last desperate attempt to maintain some control over their lands and fate was made by the Fourth Regional Muslim Congress in Kokand in December 1917. They declared the autonomy of Turkestan (incorporating all the provinces of Turkestan, except Semirechye which remained under a Soviet yoke) and professed their aims of education, westernisation and modernisation of religion.

On the basis that the Tashkent Soviet was not acting with the authority of the central government, the congress appealed to Stalin for assistance. No help was forthcoming, however, and within three months the Tashkent Soviet, realising the extent of the threat of Kokand, announced the Kokand government to be counter-revolutionary and declared war on it, capturing the city with ease and slaughtering some 5,000 of its people. This was a crippling blow to co-ordinated Muslim resistance, from which it would not recover.

By September 1919 the White Army, whose war against the Bolsheviks had effectively isolated Central Asia from Russia for two years, was finally defeated and Pishpek's native Mikhail Frunze arrived to head the new Turkestan Commission, which had been appointed by Lenin to curb the excessive power of the Turkestan government and to ensure the participation of Central Asia's Muslims.

Meanwhile, Pishpek had been reduced from a healthy trading city to a skeleton town. The cowboy Bolsheviks had proved worse than the Tsarist Russians, requisitioning men and horses to work on Russian farms, effectively as slaves, under penalty of death.

By 1920, the tyranny of these adventurers and opportunists had come to an end and relative order had been established. Turkestan was declared a Soviet Republic and for a while at least, the stunned population could breathe a sigh of relief.

BASMACHI

Following the brutal suppression of the Kokand government in February 1918, some of the Muslim leaders fled the city and, rallying supporters, formed a guerrilla group dubbed 'Basmachi' (meaning bandit or marauder) by the Russians. In 1918–19, under the leadership of Muhammed Amin (Madamin), they seized Osh and Jalal-Abad and were joined for a period by the Russian 'peasant army', settlers from around Jalal-Abad. But as Red Army reinforcements arrived the towns were reclaimed. In 1919, Pishpek-born Mikhail Frunze arrived in Tashkent to head the Turkestan Commission. As well as stepping up military operations against the freedom fighters, he wooed their supporters with the distribution of food and seed. As a result, the Russian 'peasant army' and later their leader, Madamin, defected.

However, Soviet requisitions of land and labour continued to ensure popular support for the Basmachi. Under their new leader, Kurbashi Shir Muhammed (Kurshirmat), the Basmachi, well armed and well mounted, gained control of part of what is now the Uzbek Fergana valley and destroyed railway lines and cotton mills. The Red Army received reinforcements and after fierce fighting in September 1921 Kurshirmat was defeated and fled to Bukhara.

In October, the movement was joined in Bukhara by the colourful and charismatic character, Enver Pasha. Thousands rallied to his call and by May 1922 he had inflicted telling defeats on the Red Army and made contact with the Fergana Basmachi. The organisation was weakened, however, by internal rivalry and mistrust. With the treachery of other Basmachi leaders, Enver Pasha was cornered and killed in the Pamirs in August 1922 and the movement began to dwindle. Sporadic activity continued into the 1930s but, without strong leadership, efforts at resistance were uncoordinated and ultimately doomed.

THE DAWN OF THE SOVIET ERA

History cannot be written unless the historian can achieve some kind of contact with the mind of those about whom he is writing.

E.H. Carr, *What is History?*

As the Soviet Union eyes us from its grave, the West stares back, wide-eyed, to see what will happen next in the space it once occupied. Views into life in the Soviet Union have been so bound up with images fed by Western propaganda machinery that it is difficult to get a balanced picture of Soviet life. Rather like going through the papers of a dead relative and discovering an exciting secret life, so now visitors to the countries of the former Soviet Union encounter a very different and much more complicated picture than had been imagined.

Looking back over the relatively brief period of Soviet occupation, two legacies stand out: the vast improvement in living conditions that has taken place in the region but also, ultimately, a people robbed of the spiritual and cultural basis to their lives.

THE NATIONALITIES QUESTION

Following the chaos of revolution and civil war, the new government sought an effective means to rule and exploit the Muslim borderlands. Any initial hopes of independence fostered by the Kyrgyz were pipe dreams. Central Asia's role as a resource to feed the Russian economy was clarified at a party congress in 1921: 'if the strengthening of the centre required it, a policy of plunder in the borderlands would be proper and correct'. The Bolshevik government had a morbid dread of the spectres of pan-Turkism and Islam, the two main forces around which the Central Asian peoples could unite to drive out the legacy of imperialism.

During his brief leadership of the Basmachi, Enver Pasha, self-styled 'Commander-in -Chief of all Muslim peoples', had succeeded in uniting Turkic opposition to the Bolsheviks. Meanwhile, in Russia, an influential Tatar Muslim Communist, Sultan Galiyev, was planning to set up a Muslim Confederation on the basis that the German and Russian interpretation of Marxism was unsuited to the Muslim world and to agrarian societies and therefore would need to be modified before being successfully applied to Central Asia. He was arrested and dismissed from the party in 1923.

The expediency of containing these forces gave birth to the Nationalities Policy, implemented in 1924. The first step was to carve up the area along broadly linguistic lines into five nations. Principally a mechanism to divide and rule, the artificial parcelling of the region has proved disastrous to trade and ethnic relations since independence, especially in the Fergana valley. Uzbekistan was handed the valley floor and a few awkward enclaves in the mountains around it (as well as the Pamirs, which did not become Tajikistan until 1929). The mountains to the north became part of Kyrgyzstan in 1926.

The party was also faced with the awesome task of sowing the seed of Marxist-Leninist thought amongst the people of Kyrgyzstan and inspiring them to build a new socialist world, 'to escort the Kyrgyz from the dark ages of superstition into the sunshine of the modern rational world'. One method the propagandists employed was mass rallies: red *chaikhanas* (teahouses) were set up and people were fed propaganda along with their tea and *shashlik*. Another was to redefine the traditional religious and cultural foundations to people's lives. The new republics were to be 'national in quality, socialist in essence'. In the 1930s, Party officials recruited *allahsizlar* (Godless people) to assist the Movement of the Godless in the eradication of 'mediaeval hangovers'—anything that pertained to the past, whether it be Islam, superstitious beliefs or even *shyrdak* patterns. National cultures were homogenised, cleansed and packaged into a caricature of their former selves, and then fed back to the people through schools and propaganda as 'culture'.

Borders were closed, sealing the area off from the outside world, and any whisper of opposition was swiftly stamped out by the Red Army.

INVESTMENT IN SOCIAL INFRASTRUCTURE

For now, Kyrgyzstan's lot was in with the Soviets and they had to make the best of it. To be fair, Central Asia was not used solely as Russia's bread, wool or cotton basket; money was poured into the country's social infrastructure and the standard of living rose dramatically. The people were not denied, in Stalin's words, 'a taste of the material good of the Revolution'. From the 1920s to the 1940s the Kyrgyz made an extremely swift transition from a nomadic to a settled lifestyle. A shrewd early move by the Russians was to redistribute land. In Kyrgyzstan, unlike in Russia, there were few of the grievances of the 'have-nots' against the 'haves' but the Bolsheviks wisely dealt with the existing well-earned hatred of the Kyrgyz for the Russians. On March 4 1920, 687, 841 acres were confiscated from ethnic Russians and returned to 13,000 native households.

From 1925, a new infrastructure was grafted in place remarkably quickly. The whole republic saw the rapid construction of roads, communal facilities, schools and medical stations, followed by electricity, sewers and telephone links. Ethnic Kyrgyz were appointed to local government posts. Still, in the 1930s, the traveller Ella Maillart met an exiled Russian Trotskyist who confirmed that 'the Kirghiz so far have had little say in the government. The positions to which they are appointed are purely honorary ones'.

Education was a key tool in the process of Sovietisation. The Kyrgyz devoured education and many went on to attend vocational and academic institutes and universities in Bishkek, Almaty and Moscow. For the law-abiding and, more importantly, ideologically correct, opportunities for study were superb. The rapid spread of literacy and higher education undoubtedly distracted people's attention from the rigours and oppressions of the regime, reducing their susceptibility to the infiltration of nationalist ideas.

COLLECTIVISATION

The unfettered nomadic life of the Kyrgyz was ultimately incompatible with the ideology and spirit of the Soviet regime. The Kyrgyz were cheered by the early redistribution of land but this was only a forerunner to the settlement and collectivisation of the nomadic peoples of the USSR.

The trauma of collectivisation began in 1928 and was completed by 1932. The aim was to divorce the herders and farmers from their traditional ties and turn them wholesale towards the Soviet system, their new provider and arbiter. Nomads and semi-nomads were forced into settled collective farms. Striking as it did at the activity around which their traditions and culture were built, collectivisation was the kiss of death to their nomadic lifestyles. Rather than see their herds absorbed by the state, Kyrgyz and Kazakh herders slaughtered millions of beasts and ate all that they could. Many fled to China. Opposition to collectivisation was branded reactionary and dealt with ruthlessly.

Farms were under the supervision of the local party committee and generally managed by Russians. Nevertheless, they had a considerable degree of autonomy and clans tended to congregate in one farm, thereby allowing traditional social relationships and customs to be covertly maintained. There was also some limited scope for the private ownership of land and stock.

Traditional nomadic lifestyles were branded reactionary by the Soviets

THE PURGES OF THE 1930S

Kyrgyzstan did not escape the purges that shook the Soviet Union from 1936 to 1938, initiated by Joseph Stalin with the purpose of ridding the state of 'enemies of the people'. Anybody showing nationalist or bourgeois tendencies was liquidated. In Uzbekistan, hardly a family was left untouched by the purges. The Kyrgyz were accused primarily of ultra-nationalism and having links with China. In 1937, at Chong Tash, near the mouth to Ala Archa valley, around 138 people were murdered by secret police

Soviet-era housing at Karakol overshadowed by the Tien Shan mountains

and buried in a common grave. It is thought that the entire legislative central committee were among the victims, including the father of the famed Kyrgyz writer, Chinghiz Aitmatov. All intellectuals were under suspicion, as were an entire generation of *akyns*, traditional performer-songwriters and *manaschi*, singers of the Manas epic. According to the writer Ahmed Rashid, fewer than two per cent of the rank-and-file delegates to the Communist Party of the Soviet Union congresses in the 1920s still held their positions in 1939. The historian R Pipes (1990) expressed it thus:

> *The Red Terror gave the population to understand that under a regime that felt no hesitation in executing innocents, innocence was no guarantee of survival. The best hope of surviving lay in making oneself as inconspicuous as possible, which meant abandoning any thought of independent public activity, indeed any concern with public affairs, and withdrawing into one's private world.*

WORLD WAR II AND INDUSTRIALISATION

Many thousands of Kyrgyz men died fighting Nazism. Uzbek historian, Dr Hiyatt, asserts that half of the Central Asian forces at the front defected to the German side. As the Soviet Union launched itself into the Great Patriotic War (as the Soviets termed it), scores of factories were evacuated to Kyrgyzstan from European Russia, many complete with their staff. In general, the war marked a watershed for Soviet Kyrgyzstan; people had resigned themselves to the status quo. An entire generation had now grown up under the Soviet system. The country's embryonic industry received a boost, enabling for the first time, the possible appearance of an industrial proletariat. Between 1959 and 1970 there was a 30 per cent increase in the number of Russians settling in Kyrgyzstan. They took key managerial and technical jobs: European tutelage over Asian subjects persisted and Lenin's nightmare of Great Russian Chauvinism had come to pass. Just as today the Russians complain that the Kyrgyz are pushing them out of their jobs, so in the 1940s–80s, jobs with status and good wages were monopolised by the Russians.

The 1970s and 1980s were the 'Golden Years', when the spectre of famine finally disappeared. In 1971, Brezhnev made the bold claim that 'a new historical community of people—the Soviet people—had emerged', a people that was united. Yet it appears that the reverse was true in Central Asia, which saw a revival of local cultures and Islamic heritage by a new generation of intellectuals. Some writers claim that even the party leaders were nationalistic and Islamic at home, while donning an international Communist face in Moscow.

INDEPENDENCE

Party politics in Kyrgyzstan were characterised by clan and regional loyalties. During the preamble to independence the Kyrgyz people remained the least politicised of the Central Asian peoples; by 1989 Kyrgyz and Russians were still equally represented in parliament at 37 per cent each, even though the Kyrgyz population was much larger.

As the rest of the Soviet Union buzzed to the economic and political reforms of the Gorbachev years the Central Asian governments remained deeply conservative; Gorbachev's twin policies of *glasnost* (openness) and *perestroika* (restructuring), were never allowed to gain a foothold.

Housing and land, at the root of most of Central Asia's strife, were becoming increasingly serious problems in Kyrgyzstan. A number of pressure groups were set up by young Kyrgyz intellectuals to address the problems; they took the initiative of claiming vacant land and building mud huts to alleviate the problem of homelessness.

The Kyrgyz people witnessed a bloodless revolution on their smooth journey to independence. A standard rubber-stamp style Soviet election was held in February 1990, with the Kyrgyz Communist Party (CPK) taking most of the seats.

In June 1990, however, riots erupted in Osh like a volcano, decisively changing the course of Kyrgyz politics. Latent discontent and ethnic hostility was sparked off by the allocation of an Uzbek-run collective farm to a Kyrgyz group for housing. A horrific wave of atrocities on both sides spread to other towns, the most brutal being in Ozgon, where it is claimed that three quarters of the town's residences were burnt down. The official death toll was 200 but unofficial sources suggest more than 1,000 were killed.

As a sop to increasing demands from the newly formed Democratic Movement of Kyrgyzstan for the CPK leadership to resign, the new (powerless) post of President was created. Askar Akaev, a highly respected 46-year-old physicist and head of the Academy of Sciences, was elected president by the Supreme Soviet on 28 October 1990, the first non-communist Central Asian leader. On 12 December 1990 Kyrgyzstan announced its sovereignty.

From the start Akaev cast himself as a liberal. During the coup of August 1991 in Moscow, unlike other Central Asian leaders, Akaev did not sit tight awaiting the result of the coup but put tanks on the streets of Bishkek to prevent a hard-line communist uprising at home. Once the coup was crushed Akaev banned the CPK and on 31 August 1991 the Supreme Soviet reluctantly voted to declare Kyrgyzstan's independence. Shortly after, Askar Akaev was re-elected unopposed in full presidential elections.

The new republic was born. The government was thrust out onto the stage with no lines. They were totally unprepared for independent rule.

BEYOND INDEPENDENCE

Although proud to be independent, the last few years have presented serious challenges to the people of Kyrgyzstan. In spite of some positive developments in the economy, the country is severely limited by its lack of natural resources. Some people have benefited from Kyrgyzstan's engagement with capitalism and a tenuous middle class is emerging. Nevertheless, most of the population is forced to rely increasingly on an informal economy, in which people support each other.

Frustration with the slow pace of economic reform, which had failed to relieve the stark poverty with which most people struggle, led to calls for President Akaev's resignation in 2002. In the turbulent years that followed, the government was bedevilled by internal strife and power battles. Opposition parties became more vociferous and popular unrest grew.

Matters came to a head with the parliamentary elections in 2005 from which many opposition candidates were barred and Akaev claimed a victory for his party. This sparked the so-called Tulip Revolution; protests, which first paralysed the south, escalated to Bishkek and demonstrators seized government buildings; Akaev fled to Moscow and resigned on 7 April. In June, Kurmanbek Bakiev was elected President.

Bakiev made a good start, significantly raising some public sector salaries. In November 2006 and April 2007, demonstrators took to the streets demanding among other things, a faster pace of reform. In October 2007, citing irreconcilable differences with the legislature, President Bakiev dissolved parliament. Elections were held in December 2007; the ruling party, Ak Zhol, swept to victory however, Kyrgyzstan's main opposition party, Ata Meken, rejected the result and rumbling unrest continues; such are the growing pains in most young democracies.

Geography

With an area of 199,000 square kilometres (76,641 square miles) Kyrgyzstan is about the size of Great Britain. The altitude ranges from 401 metres in the Fergana valley to 7,437 metres at the summit of Jengish Chokosu, formerly Peak Pobeda. Just over 90 per cent of the territory is above 1,500 metres and 41 per cent is above 3,000 metres. About a third of the country is permanently under snow. Water covers 4.3 per cent of the land and forest 5.1 per cent. The main mineral resources are antimony, gold, coal, lead, mercury and uranium. Kyrgyzstan is in the north-east of Central Asia and shares borders with China to the east, Tajikistan to the south, Uzbekistan to the west and Kazakhstan to the north.

Kyrgyzstan's dominant feature is the Tien Shan ('Mountains of Heaven'), which cover around 100,000 square kilometres and extend some 2,500 kilometres from north-

The national flag of the Kyrgyz Republic

west China through Kyrgyzstan to its western borders with Kazakhstan and Uzbekistan. Its maximum width reaches 480 kilometres. Its icy fortress is the Central Tien Shan, where the South Inylchek Glacier, one of the biggest in the world, stretches 62 kilometres. The Tien Shan chains sprawl across Kyrgyzstan; the Terskiy and Kungey Ala-Too flank Lake Issyk Kul to the south and north respectively; the Kyrgyz Ala-Too fringe the south side of the Chui valley.

In the south the Fergana valley cul-de-sac is entrapped by the Fergana range to the east, the Chatkal range to the north, which extends also into Uzbekistan, and the Alay range to the south. The eastern end of the Tien Shan is mostly crystalline and sedimentary rock, created when the land folded about 540 million years ago, whereas the softer western end was formed under heat and pressure around 245 million years ago.

Kyrgyzstan's southern border with Tajikistan skirts the northern edge of the Pamir. This dramatic bastion lies mostly in Tajikistan and culminates at the Pamir Knot, a melée of peaks, topped by Kuh-i-Samani (formerly Peak Communism) at 7,495 metres. 'Pamir' in Turkic refers to the high rolling grassland that is a feature of the mountains. The Kyrgyz Alay and Turkestan are sub-ranges of the Pamir, and popular with climbers.

The republic boasts about 1,923 lakes, of which the pièce de resistance, Lake Issyk Kul ('warm lake'), lies in a basin at 1,600 metres. One of the deepest (702 metres) and largest (6,280 square kilometres) mountain lakes in the world, it derives its fame from its sky blue colour, high mineral content and the fact that it never freezes.

Water plummets constantly from Kyrgyzstan's mountains and glaciers into a myriad of streams which converge to form some of Central Asia's major water sources. The Naryn river, the most important, rises in the At Bashy Range and joins the Kara Darya

The majestic peaks of the Tien Shan run east to west for the entire length of Kyrgyzstan

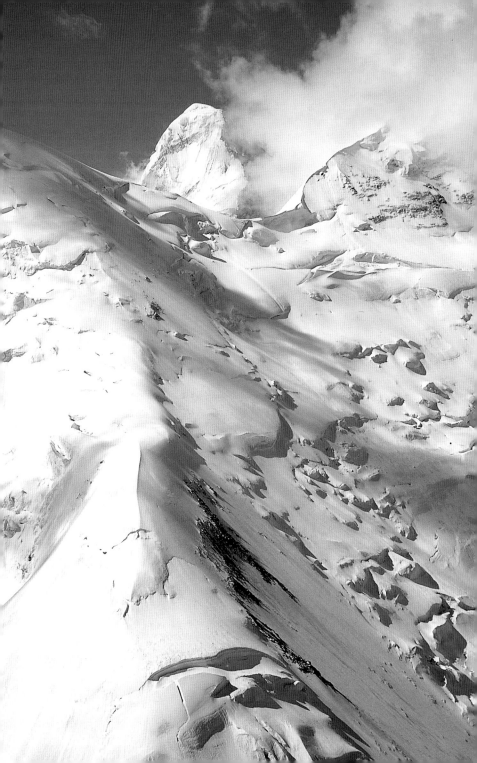

in the Fergana valley to become the Syr Darya, which waters Uzbekistan. The Naryn river supports seven power stations. The Chui river is channelled into a major irrigation canal along the Kazakh border, before fanning out into the arid Kazakh steppe. The Sary Jaz, Inylchek and Ak Shyrak rivers flow east to China's thirsty Tarim basin.

Environment

> *One should not treat badly a snake that has not done harm to you. Let even small insects live their own life.*
>
> Asan Kaigy (Kyrgyz *akyn*)

Kyrgyzstan is an unusual land. Despite its small size, it has a large variety of plants and animals, possessing nearly one per cent of all known species in just 0.13 per cent of the world's land mass. The country is particularly rich in medicinal herbs, which were sold throughout the Soviet Union. Kyrgyzstan's ecology is fragile, and depends on the specific combition of species which have evolved here and which play an important part in processes such as the creation and preservation of soils, water distribution, cleaning of surface waters, and atmospheric composition. The high level of adaptation to the extreme conditions means that once extinct, these species and the functions they provide cannot be replaced by other types of organism.

Preservation of the environmental ecosystem took a low priority in Soviet planning and the Kyrgyz government inherited a slew of Soviet-era problems. There are 50 functioning enterprises using highly poisonous substances but no suitable storage sites. There are also 49 uranium dumps, containing 145 million tons of radioactive and toxic wastes, many of which are situated close to villages. Some 6,000 hectares of land have already been exposed to radioactive pollution. Over 90 per cent of land in the Osh region is contaminated by DDT and smaller, though still significant, percentages are common throughout the country.

The other major hangover from Soviet production schedules is the serious erosion of land as a result of overgrazing (one third of grasslands have become unusable). This has, however, been less of a problem since independence, as a result of the drastic drop in numbers of livestock.

Most worrying of all is the absence of adequate legislation to control the potentially damaging activities of private businesses. On several occasions, lorries carrying cyanide for use in the Kumtor gold mine crashed, spilling their cargo into river systems leading to Lake Issyk Kul.

Kyrgyzstan has lost half of its forest cover in the last 50 years. The economic difficulties since independence have driven people to live more directly from the environment: households fell trees for fuel and have encroached upon the fragile forest ecosystems of Sary Chelek, Talas, Fergana and Besh Aral just to survive, causing irreparable damage. Attempts at reforestation have failed due to the vulnerability of young trees in such a harsh climate; research shows that only ten per cent of trees transplanted since 1997 have survived.

Extinction of animal and plant species has resulted from over-hunting, degradation of soil and water, and loss of habitat. Research suggests that global warming is likely to destroy 70 per cent of the world's colder habitats by the end of this century, resulting in the extinction of several more plant and animal species.

The future holds some promise, however. The government recently developed a National Biodiversity Strategy which will lead, in the coming years, to a series of wide-ranging projects to address the interrelated ecological and social issues of environmental degradation and poverty. The West Tien Shan Inter-State Biodiversity Project, covering Sary Chelek, Chatkal and Besh Aral as well as connected areas of Uzbekistan and Kazakhstan, is a comprehensive programme with elements addressing conservation, education and the creation of alternative livelihoods through grants and training.

FLORA AND FAUNA

Kyrgyzstan boasts a rich diversity of habitats. Much of the country is dominated by mountain and high plateau ecosystems, with habitats ranging from alpine meadows to tundra and glaciers. The lower slopes of these mountains support globally important areas of forest—including the rare walnut and pistachio forests of the south (currently under threat from a foreign firm), and important stands of juniper and Tien Shan pine in the north.

This diversity of Kyrgyzstan's habitat underlies its variety of plant and animal life. The botanical diversity of the country is particularly astounding—including about 400 species found only in this country—often with highly restricted distributions in high mountain areas. Of particular note are a range of endemic tulips (*Tulipa spp.*) and wild onions (*Allium spp.*), as well as other bulbous species such as anemone, crocus and colchicum. The high meadows support a number of alpine specialities including wild-flowers such as edelweiss (*Lontopodium alpinum*) and the rare Aigul (moon) flower found only on the Turkestan range. The forests to the south of Kyrgyzstan support a wide range of wild relatives of fruit and nut species, including walnuts, pistachio, almond, apples, pears, cherry and pomegranate.

The animal life of Kyrgyzstan is equally varied. Insect life is abundant throughout the country (over 10,000 species have been documented). The dry, open steppe lands support species such as the goitred gazelle (*Gazella subgutturosa*), great bustard (*Otis tarda*), and corsac fox (*Vulpes carsac*), although in much lower numbers than before. In addition, ground squirrels (*Spermophilus spp.*) are commonly seen (often from a car window). European red squirrels (*Sciurus vulgaris*) occur even in urban parks.

The mountain habitats are typified by wild goats or ibex (*Capra ibex*) and the now rare Marco Polo sheep (*Ovis ammon*), with its distinctive coiled horns. Only the very lucky will come across signs of the snow leopard (*Uncia uncia*) which still stalks the snow-capped peaks of the Tien Shan. In contrast, one of the most common animals to be seen in the mountains are the marmots—a medium-sized rodent—often visible as bundles of pale fur sitting outside their burrows. Various species occur in Kyrgyzstan, and if you are lucky you may come across one of the rarer long-tailed marmots (*Marmota caudata*) or the giant Menzbier's marmot (*Marmota menzbieri*), which is restricted to the Tien Shan mountains.

Tigers and cheetahs once roamed the forests and plains of Kyrgyzstan, but these are long extinct. The only remaining big cat species is the elusive snow leopard. Other carnivores include wolves (*Canis lupus*), foxes, declining populations of Asiatic wild dog (*Cuon alpinus*) and the Tien Shan brown bear (*Ursus arctos isabellinus*). Remnant populations of European otter (*Lutra lutra*) are found in the Alay valley in the south-west.

Of particular note is the birdlife of Kyrgyzstan—a birdwatcher's paradise with over 360 species recorded, including an intermingling of European species with more unusual birds from Asia and China. A wide range of raptors is visible—including vultures and eagles (such as the rare black vulture (*Aegypius monarchus*) and imperial eagle (*Aguita heliaca*)). The wetlands of the country support a wide diversity of wildfowl, especially during the migration periods.

Nature is important to Kyrgyz culture; handicraft designs take inspiration from the patterns of the natural world, while folklore and music rely heavily on a spiritual association with nature, reflecting the Kyrgyz people's nomadic roots.

Around Arslanbob lush valleys and hillsides give way to harsh craggy peaks

People

ETHNIC GROUPS

The population of Kyrgyzstan at the end of 2006 was 5.2 million, giving a density of 26 people per square kilometre. Over half the population live in the Fergana valley (just 15 per cent of Kyrgyzstan's territory). An estimated 65.1 per cent of the nation live and work in rural areas. Kyrgyzstan is a multi-national society comprising at least 23 national groups. The ethnic Kyrgyz make up 66.3 per cent of the population but figures change constantly due to the continued exodus of Slavic peoples since independence.

Uzbek boy with herb tea

Large-scale migration has been a major problem since independence. According to UNDP statistics, one seventh of the population of Kyrgyzstan moved into, out of or around the country between 1991 and 1998. Minority populations in particular have taken the opportunity to return to what is still regarded as their homelands; Russians, Ukrainians and Germans are drawn by higher salaries in their land of origin. In spite of the president's stated commitment to an equal society, inter-ethnic tensions are very real. Russians in particular feel they are being pushed out of jobs and denied opportunities to enter government. Between 1989 and 1999, the Russian population reduced by some 34 per cent (273,000) and the German population by around 79 per cent (61,000). The exodus continues.

About 14 per cent of Kyrgyzstan's people are **Uzbeks**, who live principally in and around the Fergana valley, a natural extension of Uzbekistan. Firm believers in Islam, they are traditionally settled people and culturally quite distinct from the Kyrgyz. Typically, they are traders and farmers and dominate the cotton farms in Kyrgyzstan.

The **Russians** are the largest Slavic minority, accounting for about 11.2 per cent of the population. Most live in Bishkek, along the north shore of Lake Issyk Kul and in Talas. They began to arrive in Kyrgyzstan in the latter half of the 19th century in response to Russian government promises of land grants and tax breaks and many communities were moved wholesale during World War II. They work as settled farmers, technicians and academics and formed the Soviet intellectual elite; thus their mass departure is a serious brain drain for Kyrgyzstan.

The **Ukrainians** are a dwindling population and now account for only 0.8 per cent of the population. Some 53 per cent (36,000) have left since independence.

MARRIAGE PROPOSAL

*O*ne day Fate, in the form of the aqsaqal, approached me. He came into my yurt one evening, sat down by the fire, and began to take long draughts of the tea I offered him. Then he let fly:

'You are no longer a stranger and an urus [outsider] in our aul!' I guessed what the wily old man was trying to get at, and as I had long foreseen some such proposition I had an answer ready: 'You speak truly, O my father'.

'At home in your own country have you a lady wife who waits on you?' Manfully I lied: 'Yes, my father.'

'It isn't right that you should live alone in your yurt. The days are short and the nights are long. Your lady will understand if you take a servant girl to bed.'

'In my country that isn't done, father. Besides I am poor. I have neither camel nor horse to offer as a bride-price.'

'No one will think of expecting a bride-price from you. The bigger girl who is serving you has no relations but a grandmother. She is willing to let you take the girl for nothing. I have talked the matter over with her.'

'I'll think about it father.'

For a few days I was left in peace, then the aqsaqal paid me another call. Again he sat down by the fire, put salt and fat into his tea, and swallowed it with noisy grunts:

'I was a guest in your yurt the other day.'

'Indeed I remember, father.'

'I then spoke to you about Maimakha!'

'Yes, father.'

'Her grandmother says that Maimakha is fifteen and the girl says she will no longer be unwed, for she feels it is a disgrace.'

'She must marry another then.'

'But she wants to marry you, my brother.'

'Since when is it the custom amongst the Qirghiz that the girl should seek out for herself the man she wants to marry?'

For a long time the old man sat silent, staring into the fire. 'Take a whip and thrash the idea out of her head. Thus you will have peace.'

'You forget, my father, that I am, after all, an urus. In my country no man strikes a woman.' Another lengthy pause. I filled the chilim with Farghana tobacco and held it towards my guest. Then I gave tongue again to make an end of the business. 'Father, do you know what a kafir is?'

'Yes, an Unbeliever.'

'Well, look you, I am an Unbeliever, and moreover I am a penitent and I have taken on me a vow not for three years to touch a woman. Am I to break my vow for Maimakha's sake? That you could not ask of me.'

Shaking his head, the old man stood up, wrapped his fur mantle about him, and went out. After that evening I heard no more of marriage and a few weeks later I learned that Maimakha had consoled herself and was going to be married in a few days, not to a poor penniless devil like me, but to a fine young Qirghiz, who was able to pay a handsome bride-price for her.

Gustav Krist, Alone Through the Forbidden Land, 1939

(*above*) *At-Bashy family*
(*below left*) *Kyrgyz horseman; (below right) Kyrgyz man sporting a* kalpak

(*above*) A manaschi *at work*
(*below*) *Uzbek girl*

About one per cent of Kyrgyzstan's population is **Uighur**, living mainly around Bishkek, Ozgon and Jalal-Abad. Uighurs are a Turkic people related to the Uzbeks and based in Xinjiang, China. Most of the Uighurs in Bishkek are descendants of refugees who have fled persecution at the hands of the Chinese since 1881. The Uighurs in the south are a far older community: some families date as far back as the tenth century Karakhanid Dynasty. Intermarriage with the Uzbeks is relatively common. The Uighurs are mostly active in trade and farming.

The **Tatars** currently number 51,700 and are another Turkic people. They tend to live in Bishkek and Osh. The Tatars came to Kyrgyzstan from the Volga region of Russia during colonisation to work as traders, clerks and clerics; further groups were deported from the Crimea in 1944. Some 25,000 have left the republic since 1991, mainly to return to the Crimea or to Russia.

The **Kazakhs** (about 1 per cent of the population) live along the border with Kazakhstan, at Talas, in the vicinity of Karabalta, and at Tokmak and the Karkara valley. Their lifestyle and economy are similar to those of their Kyrgyz cousins.

Around 0.6 per cent of Kyrgyzstan's population is made up of **Turks**, who live around Bishkek, Tokmak and in the south. They are mostly Shia Muslim Meskhetian Turks who were moved from Georgia and Azerbaijan in the 1940s and eke out a living as small farmers, in technical professions or trade.

The settlements around Bishkek, especially Karabalta, Alexandrovka, Kant and Ivanovka, are home to Dungan and Korean communities, who jointly make up about 1.5 per cent of Kyrgyzstan's population. The **Dungan** (Muslim Chinese, known in China as Hui) are descendants of refugees from Xinjiang who fled persecution in the 19th century. Karakol also has a significant Dungan population.

The **Koreans**, totalling around 19,800, were deported from Sakhalin and Vladivostok in the Russian Far East between 1931 and 1945 by Stalin, who feared they might become a 'fifth column' for the Japanese, who at the time occupied neighbouring Manchuria and Korea. Both the Dungan and Korean people are predominant in specialized agriculture and technical professions, and belong to the most dynamic and prosperous communities in Kyrgyzstan.

Finally, there are 40,500 Persian-speaking **Tajiks**, most of them farmers in the far south. After civil unrest began in Tajikistan in 1993, some 13,900 refugees from Tajikistan took refuge in the country. Initially they set up camp around Osh and Jalal-Abad, but after tensions arose with the host communities, many were resettled in northern places such as Karabalta and Ivanovka where they were given the houses of emigrated Slavs. Many have since returned but the ethnic Kyrgyz Tajiks have stayed.

CLANS IN KYRGYZSTAN

Legend has it that long ago two children, the only survivors of a war with a neighbouring tribe, were brought to Issyk Kul and cared for by a deer and that their offspring were the forefathers of the various Kyrgyz tribes. Tribal and regional origins remain a central part of Kyrgyz identity and society. As one author put it: 'If two Kyrgyz, even Russified ones, sit together, in no time they'll find out where the other comes from and what his or her lineage is.'

Today, there are some 30 Kyrgyz tribes or *sanjira*. They are grouped into two main regional blocks, which do not only have distinct identities but also compete for political power: the northerners or Tagai, who also include the tribes of the central plateau and the Kyrgyz of Kazakhstan; and the southerners, or Ich Kylyk, who include the Kyrgyz living in Tajikistan and China.

In the north, running roughly from Sary Chelek in the south-west to the eastern end of Lake Issyk Kul, the major tribes are the Sary Bagysh (to which the president and his entourage belong), the Solto, the Bagysh and the Bugu. Because they have lived with Slav settlers for almost one and a half centuries the northern Kyrgyz tend to be more Russified than their kinsfolk elsewhere in the country—even though the rates of Kyrgyz–Slav intermarriage have always been low.

In the southern Fergana and Alay regions the main tribes are the Adygene (around Osh), the Kadyrsha, Kara Teit, Naiman, Bostan, Kesek and many others. The mountains close to China and Tajikistan are home to half a dozen of clans collectively nicknamed Kara ('black') Kyrgyz. As a result of increased contact with the sedentary Uzbeks, Uighurs and Tajiks, the southern Kyrgyz (who were once goverened by the Kokand khanate) have taken on board more Islamic culture than their northern cousins. The dialects are also quite distinct (the southerners have absorbed some Farsi into their language), to the extent that they sometimes have difficulty understanding one another.

Finally, a collection of tribes live in the central plateau, covering Song Kul, Suusamyr and southwestern Issyk Kul. Here the Sajak are dominant. In the At-Bashy and Torugart area live the Cherik. Since these regions are more isolated and ethnically homogenous, the Sajak are often considered as the 'purest' Kyrgyz.

Of course, due to numerous migrations and deportations, the picture is far more complex than this. Nevertheless, tribal and regional networks remained strong throughout the Soviet period and continue to do so today, especially since many people now depend on the informal economy. So, whether it is about political power or a spot in the bazaar to sell your produce, much functions on the basis of 'kin helps kin'.

THE LANGUAGE PROBLEM

Language is a powerful political tool that is still being wielded today. In the Soviet era Russian was the dominant language, a passport to education, professional information and the State, whereas Kyrgyz was used socially.

Following independence in 1991, Kyrgyz was established as the state language. In reality, though, language use continued as before, with many urban Kyrgyz shocked to discover how patchy their knowledge of their native tongue was. The Russians and other minority nationalities were suddenly faced with the need to learn Kyrgyz. In order to formalise its position as the language most commonly used in government and official business, and to try to retain the Slav community, in May 2000, Russian was made a second state language, on an equal footing with Kyrgyz. Later in the year, a Kyrgyz language exam was instituted for presidential candidates.

When Kyrgyz was adopted as the state language, tensions emerged between the urban Russian-speaking Kyrgyz youth and the young rural Kyrgyz-speakers who moved to Bishkek from all over the country in search of better opportunities. This sometimes violent confrontation between the children of a single nation, divided by language, sometimes disguised the reality that most citizens don't really care whether or not their leader can reproduce a few set texts in Kyrgyz—their dream is of an intelligent, pragmatic leader who will strive to improve living standards, stamp out corruption and safeguard the constitution.

In spite of this politicisation of language, many Kyrgyz people have a deep appreciation of Russian which has given them access to Russian and world literature. There has been an enrichening exchange between the two cultures of the complex heritage of jokes, stories and, above all, songs that both peoples value so highly.

Kyrgyz Culture—Past and Present

TRADITIONAL CULTURE

The cities and towns of Kyrgyzstan greet you with a very Soviet face. At first glance you might get the impression that little remains of Kyrgyz culture from the 150 years of Russian occupation, but a closer look will reveal that the fundaments of pre-Russian nomadic society are alive and kicking.

The fluid nature of tribal society has been ideally suited to adapt to the ebb and flow of humanity surging into the region over the last two millennia. The people we know today as the Kyrgyz are actually a mix of the original groups that migrated from the banks of the Siberian Yenisei River, overlaid with Mongols and a host of smaller tribes whom they absorbed over the centuries. The national hero, Manas, is credited with uniting the warring tribes.

Early travellers to the region commented on the Kyrgyz camps, numbering 50 or more yurts. These were *ails* (villages) and comprised one man (the chief), his married sons and unmarried daughters. Sons were given a yurt on marriage (nor-

At the central bazaar in Osh

mally provided as part of the girl's dowry), except for the youngest who stayed to look after his parents and eventually inherit their yurt. Wealthier chiefs might temporarily take in orphans, hired workers and destitute men who would live as part of the family, receiving animals, food and clothing as payment.

A group of *ails* was headed by a *bi*, (or *manap*), an elder who made decisions about the general welfare of the group with the help of a committee of advisers (*aksakals*) from the *ails*. The *bi* was not elected but was the most senior man by birth in a group of *ails*. In reality, however, a leader's influence depended on the respect he inspired amongst his people so the inherited position had also to be earned. Respect for elders was imbued into children from birth. The *bi* had the job of resolving dis-

Shyrdaks *provide yurts with warm, decorative lining*

putes and difficulties; if the people had no confidence in his wisdom they would take their troubles to another elder. A *bi* had not only to be wise but also wealthy enough to fulfil his duties of hospitality and assistance.

The Kyrgyz have always been intolerant of authoritative leadership (to their cost in Soviet times) and if a *bi* became too autocratic, the *ail* could move away to join another group of tribes—one of the advantages of being nomadic. Soviet literature seized on the social hierarchy of the Kyrgyz nomads, deriding the *bi* for their cruel exploitation of the Kyrgyz masses, but 19th century reports corroborate the Russian Turkic scholar W. Barthold's statement that 'the Kara Kirghiz [Kyrgyz] had neither princes nor nobles; the elders... were not chosen by any kind of election, but owed their position entirely to their personal influence'.

By the end of the 19th century, the Kyrgyz still celebrated their unity as a people every year when a khan was elected amid horseback games and great festivities, where *akyns* (bards) wove local characters and events into their stories and songs. The khan's appointment was symbolic only, as real power lay with the clan leaders.

It would be a mistake, however, to imagine an idyllic nomadic life; yurts were damp and smoky, herders were constantly involved in sheep raids and inter-tribal battles. One punishment common on the pastures was to tie the guilty party face-upwards on the ground and watch him be trampled by a flock of sheep.

The shaggy sturdy horses of the Kyrgyz had none of the fire of the Turkmen's elegant steeds. Nonetheless, they formed the backbone of the economy, providing transport, meat and *koumys* (fermented mare's milk), to the extent that something of a cult grew up around horses in Kyrgyz culture (see page 262). The size of a man's herd of horses was an indication of his status far beyond the herd's actual economic value. In spring, the birth of the first foal meant the first batch of *koumys*, cause for celebration and feasting. Other livestock included goats, two-humped Bactrian camels, yaks, typical Asian fatty-tailed sheep and the inevitable scraggy dog whose descendants are still today serving the dual purpose of protection and herding.

Cattle only began to appear with the Russians. Grazing patterns were efficient and made the most of available fodder: in spring, horses would be released onto pasture first to break up the ice and snow with their hard hooves; they would be followed by camels and finally the sheep who nibbled grass down to the roots. On the steppes a thaw followed by a very heavy freeze would sometimes cause a *dzhut*—covering the land with unbreakable ice, which prevented grazing and killed off many animals.

Some tribal groups had winter quarters made of stone or clay, where they grew wheat and barley. As spring dispelled the snows, some of the men would stay to tend the crops while the families dispersed into the mountains. The group did not rove arbitrarily but each within a territory tacitly acknowledged to be for their personal use. They stored only limited fodder so it was crucial that animals fattened up sufficiently by autumn to make it through the rigours of a harsh winter. Animals unlikely to survive were killed for food in the autumn. Whole herds were occasionally wiped out during harsh winters.

Like today, the traditional diet consisted of meat and dairy products. *Koumys*, fermented mare's milk, was considered a treat; families who could not afford this added water to curds made of boiled sheep's milk. Winter stores of food included little hard balls of cheese (*kurt*), still found today, smoke-dried meat, sausages made with horses' intestines and the preserved tail fat of sheep. They ate few vegetables.

The Kyrgyz welcomed any occasion for a celebration, which usually involved feasting, improvising witty songs, storytelling and horseback games. Marriage had an important social funcion, establishing social and financial ties between families. An arrangement was usually made between parents early, when the boy was aged 12–15 and the girl prepubescent. An early marriage ensured the girl's virginity, secured a bride price (*kalym*) for the young woman's parents and reduced the likelihood of young people falling in love and eloping. The bride price was (and still is) high, and generally paid in livestock. Poorer men would have to save up for years before being able to marry, or would earn their bride by working for her father.

The bride price was seen not as payment for chattel but as part of a contract, strengthening the marriage and indicating the groom's family's intention to care for the woman and her children. The young woman's dowry to her new family normally included a yurt, household equipment and jewellery, which could be inherited by her children only (polygamy was common).

Kyrgyz women undoubtedly occupied a lowly position but they had more freedom than the settled women of Central Asia. In games and celebrations, young men and women associated freely. A woman could divorce her husband and, on his death, had the right to remain single or marry outside the family, rather than be forced into a marriage with his brother. In her husband's absence and after his death, she was the boss.

THE YURT

For centuries, the superbly portable yurt has been a cornerstone of nomadic life throughout Central Asia, including Kyrgyzstan. Today, it has been replaced as the main form of dwelling by brick houses or Soviet-style concrete apartment blocks, but it retains a special place in Kyrgyz hearts, as both a tangible link to their nomadic past and a symbol of their national identity. The *tunduk*, the circular frame with wooden batons around the smoke hole at the top of the yurt, is even represented on the national flag. During birthdays, funerals and other special occasions, people often set up a yurt and invite friends to the *dastorkon* or feast. And in summer the yurt comes into its own again when shepherds take their flocks high in the mountains to graze.

In Kyrgyz the yurt is known as the *bozuy*, or 'grey house', after the black or grey wool used by ordinary shepherds. Only the clan chiefs could afford to use costly snow-white yurts called *ak-orgo*.

Yurts are believed to have been around for thousands of years and their structure has changed little. They consist of a framework of poplar poles (*kanats*), bent and fixed with leather nails and rawhide straps, around which a circular trellis wall (*kerege*) is erected. This collapses easily, concertina-like, for swift dismantling. Woven mats made of a reed, *chiy*, line the walls, and the whole structure is covered with several thick layers of felt (*kiyiz*), each of which is tied to strong poles dug into the ground. The top has a smoke hole (which is covered during rain) but today people use stoves with chimneys. Wealthy people line their yurts with brightly coloured *shyrdaks* (rugs) and use richly embroidered woven strips decorated with tassels to tie the yurt to the *kanats*.

Inside, space is allocated according to tradition. The left hand side (*er jak*) is reserved for men and contains horse and hunting gear, and the right hand side (*epche jak*), where the stove and cooking utensils are stored, is for women. At the back, opposite the entrance, is the *juk* where blankets and carpets are kept, usually on top of a richly carved or painted chest; the higher the *juk*, the richer the family. At night the blankets are spread out on *shyrdaks* (rugs) on the ground for beds; newly-weds usually sleep behind a curtain for extra privacy.

Maintaining the yurt and family involved a lot of work and, like today, women did most of it. Men and women both worked leather to make bags, clothing and saddles. Men tended the livestock while women milked the animals, looked after the food and children, made the clothes and bedding and saddled their husbands' horses. Women were meant to be expert at decorative needlework and started at an early age, turning out embroidery, appliqués and colourful felt *shyrdaks*, as well as making plain felt, to line yurts with in the autumn. The *ail* was largely self-sufficient, depending on itinerant craftsmen for iron pots, cooking utensils, bridle bits, jewellery, wooden saddles and yurt frames, and to decorate headstones for the dead.

Mazar Ukok jailoo where for generations herdsmen and their families spend the summer

Traditionally, the building of a new yurt was celebrated with great festivities. A ram's head would be tossed up with the words: 'May smoke always rise from this yurt! May the fire never go out in it!' A clan chief (or *manap*) measured the number of his subjects by counting the number of *tyutyuns* (columns of smoke) rising from a group of yurts. This word is still used in Kyrgyz villages to count the number of households. Dismantling an encampment was done in a few hours, with belongings and yurts rolled up into *shyrdaks* and packed on horses. The departure was a great event and took place ceremonially, in a particular order and accompanied with special songs.

The Soviet writer Victor Vitkovich described the valleys around Naryn in the late 1920s and early 1930s, in scenes that had changed little for generations:

> *In the middle of the valley, near a swift river with waters swirling from one bend to another and filling the air with the rattle of stones, there usually was the big, white ornamented yurt of a manap ... Close to the yurt of the feudal prince stood his winter clay house, the yurts of his wives and the yurts of the menials. Some of the latter were so poor that instead of a yurt they had an alachik: four posts covered with a piece of felt. The families of the labourers made and embroidered the felt for their manap, prepared the koumys for his table, smoked horseflesh sausages over the fire-places, made cheese and sweet curds from the sheep's milk, cooked mutton in soot-covered pots and distilled liquor from koumys, sometimes adding camels' milk to make it stronger.*

Not everyone extols the virtues of yurts, however. The Kyrgyz poet Aaly Tokombayev revealed the misery of a yurt in winter with the following lines:

How can they breathe in smoke so thick?
How keep together body and soul?
The young housewife takes a stick
To open up the chimney hole.
In vain—the wind drives back the smoke,
Tears blanket up our smarting eyes.
And what a cough! More troubles here
Than anyone can realise.
The wind, run amuck, tears the felt
With all its ever-growing strength.
Like the eagle's wings, the tatters flap
As if to fly away at length.
To keep the yurta from crashing down
We go and prop it up with poles.
The guests extend their freezing hands
To warm them at the hearth, poor souls.

In the epeche jak, woman's area of the yurt, a mother makes kaimak

HINTS ON ENJOYING A HOMESTAY OR YURT STAY IN KYRGYZSTAN

Hospitality is pivotal to Kyrgyz identity and culture—historically, it's a code for nomadic survival in a harsh terrain. As a result, behaviour around eating is much more ritualised than in western cultures; indeed, our casual attitude to eating could be seen as quite offensive.

Seating at mealtimes is important—the host would be failing parlously in his duty if he allowed a guest to sit with their back to the draught and danger of the door. That is his place, with his wife or another woman to his right—she will serve the food and ensure that teacups are replenished.

Most families perform the *omin*, a prayer in which cupped hands receive the blessing of God and are passed over the head and face, before and after meals. There's much debate about how visitors fit in to this; some argue that there is no point in doing it unless we understand and believe the significance of it, while others suggest that non-believers can perform the *omin* out of respect to the host and to honour their own spiritual beliefs.

Living cheek by jowl with people whose lifestyle is very different from our own means a certain amount of compromise is needed on both sides.

For most of us, this means adjusting to less comfort than we're used to. Accommodation in houses may be provided on beds with thick duvets or on a pile of traditional mattresses warmly stuffed with cotton or wool, laid on *shyrdaks* on the floor. In yurts it is invariably the latter—bring a sleeping bag.

Washing facilities are generally limited to a hand basin (increasingly with soap and towel), but not in a private space. Toilets are usually traditional long-drop, a hygienic minimum of 20 yards from the house—which can be a challenge if you become unwell. Toilet paper is now supplied in CBT households, whereas previously you'd be likely to find an old Russian novel to tear up and use for the job.

The hosts ask that we respect their culture and religion and avoid giving to begging children or paying for photos, as this breeds a dependency culture. Essential courtesies include always taking your shoes off at the entrance to a house or yurt; keeping feet clean or covered and never pointing the souls of your feet towards people or food. CBT also asks visitors not to smoke in people's homes and if you need extra blankets, to ask for *joorkan* rather than helping yourself to the large stack in the room.

See also Customs, page 100

FESTIVALS AND GAMES

Spurred on partly by tourists, the Kyrgyz are beginning to rediscover their love of festivals and games. Most are organised by CBT but they are still enjoyed by their Kyrgyz participants and are not yet jaded parodies of traditional culture. For up-to-date details, check www.cbtkyrgyzstan.kg; www.advantour.com and www.fantasticasia.com. In 2007 the following were held:

March: **Kok Boru**, Bishkek Hippodrome, government-organised traditional horse game involving two teams and a goat carcass.

May: **National Applied Arts**, Kara Alma, 55 kilometres from Jalal-Abad: CBT-organised displays of patchwork and loomwork, Kyrgyz cuisine, games.

June: **National Cuisine and Utensils**, Sarala-Saz *jailoo*, 65 kilometres from Kochkor: CBT-organised music, games and Kyrgyz cuisine.

July: **Manas at Song Kul**, Lake Song Kul: government-organised cultural festival with story-tellers, music, traditional cuisine, horse games.

July: **National Horse Games**, Cholpon Ata, Novinomad-organised horse games, handicrafts.

July: **National Horse Games**, Sarala-Saz *jailoo*, 65 kilometres from Kochkor: CBT-organised games, folklore show, Kyrgyz cuisine, handicrafts.

July: **International Oimo Festival**, Tamchy, Lake Issyk Kul: CACSA-organised Central Asian crafts fair, also music and national cuisine.

July: **Felt festival**, Kara-Too village, near Kochkor: CBT-organised demonstrations of wool-dying and felt-making.

July: **Cleaning up at Lake Song Kul**, northern shore of Lake Song Kul: CBT-organised games, folklore show, horseback riding (optional).

July: **Festival of Folklore and Cuisine**, Jeti-Oguz valley, near Karakol: CBT-organised felt-making, music, tasting of national cuisines.

July: **Kyrgyz National Ceremonies and Traditions**, Tash Rabat, Naryn oblast: CBT-organised display of Kyrgyz traditions, eg the wedding ceremony, folklore.

July: **National Horse Games**, Cholpon-Ata, Lake Issyk Kul: CBT-organised games, folklore show, Kyrgyz cuisine, handicrafts.

August: **Birds of Prey**, Manzhyly-Ata area, near Bokonbaevo, Lake Issyk Kyl: CBT-organised demonstration of falconry, yurts, handicrafts.

August: **Kyrgyz Kochu**, from the southern shore of Lake Song Kul to Jangy Talap village, Naryn oblast: CBT-organised games, music and dismantling of yurts.

August: **National Horse Games and Traditions**, from Bel Tam to Jai Chi, southern Lake Issyk Kul: CBT-organised games, folklore, Kyrgyz cuisine

Autumn: **Central Asian Crafts Fair**, Bishkek: CACSA-organised exhibitions and demonstrations of handicrafts.

AT CHABYSH HORSE FESTIVAL

This is one of the most exciting annual events and takes place in late October/early November. This four-day mix of sport and culture, organised by Kyrgyz Ate, whose aim is to preserve the Kyrgyz horse (see page 7), begins with a day of culture in Bishkek, then moves to Ak Tuz, close to Barskoon on the south shore of Lake Issyk Kul.

As well as traditional horse games and races, there are *akyns* (bards), eagle and falconry displays, handicrafts, music and international guests which in 2007 included the Sioux of Dakota and craftsmen from Tajikistan. There's also an astonishing 47-kilometre, high-altitude endurance race, *Bash baïgue*. It attracts thousands of visitors, mostly Kyrgyz, and is probably the closest you're likely to get to a genuine celebration of traditional culture.

KYRGYZ CULTURE UNDER ATTACK

When money made its appearance, the well-being of the people went away.
Moldo Kylych, *akyn*

How far did Kyrgyz culture survive Russian occupation and Soviet indoctrination? The answer has to be complex and highly subjective. What is certain is that, in many respects, it is the traditional values and patterns that determine social conduct today.

By the end of the 19th century, Kyrgyz society was already undermined. The growth of mining and trading under the Russians, and an increased reliance on bazaars, meant the traditional Kyrgyz economy of self-sufficiency and barter was being dismantled. At the same time the social structure was dislocated: the *bi* were drawn into the Russian administration, away from their traditional role, and increasing land ownership weakened tribal and kinship ties. The authority of the *bi* was challenged by the Russian courts, whose rulings were biased, arbitrary and generally ignored. Social harmony came under pressure as the gap between rich and poor widened.

Determined to create 'Soviet Man', the Soviet authorities mounted a multi-layered assault on local cultures and beliefs. After the trauma of collectivisation and the horrors

of Stalin's purges, in which the revered *Manaschi* (reciters of the Manas epic) and *akyns* (song-story-tellers) were all but wiped out, the Kyrgyz adopted a dual life, outwardly complying with the Soviet system while continuing many of their old practices in private. Bride price, designated a 'crime against the state' (along with polygamy and marriage below the age of 18) dwindled in popularity but was still paid. In 1928 it averaged one horse and 30 sheep, though livestock was gradually being replaced by cash. Dowries were given, though now in the shape of European style furniture—the new status symbol.

It seems almost miraculous that so much of Kyrgyz culture survived. In Soviet days the Kyrgyz excelled in finding ways to circumvent the regulations. Within the collective farms

Bread did not appear on Kyrgyz tables until the 19th century

(*kolkhoz*) a small number of animals were allowed for private ownership. The Kyrgyz took this so much to heart that, in 1961, one farm counted 560 *kolkhoz*-owned and 10,470 privately-owned goats.

In the 1960s, Nikita Khrushchev decided that the nomadic lifestyle was, after all, an efficient means of farming steppe and mountain, and that the Kyrgyz and Kazakhs showed considerable knowhow in this field, so a semi-nomadic life re-emerged in which the family groups of the collective farms took to the mountains in the summer months. Mobile adult education units were set up in so-called 'Red Yurts' to ensure the 'correct thinking' of the nomads.

In this turbulent time the only traditional craft to survive truly intact was felt-making, although artificial dyes introduced new harsher colours. Silverwork skills were lost and traditional embroidery was replaced by Russian, Uzbek or Ukrainian designs.

While the Kyrgyz have undoubtedly absorbed Russian elements into their lives, many of their non-traditional accoutrements are foreign, not just Russian. Bread only started to appear on a Kyrgyz '*dastorkon*' (table) in the late 19th century, but as Uzbek *nan* rather than Russian *khleb*; the Kyrgyz adopted Russian samovars, but only at the same time that tea was adopted from China.

Although nomadic life is firmly a thing of the past, the yurt still holds a fond place in people's hearts. Those who can afford a yurt put one up in the garden every summer, while many rural people are still semi-nomadic, spending the summer months in yurts on the high pastures with their livestock. However, ask them if they would like to go back to living in a yurt full-time and the response is a resounding 'No! It's damp, there's no heating and no TV!' A Kyrgyz journalist recently summed up 20th century changes thus:

> Now, looking back at our paradoxical past, with all our hatred of the social-ist-type command administration system, we nevertheless should do justice to it, first of all for the excellently exercised policy of transition from a nomadic to a more settled life.

Religion

ISLAM

Islam first appeared in Central Asia in the seventh century but was not declared the official religion of what is modern-day Kyrgyzstan until the tenth century, under the auspices of the Karakhanid empire. It was the Silk Route merchants who were responsible for spreading a veneer of Islam amongst the mountain nomads (see page 14).

The Kyrgyz never converted wholesale to Islam. Certainly they did not adhere to the 'five pillars' of Islam: biblical names were invoked alongside Allah's in shamanistic practices; they prayed when the mullah visited, but not in mosques; they had no need for almsgiving, as the unfortunate were already catered for within their own society; and there was no fasting during Ramadan, nor pilgrimage to Mecca.

A number of Muslim practices, such as circumcision and commemorating the first anniversary of a person's death, were grafted on to existing shamanistic rituals, though the associated festivities remained Kyrgyz in style. Weddings and funerals came to be conducted by a mullah if one was present; otherwise they went ahead just the same.

In the early 19th century much of Kyrgyzstan was incorporated into the Islamic Khanate of Kokand and a more thorough attempt at conversion was made. This was much more successful in the south of the country, due to its proximity to the devout Uzbeks of the Fergana valley; greater industrialisation and Russianisation on the north side of the Tien shan barrier combined to reinforce their more secular outlook. This factor exacerbates the serious north-south divide in the country today.

After 1917, Islam grew in popularity in Kyrgyzstan, amid the horror of violent change and, no doubt, due partly to the newly adopted settled lifestyle. Shrines were visited by more prilgrims than ever before and hundreds of people attended Friday prayers at mosques. Stalin's 'Movement of the Godless', which was particularly intense in the 1930s, effectively pushed Islam underground, where it was kept alive by the Sufis, Islam's mystical ascetics. To boost morale during World War II, rules on religion were relaxed; judging by the intensification of atheist propoganda in the 1950s this led to an Islamic resurgence. In 1951, the Tien Shan Komsomol (communist party youth) held nearly 3,000 anti-religious lectures in Kyrgyzstan and southern Kazakhstan and in Kazakhstan a special leaflet was produced entitled, 'What an Atheist Should Know About the Koran'. As is common with peoples under seige, their worship and beliefs turned inwards, invisible to the prying eyes of the KGB.

In the Gorbachev era of *glasnost* in the late 1980s, Islam resurfaced even before the Central Asian countries had shuffled off their Soviet mantle. Today Islam is far less visible in the north than in the south of Kyrgyzstan but it is making a silent comeback there as well, especially on the streets of suburban Bishkek and nearby villages.

Today, Kyrgyzstan is a secular state and the government preaches a policy of tolerance for all religious beliefs. Since the 11 September 2001 attacks on the World Trade Centre in New York, there has been increased scrutiny of Islamic groups in Kyrgyzstan, especially the Khizb ut-Tahrir, which has now been banned. While the organisation's aim is to establish an Islamic state in the Kyrgyz and Uzbek Fergana valley, it espouses non-violent means, but is considered vulnerable to infiltration by more radical elements. Nevertheless, Islamic fundamentalism is extremely unlikely to gain a firm foothold in Kyrgyzstan. (See Geo-Political Position on page 58).

Most of the shiny new mosques which have sprung up around Kyrgyzstan were funded by Turkey or Saudi Arabia; some were built by local people themselves, often by the system of *ashar*, whereby villagers donate money or voluntary labour for public works.

Today Islam is jostling for position with Christian groups all vying for converts amongst a people in spiritual disarray. However, most Kyrgyz people consider themselves Muslim and respect the mores of the religion, even if many don't practise it. Ask virtually any Kyrgyz man or woman if they are Muslim and they will say 'of course'. Ask them if they go to the mosque or observe Ramadan, however, and most will say 'no'. Perhaps Islam's most important role in modern-day Kyrgyzstan is as a source of cultural and ideological identity in the vacuum left by the discrediting of communism. Given the rise of social ills and the increasing desperation and exploitation of the vulnerable sectors of society, many argue that religion provides a necessary moral base.

SHAMANISM

Neither religion nor belief system, shamanism is the ancient practice of drawing on the power of the spirits of the earth, the animal kingdom and the heavens for the benefit of groups or individuals. Shamanism came to Kyrgyzstan with the earliest invaders from the Siberian region and is thought to have emerged initially in the Neolithic period. The word shaman comes from the Tungus-Manchurian word *saman* meaning 'he who knows' (the equivalent in Kyrgyz is *bakshi*). Women may also be *bakshi*, and in fact there are said to be more female than male practitioners nowadays.

In nomadic times the shaman was central to the life of the tribe, providing auspicious dates and rituals for important events, and dispensing solutions to a range of spiritual and medical problems. Central to the practice is the belief in many levels of spiritual consciousness and that our souls ultimately belong to a spirit world which ordinary mortals cannot access. The shaman is the messenger between the physical and spiritual universes and the link with all supernatural phenomena. He once performed ritual sacrifices for warriors going into battle in order to harness the powers and strengths of particular animals. Both medicine man and prophet, the shaman escorts the soul of the dead into the next world. Indeed, descriptions of these journeys provide the most dramatic accounts of shamanistic missions.

The shaman at work enters a trance state, while retaining control over his consciousness as it leaves his body and travels to other spheres. He does not become 'possessed' by another force or being. The spiritual journeys he recounts appear in Kyrgyz epics and songs. His most common role is as healer. The soul of a sick person is considered to be missing, having either wandered off by itself or been stolen by demons. The shaman's job is to ascertain which, and to find and escort it back.

The shaman, who is believed to be 'appointed' by the spirits, often has special physical characteristics (for example, an extra finger) and is assisted by a group of spirits, with a particular spirit guardian who may be in the form of another person or an animal.

Some remnants of shamanist practice are still alive in Kyrgyz life today: many will call a shaman as well as consulting a doctor. The smouldering branches of the *archa*, a kind of juniper, are waved around a house to rid it of evil spirits or to exorcise the lingering vibes of a disliked visitor. In the 1950s, the Russian writer Victor Vitkovich witnessed (with much Soviet scepticism) a *bakshi* invoking shamanist rituals to cure a sick boy:

> *He rubbed spruce resin on the sheep-gut of his komuz and ran his fingers across them. It seemed as though a whole swarm of wasps were droning softly … The Bakshy sang a song: 'O insect with a camel's head, I'll force you out, don't joke with me! Be gone, jinn, be gone, before the breath of Suleiman!'*
>
> *The jinn was in the yurta! The Bakshy seized a whip and began to flog the invisible jinn … With the knife the Bakshy began to prick the [boy] in the belly, chest, feet, head and arms. This meant the jinns were rushing back and forth in his body. A whistle came from the witch-doctor's lips, which had turned blue from the tension … The boy groaned and twisted … the jinns had darted out of the boy's body through his mouth.*
>
> Victor Vitkovich, *Kirghizia Today*

Arts

MUSIC AND STORYTELLING

Central to Kyrgyz culture are the songs, poems and stories performed by *akyns* (itinerant bards). The Kyrgyz word, *yr*, encompasses all these styles.

Akyns had a repertoire of lyrics which they adapted as the occasion required; they were hired for weddings, anniversaries and other festivities to bestow a blessing with their witty elegant verse. A particularly revered group of *akyns* were *Manaschi*, the narrators of the Manas epic (see the Manas Special Topic, page 50).

Yr carried an ethical, philosophical and moral message, giving guidance, hope and courage in the face of constant war, upheaval and inter-tribal strife. Some *akyns* became famous, such as Toktogul, Togolok Moldo and Bokonbaev Joomart, whose names grace streets and towns throughout Kyrgyzstan today.

Early travellers to the region were astonished at the eloquence of the Kyrgyz, their capacity to improvise songs and the fluency of the language. The 19th century Russian anthropologist, Radlov, wrote 'one cannot but admire how the Kyrgyz people master their language… He expresses his thoughts exactly and understandably, making his speech somewhat graceful… That is why folk poetry of the Kyrgyz has reached such a high level'. Even today language is highly respected and great value placed on being articulate and circumspect in one's use of language.

It is said that long after the Tower of Babel spread confusion and misunderstanding between peoples, music brought the world together in a common language. It is central to Kyrgyz culture, and *akyns* were accompanied by the *komuz*, a three-stringed plucked instrument or by a *kyyak*, played with a bow. Wood, brass, horn and clay instruments create ethereal sounds while percussion reproduces chimes and the all-important sound of animal hooves on the hard earth.

LITERATURE

The only renowned modern Kyrgyz author is Chinghiz Aitmatov, born in Sheker in the Talas valley in 1928. Writing initially in Kyrgyz and later increasingly in Russian, he first achieved major literary recognition for his collection of short stories, *Tales of the Mountains and Steppes*, published in 1963. The collection won him the Lenin Prize and explores the themes of love and friendship, and the conflict between Soviet ideals, individual aspirations and traditional life. Although some are firmly located in the Soviet context many of his works make an accessible and compelling read.

A major Soviet writer, Aitmatov was on the governing board of many intellectual and cultural institutions. He continued to write ideologically acceptable literature throughout the 1960s and 70s and won the Soviet State Prize for Literature in 1968.

In 1973 he co-wrote a play, *The Ascent of Mount Fuji*, with a Kazakh, Kaltay Muhamedjanov, addressing the moral compromises made during the rule of Joseph Stalin. It was received with ambiguity in Moscow and popularity abroad.

During the 1980s his work became more overtly critical of government hypocrisy and the restrictions it placed on the individual. *The Day Lasts More than a Thousand*

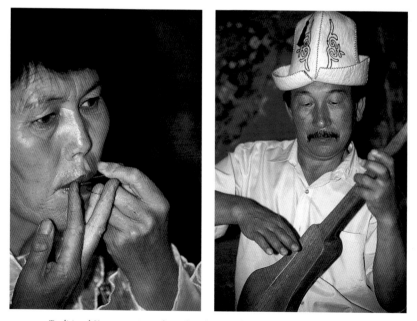

Traditional Kyrgyz music performed on the timir komuz *(left) and* komuz *(right)*

Years (1980) concerns a Kazakh worker who takes on the heroic task of burying a friend according to traditional Muslim rituals. *The Place of the Skull* (1986) explores the drain of youth into the drugs trade and the role of religion in providing a source of hope.

In spite of his implied criticism of the state, Aitmatov remained a member of the Supreme Soviet from 1966 until the demise of the USSR. He is currently Kyrgyz Ambassador to the European Union in Brussels.

Government and Politics

The president of the Kyrgyz Republic holds considerable authority and is directly elected every five years. There are effectively three arms to government: the Executive Branch, led by the President, Prime Minister and cabinet of ministers (appointed); the Legislative Branch (*Jorgorku Kenesh*), elected to serve five-year terms; and a Judicial Branch, headed by the Supreme Court whose judges are appointed for ten-year terms by the *Jorgorku Kenesh*.

Following the constitutional reform of 2006, the Prime Minister is appointed by the party which won most votes in the most recent parliamentary election—which has at times led to conflicts between Prime Minister and President.

The country is divided administratively into seven *oblast*, (provinces) plus the capital: Chui, Issyk Kul, Naryn, Osh, Jalal-Abad, Talas and Batken. Each *oblast* has a governor and is divided into *rayon* (districts), which further divide into *ayil okmotu*, city, town or village councils.

The government is committed by its constitution to a democratic, secular society with freedom of worship and expression and an uncensored press. Certainly, Kyrgyzstan's press is the freest in Central Asia. Observers are concerned whether the Kyrgyz language exam, introduced to ensure the president has a good working knowledge of Kyrgyz, is being applied equally and fairly.

The binding clan and regional affiliations that have dominated politics to date remain a powerful force.

KYRGYZSTAN'S GEO-POLITICAL POSITION

The establishment of a long-term US military base outside Bishkek in 2002 changed power dynamics in Central Asia. World powers have been pacing the region since independence in 1991, drawn by its rich resources—oil and gas in Kazakhstan, Uzbekistan and Turkmenistan and water in Kyrgyzstan. Equally, they have been perturbed by the global impact of its problems—the flow of drugs and Islamic fundamentalism from Afghanistan to Central Asia and beyond. The attacks on the World Trade Centre and the Pentagon in the United States on September 11, 2001 and the subsequent war in Afghanistan have not changed the issues, but have raised the stakes in the region. Central Asia has been of key strategic importance to China for centuries and more recently considered 'Russia's back yard', as well as being courted, chastised and cajoled by the West and Middle East, by means of loans, new mosques and educational establishments, and humanitarian and military aid.

The destabilising effects of drug trafficking in Central Asia cannot be overestimated. Afghanistan is the largest source worldwide of heroin and opium, and the bulk of it is transported through Central Asia, broadly following the old Silk Routes. Analysts' predictions that the drug problem would not disappear with the Taleban have been proved accurate, and trafficking is now funding the Islamic Movement of Uzbekistan, the major guerilla group of the area (see below). Regional instability is further exacerbated by the fact that the Central Asian states are still struggling with weak economies, rampant corruption and minimal neighbourly co-operation—all factors that underpin growing poverty and social unrest.

Kyrgyzstan has bigger brasher neighbours with more resources and greater political muscle than itself. Its vulnerability locally is exacerbated by its long, hard-to-police mountain border with Tajikistan, which is traditionally seen as the buffer zone from turbulent Afghanistan. Kyrgyzstan's relatively weak standing within Central Asia is particularly galling given the importance of its rivers in supplying water to its neighbours; Kyrgyzstan uses only 25–30 per cent of the run-off from its rivers with the bulk supplying the other central Asian countries. Its hydro-electric stations along the Naryn river generate much of the electricity used by the region.

Water is set to become the most hotly contested resource in the coming decades. Commentators suggest that the Kyrgyz government could exploit the country's resources more fully to give it greater political clout in the region. Kyrgyzstan imports the vast majority of its gas, oil and coal supplies from local giants Uzbekistan and Kazakhstan but has been unable to negotiate favourable terms with either government. As a result of Kyrgyzstan's inability to meet payments, the Uzbekistan government frequently cuts off its supply of gas. The gas problem led to the bankruptcy of Kyrgyzstan's gas monopoly, Kyrgyzgazmunaizat, amid accusations that millions of dollars had been laundered. Many people lost their prime source of energy and it is now not unusual to see Bishkek people cooking on open fires in their courtyards.

Kyrgyzstan's political and economic difficulties are compounded by the stark division of the country into north and south by the mighty Ala-Too mountain range. This geographic separation has been reinforced by tension in the south between the Kyrgyz and the majority Uzbek communities. While the north has had a stranglehold on political influence and industry, the south has provided the nation's raw materials. Tribal and ethnic divisions in the south are exacerbated by unemployment, the collapse of crucial cross-border irrigation infrastructure, demographic pressure and the low allocation to the south of resources from IMF and other international loans. Resentment ferments as the Uzbek/Kyrgyz border dispute interferes with trade routes which have for centuries linked China and the Caspian Sea through the Fergana valley; people who depend for their livelihoods on cross-border activities run the daily gauntlet of violence and extortion at the hands of the border guards.

Although Islamic funda-
mentalism is unlikely to
become a problem for Kyrgyz-
tan generally, these conditions
provide fertile ground for
Islamic movements in the
Kyrgyz and Uzbek Fergana
valley. Of particular concern is
the Islamic Party of Turkestan
(IPT), formerly the Islamic
Movement of Uzbekistan,
widely considered to be an
international terrorist organisation. Its declared aim is to
establish an Islamic caliphate in
all of Central Asia.

Much of Kyrgyzstan's arable farmland depends on irrigation

In May 2003, Kyrgyz security forces foiled an IPT plan to bomb the US embassy and a hotel in Bishkek. In the summers of 1999 and 2000, the then IMU crossed into Kyrgyzstan's south-westerly province of Batken from Tajikistan, occupying villages and taking hostages, but each time withdrawing before winter snows sealed the mountain passes. They were demanding free passage to Uzbekistan which both offered no military support to Kyrgyzstan to repel these forces and, at the same time, threatened dire consequences should they be allowed to cross over its borders.

The summer of 2001 saw a number of lesser attacks on Kyrgyz border guards for which the IMU claimed responsibility, though locally these were felt to be linked to drug smuggling activities. Uzbekistan's response has been the unilateral land mining of its Kyrgyz and Tajik borders, causing many civilian and livestock deaths.

After the defeat of the Taliban in Afghanistan in 2001, the IMU/IPT was weakened but regrouped in 2003 and is still considered a danger in the region. Some commentators suggest that international and regional governments might be tempted to exaggerate the risk from terrorism to further their own aims: it ensures foreign powers a foothold in the region and, for local administrations, continued economic and military support from abroad.

Attention has since shifted to Islamic group Khizb-ut-Tahrir (now banned in Kyrgyzstan), which shares the objective of an Islamic state but through grassroots activism and, it is claimed, peaceful means. However, observers report the emergence of KT splinter groups with a more radical agenda. KT has gained popularity for its criticism of government corruption and failure to address poor living conditions. It is seen by some as a champion of social justice but is also regarded as having serious potential to destabilise the area.

The arrival of US air bases throughout Central Asia met with ambivalence from the people who voiced two main concerns: firstly, it was widely hoped that the US would step up pressure on local governments to address these crucial social and political issues as well as the worsening human rights situation; however, in Uzbekistan regular and serious human rights infringements continue to be overlooked. Secondly, people feared that the US presence would compromise Kyrgyzstan's relationship with its two powerful neighbours, Russia and China.

The US has been accorded very favourable conditions at its air base at Bishkek's Manas airport and has established a long-term military presence in the country. Relations were soured by the Kyrgyz Government's siding with Russia in its opposition to the US-led invasion of Iraq in March 2003 and by its refusal to authorise use of the air base for the war.

Speculation about US intentions in Central Asia include a desire to undermine Russia's hold on its traditional sphere of influence, to secure the safety of potential oil pipelines in the region and to encircle China. According to a CIA report, China is expected to have around 1,000 long-range missiles aimed at the US by 2015.

Local analysts fear offending China, whose long-standing interest in its westerly neighbours is no doubt motivated partly by its increasing reliance on oil imports. China's involvement in the region was formalized in the Shanghai Co-operation Organization (SCO), set up in 1995, comprising China, Russia, Kyrgyzstan, Kazakhstan and Tajikistan, to address Islamic fundamentalism and improve trade, but is seen chiefly as a vehicle to further Chinese ambitions. In June 2001 the 'Shanghai Five' were joined by Uzbekistan and now aim to become a cornerstone organization for the maintenance of stability in Central Asia. However, the inability of the SCO to respond effectively to security and drug trafficking issues left a vacuum that has naturally been filled by the new player in the region, the US. Furthermore, the battle between twin bullies Uzbekistan and Kazakhstan for dominance in Central Asia undermines the area's cohesion and makes it more vulnerable to exploitation by world powers.

Wooed by Washington, with its wealth and global influence, the Central Asian states are avidly courted by the SCO and Russia.

Nevertheless, public anxiety is mounting in relation to the diplomatic and domestic implications for Kyrgyzstan of alienating China or Russia. While some in Kyrgyzstan are in favour of developing security relationships with all three superpowers, the sceptical express concern about its potential loss of sovereignty as the rivalries between Russia, China and the US are played out on its soil.

It is generally agreed that now, more than ever, the Central Asian states need to forge genuine solidarity amongst themselves to protect their mutual interest, and that only through regional co-operation and economic integration will it be possible to defeat extremism and organized crime and retain some control over their own destinies.

The Economy

The task facing the Kyrgyz government at independence was monumental. The dissolution of the Soviet Union revealed the depth of its economic problems. Kyrgyzstan had played the historical role of the colonised: its economic activities were based on agriculture and the extraction of raw materials for processing elsewhere in the Soviet Union and the country depended entirely on Moscow for trade and for access to capital and technology. All communication and transport systems revolved around Moscow, at the expense of ties with other, closer trade partners. Financial arrangements belonged to the enclosed world of the Soviet system and were unsuitable for use in world trade.

During the first five years of independence, the Kyrgyz Government courageously undertook major reform and restructuring of political, economic and social systems and institutions, with a view to building the infrastructures required by a market economy and democracy, and to allow international trade and investment. This commitment has been less visible since 1995. Kyrgyzstan saw little return for its efforts. Its better resourced neighbours did not follow suit, hindering regional trade which is crucial to Kyrgyzstan's survival.

From 1992 to 1995, Kyrgyzstan reeled as subsidies from Moscow (up to 50 per cent of the country's budget) were cut and the country left the rouble zone to set up its own currency. Food prices soared, fuel became scarce and wage increases failed miserably to keep pace. Agricultural and industrial privatisation led to massive job losses. During this period, industrial output declined by 63.7 per cent—disabled by the energy crisis and large scale emigration by the Russians—and agriculture fell by 83.3 per cent. Inflation rocketed, hitting 1,300 per cent in 1993, although it thankfully fell back to a mere 300 per cent in 1994.

By the mid-1990s, people were developing a familiarity with the new systems and by 1996, Kyrgyzstan was on the road to partial economic recovery. By 1997, Kyrgyzstan was boasting a GDP growth of ten per cent, while industry grew by 35 per cent and agriculture by 10.7 per cent. This was largely due to foreign investment, in particular into the Kumtor gold mine. Inflation dropped to 14 per cent by the end of 1997. Through sterling efforts, the Government got it down to 5.2 per cent by 2005.

Optimism began to appear on the streets and pastures of Kyrgyzstan but in 1998 disaster struck: the Russian financial crisis dealt a severe blow to the fragile and still very dependent economy. By late 2002, the GDP was still only 66 per cent of its pre-independence level. Through sterling efforts, the Government got it down to 5.2 per cent by 2005.

Another factor impacting heavily on the economy is the 'brain drain'—the exodus of the Slavic community, which boasted the majority of the country's most qualified people. In 1993, the exodus peaked at a rate of 250 people a day. Russians were still leaving the country at a rate of 15,000 a year in the early 2000s and the gap in technical expertise will take decades to fill.

Kyrgyzstan's difficulties stem from being a remote landlocked country with scant resources. Kyrgyzstan barters hydro-electric power for fossil fuels from Kazakhstan and Uzbekistan. But the government has been criticised for failing to exploit fully its abundant water resources and hydro-electric potential, which in the early 2000s was being exploited to only one tenth of capacity. In addition, Kyrgyzstan loses significant amounts of water due to its antiquated infrastructure and almost half of electricity generated is lost to leaks and theft.

Kyrgyzstan's other resources are hard-won mining and agricultural products rather than the free-flowing fuels enjoyed by its neighbours. The economy has been heavily dependent on foreign aid since independence, but this has dropped off dramatically since 1999.

Gold has become increasingly important as Kyrgyzstan's chief export to countries outside the CIS. Kumtor sits on one of the largest gold deposits in the world but is expected to close by 2010, with a resulting impact on GDP.

Kyrgyzstan is already crippled by an external debt of US$2.4 billion (as of the end of 2004), although it has managed to renegotiate some of its debt with Russia and the West.

AGRICULTURE

Agriculture is the core sector of the Kyrgyz economy. The fact that 55 per cent of workers are employed in agriculture and only 15 per cent in industry illustrates starkly the difficulties facing Kyrgyzstan. In Soviet times Kyrgyzstan apparently produced enough buttermilk, yoghurt and cheese to feed the whole of the Soviet Union, but much of today's agriculture consists of subsistence farming. Indeed 55 per cent of agricultural output comes from private household plots. Farming (animal husbandry and arable) is possible on only 60 per cent of land in Kyrgyzstan, of which just seven per cent is suitable for arable use while the remaining 53 per cent supports hayfields and pastures. Main exports are wool, meat and cotton. The world's largest natural walnut forest lies around Arslanbob in the south; conservation and sustainable exploitation of the forest is just beginning.

After independence, swift moves were made to privatize state-owned land. By the end of 1992, 165 state farms had been reorganised into 17,000 agricultural enterprises and by 1998 over 50 per cent of land was owned by individuals or cooperatives. Land was leased for a period of 99 years, with distribution based on the number of members in a household. Since then, land reform has proceeded very slowly.

Much confusion followed privatization and production was disrupted. Most noticeable was the reduction of livestock herds, especially sheep and goats, whose numbers fell from 8.7 million in 1992 to 3.8 million in 1998, with serious implications for the wool market. Most of these animals were killed for food during severe shortages. Nevertheless, pressure on grazing has led to a serious problem with top soil erosion.

GOLD IN KYRGYZSTAN

Kumtor, one of the highest gold deposits in the world, is situated in the southern region of the Central Tien Shan at an altitude of 4,000 metres above sea level in a permafrost zone. The deposit is located 425 kilometres from Bishkek, the capital of the Kyrgyz Republic.

The deposit was discovered in 1978, its total gold reserves being estimated at approximately 716 tonnes.

The deposit is being developed by the Canadian Kumtor Operating Company, a wholly owned subsidiary of Centerra Gold Inc., an international company engaged in gold mining projects in Kyrgyzstan and Mongolia and in an exploration project in the USA.

The **Kumtor Operating Company** (KOC) was established in 1992 as the operator of the Kumtor Gold Project responsible for financing, production and sales. Today, it is the first and by far the greatest investment project in the mining sector of Kyrgyzstan. Total investments in the Kumtor Gold Project have exceeded 450 million USD.

The Kumtor mine was built within a record time: commencing in 1994, the project was commissioned in 1997. Currently, KOC employs over 2,600 people of whom 96 per cent are Kyrgyzstan citizens. To date, the project has produced approximately 191

tonnes of gold. Since the project start-up in 1997, KOC's output has averaged 10 per cent of the Kyrgyz Republic's GDP. Kumtor's gold constitutes over a third of national exports of goods and services. Since 1994, the Kumtor Gold Project's cumulative payments within the Kyrgyz Republic have exceeded 854 million USD.

Continual technological improvements and innovation practices, proactive exploration program and investments in the development of the mine enable the Company to maintain high growth rates and lead the field in Kyrgyzstan's mining sector.

KOC proactively engages in sustainable development and community investment programs in the regions of the Kyrgyz Republic where it operates and most of its employees live. Environmental protection and safety remain Kumtor's top priorities. KOC activities adhere to environmental standards effective in the Kyrgyz Republic, Canada and to those accepted by international lending institutions, such as The World Bank.

Many of the recipients of land had neither the capital nor equipment to succeed at independent farming and so sold off their land for immediate cash needs. Collective farm managers often appropriated the machinery of the former state farm and sold it for their own profit, or hired it out to smaller farmers, laying the foundations of a new form of feudalism.

Overall, in spite of the general economic decline, agricultural production is now growing. Partly to thank for this are the government's bold moves to provide a range of support services and reduce and simplify the relevant tax system. Crucial measures yet to be taken include the fair distribution of remaining assets. Many farmers, initially resentful about the dissolution of the collective farms, are warming to capitalism, pointing out that they can now earn more in a day than they previously could in a month, however hard they worked.

INDUSTRY

The days of the Soviet Union saw the high-tech manufacturing of electronic parts, semi-conductors and specialised instruments for spacecraft—apparently the gamma radio telescope used to photograph Halley's Comet was made in Kyrgyzstan. These businesses depended heavily on supplies from other republics; this, coupled with the energy crisis, the collapse of the Russian market, and old, worn out equipment, has meant the almost complete closure of Soviet industries. Whole factories lie in gloomy rusted ruin. The government now owns only about 5 per cent of all industrial output.

The potentially enormous business of hydroelectric production is hampered by antiquated machinery and methods. Two new hydro-electric stations on the Naryn, started in Soviet times, are currently under construction, financed by two big Russian companies, but more money is needed. Bishkek and Beijing are in talks over the possibility of widescale Chinese investment in Kyrgyzstan's power industry in exchange for electricity, iron and precious metals. Kyrgyzstan's coal extraction, based in the south and centre of the country, has fallen dramatically and the country now imports most of its coal from Kazakhstan and Russia, although the Government plans to step up exploitation of its considerable remaining reserves.

The most high profile foreign investment is the Kumtor gold mine, a Kyrgyz-Canadian joint venture south of Lake Issyk Kul, which opened in May 1997, and currently contributes about ten per cent of GDP. Other mining possibilities include antimony, mercury and uranium oxide, although currently exploitation of these resources has almost completely ceased.

The Kyrgyz Government continues to meet with some success in its endeavours to attract foreign investment to Kyrgyzstan, but the shadow economy still thrives.

The climate for small and medium-sized businesses is seen as much less favourable in Kyrgyzstan than in Uzbekistan, although corruption and bribery are commonplace there too. The traditional traders of Central Asia, the Uzbeks continue to thrive in this field, whereas Kyrgyz entrepreneurs are bedevilled by over-regulation, high taxation, government interference and the constant demand for bribes from government officials. Not surprisingly most small business people prefer to stay in the shadow economy.

TOURISM

Tourism has the potential to be a good source of income, both to the government and to local communities. Kyrgyzstan has always been popular with visitors from CIS countries: current figures suggest that 60 per cent of holidaymakers come from Kazakhstan, 15 per cent from Russia, 20 per cent from within Kyrgyzstan, three per cent from Uzbekistan and just one per cent from outside the CIS, although the latter figure is growing. Eighty per cent of CIS tourists came to visit friends, with many using health resorts and a growing few choosing adventure tourism. The government is taking steps to encourage tourism, such as simplifying the visa system, but its best efforts are hindered by crippling taxes and the increasingly restrictive border regulations of its neighbours. Although efforts at analysis of tourist activity are being made, reliable statistics are hard to come by. The main impediments on the growth of tourism appear to be appalling roads and the lack of an independent information service in Bishkek.

New types of caravanserai are opening to serve modern tourists on the old Silk Routes. Some are foreign-owned or joint ventures, which place business control and the majority of the profits firmly with the investor, leaving minimal financial benefit for Kyrgyzstan and, more particularly, the local community.

Tourism is a powerful and unpredictable beast, as other parts of the world can testify: its capacity to ravage communities and environments and distort local economies is frightening. Harnessed and managed carefully, however, and placed in the hands of local people, it can bring considerable economic benefit, as well as providing a friendlier, more authentic experience to visitors. Furthermore, it improves the chance of local cultures being presented to visitors in an accurate and respectful way. Throughout the world a new kind of tourism is coming to life; it is taking a sceptical second look at corporate ownership and placing control in the hands of local communities.

In the vanguard of this new trend in tourism are two successful organizations: Community-Based Tourism (see box page 292) and Shepherd's Life give travellers the experience of staying with local families and the satisfaction of knowing that income goes straight into village households, relieving rural poverty. Ecotour promises its visitors 'nature and culture', a package that is both eco-friendly and respects the local community.

Kyrgyzstan has the freedom to choose the kind of tourism it adopts: a privilege that many countries, spoilt by uncontrolled tourist development, sorely envy.

Surviving Transition

Under the Soviet Union everyone had a job and a good life but I think independence is better for Kyrgyzstan; right now things are hard because young people don't know how to live in a market economy, but they will learn.
Teacher, turned politician, turned farmer

Ecotour's yurt camp at Jeti-Oguz

It is impossible for us to appreciate fully how deeply the collapse of the Soviet empire devastated the Kyrgyz people. Many visitors are surprised to hear of the thoroughness with which the Soviet people's needs were catered for, particularly since the 1940s, and of the educational and sporting opportunities it offered free of charge to everybody, regardless of their financial status. By and large oppression seems to have been more of an issue for outsiders; in Kyrgyzstan people got on with life. 'It was better then...' is a common refrain, as a whimsical look clouds the eyes. Today's hardships doubtless add a glow to fond memories.

While most express gratitude for the improvement in living conditions and opportunity brought by the Soviet system, now that the party is over, the tragedy of the Kyrgyz people's cultural loss has hit home. The Kyrgyz are doubly bereaved; not only have they lost their Soviet-era security, but also much of their nomadic identity. As the system and ideology which so totally engulfed their lives crumbles into history, the people of Kyrgyzstan are grappling with how to restore some dignity to their nomadic roots.

Since independence, Kyrgyzstan has been in social and economic turmoil. For

End of an era: Lenin's statue being moved from the front to the back of the Kyrgyz State Historical Museum [Saffia Farr]

Lady selling lepioshka to babushka at Ortosai bazaar [Saffia Farr]

years, incomes were impossibly low and today life remains very tough, especially in rural areas. However, recently average monthly wages have increased to US$110, partly because of the economic boom in Bishkek and partly because the Government hiked salaries of teachers, social workers and medical staff by 30 per cent.

The World Bank estimates that unemployment is at 20 per cent. It is more prevalent, but not so serious in rural areas as people can normally eke a living from the land. Many people survived the transition period by falling back on their traditional ways of subsistence.

Many people find ways to make a little money. The better off become 'shoptourists', flying to Delhi, Istanbul, the United Arab Emirates, or bussing to Kashgar for supplies, which they sell in the markets.

Unemployed migrants who are not registered as Bishkek residents cannot use educational or health facilities. Training programmes are beginning to appear for the registered unemployed and those who have paid a minimum of a year's contributions to the Employment Fund receive small benefits. Registered businesses pay up to 40 per cent of each employee's salary to a social fund but many flee this responsibility by operating in the shadow economy.

Pensioners are arguably the worst off in the post-Soviet chaos. They receive minute pensions although the Government has just increased pensions by ten per cent. With the Soviet mindset well engrained, many do not even try to understand the new system. Those who are not supported by their families and cannot find work resort to begging; these are almost exclusively ethnic Russians whose children have left Kyrgyzstan.

Around 46 per cent of the population lives in poverty according to the latest government figures. A flurry of non-governmental development organisations have appeared in recent years, the most effective of which are started by women locally to promote economic development and improve social status. Women represent 70 per cent of those living below the poverty line.

HEALTH

Kyrgyzstan, particularly the south, has seen a resurgence of poverty-related diseases, especially tuberculosis which, largely under control in Soviet times, increased by 50 per cent in just three years after independence. Government spending in the health sector has fallen dramatically; there is a shortage of medical personnel and pharmaceuticals, which are imported. Women's health in particular has been affected by the loss of maternity and antenatal care. Much of this is now covered by non-governmental organisations, which are also eagerly promoting contraception. As a result of a public information campaign and widely available free contraception, use in urban areas is on the increase and abortion rates have reduced. The reception in rural areas has been less enthusiastic.

Official HIV figures suggest there are just over 1,000 cases as of January 2007 but some estimates put it at closer to 8,000, mostly in the south and mostly related to drug use.

EDUCATION

Education in Kyrgyzstan is compulsory for nine years and nominally free but families are asked to contribute. Kyrgyzstan has an impressive literacy rate of 98.7 per cent but school attendance is falling, particularly in rural areas. Private schools are beginning to appear, such as the American University in Bishkek and the Turkish 'Silk Road' primary schools, but only children of well-off families can afford to take advantage of these.

In general, schools are desperately short of good teachers due to the very low salaries (which are always paid late). Higher education facilities have increased three-fold since independence, some with foreign money, such as the Turkish University in Bishkek. On the whole, though, the quality of education is falling throughout the system. In Soviet times girls accounted for over half the students in higher education but this has fallen in recent years.

SOCIAL ILLS

As the shock waves of such enormous change reverberated through a society racked with moral and ideological confusion, increasing hardship, unemployment and uncertainty, it is no surprise that many people have taken refuge in drink, drugs and even suicide.

Vodka, introduced by the Russians, has long been abused all over the Soviet Union. However bare of food shop shelves became, the trusty bottle of vodka was always available. Today its use is undermining all aspects of economic and family life, with no 'sobering up' centres to act as a deterrent as in Soviet days.

Drug use and trafficking are serious problems in Kyrgyzstan, undermining public health, security and the economy. There are 6,327 officially registered drug users, but observers believe the true number could be as high as 85,000.

In spite of all this, people assert that life is easier than in the early years of independence and few would trade in today's hardships and freedom for the predictability and security of the Soviet days. The resourcefulness and resilience of the Kyrgyz people have seen them through centuries of war and cultural and social dislocation; they are not about to be beaten by 'transition'.

Facts for the Traveller

The bureaucratic hurdles to visiting Kyrgyzstan are gradually being dismantled, making the country more accessible to travellors than ever before. It was closed to foreigners during the Soviet period largely due to its proximity to China and its role as top-secret Soviet military research centre. It was, however, one of the foremost destinations for Soviet workers on their statutory free holidays, thanks to the long sandy beaches of Lake Issyk Kul and the best mountaineering, rock climbing and trekking the Soviet Union had to offer.

In addition to these attractions, a vast array of other possibilities have emerged in recent years enabling visitors to explore the culture and history of the country as never before. A network of locally owned home-stay, transport and guiding services are available in villages all over the country, offering an introduction to authentic Kyrgyz life and tradition, and reducing dependence on tour operators. Where Silk Route caravans once traversed Kyrgyz highways between modern-day China and Uzbekistan, today's travellers wanting to extend their tour of Uzbekistan or cross to China will find in Kyrgyzstan a welcoming and stunningly beautiful land.

Getting There

Pursuing its traditional crossroads role, Kyrgyzstan has good road links with all its neighbours and offers a gateway to the rest of Central Asia, Russia and beyond. Roads go to China (allowing onward travel within China or along the Karakorum Highway to Pakistan), Uzbekistan, Kazakhstan (and an alternative crossing to China) and Tajikistan.

AIR

British Midland International currently operate four weekly flights between London and Bishkek, with one stop in the Caucasus. Flights take about nine hours and connections are available. These flights are generally cheaper if booked through a tour operator.

In late 2007, China Southern Airlines launched a twice-a-week service from Urumqi to Osh. They also fly between Urumqi and Bishkek four times a week.

Turkish Airlines fly daily between Istanbul and Bishkek, taking five hours and ten minutes. Aeroflot operate daily flights between Bishkek and Moscow. Both offer onward connections worldwide. A visa is required to transfer between airports in Moscow. Local airlines run two weekly flights to St Petersburg, one to Novosibirsk and Ekaterinburg. Several weekly flights link Bishkek with Tehran and Mashad in Iran, Dubai and Sharjah in the United Arab Emirates, Delhi in India and Seoul in South Korea.

Good onward connections to Beijing, Moscow, Frankfurt and London are available with Uzbekistan Airways, who operate five weekly flights between Bishkek and Tashkent. Several airlines link Bishkek with Dushanbe, Almaty and Tashkent.

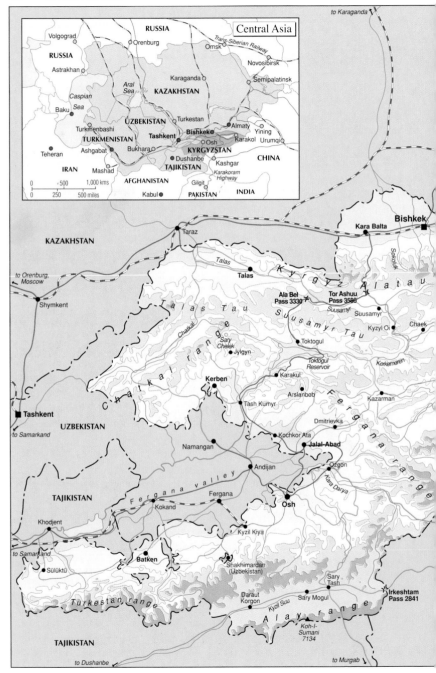

Central Asia

to Karaganda

Volgograd
RUSSIA
Orenburg
Omsk
Trans-Siberian Railway
Novosibirsk
RUSSIA
Astrakhan
Aral Sea
Karaganda
KAZAKHSTAN
Semipalatinsk
Caspian Sea
Baku
Turkestan
Almaty
Yining
UZBEKISTAN
Tashkent
Bishkek
Karakol
Urumqi
Turkmenbashi
TURKMENISTAN
Osh
KYRGYZSTAN
Teheran
Ashgabat
Bukhara
Dushanbe
Kashgar
CHINA
IRAN
Mashad
TAJIKISTAN
Karakoram Highway
AFGHANISTAN
Gilgit
INDIA
Kabul
PAKISTAN

0   500   1,000 kms
0   250   500 miles

KAZAKHSTAN

to Orenburg, Moscow

Shymkent

Taraz

Talas

Talas

Talas Tau

Kyrgyz Alatau

Sokoluk

Kara Balta

Bishkek

Ala Bel Pass 3330
Tor Ashuu Pass 3586
Suusamyr
Suusamyr
Suusamyr Tau
Kyzyl Oi
Chaek

Chatkal range

Chatkal

Sary Chelek

Jylgyn

Toktogul

Toktogul Reservoir

Kerkemeren

Tashkent

UZBEKISTAN

to Samarkand

Kerben

Karakul

Arslanbob

Tash Kumyr

Kochkor Ata

Kazarman

Dmitrievka

Jalal-Abad

Fergana range

Namangan

Andijan

Özgön

Kara Darya

TAJIKISTAN

Fergana valley

Fergana

Kokand

Khodjent

to Samarkand

Sülüktü

Batken

Kyzyl Kiya

Shakhimardan (Uzbekistan)

Osh

Sary Tash

Daraut Korgon

Kyzyl Suu

Sary Mogul

Alay range

Irkeshtam Pass 2841

Turkestan range

Koh-I-Sumani 7134

TAJIKISTAN

to Dushanbe

to Murgab

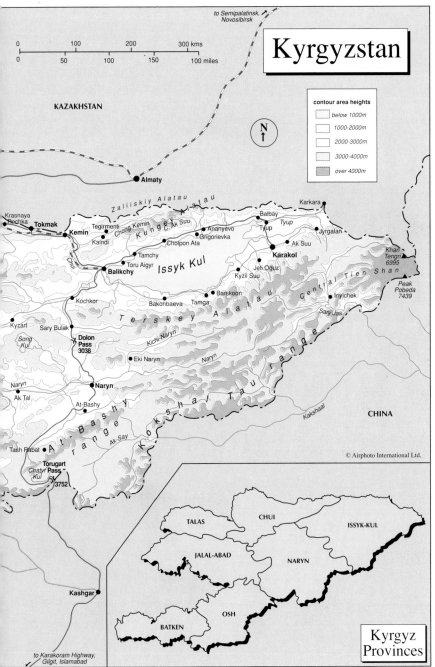

to Semipalatinsk,
Novosibirsk

Kyrgyzstan

| 0 | 100 | | 200 | | 300 kms |
| 0 | 50 | 100 | 150 | 100 miles | |

KAZAKHSTAN

N
↑

contour area heights

	below 1000m
	1000-2000m
	2000-3000m
	3000-4000m
	over 4000m

Almaty

Zaliiskiy Alatau

Kunge Alatau

Krasnaya
Rechka   Tokmak
Kemin   Tegirmenti
Chong Kemin   Ak Suu
Kaindi
Cholpon Ata
Chui
Tamchy
Toru Aigyr
Balikchy   Issyk Kul

Karkara
Balbay
Tyup   Tyup
Ananyevo
Grigorievka   Ak Suu   Jyrgalan
Karakol
Jeti Oguz
Kyzil Suu

Khan
Tengri
6995

Terskey   Alatau

Barskoon
Kochkor   Bakonbaeva   Tamga

Central Tien Shan

Inylchek
Sary Jas

Peak
Pobeda
7439

Kyzart   Sary Bulak
Song
Kul   Dolon
Pass
3038
Eki Naryn   Kichi Naryn   Naryn

Kakshaal

CHINA

Naryn
Ak Tal   Naryn

At-Bashy
At Bashy range
Ak-Say
Kokshaal Tau range

© Airphoto International Ltd.

Tash Rabat   Torugart
Chatyr   Pass
Kul   3752

Kashgar

TALAS   CHUI

JALAL-ABAD   NARYN

ISSYK-KUL

OSH

BATKEN

Kyrgyz
Provinces

to Karakoram Highway,
Gilgit, Islamabad

Kazakh airline Astana Airways fly twice, KLM four times and British Airways three times between London and Almaty in Kazakhstan—just five hours' drive (US$200 for a car) from Bishkek—but, frustratingly, for these options you need a Kazakh transit visa. Return flights from Bishkek to Osh operate four times daily and to Jalal-Abad twice weekly. For international flights, see pages 71 and 130–131.

When taking spectacular helicopter flights over the Tien Shan, it is worth bearing in mind that helicopters are not subject to international-standard regular checks. Tickets can also be booked through Kyrgyz Concept and CAT

TRAIN

Train connections with Almaty and Tashkent are poor and the bus is a better option. Three trains a week run to both Tashkent and Almaty, taking 16 hours. Trains run twice a week between Moscow and Bishkek (72 hours), and once a week to Novokuznetsovsk in Siberia and Ekaterinburg in the Urals. Timetable and prices are vulnerable to change and locals warn of crime, delays and smuggling en route. A Kazakh transit visa is required for travel on all of these routes.

BUS

Long distance bus journeys start at Bishkek's new or West bus station, linking the capital with Tashkent, Almaty and, in theory, Kashgar. Several buses depart for the ten- hour journey to Tashkent after 5pm and cost the equivalent of about US$8. The bus goes through Kazakhstan and foreigners need a Kazakh transit visa. Minibuses also leave Osh Bazaar Bishkek for Tashkent and cost a little more but take about eight hours.

Buses to Almaty leave every hour or two all day and take about five hours, for US$6. The minivans by the gates of the West bus station leave for Almaty when full. From Almaty you can fly, catch the train or bus to Urumqi in China.

In theory, buses leave the West bus station for Kashgar and Artysh in Xinjiang four times a week, with tickets costing US$50. However, this does not seem to be the case. Be aware that foreign nationals cannot travel beyond the Kyrgyz/Chinese border on public transport and must pre-book a private vehicle from the border to take them to Kashgar. For more details see the Torugart section of the Central Kyrgyzstan chapter.

Visas and Red Tape

Unique among central Asian powers, the Kyrgyz Government made a commitment to unravel some of the cumbersome bureaucracy around travel to Kyrgyzstan.

Until 2002 an invitation letter was required from a registered tour operator, but today this is no longer needed for nationals of 28 countries—including Australia, New Zealand, the USA and most of Europe. Now these nationals may obtain their tourist or business visa on arrival at Bishkek Manas airport, although it is advisable to get it in advance.

At the time of writing, the Embassy of the Kyrgyz Republic in London was issuing visas at the following costs: one-month single entry visa—UK£45 and one-month multiple entry visa—UK£60. The application form may be found on the website; enclose a pre-paid return envelope for your passport. Processing takes five working days and there is no express service.

On arrival in Kyrgyzstan ensure that your visa is stamped to show the date you entered the country. A recent complication is that internationals must enter and exit the country at staffed border crossings only. Entering the country by the trekking routes from Kazakhstan and Uzbekistan may, therefore, lead to difficulties on leaving the country as you won't have an entry stamp to validate your visa.

Kyrgyz consulates abroad include:

Austria: Invalidenstrasse 3/8, a-1030 Vienna. Tel. (431) 5350379
fax. 5350313; email: kyrbot@nnweb.at
Belgium: 47 Rue de L'Abbaye, 1050 Brussels. Tel. (322) 6403883
fax. 6400131; email: aitmatov@photohall.skynet.be
China: 271, Tayuan Diplomatic Office Building, Beijing. Tel. (8610) 65326458
fax. 65326459; email: kyrgyzch@public2.net.cn
Germany: 146 Otto-Suhr-Allee, 10585 Berlin. Tel. (4930) 34781338
fax. 34781362; email: 101477.1160@compuserve.com
India: C93 Anand Niketan, 110021 New Delhi. Tel. (9111) 24108008
fax. 24108009; email: welcome@kyrgyzembassyindia.org
Iran: 12, 5th Naranjestan Alley, Pasdaran St, Tehran. Tel. (9821) 2830354
fax. 2281720; email: krembiri@kanoon.net
Consulate in Mashad: tel. (98051) 818444
Kazakhstan: 68a Amangeldi St, Almaty. Tel: (7727) 632565
fax. 633362; email: Alche@kyrgyz.almaty.kz
Russia: 64, Bolshaya Ordinka St, 109017 Moscow. Tel. (7495) 2374601
fax. 2374452; email: 3235.g23@g23.relcom.ru
Switzerland: Switzerland: Rue Maunoir 26, 1207 Geneva.
Tel. (4122) 7079220; fax. 7079221
Tajikistan: 3 Proesd Chekova 41, Dushanbe. Tel. (99237) 2830354; fax. 210843
Turkey: 7 Lamartin Caddesi, Taksim, Istanbul. Tel. (90212) 2518370;
fax. 2359293; email: genkon@anet.net.tr
United Kingdom: 119 Crawford Street, London, W1H 1AF. Tel. (44207) 935 1462
fax.935 7449; email: embassy@kyrgyz-embassy.org.uk;
USA: 2360 Massachusetts Avenue, Washington DC 20008.
Tel. (1202) 3385141; fax. 3867550; email: consul@kgembassy.org
web: kyrgyzstan.org. Consulate in New York: 866 UN Plaza, Suite 514
Tel. (212) 3192836; fax. 3192837; web: kyrgyzconsulate.org
Uzbekistan: 30 Samatova St, Tashkent. Tel. (99871) 1374794; fax. 1374791
email: krembas@globalnet.uz

REGISTRATION

In November 2002, the Government abolished the requirement to register with OVIR (Visa and Registration Department of the Ministry of Internal Affairs) within three working days of arrival for nationals of 28 countries, including most of Europe, Canada, Australia, New Zealand, Israel and the USA. However, should registration be re-introduced, it can be done in Bishkek, Karakol, Osh and Naryn (see the relevant chapters for details).

For those who do have to register, you might find the OVIR desk in the airport terminal building open. If not you should, in theory, register at the OVIR office in the district you are staying in, having first made payment at the AKB Bank. Many travellers find that the OVIR office in Bishkek at 58 Kievskaya (second floor, take the left hand door) will take the money and register you on the spot. The office is open Monday to Friday from 9–12am and 2–7pm. Hotels and tour operators will assist their clients with registration for a small fee.

For visa extensions, apply to the Consular Department at the Ministry of Foreign Affairs on Togolok Moldo. All or any of the above procedures may change, so check with the Kyrgyz Consulate before you travel.

PERMITS

Military border permits are needed for certain sensitive areas, in particular within 50 kilometres of the border with China and Tajikistan, including in the Pamir Alay valley. They should be arranged at least four weeks in advance through a tour operator (see the Bishkek section), which will need your passport details and exact itinerary. It is also possible to buy permits in Karakol and Osh (see pages 167 and 239).

Thankfully, foreigners were liberated in 2002 from the requirement to purchase a **trekking permit** to visit certain areas. However, should this be re-instated, permits can be bought on the spot from the Ministry of Sport and Tourism in Bishkek at 17 Togolok Moldo, tel. (0312) 220657, 212843 (9.30am–5.30pm). From the street, go through the arch and to office 36 on the third floor of the building to your left. Ask for a *razresheniye na trekking* and be prepared to wait.

EXPORTING SOUVENIRS

Unfortunately, regulations relating to the export of antiques and handicrafts are unclear and no comprehensive list of prohibited items exists. However, as a general rule any object over 30 years old, all *tush kyiz* and large quantities of other items (say, five or more *shyrdaks*) will require an export certificate. This is easier said than done, as the whole process can take up to one week, but normally just a couple of days, costs approximately US$30 (depending on the nature of the item you wish to export, not its value) and involves the exporter completing paperwork in Russian only. Two 10cm x 13cm photos of the item must be submitted to the Ministry of Culture for consideration, before one is attached to the export certificate and signed personally by the Minister. Many Bishkek tour operators and hotels will provide assistance for a small fee and

Taxis are the best way of travelling around the back roads of Kyrgyzstan

may be able to speed up the process a little. The higher prices charged in some hotels and upmarket souvenir shops often include the cost of the export certificate and assistance with paperwork—check when buying. It is not possible to buy certificates in advance, so look out for souvenirs sold with bogus ready-attached documents. Also, it is strictly forbidden to export military uniforms and coins over 100 years old.

EMBASSIES AND CONSULATES IN BISHKEK

Visas for other countries can be obtained in Bishkek, but the process is often more time consuming and expensive than in your home country. The Kazakh and Uzbek Embassies in Bishkek open erratically and are particularly slow and unhelpful. Buy visas in advance where possible. Until such time as a British Embassy opens in Bishkek, British citizens should refer to the UK Consulate in Almaty or the UK Embassy in Astana (see below).

Canada: 189 Moskovskaya. Tel: (0312) 650202; fax: 650204

China: 196 Toktogul. Tel: (0312) 610858; fax: 663014; chinaemb_kg@mfa.gov.cn

France: 49 Razzakova. Tel: (0312) 660053, 660364; fax: 660441

Germany: 28 Razzakova. Tel: (0312) 666624, 666634; fax: 660207
info@bischkek.diplo.de

India: 164a Chui. Tel: (0312) 210863, 661499; fax: 660708
ss@indemb.bishkek.su

Iran: 36 Razzakova. Tel: (0312) 226964; fax: 620009

Kazakhstan: 10 Togolok Moldo. Tel: (0312) 660415, 660164; fax: 225463
kaz_emb@imfiko.bishkek.su

Pakistan: 308 Panfilova, Bishkek. Tel: (0312) 227209; fax: 621550
pakemb@asiainfo.kg; web: pakemb.kg
Russia: 17 Razzakova. Tel: (0312) 221775, 624736; fax: 221823
ruscons@imfiko.bishkek.su
USA: 171 Mira. Tel: (0312) 551241; fax: 551264; web: usemb-bishkek.rpo.at
Uzbekistan: 213 Tynystanova. Tel: (0312) 662065; fax: 664403
UK: Closest embassy is in Astana, Kazakhstan at 62 Kosmonavtov St, Renco
Building 6th Floor. Tel: (73172) 556200; britishembassy@mail.online.kz;
a UK Consulate can be found much closer in Almaty at 158 Panfilova St.
Tel: (7) 573 1502200; almatyvisageneral@fco.gov.uk
For Bishkek, **British Honorary Consul**: 2nd floor, 115 Ibraimova, Bishkek (next to
Dordoi Plaza Business Centre). Tel: (0312) 652855; mob: (0312) 584245;
gbhoncon@mail.kg.
Many embassies ask for a photocopy of your passport when applying for a visa, so
come prepared.

Organised Tours and Independent Travel

The pleasure of travel in Kyrgyzstan is becoming ever more accessible. With a wave of
new tour operators and tourist facilities throughout the country, you are increasingly
able to customise your trip according to your own interests, time and budget, and the
degree of comfort and predictability you require. It is possible to book as little or as
much of your trip as you choose, anything from a fully-escorted tour to travelling
completely independently, with your own transport if you prefer—jeep, bicycle or
horse. Most people's travel arrangements fall somewhere between the two.

Kyrgyzstan welcomes all: while it glows as a paradise in the hearts of trekkers and
mountaineers, you don't have to be super-fit and take to the hills to view the luxuriant,
delicate, sometimes stark beauty of Kyrgyzstan. Many places are accessible by car or
jeep as a day trip from good hotels.

Most **group tours** combine Kyrgyzstan with neighbouring Uzbekistan and/or China
so don't offer the opportunity to explore the country in much depth. If you plan to
travel **completely independently**, you will be richly rewarded but will need time,
patience and some flexibility. While transport along the main routes (Bishkek to
Karakol, Naryn or Osh) is frequent and reliable, if you wish to visit the wilder areas of
Suusamyr valley, Tash Rabat, Lake Song Kul, the petroglyphs at Saimaly Tash, the Naryn
to Jalal-Abad road, Chatkal or Sary Chelek, bus services are crowded, irregular or non-
existent. To reach some of these areas independently you will need to negotiate a deal
with a local taxi, which can be time consuming; if you have limited time, you might
consider hiring a car and driver through a local tour operator.

An innovative network of community-based tourism initiatives (see CBT   page
292), is blossoming throughout the country, making independent travel safer and easier

than ever before. These village-based projects offer homestays and yurt stays, transport, guide services and horse hire; they enable you to venture further into the mountains and come closer to ancient nomadic traditions. You can now book from abroad and you have the satisfaction of knowing that every much-needed penny you spend will go direct to the host community.

If you want to book through a tour operator which offers tailor-made trips, your best bet is to decide your own ideal itinerary, in order to get off the beaten track.

UK-BASED TOUR OPERATORS

Audley Travel: New Mill, New Mill Lane, Witney, Oxfordshire, OX29 9SX, UK. Tel:01993 838 000. www.audleytravel.com.

Eastern Approaches: 5 Mill Road, Stowe, Galashiels, TD1 2SD, Scotland, UK. Email: info@eastern approaches.co.uk. www.easternapproaches.co.uk.

Regent Holidays: Mezzanine Level, Froomsgate House, Rupert Street, Bristol BS1 2QJ. Tel. (0845) 2773317; fax. (0117) 9254866; email: regent@regent-holidays.co.uk. www: regent-holidays.co.uk.
Offer tailor-made tours in Kyrgyzstan and throughout the five central Asian countries and on to China via the Torugart and Irkeshtam passes.

Steppes East: The Travel House, 51 Castle Street, Cirencester, GL7 1QD. Tel. (01285) 651010; fax. 885888; email: east@steppestravel.co.uk; www: steppeseast.co.uk.
Experienced operators, offering up-market guided and tailor-made tours throughout Central Asia. Can do off the beaten track itineraries on request.

Wild Frontiers Adventures Travel Ltd: Unit 6, Townmead Business Centre, William Morris Way, London, SW6 2SZ. Tel. (0207) 736 3968; fax. (0207) 751 0710. email: info@wildfrontiers.co.uk; www: wildfrontiers.co.uk.
Owned and run by travel writer Jonny Bealby who rode on horseback from Kashgar to Turkmenistan. Small, relaxed adventure group or tailor-made tours with a mix of trekking, on foot or horseback, and jeep travel. An emphasis on local culture. Now running horsetreks from Sary Chelek to Talas, Song Kul to Tash Rabat and others.

The Adventure Company: 1 Cross and Pillory Lane, Alton, Hants, GU34 1HL. Tel. (0845) 4505312; email: sales@adventurecompany.co.uk; www: adventurecompany.co.uk.
Kyrgyzstan features briefly as part of a Silk Road tour. Highlight is a horse trek with Bishkek-based Shepherd's Way Trekking.

Great Game Travel: 112 High St, Holywood, Co. Down, BT18 9HW. Tel. (028) 9099 8325; fax. 9099 8951; www: greatgametravel.co.uk.
Tours through Afghanistan and Tajikistan touch on Kyrgyzstan and may expand.

Himalayan Kingdoms: Old Crown House, 18 Market Street, Wotton-under-Edge, Gloucestershire, GL12 7AE. Tel. (0845) 3308579; fax. (01453) 844422 email: info@himalayankingdoms.com; www: himalayankingdoms.com.
Catered group cultural and trekking tours throughout Central Asia.

Ride World Wide: Staddon Farm, North Tawton, Devon, EX20 2BX. Tel. (01837) 82544; fax. 82179; email: info@rideworldwide.com; www: rideworldwide.co.uk. Offers well-supported but challenging riding holidays to Song Kul from the north, from Kochkor, from Tash Rabat.

Explore Worldwide Ltd: Nelson House, 55 Victoria Road, Farnborough, Hants, GU17 4PA. Tel. (01252) 391110; email: info@explore.co.uk; www: explore.co.uk. Old hands at running action-packed group tours, they offer interesting tours of Kyrgyzstan in combination with its neighbours.

IntrepidGuerba: Wessex House, 40 Station Road, Westbury, Wiltshire, BA13 3JN. Tel. (01373) 816611; fax. 858351; email: enquiry@intrepidguerba.co.uk. www: intrepidtravel.com. Veterans in group tours, they touch on Kyrgyzstan on trans-Central Asia routes.

Sundowners Overland: 1 St George's Court, 131 Putney Bridge Road, London, SW15 2PA. Tel. (0208) 877 7660; email: europe@sundownersoverland.com. www: sundownersoverland.com. Well-established company offering small group and tailor-made tours.

US-BASED TOUR OPERATORS

Abercrombie & Kent: Many offices, including USA, UK, Australia and Hong Kong. www.abercrombiekent.com.

Geographic Expeditions: 1008 General Kennedy Avenue, PO Box 29902, San Francisco, CA94123. Tel. 800-777-8183; fax. 415-346-5535; email: info@geoex.com; www: geoex.com. Long-time operators offering group tours flitting through Kyrgyzstan, or more in-depth, tailormade trips.

MIR Corporation: 85 S. Washington Street, Suite 210, Seattle, WA98104. Tel. 206-624-7289; fax. 206-624-7360; email: info@mircorp.com; www: mircorp.com. Tailor-made holidays and small group tours taking in most of the 'stans'.

AUSTRALIAN TOUR OPERATORS

Sundowners Overland: Suite 15 Lonsdale Court, 600 Lonsdale Street, Melbourne, Victoria 3000. Tel. (03) 9672 5300; fax. (03) 9672 5311. email: info@sundownersoverland.com; www: sundownersoverland.com. Well-established company offering small group and tailor-made tours. Also has a London office.

SWISS TOUR OPERATORS

Horizons Nouveaux: Rue de Medran 6, Case Postale 196; 1936 Verbier. Tel. (27) 7717171; fax. 7717175; email: infos@horizonsnouveaux.com. www: horizonsnouveaux.com. French-speaking small group riding holidays.

TOUR OPERATORS IN BISHKEK

Now that email has shrunk the world, you might prefer to contact Kyrgyz tour operators direct. This is preferable to just showing up, as in the busy summer months arrangements may take a few days to make.

Tour Operators have mushroomed in recent years. The predominantly Russian operators, mostly former mountaineers, who launched tourism post-independence, have been joined by a plethora of newcomers, each with their own specialisms. Although they appear to serve the same dishes—Silk Road tours, trekking, Issyk-Kul, 'cultural'—they each have their own specialism. However, as trip possibilities are so numerous and levels of comfort vary greatly, tour operators will best be able to help if you are clear about the kind of experience you want; hospitality is key to local culture and trip organisers want you to enjoy your visit.

Most operators can now organise folklore programmes, demonstrations of felt-making, falconry or horseback games.

Ak Sai Travel: 65 Baitik Batyr (Sovietskaya). Tel. (0312) 544277; fax. 544219. email: info@ak-sai.com; www: ak-sai.com.

A dynamic young company offering an all-round service, it also runs a mountain club. Basecamp at Inylchek Glacier and at Achikh Tash for Peak Lenin. They specialise in mountaineering and adventurous trips and can organise the Sary Chelek to Talas trek.

Alltournative: 88/1, 308 Turusbekova. Tel/fax. (0312) 900199, mob. (0555) 536373, (0775) 586373; email: tripstours2@gmail.com; alltournative@elcat.kg. www: alltournative.kg.

Also run an **Information Office** at 6 Togolok Moldo, tel. 956373.

This friendly company, with excellent guides, organises day and weekend horseriding, trekking and rafting trips into the mountains around Bishkek, adventure trips in Kyrygzstan and tours of Uzbekistan. Also horseback treks around Sary Chelek, Talas and Tash Rabat. Their emphasis on culture and use of homestay and grass-roots services appeals to the adventurous. They also hire out a variety of good cars.

Asia Mountains: 1a Tugolbai Ata (formerly Lineinaya). Tel. (0312) 694073; 694075; fax: 694074; email: aljona@mail.elcat.kg. www: asiamountains.elcat.kg; asiamountains.net.

This well-established, competent company offers wilderness and adventure tours (including caving) and aims to reach rarely visited parts of the country.

CBT: 58 Gorky. Tel. (0312) 540069; tel/fax. 443331; email: cbttours@mail.ru. www: cbtkyrgyzstan.kg, cbttours.kg.

A network of community-based tourism services (see CBT page 292).

Celestial Mountains Tour Company: 131/2 Kievskaya. Tel. (0312) 212562; fax. 610402. email: ian@celestial.com.kg; www: celestial.com.kg; www: tours.kg.

Friendly and reliable British-owned company with experienced team offering tours anywhere in Kyrgyzstan, on to China and along the Karakorum Highway in Pakistan; also Silk Road tours through the other central Asian states and Russia. Professionalism and flexibility are key—will arrange skeleton or full package tours. Special interest in Kyrgyz culture. They run high quality hotels in Bishkek and Naryn and can organise car hire using excellent vehicles and reliable drivers. Their highly informative and wide ranging website is well worth checking out.

Central Asia Tourism Corporation (CAT): 124 Chui Prospect. Tel. (0312) 663664, 663665; fax. 900420; www: cat.kg.
Reliable Kyrgyz-Kazakh joint venture and one of the leading tour operators of Central Asia, offering tours along the Great Silk Road, cultural, eco and horseriding tours to groups and individuals. This company is the agent of all international and domestic airlines where you can buy tickets. They also offer quality transport hire with a driver and transfers. They also have an office at Manas airport, Tel.: (0312) 603595.

Dostuck-Trekking: 42–1 Igemberdieva. Tel. (0312) 503082, 545455; fax.443090 email: dostuck@saimanet.kg
Kyrgyz-British joint venture firm offering a reliable and comprehensive service. As well as mountaineering and heli-skiing throughout Central Asia, they run professional and well-supported treks, mainly in the Kyrgyz Ala-Too, and will arrange rafting, horse riding, cycling, skiing and sports tours.

Ecotour: 46–A Donskoi Pereulok. Tel. (0502) 802805, (0502) 913245. email: info@ecotour.kg; www: ecotour.kg.
Friendly and professional, Ecotour offer culture, horseriding and walking tours with their own particular flavour. Their vision is to introduce visitors, with a good level of support and comfort, to the traditions, lifestyle and hospitality of the Kyrgyz. Small groups are well catered for in yurt camps located in areas of great beauty and equipped with long-drop toilet and solar-heated shower. Food is abundant and high quality. They also run stunning horseback tours to Song Kul. Ecotour actively promote sustainable tourism.

Edelweiss: 68/9 Usenbaev. Tel. (0312) 280788, 284254; fax. 68003. email: edelweiss@elcat.kg; www: edelweiss.elcat.kg.
An all-round team offering standard tours in central Asia plus mountaineering and trekking. Downhill and heli-skiing specialists with ski and mountaineering equipment for hire.

ITMC "Tien-Shan": 1–A Molodaya Gvardia. Tel. (0312) 651221, 651404; fax. 650747; email: itmc@elcat.kg; web: itmc.centralasia.kg.
Reliable and friendly and run by a veteran mountaineer, ITMC are competent all-rounders, and specialists in mountaineering and trekking. They organise travel throughout Kyrgyzstan and the Silk Road, heli-skiing and mountain biking. From June to September they run a basecamp at Achikh Tash (for Peak Lenin) and on the North Inylchek glacier (for Khan Tengri).

Kyrgyz Concept: Block 1,42/1 Isanoya. Tel. (0312) 692727, 692929; fax. 660220; email: tours@concept.kg; web: concept.kg. Also at 126 Chui Prospect. Tel. 666006; fax. 661011; and for air reservations at 69 Kievskaya, tel. 600404; email: ticketing@netmail.kg.
This Kyrgyz-owned company offers a high quality service to groups and individuals, tourists and business visitors. Their tours are lowland cultural tours throughout Central Asia. At present this is one of the best places to buy domestic and international flights. They also offer car hire (with driver) and transfers, conference management and translation services.

Kyrgyz Land (formerly Kyrgyz Travel): 237 Elebosova. Tel/fax. (0312) 678444 email: d-sasha@elcat.kg; www: kyrgyzland.com.

This friendly, family firm are trekking specialists, also offering mountain biking, bird watching and wildlife trips with their personal, in-depth knowledge of the mountains south of Lake Issyk-Kul. Also tours throughout Kyrgyzstan. They also have a comfortable guesthouse at Tamga.

Muza: 107 Kieveskaya. Tel. (0312) 210752; fax. 610620; email: info@gocentralasia.com; www: www.gocentralasia.com.

As well as Kyrgyzstan and Silk Road tours, Muza offer treks and cultural trips off the beaten track. Also sell airline tickets.

NoviNomad: 28 Togolok Moldo. Tel. (0312) 622381; fax. 622380 email: novinomad@elcat.kg; www: novinomad.com.

This dynamic, reliable company offers general tours, using primarily home and yurt stays. They are particularly involved in the development of the trekking sector, providing training to guides and porters, and opportunities to young local people to get a taste for the mountains. They work closely with Ecotrek in Karakol. They have 'yurt inns' at Jeti-Oguz and Song Kul.

Shepherd's Way Trekking: PO Box 2032. Tel. (0312) 297406, 667371; mob. (0502) 518315; email: shepherd@elcat.kg; www: kyrgyztrek.com.

This friendly, professional family firm offers fully supported horse treks and comes highly recommended. The owners spent childhood summers on the jailoo with their shepherd parents. Their intimate knowledge of the mountain world behind Barskoon, their love of their culture and of horses are central to their company ethic. The village benefits from a portion of company profits. They organise a multitude of horse-treks at all levels (including beginners); unusual ones include the Alay valley and Barskoon to Tash Rabat.

Silk Road Water Centre: 104 Musa Jalila. Tel/fax. (0312) 284142 email: kyrgyzraft@infotel.kg; web: swcenter.nm.ru.

An experienced rafting firm which offers the full range of tours. Little English is spoken in the office. They provide equipment, including dry suits, helmets and life jackets.

Tien Shan Travel Ltd: 127 Scherbakov. Tel/fax. (0312) 270576 email: travel@tien-shan.com; www: tien-shan.com.

Mountaineering experts, this experienced company offers mountaineering, trekking and rafting and runs base camps on the South Inylchek Glacier and at Achikh Tash.

Top Asia: 175 Toktogula. Tel/fax. (0312) 211644; email: topasia@mail.kg. www: bishkek.su/TopAsia, topasia.kg.

Friendly with an emphasis on Kyrgyz culture, offering standard tours.

Turkestan: 273 Toktogula, Karakol. Tel. (0312) 511560; mob (0543) 911451 email: psi61@mail.ru .www.turkestan.biz. Friendly and flexible, they offer all kinds of tours nationwide and logistical support.

Transport

ROAD

As elsewhere in the former Soviet Union, ageing trusty red Ikarus **buses** still ply the roads of Kyrgyzstan running to an approximate schedule. They are state-owned and serve all but the remotest parts of the country. They are being superceded by **Mercedes Princess** buses, which are faster and more comfortable, on the main routes. Tickets for passengers and stowed baggage are bought at bus station booths. It is advisable to arrive early as buses get crowded or

Bus stop shaped like a kalpak

leave early when full. Services to some rural areas are not daily so check these in advance. Buses will carry any form of luggage, including bicycles and livestock.

In competition with the public buses are a growing number of privately run **minibuses**. They generally congregate at the bus station gates and are faster, more expensive and cover some of the remoter areas missed by public buses. Prices are fixed and tickets bought from the driver. Get there early to ensure a seat.

Shared taxis, found outside the bus station, are usually quicker still and will depart on fixed routes, with fixed prices, when full. For journeys to some of the most interesting places in the country you will need private transport, which can be arranged with any of the tour operators or with Community-Based Tourism co-ordinators (see page 292) or with a taxi driver. Key qualities in negotiations with taxi drivers are patience, fair-mindedness and determination!

Given the appalling state of many of the roads, it is worth taking careful note of the condition of the tyres and the driver's sobriety before making a decision, particularly in winter. In winter, the public buses' more leisurely pace is often safer over the icy passes. It is worth noting that accident rates are spiralling with the increasing numbers of cars, deteriorating roads and appalling driving. On the road to Balykchy, crashed cars are mounted on concrete blocks as a graphic road safety warning to drivers.

SILKROAD VOYAGER
Via Karakoram Highway
PAK CASPIAN is operating a scheduled service by 8 seater minibus from Islamabad to Kashgar, China via the Karakoram Highway connecting to Bishkek, Kyrgyzstan, via Osh, from 24th May to 1st October 2008.

Departures are guaranteed if at least one passenger is booked. The average driving time per day is about 6 hours. Passengers may book a stop over and continue on another bus. Reservations must be made at least 2 weeks before departure.

Email: kkhbus@gmail.com

RAIL

Kyrgyzstan's terrain does not lend itself to train travel. From Bishkek they run to Balykchy, Moscow, Novosibirsk, Tashkent and Almaty. The only seriously used route is to Moscow; for others, a bus is quicker and safer. Unlike Russia's excellent railway network, Central Asia's trains are riddled with crime and best avoided. Bishkek to Osh and Bishkek to Kashgar lines are mooted but unlikely to materialise in the near future.

In summer 2007 the Kyrgyz and Chinese governments agreed, in principle, to construct a new railway line to link Kashgar with Osh.

BICYCLE

The bike, rivalled only by the horse, offers the most rewarding means to travel through some of the most scenic mountain terrain in the world. Unmade or broken roads and tracks, inaccessible to cars, disappear into the mountains; CBT homestays and yurt stays offer a respite from camping in remoter areas. Increasing numbers are pedalling across central Asia, while shorter trips in Kyrgyzstan can be done independently or well-supported through a tour operator.

However, cyclists are vulnerable. Bike parts are almost non-existent; few people outside the main towns speak foreign languages; drivers can be drunk; and roads are pot-holed, dusty and rock-strewn, which can be hard going. Be flexible and be prepared for all weathers.

Activities

As a cyclist said when lost somewhere between the Dolon pass and Karakol, 'it didn't really matter, for in Kyrgyzstan all roads led to majestic vistas and encounters with friendly people'. Kyrgyzstan's natural paradise can be enjoyed by all: from those who prefer to travel with the comfort of a car and a short day stroll to serious mountaineers, you have a vast menu to choose from: walking, horse-riding or cycling through canyons and pasturelands strewn with alpine flowers; trekking amongst snowy peaks; scaling walls of rock or ice at sub-zero temperatures; relaxing by turquoise lakes high in the mountains, surrounded by juniper, maple and Siberian pine forests; or careering in a canoe or dinghy down one of Kyrgyzstan's many glacier-fed waterways. For most of these you will need some level of support—see local operators for each area and Bishkek-based tour operators.

MOUNTAINEERING AND ROCK CLIMBING

Peak-baggers head for the giants of the Central Tien Shan, a knot of peaks where the massive ranges of Kokshal Too, Sary Jaz, Tengri-Tag, Inylchek and Kaindi come together. The highest and toughest is Jengish Chokosu (7,439 metres), formerly called Peak Pobeda, which can be climbed from 25 July–25 August. Khan Tengri (6,995 metres), claimed by both Kyrgyzstan and Kazakhstan but more easily and commonly ascended from Kyrgyzstan, looms above the others and has a haunting beauty as its snowy face runs through all known tones of red and orange in the setting sun. The most commonly used of the ten or so ascent routes start from the Inylchek glacier though there are still several untried routes. The climbing season is mid-July to mid-September.

Near Kyrgyzstan's southern border with Tajikistan, Kuh-i-Garmo (7,134 metres), previously known as Peak Lenin, is in the Pamir range and popular as one of the easiest 'seven thousanders' in the world, although the extreme and unpredictable weather it attracts still presents a significant danger to climbers.

The Kyrgyz Ala-Too, conveniently situated half an hour's drive from Bishkek, offer a wide choice of high-altitude fun for mountaineers and rock climbers. The most popular areas are Ala Archa (4,875m), the Ak Sai glacier and around the Alamyedin valley. Hundreds of virgin peaks throughout the country are still waiting for their first ascent.

Tien-Shan RTM (Rescue Transportation in Mountains) has been rescuing injured people in the mountains for more than a decade. A not-for-profit foundation, **Mountain Rescue**, tel. (0312) 651404, is currently undergoing registration which is expected to be complete by December 2007. Tien-Shan RTM will then hand over operations and equipment. The new foundation will arrange search and rescue, medical and repatriation services to those with payment guarantees. They prefer mountaineers to register before departure, leaving names, itineraries and insurance details.

TREKKING

Trekking possibilities in Kyrgyzstan tempt more superlatives than would be decent in a guidebook. The variety is immense and there is something, with spectacular views, for everyone, from a picturesque two-hour stroll to a three- or four-week trek through demanding terrains. Unlike many other trekking destinations (Nepal, for example), the trekking infrastructure of Kyrgyzstan is poorly developed and deluxe or tea-house treks are not yet available. You pass through very few villages (though you may encounter summer yurt camps) and equipment and service are more basic.

Most treks take you through pastures with shepherds' yurt camps, to mountain lakes, forests, canyons and waterfalls. Even the shorter and easier treks can keep lofty white peaks in view, particularly in the Ala Archa and Sokoluk valleys of the Kyrgyz Ala-Too. Around Karakol, at the feet of the mighty Tien Shan, day strolls in the Altyn Arashan or Jeti-Oguz valleys are rewarding, while three- and four-day treks take you high into the mountains and demand only a moderate level of fitness. On the fabulous, remote routes from the south shore of Lake Issyk Kul to Naryn or Lake Song Kul, you can see eagles and relax in hot water springs. One of the many trekking highlights is the gracefully beautiful mountains of Sary Chelek Biosphere Reserve, famous for its seven vivid blue lakes and its pristine ecology. From here, routes across the Chatkal range claim bird's eye views of the Reserve and take you to the Chatkal valley and Besh Aral Reserve.

If you enjoy vast open spaces and a wild west feel, head for the plateaux and arid hills of central Kyrgyzstan, around the Ak Tala and Terek river valleys and, to combine this with lush pastures, the At-Bashy range east of Naryn.

Safety in the mountains deserves serious thought and preparation. Adequate clothing, with layers for warmth, sturdy water- and wind-proofs and good walking boots are a must, even at the height of summer. You should stock up on food at the local town, allowing for the occasional purchase of eggs and dairy products from farms en route. Tour operators can arrange any level of support for your trek, including porters, cook and food drops if you prefer to trek in comfort (and pay the price!). Some hire camping and mountain gear. Contact them in advance to ensure the best use of your time.

GUIDES

It is always safer to hire a guide for even a short trek as trails are generally unmarked and maps are poor. It also provides much needed local employment. The larger tour operators often import guides from Bishkek. Wherever possible, it is best to hire a guide locally (although check the language situation—some local operators have interpreters): they will give more of an insight into local culture, have a better knowledge of the terrain and wildlife and will know the best places for unofficial refreshment en route.

Currently no guide accreditation scheme exists in Kyrgyzstan. However, with support from European mountaineering organisations, tour operators are beginning to provide training for guides and other trekking support workers. Before heading into hazardous mountains, it is advisable to check your guide's credentials, training and experience.

Horse-Riding

The best way to glimpse Kyrgyzstan from the locals' perspective is on horseback. A Kyrgyz saying sums it up: 'Our grandfathers were born on a horse and they died on a horse'. Kyrgyz horses are hardy, wiry beasts, purpose-built for high altitude, rough paths and scant food. Extremely sure-footed, they will have a go at almost anything. Particularly recommended areas to explore on horseback are day treks near Bishkek (Alltournative), the routes from the south shore of Lake Issyk Kul (Shepherds Way), Bokonbaevo to Lake Song Kul (Ecotour). For more experienced riders, At-Bashy mountains and Sary Chelek.

Horse-treks should be arranged in advance where possible. No hard hats are available. At Community-Based Tourism villages, you might have to wait a day for horses to be available for longer treks at the height of the farming season.

Rafting and Canoeing

Possibilities in Kyrgyzstan range from Levels 2 to 4. For trips starting at half a day there is the Chui river, which flows through the austere scenery of the eerie Boom canyon, just two hours from Bishkek by car, and also the nearby Chong Kemin river. Further afield and more rigorous, involving camping, are trips on the Suusamyr river (Levels

2–4), through fast-changing landscape at the western edge of Suusamyr valley. To the west of Naryn, rafting trips go through the dramatic gorges of the Naryn river (Levels 3–4). In the autumn of 1999 a group of death-wish rafters from Russia took on the magnificent marble canyons of the perilous Sary Jaz river—and lived to show the video. The Song Kul river flowing from the lake is said to offer appealing and technically fairly manageable canoeing. Trips can be arranged through Silk Road Water Centre in Bishkek (see page 83).

SKIING

Heli-Skiing (October to March) on fresh powdery snow is magnificent in the mountains around Bishkek and Karakol. Skiing is from a maximum of 4,200 metres. You ski with two guides and carry radios and avalanche detection equipment. The avalanche threat is assessed as moderate. Accommodation is in chalets or sanatoria (see Edelweiss, page 82).

Downhill skiing is available in the Karakol valley (see page 175) and at Kashka Suu in the Kyrgyz Ala-Too (see page 135).

HUNTING

By 1985, 15 per cent of native Kyrgyz mammals and ten per cent of birds were threatened with extinction. Even animals listed in the 'Red Book', a Soviet catalogue of endangered species, have been poached mercilessly over the years. Recently this situation has been exacerbated by foreign hunters, who consistently flout regulations devised to protect biodiversity and who offer bribes to local firms willing to poach.

Climate

Kyrgyzstan's position near the middle of the Eurasian land mass creates a continental climate with sharp local variations. In January the average lowland temperature is -5°, a little warmer in Osh and around Lake Issyk Kul which, as its name 'warm lake' would suggest, does not freeze in winter. Mountain valley temperatures typically fall to -30°C or lower, the record being -53.6°C. In winter, Bishkek temperatures range from +4°C in the sun to -20°C at night. Freezing fog sometimes closes the airport and makes roads perilous. In the lowlands, the thaw begins in February or March. However, many mountain passes and some sections of the Bishkek to Osh road are still under snow in May. Spring weather tends to be changeable and temperatures can drop suddenly. Most of the rain falls in April, May and June, resulting in avalanches, land- and mud-slides.

Trekking is best from May to September (depending on the area), although in the mountains rain and snowstorms are possible at any time. The average lowland temperature for July and August is 26–30°C although it can creep over 40°C. Highland temperatures average at 8–12°C. The higher valleys see sub-zero temperatures at night even in summer. Weather in the mountains changes constantly, taking you through the

Scenery at Tash Rabat

WOMEN AND MARRIAGE

If your wife is shrewish and nasty, it matters little that she is pretty.   Kyrgyz saying

In many ways, Kyrgyz women are much better off than most of their Central Asian sisters. The casual nomadic attitude to Islam has been traditionally favourable to women and the years of Soviet rule brought them greater opportunities than they'd had before. Soviet education statistics show that both Kyrgyz and Kazakh women achieve higher levels than those from traditionally sedentary societies.

That said, the patriarchal system which governed traditional nomadic society for hundreds of years never truly disappeared under the Soviets and has been strongly revived since the fall of communism, to the detriment of women.

That much was made clear by the international watchdog, Human Rights Watch, in its first report on Kyrgyzstan in 2006 in which it accused the government of not taking domestic violence and bride-kidnapping seriously. While Kyrgyzstan had progressive laws on violence against women, the report said it failed to implement them.

The levels of domestic violence uncovered by Human Rights Watch are partly a symptom of the rise in poverty, unemployment and alcohol abuse in recent years; women have born the brunt of men's frustrations and stress. But some of it arises from an ancient custom, *ala kachuu* ('grab and run'). The authorities like to portray bride-kidnapping as a rare and harmless ancient ritual but women are genuinely afraid of it and the practice seems widespread, especially in rural areas. According to some estimates, close to a third of married women were snatched off the street.

In its worst form, the woman is forcibly kidnapped by a stranger or acquaintance and taken to his parents' home where his family puts huge pressure upon her to accept the marriage. In the most brutal cases, she is beaten and raped. Even if she rejects the marriage, her family may refuse to take her back, especially if she has spent a night away, something considered deeply shameful. Many feel they have little choice but to marry their kidnapper. One woman, in her mid-20s, kidnapped five years beforehand, shrugged and said: "What can I do? It's our tradition." In urban areas, however, women are increasingly unwilling to submit meekly to a marriage they have not sought.

Not all 'kidnappings' are forced; they may be planned jointly by the couple. An elderly shepherd in his 70s, when asked why he had kidnapped his wife, laughed and said, 'Simple answer: do you know such a thing as love? I stole her but she knew about it. We made an appointment and I took her to my house.'

Simply 'running away together' is a common way of arranging a marriage. The prospective husband takes his bride-to-be to his parents' home. In the evening his parents contact her family to tell them they no longer have a daughter: 'She is with us, she's our daughter now.' According to tradition, her family then asks her if she really wants the marriage, and urges her new family to look after her.

All marriages are conducted by the imam (Islamic clergyman). Before the ceremony the bride spends three days veiled behind a curtain at the home of her new parents-in-law. Friends and family make congratulatory visits. Anyone wishing to see the bride must pay a small sum, US$1 or less, in a custom called *gorunduk* (the word also applies to seeing a newborn baby). Meanwhile the husband pays the *kalym*, or bride price, to his bride's family. There is no fixed sum but it is supposed to reflect the value he places upon her. Her family usually gives a bed, blankets and pillows as a wedding present.

After the marriage the couple traditionally lives with the groom's parents. One man, explaining why he was so keen to have a son after five daughters, told us: 'My daughters are not my children, I am raising them for someone else.' This does not mean Kyrgyz parents don't love their daughters, more that it reflects the sense that a woman's allegiance is to her husband and his family after marriage.

In the family hierarchy, the daughter-in-law has the lowliest place, at least until the birth of her first child. She is never allowed to sit in the *tyor*, the place for honoured guests; her role is to serve guests and attend to domestic chores. She must behave with decorum in the presence of her husband's parents, which includes always wearing the headscarf adopted in public by married women. Traditionally she must never refer to her husband's senior male relations by name but by their position in the family: 'Your father's eldest brother' and so on.

Despite such strict social conventions, Kyrgyz women are much more active in all walks of life than in neighbouring Central Asian countries (apart, perhaps, from Kazakhstan). Today, women go to university, run their own businesses and are increasingly asserting themselves in personal relationships (one reason for the rising divorce rates). In many ways they are the backbone of modern Kyrgyz society. One woman politician told us: 'When we changed to the market economy, all the difficulties were placed on women's shoulders.'

When it comes to political participation, however, women are sliding backwards. In 2001 they were elected to 6.6 per cent of positions; after the 2005 elections, that figure dropped to 1.3 per cent. Currently there are just two female ministers and no women hold regional governorships. And since independence, the political representation of women in state agencies has plummeted from 40 per cent to four per cent.

Some of those who have tried to participate in political life have been threatened with losing their jobs; others have come under attack by unofficial but influential councils of village elders convened to persuade them to stay out of political life and 'not to engage in a contest with men'.

Despite this dismal situation, there are many inspiring women in Kyrgyzstan who are taking a lead as activists or leaders of non-governmental bodies. They include Tolekan Ismailova, who heads Citizens Against Corruption, and Byubyusara Ryskulova who started the first anti-domestic violence organisation in Kyrgyzstan. Both, along with four others, were nominated to the 1,000 Women for the Nobel Peace Prize list in 2005.

even in summer. Weather in the mountains changes constantly, taking you through the extremes of winter and summer in one day. Although clouds tend to collect over the mountains, Kyrygzstan is generally sunny, with an average of 247 sunny days a year.

Snow usually falls by September in the mountains, and by November in the lowlands. By October, the average temperature in Bishkek has dropped to 10ºC.

Maps

The maps available outside Kyrgyzstan are general and cover the whole of Central Asia. More detailed maps in Cyrillic and Roman script are available from the Bishkek Cartographic Agency at 107/4 Kievskaya (third floor); email: geodes@elcat.kg.

Arguably the best country map currently available is the State Department of Geodesy and Cartography Kyrgyzstan map published in 2006, but this is a political map and does not show mountains. A physical map is also available but, unfortunately, not one combining the two. Novinomad, Bishkek, and CBT and Ecotrek, Karakol, stock maps, but none has sufficient detail for trekking. Another good option is the Kyrgyzstan Travel Map published by Rarity Firm Ltd (aka 'Raritet' bookshop in Dom Druzhba off Ala-Too Square), which has some country information on the back. Novinomad have produced a series of maps of the region, the country (1:1,000,000), and specific areas: Karakol and Inylchek Glacier; northern Issyk Kul and Chong Kemin valley; southern Issyk Kul west of Barskoon, all with a scale of 1:100,000.

Street names in all towns are changing from Soviet to Kyrgyz; a confusing collection of old and new are used by locals and marked on street signs. In Bishkek, for example, Sovietskaya now has three new names: Baitik Baatyr (south), Abdrakhmanova (centre) and Bakinskaya (north). A variety of Bishkek maps are now available; be sure to choose one showing old and new street names.

Useful, but not sufficiently detailed for trekking unguided, is a series of topographic maps on a scale of 1:200,000, covering the whole country in 14 sheets for U S$3 each.

Safety

Overall, Kyrgyzstan is a hospitable, tolerant and safe country and you are far more likely to come away feeling bloated on hospitality than cheated or abused in any way. The reaction of Kyrgyz people to the terrorist attacks on New York and Washington in September 2001 was one of genuine shock, compassion and dismay. Most of the ex-pat businesspeople and aid workers who left Kyrgyzstan during the panicky weeks after September 11 quickly returned, realising that they faced no special risk.

Still, the low crime rate is growing and sensible precautions need to be taken, as anywhere else in the world. Drunkenness is common at all times of the day and drug use is rising. This has led to an increase in opportunistic street crime in cities, particularly

(right) Early dusk at Sary Chelek

Bishkek, around nightclubs, casinos, money change booths and the station. Growing numbers of street children pick pockets. After dark, avoid parks and poorly lit areas and choose your taxi with care—see Bishkek transport section for taxi services. Probably the biggest hazard comes from uncovered man-holes in the street—bring a torch.

Beggars are increasingly common. They are mostly street children, alcoholics, refugees and, perhaps most tragic and sincere of all, Slav pensioners who can no longer survive on a minute pension.

Women travellers do not appear to face any particular danger. General harassment is extremely rare. It is customary for people to befriend only their own sex; innocent friendly gestures towards a man can be misinterpreted.

With an intensification of terrorist and drug activity on Kyrgyzstan's Tajik border, police are becoming more vigilant. Some are just doing their job while less scrupulous officers are looking for documentation irregularities that warrant a 'fine'. Always carry your passport; police have the right to see your documents and to search you. In Bishkek the prime spot is outside Zum, although the situation appears to be improving.

If you are stopped, maintain a friendly, confident air and say 'salaam aleikum', the traditional Muslim greeting. Before co-operating with document inspection, ask to see the officers' ID, and refuse further contact if none is available. Politely insist that you stay where you are and never get into a car; public tolerance with police harassment is wearing thin and locals have been known to help foreigners in difficulty, so make a scene if necessary.

If you have to pay a fine, remember that the official policy is that all fines should be paid at a bank, not direct to officers.

Some scams are about in Bishkek and the general rule is if someone drops something, don't pick it up. Take particular care when changing money and preferably use an office, ie off the street. Don't be tempted by apparently better rates offered by individuals on the street—a sleight of hand will almost certainly leave you short.

Finally, always keep details of your embassy or consulate to hand and check their website for up to date safety advice before travelling (see page 77). Civil protest has become increasingly common and can be volatile—keep your distance. Emergency numbers: police 102, city ambulance 103, commercial ambulance 548666, fire 101.

Warning—Terrorism is a possibility anywhere in Central Asia—be vigilant.

Tension is inevitable at the junction of Kyrgyzstan, Uzbekistan and Tajikistan in the Pamir Alay. The area to the south and west of Osh remains volatile and unpredictable and as a result, since 1999, the British Government has frequently advised travellers to avoid the area entirely. At the time of writing, the warning has been lifted, but it is advisable to check.

The area is problematic for a number of reasons. For a start it is the main route for opium from Afghanistan, headed for the streets of Russia and western Europe, and so has prompted the interest of organised criminal gangs.

At the turn of the century there were a number of incursions by Islamic militants which, in 1999 and 2000, involved localised fighting and hostages being seized. Less serious incursions into Batken have occurred since then, most recently in 2006; due to its porous borders, this part of Kyrgyzstan remains vulnerable to the influence of extremist Islamic groups from outside the country. The security forces have been accused of heavy-handed tactics and the situation remains tense. However, instability in this strip of land is localised and doesn't suggest a wider problem with anarchy or extremism.

Health

Your most valuable document after your passport in Kyrgyzstan will be your travel health insurance, complete with evacuation clause. The health service is generally agreed to be in an abysmal condition and is paralysed by corruption and lack of funds. Only use it if unavoidable. The service is free to locals but the kind of attention you get depends on the amount of money you can afford to slip to medical staff. Horror stories abound of foul play, such as doctors refusing to complete an operation until relatives pay more money.

No immunisations are mandatory but polio, tetanus, hepatitis 'A' and typhoid fever are recommended. Malaria is present in the south and in a ring around the outskirts of Bishkek. Rabies is said to be on the increase. Dogs cover the whole range from utterly pathetic to pretty fierce but don't tend to attack. If in doubt, pick up a stone; they understand this gesture.

The sun represents a serious threat in summer: a hat and sunscreen should be worn for protection. One of the most common causes of diarrhoea is dehydration, which sets in particularly quickly on the plains and at higher altitudes, so ensure that you drink plenty of clean water. Bottled water is readily available all over the country.

Fridges are rare outside the cities so the culinary delights of the country can carry bugs to which unaccustomed stomachs are particularly susceptible. Dairy products are not pasteurised and meat frequently hangs uncovered. The rule of thumb is that if you can't peel it or cook it, then leave it. However, this would deny you the tasty range of dairy products, topped by the traditional Kyrgyz drink, *koumys* (fermented mare's milk), which would be a shame.

Equally tempting are the luscious mounds of fresh and dried fruits that hit the bazaars in summer. Try to avoid cooked food that has been sitting; *laghman* and *shorpa* are generally reasonably safe as they have been boiled. When struck by the inevitable bouts of diarrhoea, it is crucial to rehydrate with green or black tea, bottled, boiled or purified water, rehydration solution and soft drinks allowed to go still.

Your medical kit might include: disposable needles, painkillers, diarrhoea pills, rehydration powders, water sterilisation tablets, antiseptic spray or wipes, plasters, dressing pads, bandages, tweezers, scissors, insect repellent and sting relief in summer.

The Family Medical Clinic is at 144a Bokonbaeva, tel. 660644. A list of clinics, hospitals and dentists can be found on http://bishkek.usembassy.gov/medicalinformation.htm. The Republican Diagnostic Centre at Kievskaya 27 (near Shopokova) in Bishkek is used by the UN for medical checkups. If you don't speak Russian take an interpreter. For urgent dental treatment, try the improbably named Hollywoodskaya Ulibka at Kievskaya 112, tel. (0312) 666522.

Altitude sickness can affect anybody above 2,500 metres. The symptoms are breathlessness, headache, nausea, loss of appetite and quickened heartbeat. Try to ascend slowly to allow your body to acclimatise—500 metres per day is the basic rule, drink plenty of fluids (no alcohol), eat well and don't smoke. If the symptoms persist beyond a couple of days or if you begin to turn blue, descend immediately as fatal conditions develop quickly.

Accommodation

The kind of accommodation you opt for will, in large measure, dictate the nature of the experience you have in Kyrgyzstan. There is a danger that, staying in hotels and travelling with a car and driver, you could largely by-pass Kyrgyz culture altogether.

Accommodation options have mushroomed all over Kyrgyzstan. In Bishkek the visitor can pick from the whole range, from a five-star Hyatt hotel to budget options and family stays. Osh, Naryn, Karakol, Jalal-Abad and the north shore of Lake Issyk Kul all have comfortable modern hotels. Hotels, along with other buildings, are often ridiculously hard to find. It's as if a shroud of Soviet secrecy still clings to the streets—few guesthouses have a name and virtually none has a sign outside, or even a street number by which to locate them. Even very small towns have once-gleaming and proud **Soviet-era hotels**, now suffering general dilapidation, water problems (or absence) and prostitution.

An exciting development in recent years has been the growth of the network of **Community-Based Tourism (CBT) homestays**, incorporating Shepherd's Life, set up by villagers with the help of Swiss development agency Helvetas. This means, for the first time, that you can travel well off the beaten track in Kyrgyzstan, in the confidence of finding safe and comfortable accommodation.

CBT provides food and lodging in private homes in villages, and in yurts on summer pastures. They are not professional tourism workers but communities of farmers and villagers. The scheme offers a great way for visitors to meet local families and learn about their lives, but there are compromises to be made. Washing facilities are usually limited to a hand basin, although increasingly families have a shower or a *banya*, a Russian-style sauna; this needs to be ordered in advance. Toilets are long drop, usually a hygienic minimum of 20 metres away from the house, and are often not very clean. Bring a torch. Toilet paper is normally provided; gone are the days when the pages of an old book were left in there, to be used as toilet paper, not reading material. For yurt stays bring a sleeping bag. (For more information on CBT see page 292).

Playing Nardy, a traditional board game

A number of 'Yurt Inns' are appearing in some regions, run by various Bishkek-based tour operators. They normally consist of a cluster of yurts offering dormitory-style accommodation, a yurt kitchen, a separate toilet and non-private washing facilities.

The whole country is a campsite. When **camping** in rural areas, for safety pitch the tent near a village or shepherd's yurt camp and ask permission beforehand. Local dogs may be noisy but they keep wolves away. It is better not to camp in towns, as poverty and drinking are increasing petty crime. When camping wild, be aware of damage to the environment from detergent soaps, and ensure all rubbish is removed, not buried. There are currently no official campsites, other than at Turkestan Yurt Camp in Karakol.

Media

An excellent English-language newspaper, *The Times of Central Asia* (www.times.kg), is produced twice weekly providing fairly thorough coverage of the main issues and events in Central Asia. It is sold at news stands and is free of charge at some hotels and restaurants. The other English-language paper, the weekly *Bishkek Observer*, focuses mainly on Kyrgyzstan with a couple of pages of world news.

Respublika is a privately-owned Kyrgyz-language daily; the very popular daily, *Vecherniy Bishkek*, is a privately-owned Russian-language paper; *Slovo Kyrgyzstana*, a government-owned Russian-language paper, comes out three times a week.

Foreign newspapers, a couple of days old, can sometimes be found at news stands and hotels.

Internet news agencies reporting local and international news include Eurasianet (www.eurasianet.org), Institute for War and Peace Reporting (www.iwpr.net), Kabar news agency (http://en.kabar.kg) and Aki-Press (www.akipress.com).

Discovery Kyrgyzstan (www.silkpress.com) is an English-language magazine published four times a year featuring articles on tourism and other matters. *Steppe Magazine* (www.steppemagazine.com) is twice-yearly glossy with interesting articles and fine photography, focusing mainly on the arts and culture of Central Asia.

The Kyrgyz National Television and Radio Broadcasting Corporation is state-run and has two networks in Kyrgyz and Russian. Pyramida and NTS in Bishkek, Ecological Youth in Issyk Kul and Osh TV in Osh are all private channels and there are several more. Cable TV is available in Bishkek offering a large number of foreign stations.

Money and Costs

In August 1993, Kyrgyzstan was the proud, if nervous, first Central Asian country to break out of the rouble zone and introduce its own currency, the *som*. It appears in notes only and is divided into 100 *teen*, which are rarely used.

The preferred foreign currency is US dollars, although euros are increasingly popular. US dollar bills should be in pristine condition and printed post-1995.

Cash can be exchanged in banks and some hotels but most convenient and profitable are the **exchange booths** (*obmyen valyoot*) found in most towns. Be vigilant when changing money in the street; and don't expose tempting wads of dollars in public. You may receive a less favourable rate for low-denomination dollar bills (US$20 and under).

Throughout this book, prices are approximate and are quoted in US dollars to make allowance for the fluctuations of the som, but all payment should be made in som, except to large tour operators and hotels. The cost of living, extortionate for locals, is currently very low for those from hard currency countries. Please note that prices quoted are guidelines only and will increase over time.

Traveller's cheques can be exchanged at most banks in major towns.

Credit cards are increasingly accepted in the major cities, and some banks give credit card cash advances. Bishkek has a growing number of ATMs allowing cash withdrawals, including at Zum and Dordoi Plaza.

Communications and Post

Local phone calls are free from people's houses but to use a public booth you will need a token (*zheton*) costing a few som. The old booths are quickly being replaced with card-operated phones (*taksofon*). The cards (*taksofoniy cartiy*) and *zheton* are available from street kiosks. It is now possible to make international calls from some of these card phones, although it would be cheaper to call from KyrgyzTelecom (10 som per minute to Europe and US) or internet cafés, which now have phone booths. Calling from major hotels is another, more expensive, option.

Kyrgyzstan's country code is 996. For an international line dial '00' and the country code. For Almaty, dial 00 7 3272 and for Tashkent dial 00 998 71 for seven-figure numbers or 712 for six-figure numbers. To call the operator in Bishkek call 107 (162 for the international operator). **Emergency** numbers in Bishkek are: Fire 101, Police 102, Ambulance 103.

Mobile telephone coverage is increasing. You can buy a phone from a department store to use within Kyrgyzstan—BITEL is currently considered the most reliable provider. Top-up cards are readily available—look for the MobiCard sign. **Satellite** phones may be hired from Aylesbury Satellite Systems, tel (0312) 650880, email info@globalasia.ru.

Thanks to Soviet telephone line networks and improvements made by KyrgyzTelecom, **Internet** services are found in most towns of any size, either in cafés, libraries or tour operators' offices.

The **postal service** is reliable, with letters taking about ten days to two weeks to reach Europe. Parcels can be posted from the main post office in each town. Packages should be left open for the clerk to inspect the contents, with books and papers packed separately from clothes and souvenirs. Take a length of linen so that the parcel can be sewn up and sealed afterwards. Any customs requirements must be cleared beforehand.

Express Mail can be sent from Bishkek and Osh by DHL and Federal Express. **Shipping Companies** include ARICargo, in Bishkek and Osh (see relevant sections).

Electricity

In common with the other Central Asian states, Kyrgyzstan uses European style two-pin plugs for 220v, 50Hz. There is no shortage of water for the country's hydroelectric stations but cross-border fuel agreements (or disagreements) lead to power cuts. Bring candles and a torch. If you are travelling to China, Zum and Beta Stores stock converter plugs.

Time and Opening Hours

Kyrgyzstan is six hours ahead of Greenwich Mean Time and two hours ahead of Moscow time. Daylight Savings Time is no longer in operation. Regular retail hours are 9.00am–5.30pm Monday to Saturday, but many places close for an hour at lunch time.

Shopping

It is with bemusement, turning to delight, that Kyrgyz women are discovering the Western penchant for their functional felt handicrafts.

Traditional brightly coloured *shyrdaks*, used as rugs and wall hangings, are now being produced in a variety of sizes and more muted colours to meet the tastes of the foreign market. Felt bags, cushion covers, slippers for all members of the family, miniature yurts, little statues and figurines to be hung from the car mirror are all churned out in felt and lined up in souvenir shops. Leather goods, used for transporting milk or making *koumys* are also for sale, along with musical instruments and *kalpaks*, the traditional conical felt hat once worn by all self-respecting Kyrgyz men.

A rare and beautiful item is the *tush kyiz*, a large piece of cloth embroidered with stylised patterns round the edge. Made by a grandmother for weddings, it is hung over the marriage bed for good luck. These beautiful objects are rarely found for sale so if you come across one in reasonable condition it is well worth snapping it up. Prices increase with age: for a 15-year-old *tush kyiz* you would pay around US$150. *Shyrdaks* range in price from US$25 to US$100, depending on size and condition; the pressed felt carpets, *ala-kiyiz*, are cheaper.

With all handicrafts, check for machine-made interlopers; you should see the discontinuities of thread on the back and a neatly sewn border.

Felt products bought at co-operative outlets support rural income-generation initiatives. These include **Altyn Kol** (Golden Hands), found in 'Shepherd's Life' villages; **Altyn Oimok** (Golden Thimble), a creative handicraft project in Bokonbaevo on the southern shore of Lake Issyk Kul; and **Kyrgyz Qorku** (Kyrgyz Style) in Bishkek. While still an important source of income (one recent workshop on making a *shyrdak*, traditionally women's work, included an unprecedented two men), these co-operatives seem to be evolving into more commercial operations.

In an attempt to prevent their cultural heritage from ending up in American and European homes and museums, the authorities require a certificate from the Ministry of Culture to export anything looking as though it might exceed 30 years. This costs approximately US$30 and can take up to a week.

Customs, Dress and Conduct

A guest is sent from God. Even if he stays a short while, he will see a lot.

Kyrgyz Saying

Both at home and as a guest,
Eat and drink as others request.

Kyrgyz Saying

These old Kyrgyz sayings sum it up: guests are placed on a pedestal but also have an obligation to behave in a prescribed fashion in order to avoid offence. Ever since the days of the Silk Road, survival in the deserts and mountains of Central Asia has depended on the generosity of others. Now that many people depend on the informal economy and mutual favours, this sense of duty towards a guest is truer than ever. After so many years of isolation, Kyrgyz people are particularly glad to welcome foreign guests into their homes. Following are some hints to help you carry out your visitor duties and enjoy the partying (see page 292).

It is polite to bring a small gift (fruit, nuts or bread, for example) and, if the family have children, a souvenir from your home country—a postcard, key ring or badge. People are always interested in photos of your family and friends and your home, as long as it does not look too luxurious. When you enter someone's home, take off your shoes. Handshakes are between men and never across the sexes; shaking hands through a doorway brings bad luck. In an Uzbek home, never refuse when offered water poured from a ewer to wash your hands.

Handmade shyrdaks on sale at the Altyn Kol co-operative in Kochkor

Meals, especially in Uzbek households, often begin and end with a prayer, the *omin*, in which the cupped hands are held out to receive God's blessing and then lowered over the face. Guests must wait for the host to offer the *omin* to signal the end of the meal.

Meals are served on a cloth (*dastorkon*) set on the floor or a very low table. Be sure to keep feet well away from the cloth. It is considered polite for women to cover their bare feet—with socks for example. As elsewhere in Asia, the left hand is traditionally used for washing after defecating so should be kept well away from food. To offer, receive or handle food with your left hand is most insulting.

Bread is treated with the utmost respect: when offered, you should always take and eat a little bread even if you leave some; it is a way of accepting the host's hospitality. Bread should always be placed with the patterned side up and never thrown away in the street.

(above) Sewing a shyrdak
(below) Koumys jug

Food will be lavished on you—trying to decline it politely is normally ineffective. Whereas in Europe it is polite to refuse refreshments offered, in Kyrgyzstan it is considered an insult. You are not expected to finish what you are offered; in fact an empty bowl will be refilled. A little tea is normally served to the guest first and then thrown away and refilled to about half way, leaving room for the host to replenish it later.

A good 'guesting' will end with an army of empty vodka bottles. Women are not expected to drink much, but men come under considerable pressure to empty their glass. Watch your host: especially in Kyrgyz households, whereas Westerners tend to sip drinks and Russians down them in one, the Kyrgyz tradition is to drink half of the glass, leaving the second half to be topped up. The host won't consider that he has fulfilled his duties until the bottle is empty. It is easier to politely decline drink from the start, saying you have been ill or are teetotal. Once you start, everyone seriously expects you to go on to the bitter end. Starting to drink and then stopping earlier than the rest will be taken very badly. So it's either full abstention, or the whole cure. You will also be expected to take your turn in the toasting rounds; your hosts, friendship, the family and world peace are popular subjects.

The eye of the sheep is always given to the guest or someone you want to be friends with, so your particular honour will be to eat it without grimacing—quite a challenge for some. Women are advised to take a man along as this pleasure will then invariably fall to him. Other symbolic parts of the sheep are traditionally distributed as follows: the head is given to special guests or old people to whom you want to show respect. In a regional variation, around Naryn, the head may be given to a young boy as he will grow up to be head of the household. The foreleg is given for services rendered, so this usually goes to the daughter-in-law as she does most of the housework. The ear is given to young boys so that they will listen to their mothers. The roof of the mouth goes to brides and young women so that they will be good at embroidery (it is ridged so is said to resemble embroidery). The foot goes to children.

Sometimes, overwhelming hospitality can be hard to deal with, especially if you cannot face more food or if the host family is so poor that they have to borrow from the neighbours or slaughter their last chicken to give you a meal. Good justifications to drop into your jovial refusal are that you still have a long way to go, that you have already eaten a lot or that you do not have much appetite due to the altitude. Thank the potential host with *chong rakhmat* ('thanks a lot') and your right hand on your heart with a slight bow.

If you eat in a yurt, you might notice the strict allocation of seats. The guest's or oldest person's place around the mat is opposite the door, in the warmest spot. Seating progresses along the table in order of age and seniority until you reach the host, who sits with his back to the entrance, with his wife or daughter-in-law on his right hand side to serve food. Men and women have very specifically defined roles. Men are still regarded as the head of the family, except in some city households. The woman's realm is the yurt, the children and usually the milking.

Many Kyrgyz women seem to agree with the old grandmother who told us, 'I don't want him (her husband) in my kitchen. He's got his own work, outdoor work, and he knows his responsibilities. I have my work in the home and I have children, they can help me. Of course, if there is no one around, it's okay if he helps me a little. But the man is the head of the family and should take care of global matters, it's not right that they should deal with little things like the washing up.'

Although the Kyrgyz have been very selective in their application of Muslim tradition to their lives, they tend to apply Islamic dictates to cover up flesh, though to a much lesser extent than other Muslim societies. Minimally dressed visitors cause offence and imply a lack of respect for the culture. Visitors should not wear shorts or short skirts, 'vest' tops, or go barefoot, though short-sleeved tops are acceptable. In rural areas tight trousers should not be worn. It is respectful for women to cover their heads when visiting a mosque or holy place, including a Russian Orthodox church. You will undoubtedly see young people scantily clad; in Bishkek many women stroll the tree-lined avenues in skin-tight mini dresses, offering no concession to traditional notions of decorum, but foreigners doing the same will be looked down upon and accorded little respect. If they take your fancy, the colourful headscarves worn by Kyrgyz and Uzbek women protect your head from the sun and dust in the countryside. It is not customary for women to go to gravesides or mausolea.

There is no taboo amongst Kyrgyz people about asking what we would consider blunt personal questions. Women will frequently be asked where their husband and children are; any explanation of childlessness will be met with incomprehension and pity. A more difficult question is 'Skolko zarabatyvaesh?'—how much do you earn? The best thing to do is to 'translate' your income to Kyrgyz standards, relating it to the the high cost of living in the West.

Food and Drink

> While the besh-barmak is cooking, the wise man looks after the fire while the fool looks in the pot.
>
> Traditional Kyrgyz Saying

Although Kyrgyz cuisine is unlikely to achieve international renown, if you resign yourself to a limited choice and a lot of mutton, the Kyrgyz and Russian dishes together provide a tasty and sustaining menu.

The pièce de resistance of Kyrgyz cuisine is besh-barmak ('five fingers'), reserved for special occasions and really only worth sampling in a yurt. The ritual preparation is precise, from the killing of the sheep to its presentation.

Daily dishes reflect the nomadic focus on meat (mutton) and dairy products. There are few vegetables but delicious mounds of fruit appear in summer and autumn in the bazaars. Laghman is mutton stew with noodles and vegetables, often eaten with shredded cabbage, carrot or onion. Shorpo is laghman without the noodles. Manti, a steamed dumpling filled with meat, requires caution at unknown venues as meat quality varies wildly. Plov, is an Uzbek dish, with bits of meat and shredded parsnip or carrot thrown in. Shashlik, eaten with onions, is mutton kebab and delicious when fresh.

Russian restaurant meals can make a welcome change and often involve salad. Dishes include pirozhki, fried flat dough filled with potato or meat, a Russian pastry; blini are rolled pancakes filled with meat, Russian cottage cheese or jam. Ganfan, a Dungan dish of cut meat and vegetables over rice is frequently sold in markets. Ashlan Fuu is a Korean dish of spicy soup with vegetables and a kind of 'tofu'.

Lepyoshka and Kyrgyz *nan* bread are delicious straight from the clay oven. Food is generally served with tea (*chai*), either green (herbal) or black.

The best known of Kyrgyz drinks is *koumys*, made from fermented mare's milk, alleged to cure ailments and perk up your sex life. It has a strong taste not to everybody's liking but the less fermented varieties are easier on the unaccustomed palate. *Ayran*

(above) Shashlik; (below) Traditional Kyrgyz meal

(*kefir* in Russian) is runny yoghurt; *maksym*, a thick wheat-based drink that the Kyrgyz consider healthy in summer, is sold at street stalls under the brand name of Shoro (who also make *koumys*).

Alcohol arrived with the Russians at great social cost. Vodka (*arak* in Kyrgyz) is the favourite; its homemade counterpart, *samogon*, sold surreptitiously in kiosks, is lethal. Foreign beer is present in force, but tasty local brews are Bars and Steinbrau, brewed by a local German in Bishkek. *Kvas* is a yeasty Russian drink made from bread. Kyrgyz, Russian and foreign wines are now found in most restaurants and, occasionally, Russian champagne which is cheap and delicious.

Major towns have restaurants, *chaikhana* (teahouses), cafés and *stolovaya*—a basic café. Markets are stocked with seasonal produce and fresh dairy and kiosks sell salami, cheese, bread, Turkish biscuits and beer. Out on the road, pickings are slim, so plan ahead. Empty railway carriages in small villages and at major junctions house small counters stocked with Snickers bars, cigarettes, and vodka. If invited into a home, bear in mind that many people are in dire economic circumstances, struggling to put bread on the table, but will nevertheless offer you food.

Festivals and Holidays

Please note that the borders at Torugart and Irkeshtam passes are closed on public holidays and at weekends, and also from 1–7 October.

1 January	New Year's Day
7 January	Russian Orthodox Christmas
23 February	Army Day
8 March	Women's Day
21 March	Nooruz (Muslim Spring Festival)
1 May	Labour Day
5 May	Constitution Day
9 May	Victory Day (World War II)
31 August	Independence Day
November 7	October Revolution Day

The dates for the Muslim festivals of Orozo Ait (end of Ramadan) and Kurban Ait (Feast of the Sacrifice) depend on phases of the moon and change each year. Kurban Ait occurs 70 days after Orozo Ait.

Another festival which has become increasingly important since independence is the **Manas** celebration which is generally held around Independence Day, with traditional horseback games and feasting in Bishkek and Talas.

Nooruz is the main festival in Kyrgyzstan, a shamanistic rite adopted by Islam and celebrated all over Central Asia on 21 March, in honour of the spring equinox. During the Soviet years it was frequently banned. In 1989, in yet another vain attempt to distract attention away from growing Muslim nationalism in the region, the Soviet government resurrected the feast as a large official celebration. Now it is celebrated in style with dance, music and traditional games. A special meal is prepared which should include separate symbolic dishes for men and for women and seven items, all of which begin with 'sh': *sharob* (wine), *shir* (milk), *shirinliklar* (sweets), *shakar* (sugar), *sharbat* (sherbet), *sham* (candle) and *shona* (a bud). People join hands around burning juniper to ensure a good harvest.

GERMANY'S PRODIGAL SONS

If you happen to be in the Kant area (20 kilometres east of Bishkek) don't be too surprised to come across dusty villages with German names like Luxemburg, Rotfront or Thälmann. Near Talas, there is even a village called Johannesdorf. They are testimony to the fact that Kyrgyzstan was once home to a substantial German community. According to the 1989 census, there were 56,300 Germans (about 2 per cent of the population) in the republic, although the real numbers are believed to be substantially higher. They are known, or rather, remembered, for being competent, hard-working technicians, farmers and craftsmen.

Now how did German settlers end up here, a stone's throw from China? Some are descendants of Nazi prisoners of war who never made it home but this is only part of the story. The German presence in the Russian empire goes back to the late 18th century, when Catherine the Great (of German origin herself), invited farmers from Saxony and Prussia to help populate and develop the newly acquired territories in southern Russia, the Volga basin and the Crimea. Isolated from Germany, the so-called Rußland-Deutsche developed a separate culture, centred around their Protestant faith and their dialect of Saxon German, heavily laced with Russian loanwords.

In the late 19th century, when Russia conquered Central Asia, Germans from the Crimea and Ukraine were offered free land in present-day northern Kyrgyzstan. Much later, after 1941, the numbers of Germans swelled considerably when Stalin, convinced they would actively sympathize with the Nazis, had the entire ethnic German community from the western USSR deported. Many died along the way and the survivors were resettled in Siberia, Kazakhstan and Kyrgyzstan. Earmarked as 'traitors', Soviet Germans were long denied access to universities and Communist Party careers.

After 1991, the breakdown of the USSR and Germany's 'open door' policy for East European and CIS citizens of German origin offered the opportunity of a better life in the Heimat. Today, 75 per cent of the Germans have gone. The only village that has a substantial German community left is Bergtal, better known by its Soviet name Rotfront.

Bruno De Cordier

THE FINAL FAREWELL: A KYRGYZ FUNERAL

A man is helpless twice along life's road; when he begins his journey and when he has grown old.   Folk saying

The huge cemeteries on the outskirts of every town or village testify to the respect the Kyrgyz accord their dead. Funerals are traditionally large, costly affairs and the graves themselves are elaborate structures, frequently adorned with turrets or domes, decorated with marble or patterned brick tiles and topped with the Muslim crescent moon. In the past, when people had to move constantly with their herds, the Kyrgyz used to say the only proper time to have a settled home was after death. These mausoleums typically cost about US$220 (approximately the price of a horse) and the entire extended family is expected to contribute, with senior relations giving the equivalent of at least US$20 each. In January 2002, legislation was introduced to limit the amount spent on funerals. It is expected to be widely ignored.

The funeral itself lasts about ten days but the period of ritual mourning goes on for a year. Firstly, two yurts are erected; one for the women mourners and the other for the body of the dead person. Relations and close friends then gather to mourn. By tradition people express their sorrow openly, and guests will begin weeping long before they reach the home. Horsemeat, the most prestigious and expensive of foods, is traditionally served, along with *plov*.

After three days of communal mourning, the dead person is buried in a white cloth. According to one custom, a woman reads a prayer on a white horse before riding away; other than this, women are not allowed at the burial. Every day for the following seven days the men go to the cemetery to read the Koran. The Kyrgyz say that the dead person is not used to being alone in the ground yet, and needs support.

On the seventh day, and again on the 40th, the family invites mourners to the house to read the Koran. Over the next year, people regularly visit the family and the cemetery to pray and express their condolences; the idea is to keep the family too busy to grieve. After about a year, the gravestone is erected and it is said that the family starts to mourn for the dead person, 'because this is finally the end, he's not here any more'. Families also visit the cemetery on religious holidays and on 8 May (Remembrance Day) to read the Koran and clean their ancestors' graves. Sometimes they hold a feast, slaughtering an animal and eating a special kind of bread.

Bruno de Cordier

For centuries the Kyrgyz have had a very close relationship with their highly schooled horses. As one proverb goes, horses are the wings of the Kyrgyz. [Lynn M. Alleva]

Bishkek

Kyrgyzstan's capital city, Bishkek, lies at about 800 metres above sea level, just to the north of the latitude occupied by Tbilisi, Barcelona, Rome and Boston, and only 30 kilometres from the Kazakh border. It crouches in the fertile Chui river valley on the banks of the Ala Archa and Alamyedin rivers, whose waters are rigorously siphoned off through the Chui canal to the Kazakh steppe. The Chui river itself runs along the Kazakh border. Always visible above the trees and the 1950s concrete housing blocks, the snow-clad peaks of the Kyrgyz Ala-too hover to the south.

Bishkek is a comfortable, leafy city. It's hard to imagine that little over 100 years ago it was a barren, windswept, dusty backwater. The neat grid pattern on which it was arranged by 19th century Russian designers makes it easy to navigate. Its outskirts still resemble a Ukrainian village, whose Slavic houses with their carved eaves are set in gardens of blossoming apricot and apple trees, surrounded by fragile fences interlaced with vines. In the centre, poplar trees shade the broad streets and avenues, and parks of ancient oak break up the city concrete.

In recent years, Bishkek has transformed itself into a modern city; gone are the jetons used to make calls from antiquated street telephone kiosks, now everyone has a mobile phone. The fleets of battered Ladas, which once crowded the streets, are gradually being nudged off the road by growing numbers of Western cars, many of them smart four-wheel drives. Ella Maillart found a different scene in 1932:

> The ground swarms with people, bulls, outdoor eating places and carts bringing in fruit and vegetables and forage drawn by pairs of camels wearing a harness of coarse woven wool which fits closely over the hump.

The make-up of Bishkek's population of 900,000 has changed dramatically since independence. In Soviet times the city was almost exclusively Slav, but thousands have left, giving way to a nouveau riche of 'new Kyrgyz', as well as to South Asian and Turkish businessmen and a growing tide of foreign aid agencies. In response, smart new restaurants, cafés and shops have sprung up, lending a prosperous face to the centre. Although the ethnic make-up of the city has changed dramatically over the past ten years, Bishkek still remains culturally a Russian city in comparison with the rest of the country.

You don't need to step far behind the modern veneer, however, to glimpse post-independence economic hardship. Migrants from other parts of Kyrgyzstan have poured into Bishkek in search of work, crowding into poor housing on the edge of the city. In the sweltering summer sun, street vendors try to eke out a living by selling cheap cigarettes, pens and sweets. Among the most tragic are the elderly Russians who beg on the streets or scavenge the bins at night. Many no longer have family here and their situation is dire.

Bishkek simultaneously presents a dynamic picture of its recent past and its emerging future. It embodies many of the predicaments and contradictions that the people of Kyrgyzstan are living with today.

History

A *bishkek* is the wooden spoon-like utensil with which *koumys* (fermented mare's milk) is stirred. A favourite story explaining the origins of the capital's name (and perhaps reflecting the high regard in which *koumys* is held) relates how a woman left her *bishkek* behind when her people struck camp on the edge of the Alamyedin river long ago. Other stories abound, but the most likely explanation is that the Turkic Pishpek resembled its Sogdian name, Peshagakh.

The earliest signs of human habitation in the region are Stone Age implements found around the Alamyedin hydroelectric station, dating back 7,000 years. The Hun war machine, which so terrorised Europe, was replaced by the nomads of the Western Turkic khanate who, in the seventh century, mingled peaceably in the Chui valley with the Persian Sogdians, sedentary people who colonised the area from Samarkand. They established a string of trading posts which flourished and waned with the fortunes of the Silk Road. Under the streets of Bishkek lie the ruins of Jul, whose heyday was between the eighth and 13th centuries. As was typical of early Silk Road centres, Buddhists, Zoroastrians, Nestorians and Manichaeists lived and traded peaceably. In the 13th century the unforgiving Mongol storm of Jenghis Khan destroyed the city and the region returned to nomadism. For more details on the region's early history see the History section in the Introduction chapter.

Bishkek's visible past began in the 1820s when the Kokand khanate built Pishpek fort to guard the caravan routes from Tashkent to Kashgar. Apart from a military garrison, the crenulated and moated fort housed a collection of hostages, donated by Kyrgyz chiefs as peace-pledges. Settlers and traders accumulated around its walls. Such a powerful statement attracted the attention of the Russians from across the steppe but it was actually the Kyrgyz (in hindsight they might have made a different decision) who led the definitive attack on the fort in 1862. The Solto and Sarybagysh tribes joined forces under the leadership of Baitik of Solto; they invited Kokand's commandant to a feast and murdered him and his entourage on their way home, then attacked the fort. Lacking the appropriate weaponry to finish the job, however, they called on the Russians at Verniy (now Almaty) who were eager to oblige. The Russians thereafter administered Pishpek.

The bazaar that grew up around the fort was the embryo of the modern city. Adobe huts along what is now Jibek Jolu housed Cossack farmers and Sart (Uzbek) merchants and craftsmen. When Kyrgyz people took up settled farming in the area, they built adobe houses with open verandas, very different from the enclosed houses of the Sarts. Russian peasants began to arrive in great numbers, lured by fertile soil and land breaks.

The city's finest hour came in 1878 when the regional administration moved to Pishpek from Tokmak, which had been devastated by floods. The city grew in surges of civic planning. By 1898, the mayor, Ilya Terentev, counted 752 houses in the city but no sewerage, and limited health and education (for Russians only). The Kyrgyz population could be counted on one hand and the remaining population was made up of Dungans,

Bishkek

N ↑

0 — 250 — 500 m
0 — 250 — 500 yds

Miscellaneous
1 Western Bus Station
2 Osh Bazaar
3 Rariyet bookshop
4 Dordoi Plaza
8 Philharmonia
9 Guyim
11 CACSA
18 Akademkniga
20 Cartographic Agency
21 Beta Stores
24 Ministry of Tourism and Sport
29 Tumar Souvenirs
31 Consular Department
44 Asahi
50 Kyrgyz Style (handicrafts)
53 Bowling
57 ZUM Department Store
58 Central Telephone and Post Office
59 OVIR
60 Europa Supermarket
63 British Airways and KLM
65 Kyrgyz Airlines
66 Turkish Airlines

Restaurants, Cafés and Bars
5 Metro Pub
10 Cyclone
13 Classic Café
16 Jalal-Abad Café
26 Time Out
27 Adriatico/Paradiso Restaurant
28 Santa Maria Restaurant
47 Fatboy's
55 Indus Valley
56 Four Seasons
61 Pit Stop
70 Yusa Restaurant

Museums, Monuments and Galleries
6 Mineralogical Museum
7 Manas Statue
17 Russian log house
25 Academy of Artists Museum of Graphic Arts
34 White House
35 Friendship Monument
36 Erkindik Monument
37 Kyrgyz State Historical Museum
38 Monument to Labour Glory
40 Mikhail Frunze Museum
41 Marx and Engels Monument
42 Memorial to the Red Guards
46 Asia Gallery
48 Russian Drama Theatre
49 Kyrgyz State Museum of Fine Arts
52 State Opera and Ballet Theatre
62 Toktogul Literary Museum
69 Aaly Tokombaev Memorial House Museum
71 Gapar Atiev Museum

Places to Stay
14 Kyrgyz Altyn
23 The Silk Road Lodge
33 Sary Chelek Hotel
39 Business Centre and Salimar Hotel
51 Hotel Hyatt International
54 Holiday Hotel
67 Asia Mountains Guesthouse
68 Altyn Saray Hotel
72 Hotel Bishkek

Banks and Internet Cafés
12 Ai-Ka Internet Café
19 In-tel Internet Café
22 Mate nternet Café Park Net
45 Bishkek Net

Embassies
15 Chinese Embassy
30 German Embassy
32 Kazak Embassy
64 Uzbek Embassy
73 Russian Embassy

to Hotel Pinara 2.2 km,
Hotel Issyk-Kul 5 km,
Eldorado Business Centre 2.1 k
US Embassy 3 km

© Airphoto International Ltd.

to Eastern
Bus Station

9

Ivanitsina Ul.

39 33

23   24   Frunze Ul.   53
                          40   55
25   54
      26   Panfilov   Abdumomunova Ul.   51   Victory
            Park   Square
                    38   41   42   49
                                             52
                    37   56
                                    48

            Pushkin Ul.

27   28   34   35   36   Ala Tau   Dubovy
44 10 29   22   Square   Park   57
16   45 19   46   47   58   mini bazaar
                                                             59
                                                        Kievskaya Ul.

Chui Prospekt   Chui Prospekt
                                                                  4

62 61   63   60

31
32
11

Togolok Moldo Ul.
Logvinenko Ul.
Panvilova Ul.
Orozbekova Ul.
Razzakova Ul.
Erkindik Prospekt
Erkindik Prospekt
Tynystanova Ul.
Usup Abdrakhmanova Ul.

Toktogula Ul.

64

Moskovskaya Ul.

Shopokova Ul.
Ibraimova Ul.

30   72
73   71

50

70   65
69   66   Bokonbaevo Ul.

to Steinbrau
67

Railway
Station

18-Ya Liniya Ul.
Fatyanova Ul.
Baitik Batyr Ul.

Kulatova

Sarts, Tatars, Russians and Ukrainians, each inhabiting their own districts. By 1914 the population had exploded to 20,000 and cinemas, pavements and places of worship had begun to appear. Revolutionary activity came late to Pishpek. When the Pishpek Duma (a too-little-too-late tsarist concession to democracy) was inaugurated in August 1917, Bolsheviks were already staging demonstrations in the city's leafy squares. The end of 1918 saw the region in turmoil as a counter-revolution swept in from the village of Belovodsk, 30 kilometres to the west of Pishpek. After eight days of fighting in Pishpek, the Bolsheviks were victorious under the leadership of Yakov Logvinienko, whose name still graces a central street in Bishkek today.

By 1920, Pishpek had been reduced from a healthy trading city to a skeleton town. While the Red Army preached the communist message to stunned residents, an enthusiastic Czech workers collective called Interhelpa began in 1925 to build the new world: factories, institutes, hospitals, schools, street lighting and theatres went up, including many of the finer buildings you see in Bishkek today.

In 1926, Pishpek was renamed Frunze ('green leaf'), after its illustrious son, Mikhail Frunze, who had been instrumental in the Bolshevik advancement into Central Asia. It was a typically insensitive choice of name, especially given that the sound 'f' doesn't feature in the Kyrgyz alphabet.

In the late 1930s, Frunze was hit by Stalin's purges and in 1937 the secret police massacred 138 Kyrgyz bureaucrats outside the capital (see Chong Tash). World War II brought a wave of immigrants and industry, bolstering the city's development.

Otherwise, Frunze's journey to the 1980s as a socialist capital was unremarkable; development continued apace and awards were bestowed with pleasing regularity. May 1967 saw a rare anti-Soviet upsurge. Riots broke out in the central bazaar after policemen beat up a customer. The Soviet authorities blamed the unrest, which lasted days and only ceased after Red Army tanks moved in, on 'Chinese sabotage and agitation' and arrested scores of Uighur and Dungan grocers. The real reason, however, was deeply-rooted discontent about police racketeering of bazaar traders and bureaucracy.

During the 1970s and 1980s, the 'Golden Years of Stagnation', the First Secretary, Turdakun Usubaliev, constructed the monumental marble buildings which now dominate the city centre; the National History (then, Lenin) Museum, the White House, the Philharmonia and the Ala-too Square ensemble. The shortage of housing (still an issue today) sparked off mass demonstrations in January 1990, when angry residents took to the streets as rumours circulated that housing priority was being given to refugees from an earthquake in Armenia. It was the beginning of the end for the Supreme Soviet.

In October 1990, Askar Akaev became president and in April 1991, the capital reclaimed its ancient name, Bishkek. After the Moscow coup, according to Dan Prior (1994), a rich gesture, typically Kyrgyz using the medium of song, burst from the basement of the Lenin museum: the Rolling Stones song *Sympathy for the Devil* boomed out, '*Killed the Tsar and his ministers/Anastasia screamed in vain...*'

Sights

KYRGYZ STATE HISTORICAL MUSEUM

North end of Ala-too Square, tel. (0312) 626105; open Tue–Sun 10am–7pm. Entrance US$1, English-speaking guide US$5, photography US$2, video camera US$4.
This is one of Central Asia's largest museums. Founded in 1925, many of its collections are unique and of great scientific value—although the best items were spirited off to Soviet museums during the Soviet era. The museum directors are planning big changes to the exhibits, with more of an emphasis on Kyrgyz history and less on that of Soviet Russia.

Most exhibits are in Kyrgyz and Russian only so it's worth hiring a guide for a whistle-stop tour of the history of Kyrgyzstan. The story starts on the top floor where the fetching, colourful ceiling paintings celebrate the Soviet Union's cheerful ethnic mix, united as ever in their march towards socialism. Look out for the anti-US propaganda, including a skeleton wearing an Uncle Sam top hat riding a missile rodeo style.

The paucity of visible archaeological and historical remains belies a rich and varied history, with civilisations of sophistication and international importance. Although mammoth remains have been found in Kyrgyzstan, the earliest exhibits here are petroglyphs from Saimaly Tash (west of Naryn) and the Chui Valley, dating from 2000–1000 BC. Bronze Age axes, knives and huge cooking pots, found in burial mounds around Lake Issyk Kul, are displayed along with a ceremonial plate for animal sacrifices, which apparently transferred the beast's strength to men.

Silk Road relics include a third-century scrap of silk from Batken in southern Kyrgyzstan, 11th century glassware and glazed azure floor tiles from a medieval palace in Sadovoye, Chui Valley. Very little appears to have survived the destructive forces of Jenghis Khan. Burial pots, thought to date from the Sogdian period and decorated with leaves and sheep, contained the bones of the dead when excavated.

Displays from the 18th to 20th centuries include traditional Kyrgyz dress and marriage items, including jewellery (mostly silver, inlaid with turquoise) and a felt-covered belt for women who had recently given birth. There are also a fully furnished yurt, dolls woven from ribbons and 19th century photos of nomadic families.

The huge statuary on the stairs is of Lenin leading the revolutionary masses; the inevitable sizeable collection of Soviet memorabilia is still on show on the middle floor.

KYRGYZ STATE MUSEUM OF FINE ARTS

196 Usup Abdrakhmanova (Sovietskaya) just opposite the Opera, tel.(0312) 661624. Open Tue–Sun 9am–5pm, and Fri 10am–4pm. Entrance US$2. Captions are in Kyrgyz, Russian and some in English.
Built in 1974, this museum's prime function is to house temporary exhibitions of a wide variety of art, both Kyrgyz and international. Amongst its permanent exhibitions are Kyrgyz folk and applied arts, including excellent wall hangings and vast carpets, some Soviet Realist paintings and a collection of propaganda art. Women from a small

village near Tokmok, site of the Burana Tower, occasionally bring their felt-ware to display and sell.

MIKHAIL FRUNZE MUSEUM

364 Frunze, at the crossroads with Razzakova, tel. (0312) 660607. Open Tue–Fri 9.30am–4.30pm Sat–Sun 10am–4pm (lunch 12.30pm–1.30pm). Entrance US$2. Captions in Kyrgyz and Russian.

The Mikhail Frunze Museum is one of a dying breed: a eulogy to a Soviet hero. Don't be put off, though; it's well worth a visit, especially if you hire a well-informed (Russian-speaking only) guide at the museum, when the sense of paying homage at the shrine of Mikhail Frunze will be greatly enhanced.

Within the building is what is said to be Frunze's childhood home, a modest, clay thatched cottage complete with spinning wheel, rocking horse and high chair.

Frunze, born in 1885, is best known for his brutal suppression of local resistance to the advance of Bolshevik socialism into Central Asia and for giving his name to Soviet-era Bishkek. He died in 1925 in hospital undergoing an operation for stomach ulcers that Stalin insisted he undergo; a debate still rages over whether Stalin ordered his demise.

The museum contains all the paraphernalia of Frunze's life and glittering career; depicting him as, at once, brave soldier, inspired leader, accomplished academic, family man and, above all, devoted exponent of Bolshevism. Most notable are the triangular desks which he crafted while in a Siberian prison camp, his Order of the Red Banner and other awards for military activities.

OTHER MUSEUMS

The **Aaly Tokombaev Memorial House Museum** at 109 Chuikova is open from Mon–Fri 9am–5pm. It chronicles the life of Tokombaev (1904–1988) a famous *akyn* (bard) and writer, who was instrumental in standardising written Kyrgyz in its adapted Cyrillic alphabet.

He also translated much foreign literature into Kyrgyz for the first time. Most interesting are the exhibits on the 1916 uprising against Russian exploitation.

The **Toktogul State Literary Museum** is at 111 Toktogula. Open Mon–Fri 9am –5pm, closed 12–1pm. Entrance US$0.50. One of its two small halls houses temporary exhibitions about Kyrgyz writers, together

Opera and Ballet Theatre, Bishkek

with 4th–18th century rocks inscribed with Turkish, Arabic, Tajik, Sogdian and Nestorian writings. Some alphabets are indecipherable. The second hall is devoted to Toktogul Satulganov (1864–1933), the renowned Kyrgyz *akyn* who once lived in this building and gave his name to the street. For more details see page 252.

The **Gapar Atiev Studio-Museum** at 78 Tynystanova (open Mon–Fri 9am–5pm, entrance US$0.10) show-cases the life and work of Kyrgyzstan's most famous painter and sculptor. Atiev (1912–1984) specialised in painting Kyrgyz scenes and was famed for his skilled portrayal of light and air. Some of his paintings can be seen in the Fine Arts Museum (above), although many are in Moscow's Tretyakov Gallery.

The **Mineralogical Museum** (open Mon–Fri, 9am–4.30pm, closes when dark in winter. Entrance US$0.50) is at 164 Chui (opposite the Philharmonia) and houses a vast, colourful array of some of the rocks and minerals found in Kyrgyzstan. Captions are in Russian.

Statue of Manas

The **Academy of Artists Museum of Graphic Arts** (open Mon–Fri 9am–4pm, closed 12–1pm) at 50 Togolok Moldo, between Chui and Frunze, is a spacious museum exhibiting the smaller works of Tinibek Sadykov, whose public art includes the sculptures for the Philharmonia, the Martyrs to the Revolution and Victory Square.

The small **SA Chuikov Museum**, at 87a Chuikov, is dedicated to the Pishpek-born artist Semenov Afanasievich Chuikov, whose work is based on the Soviet tradition of realistic art. The Soviet sculptor Olga Manuilova is honoured at the **OM Manuilova Memorial Musum**, 108 Tynystanova St, her former home. Manuilova spent 50 years in Kyrgyzstan and produced around 800 works and designed the Theatre of Opera and Ballet.

The **Museum of Open Air Sculpture**, in Oak Park (Dubovy Park) just of Razzakova, was inaugurated in 1984 to mark the 60th anniversary of the Kyrgyz Republic. Sculptors from all over the Soviet Union submitted work under the title 'Peace and Labour' but many of the metal works have been stolen for scrap.

THE MANAS CELEBRATIONS COMPLEX

In the grounds of the Issyk Kul Hotel, on the site of an ancient nomadic encampment, stands this surreal collection of concrete flagpoles, symbols and yurts, which hosted the celebrations for the 1,000th birthday of the Manas epic. None of the colour and spirit of the event remain—the games on horseback, the feasts, flags and textiles—and the complex has the feel of an abandoned stage set. It is now used for official functions and makes for an interesting visit. It is popular with locals and the highlight is having your photo taken in full traditional head-dress in Manas' tent. In summer, horse and cart rides around town depart from next to the ticket kiosk. Costs are around US$3 per cart per hour. Round it off with a fairground ride in adjacent Flamingo Park, Bishkek's own amusement park, before moving next door to the Free Economic Zone to buy your Italian designer suit.

A STROLL AROUND CENTRAL BISHKEK

Bishkek's central area of streets and parks is a gallery of statues old and new, in a bizarre but comfortable merge of Soviet and Kyrgyz. In Tbilisi the people tore down Stalin statues, their once revered and feared forms smashing on the streets, as children ran off with a nose or finger; in Moscow they left the toppled figures to lie in the dirt for passers by to climb on. In Bishkek, however, most statues still stand, testimony to a philosophical decision on the part of the Kyrgyz not to obliterate their Soviet heritage but to grant it a place in their people's history. These symbols of Soviet power now loiter like the icons of a dead religion, witness to the rise of a culture they had sought to suppress.

Start at the **Erkindik (Freedom) Monument** where Lenin stood until August 2003. The Erkindik Monument was unveiled in August 1999 at its former location at the far end of Erkindik Street to mark eight years of independence. The woman is holding a flame-ringed *tunduk*, the smoke-hole in the centre of a yurt. Traditionally, a sheep's head is thrown in through the *tunduk* of a family yurt to bring good luck to the newly-weds. The statue is a fine example of the inclination to look back to nomadic traditions in the search for new symbols to represent the Kyrgyz national identity. Opposite lies the Kyrgyz Ala-too mountains and, more immediately, **Ala-too Square** (formerly Lenin Square) where all official celebrations take place. Just west of the Erkindik monument is the **official flagpole** erected in 1998. The changing of the guards is worth seeing and takes place every hour from dawn till dusk, when the flag is packed away for the night.

Walk west along Chui towards the **White House**, the parliament building, completed in 1985, where the Kyrgyz president has his offices. Behind the building, **Panfilov Park** resounds with fun, as people of all ages enjoy the rickety fair ground and its pony rides, ice cream and *shashlik* stalls. Before you reach the White House, the statue to your right is the **Friendship Monument** built in 1974 to commemorate the 100th anniversary of what Soviet historians optimistically describe as Kyrgyzstan's voluntary entry into the Russian Empire.

Walk downhill and northwards along Orozbekova, passing Lenin, who was moved from the front to the back of the Historical Museum, his face now forever in shadow, on your left. Continue to the end of the square and turn right in front of the imposing Government administrative building, topped by a Kyrgyz flag. Carry on past the **American University** on your left and the **National Historical Museum** behind the trees to your right. Ahead on the right sit **Marx and Engels** on a bench, deep in conversation. They form the northern end of Central Square, built in 1933, and look towards a collection of renowned Kyrgyz politicians at the southern end.

About 100 metres east of this, just inside the park off **Erkindik Prospect** stands the **Memorial to the Red Guards**, a red granite obelisk in honour of Bolshevik soldiers killed in the October Counter-Revolution. If you feel overwhelmed, as you are meant to, by this silent display of Soviet power, pause for a cold beer in the nearby café just next to the Russian Drama Theatre, also delightful for its impeccably clean toilets.

Continue south through the park along leafy, pedestrianised Erkindik to the spot where the Erkindik monument stood until August 2003; it now occupies the place of honour opposite Ala-too square previously enjoyed by Lenin. Before independence a statue of Felix Derjinsky (1877–1926), the first director of the Cheka, the forerunner to the KGB, stood here, sending a chill to the hearts of the public.

Now turn east up Pushkin St and pass the **Russian Drama Theatre** once more, on your left. This area is known as **Dubovy** ('Oak') **Park**, in summer full of open-air cafés and ice-cream bars. Scattered amongst the ancient oak trees are **sculptures** symbolising the main cities of the former Soviet Union. Head for Usup Abdrakhmanova (Sovietskaya) where you turn left. Continue north to the **Fine Arts Museum**, next to which sits a recent statue of **Aaly Tokombaev**, the renowned 20th century *akyn* (bard). Tokombaev helped to standardise written Kyrgyz in an amended Cyrillic alphabet and translated numerous works of world literature into Kyrgyz for the first time.

On the other side of the road behind the pillared, elegant **Opera building**, stands a large bizarre-looking **monument** to famous Kyrgyz figures from all walks of life: former President Akaev, the ballerina Bibisara Beshanileyeva and the celebrated doctor, Mamakaev. From here, head south back to Chui Prospect and finish your walk just west of Usup Abdrakhmanova (Sovietskaya) where a statue of **Urkuya Salieva**, the first woman revolutionary, stands surrounded by the awakening proletariat.

OTHER SIGHTS

Mahatma Gandhi (formerly Molodaya Gvardia, meaning 'young guard'), is a tree-lined boulevard dedicated to the young Soviet soldiers of the past. The section just off Chui is known as Hero's Lane, for fighters who died in the 1920s, 1930s and World War II. Busts of individuals still stand but their names have, sadly, been scratched off.

Once the haunt of Bishkek's courting couples, Mahatma Gandhi is today known locally as *kulbazaar* (slave market) because of the groups of men who stand around in the hope of being offered seasonal work. Most of them are emigrants from the south and central regions of Kyrgyzstan—first generation city-dwellers who live in large housing blocks on the edges of Bishkek, which receive the barest minimum of public utilities.

Pobeda Square, on Shopokova and Frunze, was built in 1985 on the site of the former central market to commemorate the Soviet Union's victory over Germany in World War II. The structure, like a half a yurt frame, is topped by a *tunduk* surrounded by a wreath for the dead. A **Russian Log House**, at 145 Moskovskaya, is a well-preserved example of the type of building prevalent before the advent of Soviet architecture.

At the intersection of Usup Abdrakhmanova (Sovietskaya) and Frunze is a one-storey building that houses the Pakistani café Lasani. This used to be the **State Savings Bank**, the first Soviet bank in Frunze. It is about the only building in Bishkek where you can still see inscriptions in the Turkish-Roman alphabet that was used to write Kyrgyz in the 1920s and 1930s. To dip back to the pre-war days, take a stroll through the city's northern neighbourhoods, in the vicinity of the **Bolshoi Chuiskiy Kanal** and the **Karagachevaya Rosha woods**. This part of the city is a maze of small, dusty streets and alleys, lined with Slavic gingerbread houses, lush orchards and gardens. Evocative of a village in Ukraine or Romania, it is just a couple of kilometres from central Bishkek.

Bishkek Practical Information

CITY TRANSPORT

Bishkek is well served by a network of trolleybuses, buses and private *marshrutka* (minibuses). The former move remarkably slowly but run frequently up and down the main axes. They are almost the number one spot for pickpockets and for this reason many people prefer not to use them anymore. Minibuses are quicker but cost a little more (US$0.10 per journey as opposed to US$0.06 on buses or trolleybuses). Useful routes include minibus 19, which travels westwards along Chui to Osh Baazar, and bus 35 or minibus 48, which run on a circular route from Moskovskaya (between Gogol and Sultana Ibraimova) via the railway station, West and East bus stations.

Taxis range from the most antiquated, ailing Ladas to swanky new German and

Japanese cars. Locals advise that you use marked taxis only, especially as poverty and crime are on the increase. After dark, choose your taxi with care; reputable firms include Express (dial 156), Super (dial 152) and Udacha (dial 154). No taxis have metres but standard fares in 2007 were US$1.85 within the city limits, US$3.20 after dark. Agree fares before you set off, with payment on arrival.

ACCOMMODATION

With increasing numbers of visitors (business people, airline staff, aid agencies, consular workers and tourists) to the Kyrgyz capital, the range of accommodation on offer is expanding rapidly.

Hyatt Regency: 191 Usup Abdrakhmanova (Soviet-skaya). Tel. (0312) 661234; fax. (0312) 665744 email: concierge.hrbishkek@hyattintel.com; web: bishkek.regency.hyatt.com.

Traditional kalpak hat

Bishkek's first five star hotel occupies the very central site of the old Hotel Kyrgyzstan next to the Opera and Ballet Theatre. It offers a delightful mix of style and comfort with 178 sumptuous rooms, grand lobby areas, restaurants and bars (including outdoor pool bar). There is also access for wheelchair users. Singles cost US$280 and doubles US$305, not including breakfast.

The Silk Road Lodge: 229 Abdumomunova, near Frunze/Togolok Moldo. Tel. (0312) 661129; fax. 661655; email: silkroad@celestial.com.kg; web: silkroad.com.kg
This superb British-owned, four-star hotel combines comfort with a central location and is the best option in the mid to deluxe price bracket. All 28 rooms have en suite bathroom, satellite TV and IDD telephone. Staff are refreshingly friendly and balance efficient service with a genuinely personal ambience. Thoughtful touches include a well-stocked library of English-language books and films, vegetarian food in the restaurant and free airport transfers. There is a business centre, downstairs restaurant/bar, saunas, indoor swimming pool and exercise room. An attractive feature is the garden area where guests can order drinks. Prices start at US$95 B&B (single) and US$105 (twin).

Hotel Dostuk: 429 Frunze. Tel. (0312) 284411; fax. 284466
The poorly lit lobby has the shadowy feel typical of Soviet-built hotels, but rooms are comfortable and clean, with homely Russian décor and leaky bathrooms, TV and phone. The nearby Circus and large casino attract prostitutes and their pimps, which has proved dangerous. Singles start from US$80 B&B and doubles from US$95.

Hotel Ak-Keme (formerly Pinara-Bishkek): 93 Prospect Mira. Tel. (0312) 540143, 540144; email: info@akkemehotel.com; www: akkemehotel.com.
This comfortable four-star Turkish-owned hotel is eight kilometres from the city with glorious mountain views. Facilities include restaurant, café, swimming pool, sauna, fitness centre and business centre. The rooms come with satellite TV and IDD telephone. Singles start at US$160 and doubles at US$220.

Kyrgyz Altyn: 30 Manas (between Kievskaya/ Toktogul). Tel. (0312) 666412, 666114; fax. 666371
Offering simple accommodation at reasonable prices in the city centre, the Kyrgyz Altyn is popular among CIS business people. A small clean café downstairs serves breakfast. A single costs US$31 and twin en suite US$61.

Asia Mountains Guesthouse: 1a Igemberdieva, off Gogol. Tel. (0312) 690235/34; fax. (0312) 690236; email: asiamountains@mail.ru; www.asiamountains.elcat.kg
This delightful hotel is 15 minutes from the centre by car, near the Steinbrau pub. The beautiful garden is well laid out with lawns, shaded relaxation areas and a swimming pool. The main building has a bar and restaurant, rooms are all en suite with air conditioning, IDD phone, TV and fridge. Singles cost US$30 and doubles US$40. The Asia Mountains tour company office has internet access.

Business Centre and Salimar Hotel: 237 Panfilova. Tel. (0312) 623107; fax. 660638
Accommodation here comes in two grades. The Business Centre Hotel on the third floor
offers shabby singles and doubles with shared bathroom and tiny beds for US$22. The
Salimar Hotel on the fifth floor offers plain, clean en suite rooms for US$60 (singles)
B&B and US$76 (doubles). The hotel is on the corner of Panfilova and Frunze. Enter
the Business School doors and turn right.

Sary Chelek Hotel: 87 Orozbekova/Frunze. Tel. (0312) 613000; www.kyrgyz-service.co.uk
This old Soviet-style building has 24 rooms (from singles to four-bed), all en suite.
There's also a large family room with sitting room. There are no frills but lux rooms have
local TV. Singles start at US$18.

Philema House was conceived and run for visiting missionaries. This clean-living
guesthouse, converted from a Slavic house, is well-designed, peaceful and homely, with
a pergola and shady garden. It's not open to the general public but Alltournative can
book it for you although probably only if you are church-connected.

Shumkar Asia Guesthouse: 34 Osipienko/Isanova. Tel. (0312) 272105; fax. 671038
email: shumkar-asia@inbox.ru
A 20-minute drive from Beta Stores, this clean, pleasant guesthouse has an outdoor
swimming pool and offers internet and IDD telephone. The en suite rooms have TV and
cost US$38 (singles) and US$54 (doubles).

Nomad's House: 10 Drevesnaya, Tel: (0312) 299955; email: nomadshome@gmail.com
This budget option is just behind the Eastern bus station and near Chui Canal. The
family home offers a 12-bedded room with bunks, one double and yurts with beds in
the yard. All share long-drop loos and showers. It offers TV, DVD, a relaxation space
outside and airport transfers. B&B costs US$5pp.

Maiman Guesthouse: Kulatova 25. Tel. (0312) 548146, (0772) 697996
email: shabdanbekova@mail.ru
This colourful, stylish and very clean guesthouse opened in 2006 and is set in a
relaxing shady garden with an Uzbek-style *tapchan*. There's no sign so look out for
Kulatova 25 written on the red gate down the driveway between Nos 21 and 31.
Distinctive for its wooden furniture, *shyrdaks*, *ala-kiyiz* and traditional costumes, it has
three doubles and a single with shared facilities. Prices start at US$25 B&B.

Hotel Altyn Saray: 541 Jibek Jolu/Frunze. Tel. (0312) 660452, 909140
This big Chinese-built hotel, ten minutes' walk from the centre, opened in June 2007
and is mainly aimed at the increasing numbers of Chinese business visitors. Reception
and rooms are on the third floor and the 12 en suite rooms have all mod cons. IDD
phone and internet are available through reception. Luxury rooms boast a jacuzzi for
US$160. Singles cost US$53, doubles US$80.

Hotel Alpinist: 113 Panfilova (off Gorky). Tel. (0312) 595647, 699621; fax: 595647;
email: alpinist@elcat.kg; www.alpinisthotel.centralasia.kg

A quiet, comfortable hotel, owned by tour operator ITMC and fetchingly decorated with climbing boots and ice-axes, Alpinist is a 15-minute taxi ride from the centre. The 18 en suite rooms are equipped with satellite TV, fridge and internet access. Outside, guests limber up at the climbing wall in the garden or recline at a *tapchan*. Bed and a smorgsbord breakfast cost US$39 (single) and US$48 (double).

Holiday: 204A U. Abdrakhmanova. Tel. (0612) 902900 and (0612) 902923 email: hotel@holiday.kg; www.holiday.kg
This excellent and fairly plush city-centre hotel opposite the Hyatt has dark curved corridors. The 18 en suite rooms have wireless internet, TV and telephone, and there is a restaurant and lobby bar. B&B costs US$95 (doubles) and US$80 (singles).

Golden Dragon Hotel: 60 Elebaev/Gorky. Tel. (0312) 902771; fax: 902773 email: GDHotel@saimanet.kg; www.GDHotel.kg
About three kilometres from the town centre, this spotlessly clean, Chinese-owned four star hotel is popular with tour groups and offers spacious en suite rooms with all mod cons including satellite TV. There are saunas, a fitness room, an outdoor swimming pool and and a business centre. Singles start at US$95 and doubles at US$115 B&B.

Guesthouse Radison, 259 U. Abdumumonova
A 10-minute walk from the centre, Radison is clean and comfortable. The air-conditioned en suite rooms have satellite TV, phone and fridge. With doubles at US$35 and singles at US$25, this is a good city centre option.

Ultimate Guest House: 185 Kurienkeva (off Togolok Moldo). Tel. (0312) 270754 mob. 0502 222634; email: ultiadv@mail.kg
A Slavic house with a large shady veranda 10 minutes by taxi from the centre, this French-owned hostel offers basic but comfortable accommodation in doubles and triples, from US$21 B&B.

Umai: 46-a, Donskoy Pereulok. Tel. (0502) 802805; email: info@ecotour.kg. This new guesthouse, belonging to Ecotour, has comfortable rooms with private bathroom for US$25 B&B per person a 20-minute walk from the centre.

Homestays in Bishkek generally mean a bed and breakfast arrangement in a furnished, uninhabited flat. With increasing financial hardship, few families have a spare room, so a genuine family stay experience is difficult to arrange in the capital. Book through one of the local tour operators, particularly Ak Sai Travel and NoviNomad (see Tour Operators page 78).

FOOD AND NIGHTLIFE

In recent years Bishkek has seen the arrival of international cuisine and a dramatic increase in the choice of restaurants catering for all budgets. Generally there are two types of restaurant in Bishkek; *chaikhanas* (cafés) serving local food, and more formal restaurants, many of which are foreign-run. Prices throughout are reasonable for foreigners but prohibitive for locals except the growing group of 'new Kyrgyz', mostly successful (and lucky) young people sporting sharp suits.

Uzbek dinner table

SNACKS AND BUDGET MEALS

Street food is available everywhere (*lepyoshka*, *manti* and *pirozhki* are a good bet) and in summer you can't do better than to relax in shady Panfilov or Dubovy Park where stalls offer snacks, *shashlik*, *laghman*, *plov*, soup and salads. It's also a chance to immerse yourself in an eclectic mix of Kyrgyz, Russians, Uzbeks, Koreans and Dungans.

The **Jalal-Abad Café**, an elaborately carved wooden Uzbek-style *chaikhana* on the corner of Togolok Moldo and Kievskaya, has drinks and light meals, while the Turkish-run **Continental Cuisine**, on Moskovskaya, near Usup Abdrakhmanov, is clean and friendly and offers tasty Middle Eastern and European food for reasonable prices. **Beta Gourmet**, in the Beta department store at 150 Chui, does good Turkish, Korean and Kyrgyz fast food. Also good for fast food is **Café Express** on Moskovskaya /Tynystanova. **Coffee Café** on Turusbekova is said to be the best place for real coffee while **Café Boulevard**, on the west corner of Erkindik Avenue and Kievskaya, is a popular ex-pat hangout.

RESTAURANTS AND BARS

Eating out in Bishkek has improved enormously in recent years, both in the number of restaurants and the variety and quality of food available. Here, in no particular order, are some of the options.

Head for **Cyclone** early or book (Tel: 0312 212866), especially on the days when they're making their special lasagne. This good quality, reasonably priced, small Italian at 136 Chui, on the corner with Togolok Moldo, is very popular and serves cheap Eastern European wines if you're seeking a change from beer.

Adriatico/Paradiso, at 219 Chui, is a plush, comfortable and pricey Italian restaurant, while the very relaxed **Dolce Vita** at 116a Akhunbaeva, is another Italian option with a genuine brick oven.

Four Seasons, with its Russian/European cuisine, on Tynystanova next to the Russian Drama Theatre, is a favourite among grown-ups and children alike. Spacious and stylish, with a delightful location under shady trees, it has a play area in one corner. It's pricey but the food is very good. Also very pleasant but busier and noisier is **Time-Out**, on Togolok-Moldo, next to the small Spartak Stadium. Outdoor dining (international and some Chinese dishes) takes place in front of a large screen playing music videos, and there's a children's play area in one corner.

Bombay Restaurant, at 110 Chui near Erkendik (downstairs from the Song Kul Restaurant) is a Kyrgyz-Indian joint venture and has a vast, excellent and affordable menu. The only snag is the loud band. **Indus Valley**, at 105 S Ibraimova, is pricey but recommended for Indian food and serves a particularly good buffet lunch.

The popular **Classico** Café, 49 Manas, a little pricey, serves mainly Russian and European food, with some Kyrgyz and Uzbek dishes. **Santa Maria**, at 217 Chui just west of Togolok Moldo, is a stylish and upmarket Korean restaurant, while **Varshova**, at 105 Ibraimova, is a plush Polish restaurant; the fish is very good.

Yusa, at 14 Logvinienko, is popular at lunchtime with foreign workers and business people for its huge selection of Turkish dishes. As their names suggest, **Pekin** at 253 Chui offers Chinese cuisine and **Tokyo** at 104 Bokonbaevo Japanese food, as does **Suiseki** on the corner of Gorky and Panfilova.

Navigator Bar, a bright, clean but pricey café at 103 Moskovskaya, serves Russian/European dishes and some vegetarian options, while **Faiza** at 555 Jibek Jolu is cheap and has good local and Dungan food. **Dasmia**, at 2 Gorky, serves Kyrgyz dishes alongside ethnographic exhibitions, music and dances, and you can also taste the local cuisine at **Caravan-Sarai**, at 136 Kurmanjan-Datka, and **Arzu**, at 311 Pobeda. **Zolotoi Fazan**, at 40 Yunusalieva, offers an intriguing mix of game dishes and live piano music.

Capita Nemo Restaurant at 130 Toktogula/Togolok Moldo is a fish restaurant done out in nautical style, while **Pitstop**, at 107 Toktogula (near Orozbekova) is decorated with chequered flags and racing memorabilia, and serves mainly Russian cuisine. For great views of the city and mountains and good food, head for the roof-top restaurant on the **Vefa Centre**, on the corner of Gorky and Usup Abdrakhmanova.

Fatboy's, in a prime spot at 104 Chui, is a popular ex-pat hangout and offers fast food (including the Full Monty Breakfast) and has a small English language library and basement bar, but the service can be dilatory. **Metro Pub**, at 168 Chui, is a social hotspot for many foreign residents. Situated in a converted theatre with a spectacular 'long bar', this venue still has a thespian charm. Food is Mexican or American style.

A family of local ethnic German brewers runs the popular **Steinbrau** pub at 5 Gertzena, where porthole windows allow drinkers to view the fermentation rooms. It serves mainly European food. The trendy Italian-owned **2x2** bar on Isanova just south of Chui, has light snacks and a huge range of liqueurs and cocktails.

Other pubs include **Planeta Holsten**, 122a Tynystanova, and **Sibirskaya Korona**, 186 Chui. Popular nightclubs include **Soho**, at 62 Orozbekova, **Galaxy** (also Bishkek's

Walnuts on sale at Osh bazaar

first ten-pin bowling club) at 338 Frunze near S Ibraimova. You can hear live rock and jazz at **Zeppelin**, 43 Chui, and jazz at **Doka Pizza** on Abdrakhmanova/Akhunbaeva and **Admiral** at 42 Manas. For more live music, see page 129)

It's not in Bishkek but is considered one of the best places to eat in the area. Around 30 minutes' drive from the centre, the **12 Chimneys Restaurant** enjoys a tranquil spot on the banks of the Alamyedin River at the mouth of the Alamyedin Valley (see page 133). It is hugely popular, as much for its gorgeous location (diners eat outside, surrounded by the 12 tall chimneys, or ovens) as for the quality of its European/Russian cuisine.

VISAS AND RED TAPE

Some nationalities must register with the OVIR office within three working days of arrival in Kyrgyzstan (see page 76). The easiest way to do so if arriving by air is at the OVIR office at the airport. Otherwise, head for the Central OVIR office at 58 Kievskaya, just west of Shopokova, (second floor, take the left hand door). Bishkek tour operators will help, for a small fee. To extend your visa, see page 74.

COMMUNICATIONS

The main **telephone office**, marked **KyrgyzTelecom**, is on the corner of Chui and Abdrakhmanova (Sovietskaya) and open daily from 7am to 11.30pm. Local calls can be made from the phone boxes outside. National and international calls are made from the booths. Queue at the counter to pre-pay for your call. Dial 00 for an international line; when your call is answered, dial 3 to start talking. Return to the counter for your change. US and European network standard mobile phones work in Bishkek. Alternatively buy a mobile phone at a department store (Bitel is considered the best provider) and top up using Mobicards. Most internet cafés also offer IDD telephone calls.

The **post office** is next door to KyrgyzTelecom and is open daily 7am–7pm or 8am–7pm on Sundays. Leave parcels open for inspection, allow plenty of time to complete customs declarations and bring a length of linen so that the parcel can be stitch-sealed afterwards. To **courier** items abroad try DHL at 107 Kievskaya (west of Isanova), tel. (0312) 611111, or Federal Express at 217 Moskovskaya, tel. (0312) 650012.

To ship goods by land or air, try ARI Cargo (American Resources International) at 35 Erkindik, near Toktogula: email: bishkek@aricargo.com, tel. (0312) 660077.

INTERNET ACCESS

Internet cafés are springing up rapidly all over Bishkek and closing down again just as fast. US$1–US$2 per hour seems to be the market rate.

The **Ai-Ka** internet café on Isanova, on the west side of Beta Stores, is open 24 hours a day. **In-tel**, at 90 Kievskaya, is open from 8am–11pm, as is its neighbour at 88 Kievskaya, close to the junction with Erkendik. Meanwhile the **Mate** internet café at 128 Chui operates from 10am to 8pm. Also try the outlets in **Zum's** basement and the **Central Post Office**.

MAPS AND GUIDES

Bishkek and Suburbs by Victor Kadyrov, published by the Bishkek publisher Rarityet in 2007, is a handy guide to the city and surrounding areas and contains cultural as well as practical information. Check out Zum department store, Europa, Beta Stores, Rarityet at 271 Chui and hotel shops for other guides and also for up-to-date maps of Bishkek. The best purveyor of maps is the **Cartography Agency** at 107 Kievskaya, third floor; tel. (0312) 212202. Open Mon–Fri (Sat in summer), 8am–12 noon, 1pm–6pm. Near Togolok Moldo, it is set back from the road in a large building. Say *kartii* (maps) to the rather keen doorlady who filters visitors.

Street names in Bishkek are changing from Soviet to Kyrgyz: a confusing collection of old and new are used by locals and marked on street signs. Sovietskaya now has three new names (for north, south and central sections) but is still widely known by its old name (see page 92).

A variety of street maps are now available which also show some much needed tourist information. (For information on country and trekking maps see page 92).

Used and new maps and books are available through Silk Road Media Publishing House at Ak Sai Travel and Alpinist Hotel.

SHOPPING

After years of communism, Kyrgyzstan is embracing the new consumer age with gusto, and nowhere more so than in Bishkek. There are more shops, supermarkets and posh shopping centres than ever before, even though only a minority of people have the money to spend in them. They're better stocked, too, albeit often with the cheap Chinese imports now flooding into the country.

Zum, once Bishkek's flagship seven-storeyed 'Central Department Store' on Chui/Shopokova, is now looking distinctively tatty by comparison with the new malls. It will be getting a much needed facelift, thanks to new Kazakh investors, who plan to build two new shopping plazas on its west and northern sides, but you can still buy just about anything you want here, from household appliances to clothing and shoes.

The new shopping malls include **Dordoi Plaza** (not to be confused with Dordoi Bazaar, of which more later), near Zum at 115 Ibraimova, which has a range of smart shops selling clothes, electronics, mobile phones (and top up cards), cameras, DVDs, CDs and computer games on two floors. There's an excellent indoor children's play area on the second floor.

Even smarter is the **Vefa Centre** on the corner of Usup Abdrakhmanova (formerly Sovietskaya) and Gorky where the shops stock some very upmarket labels including Cacharel, Pierre Cardin, Levi, Ecco and Benetton. The second floor has a Russian bookshop, a cinema and a Wellness Centre, while the basement has an excellent handicraft stall. There's also a very posh supermarket next door.

Some of the best fun, however, is still to be had in Bishkek's markets and there are three main bazaars. The largest is the **Osh Bazaar** on Kievskaya/Beishenalieva. Trolleybuses trundle along Kievskaya from the centre and minibuses depart from the Manas statue for the bazaar. It's heaving with life and is the place to stock up on clothes, fabric and fresh fruit, vegetables and spices, typically piled high in pyramid-shaped displays.

Alamyedin Bazaar offers a smaller range of similar goods and makes a good last minute stop en route to Almaty. It's in the north east of the city, on Jibek Jolu, east of the Alamyedin river. Close to the centre is the huge Chinese market, **Guyim**, at Jibek Jolu/Abdrakhmanova selling everything from Chinese herbs to kettles and top of the range electronic goods.

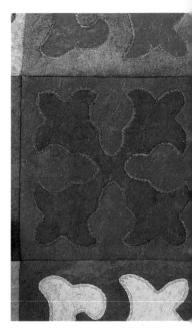

Shrydak detail

The **Dordoi** (also called Tolchok) **Bazaar** sells mainly Chinese-made clothes and household items at knock-down prices. Pick pocketing is rife. It's about 7km north of the Usup Abdrakhmanova/Moskovskaya intersection, from which minibuses run regularly to the bazaar.

Handicrafts, artefacts and souvenirs are more widely available than ever before, although of varying quality so it pays to look around. Every shopping mall will have at least one handicraft stall. Other shops well worth checking out include the **Tumar** (meaning 'Talisman') **Art Salon** on Chui/Togolok Moldo, which has one of the most interesting and contemporary collections of felt accessories, carpets and hangings. Most comes from their own workshops but they also stock work by well-known Kyrgyz and Kazakh jewellers as well as ceramics from the region. They have a website, tumar.com.

Next door, on Chui, is **Asahi** with an unusual (albeit somewhat pricey) collection of 'art handicrafts' ranging from antique silver earrings to felt slippers in funky colours. They specialise in vegetable dyed, handmade *shyrdaks* and *ala-kiyiz* carpets and handbags and offer good quality Afghan *kilims*. There's a 10 per cent discount for cash purchases.

There are several small handicraft shops opposite the White House on Chui, such as **Kyrgyz Souvenirs** and **Iman**, which sell artefacts such as paintings, statues, chess sets, Soviet pin badges and other nick-nacks.

A must for anyone looking for the genuine article is **Tabernik**, at 134 Chui, a small two-room shop selling souvenirs and antiques. The first room has the usual tourist stuff while the second looks like an antique jumble sale. There are some real treasures to be found here if you have time to search through the old carpets, embroidered hangings, saddles, leather water carriers and metal ware. **Kyrgyz Style**, pricey but stylish, is at 133 Bokonbaeva.

The **Central Asian Crafts Support Association** is at 162 Manaschy Sagynbai, on Togolok Moldo between Moskovskaya and Toktogula—the address is in Russian on a blue gate; tel: (0312) 662445. This professional organisation works with artisans throughout the five central Asian countries and Mongolia, helping to revive and develop traditional crafts. As one of the few handicrafts organisations experimenting with new designs, CACSA acts as an interface between designers and craftspeople. Artisans sell their wares via the internet, in local stores, at craft fairs and in the small shop at the CACSA office.

For camping, mountaineering or trekking gear, head for **Ak Sai Travel**'s basement shop at 65 Baitik Baatyr which mainly stocks the popular Russian label, Red Fox; or **Limpopo** (formerly known as Extreme) at 129 Kievskaya. This is at 129 Kievskaya on the corner of Isanova, not far from Beta Stores. It's in the basement and you enter via Isanova. **North Face** gear can be found at the Vefa Centre and, in a smaller shop at the Dordoi Plaza, but check the quality before you buy.

One of Kyrgyzstan's best known fashion designers, Dilbar Ashimbayeva, has a boutique, called **Dilbar**, at 88 Turusbekova, just north of Chui; tel: (0312) 611708. This stylish, upmarket shop will be well beyond the budget of many travellers and has a museum-like air with ancient artefacts on the walls. Dilbar used to design theatre costumes before opening her own fashion house in 2004 (www.dilbarfashion.com) and her beautiful, lavishly embellished and hand-embroidered clothes and accessories are strikingly individual.

Supermarkets have also sprung up all over Bishkek: **Beta Stores**, at 150a Chui on the corner with Isanova, is the most convenient, **Narodniy**, open 24 hours, is an up-market (and expensive) chain found all over Bishkek, while **Caravan** is less flashy—a store has recently opened on Kievskaya.

MONEY

The days when exchange bureaux were few and far between, and it was hard to change currencies other than dollars and euros are long gone. There are numerous exchange booths in the centre, taking all the main currencies including Chinese yuan, Russian roubles, Uzbek som and Kazakh tenge.

It's worth shopping around to find the best rates (we found these were from the booths along the southern end of Usup Abdrakhmanova, between Moskovskaya and Bokonbaevo). Ensure the notes you are changing are new (post-1995 if possible) and unblemished; if you try to exchange a torn note, you'll probably have it refused.

Several banks will cash travellers cheques, especially American Express, as well as provide credit card advances; several also offer Western Union Money Transfer services. There is a growing number of ATMs offering international withdrawals; Beta Stores has one, as do Dordoi Plaza and Zum.

ENTERTAINMENT

The years since independence, Kyrgyz performing arts have flourished but it's not easy for outsiders to find out what's going on. Performances are not held every night and are not publicized in English-language papers. Visit the box offices or ask tour operators, such as Celestial Mountains, tel. (0312) 212562 or Kyrgyz Concept, tel. (0312) 661331.

The beautiful **Opera and Ballet Theatre** at 167 U. Abdrakhmanova has its own opera and ballet companies and hosts visiting companies, but the season usually runs from autumn to spring. The **Philarmonia**, at 253 Chui, stages classical and modern Kyrgyz and Western music performances.

The **Kyrygz Academic Drama Theatre**, at 273 Panfilova, performs plays in Kyrgyz and Russian, while the **Russian Academic Drama Theatre**, at 122 Tynystanova, stages performances in Russian in Oak Park. The **Puppet Theatre** at 230 Usup Abdrakhmanova has performances on Sundays at 11am.

Cinemas are springing up all over Bishkek, although generally featuring Russian (or Russian dubbed) films. **Dom Kino** ('the House of Cinema') at 13 Logvinenko, hosts seasons of international films and often shows films twice—in their original form and then dubbed into Russian. Jazz concerts and poetry readings also take place here. The multiplex **Russia**, at 213 Chui, has the largest screen in town.

There's more **live music** in Bishkek than ever before, particularly jazz which sounded its first notes here in the 1940s and has seen a resurgence in recent years. Bishkek held its first international jazz festival in April 2006 and another in 2007; organisers hope it will become an annual feature.

Bishkek's original live rock bar, **Zeppelin**, is still going strong at 43 Chui but now has competition from a host of others. One of the most popular is the **Promzona Club**, at 16 Cholponatinskaya, considered one of the best places to hear live music, mostly Russian rock.

Another lively and very popular rock music venue is **Golden Bull**, near the White House at 209 Chui, but beware the pickpockets and the occasional dodgy taxi driver waiting outside to mug drunk foreigners in the early hours. **Jazz Club**, on Akhunbaeva, just off Manas, plays live music seven days a week and has a lovely interior decorated with posters of all the jazz greats.

OTHER ACTIVITIES

Golf has come to Bishkek in the shape of the Canadian-run Maple Leaf Golf and Country Club, tel. (0517) 790877. Just 20 minutes by car from the centre, it enjoys a spectacular view of the Tien Shan mountains and boasts a nine hole course, beginners' driving range, pro shop and club house. A visit also offers a chance to stop at the gorgeous 12 Chimneys Restaurant at the mouth of the Alamyedin Gorge (see Restaurants and Bars).

Bishkek has several open air **swimming pools**; one at Sports Palace, on Togolok Moldo/Ryskulova and two at the Dolphin Sports Complex, at 304 Chokmorova, at the intersection with Mahatma Gandhi (Molodaya Gvardiya). There are **tennis** courts behind Spartak Stadium on Togolok Moldo and you can also brush up on your **riding** skills at the Equestrian School at 204 Bakinskaya, tel. (0312) 279698.

TRANSPORT

AIR

Manas airport is one of the biggest and most modern in Central Asia, with 11 airlines transporting nearly 400,000 people through its doors each year. It possesses the longest artificial runway in the region thanks, no doubt, to the presence of the US Air Force Base at Manas, which provides logistics support to the forces in Afghanistan.

The number of flights, both domestic and international, has increased enormously in recent years. Depending on the time of year, there are 85 flights a week to Osh alone—a staggering improvement on the four weekly flights to Kyrgyzstan's southern capital available just four years ago.

Together with the 12 weekly flights to Jalal-Abad and several to Batken, links with the south have been dramatically improved. There is also one flight to Karakol each week.

Manas airport is 23km to the northwest of Bishkek. Bus no 153 runs every 30 minutes between the airport and the Beishenalieva bus stop on the corner of Chui and Mahatma Gandhi (Molodaya Gvardiya), also stopping on Chui just west of the Manas statue. The journey costs US$0.30 and takes 45 minutes.

Minibuses plying the same route cost twice as much and take 30 minutes; alternatively two taxi firms operate officially from the airport, charging around US$9. You can order one 24 hours a day from the Business Centre on the first floor of the airport's north terminal (there have been warnings about taking private taxis from the airport).

The journey from the airport makes a seductive introduction to the country in summer, as you pass avenues of tall poplar trees, fields of sunflowers and men on horseback herding dusty brown cows. People en route to Osh Bazaar often carry buckets of raspberries, strawberries and currants, held in place by cloths fetchingly tied like scarves around the top.

There's a useful and comprehensive airport website (www airport.kg) in Russian and English.The following airlines have offices in Bishkek or Manas airport:

British Midland International is based at Manas airport, tel (0312) 664220 email: mariana.kazantseva@flybmi.com; www.flybmi.com.

Kyrgyzstan Airlines is also at Manas airport, tel (0312) 603410 email: office@kyrgyzstanairlines.kg

Kyrgyz Air is at 129 Abdrakhmanova, tel (0312) 622123 email: KyrgyzAir@aviareps.co.ru

Aeroflot is at 230 Chui, tel (0312) 651422; email: aflfruto@elcat.kg

Altyn Air is at 195 Abdumomunova, tel (0312) 225446; email: altynair@elcat.kg.

China Xinjiang Airlines is at 128/3 Chui, tel (0312) 664668; email ebin999@sina.com.

Enkor is at 86/1 Moskovskaya, tel (0312) 223355; email: 7777@imfiko.bishkek.su.

Uzbekistan Airways is at 107 Kievskaya, tel (0612) 600123; email: uzb-air@elcat.kg.

Botir Airlines is at 14 Suyumbaeva, tel (0312) 2858444; email: baarlines@infotel.kg.
Itek Air is at 128/10 Chui, tel (0312) 664057; email: itek@infotel.kg.
Turkish Airlines is at Manas airport, tel (0312) 660008; email thymanas@airport.kg.
Be aware that most Kyrgyz airlines are banned from flying over or to the European Union. Glavtour, at 93 Toktogula, tel. (0312) 663232, 660313; email: glavtour@infotel.kg acts as an agent for several airlines including Lufthansa, KLM, Indian Airlines and Kazakh Air. You can also buy air tickets through some of the city's tour operators.

TRAIN
There is a very limited train service in Kyrgyzstan. Trains depart from Bishkek II station for Balykchy and Kaindi (sporadically in winter), but the bus is quicker and safer. There is a five som charge for information at the central Bishkek railway station. For international train services see page 74.

BUS & CAR
Ancient, bald-tyred and decrepit Soviet buses are being replaced by Mercedes Princess buses. They run frequently and travel all major routes in all weathers so they provide the ideal transport. Short-distance buses and private minibuses depart from the old or East bus station on Jibek Jolu. From here, daily buses trundle to **Tokmok**, **Kant**, **Kemin**, **Issyk-Ata** and **Chong Kemin**. Private minibuses whiz along many of the same routes poaching some of the passengers from the scheduled buses.

Long distance and international buses depart from the new or West bus station on Jibek Jolu/Akmuz. There is a left luggage here and some signs are in English. Unfortunately, displayed timetables are unreliable. Go upstairs for information and downstairs to buy tickets. Buses and minibuses leave for **Almaty**, **Tashkent** (foreigners need a Kazakh transit visa), **Balykchy**, **Karakol**, **Naryn**, **Talas** (via Kazakhstan) and everywhere in between. Buses depart several times daily to **Almaty**, **Karakol** and **Balykchy**.

From here, Karakol buses speed along the northern shore (seven hours) and creep along the southern shore of Lake Issyk Kul, so choose your bus with care. Two buses a day take the southern shore route (*yoozhnaya doroga*), departing before midday, but rarely stick to their schedule so check before you intend to travel. The public bus to **Naryn** often doesn't run so a minibus or private taxi is probably your best bet for this route. Wherever you are headed, arrive early. Get a separate ticket for stowed baggage, but if possible keep it with you as the hold is often used for animal fodder, cans of petrol or sheep with all four legs tied together (some Peace Corps friends once shared a bus with a cow and her calf). Toilets, food and money exchange (at unattractive rates) are available at both bus stations.

Minibuses to **Osh** (15-16 hours) and **Jalal-Abad** (13–15 hours) and shared taxis now zoom down the recently repaired and excellent Bishkek-Osh road, departing from Osh bazaar.

You can arrange a car and driver through one of the local tour operators (see page 81) or, for a fraction of the price, pay for a seat in one of the shared taxi waiting outside bus stations. Alternatively, negotiate a price for a specific journey.

One of Kyrgyzstan's fine avenues; sadly, many are losing their trees to firewood

Around Bishkek

To the west and south of Bishkek loom the Kyrgyz Ala-Too, an outer chain of the northern Tien Shan which stretches 400 kilometres from the western end of Lake Issyk Kul towards Kazakhstan and boasts around 480 glaciers. The highest peaks of the Kyrgyz Ala-Too range crowd between the Ala Archa and Alamyedin valleys. Together they are known as the Ak Sai Knot and are dominated by Semyenov-Tienshanskiy at 4,895 metres, named after the 19th century Russian explorer-scientist, (and some say spy). The main rivers which cut through the mountains are the Karabalta, the Ak Su, Sokoluk and Alamyedin. Be warned that the Kyrgyz Ala-Too receive most of their rain in May and June.

ALAMYEDIN VALLEY

Just 25 kilometres from Bishkek and boasting healing mineral spa waters, Alamyedin valley is the place to see Bishkek city folk at play. Keen to escape the heat of the capital, they head for one of the three accommodation options on offer in the valley. The Tyoplo Klyucho Sanatorium is 12 kilometres up the valley from Koy Tash. They flash through the village in their shiny new Audis and Mercedes, past failing farms and families struggling to survive. City children are disgorged daily from coaches into the clean air and, rather charmingly, return clasping bunches of wild flowers.

Though Alamyedin can't quite rival Sokoluk or Ala Archa valleys for beauty, it has the advantage of comfortable chalet-style accommodation with fabulous walks right from your front door. The sanatorium, opened in 1984 for employees of the Ministry of Energy, is now a shadow of its former self but still offers a swimming pool, massage services and baths at 54°C, fed by underground hot springs (due to radon levels a maximum of ten minutes per session is recommended).

The chalets and dining room are a 15-minute walk up the hill. Two four-bedded rooms share a grubby bathroom with a fairly reliable supply of hot water. Regular visitors in the know bring their own salads, fruit, cakes and vodka to supplement the scanty meals. Overall, a visit to the sanatorium is a veritably Soviet experience, enhanced by fine, if dilapidating, examples of Soviet kitsch architecture.

12 Chimneys Restaurant, tel. (0312) 960690, offers comfortable, if pricy, accommodation in cottages at a tranquil spot on the Alamyedin River at the mouth of the valley. En suite doubles B&B cost US$54. A cheaper alternative is in the village of Koy Tash itself.

TRANSPORT
To get to the sanatorium you first have to catch a bus from outside Bishkek's Alamyedin Bazaar to the village of Koy Tash. Several buses for other destinations go through the village so it is best to ask for the earliest bus. Koy Tash, dotted with new dachas, straggles for a couple of kilometres as the road climbs the 12 kilometres up valley to the sanatorium. You'll need to hitch or get a taxi in the village for this stretch.

If you have your own transport, the Golubini (Pigeon) Waterfall, up the river valley from the village of Tatyr, makes a pleasant detour. To reach Tatyr (about three kilometres from Koy Tash) cross to the west side of the river in Koy Tash and follow the road south up a tributary to the Alamyedin river.

ALA ARCHA NATIONAL PARK
The wide beautiful valley of the Ala Archa river (45 kilometres from Bishkek) sweeps up to the highest peaks and largest glaciers of the Kyrgyz Ala-Too range. To protect its tremendous natural diversity it was made a national park in 1976. The valley's steep wooded slopes, pristine water meadows and craggy cliffs provide habitats for over 170 animal species, including eagles, shy Marco Polo sheep, bear, lynx, wild boar, wolves and, in its upper reaches, rarely spotted snow leopards. It also supports over 800 plant species; a dream-come-true in spring for alpine flower enthusiasts. To the casual observer, the hills appear clothed in junipers, rowan trees and birches.

The valley's charm and accessibility from Bishkek attracts the crowds so try to avoid weekend visits if possible. Once you've left the suburbs of Bishkek you pass through an arch entitled 'Alamyedin'. The cemetery to the right contains the memorial tower to **Baitik Khan** (though he was buried elsewhere) who went quietly to his grave without knowing how profoundly his actions would affect his land. Leader of the Solto and Sarybagysh tribes, he rebelled against the tyrannies of the Khokand khan, killing him in 1862. He asked Russian troops for assistance, they successfully stormed the Pishpek fort and Tsarist rule was introduced in the region.

The entrance to the park lies ten kilometres beyond the village of Kashka Suu. Entrance fees are around US$1 per person, plus a levy on cars. The small museum near the entrance exhibits local species, including a sad array of stuffed animals. The ten and 30 minute guided tours appear to contain the same information, but delivered at different paces. The *turbaza* is a further 12 kilometres.

There are plenty of options for **walking and trekking** in the valley and it is best to bring your own food and camping equipment, although you can sometimes get a bed at the *turbaza*. The starting point is at this unsightly building, 12 kilometres from the park gates. It was well maintained for climbers in Soviet times but is now principally a restaurant and bar. At this altitude (2,150 metres) the weather can change swiftly so come prepared for cold and wet. A popular, fairly gentle walk heads downhill from the *turbaza*, across a footbridge and south-west for eight kilometres below the Andygene glacier. You pass a cemetery for fallen climbers; a solitary grave outside its boundaries is for the man who 'committed suicide' by cutting himself free in order to save his comrades. A new comfortable hotel after the second gates charges around UUS$50 B&B.

Another popular, but tougher, walk takes you within view of the Ak Sai glacier. The path climbs steeply to the east above the *turbaza* to a meadow at the entrance to the Ak Sai canyon. A little further up is a waterfall. The path beyond is rough and steep and climbs high above the river to a stone hut at 3,300 metres, a popular camping spot. Beyond lies the terrain of the experienced mountaineer with equipment and a guide. Unless you have climbed very gradually to this point it is quite possible that you will suffer from some form of altitude sickness here so it is worth leaving enough time to return to the *turbaza* if your symptoms are bad.

Public transport from Bishkek's Osh Bazaar goes only as far as Kashka Suu, ten kilometres from the park entrance and 22 kilometres from the *turbaza*. If you plan to hitch out of the valley you should leave early. The most convenient option is to hire a car and driver from a tour operator or negotiate the day trip with a taxi at Osh Bazaar.

KASHKA SUU TOURIST CENTRE

A poor jeep road runs seven kilometres up the Kashka Suu valley from Kashka Suu village to the **Tourist Centre** (tel. 211141, 434835, 219974 in Bishkek), a hostelry consisting of three chalets, a restaurant, a sauna and two ski lifts. Popular with skiers in winter, the hotel is mainly used for conferences. However, high up in the cool of the hills overlooking the Chui plain, it makes a good base to escape summer Bishkek and stroll or trek into the mountains. The centre is also used as a base for heli-skiing (see Activities in the Facts for the Traveller chapter).

No guides or horses are available here but day walks are easy and plentiful. Those intending to trek into the mountains are advised to hire a guide in Bishkek.

From January to March, conditions on the 3.5 kilometres long slopes are perfect for downhill skiing. The 1,500 metre chair lift carries you to a red run; beware that the drag lift serving an easier slope has no T-bar attachment. The centre is not ideal for the passing skier, largely because you cannot hire skis here, but you might have luck with the Edelweiss agency in Bishkek (see Tour Operators section in Facts for the Traveller).

Chalets contain three rooms, each with two or three beds. There is one bathroom per chalet with occasional hot water. Rooms cost US$10–15 per day, plus US$5 for meals. A lift pass costs US$5 per day.

Public transport will take you from the south-west side of Bishkek's Osh Bazaar as far as Kashka Suu village; from where you could try to hitch or, better still, try to find a taxi in the village.

SOKOLUK VALLEY

Some 40 kilometres south-west of Bishkek the Kazakh steppe erupts into smooth rounded green hills. Treeless, and grazed by elegant horses, the distant scene resembles a Gainsborough painting. The dancing Sokolok river rushes down from snow-clad peaks, visible at the head of the valley. Between the two lies a jumble of alpine, valleys filled with meadow flowers, medicinal plants, wild birch trees, waterfalls, wolves, foxes, snow leopards and a variety of deer, all vigilantly watched over by eagles.

In the cool of the foothills, 55 kilometres from Bishkek, lies the village of **Tash Bulak** ('stone spring' in Kyrgyz), which locals still sometimes call by its Soviet-era name, Belogorka.

Strung for about two kilometres along a straight road, Tash Bulak is an attractive village of handsome Slavic houses, square and squat, and set in well-kept gardens alive with flowers, vegetables and birch trees. The roofs of many houses are decorated with tin reindeer, sunflowers, cockerels and horses. The population has now stabilized at around 2,500 but in Soviet days it was larger, with equal numbers of Kyrgyz and Slavic people. Many Russians and Ukrainians left the village in 1990 and some have since returned. You can see why: with fertile land and plenty of clean water from the glacier-fed river, it is possible, with hard work, to scrape together a reasonable living here.

In Soviet days, a huge collective farm operated from Tash Bulak, one of the richest in the USSR. Many locals still receive a slightly raised pension in honour of past agricultural glories. The farm provided full employment and, as whimsically pointed out by villagers, all necessary amenities and shops. In stark contrast, today's one small kiosk store sells only noodles, vodka and Turkish biscuits. For anything beyond this, it's a 24-kilometre trip to the market town of **Sokoluk**. The collective farm also encompassed summer pastures in the Suusamyr valley to the south, to which large numbers of livestock were herded over the snowy pass each spring.

Wildflowers carpet the Kyrgyz grasslands in May and June

On the break-up of the farm, many Tash Bulak residents were awarded land in the Suusamyr valley, which they have never seen and cannot use. With minimal farm machinery and disintegrating irrigation systems, farming the private plots of land is labour intensive. Nevertheless, relative to much of Kyrgyzstan, Tash Bulak is reasonably prosperous.

WALKING AND TREKKING

From the village, a multitude of easy day walks lead into the foothills of the Kyrgyz Ala-Too, either on foot or horseback, taking in rivers and lakes en route. There are beautiful camping spots but, as a matter of courtesy and security, it is best to check with locals before pitching a tent. If you plan to camp or trek, bring plenty of dried and canned food to supplement the eggs and *kefir* (yoghurt) you can buy at the farms.

If you want to get into the mountains, it is advisable to hire a guide (see Practical Information later in this section). From the village, the road runs for 20 kilometres up the Sokoluk valley. For quick access to the mountains simply hire a car and driver from the village. An hour's walk along a clear path through woods from the end of the road takes you to a waterfall, its waters vaporising as it tumbles 20 metres from the cliff above. This can also be done as a half-day trip. Just before the outflow, a small clearing on the left provides an ideal **campsite**.

From here you can walk further up the Sokoluk valley into the snowy mountain peaks; the most straightforward route follows a faint path along the river (keep it to your left) through occasional wild birch groves. A higher path involves a scramble along the steep hillside, where luscious plants and twisted trees cling optimistically to the loose earth and an abundance of flowers blossom throughout late May and June. In many places the path has been swept away by frequent springtime landslides.

After two or three hours, the valley narrows considerably and is joined from the right by a steep river valley topped by a waterfall. If you make your way to the grassy saddle at the top of the side-valley you will be rewarded with a view of snowy scree and peaks beyond. For those with less of a head for heights, keep to the right of the river and half way up the valley turn to the right for the short steep climb to the ridge above.

From here you get a glimpse of high pastures too inaccessible to be used as grazing and untouched by humans, except for the occasional hunting jaunts. Rumour has it that some pearly lakes appeared in these peaks following an earthquake in the mid-1980s but their location is vague and it is unclear whether anyone from the village has actually seen them. It is inadvisable to trek beyond the end of the road without a local guide.

In theory it is possible to trek over the 3,775-metre Sokoluk pass into the Suusamyr valley. The route heads up the side valley to the right just before the end of the road. There was a well-used trail in Soviet times but after independence the smaller numbers of livestock diminished the need for additional summer grazing.

When the snow over the pass was regularly trampled by hundreds of hooves the crossing remained manageable, but for nigh on ten years successive snowfalls have lain undisturbed. For trekkers with sufficient experience, fitness, equipment and food this route is a possibility in July and August only. The route descends to Karakol (for accommodation at Karakol on the other side of the pass see the Suusamyr valley section in the Central Kyrgyzstan chapter). Avalanches, landslides and deep snow make the route prohibitive even in June.

The crossing would take a minimum of three days from the end of the road. For the foreseeable future, at least, it will not be possible to take pack horses over the pass. It would be unwise to travel without a guide from the village, though it can be hard to find someone prepared to go; generally the Kyrgyz do not share our enchantment with their mountains, seeing them as harsh and unpredictable, vengefully taking lives with avalanches, landslides, swollen rivers and perilous glacier crevices.

PRACTICAL INFORMATION
CBT partners, **Tourism Group Sokoluk** (Asylbek Kushchugulov, tel. (0312) 781596, mob (0517) 781596), offer homestays, yurtstays, guides and horses for trekking and horseback trips. Find them at Chetindi, three kilometres from Tash Bulak.

Kenjibek Degembaev, at 2 Bulana, in Tash Bulak is a good contact in the village for **accommodation**, **guides** and **horses**. It is not necessary to pre-arrange, but arrive before 6.30pm. Kenjibek can be found during the day at his office in the Tash Bulak municipal administration (*ail okmotu*) on Ulitsa Batik Batyr (Sovietskaya). The **homestay** accommodation is clean and friendly but basic, comprising a mat on the floor (it is best to bring your own sleeping bag) and plenty of good, simple food. There is a long-drop pit toilet but no private washing facilities.

Basic accommodation for about US$6 a night can also be found at what was once the **Yuri Gagarin Pioneer Camp** at the southern end of the village. These once fine facilities for city children ('Young Pioneers building socialism') are now crumbling into the hillside.

Bus no 253 leaves from 'The Schlagbaum' at Bishkek's Osh Bazaar three times a day, in the morning, and takes two hours. Failing this, buses go more regularly to Sokuluk, 30 kilometres west of the capital, from where you can jump on a local bus heading for Tash Bulak. Alternatively, a taxi from the '*schlagbaum*' at Osh Bazaar should cost around US$14 one way. Once in Sokuluk, look for the Orthodox church and turn left towards the mountains. For the return journey the bus leaves Tash Bulak for Bishkek from the far (mountain) end of the village at 8.30am, 11am and 2pm. In addition, cars stop at the bus stop to take people to Sokuluk, from where there are fairly regular buses to Bishkek.

En route to Sokuluk the village of **Gavrilovka**, 16 kilometres from Bishkek, is famous for its very sweet grapes. In summer huge bunches are sold along the roadside. The **Svetaya Dusha** (Holy Spirit) **Orthodox church** in Sokuluk is worth a visit, especially on Sundays. It was built in 1993 with materials and funds donated by Sokuluk's still substantial Slav community. Its lavishly decorated interior wall paintings and icons are typical of rural Orthodox churches all over Eastern Europe and the CIS. Orthodox choirs perform during mass. It is normal for women to cover their heads when entering an Orthodox church.

Look out for **Lenin**; his statue still stands in the town centre. The **Safeze Dungan** café on Sokoluk's main road, just before the church and the turning to Tash Bulak, offers a delightful summer terrace and a wide variety of oriental dishes for approximately US$1 each. Continuing five kilometres past the turning, the Dungan village of **Alexandrovka** has a renowned selection of good cafés.

ISSYK ATA

Issyk Ata (Father Heat) used to be a place of pilgrimage but is now synonymous with its popular health resort, which offers the full package of medical examination and mineral spring-fed hot baths. Until the early 19th century, villagers grateful for the healing properties of the water expressed their thanks by smearing sheep grease onto the large rock, which has a depiction of Buddha on it (the rock can be seen behind the dining room). Doubles with en suite facilities at the spa cost US$6. There are walks into the hills behind the resort. One bus leaves daily at 5pm from Bishkek's East bus station; arrive early.

SHAMSHIY VALLEY

Due south of Tokmok (60 kilometres east of Bishkek) is popular for short treks on foot or horseback (see Alltournative page 81), and is the start of a magical five-day trek to Lake Song Kul, run by Ride World Wide (see page 80). Routes take you through valleys rich in wildlife, wooded with larch, spruce and juniper.

KEGETI GORGE

Ninety kilometres east of Bishkek, Kegeti valley is very beautiful with steep forested slopes. A two or three day trek takes you to turquoise Lake Kul Tor, surrounded by beautiful waterfalls. From here yurt accommodation is available at Bel Saz jailoo.

KONURCHEK CANYON

Around 125 kilometres from Bishkek, this starkly dry canyon (it sees virtually no rain or snow) with red walls, is a silent world apart of towering pillars, an extinct volcano and extra-large plants.

CHUMYSH PETROGLYPHS

Frustratingly, these wonderful petroglyphs, only 20 kilometres from Bishkek, are just over the Kazakh border. If you have Kazakh visa or are travelling to Almaty, they make a worthwhile excursion. The Iron Age drawings depict hunters, sheep, dogs, horses and dancers. At the border post closest to Bishkek, turn right after passing Kazakh inspections but before the final STOP gate. Continue for approximately four kilometres along the road that hugs the river. Backing on to the first large village is a rocky hill; the petroglyphs are scattered along its brow. A road leads to the top of the hill from the eastern end of the village.

The Chui Valley and Issyk Kul

To a large extent the history of the Chui valley and Issyk Kul is the history of Kyrgyzstan. The first evidence of human settlement in this fertile, well-watered plain dates from the early Stone Age, some 7,000 years ago. In the early Iron Age, nomadic groups known as the Saks lived in the Chui valley region, followed by the Usuns, who flourished until the third century AD. Sixth-century eastern Central Asia was dominated by the western Turkic Khanate, which was based at Suyab on the river Chui, straddling a flourishing branch of the Silk Route.

The Chui valley became a centre of learning in the 10th and 11th centuries when the enormous Karakhanid empire had a thriving capital at Belasagun (see the Burana Tower entry later in this chapter). Nourished by the Silk Routes, previously half-hearted attempts at sedentarism now solidified into flourishing commercial and cultural centres in the valley.

In the 18th century the valley became the property of the exploitative Kokand khanate, which ruled from the Fergana valley. Little over a century ago only a few small fields were cultivated in the valley and much of the area was marshland, stalked by tigers which are long since extinct.

Russian advancement in the mid-19th century was relentless, and their early actions in the land of the nomads did nothing to win them the favour of the local population. A Cossack General explains:

> The worst land was left to the Kirghizes, the best was taken from them and given to the Russian settlers who, instead of cultivating it themselves, found it more profitable and convenient to lease the land to the Kirghizes it had originally belonged to or hire them to work it for pitiful wages.

Robbed of land and livestock, a fierce struggle ensued in the Chui valley and many Kyrgyz fled to the mountains and to China. A Kyrgyz petition to the Tsarist consul in early 1916 read as follows:

> Our lands were taken from us on the pretext that we do not serve in the Army, and we were driven to the mountains. But the mountains, covered with forest, turned out be the property of the state. Taxes were imposed on our livestock and yurtas. The land went to the settlers, the mountains to the Treasury, and we were left with nothing.

The new arrivals planted sugar beet, wheat and potatoes and built the square white-washed houses and fenced-in gardens that still give the region its Russian village feel. In

Kyrgyz summer yurt

the 1870s and 1880s Dungans and Uighurs arrived at the lake, fleeing suppression in the wake of Muslim uprisings in China's Xinjiang, Gansu and Shaanxi provinces. Victor Vitkovich, the Soviet writer, describes the colourful ethnic variety of the pre-collectivised 1920s:

> There were Ukrainian villages: cherry gardens ... brightly painted window frames; moist-lipped, lop-eared bullocks drawing long, canvas-covered carts ... There were villages of the Dungan: gay poppies blossomed on the flat roofs, vegetables were grown and the green tips of rice peeped out ... There were Kirghiz villages of ... clay-walled houses. Behind were the grey outlines of patched yurtas that in those years were still dear to the hearts of the nomads of yesterday.

The Soviet era swept all before it. The Chui river was harnessed, along with others, to create the Grand Chui Canal, part of a massive irrigation scheme which watered the region as far as the arid Kazakh steppe. Wheat and sugar beet production was boosted. One farmer was heralded 'the magician of Kyrgyz wheat' for developing a variety that was drought resistant and fast ripening. Melon fields ousted local wildlife and the *mykan* (quagmire) marshes, home to bitterns and herons, were turned into fields of buckwheat, flax, tobacco, fruit, maize and rice, even subtropical persimmon and fig.

From 1930, Soviet Kirghizia developed sugar beet with a passion, claiming the best yield in the Soviet Union (the sugar factory at Kant just outside Bishkek, is still in operation). They lined their roads with Lombardy poplars and planted mulberry bushes and elm as protection for crops. Local Russians will tell you that there were no horse and donkey carts on the roads during the Soviet era, but these have begun to creep back with the economic hardship brought by independence.

National differences were tidied up but what Victor Vitkovich says of the 1950s is probably still true today. On national holidays:

> Ukrainian housewives serve cherry dumplings with sour cream, in the Kirghiz home the family sits down to besh barmak (boiled mutton), while in a Dungan home guests eat Chinese puff cakes. In the evenings you will hear the strains of a concertina in a Russian village, the characteristic muffled notes of a Kyrgyz komuz (two-stringed guitar) and the liquid notes of the Chinese flute.

Still, today, Chui *oblast* (province) has the largest mix of peoples and religions, and a refreshing lack of ethnic tensions.

The Chui Valley

The wide, fertile Chui valley stretches from the Kazakh steppe in the west to the Boom canyon in the east, ranging from 500 to 1,300 metres above sea level. It is the largest of Kyrgyzstan's valleys, supporting a population of 770,000. As you head east from Bishkek towards Issyk Kul, it is hard to believe that the picture before you of rural harmony and productivity is largely a Soviet creation. The valley has always been known in Kyrgyzstan as a 'land of milk and honey', surrounded by a ring of fierce, unpredictable mountains. It is said that you can drop camel dung on the earth here and it will grow cheese!

Today, Chui *oblast* remains the most prosperous and productive region of the country, with poverty levels of 25 per cent, compared with the national average of 62 per cent. In recent years its economic growth has slowed, sparing the environment from the excessive use of fertilisers.

NAVEKAT AND KRASNAYA RECHKA

Krasnaya Rechka is 30 kilometres east of Bishkek, on the road to Balykchy. Two kilometres beyond the village is the Ala-Too petrol station. About 1.5 kilometres after this, turn left down a track marked with a stone cairn. Accessible by four-wheel drive or a 15-minute walk from the road, the series of irregular mounds hinting at dwellings and boundary walls are all that is left of the Sogdian town of Navekat, the largest settlement in the valley from the sixth to the 12th centuries.

Whilst ploughing the fields that surround these ruins, a Soviet tractor driver turned up a golden burial mask, stamped with curious patterns and with a precious stone in each eye socket. Investigation revealed that the mask had been buried on a middle-aged woman in the fourth or fifth century; the linear patterns were thought to represent her ancestors, children and grandchildren. Archaeologists have unearthed remains of a Buddhist temple, a Karakhanid palace and Buddhist and Nestorian Christian cemeteries. On the summit of the citadel (the largest mound) are a series of collapsed chambers, now taken over by mice and lizards. They are reminiscent of similar remains at Topraq Qala in Uzbekistan (albeit on a smaller scale). Look for the preserved sections of mud brick walls and for fragments of pottery. From the top of the citadel you can also see the Kazakh border to the north, marked by the Chui river.

TOKMOK

Sixty kilometres east of Bishkek, Tokmok is the commercial centre of the Chui valley. It was an important link in the string of forts erected by the Kokand khanate in the 18th century to protect the lucrative trade routes between Kashgar and Tashkent. It was the regional administrative centre until 1878, when a series of floods destroyed much of the town and drove the exasperated bureaucrats to relocate to Pishpek (present-day Bishkek).

The tiny **Tokmok Museum** at 146 Tryasina (open Mon–Sat 9am–5pm; entrance US$0.5) is worth a quick visit since it contains artefacts from many of the region's archaeological sites. A selection of enormous clay wine vessels and some Zoroastrian ossuaries come from Navekat and Krasnaya Rechka. From Burana (see below) are oil lamps, pipes and prehistoric tools used by the Sak and Usun peoples in the seventh to third centuries BC. The petroglyphs and mammoth horns were found in Ala Archa valley, south of Bishkek. A poignant display of war memorabilia honours the local heroes of World War II and the 1980s Soviet war in Afghanistan. Exhibits are labelled in Russian only.

Tokmok has a small hotel, the **Aliya Hotel** at Kirova/Pionerskaya near the station (US$7 per person). Clean but noisy, all rooms have a leaky private bathroom but no hot water. The **Bonu** café/restaurant complex (on Lenina, 50 metres east of an intersection dominated by a MIG fighter plane) is easily the plushest eatery in town. It boasts a relaxing, shady courtyard with a fountain. The large indoor restaurant serves standard local and Russian fare for approximately US$1. Internet is available in the games room.

Any bus from the West bus station bound for Balykchy or beyond will take you to Tokmok.

BURANA TOWER

This 10th century tower is just outside Tokmok, 13 kilometres from the main road, so hop in a taxi or, if you are really short of cash, catch a bus to the village of Burana, just six kilometres from the tower. There is a nominal entrance fee.

The word 'Burana' is thought to derive from the Turkic word for minaret, *munara*. The renovation of the tower you see today, banded with intricate brickwork, was completed in 1974. The ruined structure, originally 45 metres tall, was further weakened by Russian settlers, who stripped the tower of its bricks as high up as they could reach.

The Burana Tower marks the original site of the Karakhanid town of Belasagun, founded in 960. The loose-knit Turkic Karakhanid empire sprawled over much of Central Asia, covering an area larger than modern India, and had another elegant capital at Mavarannahr, now Ozgon, and a highly cultured and scientific centre at Kashgar. The Silk Routes, splintering through the valley, deposited a flotsam of trade and knowledge at Belasagun and the busy market town blossomed.

Jenghis Khan was so impressed by the settlement that he spared Belasagun and renamed it Gobilik ('good city'). Excavations of Chinese coins, bracelets of Indian cowrie shells, iron swords, bronze lamps and amulets, and stone Nestorian crosses have confirmed the international nature of the trade routes. By the 15th century the town had dwindled to nothing. The finds can be seen in the small **museum**, which is open 9am–5pm daily. If the museum appears closed, just call at the house next door as there is always somebody around.

The Kyrgyz tell a different version of history. Long ago there lived a wise and famous king who loved his clever and beautiful only daughter more than anything. Afraid that he would not live to see her bright future, he summoned all the fortune tellers and clairvoyants to reveal his daughter's fate. All foretold a happy life except one, who predicted that before she was 16 the princess would be bitten by a spider and die.

The king was angry and built a tall tower that touched the sky; the old fortune teller was thrown into the dark dungeon in the basement, while his daughter lived safely in a bright room at the top. All her servants and food were inspected for poisonous insects. She grew ever more beautiful and intelligent. On her 16th birthday the king brought her a large plate of vines to congratulate her. As she took the plate, she fell to the floor, dead. The king looked at the tray to see the spider which had killed his beloved daughter. He died shortly after, grief stricken.

Belasagun is also famous for the poet Jusup Balasagun, born here in about 1015. His only surviving work is a didactic poem, *Kutadgu Bilig*, roughly translated as 'The Knowledge which Brings Happiness'. It was written in Jusup's native Uighur (Turkic) in Arabic script and won him the favour of the Khan of Kashgar. The poem is a fine example of the high Islamic culture of mediaeval Central Asia and is still popular today. In a rush of nationalism, some academics are endeavouring to discover Kyrgyz roots for the poet.

Sheep herding in the Altyn Arashan valley

You can climb rickety stone steps inside the tower for Kyrgyzstan's readiest commodity—a mountain-fringed view. In the surrounding fields stand about 80 burial stones from the Western Turkic khanate (sixth to 10th centuries); ancient effigies whose fierce visage depicts either the fallen hero or somebody they have killed. They were brought here from throughout Kyrgyzstan and Kazakhstan. The finishing touch to the site is a slightly crude pictorial account of the town's history, with accompanying Russian text. Even if historical sites were not so rare in Kyrgyzstan, the Burana Tower ensemble would still be well worth a visit.

Trekking in the Chong Kemin Valley

The Chong ('Big') Kemin valley runs east-west for 80 kilometres between the Kungey and Zaliiskiy mountain ranges. Parallelling the border with Kazakhstan, the valley landscape of green pastures, ochre mountains and steep pine-covered slopes, used in summer by herders, offers a fine backdrop for hikes ranging from a long day-walk to cross-border treks lasting up to a week.

The population of the valley (about 4,000) is overwhelmingly Kyrgyz, of the Sary Bagysh tribe. Most people live in eight villages, scattered along the deep blue Chong Kemin river, the most remote of which are Kaindi and Tegirmenti. In the Soviet era, a collective farm and mining concern in the nearby Kichi ('Lesser') Kemin valley guaranteed full employment but these collapsed with the USSR.

On independence the local population lived in hope of receiving privileged government assistance, as Chong Kemin is the birthplace of Kyrgyzstan's former president, Askar Akaev (his brother still lives in the village of Kyzyl Bairak). In recent years, however, they have wisely switched to collective self-reliance initiatives and diversified agriculture, with the assistance of several United Nations development initiatives. Today, potato growing and cattle breeding are the main sources of income.

The small, modern mausoleum next to the village of Kyzyl Bairak (paid for by wealthy locals) is dedicated to Shabdan Batyr, a 19th century chieftain of the Sary Bagysh tribe who ruled the valley as his fiefdom. He is revered by his kinsfolk as a great patriot.

ROUTES

Note that this area suffers from a cross-border cattle theft problem. Foreigners are most unlikely to become involved, but, where possible, it is wise to camp close to a village, farm or shepherd's camp with the elders' permission. If you plan to trek and camp by yourself, bring enough canned and dried food to supplement the bread, eggs and milk products that you can buy in farms or shepherd camps. It is advisable to hire a local guide for all the treks in this section as maps are not sufficiently detailed and paths are often faint or confusing.

An attractive option is simply to head up the Chong Kemin valley for a few days. High up at the eastern end of the valley, Lake Jassyk Kul is one of the loveliest spots in these mountains. At this end of the valley people are less beset by cross-border cattle rustling and are very friendly. The closure of the mine at Ak Tyuz, north of Kaindi, near the border with Kazakhstan, dealt a severe blow to their livelihoods, however.

There are a number of possible routes over the mountains to Kazakhstan or to Issyk Kul. Kaindi is the obvious starting point but the early section of the valley makes for less interesting walking; it's better to hire a vehicle in Kaindi to the *koshara* (stables) at the junction of the Chong Kemin and Kashka Suu rivers (40 kilometres from Kaindi) and start walking from there. Jassyk Kul is approximately 50 kilometres further up the valley on rough tracks, dwindling to paths, along the Chong Kemin river.

For people with suitable fitness, equipment and some experience of glacier walking, the main trek is about 120 kilometres long (about six days) from **Kaindi to Grigorievka**, a village roughly half way along the north shore of Issyk Kul. Follow the Chong Kemin river nearly up to the head of the valley. Turn right (south) and climb steeply up the Zapadniy (western) Ak Suu stream and follow it to the Ak Suu glacier and pass (4,052 metres). Here you join the tough, though once popular, route from Bolshoe Almatynskoe Lake in Kazakhstan, to Grigorievka. From the pass, follow the Chong Ak Suu river down to Grigorievka.

A shorter and easier trek to Issyk Kul leads from **Kaindi to Toru Aigyr** on Issyk Kul. This trail is about 45 kilometres long and can be done in three days. From Kaindi, follow the Chong Kemin river eastwards until you cross a stream called the Toru Aigyr. Hike up alongside this to the Kyzyl Bulak pass at 3,800 metres. The descent takes you through Nevada-like rock desert that rolls all the way to the lake and Toru Aigyr village, so stock up with plenty of water. Not far from Toru Aigyr is a hamlet called Ulan, next to which is a *turbaza* where you can spend the night after your trek.

A local legend tells how the village of Toru Aigyr got its name. The story concerns a horse named Toru Aigyr who was very brave and intelligent. His master was a great warrior and fought all the enemies of the Kyrgyz people. After one such battle the villagers were surprised when their hero didn't return. Gazing at placid Issyk Kul one afternoon, a villager saw a horse swimming through the water. Eventually the horse reached the shore and shook itself. It was Toru Aigyr. The horse galloped off towards his master's house where he hung his head and neighed before racing off into the mountains. In gratitude for telling them that their beloved hero was dead, they named the village after his horse.

A slightly longer route (three to four days) would take you to **Chong Sary Oy**, further east along Issyk Kul lake. Starting at the stables, walk east up the Chong Kemin valley to the Orto Koy Suu river, which you follow to the Kok Ayryk pass (3,889 metres) on the Kungey Ala-Too ridge, then descend along the Orto Koy Suu river to Chong Sary Oy, about 20 kilometres west of Cholpon Ata.

Kyrgyz grandmother and grandson outside the traditional Slav-style family home

If you are heading for **Kazakhstan**, two alternative routes (each about four days) branch north from the Chong Kemin river. The first turns north at the Almaty river to take you over the Almaty pass (3,599 metres) on the Zaliiskiy ridge and down to Kokshoki. The second turns north a little further east, up the Kol Almaty river to the Ozerny pass (3,503 metres), also on the Zaliiskiy ridge, and descends down a good path following the Ozerny river to Bolshoe Almatynskoe Lake and Kokshoki, from where you should find transport to Almaty.

PRACTICAL INFORMATION
Ashu Guesthouse: 22 Borueva, Kalmak-Ashu; tel: (03135) 28108, (0312) 661331 (Kyrgyz Concept), mob: (0502) 524037; web: ashuctc.kg. An innovative combination of traditional Kyrgyz crafts and modern design, this friendly, family-run guesthouse offers rooms, some with en suite, some with shared clean bathrooms. The cosy dining room has an open fire and there's a garden for the summer. Singles US$40/doubles $60 full board. They can arrange treks on foot or horseback in the valley or horse and cart-rides around the village. It comes highly recommended by ex-pats and is signposted from the main Bishkek to Balykchy road.

CBT co-ordinator, Janibek Sariev, Karool Dobo village, tel: (0502) 832065, arranges homestays, guide services and horses. In Kaindi, schoolteacher **Sabish Chechebaev** (2 Shaibekova) might be able to organise homestays.

The blue waters of Issyk Kul

Buses from Bishkek's East bus station run to Kaindi and Tegirmenti. Minibuses go as far as Kemin, 55 kilometres from Kaindi. Bear in mind that if you're trekking from Kazakhstan, you'll need to get an entry stamp in your passport to avoid problems on leaving the country.

Tokmok to Balykchy

As you travel east from Tokmok the road creeps ever closer to the mountains. The Chui river which, from the south, seems to be heading straight for Issyk Kul, suddenly swerves to the west, as if in fright, and plummets towards the plain. Just after the small town of Kemin and before the road dips south into the Boom canyon, it merges with the Chong Kemin river which flows from the Kungey Ala-Too.

The stretch of the river between here and Balykchy is popular for easy one-day **rafting** trips organised direct with the Silk Road Water Centre or through Alltournative or other tour operators (see Tour Operators in the Facts for the Traveller chapter). A day trip from Bishkek involves a three-hour transfer to near Balykchy and about five hours of rafting on a 25-kilometre stretch of river classed at level 2, with a break for lunch. A slightly longer day would take you on level 4 waters through the Boom Canyon.

The main Bishkek to Balykchy service station, Kholodnaya Voda ('cold water'), is a row of yurts near the confluence of the rivers. As you pull up, restaurateurs will compete loudly and vigorously for your custom. Standard Kyrgyz and some Russian fare is available—*laghman, shorpa, shashlik*, meat or potato *pirozhki* and, of course, tea.

As you climb into the dry Boom Canyon, the road is lined with Soviet statues of snow leopard, eagle and stag. Walls designed to prevent landslides from pulverising the road look unnervingly flimsy. Once over the pass, the Issyk Kul basin opens out before you: a 192-kilometre corridor of sky-coloured water at the foot of a snowy mountain fortress. The descent to Balykchy and the lake takes you past a statue of Semyonov Tien-shansky, the Russian explorer, and a newer monument to Manas—an odd but common juxtaposition neatly summing up the current struggle to put a stamp of Kyrgyz cultural heritage on the vision of the future as well as on the uncomfortable reality of the past.

Issyk Kul

A sea is not just scenery. It is an expression of eternity, an expression of death, a metaphysical dream.

Thomas Mann

Issyk Kul *oblast* (province) makes up 20 per cent of Kyrgyzstan's territory, an area of 43,500 square kilometres, but is populated by only 410,000 people. Prospects for economic prosperity here are bright. The closing down of production enterprises has caused poverty but tourism provides significant employment along the north shore of Issyk Kul. The tourist sector, already substantial, promises to become increasingly important to the local economy, though this will depend on sustainable and careful management of tourism development in the coming years to ensure the protection of the region's natural resources.

Synonymous in the Soviet mind with relaxation and fun, this 6,236 square kilometre expanse of sky-blue water with its sandy beaches is the pride of the Kyrgyz people. Strike up a casual conversation with your taxi driver or the person sitting next to you on a bus and one of the first questions, posed with a certain glee, will be whether you've visited Issyk Kul. At an altitude of 1,608 metres it is the second largest mountain lake in the world.

An air of mystery and legend surrounds this great inland sea. The official depth of 702 metres is disregarded by locals who know it to reach to the hot centre of the earth. Legends of ruined cities nestling on the lake floor were confirmed when the ruins of Chegu ('red valley'), a former Usun town, were discovered under the water near Tyup. Fishermen in Toruagyr, near Balykchy, also speak of seeing submerged buildings in waters just off their village.

Dusted with clouds and dotted with villages on the north shore, the lake runs east-wards for 182 kilometres and is up to 61 kilometres wide. Minerals give the salty lake its curative properties and colour, and make it unsuitable for drinking or irrigation, though cattle are sometimes watered here. Visibility in the clear water is unusually high at 20 metres. The lake's western and eastern shores serve as a wintering place for water-fowl: the pochard duck, mallard, bald coot and teal are the main visitors. Hare, fox and muskrat live in the thickets around the lake. Supporting some 40 kinds of mammals and 200 types of birds, the lake and a 1.6-kilometre-wide zone around its shore were made the Issyk Kul preserve in 1948 and hunting was banned within its limits.

When Pyotr Semyonov and his army arrived at the lake in the 1850s they caught 400 pounds of carp by simply slashing in the shallows with their sabres. By the 1920s carp, bream (whose species are unique to the lake) and herring were perilously depleted. To boost levels of edible fish, trout were brought from Lake Sevan in Armenia in 1928 to little avail. A second attempt was made in 1936, which also seemed to fail until, during World War II, a monster version of the trout appeared, at least three times its normal size and weight. More bream were later introduced from the dying Aral Sea but the outsize trout are said to have unbalanced the fish species of the lake.

Colin Thubron (see Recommended Reading), travelling in the early 1990s, describes an encounter with fishermen who called from their boat 'England!...Football!... Hooligans! Better off here, fishing!' Bad news travels far. The lake's serene face can change in a moment to mountainous waves, whipped up by winds from one or more of the ravines, chasing even large ships into the shelter of a bay.

Around Issyk Kul, snow-clad mountains hover at over 4,000 metres on all horizons, disembodied by the intervening haze. To the north the Kungey ('facing the sun') Ala-Too are green, fertile and populated, while the Terskey ('one who turns away from the sun') Ala-Too to the south are baked and barren, fed by very little rain or snowmelt, and hence less populated and very poor. The western part of the basin consists of rocky desert shores with sparse, saline vegetation while in the east are well-watered steppes and meadows and an unusual variety of elm, which thrives in the black chestnut soil.

As well as more conventional crops, the north-eastern shores were famed for their huge harvests of raw opium, though this has now been banned. Bizarrely for a lake fed by scores of rivers and streams and drained by none, the level of the lake has fallen by two metres in the last 500 years.

THE LEGEND OF HOW THE KYRGYZ PEOPLE CAME TO ISSYK KUL

Long ago when the world was covered in forests, grasses and rivers, there lived a Kyrgyz tribe on the banks of the Yenesei river. They were in constant battle with neighbouring tribes. One day a beautiful bird appeared to them, declaring 'there will be a disaster!' Just then a great noise erupted and they found themselves under attack.

Everybody was killed, except for two children, a girl and a boy, who ran away in horror. But eventually, desperate for food, they came across the camp of their enemies. An old woman gave them food but others recognised them as Kyrgyz and ordered her to kill them. Reluctantly she took the children off, planning to throw them over a cliff. To the crying children she pleaded, 'forgive me, please!'

Just then a beautiful white cow with black eyes, her udders full of milk, approached. Her calves had been killed by humans and she begged the old woman to give her the children. She took them to Issyk Kul where she raised them until they were old enough to marry. Their two sons were the firstborn of two Kyrgyz tribes.

Balykchy

Known today as a town of wind, truckers, vodka and prostitutes, Balykchy is indeed an uncomfortable place, with little to interest the visitor beyond a change of buses. Its name means 'fisherman' in Kyrgyz, just as its former name, Riybachye, did in Russian. Once the proud centre of the Kyrgyz fishing, shipbuilding and transportation industries, it has now dwindled to an important transport junction.

Buses depart for Karakol via the north shore (several times daily) and the south shore (twice daily), and also run to Naryn in the summer. Minibuses and shared taxis are quicker and cost about 30 per cent more, but lack of maintenance and high driving speeds can make these more hazardous options, particularly in bad weather.

If you are passing through, the **Ak Joltoy** on Kydyk Kaldibaev/Komsomol is the best café in town; open daily from March to October, it is clean and serves Russian and Kyrgyz food. With a handy *univermag* (general store) on the ground floor and hygienic toilets outside, expect to pay around US$1 for two courses.

If you need to stay, **Kairat**, 196 Frunze, tel. (03944) 21946, offers unoccupied flats. **Hotel Meder** on the corner of Gagarina/40 lyet, tel. (03944) 24126, is clean, open all year and offers rooms with shared facilities. Both hotels cost US$4 B&B. Another option is the **DOTS Ulan** (tel. 0773 816459) at Kyzil Uruk, just west of Toru Agyr, 23 kilometres from Tamchy and 18 kilometres from **Balykchy**. Now a children's camp, you can stay in basic rooms with outdoor facilities for about US$9 full board. This could be a convenient stop at the end of a Chong Kemin valley trek.

Lake Issyk Kul—The North Shore

In Soviet times the lake was considered one of the best health resorts of the USSR, a playground and convalescent centre for workers and dignitaries alike.

Today, the north shore of Lake Issyk Kul is saturated with tourism; a new generation of hotels, typically with discos, bars and karaoke, has risen from the ashes of post-Soviet decay to complement the renovated Soviet-era sanatoria. Hotel building continues apace but little suitable space remains, while resources and infrastructure, especially sanitation, are stretched almost to breaking point. The incidence of disease is on the increase around the lake, and over-development is sited as a possible cause.

Many hotels block-book a year in advance to Kazakh and Russian travel agencies. It is almost impossible, now, to book a lake break during the season. Flights to Issyk Kul airport, five kilometres from Tamchy, make the lake more easily accessible to people from CIS countries and the road—long-planned and likely to open soon—from Almaty to just west of Cholpon Ata, will swell numbers further.

Tourism revenue is crucial to both the local and national economies. However, although research shows that holidaymakers generally return home satisfied, there is increasingly stiff competition from Turkish resorts so it is essential to preserve Issyk Kul as an attractive and reasonably-priced holiday destination.

If you would like to include a little sun and sand on your visit, your best bet would be the south shore, in particular around Kaji Sai (see page 188).

Of the myriad of accommodation options along the north shore, the following (arranged from west to east—see also Cholpon Ata) are just a few. For a fuller list, see websites for Kyrgyz Concept, concept.kg or CAT, cat.kg. Prices vary with the season; those quoted are full board per person in peak season.

ACCOMMODATION
Villa Stariy Zamok ('Old Castle'): 1 Baytikov Turdakun, Tamchy. Tel. (03943) 42363, mob (0502) 615568. Follow the large sign advertising 'Willa' from the main road.
A surreal experience of kitsch and comfort, the three main buildings each attempt a distinct architectural style—Chinese, French, English. 'Lux' rooms, with thick carpeting over floors and walls, sport mock Victorian furniture and outsize beds and TVs. An underground cavern, houses the bar, swimming pool and sauna. Outside are another swimming pool and tennis courts. Costs are US$30–80.

Royal Beach Hotel: Chok Tal, east of Tamchy. Tel. (03943) 23176, (0312) 663232, (0502) 358375; email: royalbeach@mail.ru; web: royalbeach.kg
Its red roofs unmissable from the road, this tasteful, mostly low-rise hotel claims a prime spot on the lakeshore among trees. Eateries include the glass-walled restaurant and beach cafés. Also offers a sports complex, business centre, conference facilities and boat trips around the seashore. Cost is US$45.

Akun: Kara Oi. Tel. (03943) 54135, (0502) 571272, (0312) 240997 email: akun_mrk@elcat.kg; web: akun.kg
Set in its own parkland, the hotel offers all grades of room with en suite; as well as a bar, disco, tennis, other sports and a sandy beach with water-skiing. Cost is US$35.

Kyrgyz Vzmorye ('Kyrgyz Seaside'): Bosteri, ten kilometres east of Cholpon Ata. Tel. (03943) 35648, (0312) 790738, mob. (0502) 574633.
This 1970s sanatorium is set in parkland with a sandy beach offering parachute jumps, boat trips and a variety of sports. Renovated, it's now modern and comfortable with en suite and is renowned for its salt cave which is particularly beneficial for respiratory problems. Cost with treatments is US$48.

Hotel Alma Ata: Bosteri. Tel. (03943) 35733
This vast, modern, international-standard hotel is Kazakh-owned. It offers small standard rooms to plush apartments, all en suite. With its own sandy beach, the full range of sports is available as are conference facilities and business centre. Cost is US$50.

Talisman Village: Bosteri. Tel. (03943) 36527; email: tvillage@mail.kg.
A newly built, relatively small complex of cottages, with a sandy beach and beach café. Comfortable rooms have en suite. Prices US$50.

Issyk Kul Sanatorium (known as 'Avrora'): Bulan Sogotuu, 20 kilometres east of Cholpon Ata and just west of Korumdu. Tel. (03943) 37215, (0312) 662571; email: aurora@ktnet.kg; www. aurora.kg. Built to simulate the *Aurora* cruiser of revolutionary fame, this was once the haunt of presidents and dignitaries, and retains some of its old prestige. It is set in landscaped wooded gardens which run down to the beach where water sports are available. There's also an indoor lake-water pool and the full range of health facilities, and internet access. Simple rooms have en suite bathroom and lake-view balcony. Prices US$70.

Hotel Sinegorie: Korumdu. Tel. (03943) 42552, (0312) 660378. A large modern hotel, with en suite facilities. Particular attractions are its own sandy beach with boats and catamarans for hire, bars, sports and water entertainments and special facilities for children. Costs US$40.

Solemar: Korumdu. Tel. (03943) 30438, (0312) 622407, mob. (0502) 329090. www.solemarkg.com. The hotel consists of cottages set in its own parkland on the beach. The top feature here is a bar/restaurant at the end of the pier. Rooms are en suite; disco, karaoke, sports and children's playground are all available along with internet access and conference facilities. US$60.

TAMCHY

Half way between Balykchy and Cholpon Ata, Tamchy is a pretty village, known for the excellence of its felt handicrafts. A big crafts fair was held here in July 2006 and 2007, organised by the Central Asia Crafts Support Association, and this is expected to become a regular event. CBT have their only north shore office here, offering beach-side accommodation. The beach, though beautiful especially in the early morning, is disappointingly gritty and used by cattle and donkeys. The CBT contact is Baktyrgul Asanalieva, 47 Manasa, (03943) 21272, mob. (0503) 355611.

CHOLPON ATA

The main village between Balykchy and Karakol, Cholpon Ata is 254 kilometres from Bishkek and straggles along the main road for miles. Athletes used to come from all over the Soviet Union to train at altitude but today its chief attractions, other than sand and sea, are a field of petroglyphs from the sixth century BC to the Middle Ages, and the best museum in Issyk Kul.

On the short journey from Tamchy to Cholpon Ata, the vines you see between the road and the lake were a source of controversy. Government plans to plant opium for medicinal purposes were subverted by international institutions active in Kyrgyzstan, which instead gave funds to develop tourism and plant vines brought from abroad to expand Kyrgyzstan's embryonic viniculture industry.

CHOLPON ATA MUSEUM

69 Sovietskaya. seven days a week in summer 9am–6pm; in winter closed Sun. Entrance US$1. Exhibits in Russian and Kyrgyz.

This museum displays the majority of the archaeological finds from around the lake and the Chui valley—the little that, excavated in Soviet times, was not shipped off to St Petersburg. The museum presents a well-arranged walk through the history of Kyrgyzstan. If you understand Kyrgyz or Russian, it is worth hiring a museum guide who will breathe life into the display with the energy and knowledge of the enthusiast.

Amid the familiar bronze and clay pots and agricultural implements, you find unique ancient embroidery, made with vegetable-dyed silk on cotton, a variety of stones bearing inscriptions from the earliest petroglyphs to Tibetan examples found near Tamga. There are also musical instruments and exhibitions devoted to the Manas Epic, Akaev (President 1991–2005) and writer, Chinghiz Aitmatov. For a nation deep in the process of evaluating and rewriting its past, the museum is a valiant effort to capture and interpret history.

PETROGLYPHS

Star attraction at Cholpon Ata is the **Issyk Kul** Historical State Museum—a remarkable open-air art gallery sprawling on the lower slopes of the Kungey Ala-Too just north of Cholpon Ata. The Soviets attempted to document and preserve the petroglyphs and, after a period of neglect, it is now a **Unesco** project, sponsored also by Novinomad. The site is three kilometres from the main road; to get there, head west from the centre for about a kilometre and take a right turn by a 'militsia' sign, fork left and pass a mosque. Meandering through these huge fields, you come upon pictures carved on rocks of all sizes. They depict hunting scenes and sacrifices, wolves, long-horned ibex, goats, horses and snow leopards. Probably dating from 500 BC to 100 AD, their creators are thought to be the Sak and Usun peoples. In addition, on the upper slopes stand stone circles, tombs and *balbals*, and there is a spectacular panorama of Cholpon Ata bay.

STUD FARM

The horse breeding centre here was once a leader in its field. The skinny, sinewy Kyrgyz horse was perfect for its hard mountain job—strong, with rock-hard hooves and incredible stamina, managing with no food for three days when necessary, and sure footed as a mountain goat. The Soviets were determined to 'improve' this revered beast; they wanted it taller, faster and sturdier, tough and tenacious but with more graceful lines. A Kyrgyz-French organisation, **Kyrgyz Ate**, run by Jacqueline Ripart is working to find and breed the original Kyrgyz horse (see page 262).

Travel Agency Novinomad organises horse games at the Hippodrome here every year. They are planned for August 2, 2008 and August 1, 2009 (www.novinomad.com)

Petroglyph of ibex at Cholpon Ata

BOAT TRIPS

The Yacht Club, known as **Cruis**, is on 22 Akmatbai, tel. (03943) 43373, mob: (0772) 271366. They run boat trips around the lake in summer for about US$8 per hour and cross the lake to the south shore, taking one to three days. They also hire out yachts of different sizes. The cost of a six-berth yacht would be US$32. Life jackets are included.

PRACTICAL INFORMATION

In summer, Cholpon Ata is teeming with holiday-makers, Costa del Sol style. As a result, every other building appears to be a guesthouse. We list a few here. More can be found on the websites of tour operators such as Celestial Mountains, CAT and Kyrgyz Concept (see page 82). New in Cholpon Ata is **Castle Hotel**, tel. (0502) 214854; email: nbrowne174@yahoo.co.uk. British-owned and run, this friendly and spotlessly clean hotel opened in summer 2007. It offers comfortable modern rooms, with impeccable en suite bathrooms, a garden café and a café/restaurant roof terrace with panoramic views. Just a ten-minute walk to the beach, it welcomes families and has toys and a sandpit. Conference facilities and transport within Cholpon Ata and further afield complete the package. B&B from US$25 per person in peak season.

For a truly Soviet experience, and a therapeutic mud bath, try **Goluboy Issyk Kul** in the centre of town, tel. (03943) 43858 for US$23 (east of the centre near the new bazaar). **Ala-Too Sanatorium** west of Cholpon Ata, tel. (03943) 44560, (0312) 645406. Set in its own parkland, it has the best beach in town, welcomes families and offers the usual range of sports. Accommodation is in cottages among Tien Shan fir. Cost US$17.

Cholpon Ata's privately owned guesthouses tend to provide better value for money but phone ahead where possible. **Pensionat Regina**, at 42 Gorkova, tel. 03943 42823, mob (0772) 387762 (opposite a car parts shop and cinema), offers 12 simple, spotless twin rooms all with en suite bathroom. It has a pretty orchard garden. B&B costs US$12 per person.

Another clean, cheerful place is **Liubov Vassilevna's Guesthouse** at Pravda 2 and 3, tel. (03943) 42102. Take the road opposite the Regional Administration building and then first right. The chocolate-box wooden house overlooks a pretty currant-bush garden. Each room has a toilet and cold water; showers are shared. Full board costs US$20. The two families jointly own and run **Chastniy Pensionat**, nearby at 87

Sovietskaya (the main road), tel. (03943) 43794. It is clean but more basic and open May to September only, costing US$19 B&B per person.

El Noor Bazaar is well-stocked with beach must-haves (no buckets and spades in Kyrgyzstan) and fresh food—breads, cheeses and tomatoes, with particularly lush piles of fruit in autumn. In the central area (at the western end of town, near the museum and Central Post Office and Telephone Exchange) a range of shops, sell necessities. The Internet is available at two shops on the south side of the road and, sandwiched between them, is attractive Oosys café. Due to the large Russian population in Cholpon Ata, cafés and restaurants serve Russian food as well as normal Central Asian fare. There are a number of exchange booths on both sides of the road around the bazaar and one in the Post Office.

There is a clean, flower-filled park just west of the centre with an excellent children's playground and café.

Along the road between Cholpon Ata and Bosteri, ten kilometres to the east, are attractive eateries and signs announcing rooms in houses. Some nice stretches of beach provide good picnic spots for passers-by. Bosteri is home to many sanatoria. Issyk, tel. (0503) 207648, (0503) 215358, a backpackers' hostel (B&B US$15) has recently opened in Bosteri.

TREKKING ROUTES TO KAZAKHSTAN

See also the earlier section on Chong Kemin valley. Please be aware that trekkers have been robbed in these mountains—you'll be safer with a local guide. The Kyrgyz government has decreed that internationals must enter and exit the country at staffed border crossings only. Entering by trekking routes from Kazakhstan may therefore lead to difficulties on leaving the country as you will not have an entry stamp to validate your visa. This also applies to Kazakhstan. The area is criss-crossed with trekking routes so it's not necessary to cross the border.

Probably the best known valleys in the Kungey ('One Who Turns Towards the Sun') Ala Too are Semyenovka and Grigorievka, cut through by the Ak Suu ('White Water') and Chong Ak Suu ('Big White Water') rivers respectively. Fifteen kilometres into Semyonovka valley, the road leads to a *jailoo* at 2,010 metres. Here, an unusual yurt camp enjoys beauty, tranquillity and excellent views. From June to the end of September, you can stay in this traditional (as opposed to the 'tourist') yurt camp with normal Kyrgyz culinary, sleeping and bathroom arrangements. The activities on offer give an insight into the history, culture, crafts, horse games, music and lifestyle of the Kyrgyz. You could stay for a while or visit on a day trip from Ananyevo.

The five or six day trek from Grigorievka to Kokshoki was a popular route in Soviet times but now the trail is not always visible so it is advisable to hire a guide. This trek should be undertaken only between June and mid-September by people of good fitness with experience of walking on glaciers. You will need your own camping equipment and food. The trek starts from Grigorievka village, 40 kilometres east of Cholpon Ata, and follows the Chong Ak Suu river (not to be confused with the Ak Suu river) north to the Ak Suu pass (4,052 metres), on the Kungey Ala-Too ridge. On the northern side you have to cross a two-kilometre long glacier. Descend northwards alongside the Zapadniy (western) Ak Suu river to the Chong Kemin valley.

On reaching the valley floor you might want to make a detour eastwards to Lake Jassyk Kul, in a beautiful setting high up in the valley, surrounded by pastures used by shepherds. The walk continues down the Jassyk Kul valley to climb into the Zaliiskiy Ala-Too mountains just to the east of the Kol Almaty river. Cross the Ozerny pass (3503 metres) to Kazakhstan and descend alongside the Ozerniy river to the Bolshoy Almatyn-skoe Lake and the tarmac road to Kokshoki. Here you should be able to pick up transport or a ride to Almaty. Detailed maps of this area can be bought in Bishkek only (see page 127).

The fairly undemanding trek from **Sary Bulak to Saty** in Kazakhstan via the **Kolsai lakes** can be done on foot or on horseback and takes around four days. From the tiny village of **Sary Bulak** at the eastern end of Issyk Kul, you climb to the 3,274-metre Sary Bulak pass on the Zaliiskiy ridge and then descend past the three colourful Kolsai lakes in Kazakhstan to the village of Saty, a five-hour drive from Almaty. Travel agencies Turkestan and Ecotrek in Karakol (see pages 168–9) can arrange horses and a guide for the trip, and the former usually keep kayaks at the Kolsai lakes.

ANANYEVO

As you drive eastwards from Cholpon Ata, the mountains close in on both sides and you appear to be heading for a white peaked cul-de-sac. The villages along the roadside are refreshingly low-rise and the hills become softer and more wooded. The old Cossack settlement of Ananyevo, 50 kilometres east of Cholpon Ata and 85 kilometres from Karakol, is a good place to relax and enjoy the mountains and lake away from the sanatoria. It also has the advantage of cheerful, reasonably priced accommodation.

The village has 12,000 inhabitants, roughly 60 per cent of whom are Slavs and the rest Kyrgyz with a few Dungan families. Ananyevo was founded in the 1890s but acquired its present name after World War II, when it was named after Captain Nikolaï Ananyev, who perished along with some 700 conscripts from this area—almost its entire male population—defending a small village outside Moscow. After the war migrants from the Russian Far East were moved in. There is a poignant memorial to the men beside a statue of Lenin, on Ulitsa Lenina, which runs north off the lakeside road from the village's only set of traffic lights. The small, charming Orthodox church and the local museum, housed in the school, are also worth a visit.

Besides agriculture and cattle farming, Ananyevo's main employer is forestry in the mountains to the north along the Kazakh border, as well as the sawmill and joinery.

The Swiss-funded **Lesic Forestry Programme** runs a friendly guesthouse at 76 Almatinskaya. It offers modern rooms with shared facilities and a lounge-diner with TV, video and music centre. The pretty orchard outside has a *banya* and barbeque area. Costs are US$16 per person full board. Book in advance through Natalya at the Lesic office, 23 Oboronnaya, tel.(03943) 61694, mob (0773) 707828, email: ananyevo@elcat.kg; or through Galina at the guesthouse on (03943) 61888. The office is first left after the war memorial on Ulitsa Lenina. Almatinskaya is the fourth road east of Ulitsa Lenina.

Most buses from Bishkek or Balykchy to Karakol stop at Ananyevo.

SVETLY MYS

Svetly Mys, a hamlet 48 kilometres from Karakol, is reputed to be the burial place of the apostle Matthew. This secluded site has attracted a succession of believers, pilgrims and eight monastic communities over at least 16 centuries, including a Nestorian Christian and two Armenian monasteries, and a Russian Orthodox monastery in the 19th century. Roads in the village are arranged to represent an Orthodox cross.

In the 1916 uprising (see page 21) the monastery was attacked and all but two of its 26 monks were skinned alive, boiled or otherwise horribly murdered. The two survivors have since been canonised.

Graves from an earlier monastery were uncovered in the 1950s, when foundations for an agricultural college hostel (on your left as you enter the village) were dug. An intricate silver crucifix was stolen from around the neck of one of the skeletons, at which point the fragile grave collapsed into dust. Local women are still working to find the cross and return it to the church. Rumour has it that some Kyrgyz fishermen found an icon of the Madonna and child floating in Lake Issyk Kul; they took it to the cathedral in Karakol where it now has pride of position.

Complexes of catacombs, said to be the cells of fourth or fifth century Armenian monks that were inhabited by subsequent communities, can be found on lakeshore peninsulas close to the village. Most are overgrown and filled with silt; elderly villagers talk tantalisingly of childhood games in 50-metre long corridors of cells, long since collapsed. One surviving site is on the shore south-west of the village.

Just west of the village of Ak Bulung, formerly Belovodsk, and its turn-off to Svetly Mys are a series of large, grassy mounds, laid out in perfectly straight lines between the mountains and Lake Issyk-Kul. These are *kurganii* (tumuli), the burial chambers of Scythian warriors and nobles. Some are said to be unexcavated. Similar mounds in Kazakhstan and to the south of the lake were found to contain armour, weapons and intricate golden jewellery, including the famous 'Golden Man', now displayed in an Almaty museum.

Karakol

Karakol is sandwiched between Lake Issyk Kul and the awesome wall and jagged fangs of the Tien Shan, the mighty mountainous barrier that rears up between the former Soviet Union and its powerful neighbour, China. For many centuries the Tien Shan, enveloped in legend and strictly out of bounds in Soviet times, remained one of the most unexplored and remote places in the world. The seventh century Chinese traveller-monk, Xuan Zang, reported:

> *These mountains stretch for thousands of leagues: among them are several hundred tall peaks which reach to the very sky; the valleys are dark and full of precipices. The snow that has accumulated here since the creation of the world has changed into ice rocks that do not melt either in spring or summer. There is a strong cold wind and travellers are molested by dragons.*

Upper-class 19th-century Slav house, Karakol

And yet at its feet the land is fertile and the climate mild. As a series of brave Russian explorers gave modern names to these valleys and peaks, Karakol, initially a military garrison, burgeoned as a town of explorers, professionals and merchants.

A quaint story surrounds its founding in 1869. The cartographers appointed to survey the site had just finished their work when a ferocious storm swooped in from the mountains, sweeping away the contents of their yurts, including the precious maps and plans. The following day the local Kyrgyz people offered to lend a hand and, together, they and the Russians formed a line towards the Jergalan river to comb the valley in the direction the storm had taken and found all but a few pages of the surveys. Thus the friendship between Kyrgyz and Russian inhabitants is said to spring from the very founding of the town. The population swelled considerably in the 1880s with the arrival of Dungan, Chinese Muslims, fleeing persecution in China. At this time Karakol was a town at the edge of the world.

The town was named Karakol until 1888, when the Russian explorer Przhevalsky died here while preparing for an expedition to Tibet. The town was graced with his name until 1921 when Lenin, in response to local sensitives, returned the town's original name. In 1939, at Stalin's behest, it reverted to Przhevalsky which it remained until the fall of the Soviet Union, when it resumed its Kyrgyz name—Karakol, or 'black wrist'.

Karakol is 1,770 metres above sea level and has a population of 75,000 people. It is the administrative centre for Issyk Kul *oblast* and boasts three bazaars, a small one for the town, a regional one on the outskirts and an animal bazaar every Sunday—not to be missed.

The town still has its frontier feel but also a cosy air, maybe emphasised by the rigours of the mountains beyond. Watered by rain blown west by the prevailing winds, it is a fertile garden town, famous for the sweetness of its apples. Its gardens overflow with plums, pears, cherries, peaches and apricots as well as flowers. The streets are shaded with unusually high poplar trees, and Tien Shan spruce, tall and magnificent, stand with dainty Siberian birch in Pushkin Park.

But it is the mountains that make Karakol really special. Just outside the town they entice you with possibilities: all abilities of biking, climbing, riding, skiing and more hiking than there are days in a lifetime. Karakol is fast becoming an important outdoor activities centre, but its success depends on continued investment in infrastructure and sustainable tourist facilities.

SIGHTS

HISTORICAL MUSEUM
Assanbay Zhamansariev near the crossroads with Toktogul. Open Mon to Fri 8am–4pm. Exhibits in Russian and Kyrgyz, many also in English. Entrance US$1.

Karakol's small museum is worth a visit for its splashes of information on a variety of topics. Kumtor, the joint venture Kyrgyz-Canadian company which is exploiting gold reserves high in the Tien Shan mountains, exhibits photos and information on its activities, with a slightly familiar Soviet propagandist emphasis on high local employment and skills transfer. A small section recounts the history of the Russian community in the region and another section is devoted to the story of the revolution.

More traditional exhibits include vast Scythian bronze pots apparently retrieved from Issyk Kul and measuring one metre in diameter, large beautifully decorated leather *koumys* (fermented mare's milk) containers, 14th century pottery jugs, musical instruments, jewellery of silver and semi-precious stones and a display of Kyrgyz applied art; costumes, felt wall hangings and yurt doors. The surrounding streets of pretty, Slav-style houses are also worth a stroll.

RUSSIAN ORTHODOX CATHEDRAL
This pretty little church, built originally of stone in 1872, replaced the new town's first Christian place of worship, a yurt. Destroyed by an earthquake in 1890, a new cathedral was completed in 1895, of wood on a brick base. The ravages of communist secularism stripped the Cathedral of its domes. Rebuilding was completed in the early 1990s for

re-consecration in 1991 and 1997. Today, the *Batiushka* (Father) oversees the entire Issyk Kul diocese. The Cathedral's greatest treasure is an icon of the Gentle Virgin Mary. During the anti-Russian uprising of 1916, the icon hung in Svetly Mys monastery (see page 159). Here, it apparently shed tears and blood whilst the monks were brutally murdered, shone with an ethereal light and repelled bullets. Copies of the icon are said to have healing powers. Visit the church on Sundays before 10am, when the choir's chanting adds to an incense-and-candles fuelled Old Russian atmosphere.

DUNGAN MOSQUE

This distinctly Chinese building looks bizarrely out of place in Karakol. It is a masterpiece of Dungan architecture, featuring a carved frieze of fine workmanship.

Inside its imagery is an eclectic mix, testament to the Dungan's pre-Islamic Buddhist past, combining a pomegranate (a folk symbol of longevity) with Buddhist imagery such as the shell and wheel of fire. Completed in 1910 it was built entirely without nails, using an uncommon grey-blue brick. Instead of a minaret, the mosque has a wooden pagoda. Like many religious buildings in the Soviet Empire, it has had a turbulent century; it twice lost its roof and was closed from 1933 to 1943. Non-Muslims are sometimes allowed inside the mosque; women are asked to cover their heads.

SUNDAY LIVESTOCK BAZAAR

If you can contrive to be in Karakol on a Sunday, the *skotniy bazaar*, as it is known in Russian, will be a highlight of your visit. While Kashgar's Sunday bazaar reflects the

At the Sunday livestock bazaar

increasing modernisation and motorisation of life in China, Karakol's bears witness to a growing reliance on traditional livelihoods. Villagers and nomads often travel for days to get here, bringing fine fleeced herds of sheep and sturdy horses from high altitude summer pastures. It is an atmospheric place; stallions whinny and flex muscles as potential buyers test-ride horses with great élan, scattering the crowds. People lift sheep by the rear to assess their *kordyuk*, rump fat. You can expect to pay around US$40–90 for a sheep, depending on the size of its *kordyuk*, and up to US$1,000 for a ten-year-old horse. Horses intended for meat are slightly more expensive.

The action starts around dawn and is over by 10am. The car market opposite now does a roaring trade.

MEMORIALS

In typical Soviet fashion, Karakol contains some interesting and poignant war memorials. The biggest, in Park Pobeda (Abdrakhmanova about two kilometres

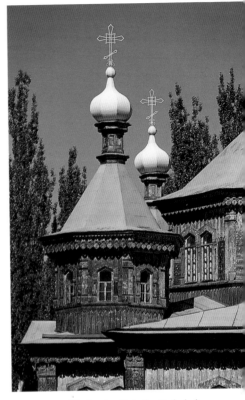

The Russian Orthodox Cathedral

south of Toktogula), is to those killed in the Great Patriotic War (WW2), and is marked by a sculpture of Mother Russia. Nearby is an alley of busts of 'Heroes of the Soviet Union'. In Pushkin Park, near the children's fairground, are two monuments: a statue of a border guard with a dog for the soldiers lost fighting the Basmachi uprising in the 1920s, and a tank commemorating those killed in the Afghan war (1979–1989).

PRZHEVALSKY MUSEUM AND MEMORIAL

Open daily 9am–6pm. Closed 12–1pm. Exhibits in Russian and English. Entrance US$2. If the door is locked just call and the caretaker will let you in.

Seven kilometres from Karakol, the museum lies on the road to Pristan (Pier) Przhevalsk and Mikhaylovka, summer playground of beaches and dilapidated dachas. Until recently, it was closed to foreigners (some have been arrested) due to its Soviet-era importance as a former torpedo research centre. Gritty and littered, the beach has little appeal compared to others around Lake Issyk Kul.

The museum and formal park dedicated to Nikolai Mikhaibvich Przhevalsky was completed in 1957. With a cavalier disregard for local sensibilities, a village graveyard was removed to make way for it. Recently, the park has again been used as burial ground, this time for local Kyrgyz dignitaries. The park is said to be planted with over 30 kinds of tree, among them Kyrgyz blue poplar, Tien Shan spruce and Siberian larch.

Explorer, botanist, zoologist and spy, Przhevalsky's only connection with Karakol is that he died here in 1888 (see page 176). Past the inevitable roll-call of Russian explorer-heroes you are taken on a tour through his life, with enough written information, in English to make it of considerable interest. An elderly Russian museum guide will share with you her knowledge about and passion for Przhevalsky (a small tip is appreciated).

Displays show Przhevalsky's early fascination for maps and exploration and the cunning deals he struck with the army to allow him to travel, as well as some harrowing details of the tribulations and hardships undergone by early travellers, along with pictures of a Chinese torture scene he witnessed. Exhibits include an array of stuffed animals including the tiny Mongolian wild horse to which he gave his name in 1885 (and which is now being reintroduced to the Mongolian steppe from zoos, having disappeared from its natural habitat) and several items of his equipment.

Conspicuously absent are details of the significant part Przhevalsky played in the 'Great Game' or 'Tournament of Shadows', as the Russians called the complex silent dance of espionage that was the cold war of the 19th century. His memorial, when erected, stood on the lake shore as he had requested. It was constructed using 21 stones to represent the 21 years of his travelling life and topped by the jubilant eagle, with a three-metre wingspan, which holds the branch of peace in its beak and a scrolled map under its claw.

To get to the museum, take a bus marked *dachi* from the bus stand outside the small bazaar in the town centre. These run frequently in summer. Alternatively, take a taxi from the same place for about US$10 return in som, including waiting time.

PRACTICAL INFORMATION
ACCOMMODATION
Hotel Issyk-Kul: 38 Masalieva, formerly Fuchika; tel. (03922) 20710; fax 59000 email: ngoshaiy@rambler.ru
Set in woods in the southeastern end of town, the two buildings that once comprised Hotel Issyk-Kul now operate separately. Hotel Issyk-Kul offers comfortable but no-frills rooms with Soviet-era private bathroom for US$25–30 per person including breakfast and dinner. Internet and IDD telephone are available. The Government Hotel (tel. 03922 59030), large and sterile, has no fixed prices.

Community Based Tourism (CBT): 123 Abdrakhmanova; tel. (03922) 55000 mob. (0502) 203087; email: cbtkarakol@rambler.ru

CBT offer their full range of homestay accommodation (see page 292 for details). From June to August it is advisable to book in advance. They can also arrange a yurt-stay with a herding family in Jeti-Oguz valley (see page 175).

Jamilla's House: 34b Shopokova; tel. Jamilla Tunaeva (03922) 43019 mob. (0543) 980981
A three-edelweiss member of the CBT group (see page 292), Jamilla offers friendly and comfortable homestays with impeccably clean shared bathrooms. Carpets on the walls, sitting room with TV, a yurt in the front yard and a shaded patio all add to its charms. In a wooded suburb by the river, it is 20 minutes on foot from the centre. At the southern end of Toktogula, turn left into Kurochkina just before the river, go right at the end, past the shops and fork left. The unmarked house is near the end of the road. Book in advance if possible direct or through CBT.

Turkestan Yurt/Camp Site: 273 Toktogula, between Moskovskaya and Assanalieyeva; tel.(03922) 59896, (0312) 511560; mob. (0543) 911451; email: psi61@mail.ru; www: karakol.kg
Operated by the travel agency of the same name, this central but quiet site is delightful and has proved very popular with travellers, and is undoubtedly the best budget option in Karakol. Set in a walled garden of pear and plum trees, it offers four grades of accommodation: comfortable rooms with TV and en suite bathroom for US$14; rooms with shared facilities (US$10); a bed in a yurt (US$8.5); and a campsite area, the latter three sharing toilets and showers. Prices per person room only. Breakfast costs US$7. Dinner can be ordered in advance. A bamboo seating area, laundry, baggage storage, security and a climbing wall complete the package. For a fee, they can arrange a performance by local musicians.

Hotel Neofit: 166 Assanbay Zhamansariev, next to Museum; tel. (03922) 20650 email: neofit@issyk-kul.kg
Its price and location sell this town-centre hotel. No frills rooms come for US$7 per person with shared facilities, or US$11 with a private toilet. Breakfast is an additional US$3.

Yak Hostel: 10 Gagarina; tel. (03922) 22368, 56901
Run by Yak Tours, this fairly central hostel offers basic dormitories and doubles with shared facilities for US$5–10 per person.

A&K Guesthouse: 121 Masalieva, formerly Fuchika; tel. (03922) 52288
Owned by a Bishkek retailer, this five-roomed guesthouse with shared bathrooms is in the outskirts. Facilities include billiards and a sauna. B&B and dinner cost US$20 per person.

Hotel Amir: 78 Amanbaev/Abdrakhmanova. Tel/fax: (03922) 51315, Bishkek (0312) 622381, fax 622380; email: info@hotelamir.kg; www: hotelamir.kg
Karakol's swanky new hotel is a welcome addition to accommodation options here. The Swiss-Kyrgyz joint venture, opened in 2005, has a quiet, relaxed air and provides well-decorated, comfortable en suite rooms. The dining room/coffee shop serves local, international and vegetarian dishes all day. Other facilities include IDD telephone, internet access, laundry and a sun terrace. All is modern and sparklingly clean. B&B singles from US$33, doubles from US$48

Ala Too Hotel: 159 Azalea (formerly Fuchika). Tel: (03922) 51130, mob (0772) 801442
This distinctive building, like an alpine lodge with steep wooden roof, is easily visible on the same road as Hotel Issyk-Kul and A&K. A popular resort in Soviet times, it has fallen into disrepair but is now under renovation, with plans to open it in 2008 as a budget hotel. No prices available yet.

FOOD
Visitors from Bishkek denigrate Karakol's eateries, but a good meal can be found at the following: **Kench** on 225 Telmana, clean and quiet, is the most upmarket restaurant in town and serves standard international, Kyrgyz and Russian dishes with a range of beers and wines. Another newish café, (imported from Turkey), **Fakir**, meaning 'poor' is more central, on Gorky. Open 8am to midnight daily, it is clean and modern and food is fresh.

Enjoying the sun at Lake Issyk Kul

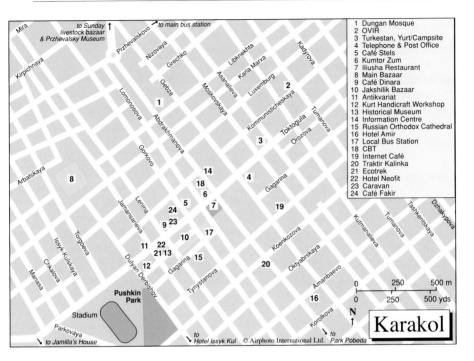

A good variety of tasty snacks and meals, including vegetarian and Chinese options are served for reasonable prices. For added entertainment, a large window into the kitchen shows the cooks at work. Opposite, **Café Stels** also has a good reputation but we never found it open.

Don't miss **Kalinka** on Usup Abdrakhmanova/Koenkozova. Its tasty all-Russian menu is served in a pretty, carved, Siberian-style log cabin, with gold wallpaper. Despite the large Dungan population, Dungan dishes are rare in Karakol. **Café Dinara** at 160 Lenina offers some. **Iliusha**, on Toktolgula opposite Kumtor Zum, serves fresh food for good value. Sit upstairs away from the karaoke. **Termirlan Complex** on Krupskoy/Toktogula is now rather dingy and overpriced. Alternatively, during the day, head for the food stalls at the **Jakshilik Bazaar**.

VISAS AND RED TAPE

Until November 2002 it was obligatory for all foreigners to report to the **OVIR** office within three working days of arrival in Kyrgyzstan to have their visa stamped. Thankfully, this is no longer required for nationals of 28 countries (for details see page 74). This could change at any time so check with a consulate before you travel.

A recent Government decree affects those wishing to trek to or from Kazakhstan; foreigners must now enter and exit Kyrgyzstan at staffed border crossings only, so trekking in from Kazakhstan may lead to difficulties on leaving the country as you will not have an entry stamp to validate your visa. The OVIR's office (*pasportniy stol*) is in the old KGB headquarters at 146a Tumanova, Room 114, tel. (03922) 28439. The office is open Tuesday–Friday 9am–1pm and 2–5pm.

Foreigners were also liberated in 2002 from the requirement to purchase a **permit** to visit the valleys to the south of Karakol. However, you will need a **border zone permit** if you plan to cross to China or to trek in the Central Tien Shan beyond Inylchek town. Obtaining this is a complicated process, so it's best to arrange it through a local travel agency. Contact them at least four weeks before you plan to arrive in Karakol, giving your passport and trip details.

TOUR INFORMATION AND OPERATORS
Tourism Information Centre, 103 Usup Abdurakhmanova. Tel. (03922) 23425. Heralded by a large sign on Toktogula, this much-needed centre was opened in June 2003 by Issyk-Kul State University Tourism Department with the help of TACIS, a development arm of the European Union. They should give impartial advice on the vast array of possible activities that the region offers, but we never found it open.

Radio LW, a community-based local radio station committed to press freedom, can be found at 101.8FM. It has some programmes in English. Topics include politics, the law, health and local events.

As with all tour operators, be crystal clear about what is included in a trip price before signing up. Trips can be arranged on the spot but it is far more time-effective and convenient to organise your trip in advance by email.

Community-Based Tourism: 123 Abdrakhmanova. Tel. (03922) 55000; mob. (0502) 203087; email: cbtkarakol@rambler.ru; www: cbtkyrgyzstan.kg. Closed Sunday. Located opposite the Tourism Information Centre. For detailed information about CBT (see page 292).The Karakol office is well-organised and friendly. As well as providing a wealth of information, they arrange homestays, transport, guides, porters and equipment for day-trips or treks of all lengths in the surrounding mountains. You can hire camping equipment here. Some horse treks can be organised but the terrain here limits options. See page 279 for top treks on horseback. They do not organise mountaineering expeditions or arrange permits.

Turkestan: 273 Toktogula. Tel. (03922) 59896, (0312) 511560, mob (0543) 911451; email: psi61@mail.ru; web: turkestan.biz
Founded in 1990 by Sergei Pyshnenko, Turkestan is user-friendly and comes recommended by ex-pats. The office is in the grounds of the yurt camp (see page 165). Turkestan operates nationwide. The team can provide a wealth of information, services and equipment but it is best to turn up with a fairly clear idea of what you want to do.

The company's speciality is its flexibility. They can put together treks of any length in the Central Tien Shan, Kungey and Terskey Ala-Too and will arrange rock-climbing and mountaineering trips. For day-trippers they can arrange transport into the foothills, eagle hunting shows, *manaschi* or folklore concerts, and can book helicopter flights over the peaks of the Tien Shan. They have five kayaks and also hire out camping and trekking equipment.

Sergei is also president of 'Freund', a Relief Fund for Karakol Zoo, set up in conjunction with wolf expert Werner Freund from Germany. The fund is for the general upkeep of the zoo and its inmates, though Werner Freund is an expert on 'the wolf in the wild'.

Ecotrek: Trekking Workers Association: 112a Toktogula. Tel: (03922) 51115
email: karakol@rambler.ru
This dynamic young company aims to provide high grade trekking guides, porters and cooks for individuals and tour operators. They hire out camping and trekking gear and map out new routes in the mountains. They work closely with Novinomad and are involved in a number of their projects (see page 83). Email in advance or call in to arrange a trek.

In an effort to raise the standard and professionalism of trekking services locally, they arrange training and support for trekking workers and operate a fund which enables porters and cooks, in particular, to buy suitable clothing.

Yak Tours: 10 Gagarina. Tel/fax. (3922) 22368/56901; email: yaktours@infotel.kg
Valentin and Galina Derevianko, who speak a smattering of English, offer accommodation in Karakol and Altyn Arashan valley, as well as lowland trekking support services. However, for years travellers have complained that paid-for services were sometimes not provided, agreed prices change unpredictably and tempers can be volatile.

Tour Khan Tengri: 114 Lenina. Tel. (03922) 20322
email: tour-khantengri@issyk-kul.kg; www: tour-khantengri.kg (Russian only)
This company run a log cabin hostel in a beautiful spot in Inylchek valley—an oasis for trekkers and mountaineers coming off the glaciers and a good place to explore the area and acclimatise to altitude.

Neofit Tourist Company: 166 Gamansariev. Tel. (03922) 20650; fax (03922) 21902
email: neofit@issyk-kul.kg; www: neofit.kg
Owners of the budget hotel in Karakol, Neofit offer local tours, transport to Bishkek, Almaty and the surrounding mountains, will obtain trekking and border zone permits and book flights.

Avante: 75 Issyk-Kul. Tel. (03922) 51809; email: t75@yandex.ru; web: avante.to.kg
A small firm offering cultural tours around Lake Issyk Kul. They are renovating a hotel in Jety-Oguz valley which should be open in 2008.

MONEY

Numerous **kiosks** which exchange US dollars cash can be found at locations around the town, in particular on the main drag, Toktogula.

The **Kyrgyzstan Commercial Bank** on Gebze/Toktogula exchanges a wide range of traveller's cheques, all at three per cent. They are trying to set up cash advances on credit cards but this is not yet operational. Carrying sufficient US dollars cash is still advisable.

COMMUNICATION

The Internet is available at **Tsentralniy** on Toktogula north of Abdrakhmanova—open 24 hours a day—and at **Molodyozhnoye**, 263 Toktogula, open 8am to midnight. Both charge by the hour and for megabytes used. Their main clientele is young people playing computer games. Try also **KyrgyzTelecom** on the corner of Toktogula and Gebze.

You can make local and international calls at **KyrgyzTelecom**, and the central **Post Office** is on Gebze, overlooking the main square.

SHOPPING

Post cards, local maps (with insufficient detail for trekking) and handicrafts are sold at most tour operators' offices.

Kumtor Zum (Government Department Store, owned now by Canadian Gold mining company, Kumtor) sells camera film, torches, batteries, toiletries, converter plugs and almost anything else you can think of. The

Timur's Mound at San Tash

best range of provisions for the mountains will be found in the **main bazaar** at the end of Krupskoy. Besides pasta, noodles, rice, vegetables, sausage, try fresh or dried fruit and nuts, and vats of honey, for which the Issyk-Kul region is famous. **Caravan** (part of a new chain), on Toktogula opposite Jakshilik Bazaar, stocks everything else you're likely to need.

The **Jakshilik Bazaar** is also worth a visit. Outdoor food stalls, in the thick of the bazaar action, are the place to try out your basic Kurgyz. Each stall has its speciality, served with milky tea or *ayran* (*kefir* in Russian), a yoghurt drink.

Locally-made handicrafts are on sale at **Kurt** at the south-eastern end of Jakshilik Bazaar, at the Turkestan Yurt Camp **handicrafts yurt** and, for inflated prices, at **Kumtor Zum**. **Antikvariyat**, on Derzhinskovo between Toktogula and Kommunisticheskaya, sells Soviet memorabilia, including a seemingly endless supply of badges, as well as antique Chinese coins, Kyrgyz and Russian jewellery, Russian Orthodox icons and embroidery. **The Information Centre** sells postcards and a small range of handicrafts.

ENTERTAINMENT

Karakol's streets are largely deserted by 8pm. A couple of nightclubs, including Arashan on Tynystanova and Iliusha on Toktogula, stay open until midnight. There used to be regular horse races and other sporting activities at the **hippodrome** (the first in Central Asia), but such luxuries have shrunk with the downwardly spiralling economy. Occasional celebratory horseback games take place on Independence Day, Nooruz and at other festivals, at short notice. The local and regional traditional horseback games leagues sometimes play here—ask local tour operators. Folklore concerts sometimes take place at Turkestan Yurt Camp.

(left) Aerial view of the Karkara valley

TRANSPORT
The main bus routes from Karakol head for Balykchy (via the north and the south routes) and Bishkek serving all the villages along the way. For Naryn, change at Balykchy and for Almaty, change at Bishkek. The north route is the main road and a lot quicker than the south. The bus station is at the northern edge of the town. Access is through the gauntlet of minibus drivers, exercising a variety of ploys to entice you away from the public bus. The privately owned minibuses are faster and about 30 per cent more expensive than the public buses but it's worth fixing the price and checking the tyres before committing yourself.

As schedules and prices change frequently, check before you intend to travel. The sedate public buses line up at the back of the bus station building. Signs above the platforms, now in English, indicate their final destinations. Princess Mercedes buses, which are fast replacing the ancient Ikarus, operate from 6.30am until 11pm along the northern road to Bishkek and towns en route, taking about eight hours and costing about US$8. Minibuses leave approximately every hour, depending on demand. Buses travelling the southern route to Balykchy and Bishkek, serve villages along the way and depart from 8am until 2.40pm. It's about two hours to Tamga/Barskoon and four hours to Bokonbaeva.

Shared taxis run on the northern and southern routes to Balykchy, where you change for Bishkek. They depart from outside the bus station when full. A place in a shared taxi to Bishkek costs approximately US$15. Otherwise, hire a taxi or a private car and driver to take you anywhere; bargaining is expected. Private transport can also be arranged through the tour operators. Local buses and minibuses leave from the local bus stand in the town centre for local villages.

Around Karakol

The valleys and mountains around Karakol are a playground for anyone who loves stunningly beautiful scenery and have something for everyone: day-trips by car; camping; day hikes; treks of a few days; hard-core trekking on glaciers; and mountaineering.

These are large majestic valleys with ever-changing landscapes: the red sandstone and grey granite walls of the canyons form impressive backdrops to smooth green hillsides, deeply cut by charging rivers. Forests shroud the slopes: Tien Shan spruce whose green clothes sweep to the ground, stretch tall and silent to the sky; Siberian larch and walnut shelter the occasional red squirrel, now almost extinct due to the introduction of grey squirrels early in the 20th century. The mountain pastures are scented with wild flowers and plants used in medicine and distilled to essential oils for use as perfumes.

From April to July, spring strides up the mountains as the sun warms the slopes. The Soviet botanist, IV Vykhodtsev, describes the multitude of spring and summer flowers:

> *A wave of tulips gives way to fields of scarlet poppies, ... and cornflower-blue ixylirion and golden Arabian primroses ... and pale pink eremurus form a veil on the foothills ... Spring reaches the sub-alpine belt where the meadows turn into gorgeous, lush, green carpets into which are woven white anemones, blue forget-me-nots, orange and golden poppies, flaming fleabane, lilac asters, deep purple geraniums ...*

KARKARA VALLEY

The Karkara valley, smooth and fertile, sweeps through the eastern pincer grip of the Central Tien Shan and the Kungey Ala-Too ranges, to Kazakhstan and China. The Kyrgyz-Kazakh border slices the valley in half but nowhere is this arbitrary border more irrelevant, disregarded by herders from both sides who, in summer, erect yurts in the valley while their animals disappear into the long lush grass.

On an unfixed date around mid-June, the valley is the site of some of the best festivities in the country; a gathering of the great horsemen and women of these two nations, with a series of horseraces, wrestling on horseback, and *baiga* (horseback fight over a headless goat), only interrupted for feasts of *besh-bermak*, exquisite haunting music or recitals of the epic poem of Manas. The date and venue change each year but it's worth asking around if you are in the region.

Karkara means 'black crane', and is named after the birds that use the valley as a resting place on their long journey between Siberia and South Africa in June and September. At its eastern end, in Kazakhstan, the Almaty-based travel agency, Kan Tengri, operates a camp which looks very much like an army base of Jenghis Khan, with clusters of tents, fluttering flags and grazing horses. What the Mongols never had is a well-equipped kitchen and bar, a sauna and a heli-pad, from where flights can be made to the Mount Khan Tengri basecamps or over the awesome peaks of the Central Tien Shan. Flights can be arranged directly through Kan Tengri or through Turkestan in Karakol.

Just within Kyrgyzstan, an unsightly mound of stones, known as **San Tash** ('counting stones'), is said to have been the means whereby the 14th century conqueror Timur (Tamerlane) counted his military losses; each departing soldier added a stone and on return removed one—the dead thus built a monument to themselves.

In Soviet times the valley was known as 'milk valley' due to the herds of dairy cattle grazing here as part of a large butter and cheese works situated near the San Tash pass. There is no public transport through the valley so you will need to hitch from Tyup (which is served by the Bishkek buses), hire a car and driver from a travel agency or, for a fraction of the price, negotiate a deal directly with a taxi driver.

The round trip via Novovosnosenovka, prettier though rougher than the main road, is about 150 kilometres.

ALTYN ARASHAN VALLEY

This outstandingly beautiful valley, alive with hot springs (its name means Golden Spa), is the ideal spot to relax and take day—or overnight walks. It is also the end point of the Ala Kul trek—see the Trekking Around Karakol section.

At an altitude of 3,000 metres, the valley is smooth, rounded and partially wooded—prime mushroom country in July and August. It is also bear country. Goats are a favourite snack for bears; locals say there have been no attacks on humans. Within the valley, the Arashan State Nature Reserve is used for botanical research. Hot mineral springs bubble to the surface and are captured in a pair of concrete bath-houses; the perfect place to rest aching limbs after a trek. Another hot springs, open-air but con-creted, lies just off the track, about 25 minutes walk towards Ak Suu village.

One of the Seven Bulls in the Jeti-Oguz valley

PRACTICAL INFORMATION

Buses leave several times a day from the local bus station in Karakol town centre for Ak Suu. Beyond the village you'll need a four-wheel-drive; the road snakes perilously into the mountains, each winter claiming several trucks which lie snow-bound until the spring thaw.

Yak Tours (see page 169) sell seats on their regular jeep run from Karakol to their cabin in the valley.

Alternatively, tour operators in Karakol will arrange a private vehicle for about US$65. It's a 17-kilometre, five-hour hike up to the valley from Ak Suu.

Accommodation in the valley is basic. Bring your own food. Altyn Arashan Cabins cost about US$10 including swims in the spa pool but without food. You can prepare a meal in the kitchen there and perhaps bring tea, sugar, salt or newspapers for the caretaker. **Yak Tours** run a cabin in the valley for a similar fee. Just outside Ak Suu village is a run-down **sanatorium**.

Excellent **camping** is to be had under two hours' walk up Altyn Arashan valley from the bath house, at the junction with Kol Dooke valley, or in the trees further up Altyn Arashan. The area is used by summer herders so it might be possible to buy *koumys* but keep an eye on the dogs!

Unfortunately, but perhaps inevitably, there have been reports of local youths causing mild harassment and stealing items left unattended. Tents have even been known to disappear during the day.

KARAKOL VALLEY

A ski resort in winter, the summer turns Karakol valley into a series of flower-strewn meadows, used by herders as summer grazing. The valley has no villages and is a national park. Entrance costs US$7 plus US$3 per night to pitch a tent. Be sure to get a receipt as park rangers might check up.

To get there, catch bus 101 from Jakshilik Bazaar or take a taxi for about US$6. If you go by car, you can save yourself an uninspiring 45-minute walk from the entrance by driving as far as the bridge. From here a track rises gently up the wooded Karakol valley, offering views to Przhevalsk Peak at the head of the valley, and skirts a couple of marshy pools where the river widens. The third broad meadow, where there is an old Soviet tented camp, is a good camping spot, from where you can explore the valley. This is about three hours' walk from the lower bridge (or five and a half hours from the end of the bus line).

Another two and a half hours' walk will take you to Seer Ata campsite. Follow the path for about half an hour up a steep hill behind the Soviet camp to a twin-log bridge over the river. From the bridge a well-marked path climbs steeply through woodland, then flower meadows, to a rocky crest overlooking the campsite. The site huddles under trees by the river between rock faces and distant peaks. There is a little cabin for cooking and eating and plenty of camping spaces. This is the first section of the Karakol–Ala Kul–Altyn Arashan trek (see below). It's well worth adding a day to trek to the upper Karakol valley for fabulous views of Karakol peak.

In winter the slopes of side-valley Kashka Suu are alive with skiers and sledgers. The new **Mountain Lodge** (tel. for info 0502-534081; to book 0312-531870; email: pmz@exnet.kg; www.karakol-ski.com) is renowned for its comfort, peace and excellent cuisine. You can only use the restaurant if you book in advance.

The 'ski-base', as it is called locally, offers three new T-bar lifts and over 20 km of runs for beginners and experienced skiers alike. Rossignol ski gear in good condition can be hired for about US$14 per day while a lift pass costs US$7. Alternatively, take a picnic and hire a sledge for peanuts and lots of fun.

JETI-OGUZ

The Jeti-Oguz canyon is one of the prettiest trekking and camping spots around Karakol. Defying superlatives, it is of the chocolate box variety, with pine-covered hills, lush pastures filled with wild flowers and an impressive waterfall. It lies about 15 kilometres south-west of Karakol, it is the most accessible beauty spot in the area, demanding no four-wheel-drive, no entrance fee and no permit.

NIKOLAI MIKHAILOVICH PRZHEVALSKY

Nikolai Przhevalsky was Russia's premier 19th-century explorer. Inspired by his boyhood hero David Livingstone, his dream was to explore the undiscovered wildernesses of the world. As he struck east across Siberia, through Central Asia, Mongolia and China, his sights began to focus on Lhasa, the hidden and much coveted capital of Tibet. En route he left his mark on Kyrgyzstan.

Born on 12 April 1839, part Cossack, part Polish nobility, Nikolai enjoyed a wild, free childhood in the woods of the family estate near Smolensk. He never really felt at home in settled society: neither the claustrophobia of the classroom nor the drunken debauchery of his army colleagues suited his independent puritanical nature. He used his early army years to study zoology and botany, assisted by his near photographic memory. Whenever possible he indulged his almost insatiable passion for hunting: he appeared to see no contradiction between this slaughter and his love of nature, just as he happily signed a protest in support of the Poles in 1862 and then went with the Russian army to suppress a Polish uprising in 1863.

Przhevalsky struck a deal with the Imperial Geographical Society of St Petersburg, led at the time by another great Central Asian explorer, Pyotr Semyonov (who had been honoured with the suffix, 'Tienshanskiy'): the Society agreed to fund Przhevalsky's pioneering trips in return for detailed reports of his findings.

In 1873, having left Russia a promising young officer, he returned from his first major journey a conquistador. He was the first European to attempt the northern approach to Tibet where, en route, people had assumed him to be a saint on his way to visit the Dalai Lama and had knelt in prayer before him. Long before he neared the capital, though, the rigours of winter forced him to turn back.

His second trip had a more political flavour to it; he was commissioned to make links with Yakub Bek, who had led the Uighurs in a rebellion against China and declared an independent state in Kashgaria, in south-eastern Xinjiang on the border with Kyrgyzstan. Russia was keen to amend the border in her favour before China reclaimed these lands. It was on this trip that Przhevalsky became the first European to see the small horse that would later be named after him (known as the *takhi* in Mongolian). The wily herds evaded his attempts to kill them, so he accepted the gift of a skin from a Kyrgyz hunter and sent it to St Petersburg for analysis, which confirmed his suspicion that it was a wild forerunner to the modern horse. Today there are only a few left and only in captivity.

By the time he embarked on his next trip for Lhasa in 1879, he enjoyed the full support of the Tsar and was determined to reach Lhasa. He took with him Cossacks (expert mounted soldiers) for protection and two and a half tons of baggage, including 25 bottles of brandy, 70 pounds of Turkish Delight and assorted geographic equipment—chronometer, theodolite, humidity and altitude instruments. His gifts for local dignitaries included a telephone (received with disappointment) and photos of a Russian actress (which proved much more popular).

But he was to be foiled again. Rumour spread that Przhevalsky's mission in Lhasa was to kidnap the Dalai Lama or to preach Christianity, and Tibetan officials decreed that any farmers found selling supplies to foreigners would be executed. Having survived the mountain passes and just 250 kilometres from Lhasa, he met with Tibetan officials who refused to let him pass. With typical determination, he argued his case and waited three weeks for news from Lhasa but an envoy conveyed a message that he was to leave Tibet at once. He knew he was beaten.

Przhevalsky's final journey (now as a Major-General) took him to Tashkent and Bishkek (Pishpek at the time) en route, he hoped, for Lhasa. Near the Chui river, where the marshes were full of reeds and wildlife in those days, he enjoyed a day's shoot. Against advice he drank the river water and caught typhoid. By the time the expedition had made its way along the southern shore of Lake Issyk Kul to Karakol, the disease had taken hold and Przhevalsky died in a military hospital on 20 October 1888. He had asked to be buried wearing expedition clothes, in a simple coffin on the shores of the lake. For someone who had survived the perils of exploration, it seemed a careless end to his life.

An ardent tsarist who embodied the chauvinist attitudes of the day—he called the Central Asian peoples 'laggards on the evolutionary process'—he was not mourned by the intelligentsia of the day. But he had started something that could not be stopped: the race through some of the world's most inhospitable mountains to Lhasa.

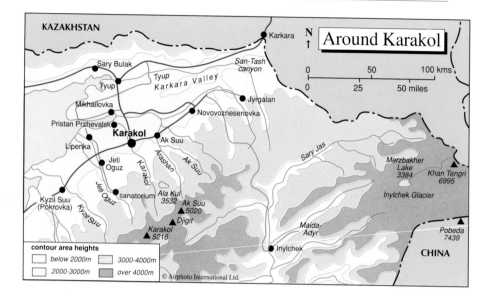

The valley owes its name (which means 'Seven Bulls') to the wall of burning red sandstone cliffs jutting proudly at the canyon entrance. The legend about how these Seven Bulls came to be here relates that although Kyrgyzstan was always a scenic place, its rulers were not always content and often waged war against each other for more land and riches. One day a king stole the wife of another. The king whose wife had been stolen was furious and wanted to inflict as much pain as possible upon the other king, so he sought the advice of a local *aksakal* (wise old man). At first the *aksakal* was reluctant to give such ill advice but eventually he told the angry king: 'You must kill your wife and give him her dead body. Let him own a dead wife, not a living one.'

After a few days had passed, the angry king decided to carry out the evil scheme at a funeral feast to be held in the mountains. During the feast he positioned himself next to his stolen wife. As the last bulls were being slaughtered, he reached for his blade and plunged it deep into his young wife's heart. Blood gushed from her heart and into the mountains and valley, taking the seven bull carcasses and the murderous king with it. The seven bulls formed into seven mountains, and thus gave the name Jeti-Oguz to the area. The lesson from this legend, say Kyrgyz people, is: 'Do not dig a pit for someone, lest you yourself should fall into it.'

One of the most striking features as you approach the canyon, just before the Seven Bulls, is a large hill, fractured in two, called the **Jaralangan Jurok**, or **Broken Heart**. According to legend, it is the heart of a beautiful woman, who died of sorrow after two suitors killed each other in a fight over her.

PRACTICAL INFORMATION

To get to the valley take a bus from Jakshilik Bazaar in Karakol to Jeti-Oguz village and hitch or walk the two or three kilometres to the sanatorium.

You can stay at the ugly concrete **Jeti-Oguz Sanatorium**, dating from the 1930s, in a pretty setting between pine-covered hills and the Seven Bulls. It's famous as the site of the first meeting between Presidents Akaev and Yeltsin in 1991 just after the abortive coup. Inside it is rather grim, with bustling white coats and unwell-looking guests seeking relief in spa treatments. Full board costs US$13 per night. Karakol-based tour operator, Avante, are rebuilding a hotel nearby which might be open by 2008 (see page 170). The alternative is yurt and hut accommodation on the *jailoo* (meadow) above.

The tarmac road ends at the Sanatorium and a stony track climbs for four kilometres through the canyon along the east bank of the fast-flowing river. Just before the fifth bridge you emerge into a massive *jailoo*. You can either continue up the river (there are good tracks on both sides) to find an excellent camping spot or follow the main track over the river and up the hill. Before you lies *Dolina Tsvetov* (Valley of Flowers), so called for its carpets of wild flowers in spring and early summer, starting with poppies in May; it is a beautiful and huge green bowl, divided into different areas by clusters of tall pines and surrounded by snowy peaks.

The track forks here. If you follow the left fork you see first the CBT yurts (up across the grass to the right), with a 'Saltanat' sign in Russian. Basic B&B costs US$9. Further along the track is the Novinomad camp (B&B US$16; book through Biskek office).

Pristine Lake Ala Kul, high in the mountains

Return to the fork by the bridge and follow the other track through trees, fork left again to reach three spartan huts. Beds can be hired for US$3 per night. The caretaker next door will cook for you—bring your own food.

This is the starting point for the 45-minute walk to a 300-metre waterfall, which attracts mini-buses full of CIS tourists staying on the shores of Lake Issyk Kul. Locals with horses offer you a ride most of the way up. Cross the river behind the huts through a rash of yurt camps, including one run by Ecotour (see page 82), which has a solar-heated shower and sit-down toilets.

Follow the obvious path up the hill where you are richly rewarded with views up Jeti-Oguz valley. The latter section of the walk is along a perilously narrow gritty path with a sheer drop (inadvisable with a young child); when we were there, some people struggled with this while others in high heels and carrying a bottle of Russian champagne were nonchalant.

TREKKING AROUND KARAKOL
Rivers from the glaciers which envelop the peaks of the Terskey Ala-Too rush towards Issyk Kul, cutting deep valleys in the flanks of the mountains. Several treks cross these ridges, parallel to the lake, at two levels; the higher involves some glacier walking, reaches 4,200 metres and passes beneath the great walls of the peaks, while a lower one (described below) is less demanding, peaking at 3,860 metres and takes in pristine turquoise Lake Ala Kul. Conveniently, the treks range from three to 12 days, depending on which valley you choose to start in.

Crucial factors are your fitness, response to altitude and the weather—you could easily see burning sun, a hail storm and snow blizzard all in one day. Bring adequate layers for warmth and full water and windproof gear. They should not be attempted without a good map and, with the possible exception of the Karakol to Altyn Arashan trek, preferably a guide. Routes are marked only spasmodically.

KARAKOL VALLEY–ALA KUL LAKE–ALTYN ARASHAN
This is a popular route, taking in the Ala Kul Lake in four to six days (minimum three nights). See the Karakol valley section above for the route to the Seer Ata campsite. From this camp you leave the Karakol valley and head east. The path climbs steeply, close to the river, for about two hours, past rock walls to a waterfall, gushing from Lake Ala Kul. Traverse south, above the waterfall, for about half an hour to a rocky bluff overlooking the lake. Descend to Lake Ala Kul (3,523 metres high, 600 metres wide and 2.3km long), keeping it on your right.

The choice is to camp here early in the wild barren beauty of the lake or to slog on over the Kol Dooke pass (3,860 metres), making a very long day. The path all but disappears here. Follow the lake to a crest which rises at its central curve; from here you can see to the far end of the lake and other tempting camping spots (one hour's walk) near the base of moraines and glaciers.

From the central point of the lake, head north-east across scree slopes up to the Kol Dooke pass and descend steeply to a number of possible camping spots in the Kol Dooke valley or the junction with the Altyn Arashan valley (about three hours from the pass). From here, a good trail leads down the valley for under an hour to the Altyn Arashan Cabins and bathhouses (see Altyn Arashan valley, page 174).

JETI-OGUZ–ALA KUL–ALTYN ARASHAN
Starting in Jeti-Oguz valley would add an extra two days to the trek. See the Jeti-Oguz section for details of getting to the trail head. From the Jeti-Oguz valley, follow the Teleti river up to the Teleti pass (3,665 metres) before descending to Karakol valley to join the route above.

CHONG KYZYL SUU–JETI-OGUZ–ALA KUL–ALTYNA ARASHAN
For an eight to ten day trek, start from Chong Kyzyl Suu village. The route leaves the valley to follow the Kara Batkak river then turns east to climb to the Archa Tyor pass at 3,800 metres. The trail then descends along the Asan Tukum river to the Jeti-Oghuz valley, which you descend until you reach the Teleti river and follow the route above.

Central Tien Shan

The ranges of the Tien Shan culminate at what is known to locals as Muztag ('Ice Mountain'), and to geographers as the Central Tien Shan. It is a mighty citadel of ice, fortified by a series of impressive chains including the Kokshal-Too (the highest range of the Tien Shan), in the shadow of Peak Pobeda (7,439 metres), now called Jengish Chokosu, on the border with China; Tengri Too, crowned by Khan Tengri (6,995 metres), on the border with Kazakhstan; and Inylchek Too, to name just a few. Viewed from an aeroplane, they have a sculpted elegance rare in such high mountains.

Khan Tengri ('Prince of Spirits') is the favourite pin-up; its perfect pyramid summit of marble and fluted ridges burn in the sunset with the colours of a hot coal, earning itself the local nickname *Kan Too*, or 'blood mountain'. Peak Pobeda by contrast is vast and bulky.

The total area of the Tien Shan's glaciers is around 6,240 square kilometres, of which about four-fifths is in Kyrgyzstan and Kazakhstan (the rest is in China's Xinjiang province). Inylchek glacier, which wraps itself around the Tengri Too range between Khan Tengri and Peak Pobeda, is 62 kilometres long, 3.5 kilometres wide and 540 metres deep in places. It is said that the glacier holds enough ice to cover the whole of Kyrgyzstan in three metres of melt-water.

This ice dragon gives life to the deserts of ex-Soviet Central Asia, through the Naryn river (which flows into the Syr Darya), and to China's Tarim basin, through the Inylchek and Sary Jaz rivers. It is unusual globally for the regularity of its outbursts.

Khan Tengri basecamp in the Central Tien Shan

On the North Inylchek glacier, near the junction of the glacier's two arms, lie two unique ice-locked lakes named Merzbacher, after the German explorer who travelled here in 1903. The upper lake is startlingly blue and clear. Once a year in mid-August the lower lake expands when its icebergs melt and water bursts through its ice walls, spewing icebergs onto the glacier below and massively swelling the Inylchek river.

Not until 1857 did the first known European, Pyotr Semyonov, venture into the Muztag heartland, crossing the Tyup river to find a way up the Inylchek river and on to the glacier. As reward, the Imperial Geographical Society of St Petersburg bestowed on Semyonov the honorary suffix, Tienshanskiy. He was followed by Nikolai Przhevasky (see Special Topic, page 176).

In Soviet times, even local mountaineers needed a permit to come to the border-sensitive zone and foreigners weren't allowed close until 1989. Now, climbers worldwide are making up for lost time. First climbed in 1931, Khan Tengri remains a favourite today. Soviet climbers were the first to summit Peak Pobeda in 1938, believing it to be smaller than its 7,439 metres.

PRACTICAL INFORMATION
To cater for today's mountaineers, ITMC Tien Shan from Bishkek (see Tour Operators, page 80) and the Kazakh firm, Kan Tengri, amongst others, operate basecamps on the South Inylchek glacier. The tent cities provide accommodation, food, saunas, guiding and consultation services. Their stupendous setting make the camps worth visiting even

if you are not a climber. For amateur climbers, Peak Diki (4,832 metres) can be summited in a day from basecamp. Concrete Maida Adyr is just a helicopter pad offering wagon and tented accommodation and food. In between the two camps is a new centre, run by Tour Khan-Tengri (see page 169), which consists of a log hut and some yurts providing food, accommodation, sauna, horses and guides.

To get to Maida Adyr, you could always try for a place in a helicopter taking a tour group on the spectacular flight over the peaks. Check with Kan Tengri (Almaty), Turkestan (Karakol), ITMC and Dostuk Trekking (Bishkek) to see if they have any groups going. Otherwise, hire a four-wheel drive for the five-hour drive to Maida Adyr, via the mining town of Inylchek. From Maida Adyr it is a five-day trek or 45-minute helicopter ride to the basecamps. Alternatively, you could undertake the tough four- to six-day trek from Jergalan to Chong Tash at the snout of the South Inylchek glacier, with the support of a tour operator.

If you go beyond Inylchek, you will need a border zone permit. Obtaining this is a complicated process, so it's best to arrange it through a local tour operator. Contact them at least four weeks before you arrive in Karakol, giving your passport and trip details.

The South Shore

In terms of rugged natural beauty and grass-roots adventure, Lake Issyk Kul's southern side is most rewarding and is not disfigured with clusters of decaying Soviet-era resorts like the northern shore. The lakeside itself belongs to the Issyk Kul national park and is a mix of reed fields, meadows, canyons and lagoons where you can spend hours walking, swimming or relaxing on beaches.

Red and yellow rock rises in wind-sculpted cones and castles to arid hills and the mighty snow-covered peaks of the Terskey Ala-Too beyond. Altogether different from the lush, alpine valleys around Karakol which are backed by the almost inpenetrable wall of the Central Tien shan, the south shore gives access to a jumble of wild, beautiful valleys, some rock-filled, others gentle *jailoo* (high altitude summer grazing) with hot water springs; arid plateaux and rolling steppe. Fabulous trips of any length on foot, horseback or by car (or a combination) can be arranged here. It also has enticing back door routes to Lake Song Kul, Naryn and Tash Rabat. Some of these are quite rough but all are well supported by competent local tour operators (Shepherd's Way, page 83, are the horse-trekking experts, KyrgyzLand, formerly Kyrgyz Travel, also page 83, for treks on foot) or other Bishkek operators.

Lacking the public investment, influx of tourists and fertile soil enjoyed by the communities over the water, the south shore was one of the poorest parts of Kyrgyzstan. However, as north shore facilities become saturated, tourists increasingly seek accommodation options on the south side, so old resorts are being renovated and new hotels built. Women are ingenious in finding ways to feed their families. A scheme to have offered some hope recently is the Altyn Oymok project in Bokonbaevo which helps women to earn money from making traditional felt handicrafts (see Bokonbaevo, page 189), but this is embryonic.

The presence of the Kumtor gold mine just south of Barskoon presents the people daily with the paradox of extreme wealth operating amongst poverty. While the people express relief and gratitude for the employment and financial assistance offered by the company, its apparently cavalier attitude to the environment, all too frequent spillages of cyanide, and fleets of trucks which roar up the untarmaced road to the mine, make it an irritation to the local community.

ORGOCHOR

Orgochor, a small, mainly Kyrgyz village, unravels along the main road some 30 kilometres west of Karakol. The village is birthplace of Telekmat Sartikyev (1799–1863), ambassador to China, Russia and the Kokand Khanate. During World War II, Japanese prisoners of war were incarcerated here.

A good reason to stop is the **Historical Museum of Jeti Oguz**, (open Mon–Fri 8am–3pm and sometimes on Saturday; entrance by donation), located on the main road just opposite a statue of Sartikyev and his advisor, Sart-Akye. Kalen Zhetimishbaev, the 83-year-old director, founded the museum in 1990 as an attempt to document local culture and history from an exclusively Kyrgyz perspective (making the exhibition unique amongst its Soviet-era counterparts). As the jumble of exhibits is labelled in Kyrgyz only and many require explanation, it is worth taking a tour (Kyrgyz and Russian only).

Several displays, such as an anthology of Kyrgyz clan ties and local family trees, are the result of collaborative community research and competitions. The ossuaries and rocks inscribed in Arabic and ancient, forgotten alphabets were found locally. There are stands devoted to the author Chingiz Aitmatov, notable Kyrgyz scientists and thinkers and the Soviet massacre of the local Bishkek government in 1937.

Inside the show-yurt (used at the 1,000 years of Manas celebrations in the Talas Valley in 1995 and donated by the Government) is an unusually well preserved 300-year-old leather storage trunk. A small gift representing your homeland is appreciated and will be put on display. There are five 6th to 9th century *balbal* statuettes here depicting figures bearing cups.

In summer, Kalen Zhetimishaev at the museum may be able to organise **homestays** and *jailoo* **yurt accommodation** south of Orgochor. There is a basic guesthouse at 157 Manas, Kyzyl Suu, west of Orgochor—look out for the blue bed sign.

BARSKOON AND TAMGA

Barskoon and Tamga are twin Kyrgyz and Russian villages respectively, which grew up around a military post in the 19th century. The 11th century scholar Mahmoud-al-Kashgari, best known as author of the first Turkic languages comparative dictionary and buried in a fine tomb outside Kashgar, heralded from this region. His map of the then known world has Barskoon as the global centre.

Today it is less illustrious but, with a high-grade horse trekking company in **Barskoon** and a fine guesthouse in **Tamga**, this is the place to start some spectacular trips by car, by bike, on foot or horseback. The **Kumtor road** sweeps up through the veil of mountains to a high world of immense variety and beauty—a gateway to the hidden realms that lie above the view from the road—and, for those who don't have time or inclination to trek and camp, much of it can be explored in a day by car.

Barskoon village lies at 1,700 metres. Two workshops, one producing felt handicrafts and the other yurts, are worth a visit. Ask for **Bakit**, where you can buy felt goods and may be able to watch the different stages of making a *shyrdak*—the first of which, wool beating, has now been mechanised. At Bakit ask to be directed to Miken's 'Akorg', workshop where a master yurt maker weaves his magic creating yurts over a six-week period. You may be able to watch some of the processes.

A kilometre east of Barskoon turn off the lakeside highway at a sign announcing 'Attention! Kumtor Technical Road'. The untarmaced road, maintained by Kumtor, leads up the Barskoon gorge to the gold mine beyond. An arm of the Silk Route, it climbs and twists steadily for four kilometres to a visible square of mounds on the right, the remains of an ancient caravanserai.

As the road continues past a rusting Soviet lorry, mounted on a plinth to the left, one waterfall, 25 kilometres from Barskoon, is visible ahead, frozen in winter and gushing in summer. The second, bigger fall can be visited in an hour and a half's walk. On the way down, look for the crumbling sculpture of Yuri Gagarin.

A further 25 kilometres takes you over **Barskoon Pass** (3,800 metres) to the upland world of **Arabel valley**, with its beautiful lakes, and glaciers nosing their way surprisingly close to the valley floor.

The Kumtor road swings left along the Arabel valley to the mine but they'll turn you away before you reach it. The road straight ahead leads over the **Sok Pass** (4,021 metres) to the **Taragay valley** and Kara Sai village, where there's a checkpoint; you will need a border permit to travel further. Beyond lies the trekking route—for the hardy only—to Tash Rabat.

The road used to continue to Inylchek but the bridges are now broken. A little beyond Kara Sai, a road turns south following a strand of the Silk Route towards the **Bedel Pass** (4,200 metres) on the border with China. This was the route taken by tens of thousands of Kyrgyz fleeing Russian reprisals following a fierce rebellion in 1916 (see page 22); most were killed by soldiers or fell to their death from the treacherous ice in this inhospitable terrain. It might be possible to reach the pass by bike in July and August.

A kilometre or so to the west of Barskoon is the much smaller village of **Tamga**. There is no signpost but look for a Soviet-style bus stop and a road heading away from the lake beside an orchard. Well worth seeking out is nearby **Tamga Tash** ('letter stone' in Kyrgyz), an ancient rock carved with Tibetan Buddhist inscriptions, six kilometres up the Tamga river gorge. Nobody knows exactly when the carvings were made. The inscription on the rock's northern face is still legible and reads '*Om Mani Padme Hum*'.

Difficult to translate, this 1,500-year-old mantra expresses the desire for all to reach enlightenment. It is still chanted by Tibetan Buddhists and can be seen in carvings and on flags all over Tibet. The inscription on the southern face has partly been worn away, but appears to bear the same legend. Look for the lotus flower on the edge of the rock closest to the river.

Locals talk of several more Tibetan rock carvings further into the mountains, but details are sketchy. It is possible to walk to the rock by following the river valley, or to drive by four-wheel drive—but the clay road is lethal after rain. It is best to take a guide as the stone is difficult to spot.

TREKKING

The season here is from early June to late September and treks can be partly or wholly supported by local tour operators. (See also Bokonbaevo page 189). Unlike the valleys around Karakol, these mountains have no tourist infrastructure and are rarely visited, so it would be unwise to attempt a trek entirely unsupported. Treks of anything from two days will allow you to glimpse the beauty of the Terskey Ala-Too.

Longer treks from here include a demanding 19 days to Sary Jaz river in the Central Tien Shan near the Chinese border or 30 days to Tash Rabat.

Walking or riding on horseback from the south shore, you discover the heart of the country—layer upon layer of mountains and valleys. It is possible enjoy this even with low to average fitness and no experience, but good boots and warm, waterproof gear is essential. Below are some examples of what you can do but the possibilities are endless.

A fairly easy trek over two or three days starts on the east side of **Barskoon gorge**. Trekking over the **Dongureme pass** (3,773 metres), you camp for two nights in the valley to do a day walk to **Juuka pass** (3,633 metres) for great views of Arabel valley, studded with lakes and surrounded by snowy peaks. The following day, trek down Juuku gorge and back to the road. This can be extended by taking in Jergalchak and Ak Terek gorges to the east. From Juuku gorge it is possible to trek to Jeti-Oguz (see page 175).

A slightly more rigorous, higher altitude three- or four-day trek starts on the west side of Barskoon gorge with a punishingly steep hike to **Jany-Korgon pass** (3,860 metres). In the broad flat valley beyond, flowers bloom all summer, marmots dart about and glaciers cling to nearby peaks. The valley runs westwards at around 3,700 metres past Chonkur Kul lake and Kerege Tash pass and leads ultimately to Jelu Suu (hot springs) in the Uchemchek valley (see page 206). This trek, however, swings north over the boulder-strewn **Tamga pass** (3,960 metres) into the Tamga valley, summer home to herds of horses, yaks and sheep, which descends in massive steppes to the forested Chegedek gorge and past Tamga Tash (see above) to Lake Issyk Kul.

To reach the Uchemchek valley by bike or four-wheel drive, take the road from Tosor village a few kilometres west of Tamga. It climbs shakily through rocky lunar landscapes over **Tosor pass** (3,893 metres) and descends to the Ashuuluu Tebe river. From here look left to see Jany-Korgon valley, described above. As the road descends, it

(right) Kyrgyz children

swings west into Uchemchek valley and Jelu Suu hot springs where a rough, rutted road runs on to Naryn or Kochkor (for details see page 206).

Another trekking route leads over the Ton pass back to the lakeshore at Bokonbaevo (see below).

PRACTICAL INFORMATION

Tamga Guesthouse, at 3 Ozyornaya, tel. (03946) 25333 or Bishkek (0312) 678444, is probably the best hostelry on the south shore and is owned and run by KyrgyzLand travel company. The typical Slav house with carved wooden gable offers homely and friendly accommodation in twins and triples with shared facilities. No frills rooms are comfortable and the shared showers and toilets are clean. There is a summer dining area in the shade of fruit trees. Costs to B&B US$14 and dinner US$3. The family also run a tour operator, **KyrgyzLand** (formerly Kyrgyz Travel—see page 83 for details), specialising in trekking and birdwatching tours locally and in climbing expeditions throughout Kyrgyzstan.

Guesthouse Zhak: Opposite Ozyornaya is a Slav house beautifully decorated externally with carvings of birds. Clean twins for US$16 full board.

Guesthouse Flora: 18 Issyk Kulskaya, opposite the brightly painted railway carriage which is a computer games hang-out. A welcoming hostelry with a pretty garden, advertising good food. B&B costs US$8, dinner US$3.

Guesthouse Uvalia: 24 Issyk Kulskaya. Tel. (03946) 25257. Basic with an outside toilet and sauna only. US$6 room only. The family also offer a flat in the Military Sanatorium by the market.

34 Issyk Kulskaya: (look for a green painted gateway.) Tel. (03946) 25570. Plans to open in 2008.

Turbaza Issyk Kul: signposted on the lakeside road one kilometre west of the Tamga turn-off. Steps lead up to a large resort of chalets among silver birch trees, with the deluxe cabins overlooking the lake. Full board US$11–US$25.

Ak Chiy ('Quiet Bay') Yurt Camp, run by Dostuck Trekking (tel. 0312 545455 see page 82) is 400 metres east of Tosor village and costs US$11 B&B. Drop-in customers might find beds full so book in advance if you can.

Shepherd's Way Trekking: tel. (0312) 297406, 623102; Mob: (0502) 518315 email: shepherd@elcat.kg; www.kyrgyztrek.com. This professional and friendly family firm, offers fully supported horse treks and comes highly recommended. (See page 83 for details).

SKAZKA VALLEY

Another brief but rewarding detour (20 kilometers west of Tamga) is a hidden valley of startlingly vivid rock formations. Known as Skazka ('fairytale' in Russian), the sandstone cliffs of this miniature canyon have been weather-sculpted into an ensemble of fairy-castles, pillars, crags, and human forms and faces, ranging in colour from deep red to bright orange and yellow. Travelling west, take the second turning left after the village of Tosor, and fork right immediately. Skazka is two kilometres from the main road. Shortly before the holiday resort village of Kaji Say, Khansaray *turbaza* offers basic summer-only accommodation with fabulous views of the lake.

KAJI SAI

This tiny village is on a very pretty beach and in summer has a convivial holiday atmosphere. With the north shore over-commercialised and over-booked, if you want a lakeshore stay, Kaji Sai is one of the best options. Most accommodation is in rustic Soviet-style resorts but the new modern hotel, Hidayat, introduces a discordant style of architectural design to the south shore—a sign of future?

Hidayat: tel. (03941) 92418. This Kazakh-funded Costa del Issyk Kul-style hotel opened in August 2007. It has fabulous views from upper windows, en suite rooms, hot spring baths and a sauna. Full board costs US$25–50.

Hotel Legend: tel. (0312) 662499, 211113. Large Soviet-style resort on the lakeside with an attractive outdoor café. Full board costs US$14–US$40.

Hotel Salimar: also on the shore; look out for sign with two swans. Another resort among fir trees with sauna/steam room which leaks rusty water. Costs US$10 B&B with shared facilities or US$35 full board with en suite bathroom.

Altyn Jeek (Golden Beach): yet another Soviet-style resort on the shore, with cabins among the trees and its own beach and jetty. Full board costs US$16–US$55.

BOKONBAEVO

The one-horse town of Bokonbaevo is about half way between Balykchy and Karakol. The population of about 14,000 has fallen on hard times, having gone from full employment in Soviet days to 70 per cent unemployment today. The return to traditional farming livelihoods is hampered by paucity of land and a lack of capital and training. Poverty and alcoholism are prevalent.

The best of Bokonbaevo is out of town. Various companies run yurt camps on the lakeshore and the mountain *jailoo*; it's an ideal place to relax and enjoy the scenery and Kyrgyz traditional activities, including eagle-hunting demonstrations (see below), or to trek in the Terskey Ala-Too.

However, before leaving town, be sure to visit Altyn Oymok ('Golden Thimble') at 69/70 Karimshakov (Kyrgyzskaya). It was conceived in 1996 with high ideals as a community development project and still provides valuable income to women in the area but appears now to be more of a conventional handicraft outlet.

The artist, Jyldyz Asanakunova, who from its inception helped the craftswomen of Altyn Oymok to experiment with new designs and restore the use of natural dyes, now has her own **Felt Art Studio** in Bokonbaevo, at 8 Togolok Moldo, tel. (03947) 91412, mob. (0502) 824091.

The small Bokonbaevo **Museum** (open Mon–Fri, 9am–4pm), next to the war memorial in the town centre, has a collection of paintings by local artists depicting *manaschi*, eagle hunters and other local scenes.

Mount Tastar Ata, 20 kilometres from the town, is a sacred place for the Kyrgyz. Manas is said to have lived at its summit surrounded by stone pillars that people call the 40 warriors of Manas. A stone here contains clean water; a young man wishing for strength of spirit and health should drink from the stone and ask Manas to bless him. CBT can organise a trip here.'

TREKKING

As well as the operators in Barskoon and Tamga, CBT and Bishkek-based travel companies offer a dizzying array of treks (both low-level locally and tougher routes to Song Kul or Naryn) and cultural tours.

From Bokonbaevo, the Jelu Suu valley (see page 206) is a short drive (camp at Kok Bulak or similar) followed by a long day's hike (eight-ten hours) over the **Ton pass** (4,023 metres). There are a number of starting points but from Kok Bulak it's a demanding five-hour haul to the glacier on the pass; occasionally, the snow melts and you have to struggle over ice-covered boulders. Having admired the stunning views in both directions from the pass, it's a three-hour hike down to the Jelu Suu hot springs and excellent camping

PRACTICAL INFORMATION
Hotel Raikhat: 66 Atakan/Turusbekova. Opened in 2004, the hotel provides adequate rooms with TV and fridge with shared facilities (B&B US$8) and en suite (B&B US$14). Meals are provided in the yurt in the front garden.

CBT: 30 Salieva (Lenina). Tel. (03947) 91312, mob. (0503) 960060; www: cbttours.kg; cbtkyrgyzstan.kg. The office, signposted, is on the main drag, next to Argymak café. They can arrange the usual homestay accommodation in town and run yurt camps in the area: **Manjily** is on the beach equidistant between Bokonbaevo and Kaji Sai (look out for the 'Hospitality Kyrgyzstan') sign; **Bel Tam**, signposted from the road, is 18 kilometres west of town and is CBT's starting point for treks to Ton pass; **Jai Chi** is in the Kongur Olon valley (see below), 30 kilometres west of Bokonbaevo and seven kilometres from the road, near Kok Sai.

In summer the CBT co-ordinator is often in the hills out of telephone range, so it is worth making contact in advance. CBT can also arrange trips locally and treks in the mountains. Just west of Bokonbaevo, **Ecotour** run a yurt camp at **Ak Sai**, where they keep camels. They also run treks from here to Lake Song Kul on horseback.

Eateries are few in Bokonbaevo, but you could try Argymak, Aida and Alima, all on Salieva where you will also find the shops and a small bazaar. There's an **internet café** on Atakan/Karimshakov.

Sagambay Byerkut, 28 Aitmambetova, tel. (03947) 91320, and his family are eagle-trainers and hunters. In summer, they offer **yurt camp** accommodation in the hills and can demonstrate **eagle hunting**—either a short show or a full day on horseback. He will also hire out horses. If possible, give him a couple of days notice of your arrival and be prepared to bargain (see Community-Based Tourism, page 292, for a rough price guide). He and his family speak Kyrgyz and Russian only. You can also book through several Bishkek-based and local tour operators.

TRANSPORT
Three buses for Bokonbaevo leave from Bishkek's West bus station between 8am and noon, taking three to four hours. It is best to get there early to get a seat and because the bus will leave as soon as it is full, rather than stick to its schedule. Make sure your bus goes along the southern side of the lake ('*yiuzhnya doroga*' in Russian). Buses leave Bokonbaevo for Bishkek or Karakol in the morning. Shared taxis also run the route.

KONGUR OLON VALLEY
To the south-west of Bokonbaevo lies the beautiful Kongur Olon valley, a 40-kilometre stretch of velveteen rolling hills, meadows and swamps at 2,200 metres, which offers great walking and access to the mountains. Kyrgyzstan's most famous film Beshkempir ('Five Old Women'), a rural drama which got an award at the 1999 Cannes Festival, was shot in this area and in the village of Bar-Bulak.

Villagers talk of how Charota Bulde, an 18th century *batir* (leader), and his army of 40 warriors captured the valley from foreign clutches, allowing ancestors of the present Kyrgyz residents to settle. The warriors were each accorded an elaborate clay *gumbez* (mausoleum) after they died. Some of the *gumbez* are still standing and two can be seen in the village of Kongur Olon.

If approaching the valley from the turn-off at Kara-Kor on the lakeside highway, take the first main road east after the village of Dun Talaa. Kongur Olon is four kilometres ahead, the *gumbez* are in a graveyard just west of the village itself. Dun Talaa, Kongur Olon and another main village, Temir Khanat, can be reached by an afternoon bus from Bokonbaevo or by taxi.

ACCOMMODATION

There are several yurt camps in the valley. CBT's **Bel Tam** camp is signposted at the turn-off from the lakeside road just west of Bokonbaevo. **Ecotour** run two, complete with solar-heated shower, sit-down toilet and excellent, abundant food—one above Temir Khanat at the eastern end of the valley and one near Tura Suu at the western end. They are unable to accept drop-in guests, so contact their Bishkek office in advance.

The tranquil camps are perched high above the villages with unrivalled views and are ideal spots to experience firsthand local Kyrgyz culture and hospitality, and sample Ecotour's refreshing approach to tourism (see page 82 for details). Guides and horses are available for hire for short rides (the glacier behind the camp at Temir Khanat can be reached in a day).

KHAN DOBO

In an attractive valley ten kilometres south of Bokonbaevo are the very scant remains of Khan Dobo, a large eighth century settlement that was abandoned in the 12th century.

Villagers in nearby Tura Suu call the site 'The Great Wall of China' since only Khan Dobo's fortifications remain: a disappointing kilometre-long ridge broken by what was once a gateway. On the way to the Khan Dobo or Tura Suu, a 19th century mausoleum, *Almatai Gumbez*, is arguably more interesting.

Balbals (ancient stone figures found throughout Central Asia) at Burana Tower [Saffia Farr]

Central Kyrgyzstan

The Suusamyr Valley

Plunging from the dramatic 3,586-metre Tor Ashuu pass in the west to the friendly and relaxed town of Kochkor, more than 200 kilometres to the east, the broad Suusamyr valley is one of the highest inhabited but least travelled regions in Kyrgyzstan. It is a land built on a scale for giants; a high steppe plateau averaging 2,200 metres above sea level, bordered to the north and south by the magical ice and snow kingdoms of the Kyrgyz Ala-Too and Suusamyr Too mountain ranges respectively, and with mighty rivers cutting a deep slash through its heart.

Always dramatic, the valley's ever changing landscape varies from vast open plains laid out on broad, descending shelves to narrow, jagged limestone gorges piled with massive rock falls and scree slopes. Its lush mountain pastures (*jailoos*) are filled with herbs and wild flowers in summer.

Marmots build networks of burrows deep below the grass while the majestic eagle and the even rarer lammergeier, with its three-metre wing span, soar high among the peaks. There are also foxes, mountain goats, curly-horned Marco Polo sheep and wolves, but you'd be extraordinarily lucky to see any of them.

The main routes into the valley are from the Bishkek to Osh road in the west, which has recently been extensively renovated and takes you through the spectacular Tor Ashuu Pass, and from the Balykchy to Naryn road at Kochkor. Another minor road enters the valley from Song Kul just west of Chaek, but it is impassable in winter, when deep snow blankets the high regions, and after heavy rain, which turns dirt tracks into dangerous mudslides. The best trekking is around Jangy Aryk (formerly Kyzart), particularly to Song Kul. The Suusamyr valley makes a fabulous cycling route.

This difficult combination—the mountains' inflexible embrace and the long harsh winters—makes the Suusamyr valley one of Kyrgyzstan's most isolated and poorest regions. The backbone of its economy is farming, mainly animal husbandry. For centuries the valley has been used to fatten sheep for the winter months; its lush grass was so coveted that clan wars used to break out over particular pastures. In Soviet times the area was almost exclusively given over to herds from the collective farms and up to four million sheep were herded here each summer from the foothill villages of the Kyrgyz Ala-Too to the north. But the collapse of the collective farm system and Soviet export channels has had a dramatic impact on local agriculture and the herds are now only about a fifth of their original size.

Since independence local people have switched to producing whatever vegetables will grow in such high, cold terrain (potatoes, garlic and cabbage), as well as animal fodder for winter. One of the biggest problems for locals left high and dry by the

(right) Taking the goat to market, At Bashy

collapse of the Soviet system has been adjusting to the free market. Charitable organisations specialising in micro-finance assist farmers in learning how to run a business and obtain small bank loans.

Nevertheless, the Suusamyr valley remains a magical place for the Kyrgyz in summer. The Russian traveller Victor Vitkovich's account of a trip he made there about 70 years ago could just as easily apply to life on the *jailoo* today:

> *It is night. Pressing closely around a yurt, sheep are deep in slumber, breathing evenly, their heads buried in the wool of their fellows. The lightest of sounds is heard in the stillness of the mountains ... The moon glides across the sky stumbling over clouds, and the peaks of the mountains, resembling enormous blocks of blue marble, are illumined by a mysterious inner light. Slowly the darkness is pushed back as, growing brighter, dazzling beams of morning light rise from behind the rim of the mountains ... The sun peeps out from between two boulders on a mountain top. A sudden gust of wind causes the grass to sway and gives the tulips a brighter hue. A shaggy sheepdog licks its master's hand wth its hot tongue. This is the morning of the shepherds, morning in the jailoo, in Suusamyr, in the preserves of the Kyrgyz people.*

There is an excellent network of homestay accommodation at the valley's eastern end, around Kochkor In the western end there are now limited but good options for accommodation.

Rural Kyrgyz people have a much more relaxed perception of time than most Westerners. *Azyr*, the Kyrgyz word for 'now', can mean up to two or three hours later. That means the meal you arranged or the horses you wanted for your trek might not be there exactly at the time you hoped. Be philosophical about it and try not to travel to a schedule that is too demanding.

The weather changes fast in these mountains, even in summer where temperatures in the valley average around 30ºC, black thunderclouds can roll in quickly, bringing stinging rain. Winter temperatures drop as low as minus 40° C. Bring appropriate clothing and be prepared for cool nights.

It is also a good idea to stock up beforehand with some fresh fruit and vegetables which are in extremely short supply, especially at the valley's western end (you can always give them to your host to cook for you but bring extra for the family). Other small gifts that are much appreciated include Bishkek newspapers and magazines, postcards from your home country and supplies of tea, sugar and salt. People speak Kyrgyz and maybe some Russian only so a phrasebook is handy.

FROM THE BISHKEK TO OSH ROAD

The road from Bishkek climbs to the tunnelled Tor Ashuu pass (see Bishkek to Osh Road, page 258), where you are rewarded with stupendous views of the Suusamyr valley below and the 4,000-metre snow-capped Suusamyr Too range in the distance. 'An emerald in a silver setting' is what the Russian explorer Ivan Mushketov exclaimed when he saw the Suusamyr valley for the first time.

The road divides under a huge hammer and sickle sign and heads south-west for the 13-hour marathon to Jalal-Abad and Osh, or south-east, dropping down into the wide undulating valley of Suusamyr. This is arguably one of the most beautiful sections of the long road east—where the Suusamyr, Kyrgyz and Talas ranges loom closer and valleys melt seemlessly into snow-topped peaks.

SUUSAMYR VILLAGE

This sprawling, somewhat tumble down village lies about 15 kilometres from the junction. It's not a particularly attractive introduction to the valley and there's little reason to stop, except to organise accommodation at the dacha a few kilometres further on (see below).

PRACTICAL INFORMATION

A daily bus leaves the south-west side of Osh Bazaar in Bishkek for the five-hour journey to Suusamyr. Changing at Karabalta may give you more options. Schedules change so you'll need to check before travelling.

A taxi from Karabalta to Suusamyr village will cost between US$35 and US$40. You may also be able to hire a taxi in Suusamyr itself; ask local people around the bus station.

There is no accommodation in Suusamyr village itself but there is a large **dacha** about ten kilometres further down the road. It is owned by the village administration, sleeps five people and costs about US$6 per person per night. Book it through Anara Kalykova in the Suusamyr village administration office (*ail okmotu*). If you arrive out of office hours, her home is the third on the right from the end of the village, heading east towards Kojomkul. If you miss Anara and turn up at the dacha without booking, you may still be able to persuade the caretaker to let you stay.

The dacha has an exceptionally pretty setting, on the banks of the wide, shallow, fast-flowing Karakol river. To find it, take the main road out of Suusamyr village towards Kojomkul. After about 20 minutes, the road forks; the right fork crosses a river and continues to Kojomkul. (The bus stops here for passengers). For the dacha take the left hand fork, alongside a river and after a few minutes turn right down a track through gorse bushes. The dacha is at the end of the track, in a glade of trees next to the caretaker's house. The large Slav-style building has a decayed charm, with two-foot thick whitewashed stone walls and a large black circular stove stretching from floor to ceiling.

There are three bedrooms with five uncomfortable beds, as well as a large living area. The sauna has been taken over by chickens. The only downside to this rural idyll is the mosquitoes which come out at dusk; in early summer they disappear pretty quickly but later in the season you'd be advised to take protection.

The caretaker's wife will cook for you if asked, but bring your own supplies if you want more than just bread and *kaimak* (cream).

KARAKOL

Karakol is a tiny, sleepy hamlet about six kilometres from the dacha. It shares its name with the much bigger town on Lake Issyk Kul but there the similarities end. This is the first village you will come to if you trek from the Sokoluk valley.

PRACTICAL INFORMATION

Roughly in the middle of the hamlet is a peachy pink house belonging to **Abdrasul Ergeshov**, a friendly man who offers basic but clean homestay accommodation for around US$6 per person, including meals. You can book a stay with him through Anara at the Suusamyr village administration office, although he'll try to accommodate you if you just turn up.

If you're lucky, he'll give you fresh trout (*asman* in Kyrgyz) from the river; it's so fertile that he reckons on a catch of four or five fish an hour.

KOJOMKUL

This large village of about 150 houses, about 18 kilometres south-east of Suusamyr, sprawls nonchalantly in a large bowl. It is named after a giant of a man, 2.3 metres (over seven feet five inches) tall, who became a national hero because of his ability to hoist enormous stones, and even his horse, onto his shoulders simply for fun. There is a **museum** dedicated to Kojomkul in the middle of the village; you'll find it by the small plaque on the door and the three huge stones outside, two of which were lifted by Kojomkul and one by his father. Inside, these amazing feats become easy to credit when his size is revealed in photographs and clothes—one photograph shows his coat draped around three people with room to spare. If the museum is closed you will find the key-holder in the house at the back

Villagers believe the spirit of Kojomkul, who lived from 1889 to 1955, still protects them. In 1992, when the Suusamyr valley was hit by a major earthquake, reaching nine on the Richter scale, many houses in Kojomkul were seriously damaged but no one died. Local people say that was because Kojomkul's grave on the hill above the village was the first to collapse, proof that he was still taking care of them.

His grave, which was rebuilt in 1996–97 by the grateful village administration, is behind the war memorial in the centre of the village, in a grand white domed mausoleum. The white votive rags are left to entice good luck.

On the road to Kyzyl Oi, another example of Kojomkul's superhuman strength may be seen at an elaborate, but broken down, yurt-shaped grave of a local dignitary. The large stone next to it, which according to its plaque weighs 690 kilograms, was carried there by Kojomkul in honour of the dead man.

The jagged peaks of the Kyrgyz Ala-Too viewed from near Suusamyr village

PRACTICAL INFORMATION

Geography teacher **Aibek Myrsahmatov** and his wife offer very hospitable homestay accommodation in their large, comfortable white-washed home, set back from the main road. Costs are around US$6 per person, including meals. To find Aibek take the left hand street about a hundred metres past the monument in the centre of the village, heading in the direction of Kyzyl Oi.

KYZYL OI

Shortly after leaving Kojomkul, the valley narrows and the road begins to wind through mountains rising steeply on either side. Smooth lush pastures alternate with huge rock falls and scree, and the distant mountains lie in folds like a carelessly discarded cloth of sumptuous green velvet. Here the Suusamyr and the western Karakol rivers join to become the mighty Kekemeren, which tumbles over giant boulders and swirls angrily in mini whirlpools in its rush east and is popular among rafters.

About 23 kilometres from Kojomkul the narrow gorge suddenly widens into the lovely tree-lined valley of Kyzyl Oi ('Red Earth'). The small oasis is captured by a relentless ring of granite cliffs and rocky peaks, a brief opening between two narrow, rock-filled gorges—life here is hard, but the village is nevertheless a welcoming place. The barren dusty mountain sides look about as unproductive as the moon, but over unseen ridges lie plateaux of scrubby but serviceable *jailoo* where people carefully herd their animals and cut winter fodder. Vegetable plots cover every available surface although only carrots, potatoes and cabbages will grow up here. Families make special trips to Bishkek to buy tomatoes and cucumbers for tourist salads. The village was rebuilt after the 1992 earthquake in a more Central Asian style, using mud-and-straw bricks crafted from the dull red clay that gives Kyzyl Oi its name.

It's worth loitering for a day or two at Kyzil Oi to feel its remoteness and explore further afield. Possibilities include an overnight trip to the four Kul Tor lakes in the Char valley, five hours' ride away over the Kumbel pass. A day trip on horseback takes you to a waterfall on the Burundu River, and five kilometres from the village are mountain pastures of Chet Tor with their numerous springs and summer yurt camps. The very luckiest will see the elusive and rare Marco Polo sheep, lynx and snow leopard which patrol the mountains above.

If you have only a couple of hours to spare, there's a bird's eye view of the valley from the nearest (rather spartan) *jailoo*. Take a track into the hills from near the shop on the road running parallel to the main road.

PRACTICAL INFORMATION
There is no public transport from Kyzil Oi. Villagers share taxis which depart from near the CBT office, hire a car to Suusamyr (US$8) or Chaek (US$13), the latter about 40 kilometres to the east. These are guideline prices only.

The **CBT** office, run by Artyk Kulubaev, is on Jibek Jolu (the main road), tel. (0503) 242199. He is informative and well-organised and sets up homestays, guides and horses for trips in the locality. Although this can be arranged on arrival, it is best to book in advance through the Bishkek or Kochkor offices, as horses cannot always be found for next-day trips when they are working in the *jailoo*. When Mr Kulubaev is out of the village, it's an accommodation-only service.

The very luckiest will see the elusive and rare Marco Polo sheep, lynx and snow leopard which patrol the mountains above.

CHAEK

Leaving Kyzil Oi through the eastern pincer grip of the red-walled gorge which falls sheer into the blue-green river, you emerge into a broad arid plain where tough grasses cling to the bleached soil and the only harvest is stones. However, what it loses in lushness, this journey more than makes up for in dramatic rock formations in the chiselled craggy faces of the cliffs.

About 15 kilometres before Chaek, the harshness gives way to farming country, well irrigated and packed with vegetables, livestock, and the pink and yellow flowers of winter fodder. The distant mountains are painted in the most delicate of hues—palest pinks, warm oranges, misty purples.

Chaek is an unappealing little town but has the basics if you need to stay there. You can reach Song Kul by road from just west of Chaek via the Kara Keche coal mines.

PRACTICAL INFORMATION
CBT homestay in Chaek (two-edelweiss) with Guljan Mykieva at 4 Molaliev Akal, tel. (03536) 22879, is friendly and comfortable. At the western end of town, turn left just before the public administration building—the house is ahead of you. B&B and dinner costs US$10.

Around the middle of the town, at 64 Erkinbek Mortiev, the **Government Hotel** is unmissable with its Chinese-style curved roof. Room-only in this rusting establishment by the river is US$4 with an outside toilet and no shower. The caretaker will cook for you, but food can be scarce so it's advisable to bring your own.

Song Kul Café, near the small square which is surrounded on three sides with heroic busts, is the main eatery in town.

From Chaek regular minibuses run to Kochkor but not to the west.

JANGY ARYK (FORMERLY KYZART)

The 38-kilometre run to Jangy Aryk is through well-populated, cultivated land. The village is signposted from the main road; turn right by the graveyard. The next door village is Doskulu. A word of warning to avoid confusion: the two villages are widely referred to by tour operators as Kyzart, Jangy Aryk's old name, although the villages are signposted separately using their new names. It's easy to miss your destination.

Jangy Aryk is the relaxed starting place for some beautiful treks to Lake Song Kul over two to four days, through Bazar Turuk gorge. Along the way, you stay in working yurts on verdant *jailoo*, considered some of the best in Kyrgyzstan, where you can experience traditional life with real shepherds. Beware that local time estimates have sometimes been over-optimistic—the trip is two days minimum.

PRACTICAL INFORMATION

CBT co-ordinator, Talgar Abdirazakov, at 25 Kurmanata, tel. (0502) 354586, will organise homestay accommodation in his large, clean and relatively affluent home with brightly coloured modern carpets on the walls. The family is very friendly and offers two private rooms and a sauna (order this in advance). The food is good and plentiful and much of it comes from their own garden where they grow strawberries, garlic, carrots, cabbages, sugar beet and potatoes.

Talgar co-operates with a number of villagers to provide accommodation, horses and guides for treks. It's best to book in advance as working horses may not always be readily available.

To find his house, turn right (if you are coming from Chaek) off the main road by the graveyard, left by the mosque at the crossroads. The house is on the right almost at the end of the road.

The **road to Kochkor** runs through prime pasture land and after the isolation of Suusamyr's western heights seems almost crowded with yurts and flocks of sheep, goats and horses. Roadside stalls are piled high with bottles of *koumys* for sale, reputed to be among the best in Kyrgyzstan (although every region says that about its *koumys*). Fermented mare's milk may be an acquired taste for visitorss but it is hugely important to the Kyrgyz. They have a saying: '*Koumys* is man's blood and fresh air is his soul'. Both are in ample supply here.

The **Kyzart Pass** is a hauntingly silent and windblown spot 15 kilometres from Jangy Aryk and 53 kilometres from Kochkor. A service station is housed in yurts and old railway carriages and a rusty snow plough stands in permanent readiness. **CBT** start a two-day trek on foot to Song Kul from here, through the Char Archa gorge. Treks on horseback to Song Kul start from Jangy Aryk.

Kochkor

Kochkor is a busy crossroads on the well-travelled Bishkek to Naryn road, the ideal spot to organise treks to some of Kyrgyzstan's best *jailoo*; treks or transport to Lake Song Kul; travel to Naryn along the main road or via the much more interesting but slower route through the Eki Naryn gorge; or for the journey eastwards to Jelu Suu and to Lake Issyk Kul.

A sprawling town in a cup-shaped valley, its broad avenues are lined with tall white poplars and silver birch. For years, there was a big German community here but most have left now. In the early evenings, the streets fill with cows and sheep 'guided' by four-year-olds with long switches. As one grandmother said, her cow makes its own way to and from the pastures and bellows outside the gate to be let back in. Visitors have reported tensions late at night caused by alcohol.

Kochkor was originally named after the Tsarist prime minister Stolypin, who promoted the Russian colonisation of Central Asia and opposed the October Revolution. After the revolution the Bolsheviks renamed the town Kochkorka. However, local people have another story about how the town got its name.

According to the legend, a couple of men were taking a flock of sheep to market in Andijan (Uzbekistan) when a woman asked if they would also take her sheep (the word *kochkor* means mature male sheep) and sell him, using the money to buy some good clothes. They agreed but along the way they mistreated the sheep. By the time they arrived at the market, the sheep was thin and scrawny, and no one wanted to buy him so instead they entered him into a contest of fighting sheep. His thinness became his advantage and he nimbly dodged his aggressive opponent until the bigger sheep collapsed, exhausted. Encouraged by this win, they entered the poor sheep into another contest with the same result. In the end, not only had he won a lot of money but his fame had spread wide and a wealthy merchant bought him for a price equivalent to that of 90 sheep. So the woman got her good clothing and the village got its name.

SIGHTS

It is worth seeing the small **Regional Museum**, on Kuttuseyit uulu Shamen (next to the park), for its excellent display of a yurt capable of housing 50 people, its handicrafts, tributes to local heroes and ridiculously large stuffed sheep. Bring a torch in case the electricity is out.

The Wednesday **animal bazaar** draws scores of white-bearded elderly men riding donkeys and wearing traditional *kalpaks* (increasingly spurned by younger men in favour of baseball caps). It offers a glimpse of the rural heart of Kyrgyzstan and marks a return to trading—the age-old Central Asian lifestyle which was entirely destroyed by the Soviet system.

HANDICRAFTS

There are now plenty of outlets for handicrafts in Kochkor. The first was **Altyn Kol** (Golden Hands), which is part of Shepherd's Life and has a shop behind the CBT office (see below). This region claims to produce the best *shyrdaks* because the high mountain pastures provide ideal conditions for the sheep's semi-fine wool. Altyn Kol was set up as a women's co-operative in 1996 with the help of Swiss development programme Helvetas but seems to be developing along more commercial lines.

Jailoo Tourism (see below), set up in direct competition with CBT, also runs a handicrafts shop. Look out for the 'Handicrafts' sign above Baba Ata café on the main street, Orozbekova.

Well worth a visit is the **Erkyn Felt Shop** at 15 Abubakir, tel. (03535) 22422, mob. (0502) 115105; email: kanay_zina@mail.ru. Master felt maker Norbubu and her daughter Zina are putting together a museum of ethnography, housed in a large room behind the shop. The collection includes old *shyrdaks* and *ala-kiyiz*, a 150-year-old camel's coat, a 207-year-old *tush-kiyiz* made from deer hide and embroidered silk, as well as ancient leather containers, trunks, instruments and jewellery. Norbubu says: "We hope that the collection will remind the modern generation of its Kyrgyz culture."

They also organise felt-making demonstrations by arrangement, provide lunch for groups and offer accommodation in five yurts in their garden for US$2.5 per person (shared outdoor facilities).

Jumagal Akhmadov, 58 Kuttuseyit uulu Shamen. Tel. (03535) 22453, sells high quality *shyrdaks* and other felt goods and also offers accommodation through CBT (see below).

These budding businesses are crucial for people grappling with making a living after the collapse of the Soviet Union. The downside is that women only receive money for the items they sell, so that some may wait for some time before their particular *shyrdak* is snapped up. But the importance of initiatives like Altyn Kol is proven by the fact that in 1998, just two years after the project began, the showroom was visited by 300 tourists and sold US$1,555 worth of goods—a huge amount in an economy where the minimum monthly wage was at the time US$4.50.

KOCHKOR PRACTICAL INFORMATION

Three main organisations offer homestay **accommodation**, transport and trekking services. **CBT** at 22a Pionerskaya, tel. (03535) 22355, mob. (0503) 873149; email: cbt_kochkor@rambler.ru, is the biggest and longest established, but now finds itself facing increasing competition from former members who have set up independently. They have 16 homestay guesthouses in Kochkor and can arrange folklore festivals on the *jailoo*—check with the office for details. (See page 292 for more information about CBT and Shepherd's Life.)

Sister organisation **Shepherd's Life**, tel. (03535) 22534, mob. (0502) 140376, which is next door to CBT, organises *jailoo* yurt stays in the region (see below). **Jailoo Tourism**, above the Baba Ata café on Orozbekova, tel. (03535) 21116, mob. (0502) 735188; email: jumabaeva@gmail.com, which splintered off from CBT in about 2002, offers both *jailoo* and homestay accommodation.

The town has a small but excellent fresh produce **bazaar**, testimony to Kochkor's fame as an agricultural centre, especially for potatoes. If you're heading to Suusamyr, stock up now. There are several shops in the centre including Gastronom Bereke which has a good supply of basics. **Café Visit**, just north along Orozbekova, has a charming outdoor area and, in the centre, **Café Baba Ata** is also a good option.

AROUND KOCHKOR

The upland area around Kochkor is unusually rich in beautiful *jailoo*. CBT, Shepherd's Life and Jailoo Tourism can all organise transport, guides, horses and other trekking logistics.

Sarala Saz (Yellowish Marsh), 54 kilometres north-west of Kochkor in the Kyrgyz Ala-Too range, is one of the largest *jailoo* in the region. It's an hour's drive followed by a two-hour walk, the highest point only 2,600 metres. En route to the *jailoo* look out for the enormous stones which, according to legend, were thrown ten kilometres away by Manas to round up his wandering horses. Also on the way are several *korgon*, burial mounds dating from the first to the fifth centuries. From Sarala Saz you can ride north to the beautiful Shamshi Gorge or south to Lake Song Kul on a five-day *jailoo*-hop, crossing four passes.

Terz Tor *jailoo*, 3,100 metres above sea level, is south-east of Kochkor—a half-hour drive plus four hours on horseback. A further two hours on horseback, normally done in a day-trip from Terz Tor, takes you to **Kol Ukok** ('Lake in a Chest'), an undrained lake full of colourful Savan trout.

The Kochkor region is the starting point for some fabulous **treks** on foot or horseback, using *jailoo* yurt accommodation. For Song Kul (two to five days) you can start from Jangy Aryk village, Kyzart Pass (see page 199) or Sarala Saz, visiting as many as seven other *jailoo* along the way. A tougher trek over at least six days leads to Bokonbaevo via Jelu Suu. For the seriously sturdy, it is possible to trek towards Naryn and Tash Rabat. However, all the above routes are unmarked and people have been lost on even short treks—hikers are strongly advised to hire a guide.

Locals also recommend a visit to the **Chong-Tuz** salt caves about 30 kilometres away, where rock salt has been mined for decades. Since Soviet times people have also been treated at the sanatorium here for asthma, spending up to ten hours a day in an underground chamber decorated with archaeological remains.

Lake Song Kul

It is easy to see why locals rave about Lake Song Kul; filled with fish and surrounded by lush pastureland, it's a herder's paradise and claims a treasured corner in the Kyrgyz nomadic heart.

The lake, 29 kilometres long, 18 kilometres wide and at an altitiude of 3,013 metres, lolls in a vast treeless plateau of rolling hills, like green velvet-covered dunes, and is encircled by distant snowy peaks. Bizarrely, not all visitors are enraptured by Song Kul. But the enormity and silence of this mountain world, with its silvery streams and colonies of marmots, can hardly fail to impress. The water, which seems to go on for ever, constantly changes colour with the ever-moving weather and is home to 66 species of waterfowl; deer, lynx, leopard, Marco Polo sheep and wolves also appear up here but you'd be extraordinarily lucky to see them.

It is worth spending a couple of days here to experience sunrise and sunset over Song Kul, but walking into the hills involves a long trawl across the plateau.

This ultimate *jailoo* is summer home to shepherds from early June. The families set up camp for a fee of US$27, supplementing their income by taking other villagers' animals: 2007 rates were US$0.21 per sheep and US$1 per cow per month. No strangers to hardship, the herder families, nevertheless, complain about the relentless wind, the permanent chill and the lack of even intermittent electricity—life is hard up here. As one woman said, 'Everyone must work, even the children have their jobs'.

PRACTICAL INFORMATION

Yurt accommodation is the only option here and may be booked (in advance) with CBT in Kochkor or Naryn (see page 292 CBT for prices), ITMC and Ecotour, among others, in Bishkek. Yurts are scattered around the vast shore, so get directions. There's plenty of room to camp free of charge, but bring food. For the last few years, Shepherd's Life in Naryn has organised regular festivals here—check with the Naryn office for details.

There are four main routes to Song Kul, all of them unpaved, with spectacular views. The main two can be done in under two hours. The most commonly used runs for 50 kilometres from Sary Bulak on the Kochkor to Naryn road. An initially flat run along the Terek River, it winds up through the Kalmak Ashuu valley (which got its name from the Kalmaks, frequent adversaries of the Kyrgyz).

Perhaps the most stunning runs from the Naryn to Kazarman road in the south; it leaves the main highway at Jangy Talap (formerly Kurtka—see page 224 for CBT details) and snakes dramatically up the mountainside in more than 30 hairpin bends.

A minor route runs from 19 kilometres south of the Dolon Pass on the Kochkor to Naryn road. The fourth, rarely used, climbs from just west of Chaek, past the Kara Keche coal mines. From at least late October to late May, and also in heavy rain, all of these routes will be difficult, probably impassable. Fabulous treks from Kochkor or Jangy Aryk (formerly Kyzart) are probably the best way to arrive at Song Kul. There is no public transport to the lake, but tour operators can arrange a car.

Kochkor to Naryn

There are two routes from Kochkor to Naryn: the four-hour 116-kilometre drive along the main road or a 252-kilometre trip, best done over two days, on appalling roads through open valleys and the pretty Eki Naryn gorge. You can also take a detour east to Jelu Suu (hot springs) and continue over the Tosor Pass to Lake Issyk Kul.

This well-travelled main route has some dramatic scenery as it snakes through the vast Central Tien Shan. The high point of the journey is the desolate 3,030 metre Dolon pass, about 46 kilometres south of Kochkor. There are superb views across the valleys, marred only by the lines of wonky telegraph poles on even the steepest of slopes— testaments to Soviet determination, if not their aesthetic sense.

On the other side, there's a dramatic descent through rugged limestone cliffs and steep valleys lined with fir trees into the narrow Dolon gorge. After the bleak heights, the road descends into a lush oasis, yurts, grazing herds. There are several places to stop for food and *koumys*, both at the pass and in the gorge.

About 25 kilometres before Naryn, the striking memorial on the hillside is to the Kyrgyz writer and poet, Arstanbek Bunlash Uluu, (1824–1878). He is regarded as a major poet, although few of his works survive, not surprising since he focussed on the influence of the 19th century Russian colonists upon his people and wrote about the 'dark times' ahead, urging the Kyrgyz to preserve their traditions and culture.

In bleak winters the road is lethal and maintenance workers housed in caravans near the Dolon Pass are often called upon to dig vehicles out of the snow.

In recent years, increasing numbers of Chinese lorries have been thundering at breakneck speed along this road (and beyond to the Chinese border at the

Kyrgyz cemetery at Jumgal

Torugart Pass), to flood the Kyrgyz markets with cheap Chinese goods. They return full of scrap metal (hold on to your car aerial). Such is the damage caused by the lorries that China has recently agreed to maintain the road.

The Back Road to Naryn

This is an ideal route for cyclists—bring plenty of food. At the one-beetle village of Sary Bulak, 34 kilometres south of Kochkor and really just a *chai* and fish stop for the Chinese truckers, turn east behind the Terskey Ala-Too and follow the Karakujur river. The pot-holed dirt road criss-crosses the river as you loop through the steep-sided slate gorge, climbing higher to emerge on to smoother rolling hills, populated by marmots and yaks, their frilly petticoats of hair almost trailing the ground.

About 90 kilometres from Sary Bulak you pass through a narrow gorge above the river and descend into a broad treeless plateau, the Balgart valley, renowned for its birds of prey. The right hand turn to Eki Naryn is 17 kilometres further on. After another seven kilometres you pass a right hand turn to the desolate Archali village and the route to Kyzil Bel valley. For the next 26 kilometres, the rutted road wanders through *jailoo* territory—good grazing, dotted with occasional yurt camps and huge flocks of sheep and herds of horses.

Keep the river to your right, taking particular care as you cross semi-washed away bridges.

The untouched wildness of these remote and rarely visited valleys leaves you with an indelible impression of silence, space and majestic landscapes.

Finally, you reach a beautiful spot at the end of the Uchimchek valley and see a small farmstead nestled

Kojomkul Museum

in the crook of the mountains, overlooked by a dirty glacier, at the confluence of two large rivers, the Teshik and the Uchemchek. The bridges have been entirely washed away but it is possible to forge the icy fast-flowing river on foot and by four-wheel drive at shallow crossing points.

JELU SUU (HOT SPRINGS)

Conceived in the Soviet imagination as a health resort, it never got beyond the foundations of construction. Broken concrete blocks litter your path as you cross an animal pen to the rickety shack where the hot springs are piped into a five-foot square pool of pungent sulphur waters—which might have trouble getting past health and safety in Europe.

Despite this, it makes for a quirkily charming experience and a welcome 67-degree soak; buckets are provided if you wish to cool it with icy river water. Entrance is rather pricey at US$2, though you should expect to pay less for your guide or interpreter. The caretaker family offer very basic B&B with dinner for US$3.5. Another option is to camp in a snug hollow on the opposite side of the river.

From this charmed corner of Kyrgyzstan, roads and mountain paths take you north to Lake Issyk Kul or south to Naryn. Both offer an abundance of magnificent scenery. For a pleasant day-trip, follow the Teshik river for two to three hours to reach Lake Teshik Kul. The Uchemchek (sometimes called the Jelu Suu) River flows from the Ashuuluu Tebe valley above the hot springs to the east. A rough, broken road (you'll need a four-wheel-drive) climbs into the valley before turning abruptly to the north to cross the Tosor Pass at 3,893 metres and descending to Tosor village on the south shore of Lake Issyk-Kul. An alternative, strenuous trekking route takes you over the 4,023-metre Ton Pass (eight to ten hours to the *jailoo*) and down to Bokonbaevo on the lake (see page 189).

EKI NARYN GORGE

Returning towards Kochkor, the turn-off to the Eki Naryn Gorge is 33 kilometres from Jelu Suu. The road winds south and crosses the river, entering a narrow, dramatic gorge. For the next 49 kilometres, it switches back and forth over the tree-lined river, crossing six bridges in varying states of disintegration. The road poses as a mini Karakorum Highway, with the sheer gorge walls jagging into the torrent below and, as the gorge narrows claustrophobically, boulders the size of cars litter the road—testimony to the frequent rockfalls that bedevil this route.

There's not much room for camping but good spots can be found just before the second bridge and after the fourth bridge, but for a more roomy site hold out until after the fifth bridge when the gorge briefly opens out. A glacier lake lies a ten-minute walk down a rough track from the fourth bridge

As you approach the end of the gorge, the conifer trees get taller; the road swings left over a final (sixth) bridge, leaving a dirt road to continue straight ahead for one kilometre to a pretty, red-walled, secluded valley with a **CBT yurt camp**.

Mr Kadyrakun and his wife have two yurts, sleeping up to ten people at standard CBT rates (see page 292) They can arrange guides and horses. No English is spoken. Book in Bishkek or Naryn, or turn up on spec (although the yurts may be occupied).

ONWARDS TO NARYN

Just after the Eki Naryn gorge in the Terskey Ala-Too mountains is a weird and somewhat macabre sight—three hectares of fir forest in the form of a swastika. The story (one of many) goes that German prisoners-of-war, brought to the area to work in forestry during World War II, planted the forest in this shape.

Ten kilometres beyond the bridge, the pretty, relaxed village of **Eki Naryn** has a dramatically beautiful setting on a broad, fertile plateau surrounded by snowy peaks. Very comfortable homestay **accommodation** is offered by Clara Duishevaeva and her husband in two rooms with clean outdoor long drop toilet. Costs are US$8 B&B. It is down the second road on the right as you enter the village; look out for the green, blue and white house on the right before the road veers off to the left.

The village shop, selling basics, is in the very first house on the right as you enter the village.

Just outside Eki Naryn, two great rivers, the Kichi (little) Naryn and the Chong (big) Naryn merge in a dramatic torrent of waters, one turquoise green and the other gunmetal grey, to form Kyrgyzstan's chief river, the Naryn. Crossing over, you enter a relentlessly brown, wind-blown valley—at between five and 15 kilometres wide and 470 kilometres long, Naryn valley is the longest in Kyrgyzstan.

Around 20 kilometres later, in **Tash Bashat** village, turn left by the mosque for the six-kilometre detour to a national wildlife reserve at the end of a lush, green valley. Locals say the steep road is lethal in wet weather. Established in 1983, the reserve is populated by wild goats, boar, bears and deer. Entry costs US$1.50 and there's a basic guesthouse (US$4); bring food.

The picturesque canyon of **Salkyn Tor** is halfway (15 kilometres) between Tash Bashat and Naryn. Signposted by a large Soviet entrance arch, its former pioneer camp now operates as a pricey guesthouse with beds at US$20 per person. ITMC also runs a yurt camp further up the valley. Entrance to the canyon is US$1 and offers easy and rewarding hiking and camping.

Naryn

Naryn is a long thin town, set between impressive red sandstone cliffs on one side and rolling green hills on the other, and spreads for about 15 kilometres along the broad, rust-brown river of the same name.

Although it is a town most people pass through out of necessity rather than choice, generally on their way along the old Silk Route to the Torugurt pass on the Chinese border 180 kilometres away, it is more welcoming now that CBT has arrived. About 45,000 people live in the town itself, the administrative centre of Naryn *oblast* (province). Naryn's outskirts, with their Soviet blocks, look pretty grim at first glance, but the town gets better as you head further in and becomes a rather attractive town of broad, leafy avenues. Despite getting a bad press elsewhere in Kyrgyzstan (its

Lake Song Kul

inhabitants are regarded snootily as country bumpkins), visitors have described it as 'unexpectedly fun'.

At about 2,000 metres above sea level, Naryn is known as the coldest town in Kyrgyzstan. Temperatures can plummet to minus 40°C; even the swift-flowing Naryn freezes in places in winter and people ski on the slopes above the town. In summer, however, it can be very hot and dusty (*naryn* means 'sunny' in Mongolian).

The modern town began life as a Russian garrison in 1868 and still houses an army base (which is why camping on the hills overlooking Naryn is forbidden).

Before the collapse of the economy, its main local industries were bread-making, meat-packing and dairy production. In Soviet days, mountainous regions such as Naryn received hardship salaries that were 40 per cent higher than in the lowlands.

In 2001, 26 per cent of the city's population earned less than US$3.50 per month, and a further 37 per cent earned less than US$11. Sadly, seven years later, Naryn's fortunes have not improved greatly and today unemployment is very high and there is a problem with alcohol. This tinderbox combination of soldiers, drunkenness and grinding poverty means the town can take on an ugly atmosphere after dark.

Perhaps out of resentment at their economic decline since independence, the town's citizens have kept their Lenin statue in the square on the long main street, still called Lenin Street. A flashy but impressive blue and turquoise mosque has been built with Saudi Arabian money on the town's western side.

Naryn *oblast* (province) was established in 1970 with the town of Naryn as its capital, and is one of the coldest regions in Kyrgyzstan. The population of around 270,000 is almost entirely Kyrgyz. More than 70 per cent of Naryn *oblast* is mountainous and virtually all of it is over 1,500 metres above sea level. The highest sizeable lake in the republic, 3,500-metre high Chatyr Kul, is located in Naryn *oblast*. The climate here is cold for most of the year. Winter temperatures are particularly bitter; the average temperature in January is minus 17°C and sometimes plummets to minus 40°C. This is the poorest province in the country, with 58 per cent of its population living in what the UN classes as 'extreme poverty'.

A major local industry is hydroelectricity, particularly along the mighty Naryn river, the most important of Kyrgyzstan's 40,000 rivers, which has seven power stations situated on its shores. The Naryn flows from east to west across the region into the Fergana valley where it converges with another major river, the Kara-Darya, to form the Syr Darya, which supplies more than a third of Central Asia's water. The Naryn is also a potential source of friction with Uzbekistan (which utilises the river to feed its cotton fields), because Kyrgyzstan wants to retain more of the water for its own use.

The *oblast* is overwhelmingly rural and more than 80 per cent of people work in agriculture, mainly sheep breeding. Horses are the major form of transport in the area, which again is hardly surprising when you consider the difficulty of building—and maintaining—roads in such a mountainous area, especially with the havoc wreaked every winter by the weather.

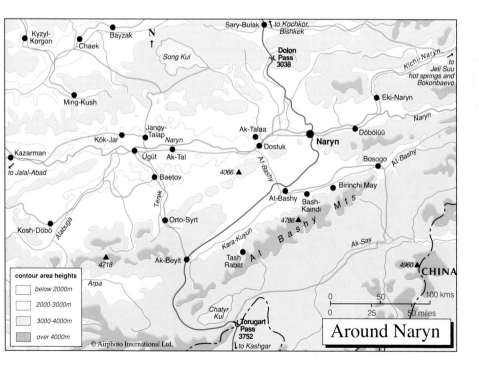

Around Naryn

Various stories about Naryn have been handed down over the generations, including one which tells how Naryn and a couple of other towns in the area got their names. Returning, exhausted, from having sold his cattle in Andijan (Uzbekistan), a herder settled down for the night on a *jailoo*, turning his horse loose to graze. The horse wandered off and ate at a place called Arpa ('Barley'). When the herder tried to retrieve it the next day, however, it ran away. The herder chased it and eventually caught it. He killed the horse and cooked its meat, leaving the head at a place he called At-Bashy ('Horse's Head'). As he continued his journey, he ate the meat until it was all finished. The herder's last meal was a bowl of *naryn*, a traditional soup dish made with thin slices of meat, which gave the town and region its name.

SIGHTS

The **Regional Museum** on Moskovskaya, just north of the eastern crossroads, is open daily from 9am–noon and 1–4pm, and is well worth visiting. There's a sign in English on the road, though not on the museum itself; look out for a building with pink doors. It has an excellent display of a yurt, neatly dissected to reveal its interior and hung with all the necessities of nomadic life, including various leather and wooden implements. There are also three fabulous *shyrdaks* hanging on the wall, lending credence to Naryn *oblast's* claim to make the best *shyrdaks* in Kyrgyzstan.

Among the other exhibits are traditional costumes, including ancient silver headdresses, belts, buttons and chains worn in the hair. In the old days women used to wear coins as decoration attached to the ends of their long plaits; in the 19th century, however, they changed to wearing Chinese coins as it was considered unseemly for the Tsar's image, on the coins of the day, to be hanging near women's bottoms. Elsewhere there are sixth- and seventh-century carved stones and a room devoted to Naryn's own Bolshevik hero, Jukeev Tabaldi Pudovkin, complete with his saddle and rather small bed.

A yurt in the main square houses a small **art gallery**. Although the square was redesigned in 1999, **Lenin** still stands nearby. **Living Fragrance Candles**, 146a Lenina (the large white building behind apartment block 146), tel. (03522) 52213; email: info@shofargroup.com; web: shofargroup.com Owned and run by Chris and Rachel Binder, a resident Anglo/American couple, the business makes a range of candles, sold mainly in Bishkek and Osh. A tour of the workshop can be arranged and you can make your own candles. In spring 2008 they plan to open a **shop** on the premises, selling their wares as well as handicrafts made locally. The statue facing the regional administrative building represents Kyrgyz youth. **Victory Park** (just off Moskovskaya) has a Soviet tank and is sometimes a venue for outdoor discos.

NARYN PRACTICAL INFORMATION

The main drag, Lenina, runs virtually the length of the town, parallel to the mighty Naryn river. Small shops and stalls selling basics are strung out along Lenina and at its western end, near the main square, are two department stores. The flashy new one, with clothes, mobile phones, electronic goods and upstairs restaurant, is located opposite the dingy old Zum. The small **bazaar** is on Orozbekova, parallel to Lenina.

If you have just arrived from China you may need to register with the OVIR (pasportniy stol, see page 76) office on Togolok Moldo, east of the centre. **Internet** is available at the Telecom office on Lenina and at the Internet Service centre at 44 Lenina.

FOOD AND ACCOMMODATION

For travellers desperate for a taste of luxury and a hot shower, there's only one option —the British-owned and operated guesthouse, **Celestial Mountains** (tel. (03522) 50412 if you speak Kyrgyz or Russian, otherwise book in advance through Celestial Mountains' Bishkek office (0312) 212562; email: naryn@celestial.com.kg or ian@celestial.com.kg). It is a little east of the Regional Museum, at 42 Razzakova (Moskovskaya), and is signposted from the road. The hotel is a modern building decked out in tiles and marble and offers a choice of rooms (some with a balcony), or communal accommodation in one of its four yurts. The main building has clean shared bathrooms, hot showers, a restaurant providing dinner and breakfast and even a TV room stocked with Western videos. Yurt residents have access to all the facilities.

Prices are US$30/36 for a single/double, or US$13 for a bed in a dormitory-style yurt where you may have to share with strangers (of the same sex). Breakfast and dinner are included in these prices.

The **Community-based Tourism co-ordinator** Kubat Abdyldaev is at 8 Lenina; tel. (03522) 50865; mob. (0502) 689262; email: kubat-tour@mail.ru. This excellent and well-organised office, which is shared by sister organisation **Shepherd's Life**, is packed with information and is a boon for travellers. CBT's homestays have transformed the budget accommodation options in Naryn, with nine guesthouses ranging from one- to three-eidelweiss standard.

Kubat, who speaks good English, can arrange homestays and yurt stays in the area, as well as trips, cars, guides and information on CBT-organised culture festivals. Shepherd's Life can organise *jailoo* stays across a wide area including Lake Song Kul, Tash Rabat (where an English speaking guide is available), Eki Naryn and Koshoi Korgon. For more information on CBT and Shepherd's Life, see page 292.

Satar's Yurt Inn, a collection of seven yurts and a brand new guesthouse, is located behind the now defunct Government Hotel three kilometres from the centre, on the airport road. The yurts have beds and clean shared facilities for US$13 B&B and dinner. En suite rooms in the guesthouse cost US$18, and those with shared facilities are US$15. The inn already does good business with tour groups and is planning to build 18 more bedrooms in 2008.

The **Hotel Ala-Too** on Lenina is worth avoiding.

The **Hotel Kunduz**, tel. (03522) 50755 or mob. (0502) 205654, opened in 2006. It is signposted on Lenina a block east of the CBT office, but the entrance is round the back up some dodgy stairs to the third floor, Appt 12. We were unable to obtain an answer.

There are a number of **cafés** offering the standard *laghman* (noodles), *shashlyk* (kebabs) and *shorpa* (soup). **Karona Café** in the centre of town comes recommended by expat residents, as does **Café Anarkul Apa**, just off Lenina, close to the Plaza.

TRANSPORT
Private minibuses depart daily for Bishkek between about 8am and 11am from the bus station east of the centre. They take eight hours.

Saudi-funded mosque at Naryn

Public buses for the seven-hour trip to Kazarman depart on Tuesdays and Fridays, returning Wednesdays and Saturdays. Public buses depart regularly for Torugart but this crossing is difficult for foreigners—see Crossing the Torugart pass later in this chapter. Buses to At-Bashy leave daily on the hour between 12 noon and 4pm and take 45 minutes. Buses to Eki Naryn depart at 8am and 4pm on Mondays, Wednesdays and Fridays.

Shared taxis are another option but the taxi drivers clustered around the bus station act as a cartel to push up prices and exploit the captive market heading for the Torugart pass or Tash Rabat. In Naryn you'll need harder bargaining skills and be prepared to pay more than elsewhere.

Close-up of a shyrdak [Saffia Farr]

At-Bashy

The road from Naryn to At-Bashy (40 kilometres) and the Torugart pass (190 kilometres) passes through yet more canyons littered with telegraph poles before climbing over the Kyzyl-Bel pass, with magnificent views of the At-Bashy range, which boasts peaks of 4,786 metres. The road emerges into a huge, flat valley of lush pastures, with the green, leafy town of At-Bashy tucked away in a hollow. The town, which is apparently built on top of settlements dating from the 8th to the 14th century, is between four and six kilometres off the main Naryn to Torugart road, depending on which of the two access roads you take.

It is a neat little town of white-washed houses and friendly people, with a lively animal market on Sundays. On either side of the plain are the magnificent At-Bashy and Naryn Too ranges, with their superb possibilities for fairly tough trekking.

At-Bashy itself has been hard hit by the collapse of the economy after independence; its collective farms collapsed and the local bread-making factory closed due to lack of wheat. Unemployment is high; one family told us that although all their adults were graduates, only one (a teacher) had a job. These are tough, self-reliant, country people born of generations of hardy farmers and herders. As one man put it: 'You could say that At-Bashy people prefer horses to people.'

At-Bashy is said to be one of the best areas of the country for *shyrdaks*. The Shepherd's Life co-operative is worth visiting.

AT-BASHY PRACTICAL INFORMATION

ACCOMMODATION
The local Shepherd's Life co-ordinator is the very hospitable Tursan Akaeva, at 25 Arpa, which is off Aity Suleymanov, four or five blocks north of the government hotel, tel: (03534) 21944. Kyrgyz and Russian only are spoken here so you can book through either Naryn or Bishkek. Her husband, Beishenbek, is an important man locally, an elected deputy in parliament and the head of the At-Bashy representatives.

The Akaev (no relation to the former president) house is clearly one of the best in town. It is set back from the road; look out for a large two-storey blue and beige building with a peaked roof and extensions on either side, like a pair of wings.

The Akaevs provide friendly and comfortable accommodation in a room with four beds at the top of the house, where *shyrdaks* from the local women's co-operative are also on display. The food is excellent, the traditional long-drop toilet is clean and hot water can be arranged for washing. They can also organise *shyrdak*-making demonstrations, and guides and horses for trekking. For prices, including accommodation, see page 292.

KOSHOY KORGON

There is very little information available about the ruins of this small citadel on the outskirts of Kara-Suu village, about eight kilometres from At-Bashy. It dates from the 10th to the 12th century and, according to one legend, is where the Kyrgyz hero Manas buried his friend Koshoy. Today all that's left is a large square filled with reeds and surrounded by crumbling walls two or three metres high.

Despite its decay, it's an atmospheric place. Stand in the middle of the citadel in the pulsating heat, with nothing but the sound of wind in the reeds to fill the silence, and you can almost sense the ghosts of long-dead warriors. To find the ruins, take the first left in the village, through the archway, past a pretty mosque and World War II monument, then left at the crossroads to the end of the road. Koshoy Korgon is in the fields on the right.

Tash Rabat

This remote, high valley on the north side of the At-Bashy range, about 75 kilometres south-west of At-Bashy, must be one of the prettiest in Kyrgyzstan. With its lush velvety pastures, winding streams and occasional yurts, it is an idyllic place to camp before or after crossing the Torugart pass. It contains a 15th century caravanserai which bears solitary witness to the massive Silk Road trading caravans that used to pour through these inhospitable mountains.

The origins of the caravanserai, which underwent some restoration work in the 1980s, are not clear. There is apparently some archaeological evidence that the site was occupied as early as the tenth century.

Today the caravanserai is a square, rather squat-looking building that is much bigger than it appears from the outside because it digs deep into the hillside behind. Inside there is a domed central chamber leading to the remains of 30 dank cold rooms including, opposite the entrance, the khan's own quarters.

One chamber contains two underground dungeons, one of which has been filled in. There is also a well and supposedly an old tunnel, possibly leading to a look-out point. The chambers on either side of the entrance each have a broad, raised ledge, which is said to be a communal bed used by the caravanserai's soldiers, who were garrisoned here to protect against bandits.

Tash Rabat is 3,530 metres high and so can be bitterly cold, despite its relatively sheltered location, so take warm and waterproof clothing. In winter and spring the wolves come right down into the snow-covered valley at night to prey on livestock; they took 45 horses alone in the winter of 1999–2000. The altitude is high enough to produce symptoms of altitude sickness, such as headaches, breathlessness and tiredness. If so, take it easy for the first day or two and give your body time to adjust before undertaking any major treks.

TASH RABAT PRACTICAL INFORMATION

ACCOMMODATION

It is possible to stay in the yurt or rather spartan house belonging to the caravanserai caretaker and his wife. She will prepare meals for you.

Shepherd's Life and **CBT** each run a six-yurt camp here. Book through the Naryn or Bishkek office or just turn up. Friday nights are particularly busy with people heading east for Kashgar's Sunday bazaar.

For some years, 75-year-old Osmon Kojo, who has been coming to Tash Rabat for years to graze his animals, also offered yurt accommodation. He and his daughters are very hospitable and if you speak Kyrgyz or Russian, he loves to discuss politics, albeit from a bygone age. He is, for example, very good on the relative leadership merits of Churchill, Roosevelt and Brezhnev!

This is *jailoo* country and bathroom facilities are a long-drop toilet and the icy river; don't follow the example of some German campers who stripped off naked while we were there to bathe in the river—you'll shock your hosts. Naryn is a long way off, so if you can bring small gifts of newspapers, tea, sugar, fresh fruit or vegetables for your hosts, this is much appreciated. B&B costs about US$10.

For more comfort and considerably higher prices, Dostuck Trekking and ITMC sometimes have yurts further down the valley—check with the Bishkek offices beforehand.

GETTING THERE

There is no public transport to the valley. About 60 kilometres from At-Bashy on the main road to Torugart, an unmarked gravel road bears south towards Tash Rabat. The turning comes just after a bizarre three kilometres stretch in which the asphalt road widens to form an emergency military airstrip, built during Soviet times but never used.

At the gate, hoot the horn and the gatekeeper will come running. It costs about US$1 for foreigners to enter the valley. Keep your ticket to show the caretaker at the caravanserai about ten kilometres further in; he or his wife will unlock it and show you around.

TREKKING AROUND TASH RABAT

The 4,000-metre At-Bashy ('Horse Head') range, which runs parallel to the road between Naryn and Torugart, makes very good hiking and horse trekking country and offers prime access to the Ak Sai plateau (see below). A local guide and adequate fitness are imperative here since maps of this area are not up to date, the landscape and climate can be treacherous and the cattle trails are often washed-out. The season is from early July to mid-September.

Trekking support in this area has still to be developed, but the caretaker at the caravanserai and CBT/Shepherd's Life, Naryn can help organise horses and act as guides for trekking (price negotiable). One German tour group he took out while we were

(above) Tash Rabat valley and pastures;
(below) Rugged At-Bashy mountains

(above) Caravanserai at Tash Rabat;
(below) Horses graze below the At-Bashy mountains

there saw the elusive ibex, a species of wild goat with huge curving spiral horns more than one metre long, which lives among crags and rocky slopes, usually above the snow-line. They also saw a lammergeier, a rare species of vulture that looks like an eagle but has a three-metre wingspan.

One good day trek from Tash Rabat is to head up to the 3,968-metre Tash Rabat pass with its views to Lake Chatyr Kul and the Chinese border. Start by going further south into the valley, crossing over the river at the caravanserai and following it upstream for an initially easy walk on springy turf amid rolling velvety hills. After about two hours the valley forks. Take the right fork for the pass or the left for an easier walk.

The route to the pass is long and strenuous, made more difficult by the altitude, and not suitable for horses, but is very attractive with dramatic limestone and quartz crags rising like dragons' teeth, and silver grey rocks covered in orange lichen. After the fork, the path immediately begins to climb steadily above the narrow gorge. After about an hour's walk, you have to decide whether to cross a small stream and bear left, or continue upwards towards the broad ridge. If you go left, there is another three hours of even steeper climbing over mossy, squelchy banks and dozens of tiny rivulets from the rapidly melting snow caps above, before you reach the boulder-strewn pass. Allow a minimum of six hours up and three hours down.

This walk can be extended to a four-day round trek via the Ak Sai valley, camping at *jailoo* on the way. The route is amongst stunning surroundings but the frequently narrow and steep zigzag track is not an easy jaunt, and for this you will need a guide.

Permits are needed for the Ak Sai valley. A border zone (military) permit can be obtained with the help of travel agencies, giving them at least four weeks' notice (see the Visas and Red Tape, page 74).

The Ak Sai Valley and Chatyr Kul Lake

The eerie, oval plateau between the At-Bashy mountains and the Chinese border (known as 'the belly of Kyrgyzstan') is the Ak Sai valley; truly the far end of Kyrgyzstan. Offering plenty of grass, water and well-protected yurt spots, the Ak Sai valley is shepherd country par excellence: about 20,000 yaks graze here and in summer, families from the villages around At-Bashy bring their livestock here. Settlement is limited to half a dozen tiny hamlets, a small meteorological station and the compound of the border guards at Torugart.

At its south-western end, next to the Torugart pass, lurks the deep blue Lake Chatyr Kul. The lake, whose name means 'lake on the roof' in Kyrgyz, is just that: at an altitude of 3,530 metres above sea level, it is the highest in the quartet of the country's main lakes (Chatyr Kul, Issyk Kul, Song Kul and Sary Chelek). Its 175 square kilometres provide breeding and resting areas for numerous migrating bird species, including the Indian bar-headed goose. The lake is a zoological reserve.

TREKKING IN THE EASTERN AT-BASHY RANGE

Another trekking possibility is to enter the Ak Sai valley from the eastern end of the At-Bashy range. With a few days' notice, Shepherd's Life co-ordinators in At-Bashy can arrange horses and guides for the very beautiful horse trek from the village of Bash Kaindy, seven kilometres east of At-Bashy. Bring a tent and provisions and consider hiring an extra horse to carry luggage, since crossing the passes is quite tough.

From Bash Kaindy the route takes you through rolling grassland and foothills to the village of Birinchi Mai (ten kilometres, two hours). From here, the track climbs moderately steeply for another seven kilometres (three hours) along a sheep track into the Jol Bogoshtu canyon. Its stunning alpine surroundings are reminiscent of the Altai or the Pyrenees, and the river and streams make a perfect spot to spend the first night. Shepherds set up camp on the *jailoo* here in summer.

From the *jailoo*, it is 20 kilometres (five to eight hours) along an old cattle track over the 3,906-metre Bogoshtu pass to the Ak Sai plateau. As you approach the pass, the mountains gradually become more barren until they open into the rolling steppe and badlands of the Ak Sai valley. The return follows the same route in reverse.

It is possible to do this trek on foot but it's a good idea to arrange transport in At-Bashy to take you to the foothills of the Jol Bogoshtu canyon and hike from there. Travel agencies such as ITMC and Edelweiss can also organise this trek for you.

Permits are needed for the Ak Sai valley. A border zone (military) can be obtained with the help of a travel agency, given at least four weeks' notice.

Across the Torugart Pass to China

As well as being the most spectacular route into or out of Central Asia (and worth a visit in its own right), the Torugart pass is the most direct route to Kashgar, arguably the most interesting corner of Xinjiang province and ideally placed for onward travel either south to Pakistan (along the Karakorum Highway) or east into China. The journey through Kyrgyzstan to the Torugart pass, whether from Bishkek or Osh, neatly encapsulates the country's scenic and cultural highlights: the caravanserai at Tash Rabat, nomadic life, the excellent display of felt handicrafts and carpets at Naryn museum and, of course, some beautiful and dramatic mountain scenery.

Finally, there's the added attraction of following a branch of the Silk Route, which wound its way from Kashgar to the Fergana valley (though it is thought that the major route crossed the modern border via Kok Art to the south).

THE AKYN

*O*ne day the aul suddenly throbbed with excitement. A troup of wandering entertainers had arrived—kumancha-players, dancers, and a story-teller. These people travel from camp to camp to cater for the nomads' amusement. That evening a great fire was lit beside the aqsaqal's tent. Carpets and felt rugs were spread round, boiling water for tea hissed in numberless kettles on their tripods, and the chilim circulated from mouth to mouth. The story-teller sat down near the fire and began to recite his tales in a monotonous voice. Though the listeners might have heard his stories a hundred times before, they never failed to thrill to them afresh. Every eye watched the old man's toothless mouth and not a sound was to be heard save his voice and the crackling of burning juniper …

'Do you know the story of Abdullah Bezdik? Nay, you cannot know it, for Allah revealed it to me in a dream. Listen, brave men! In the days of Tamerlane there lived at the court of Samarqand a certain mirza [scribe] called Abdullah Bezdik. The mirza had a great love of animals and could not bear to see them suffer. He used to go round the caravanserais of Samarqand and buy up every camel he saw come in sick or wounded from its journeyings. One day the great Tamerlane heard of the mirza's doings and sent for him. Tamerlane was seated on a throne with a circle of many imams and mullahs round him, when the mirza came in and prostrated himself again and again before the mighty Ruler of the World. Then Tamerlane asked why in the name of Allah he bought up a lot of sick camels which, after all, had no souls and were worth even less than so many women. The mirza answered that animals also had souls and suffered pain. The imams and mullahs blenched at such blasphemy and challenged the mirza to prove that the camel had a soul. If he could not prove it he must die. The mirza replied that he could not prove it, since it was not possible to prove that even men had souls.

'Tamerlane was still more enraged at this reply and bade them strike off the impudent fellow's head. Before this order could be carried out the Court Fool interposed:

"Tell me, mighty Timur, had the late Diwan Begi a soul or not?"

"By Allah," cried Tamerlane, "I shall execute any man that doubts it!"

"And shall you let the mirza go free if I prove that camels have a soul?" asked the Fool.

"By the beard of the Prophet, I promise to let him go free. But how wilt thou prove it, Fool?"

"Right easily, thou favourite of Allah! Thou hast just now declared that the Diwan Begi had a soul, and how often, oh my Master, hast thou not thyself called him a camel!"

'Tamerlane, the imams, and the mullas laughed till the roof threatened to fall in. But the mirza was free.'

Gustav Krist, Alone Through the Forbidden Land, 1939

PRACTICAL INFORMATION
BORDER REGULATIONS AND REQUIREMENTS

Bureaucracy and mutual suspicion between China and the former Soviet Union currently have the border in a stranglehold. The Torugart pass is one of those rare beasts in Kyrgyzstan around which absolutely no flexibility exists. It is designated a 'Class 2' border crossing and, therefore, technically closed to all but nationals of Kyrgyzstan and the People's Republic of China (mostly traders). The special permission (and ensuing bureaucracy) that foreigners need in order to cross the pass makes a tidy income for immigration and, especially, customs officials who are always on the lookout for irregularities. To avoid being sent back, you just have to stick to the rules. However, the situation is very fluid so check information in advance.

You need, firstly, a **Kyrgyz visa**. Secondly, if you plan to leave the road within a 50-kilometre radius of the border (to trek around the valley for example) you will need a **border zone permit** (see page 74). However, if you plan to travel straight through to Kashgar from Naryn, At-Bashy or Tash Rabat, the permit will not be necessary.

Thirdly, you need a **Chinese visa**; these can be obtained in Bishkek within three days to a week but you will need an invitation from a travel agency and the process can be problematic so, if you can, get your Chinese visa before you travel (but don't mention the Torugart). Fourthly, in the past, you have needed a fax showing that a registered Chinese travel agency has arranged a permit and a vehicle to meet you on the China side for the transfer to Kashgar. Although the car and permit are still required,

Preparing wool for use in a shyrdak

the fax of proof no longer seems to be necessary. Finally, you need to ensure that the driver of your car has permission in his passport to travel through no-man's land to the checkpoint, where your Chinese driver will wait for you.

LOGISTICS

The border is open Mon–Fri 9am–5pm, and is closed for up to three hours at lunchtime. It is closed at weekends and on Kyrgyz and Chinese (and sometimes Russian) public holidays and often, unofficially, on days that fall in between a public holiday and a weekend. It is best to arrive at the border by 9am as long queues of lorries and smaller traders slow down proceedings; you must get to the Chinese border by 5pm Beijing time (3pm Kyrgyzstan time), when it closes. People who arrive too late are sent back. Near the Kyrgyz border are several old railway wagons where you can get accommodation and food if you wish to spend the night.

The border officials will check your documents and baggage, and ask you to complete a customs declaration form; they won't let you through until they hear from the Chinese border that your vehicle has arrived. The normal place to change vehicles (something of a Glinicke Bridge experience that can make you feel like a spy) is at a Chinese checkpoint, between the two border posts. From here, you head down to Chinese immigration and customs. It is said that the purest Kyrgyz is spoken in this area as it has not been affected by the use of Russian. Once you have passed through this hurdle, you can relax—you are under two hours' drive from Kashgar.

ARRANGING YOUR CROSSING—TOUR OPERATORS

It can simplify matters to enlist the help of a tour operator in Bishkek, who can arrange your Chinese vehicle, permits and transport to the border with a reliable driver who can assist if you encounter unscrupulous border officials. They would expect the journey to start in Bishkek, which can be expensive, especially if you wish to stop on the way rather than squeeze the journey into the minimum two days. Celestial Mountains, Central Asia Tourism and Edelweiss all have experience arranging the trip. Contact the operators a good two weeks in advance.

If you wish to travel independently you could negotiate a deal with the taxis at the bus station in Naryn but they know you have little choice so prices are high—and higher still if you want to stay overnight at Tash Rabat. For a small fee, staff at the Celestial Mountains Guesthouse in Naryn (tel. (03522) 50412, though only Kyrgyz and Russian are spoken) are sometimes willing to negotiate a deal with a taxi on your behalf; the deal would remain a private arrangement between you and the driver but they can check that the driver has the relevant passport stamps and stand more chance of getting a reasonable deal. This would have to be arranged a few days in advance.

If your Bishkek travel agency arranges the Chinese side of the trip, you will probably have to pay the Chinese driver in US dollars. Alternatively, you could make the arrangements yourself through a reliable agent in China, such as Xinjiang Nature Travel Service in Urumqi—tel. (991) 2333891; fax. 2332174; email: info@china-adventure.com.

The High Road to Osh

NARYN TO KAZARMAN

Tell any Bishkek tour operator you want to travel from Naryn to Kazarman and you'll probably be told it can't be done: the mountains are too high and the road too difficult. The 217-kilometre road (288 kilometres if you go via Baetov), is certainly a rough seven- or eight-hour ride by bus and only a couple of hours less by taxi, but it is perfectly manageable, at least between early June and September. The route tracks the Naryn river through a succession of fertile valleys, crosses several passes and descends into steep-sided gorges along the way. The reasons to take this rough road are to visit the rock carvings at Saimaly Tash (a UNESCO World Heritage site) or to get from Osh to Naryn or Torugart without having to backtrack all the way to Bishkek.

The most dramatic ascent of the route comes just after the village of Kok Jar, when you climb 50 corkscrew turns to the 3,500-metre Kara-Guu pass. The superb views reveal a lunar landscape, in which the softly moulded mountains are delicately tinted in red and beige stripes. At the top, wrapped tightly against the bitter wind and a thin layer of cloud, people dart forward shouting 'koumys, koumys' at passing cars. Ironically, this chilly point marks the transition from Naryn to the generally much warmer *oblast* of Jalal-Abad.

AK TAL AND THE TEREK RIVER VALLEY

This region, west of Naryn and south of Lake Song Kul, sees few visitors but is definitely of interest for its vast, spectacular landscapes, reminiscent of the American southwest or arid parts of central Spain. It has a stunning mixture of dramatic dry rock formations, desert badlands and, scattered in the middle of it all, villages surrounded by lush trees and cultivated plots.

About 91 kilometres towards Kazarman from Naryn, turn left to take an alternative route to the Torugart pass. The high arid route follows the Terek river, climbs over the 3,268-metre Mels Ashu pass, goes through Baetovo village, 120 kilometres from Naryn, and down onto the Naryn to Torugart road.

The road to Ak Tal is so well used by cyclists that you wonder whether China's influence is encroaching on the supremacy of the horse. Seventy-seven kilometres from Naryn, at Ak Tal, you turn right, opposite Kurtka petrol station, for **Jangy Talap** (formerly Kurtka) and the most dramatic road to Lake Song Kul (38 kilometres).

PRACTICAL INFORMATION

Shepherd's Life co-ordinator, Sveta Jusupjanova, tel. (0502) 112324 at **Jangy Talap**, five kilometres from the main road, offers accommodation, will arrange guides and horses for trips locally and transport to Kazarman and Jalal-Abad. It's a convenient lunch stop, but book a couple of days in advance. B&B costs US$7.

Scenery on the Naryn to Kazarman route

KAZARMAN

Kazarman has a reputation for being a rough town, probably partly due to its isolation (it is often inaccessible by road during the winter) and partly because of the nearby gold mine and ore processing plant. Certainly it has a bit of a Wild West feel about it; its people seem a little more reserved towards strangers than elsewhere in Kyrgyzstan. In a low, flat plain about 1,230 metres above sea level, approximately half way between Naryn and Osh, Kazarman gets the worst of both their climates, with temperatures almost as low as Naryn's in winter and almost as high as Osh's in summer. The dusty town has almost no cafés.

PRACTICAL INFORMATION

Public buses leave Naryn for the seven-hour trip to Kazarman at 8.30am on Tuesdays and Fridays, returning Wednesdays and Saturdays at 8am.

There are no public buses to Jalal-Abad, but there is reputed to be a minibus, which runs occasionally: ask at the bus station. The cost of a taxi to Jalal-Abad varies widely. Some taxi drivers won't travel along the Kazarman to Jalal-Abad road as it is so rough. Find one with a sturdy car and expect to pay about US$40.

Kazarman has an airport with irregular flights to and from Bishkek and occasionally Naryn or Osh, but the schedule is unreliable.

There used to be two hotels in Kazarman but only one now seems to operate; look for an unmarked two-storey building on the square, opposite the small bus station where the bus from Naryn terminates. The caretaker turns up eventually. The rooms are pretty filthy but the sheets are freshly laundered and the beds surprisingly comfortable. There is a private sauna a couple of blocks away US$0.35.

CBT offer homestay accommodation and transport and can now arrange trips to Saimaly Tash. Co-ordinator Bujamal Arykmoldaeva is at 36 Betken, tel. (03738) 41253.

SAIMALY TASH

The magnificent 5,000-year-old petroglyphs of Saimaly Tash must rank as the archaeological highlight of any visit to Kyrgyzstan. The site, which means 'Embroidered Stones' in Kyrgyz, consists of 10,000 rock carvings and drawings strewn haphazardly over a mountain called Sulaiman, deep in the Fergana range. Although there are other major petroglyph sites, in the Ur-Maral valley west of Talas, around Aravan (see Around Osh, page 240) and also at Cholpon Ata, on the northern shore of Lake Issyk Kul, Saimaly Tash is the most complex and best preserved in Kyrgyzstan.

The petroglyphs lie scattered over two moraine slopes, which archaeologists call Saimaly Tash One and Saimaly Tash Two. About two-thirds of the images represent animals—mainly ibex, wolves, horses and, less commonly, camels, snow leopards, reindeer and even monkeys. The rest show hunting scenes, ritual dances, men ploughing fields using oxen and camels and shamanic symbols, offering a rare insight into the world of Kyrgyzstan's earliest inhabitants.

The oldest images date from the Bronze Age (3000 BC) and were drawn by pre-historic peoples so far unknown but probably of Indo-Aryan stock. Others range from Iron Age carvings (800 BC) to carvings and drawings carved as recently as the early Middle Ages by the Saks (a nomadic people of Iranian origin) and Turkic tribes. Sadly, there is also some graffiti from moronic 20th century visitors. The age of the site tells us that humans have attached strong religious significance to this spot for thousands of years. Right in the middle of Saimaly Tash One lies a small pond where shamans once gathered to conduct meditations and celebrations, and which is still a sacred spot for the Kyrgyz. The Kyrgyz believe a visit to Saimaly Tash brings good luck into their lives.

Petroglyphs at Saimaly Tash

In a country that lacks much tangible evidence of its rich and varied history, Saimaly Tash is remarkable. The only problem is that virtually no one gets to see it. Saimaly Tash's remoteness has been its saviour.

Saimaly Tash was discovered by the outside world in 1903 when the Russians built a track between Jalal-Abad and the military outpost of Naryn, (the present road via Kazarman follows this trail). A military cartographer called Nikolai Khludov became interested in stories he heard from Kyrgyz shepherds about painted stones in the mountains and organised a small expedition to search for them. He reported his findings to the Society of Archaeology in Tashkent, which organised a subsequent expedition, but Saimaly Tash was soon forgotten.

Scientific interest was resurrected in 1950 by Soviet archaeologist and petroglyph specialist Alexander Berstamm, from Frunze (present-day Bishkek). Although he only spent a month at the site, he not only scientifically documented but also dated the petroglyphs. The Institute of Archaeology in Bishkek, supported by UNESCO and the UNDP, is currently studying and mapping the stones, and also excavating burial mounds at Saimaly Tash Two. The findings from the latter may shed more light on the origins of the oldest petroglyphs.

PRACTICAL INFORMATION

Getting to Saimaly Tash is an adventure in itself. Many of the archaeologists who have visited the site have done so by helicopter; many have tried and failed to find the site alone. Saimaly Tash is certainly worth the effort but it's a big effort.

Saimaly Tash is right at the top of Mount Suleiman, at 3,200 metres above sea level. The trek itself requires no technical skills but is quite arduous so you need above-average fitness. Don't even consider trying it without a guide—you simply won't find it. The mountain is criss-crossed with sheep tracks, which are hard to follow and continually peter out. Depending on the weather, you have to make between three and seven river crossings, some of which have to be done on horseback due to the speed of the water.

The round trip is ideally done in three or four days—one or two to get there (minimum nine hours), a day at the site and a day (six hours) to return. However, if you're short of time, it can in theory be done in two days on horseback. If you decide to go to this unique spot, take plenty of food and water and be prepared for all weathers. Saimaly Tash's bizarre microclimate makes early August to early September the best time to go.

The best way to reach the ancient site is through **CBT** in **Kazarman** or **Jalal-Abad**. They will provide suitable transport, a guide, horses and food; they cannot yet hire out camping gear but might be able to in future—check with the Bishkek office. **CBT Arslanbob** offers a longer trek from the village to Saimaly Tash, taking seven to ten days.

Coming from Jalal-Abad, the journey to Saimaly Tash begins at Dmitrievka village about 50 kilometres from Jalal-Abad on the Kazarman road. Turn south to Kalmak Kirchin where locals will direct you to the honey farm (*pasik* in Russian), some 20

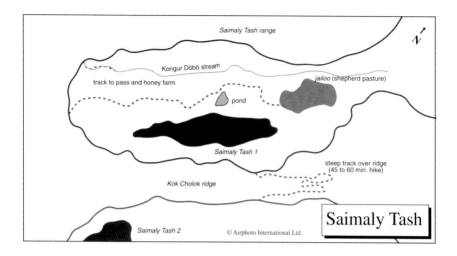

Saimaly Tash range

Kongur Döbö stream

track to pass and honey farm

jailoo (shepherd pasture)

pond

Saimaly Tash 1

steep track over ridge
(45 to 60 min. hike)

Kok Cholok ridge

Saimaly Tash 2

© Airphoto International Ltd.

Saimaly Tash

kilometres east of the village. You'll need a four-wheel drive. The people at the farm might be able to arrange a guide and horses for your trek. The packhorse will be ridden across deep, fast-flowing rivers. The hike takes you through Kok Art and Aubek river canyons.

KAZARMAN TO JALAL-ABAD

This poorly maintained 177-kilometre road across the Fergana mountain range is considerably rougher than the road from Naryn to Kazarman and is completely impassable for much of the year, sometimes closing as early as the end of August and re-opening as late as the end of May.

The road is a six-hour roller-coaster ride through red sandstone hills. At times the road hugs the mountainside, its outer edge crumbling into the void. If you're in a taxi you'll probably do no more than 30–40 kilometres per hour for the first two hours. Once over the 3,100-metre Sarygyr pass, however, the going gets much easier and your driver releases the breath he has held for the last two hours.

Once over the pass, pretty fertile valleys, with lots of rest stops and koumys stalls, give way to farms, fields of wheat, tobacco and potatoes, and acres of bright yellow sunflowers, the first sign that you have left the high mountains far behind. Hives of bees, walnut trees, apple orchards, the hot sun and houses with high triangular lofts for storing hay all reinforce the sense that you have entered a different land.

SHYRDAKS

The colourful felt carpets known as *shyrdaks* and seen all over Kyrgyzstan, are deeply rooted in nomadic culture and date back thousands of years. Portable, practical and light, they are used for both decoration and insulation.

Today, carpets made from thick, appliquéd felt (*shyrdaks*) and pressed felt (*ala-kiyiz*) offer the most tangible aspect of Kyrgyz culture. Whereas silverwork has disappeared, leatherwork is practised by only a minority, and traditional Kyrgyz embroidery designs have been pushed aside by Uzbek, Ukrainian and Russian motifs, *shyrdaks* and *ala-kiyiz* are still found in every home, just as they were 2,000 years ago.

A shyrdak is made from panels of felt, each with a stylized motif, sewn together and edged with braid. Traditionally just two colours were used but artificial dyes introduced in the 1960s have led to bold, vibrant, multicoloured *shyrdaks*. In the past, the motifs used (usually stylized representations of animals or plants) held symbolic meaning, although it is likely that interpretations varied from region to region. For example, meanings given for the kochkor mujaz, or ram's horn motif, include male potency and wealth (because a rich man has many sheep), while ram's horns used all the way around the carpet signifies a protection against evil. A bird's foot design is said to indicate a wish for happiness. Today, however, symbolic meanings have mostly been lost and people use traditional designs because their grandmothers did, not for their symbolic value.

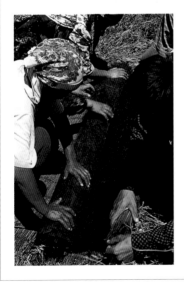

The process of making a shyrdak is laborious so groups of women work together. The first stage is to clean the wool by spreading it over a wire mesh. Two women crouch on either side and beat the wool with long thin poles so that dirt falls to the ground; this takes at least one full day.

Pressing and rolling shyrdak,
Kazarman

Layers of wool, which may have already been dyed, are then spread out on a reed mat woven from a local grass, *chiy*, and boiling water is poured over it. The mat is rolled up into a long sausage shape and tied with ropes; this is then rolled, stamped and trodden upon for two or three hours to meld the wool into one layer. The mat is unrolled, boiling water is poured over the wool a second time, and the mat is rolled up for a second time. This time, the women kneel in a row and roll the mat with their arms for about half an hour; many *shyrdak-*  makers have friction burns on their arms during the summer months when *shyrdaks* are made. Finally, the mat is unrolled and the wool left to dry.

Patterns are drawn on the felt using chalk or soap and then cut out. These are stitched together in a stiff appliqué style and attached to a piece of backing felt. No felt is wasted; the pattern's 'shadow' image will be used in another carpet, resulting in two carpets that are mirror images of each other.

Some of the best quality *shyrdaks* in Kyrgyzstan today are being made at the Altyn Oimok (Golden Thimble) workshop in Bokonbaeva, on the south shore of Lake Issyk Kul. This innovative community project is led by artist Zulaika Riskeldieva and can be found at 69/70 Kyrgyzskaya, tel. (03947) 93121, 91590. Its mission is to provide work for single women and those with large families. It has a core staff of ten with a further 32 women working from home and makes *shyrdaks*, *ala-kiyiz* and other felt goods from slippers to bags, mainly to order or for sale at the Kyrgyz Style shop in Bishkek. Other examples of innovative shyrdak design may be found around Naryn, Kochkor and At-Bashy. The museum at Naryn also has interesting examples.

As part of its community remit, Golden Thimble buys all its wool from local farmers. White wool is the most prized and expensive, at $0.80 per kilo it is twice as much as brown or black wool. The centre uses bright artificial dyes but is also experimenting with natural plant pigments, which last longer than synthetic colours. Ironically, *shyrdaks* made using the old natural pigments are now considered 'modern' in Kyrgyzstan because they are popular with tourists.

(above) Golden Thread shyrdak at the co-operative in Bokonbaeva

The Kyrgyz Fergana Valley

The Fergana valley is the huge flood plain of the Syr Darya river. The bulk of the valley, 300 kilometres long and 170 kilometres wide, belongs to Uzbekistan and is claimed as the Uzbek heartland. The valley is an agricultural oasis and is crammed with 20 per cent of Central Asia's entire population. It is also the most firmly Islamic part of Kyrgyzstan. The icy crowns of Kyrgyzstan's mountains tower around this green gem. Kyrgyz territory abuts the frilly, indeterminate border on three sides, hugging the lowlands of the Fergana range to the east, the Pamir Alay to the south and the Chatkal range to the north. This is the most populous region of Kyrgyzstan, supporting 100 people per square kilometre (compared to the national average of 25). This seat of ancient culture is soaked in history. Sultan Babur (1483–1530), a military genius who loved learning, was not alone amongst travellers to herald it a charmed land of beautiful people, its meadows sweet with flowers, its slopes rich with fruit and nut forests.

Bronze Age peoples settled around Osh's Suleiman mountain, farming the land and working stone and metal. Over 2,000 years ago, the Sogdian Davan Kingdom of Fergana was famed for its 'heavenly' horses; elegant and speedy, and said to be relatives of today's equally prized Akhalteke horses of Turkmenistan. Their images are found in rock carvings in the Aravan valley and on Mount Suleiman, as well as along the Chinese Silk Road. The Fergana valley supported one of the main branches of the Silk Route.

From the 10th to 11th centuries, the Turkic Karakhanid empire built an elegant local capital at Ozgon, then called Mavarannahr. Sultan Babur, great-great-great grandson of Timur, who was born at Andijan in 1483, inherited the throne at Osh at the age of 12. Banished by the Uzbek Shaibanids in 1504, he travelled to India where he founded the Mogul empire but was forever haunted by nostalgia for his homeland.

From 1747, the Kokand khanate ruled the whole of the Fergana valley, before being crushed by the Russians, who claimed the lands as their own. As Soviet aggression succeeded Russian colonisation, the Fergana valley erupted into the *basmachi* (anti-revolutionary bandit) movement (see page 25). In 1924, Joseph Stalin's divide and rule tactic devised today's unlikely jigsaw of borders, carving up the valley into the states of Uzbekistan, Tajikistan and Kyrgyzstan. These borders were never taken seriously until their governments began to fortify them in 1991, leaving islands of Uzbek territory adrift in a Kyrgyz sea. With Moscow's coffers in mind (and little regard for the balance of nature), the gentle beauty of the Fergana valley was churned up, irrigated and marshalled into the annual production of thousands of tons of cotton and 'Hero of Socialist Labour' awards were showered down on farmers of the silver fleece.

The cotton monoculture of the region is neither economically viable for the new republics nor environmentally sustainable. The inability of the new regimes to maintain irrigation systems has led to their collapse in many areas, particularly in highland regions, leaving whole settlements literally high and dry. As a result, many industries stand derelict and whole communities are unemployed. The result has been large-scale migration; for example, 70 per cent of the inhabitants of Kara Kulja village, which was entirely dependent on irrigation for all its water, have moved away in the last ten years. The Fergana valley is the site of most of Kyrgyzstan's mineral and oil wealth. These were located, according to the Soviet journalist Victor Vitkovich, with the help of the Soviet Kyrgyz press, who appealed to the people in the 1930s to come forward with information on the whereabouts of the country's oil and mineral reserves. The coal mine at Kyzyl Kiya (named 'Red Uphill Road' for its red cliffs) was renowned as a hotbed of regional propaganda, held responsible for spreading the Bolshevik word amongst the nomads of the region.

A large part of Fergana's fascination lies in its colourful mix of nationalities—Uzbeks, Kyrgyz, Tajiks, Kurds and Uighurs, to name just a few. But this, combined with its geographical position, also makes it one of Kyrgyzstan's most unstable areas. Ethnic unrest is exacerbated by unemployment, poor housing, population pressure and poverty, combined with the failure of the government to ensure fair and even distribution of land and resources. About 40 per cent of the population of Kyrgyzstan's Fergana territory is Uzbek; people who report feeling like outsiders in Kyrgyzstan but who are considered Kyrgyz by Uzbeks in Uzbekistan. All of these destabilising influences make people more susceptible to the influence of Islamic extremism from the south.

The Fergana region's physical isolation, both from trade routes and the power centre of the country, exacerbates the feeling of insecurity and discontent. However, this should improve following the opening of the Irkeshtam border post in late 2002, thus restoring the traditional trade route between the Fergana valley and Kashgar in China. Even the construction of a railway line between the two has also been mooted.

Osh

Osh is the oldest city in Kyrgyzstan and proudly celebrated its 3,000th birthday in October 2000. An important regional centre, around 1,000 metres above sea level, it is only five kilometres from the Uzbek border and retains a distinctly international feel; you'd be forgiven for thinking yourself, if not quite in Uzbekistan, then certainly not entirely in Kyrgyzstan either. The population of 300,000, predominantly Uzbek, is a fabulous mix of peoples. A market town to its very heart, its bazaar has apparently occupied the same spot on the banks of the Akbura river for 2,000 years.

The rich history of the oasis lies hidden beneath the avenues of socialism and little remains to be seen. History's cultures, religions and wars have disappeared from memory. The founding of the city is variously attributed to Alexander the Great, the Prophet Suleiman and even Biblical Adam. The most enduring tale is of Suleiman who, when he reached the blade of rock at its centre, shouted 'khosh' ('that's enough').

Osh was an important crossroad on the Silk Routes, rewarding camel caravans who survived the journey over the high passes of the Pamir Alay to the south and of the Central Tien Shan to the east. Their cargo of exotic items included silk from China, lazurite from modern Tajikistan, sweets and dyes from India and silver goods from Iran. Nothing remains of the palace, courts and academies destroyed in the 13th century by the armies of Jenghis Khan. Before the Russian revolution, Osh was the largest city in Kyrgyzstan, with 34,200 people, five times that of Pishpek (modern Bishkek).

Osh hit the headlines more recently during an outbreak of savage fighting between Uzbeks and Kyrgyz in June and July 1990. The hub of the discord was Ozgon but residents of both towns witnessed atrocities that they have since tried to forget. The official death toll of 300 is overshadowed by local estimates of over 1,000. The violence was ostensibly sparked off by a decision to reallocate the lands of an Uzbek-dominated collective farm to ethnic Kyrgyz; however, locals report that Russian police and militia stood idle during the violence. Both sides are inclined to believe that the riots were started by outsiders. Today there are no outward signs of tension and both Kyrgyz and Uzbeks are keen to stress that they live happily as neighbours and that inter-marriage between ethnic groups is common. In reality, an uneasy truce exists, in which both sides

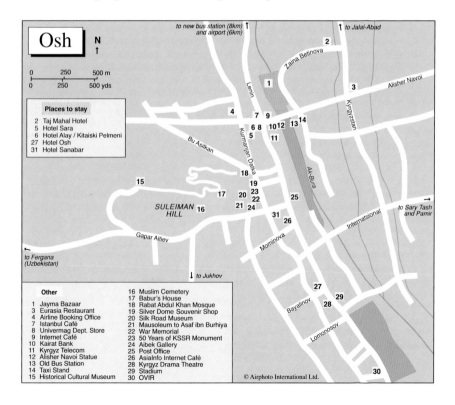

Osh

N ↑

0   250   500 m
0   250   500 yds

to new bus station (8km) ↑
and airport (6km)

↑ to Jalal-Abad

Places to stay
2 Taj Mahal Hotel
5 Hotel Sara
6 Hotel Alay / Kitaiski Pelmeni
27 Hotel Osh
31 Hotel Sanabar

SULEIMAN HILL

to Fergana
(Uzbekistan)

to Sary Tash
and Pamir

↓ to Jukhov

Other
1 Jayma Bazaar
3 Eurasia Restaurant
4 Airline Booking Office
7 Istanbul Café
8 Univermag Dept. Store
9 Internet Café
10 Kairat Bank
11 Kyrgyz Telecom
12 Alisher Navoi Statue
13 Old Bus Station
14 Taxi Stand
15 Historical Cultural Museum

16 Muslim Cemetery
17 Babur's House
18 Rabat Abdul Khan Mosque
19 Silver Dome Souvenir Shop
20 Silk Road Museum
21 Mausoleum to Asaf ibn Burhiya
22 War Memorial
23 50 Years of KSSR Monument
24 Aibek Gallery
25 Post Office
26 AsiaInfo Internet Café
28 Kyrgyz Drama Theatre
29 Stadium
30 OVIR

© Airphoto International Ltd.

fear a recurrence of violence. Whether they will be able to give up fruitless ethnic bickering for peaceful cohabitation remains a crucial issue for both local and national politics.

The centrepiece of Osh is Suleiman's Throne, a rocky mountain spine that juts out of the plain, seeming to have taken one step too far from its mountainous friends. Kyrgyzstan's second biggest city flows around the base of the hill. Sultan Babur (1483–1530) nostalgically described the city in his memoirs:

> Orchards follow the river on either bank, the trees overhanging the water. Pretty violets grow in the gardens. Osh has running water. It is lovely there in the spring when countless tulips and roses burst into blossom. In the Fergana valley no town can match Osh for the fragrance and purity of the air.

(above) Selling fruit at Osh bazaar
(below) Statue of Kurmanjan Datka

The Soviets took this last point seriously and built a convalescent rest home on its outskirts. Despite the city's antiquity, it is startlingly, relentlessly Soviet. Nevertheless, it is also a city of irrepressible Central Asian colour: flower stalls line the streets, the rainbow patterns of *atlas* silk are visible everywhere and luxuriant mountains of fruits and vegetables fill the bazaar in summer. It is well worth pausing in Osh a couple of days for its rich history, eclectic mix of peoples and to visit one of the best bazaars west of Kashgar.

Osh is a transit point for those travelling to or from Uzbekistan and a jumping-off for the valleys north of Osh and for trekking and mountaineering in the mighty Pamir Alay. You can also travel to Kashgar via the Irkeshtam Pass.

SIGHTS

SULEIMAN'S THRONE

Sacred **Suleiman's Throne** (Tacht-i-Suleiman) is the biggest of five mounds of barren limestone and quartz rock. Known as *Bara-Kuh* ('Beautiful Mountain') until the 16th century, the hill was renamed when the Muslim prophet Suleiman prayed (and some say was buried) here. It has since become one of the holiest places in Central Asia, nicknamed *Kichi-Mecca* ('Little Mecca'). The rock is bedecked with 'handkerchief' trees; tying a piece of cloth to a tree or bush is believed to bring good luck.

Pilgrims come from all over the region. Even for non-Muslims it is worth the climb to **Babur's Mosque**. Start your walk at the chrome-domed souvenir shop on Kurmanjan Datka and go through the archway to climb up the long, steep flight of steps. A 20-minute climb takes you to the top of the hill to Babur's Mosque, which marks the spot where the 14-year-old Babur first built a shelter for his *chilla*—a 40-day retreat of silent meditation with just bread and water. The shelter has been rebuilt twice, first after an earthquake in 1853 and most recently in the 1990s, after it was destroyed in 1961 by an explosion, which locals blame on the vigorous Soviet 'anti-superstition' campaign. An old Sufi will tell you stories about the place in Uzbek or Russian for a few som.

All manner of legends are attached to the hill: a tiny cave on the main path around the mount is said to have curative properties. Pilgrims come to pray there, especially in spring. Pilgrims shuffle inside, placing hands and knees in the assigned rocky dips, polished smooth by centuries of devotees. Holy men recite passages from the Koran in exchange for about US$0.50.

Legend has it that if you roll down the inclined slab of limestone at the summit you will be cured of all bodily ills. Due to the shape of the hill (said to resemble a reclining pregnant woman) some believe it to help with fertility problems, especially if you whiz down 'fertility slide' nine times!

The north face of the mount has 2,000–3,000-year-old rock carvings, depicting horses, ibex and Marco Polo sheep. Unfortunately, trying to find them is virtually a lost cause, due to the amount of graffiti. Your best bet is to look out for the blue numbers slapped on the stone, often on top of the ancient rock carvings themselves!

HISTORICAL CULTURAL MUSEUM

Open Weds–Sun, 9am–8pm (closed for lunch 12.30–1.30pm), entrance US$1.5
The steps on the south side of the hill take you down to the Historical Cultural Museum. It is housed in a cave, blasted out of the holy mountain with typical Soviet disdain. This museum has great potential, but would be vastly improved with better lighting and English translations. Of most interest are the photo exhibits and artefacts relating to local shamans and the different religions practised in Osh, past and present. Islam, Buddhism, Zoroastrianism and water faiths are presented in a respectful tone. You would get more out of the visit by bringing an English-speaking guide.

SILK ROAD MUSEUM

Kurmanjan Datka. Open 9am–6pm daily (closed for lunch 12–1pm), entrance US$1.5, English-speaking guide US$1.5. Additional charges for cameras and camcorders.

At the base of the mountain is the excellent Silk Road Museum (also known as the Cultural Museum), which opened in early 2001 to mark Osh's 3,000-year anniversary in October 2000. Exhibits are well presented (in Kyrgyz and Russian only). A photo exhibition in the entrance hall describes different aspects of life in the city. A big attraction is the broad perspective on the history of the region, covering three millennia. Archaeological artefacts, guarded by fiercely keen attendants, include Bronze Age implements and vessels, petroglyphs from Saimaly Tash, 11th and 12th century clay dishes and beautiful, glazed, azure medieval tiles. There is a measured section devoted to the Russian colonial era. There is an interesting map detailing the Kyrgyz tribes and clans. Among an abundance of exhibits relating to *manaschi*, felt handicrafts, traditional Kyrgyz songs and horseback games, it is easy to forget the region's ethnic diversity. There is a three-storey yurt in the yard.

OTHER SIGHTS

The **Mosque** of **Rabat Abdullah Khan**, built in the 16th century, lies at the foot of Suleiman's Throne, near the aforementioned silver-domed shop. One of the main places of worship in Osh, 1,000 people regularly pray here. Enter through the wooden doorways, carved with traditional Uzbek skill, to the courtyard. Men may visit three rooms with permission—cover your limbs and remove shoes; women are no longer allowed to visit the mosque.

Following the road from the Historical Cultural Museum down towards the huge Muslim cemetery, the **Aibek Gallery** is on your left on Gapar Aitiev near the Asaf Ibn Burhiya Mausoleum. The gallery, dedicated to Kyrgyz painter Gapar Aitiev (1912–84) who was born in Osh, sells paintings of varying quality, as well as art books and Russian dolls. Behind is an art college.

Lenin still occupies the **main square**, along with Kurmanjan Datka, the Kyrgyz woman general who was instrumental in liberating the Fergana valley from the Kokand khanate.

Plenty of **handicraft** outlets huddle around the Navoi/Lenina crossroads near Jayma Bazaar. Particularly recommended is **Saltanat Gallery**, tel. (03222) 24259 for its wide range of high quality artefacts.

JAYMA BAZAAR

In the north of the town, the huge **Jayma Bazaar** straddles the river. One of the best markets west of Kashgar, today it pulsates to the sounds of a vigorous trading town as buyer and seller try to outwit one another. Aurally and visually, it's very much a Central Asian mix of trading and nomadic traditions, where Soviet intrusions—the tannoy, the concrete, the music—are just a veneer. Among the green and orange headscarves of the

Pilgrims feasting at the foot of Solomon's Throne

women rise pyramids of fresh and dried fruit. There are hats for every occasion; traditional Kyrgyz felt *kalpaks*; Uzbek hats of colourful velvet, glinting with inlaid stones and mirrors; Uighur hats looking much like a 1930s European cap; and Russian fur hats for winter. Outside the bazaar, old *babushki* ('grandmothers') display their belongings on a cloth on the dust or ice, hoping to make enough for a few more meals—it helps them out to buy matches, pens or sweets.

Warning—Pickpockets are at work around the bazaar as are increasing numbers of beggars. Most are alcoholics, street kids, Tajik refugees and, perhaps the most sincere, elderly Slavs who cannot survive on an irregularly paid pension of US$3 a month. A small donation to an old person is money well spent; the children are often sent begging by alcoholic parents.

OSH PRACTICAL INFORMATION

ACCOMMODATION

Hotel Osh Nuru: 1 Bayalinova (next door to Drama Theatre). Tel. (03222) 57860, 24717; fax. 56326; email: osh_inturist@mail.ru. Previously the decaying Soviet-era Hotel Osh, the new complex includes restaurant, conference facilities, casino, a shopping mall and a Kyrygz Concept office (see below). Opposite the hotel, Demir bank cashes travellers' cheques and gives credit card cash advances. Plush but pricey rooms from US$24 per person B&B.

Hotel Crystal: 50a Navoi, (between two entrances to main bazaar). Tel. (03222) 20447, 73896; fax. 73894. Central hotel with clean, well-furnished rooms, some with en suite. Restaurant, conference facilities and casino. B&B per person from US$14.

TES Guesthouse: 5 Soyboyu. Tel. (03222) 21548; email: ghouse@list.ru Funding TES agricultural development projects, this comfortable and friendly guesthouse is done out in national style with clean en suite rooms and internet, in a quiet part of town. B&B from US$35. Very popular—book in advance.

Askar Guesthouse: two locations: 81 Nizami. Tel. (03222) 56229, mob. (0772) 324325; email: adil.kazakbaev@mail.ru; and on corner Nukatskaya/Lenina. This small, comfortable guesthouse, though pricey, fills up quickly so it's necessary to book in advance. B&B from US$30.

Guesthouse Barak Ata: 22/1 Sultan Ibraimov; tel. (03222) 55532, mob. (0772) 294941. This high quality guesthouse a little out of town is comfortable and cosy, with clean en suite rooms, sauna, satellite TV and business centre. B&B from US$25 per person.

ISLAND HOPPING
IN SOUTHERN KYRGYZSTAN

A striking feature of the map of southern Kyrgyzstan is its complex political geography and, especially, its 'archipelago' of enclaves. There are, in fact, seven of them in all. Some are little more than a former collective farm and its attached arable land. Others have real demographic and geo-political significance.

The largest of these, both in size and population, is Sokh, an autonomous district belonging to neighbouring Uzbekistan. It covers 325 square kilometres and has a 99 per cent Tajik population of 42,300. The only Uzbeks here are civil servants and the military from Tashkent. East of Sokh lies the mountainous enclave of Shahimardan, also Uzbek territory, and 91 per cent Uzbek. To the west, triangular-shaped Vorukh belongs to Tajikistan, with a population 95 per cent Tajik and 5 per cent Kyrgyz. The economies of all three enclaves rely heavily on agriculture and cross-border irrigation systems.

But how did such a bizarre geographic mosaic come into being? The classic answer is: 'Stalin's divide and rule policy'. Although this is partly the case, the story is somewhat more complex and shrouded in mystery. Officially, it was a matter of the distribution of irrigated land according to the needs of the different republics. But in reality, much had to do with the personal politics of the native Soviet leadership of the 1920s.

Jyldyz Akunbabaev, the first Soviet leader of Uzbekistan, was from Margilan in the Uzbek Fergana valley and had blood ties in the present-day enclaves. He was on good terms with his Kyrgyz colleague, Yusup Abdrakhmanova, who came from the Jalal-Abad area. It is believed that the men 'traded' the enclaves (where Akunbabaev had his kinfolk) for Jalal-Abad (where Abdrakhmanova had his roots), a predominantly Uzbek city that is still part of Kyrgyzstan today.

As one British observer put it, 'these enclaves show that history is sometimes more a matter of personal interest and negotiations around a bowl of plov in a *chaikana*, than of any geo-political master plan.'

The Batyrovs: 9/1 Suyunbaeva. Tel. (03222) 24846, mob. (03222) 59336. Small, comfortable guesthouse mostly with shared facilities. B&B US$35.

Hotel Jukhov: three locations—20a Amir Temur. Tel. (03222) 20072; email: ladaosh@mail.ru; 40 Alymbaeva. Tel. (03222) 27576; and 8 Tashkentskaya. Tel. (03222) 52328; email: stairk1961@mail.ru. Clean and friendly guesthouses, rooms have shared bathroom for US$30.

Hotel Alay: 280 Kurmanjan Datka (on corner of Navoi). Tel. (03222) 57733. Centrally located near a wide choice of cafés, rooms are clean but simple. B&B from US$9.

Hotel Sara: 278a Kurmanjan Datka. Tel. (03222) 22559. Central, friendly budget hotel above a café. Clean rooms with cheerful décor from US$7.

Hotel Sanabar: 9a Gapar Atiev (near Aravansky). Tel. (03222) 25437. Clean and simple budget option with shared bathrooms. From US$14 (no breakfast).

Hotel Jetigen: Kyrgyzstana, tel. (03222) 39910. This pleasant, modern hotel is on the ground floor of Osh's tallest building (12 storeys) near Jayma bazaar. En suite rooms cost US$16 B&B. Staff speak English and there is a sauna.

CBT Osh will arrange homestays for you in the area. Contact Asyel Ikramova, mob: (0502) 574940; email: osh_cbt@mail.ru.

FOOD

Osh's eateries are plentiful but menus vary very little. *Chaikhanas* and restaurants are concentrated around the crossroads of Navoi and Lenina and music pulsates from the brightly lit (and expensive) cafés on Kyrgyzstana. Of the former, the **Istanbul Bakery** at 22 Navoi is recommended, particularly for beefburgers, pastries and baklava. Aptly named **Richmen** on Kurmanjan Datka has good, if pricey, food and some western dishes; for a Turkish hookah and splendid outdoor eating, **Bravo Art Café** is a block down the road. For more moderate prices, the friendly **California Café**, 3/1 Suleimanova, has good pizza and pasta dishes.

Next door, **Bermet** is highly recommended for laghman and other traditional dishes, while **Naizima** on Lenina is the place for *rotisserie*. **Adanajde**, opposite the Stadium on Lenina, is a pricey Korean restaurant with in-house disco. Other restaurants with night-clubs attached are Buzeinep next to the Lenin statue in Toktogul Park, **Stelles** next door and **Parliament** on Lenina. **Nirvana Pub and Brewery** has a relaxing ambience and sells home-brewed beer alongside tasty western dishes. Bizarrely, in spite of increased trade with China, the city's only Chinese restaurant has closed.

COMMUNICATION

Osh has numerous internet cafés, most with **international telephone**, charging as little as 5 som (US$0.14) per minute for calls to Europe and the US (look for a sign for 'IP phone'). **Explorer** and **Cobweb** on Suleimanova near California Café are recommended, and there are many more along Kurmanjan Datka near Suleiman mountain. **KyrgyzTelecom**, which also has good rates, is on Lenina; goods can be mailed from here or DHL is at 44 Kyrgyzstana.

MONEY AND RED TAPE

A plethora of banks around Osh, mainly on Kyrgyzstana near the bazaar, will change money. For slightly more attractive rates but greater risk, **money changing** booths cluster around the edge of Jayma bazaar on Zaina Betinova. Beware of tricks that leave you a dollar or two short. Your best bet for changing travellers cheques and credit card cash advances is the Demir Bank at 180a Kurmanjan Datka, opposite Hotel Osh Nuru; and one of three branches of the **Commercial Bank of Kyrgyzstan**—119 Kurmanjan Datka, 312 Lenina and 28/34 Kyrgyzstana. **Eko Bank** and **Dos Bank** also offer Western Union services.

For those who need to register with **OVIR** (see page 76), the office is on the ground floor of 199 Lenina St (Mon–Fri, 8am–7pm, closed for lunch, Sat 10am–1pm). Enter on the north side of the building and it is the first door on your right. Munduz will organise registration for you.

TOUR OPERATORS

Kyrgyz Nur (formerly Alptreksport): 277/8 Lenina; tel. (03222) 24095, 23042; mob. (0555) 127647, (0543) 823709; email: kyrgyznur@rambler.ru.

Brothers Yuri and Alexander Lavrushin, competent Sovintersport veterans, formerly worked at the Pamir International Mountaineering Camp and now offer trekking and mountaineering services in the Pamir Alay and Western Tien Shan (including Sary Chelek). They will also arrange trips into the Chil Ustun caves near Osh. Border permits are needed to visit Kuh-i-Garmo, so book at least four weeks in advance. All equipment can be hired, except sleeping bags. Yuri speaks good English.

Munduz: 1 Sovietskaya. Tel. (03222) 26655, 55500; fax. 55072; email: Munduz_Tourist@hotmail.com. Branch at 180 Kurmanjan Datka, tel. 71700. Bishkek contact: (0312) 540102, mob (0543) 919953.

This is a helpful and established general tour operator, which organises general tours, trekking and rafting, transfers, accommodation and guides in the vicinity.

Kyrgyz Concept: 1 Bayalinova (inside Hotel Osh Nuru complex). Tel. (03222) 59450; email: osh@concept.kg.

A branch of the respected Bishkek operator, see page 82 for their main entry. Here they arrange flight tickets, tours locally and may be able to help you get permits for the Alay valley or Tajikistan.

Nematillo Abdulaziz: tel. (0555) 633643; email: abdulaziz18@gmail.com; nemat-18@mail.ru will organise private or shared cars from Osh to the Irkeshtam pass (nine hours on an appalling road), to Murghab in Tajikistan (13 hours)—both these trips preferably involve a night in Sary Tash. Tashkent is just six hours away—change cars at the border. He will arrange trips around Osh and might also be able to help you get a GBAO permit for Tajikistan.

CBT Osh, contact Asyel Ikramova, mob (0502) 574940; email: osh_cbt@mail.ru, can arrange transport and tours locally and might be able to help you book with CBT contacts in the Alay valley.

Chyngyz Myrbek Ametov offers interpretation andguiding services in English and French, as well as transport and excursions within Kyrgyzstan, Tajikistan, Uzbekistan and China. Tel. (03222) 33605; email: oshchyngyz@rambler.ru; oshchyngyz@mail.ru.

TRANSPORT

Flights to Bishkek run five to seven times daily, to Sharjah in the United Arab Emirates on Wednesday and Saturday, to Issyk Kul (near Cholpon Ata) on Tuesday and Friday during the summer only. From 6 November 2007 China Southern Airlines will fly on Tuesday and Friday between Osh and Urumqi in China's Xinjiang province. You can fly to Moscow on Monday, Tuesday, Thursday and Friday, returning overnight on Monday, Wednesday, Thursday and Sunday. Kyrgyzstan Airlines runs flights between Osh and Dushanbe on Sunday. The airport is 20 minutes out of town and is served by minibuses No 7A, which will take you past the bazaar and up Kyrgyzstana Street, and No 2 which passes along Lenin St. Catch minibuses heading for the airport in front of KyrgyzTele-com on Lenina or on Navoi. The Kyrgyz Airlines (*Ak Zhol*) office is inconveniently situated at 14 Razzakova. You can book Altyn Air tickets through Sputnik A travel agency (30 Kyrgyzstana St, tel. (03222) 29963; or 314 Lenina St (tel. 03222) 55490.

Minibuses and taxis leave from the **bus station** opposite Jayma bazaar for Bishkek (12–15 hours), Jalal-Abad (two hours), Ozgon (1.5 hours), Sary Tash and Daraut-Korgon in the Alay valley (five and seven hours respectively), and Batken (eight hours). You can also get taxis to Uzbekistan from here, but it's inadvisable to say you are heading for Andijan. Change to an Uzbek taxi at the border. You will need an Uzbek visa. Taxis will also take you to the busy bazaar at Kara Suu on the Uzbek border, held on Tuesdays and Saturdays.

Taxis to Batken (US$23 per vehicle) leave from the square near Alay Hotel on Navoi.

The **new bus station** is bizarrely located eight kilometres out of town and is reached by the 7A and 142 minibuses. Big buses leave here for Jalal-Abad, Ozgon, Batken, Kerben (near Lake Sary Chelek), Toktogul and Tash Kumyr (also for Sary Chelek). Buses to Kashgar in China via the Irkeshtam Pass (US$50, 24 hours) leave from here but the schedule is unreliable—check days and times before you travel. There are currently no buses into Tajikistan.

Nematillo Abdulaziz will organise cost-effective private transport—see Tour Operators above.

AROUND OSH

THE ARAVAN VALLEY AND CHIL USTUN

Remains of Fergana's long history include the **rock carvings of the Aravan valley** and the awe-inspiring Chil-Ustun caves nearby. There is only one problem; both are difficult if not impossible to find on your own. The rock carvings of the fabled 'heavenly' Fergana horse, said to date back 2,000 years, are visible only from people's back gardens and lie on south-facing cliffs where the sun makes them difficult to spot. However, the determined need not be foiled and may, with some effort and luck, discover engravings of horses and sheep. To do so, about 28 kilometres from Osh on the road through the Aravan valley, look out for a yellow arched wooden doorway on the right which gives onto a path lined with trees on one side and houses on the other. Cross a bridge towards a small rocky cliff ahead. There is a spring (dry in summer) and a shelter for pilgrims. The rock carvings can be seen high up on the cliff.

Chil-Ustun is the name given collectively to an extensive system of caves in the limestone hills near the Aravan valley. There are about 200 caves altogether, scattered across about 200 square kilometres in the almond-grove flat lands of the Ak-Bura and Aryan river basin. Most are inaccessible without a guide and ropes. Their Tajik name means 'forty columns' and derives from the caves' numerous stalactites and stalagmites. Several dozen large caves are said to measure more than 100 metres in length.

The main cave is, confusingly, itself called Chil-Ustun, and is found on the southern slope of a mountain also called Chil-Ustun. This cave consists of three large chambers connected to each other by narrow, winding passages. The first and last chambers are said to be full of light pink stalagmites and chandeliers of stalactites made of aragonite, a delicate, brittle, calcium carbonate mineral. The first chamber is 380 metres deep and contains many ancient drawings and inscriptions in various languages, including Sanskrit. The second chamber, only discovered in the 1960s, contained two skeletons. The third chamber can feel claustrophobic. A visit to the caves requires ropes and torches although apparently you do not need climbing skills to reach them.

This whole area has yet to be made accessible to the casual visitor: trips here are for the adventurous only and need to be arranged with Alptreksport or Munduz in Osh.

APSHIRSAY

Apshirsay is a valley in the foothills of the Kichi ('Small') Alay, 70 kilometres from Osh on the Batken road. A day trip from Osh can take you to the source of the Apshirsay river, which gushes from the rock some 30 metres above the ground. The waterfall is believed to be holy and curative (particularly for skin problems) and attracts pilgrims and local tourists. People stand in the spray or collect the water in a bottle to drink.

In a sacred cave nearby a holy man leads prayers from the Koran. He tells the legend (in Kyrgyz) of Idris Payganbar who allegedly turned the water to milk, and back again, 2,000 years ago. Locals say the water still tastes of milk.

Detail on minaret, Ozgon

Ozgon

The small town of Ozgon nestles on the banks of the Kara-Darya river, where the Fergana and Pamir mountain ranges converge. The area is 80 per cent Uzbek but until now the Kyrgyz have held political power. Ozgon was known by its Soviet name Uzgen until its designation was changed to conform to Kyrgyz language spelling rules. The town is known for vicious fighting between Kyrgyz and Uzbek in June and July 1990. Not many people are willing to speak about that violence but it is still fresh in their minds (see the Osh section, page 232). Coal mining used to provide employment in the Ozgon basin but poverty is now widespread, especially among the elderly.

Ozgon is an ancient settlement, mentioned as the town of Yu in the Chinese chronicles of the second century BC. More tangible glory dates from its time as Mavarannahr, a capital of the Karakhanid Dynasty, whose vast loose-knit empire ruled the region from 999 until razed by Jenghis Khan in the 13th century. Three mausoleums and a minaret are the lone relics of this cultured epoch. Standing slightly apart from the bustle of the 21st century, their position amongst the graves of their kings is dramatic against the red earth and the rise of the mountains beyond. As the 1950s Russian traveller Victor Vitkovich puts it, 'every detail of the architecture is made carefully with the delicate skill of a jeweller as though they were headpieces of ancient Eastern manuscripts'.

The mausoleums are exquisite, with engraving on terracotta slabs and relief work of up to three centimetres in depth. Intricately worked terracotta foliage swirls over doorways, pillars and facades, competing with geometric patterns and bold calligraphy. The southern mausoleum is said to be the basis on which Samarkand's tomb complex, Shah-i-Zinda, was created. The 20-metre minaret stands slightly aloof from the complex and boasts bands of fine brickwork. To find them, leave the market through the tiled gateway, walk down the road towards the bus station, and take the first left. When you come to a silver Lenin and a row of Soviet heroes you will see the site to your right.

Extremely low-grade accommodation is on offer at the **Hotel Ozgon** at 2 Gagarina Street (US$3.5 per twin room, some with washbasins but there are no working toilets in the hotel); it is better to go as a day trip from Osh or en route to Jalal-Abad.

The **bus station** on Manas Street has daily buses, minibuses and taxis to Osh, Jalal-Abad, Kara Suu and Bishkek (US$23 per taxi, divide by four if sharing).

AROUND OZGON

The village of **Ak-Terek**, north-east of Ozgon on the Yassiy river, offers homestay and trekking opportunities thanks to the UK-funded Sustainable Livelihoods for Livestock Producing Communities Project. This excellent, new initiative gives adventurous tourists access to rural Kyrgyzstan and brings much needed income into villages.

Possibilities include treks on foot or horseback along the Yassiy river through gorges lined with walnut trees and *jailoos* bordered by ancient poplars. The Kara-Shoro ('black salty water') National Park 50 kilometres or so away has mineral springs, wolves, wild boar and rare ibex. You can also trek to the 4200-metre Shilbiluu pass. Book through SLLPCP's Osh office (see Osh section page 239) or through NoviNomad in Bishkek. There's also a website—kyrgyz-village.com.kg. Alternatively, head for Ak-Terek and ask for Jengish Akmataliev. Double check itineraries before booking treks.

Jalal-Abad Oblast

This warm province in the south of the country borders the greatest valley oasis in Central Asia, the Fergana valley, which stretches more than 300 kilometres in length and 150 kilometres in width and extends over the borders of three republics: Kyrgyzstan, Uzbekistan and Tajikistan. The province is bordered to the east by the 200-kilometre long Fergana mountain range, to the north by the 120-kilometre long Chatkal range and to the south by the Pamirs. Its landscapes range from deserts and semi-arid regions to mountainous steppes; from thick forests (including its famous walnut groves) to mountainous tundra, all overlooked by the eternal glaciers and snowy peaks of its mountains.

Like neighbouring Osh *oblast*, Jalal-Abad has played host to travellers, traders and tourists for thousands of years, although there is little visible archaeological evidence left of this long history, either in its modern capital or in the surrounding area. One of Kyrgyzstan's main Silk Route branches passed through Jalal-Abad, attracting trading caravans carrying precious silk from China, sweets and dyes from India, handmade silverwork from Iran, and lazurite from Badakhshan.

The *oblast*'s capital, Jalal-Abad, lies in the foothills of the Ayub-Too mountains, near the confluence of the Kok Art and Kara Darya rivers, at an altitude of 764 metres above sea level. Like Osh, temperatures are much warmer here than elsewhere in Kyrgyzstan, averaging only minus 4°C to minus 10°C in winter and up to 40°C or 43°C in July on a bad day. The temperate climate and fertile soil means the province grows much of the nation's fruit and vegetables. Enormous fields of tobacco, sunflowers and cotton stretch around villages whose markets are piled high with fruit—melons, figs, plums, pomegranates, oranges, apples—and vegetables in summer. With so much food all around, it's hard to believe that unemployment and poverty are such big problems here.

The mighty Naryn river flows through Jalal-Abad, playing a vital role in the province's hydroelectricity industry. Coal is mined in Jalal-Abad's hills, which are also full of hot mineral springs (about 50 in total). But one of its greatest natural treasures is undoubtedly its ancient forests of wild fruit and nut trees, which are scattered across 230,000 hectares of land. Its 60,000 hectares of walnut groves are particularly important. At 800–1200 metres above sea level, they also contain apple, cherry plum, pistachio and almond trees. Alexander the Great is said to have passed this way, taking specimens of the walnut trees back to Greece. In Russian, walnuts are known as 'Greek nuts'.

The population of Jalal-Abad *oblast* is around 870,000 and is one of the most mixed in the country, comprising about two-thirds Uzbek, most of whom have lived here for generations. The rest are Kyrgyz, Russians, Ukranians, Tajiks, Uighurs, Azerbaijanis and Germans. This rich ethnic mix is more conservative and devoutly Muslim than in northern Kyrgyzstan and people tend to marry earlier and have bigger families. For that reason skimpy clothing, singlets and shorts are really not acceptable in the south.

Poverty and the growing demand for expendable labour has brought a modern form of slavery to Central Asia. In 2000 a small, mainly Uzbek village in Jalal-Abad *oblast* fell victim to a scam promising well-paid work in Kazakhstan. Altogether 82 young people, including three 14-year-olds, left to take up the 'jobs' but when they arrived, their passports were confiscated and they were told they owed their employers US$1,500 in transportation costs, requiring years of work for no wages. Four people escaped to tell their shocking story, which devastated the close-knit village: 'Almost every mother is crying. Sometimes they took two or even three people in one family.'

Jalal-Abad

Most visitors whiz through Jalal-Abad in their haste to reach Osh, which is a shame. This laid-back town of broad avenues, *chaikhanas* and hot mineral springs is well worth a visit and is also the springboard for trips into the primeval walnut forests 80 kilometres away and the Uzbek mountain village of Arslanbob. The town has a long history of attracting travellers. As well as traders passing through on the Silk Routes, sick people and pilgrims have long sought hope and healing from the curative springs of the holy Ayub-Too mountains. It is said that Jalal-Abad is named after Jalal-ad-din, who set up caravanserais and *chaikhanas* to cater for the hundreds of pilgrims who came each year.

In 1878 the Russians set up a garrison in the area, along with a military hospital. Attracted by the rich soil, warm climate and numerous hot springs, some of the servicemen settled here and are the ancestors of today's Jalal-Abad Slavs (the oldest Slavic community in southern Kyrgyzstan). Villages with Slavic names like Arkhangel-skoe and Podgornoe were originally Cossack settlements. Jalal-Abad was later linked to the so-called 'cotton railway' between the Fergana valley and Russia, and developed into an agro-industrial centre producing cotton, wheat, tobacco, walnuts, fruit, vegetables, maize and silk worms. In the Soviet era, it was also a supply centre for the now run-down local coal mining towns of Kok Jangak and Tash Kumyr.

In Soviet times Jalal-Abad was a resort town and people flocked to bathe in the nearby mineral and mud springs. The town is shabbier now but its mixture of peoples (two thirds of the population are Uzbek) gives it a unique and appealing flavour of its own.

SIGHTS

Jalal-Abad is a great place to relax and watch the world go slowly by, especially after the long trip from Naryn or Bishkek. With something like 14 universities, it has a big population of young people, many of whom may be found drinking beer, eating *shashlik*, meat kebabs, or simply chatting in street cafés such as the **Abdikar Ata** on the square on Lenina, with its fountains and huge flat-screen TV. Behind this is one of the town's most popular *chaikhana*. The eclectic **bazaar** on Lenina sells a huge variety of produce, including delicious circles of bread sprinkled with sesame seeds and warm from the oven; *samsi*, light pastry triangles filled with meat; and *manti*, dumplings filled with meat and potato or pumpkin.

Three kilometres and a 15-minute taxi ride away, on the almond-grove slopes of the Ayub-Too mountain, the run-down **Jalal-Abad Sanatorium**, tel. (03722) 23105, has been offering hot mineral baths and medicinal mud treatments for nervous disorders and skin, rheumatoid, kidney and liver complaints since 1879. Now under new management with ambitious plans for the future, its treatments include massage, colonic irrigation and sauna.

JALAL-ABAD PRACTICAL INFORMATION

The best hotel in town is the **Navruz Hotel, Café, and Disco** on Lenina, tel. (03722) 20370. The complex includes a restaurant on three levels, with a DJ from 8pm to midnight and a more locally-flavoured *chaikhana* with excellent Uighur *laghman*. Hotel rooms (from US$25–75) are spacious with spotless modern bathrooms.

Another good hotel is the **Kutbulson Hotel**, tel. (03722) 25711, next door to Jalal-Abad Sanatorium. It opened in 2002 and its modern rooms with TV, fridge, private bathroom and balconies with fabulous views cost US$42/52 singles/doubles. There is a restaurant (handy as it is pretty isolated up there).

Baking bread in a garden of sunflowers, near Arslanbob

Alternatively, the deluxe suites at the **Jalal-Abad Sanatorium**, costing US$35, have an air of faded grandeur. Some are very swanky, with modern private bathrooms, thick carpets and cable TV but they differ wildly in standard.

In Jalal-Abad itself, the **Hotel Molmol**, is on the town's main drag, Lenina, half a block up from its newly renovated, pretty fountain-filled square (tel. (03722) 55059). It is in unusually good condition for a Soviet-style hotel and offers basic but clean rooms from US$8. It houses a casino.

Tagaibe Hotel (Zhenizhok St, Sputnik suburb, (03722) 52187) is said to have basic but clean double rooms with hot water for US$8-14.

Community-Based Tourism has really taken off in Jalal-Abad (see page 292) with eight homestays, mostly of a high standard, for around US10-13 B&B. CBT co-ordinator Rukhsora Abdulaeva, 20 Toktogula, flat 3, tel. (03722) 21962, speaks English. She can arrange the trip to Saimaly Tash and services in Kara-Alma (see below).

There are a huge number of **restaurants** in Jalal-Abad, mostly on Lenina. Highly recommended for its breath-taking views over the city (and dancing on the patio) is **Panorama** near Jalal-Abad Sanatorium. **Sher Muhammed** on Lenina near the bazaar is popular. **Erkindik** (Freedom) on Lenina, next door to Hotel Navruz, is a small western-style café with burritos, pizza, hamburgers and brownies and internet downstairs. See also eateries in Hotel Navruz. **Shimkent**, next to Kurmanbek Stadium, is a popular new bar/pub with a garden, serving draught beers and tasty snacks.

Internet services have mushroomed. The two most reliable are reputedly Titan, on Lenina opposite Jalal-Abad State University, and Imex Business Centre on Lenina, next to Aigul department store. You can obtain visa cash advances from Invest Bank Issyk Kul, Ecobank and Aman Bank, all on Lenina. **International calls** may be made from the **Telecom** building opposite the taxi stand outside the bazaar and cost US$1 per minute to Europe (half price from midnight to 6am). Narodniy **supermarket** on Yusupbek Bakiev now sells western speciality foods such as Balsamic vinegar and peanut butter.

TRANSPORT

The quickest way from Jalal-Abad to Osh is through Uzbekistan but Uzbek belligerence has complicated the journey, forcing travellers to change buses at the border. Most people now take the longer route via Ozgon.

The **minibus station** is on Lenina, opposite the Aigul department store, with the **long-distance bus station** on the outskirts of town. Three minibuses a day make the 12-hour trek to Bishkek (US$20), stopping at towns along the road. In addition, three buses depart each morning for Tash-Kumyr (US$3, four hours). Buses and minibuses frequently ply the route to Osh (two hours, US$2.5), Ozgon (one hour, US$2) and Kara-Suu on the Uzbek border (US$1.2). Buses for Bazar Korgon (where you change for Arslanbob) leave every 15 minutes and cost about US$0.30 (taxis cost US$3).

Taxis gather outside the bazaar on Lenina ready to travel to Arslanbob (US$15), Ozgon (US$8), Osh (US$14), Bishkek (US$104), Bazar Korgon (US$2.3) and Tash Kumyr (US$20). Divide the price by four if you're sharing.

Kyrgyz Airlines flies to Bishkek twice a week (Tues, Sun, US$50) from **Jalal-Abad airport**; to get there, catch minibuses on Lenina. The airport is on (03722) 51301. Rail passenger services appear to have ceased.

Arslanbob

The mountain village of Arslanbob, which lies more than 1,700 metres high on the south-western slopes of the Fergana range, about 90 kilometres north of Jalal-Abad, is almost exclusively Uzbek. The minute you enter Arslanbob, you know you are in a different culture. The men don Uzbek skullcaps instead of Kyrgyz *kalpaks*; elderly men in long white beards stand chatting in groups, wearing knee-length coats, coloured sashes around their waists and calf-high leather boots, even in the heat of summer. In winter they slip on a pair of *galoshes*, like a Wellington boot cut off at the ankle.

Unlike Kyrgyz women, who only adopt a headscarf upon marriage, virtually all Uzbek women and even young girls wear them. As is common in a more devout Muslim society, the women and girls also wear narrow-legged trousers under their dresses for greater modesty. In Arslanbob many women also darken their eyebrows, creating a long thick line that meets in the middle. For all its air of being locked in sleepy tradition, however, social change is affecting the village; unmarried young women with a more modern outlook are leaving their scarves at home and going bare-headed.

Apart from its cultural interest, the main reason to include Arslanbob on your itinerary is its superb setting. Jalal-Abad *oblast*'s greatest natural treasure is its ancient forests of wild walnut and other fruit and nut trees, of which the biggest (11,000 hectares) is located around Arslanbob. A fully-grown walnut tree is an impressive sight: given ideal conditions it can reach 30 metres in height and its trunk can swell to about two metres in diameter. The route to the village is a mouth-watering vista of walnut, apple, almond, plum and pistachio trees, for which local people have a romantic explanation. They say Arslanbob was the Prophet Mohammed's servant who was sent off to find 'a paradise on earth'. After a long search he found a picturesque valley with a foaming river. It was perfect but lacked trees. Hearing of this, the Prophet sent Arslanbob a big bag of nuts and seeds, which he then scattered from the highest mountain which thereafter became known as Babash Ata ('the beginning/father of the garden').

TREKKING

There are many trekking possibilities here, including climbing in the Babash-Ata mountains, whose peaks reach 4,427 metres. Kyrgyz Nur and Munduz can arrange this (see Osh, page 239). For more modest trips you can hire horses and guides, both at US$23 per day, from the *turbaza* or, better still, from the CBT co-ordinator (see accommodation below). Nearby are two waterfalls. The 80-metre high waterfall (*bolshoi vodopad*) is two hours walk from the *turbaza*. It is said to enhance fertility and so attracts childless couples. The small waterfall (*malenkii vodopad*) is on the north-eastern edge of the village. It leaps out from a wall of foliage at 30 metres; there are prayer caves in the damp surrounding cliffs. CBT will organise a guide, horses and a picnic for a full-day ride to the waterfalls and through the walnut forest for US$44.

More rewarding day walks lead into the nearby woods and walnut groves or to a sacred rock (*svyashenniy kamen*), where apparently you can see the handprints of an 11th-century local hero, also called Arslanbob. In an echo of the Biblical Samson and Delilah story, Arslanbob could not be killed by man or weapon, except when he was praying at the rock. He told his secret to his wife but she passed it on to his enemies, who killed him as he prayed. His handprints and bloodstains are said still to be visible.

Further afield, you can make a two-day trek by horse to Kul Mazur, four small lakes in a very pretty setting. Take a guide and a tent. There is also said to be some very good walking in the nearby Kyzyl-Unkur valley, which also has a small *turbaza*, although you may prefer to camp. Bring your own supplies.

CBT co-ordinator Hayatt Tarikov can organise horse riding treks to the Kul Mazur lakes—at present tourists must supply their own tents. The Osh-based travel agency, Alptreksport, can organise one- or two-week horse riding treks along the Fergana ridge from Arslanbob, which take in walnut groves, high altitude lakes, alpine meadows and the 3,600-metre Kerei pass. The Munduz travel company, also based in Osh, has a two-day tour of Arslanbob and its forests.

ARSLANBOB PRACTICAL INFORMATION

Arslanbob is a rather conservative village so visitors should dress appropriately, but it is a warm-hearted place. Accommodation used to be pretty limited but there are now several options, from very plush hotel to run-down *turbaza*. By far the best option for those interested in gaining a closer insight into Uzbek life are the homestays organised by the **Community Based Tourism** project (see page 292). The very friendly and enthusiastic CBT co-ordinator Hayatt Tarikov, (tel.(03722) 342476; email: cbt_ja@rambler.ru), has an office in the centre of the village near the lion statue with details of the homestays available in Arslanbob and the area. Prices range from US$8–11 B&B. Hayatt can also arrange five-day horse treks to Kul Mazar ('holy lake'), the site of four azure lakes said to be a place of pilgrimage, for US$50 per day per person. Bring a tent and sleeping bag.

Just outside the village is a charming if somewhat run-down *turbaza*. Accommodation is in green and blue-painted wooden cabins with shared toilets, showers and sauna. Book the last two in advance to ensure hot water. You can order meals from the caretaker of your cabin; he'll tell you when it is ready (give him a few som for his trouble). There is also a video bar and disco, and a swimming pool which appears not to be used by women.

Much more luxurious is the **Asia Trek Hotel**, built in 2002 with wonderful views, where rooms range from US$30 for a double to US$70 for a suite. Also for hire is a private sauna, plunge pool, swimming pool and dining area. Call Fayzola on (03722) 24991.

There are a couple of teahouses in the centre of the village. Just off the village square are a general store and some kiosks, selling noodles, vegetables, rice and fruit, including enormous and mouth-watering sheets of mashed, sun-dried apricots made by local women. To get to Arslanbob from Jalal-Abad, catch a **bus** first to Bazar Korgon (see the Jalal-Abad section, page 244) and then change. Buses leave Bazar Korgon for Arslanbob every hour and take two hours. A taxi from Jalal-Abad takes three hours.

Ortok

Tourism has as yet barely touched this forest village about 60 kilometres north-west of Jalal-Abad, partly because the road there is in poor condition, but Jalal-Abad Community-Based Tourism co-ordinator Rushora Abdulaeva has high hopes for it, given its twin attractions of beautiful mountains and ancient walnut forests. One of the densest forests in Kyrgyzstan, the Ortok forest also has 170 species of plant besides walnuts, including cherry, apple, barberry, dog rose and hawthorn. Its mountain pastures are rich in wild flowers and medicinal herbs such as St John's Wort, goldenrod, sow-thistle, clover, sorrel, gentian and camomile. Feeding happily in this natural paradise are woodpeckers, eagles, partridges, badgers, marmots, gophers and the elusive wolf.

ORTOK PRACTICAL INFORMATION

The big attraction of Ortok is its scenery and there are plenty of trekking opportunities in the area, including a visit to a cave in a cliff six kilometres from Ortok. The cave has apparently never been explored; local people say its deceptively narrow entrance opens to a wide interior filled with labyrinth-like tunnels.

In the summer, villagers take their herds up to the *jailoos* four kilometres above Ortok, which may be reached by car, horse or on foot. Visitors are advised to bring waterproof boots, raincoats and warm clothing to cater for the vagaries of high altitude weather, even in summer.

Sadly, the road to Ortok has been washed away and there are no immediate plans to repair it. The forest can be visited from Kara-Alma ten kilometres away where homestays cost US$8, which may, if you're lucky, offer you some of the walnut jam for which the area is known. Book through Jalal-Abad co-ordinator, Rukhsora Abdulaeva, tel. (03722) 21962.

Buses depart from Jalal-Abad daily at 9am, returning from Ortok at 3pm.

Prayer leader at Apshirsay Cave near Osh

Western Kyrgyzstan

The far north-west of Kyrgyzstan bulges into Uzbekistan and Kazakhstan. Falling into the provinces of Talas and western Jalal-Abad, the area is dominated by the Chatkal mountain range, home to an impressive variety of animal and plant species, many of which are protected by two biosphere reserves and a series of national parks. The mountains, rising to around 4,500 metres, are of a delicate and haunting beauty, encompassing lakes, deep gorges and rare walnut and almond forests.

The Talas Valley

The Talas valley, in the north-west of Kyrgyzstan surrounded by the Kazakh border, is considered by the Kyrgyz to be the cradle of their spiritual treasures. To the Kyrgyz, every mountain, river and pasture here has a tale to tell of the great national hero Manas, for this is where the famous Manas epic said to have unfolded and where he is said to be buried. The valley's lesser hero is the 20th-century writer, Chinghiz Aitmatov, who wrote compelling fiction showing how Soviet life deprived people of their individuality.

Talas valley has a long history. The earliest traces of human life date from the Stone Age. Later, around 2000BC, the valley's ancient inhabitants left tantalising hints of their lives in rock carvings depicting scenes of hunting, ploughing and religious ceremonies. More recently, one of the greatest battles in Eurasian history took place in the valley in 751 between Chinese and Arab armies; the resulting Arab victory brought Islam to the region and changed the course of Central Asian history (see page 14).

Talas is rediscovering its traditions and is a leading member of the local and regional leagues for horseback games, played at the Manas Complex. A good time to catch a game would be around the August 31 Independence Day celebrations.

Appropriately for an area of such mythological and cultural importance, Talas valley feels like a self-contained mini-world of its own; beautiful but isolated. As you descend from the 3,330-metre Otmok pass at the valley's eastern end, it opens before you, a V-shaped vision of soft rolling hills gradually flattening to a wide serene valley through which the powerful Talas river carves its way. Open plains stretch steppe-like across the silver-green valley floor, while the distant snowy peaks of the Talas range to the south, and the Kyrgyz Ala-Too to the north and east, keep the rest of the world at bay. A major reason for the area's sense of isolated other-worldness is that it is squeezed between the border restrictions of Kazakhstan on one side and the forbidding Central Tian Shan mountains on the other.

There are two routes from Bishkek to Talas and both present obstacles. Buses take the main road through Kazakhstan via Taraz (previously Jambul). You need a Kazakh visa; this is strictly enforced by Kazakh officials eager for the chance to levy a fine. Buses depart for Talas from Bishkek's West bus station every day. The second route is via two passes: the 3,586-metre Tor Ashuu pass, on the Bishkek to Osh road, and then the Otmok pass (3,330 metres) into the valley itself, which is heavily snowbound during the long winter months. A third route is from the Chatkal valley to the south but this is open only from July to October.

Talas

Talas was an insignificant village when the Russians stormed it in 1864. One officer described it as 'a straggling, shabby looking village with almost no trees, set down on the bare steppe'. The town wears a leafier and much more attractive face today, with the added spice of a raw edge—a wild west, border feel which is confirmed by the busy trade in the bustling bazaar where, amid the stalls of clothing, shoes, crockery and food, you will also find recently decapitated horses' heads for sale. Its many avenues are lined with giant poplar trees and willow trees. The pretty Russian Orthodox Cathedral testifies to the town's Russian history and there is still a sizeable Russian community here.

TALAS PRACTICAL INFORMATION

The centre is dominated by an enormous square on Frunze, which doubles as a car park and is bordered to the north by the large, five-storey oblast administration building, complete with Kyrgyz flag. Opposite is the astonishingly upmarket **Koktom restaurant**, with its linen napkins, crystal glasses and undoubtedly the best toilet in town. It is a joy if you've been in *laghman*-only country. As well as traditional Kyrgyz fare, it has an good Russian and international menu. Despite the glamour, prices are moderate. It is open from 8am to 11pm, tel. (03422) 52890, and is on the floor above a mini-market and chemist. Enter via the external stairs on the left. Another good option is friendly Georgian restaurant, **Cholpon** on Lenina two kilometres east of the bus station, serving good tasty food.

The hospital is located at the western end of the square, and the Kyrgyzstan Bank at the eastern end; don't expect to be able to change money or travellers' cheques there. Opposite the oblast administration building stretches Saragulova (formerly Dzherzin-sky) Street, heading towards the bazaar. On the corner of Frunze and Saragulova is the **Telecom** building which charges the extorbitant rate of US$3 per minute for calls to Europe (half price after midnight). A little further at 63 Saragulova is the **Talas Net internet café**, open from 8am to 8pm. The internet is extraordinarily slow. Saragulova is also where you'll find the **post office** (on the same side as Talas Net, on the corner with Pyervayamaya) and plenty of cafés.

TOKTOGUL

High up in the western Tien Shan, one of Kyrgyzstan's most famous akyns was born, near to where the Toktogul Reservoir now lies. 'Halt! Slave of God!' is the meaning of the name Toktogul, given in 1864 to a baby boy. He became a famous *akyn* (singer-songwriter) and a symbol of the fight against oppression.

Toktogul's parents were very poor but his mother was a skilful singer and her voice remained with him all his life. He charted his life with songs; at the age of eight, he became a shepherd and sang of hardship. In his teens he entered the traditional improvisational contest, in which two singers make up derisory lines about each other, as the audience cheers on the wittier of the two. Toktogul took on Arzymat, the court singer of the local noble. The young shepherd initially won over the audience by breaking with tradition (he refused to offer a song to the *manap*), and then mocked his opponent with such panache that Azyrmat was forced to withdraw as the loser. Toktogul exchanged his shepherd's whip for a *komuz*, the traditional Kyrgyz two-stringed instrument, and became an *akyn*.

It is said that he played with such dexterity and feeling that his *komuz* appeared to speak, in Uzbek, Kyrgyz, Russian, Kazak, and imitated bird and animal calls. But Toktogul remained poor, as he played only at the gatherings of poor people. His love was married off to a richer man.

When asked by the local noble's sons to compose eulogies to them, he instead disparaged them. Not accustomed to such disrespect, they attacked him on several occasions, before falsely reporting him to the tsarist authorities for taking part in a violent anti-Russian uprising. He was arrested and, leaving behind his wife and young son, was taken to a hard labour camp on Lake Baikal in Siberia. During the 17-month journey via the Caspian Sea and Moscow he sang many songs. He escaped once but was caught and spent seven years in shackles while working on the railway line around the lake:

In loneliness, bent with despair, I sit,
Before a window that is no more than a slit.
Thirty thousand soldiers around us are strung,
They speak to me, but I know not their tongue

His wit and haunting music made him popular among his fellow convicts, who brought him a *balalaika* (Russian instrument like a guitar) with which he sang songs rich with nostalgia.

His second escape attempt was also unsuccessful but on his third attempt in 1910, assisted by his comrades who spread the rumour that he had drowned, he eventually arrived back in his beloved Tien Shan to find his son dead, his wife remarried and his mother in poverty. For the next three years his fame grew and he acquired several pupils. When he was arrested again and jailed in Namangan (modern Uzbekistan) in 1913, they were able to collect enough livestock and money to bribe the authorities to let him go.

He was heralded by the Soviets as a socialist for refusing to sing for the *manaps* and *biis* (wealthy Kyrgyz nobles) and it is said that, in Kirghizia, the birth of Soviet popular poetry dates from 1919 when Toktogul sang a eulogy to Lenin for the Bolshevik Commissar: 'Even if my jaw were to fall away I would keep on singing about the happy life that has come to my people.'

He died in 1933 having, like many, fallen into disfavour with the authorities. His most popular song reflects his pain over the death of his son:

Swans on a far-off lake
Their burning sorrow can slake.
In the steppes the grey falcon can stay
Till the wind its sorrow blows
*   ... away.*
O my son, can anyone ...
*   anywhere*
Relieve me of my
*   despair?*

Bust of Toktogul, Bishkek

ACCOMMODATION
Probably the best option is the **Community-Based Tourism** project (see page 292), run by co-ordinator Turdubek Ayilchiev, 76 Kaimova (Yuzhnaya-South), tel. (03422) 52919, mob. (0502) 643466. Email: cbt_talas@list.ru. He is very helpful, speaks some English and has a range of traditional family homestay and comfortable, though anonymous, flats in Soviet blocks. He will act as guide to the petroglyphs in Urmaral and Besh Tash gorges; in the latter, two working yurt camps accept guests. Homestays also available in Sheker (see page 257).

Tucked away behind the Talas Net internet café on Saragulova is **Hotel Erlan**. Popular with local people, it has five basic but surprisingly clean rooms with outdoor long-drop toilet; one room has a shower. **Hotel Talant**, Baitik Batyr/Panfilova, tel. (03422) 56301, offers damp basic rooms; sheet laundering appears to be infrequent. **Hotel Intourist** at 1 Janjibek Raskulova, tel (03422) 53579, offers over-priced rooms a little out of town.

TRANSPORT
The **bus station** is inconveniently located about a kilometre to the west of the town, on Lenina. Buses (taking nine hours) depart for Bishkek via Taraz in Kazakhstan (change here for buses to Tashkent) almost every hour, as do minibuses (taking six hours). A private car or taxi to Bishkek costs US$30 via Kazakhstan or about US$45 via the Otmok pass (divide by four if sharing). There are no buses south to the Chatkal valley.

SIGHTS

THE MANAS COMPLEX

Located at Tash Aryk, 12 kilometres south-east of Talas. Open 9am–8pm, captions are in Kyrgyz. Entrance: US$1.5; web: manasordo.host.net.kg

The Manas Complex is a potent statement of Kyrgyzstan's emerging sense of nationhood. Site of the impressive Manas Museum, created in 1995 to celebrate 1,000 years of Manas, it also contains the Manas Gumbez where the great national hero is said to have been buried. The Manas Complex is a place of pilgrimage for the Kyrgyz and is surrounded by the reverence and respect reserved for mosques and places of worship. For this once nomadic and disparate people, Manas has become the focus around which they have built a sense of national cohesion, a bridge between past and present.

Frustratingly for some visitors, the place is steeped in a mystique which defies an outsider's attempt to place Manas in a recognisable historical context. But, in many ways, to try to do so is to mistake the very essence of the legend and its role today. Here the various elements of Kyrgyz life and culture are bound together by the epic into a coherent whole.

As the Kazakh anthropologist, Chokan Valekhanov, said of the epic:

Manas is an encyclopaedic collection of all folk myths, fairy tales, legends brought to one period and gathered around one character—the epic hero, Manas. The way of life, customs, traditions, morals, geography, religious relations found their reflection in this great epic.

The Complex is built on an imposing scale. A huge six-metre bronze statue of Manas, perched on an 18-metre pedestal, dominates the rose gardens, fountains and fir trees that adorn the grounds. Huge as it is, it is smaller than the original version which was so heavy that it sank into the earth. The statue shows Manas' foot quelling dragons, symbolising his protection of the Kyrgyz people.

Another symbol showing his care of the nation is to be found above the Museum's large wooden doors. It is a stone plaque of three tigers, represented in the epic as Manas' guardian angels, encircling a *tunduk* (the circular smoke hole in a yurt).

Inside the large marble **Museum**, the ground floor is dedicated to Kyrgyzstan's most famous *manaschi* and the history of archaeological excavation in the area. Exhibits are in Kyrgyz only although there are plans to produce an information sheet in English.

Upstairs is the most interesting part. Amid the historical artefacts—utensils, pots and tools dating from the 10th-14th centuries and 19th century horse and camel equipment found in the Talas valley—are imaginative reconstructions of clothing, weapons and equipment based on descriptions in the Manas epic and the days of Jenghis Khan. They include a huge suit of body armour, built on a scale for a giant, said to have been what Manas would have worn. It is hard for the casual visitor to identify which items are genuine historical artefacts and which replicas. What is clear, however, is Manas' importance to the Kyrgyz. Huge, romantic paintings depict how he united the different, warring nomadic tribes into one nation and can therefore be considered the father of today's Kyrgyzstan. A few minutes' walk down one of the Complex's tree-lined paths lies the **Manas Gumbez**, first discovered in 1898. Archaeological excavation has dated the building to 1334, though it has been restored twice since then. Barely five metres square, it is made of baked red clay bricks, plain around three sides but with a richly carved facade. It bears two inscriptions: one declares in ancient Arabic that 'Power belongs to Allah'. The other is too damaged to read. The original building had no dome so historians added one based on a design common to the area.

Behind the museum is a large, man-made hill which, as well as having superb views, boasts a stone carved with an Arabic transcription, said to date from 1234, indicating the presence of a nearby fortress.

Around Independence Day, yurts, feasting and traditional horseback games breathe colour and life into the Manas Complex and it takes on the air and imposing grandeur of the ancient encampment it is designed to capture.

PETROGLYPHS

A series of petroglyphs and rock drawings lie well hidden in the canyons of the Talas valley. They date mostly from the Iron and Bronze Ages, are thought to have been drawn mainly by the Scythian (Saka) people and depict animals and ritualistic scenes. The most interesting group of drawings is on the 'Shining Rock', a huge granite wall which half blocks the Kaman Suu gorge south of Talas, and depicts galloping deers and goats. Other groups of drawings can be seen on the upper reaches of the Urmaral river and in the Besh Tash

Romantic paintings tell the story of Manas

gorge ('tash' means stone); see below. These sights can currently only be reached with persistence, private transport and a knowledgeable guide.

The Manas Gumbez with its carved facade

Your best chance of seeing any petroglyphs lies fairly close to the Manas Complex in the **Ken Kol gorge**, just a few kilometres north of Tash Aryk. On a hillside of this stony valley lies a hidden gallery of rock carvings believed to date from 1BC to 1AD. Despite this ancient history, the fragile images of animals and hunting scenes have an air of impermanence as the friable rock is gradually destroyed by the elements.

Ideally, take a guide from the Manas Complex. Take the road heading away from the Complex, which runs through Tash Aryk, soon becoming a track and entering the Ken Kol gorge. Cross the bridge and take the third track on the right, past a farm-house. When the valley narrows, look for a row of poplars on the right. Walk up the small gorge behind the poplars and search for the rocks on the left-hand hillside.

The neighbouring mini-gorges feeding the Ken Kol river are also said to be peppered with petroglyphs but only the most persistent will find them.

AROUND TALAS

Popular trips include the **Besh Tash gorge** south of Talas. This beautiful valley is a national park (with entrance fee). It is lined with silver firs and currant bushes and has a serene lake at its heart. At its upper end are petroglyphs and the five standing stones, said to be robbers petrified as punishment for their criminal activities. You can ride or hike to the top of the valley in a day and you'll find some attractive camping spots en route. Two working yurt camps here will accept guests—see CBT on page 254. The dramatic **Urmaral gorge** lies to the west of Besh Tash and is worth a visit for the adventurous; CBT co-ordinator Tudurbek Ayilchiev will act as a guide to the two valleys and can find the petroglyphs and inscriptions dating from the seventh to sixth centuries BC.

The far north-west corner of Talas valley is full of history and has an abundance of ruins, petroglyphs and other archeological traces of its early inhabitants, but information is very scant. To the west of Talas town and at the base of the revered 4,482-metre Manas Mountain lies **Sheker**, birthplace of Kyrgyzstan's renowned 20th-century writer, Chinghiz Aitmatov. The village has a small museum dedicated to its most famous son and a CBT homestay—Kulipa Kasieva, 24 Jakypek. There is said to be a guesthouse, **Baibal**, in Uzgaresh.

Further north-west, at the village of **Ak Debe** (also known as Dzhoon Debe) archeologists have discovered the site of an ancient settlement dating from the sixth to seventh centuries. Ak Debe is the birthplace of the artist Theodore Hertzen, born in 1935, who pioneered Soviet monumental art in Kyrgyzstan. He is the man to thank for all the impressive statues and stirring mosaic wall paintings eulogising the achievements of the workers. His work may also be seen in the Fine Arts Museum in Bishkek.

Submerged under **Kirovskaya Reservoir** near Kyzyk Adyr, the ruins of the ancient town of Sheljy testify to the area's pre-eminence as a central Asian metal and silver mining centre until the 16th century. Ruins can sometimes be seen as waters recede in autumn.

A bizarre and impressive sight from the north-shore dam near Bala Sary is a giant-sized face of **Lenin**, hewn carefully into the cliff overlooking the reservoir.

About 70 kilometres east of Talas and 25 from Kupyuro Bazaar, the beautiful **Karakol valley** has numerous petroglyphs which can be reached by car—the CBT co-ordinator can show you where to find them.

The Bishkek to Osh Road

Kyrygyzstan's major north-south highway is a switchback roller-coaster ride of great scenic beauty that winds for 620 kilometres over the haunches and shoulders of the Tien Shan mountains. The road takes you through landscape that is by turns awesome, harsh, dramatic or serene. It offers access to the Talas valley and to the pristine lakes of Sary Chelek. Accommodation is fairly scant, available in the Chychkan valley mid-May to September, the Suusamyr valley in the summer, and at Karakul, Tash Kumyr and Jalal-Abad. Although this might alter in the future, assume you can't change money between Bishkek and Jalal-Abad.

The road is the main 'bridge' between the north and the south of this highly divided country. The government therefore attaches top priority to this project and, for the same reason, continues to subsidise heavily the Bishkek–Osh flights. Flocks of sheep and goats have been banished as the road is plied day and night by heavily loaded vehicles of all sizes and proudly takes its place as an artery crucial for national stability, trade, opportunity and communication between the two centres. It is an essential outlet for the Kyrgyz Fergana valley, cornered by local bully, Uzbekistan.

The US$240 million upgrade of the road is now complete, including short stretches of new road in the south to eliminate the need to transit Uzbekistan; the approximately 320-kilometre stretch between Karabalta and Karakul is currently the best in Kyrgyzstan.

However, the road's mere existence is constantly challenged by nature and it needs full-time maintenance; in winter the icy stretches near the Tor Ashuu and Ala Bel passes are cleared and gritted, in spring as the snows melt the road is prone to avalanches, rockfalls and landslides. In an attempt to minimise risk and disruption, the authorities trigger some of these deliberately, causing frequent closures of up to several days. Accidents are almost daily, caused in large part by dangerous, unrealistically speedy driving —choose your driver with care. A toll of around US$1 is payable at the northern end of the road—it is worth paying a few extra som and asking for a receipt to ensure takings do not go astray.

THE ROUTE AND PRACTICAL INFORMATION

The route proceeds sedately at first, on the well-used road from Bishkek to **Karabalta** at the foot of the Kyrgyz Ala-Too. These villages are home to Dungans (Muslim Chinese), who first moved across the border about 120 years ago—look out for the distinctive Dungan roofs, topped with tiny pagodas and carved tin figures. A quick stop at Belovodsk is worthwhile to visit the beautiful old Russian Orthodox church just east of the bazaar. At Karabalta the Osh road turns south to rear over the Kyrgyz Ala-Too range, crossing it via the 1.6 kilometre-long tunnel at the **Tor Ashuu pass** (3,586 metres).

The road then slides into the **Suusamyr valley**. Eleven kilometres after the pass is the turn-off to Suusamyr village and the remote Karakol and Chaek valleys which lead to Kochkor on the Balykchy to Naryn road (see Central Kyrgyzstan). The Osh road follows the broad, flat Suusamyr valley as it meanders westwards for about 64 kilometres. Even in the winter snows, fishermen catch trout in the wide lazy river to sell at the roadside. This serene and beautiful valley, uninhabited in winter, boasts superb *jailoos* which, from June to September, are dotted with yurts and livestock.

About 16 kilometres before the western end of the valley is the turn-off for the Talas valley. **Talas** town is about 112 kilometres and 2.5 hours away. The Osh road then struggles over the Talas Ala-Too range at the **Ala Bel Pass** (3,184 metres), where it turns south to follow the Chychkan river gorge, Kyrgyzstan's chief source of marble. The tight embrace of its steep red walls relaxes a few kilometres below the pass to allow birch trees to grow alongside the river, their juice (a traditional health tonic) for sale at the roadside. The Chychkan valley is also famous for its organic honey (*myod*) harvested from mountain woods and sold along the road.

Approximately 32 kilometres south of the pass stands the **Neman Guesthouse**, owned by the engineering and pharmaceutical firm of the same name. Set back from the road among trees, it offers comfortable but unpretentious accommodation for US$14 bed and breakfast (dinner US$4) from mid-May to late September. In the middle of the Chychkan State Zoological Reserve, it is the ideal place to break your journey and spend a day exploring the gorge's side valleys. The firm is building a new café and shop at the roadside, threatening the business of the modest eatery currently housed in a former Coca Cola tanker.

On the opposite side of the road, behind locked gates, the **Chychkan Government Resthouse** nestles appealingly amongst fruit and berry trees on the river's edge. A sign declares it to be a '*Gostinitsa*' (hotel), and although it is said to be open to tourists when the caretaker is there, it is used mostly by passing officials who may not be very welcoming. Potentially, there is space to pitch a tent in this part of the valley, but you would have to ensure you were not visible from the road. Eight kilometres to the south is the main cluster of **cafés** between Karabalta and Karakul. A good option is Nurzad, the new brick house which serves good local food and is well heated in winter. Most cafés serve fresh trout.

Eight kilometres to the south, the valley loses its austerity and swoops down to the town of **Toktogul**, on the shore of the reservoir and set

Fertile pastures clothe the mountain slopes

amongst the welcome green of willows, poplars and fruit trees. Named after the much-loved 19th century *akyn* (poet-songwriter—see page 252), Toktogul was, in Soviet times, a penal colony and is still regarded with a degree of suspicion by many, so people prefer to stay in Karakul about 112 kilometres to the south. There are, however, basic guesthouses and cafés here.

The **Toktogul Reservoir** funnels the swollen Naryn river into a series of hydro-electric stations on its journey to the Fergana valley. The area provides the vast majority of electricity to the five Central Asian states. The road swings round the reservoir, through straggling villages and crosses the mighty Naryn river at its eastern tip. There is said to be good climbing and trekking in nearby Kambar Ata gorge (to get there, take the road along the Naryn river towards a hydro-electric station).

Nerve-racking as the northerly section of the journey can be, it poses none of the challenges faced by writer Viktor Vitkovich in the 1930s:

> *I first journeyed along this road in 1930 when it was only a pack trail with the suspension bridge across the Naryn, which I can never recall without a shudder. The bridge, its logs lashed together with branches and half rotted away, swung crazily over the chasm. It was frightening just to look at, to say nothing of crossing it. Coming up to the bridge Kirghiz women and old men used to pray and then crawl across on all fours. But the young jigits (courageous young men) contrived to walk across it jauntily, leading their horses by the bridles. There have been cases of horses missing their footing and crashing down against the rocks where their remains were washed away by the plunging waters of the river... It was such a horrible experience that on my way back I braved a round-about route across snow-bound passes rather than face this bridge again.*

The small town of **Karakul**, about 400 kilometres from Bishkek, is dominated by the hydro-electric station.

To reach **Hotel Tourist** on Kaskadovskaya bear west at the southern end of town and then first right. A Soviet-style hotel overlooking a garden and the river at the back, the Tourist offers standard twins and triples with balcony and private, leaky bathroom with hot water for US$8 and US$6 per person respectively. A spacious and supremely clean 'lux' comes at US$29 for the room. The hotel belongs to the hydro-electric station.

The huge spotless hotel restaurant is run by an outside company and is normally open from 8am to 1am. Food and service are excellent. The main **restaurant** in town is in the basement of the former Governor's offices, a large Soviet administration building, complete with flag, next door to the huge pink Univermag (a department store, now closed). Its cavernous dining room-cum-disco is popular with local youth and there are kiosks for a little privacy. On the menu is high quality standard local fare at good prices. An alternative eatery is the **Bermet** on the main Bishkek-Osh road.

Buses stop on the main road outside Kyrgyz Telecom. The ticket office is the blue train wagon. For safety reasons, only minibuses are permitted to run the stretch north of Toktogul. If you are staying overnight, check onward bus times on arrival as there is no fixed schedule. The 67-kilometre journey to Tash Kumyr takes about two hours and cuts through a steep-sided gorge and past the turquoise Kurpsaysky Reservoir, emerging from the mountains into a rolling green landscape of fruit trees and villages.

TASH KUMYR

The pretty town of Tash Kumyr strings out along the river for a couple of kilometres. It is one stepping off point for the Sary Chelek Biosphere Reserve. If you plan to spend the night here, your best bet is the **Chebez Hotel**, Lenina, tel. (03745) 20633 (take the grassy boulevard from the local bus station; it is the blue building at the far end). Rooms are clean and airy with private bathrooms and cost around US$5 per person. The dining room serves basic food, but you might be better off choosing an eatery on the main Bishkek to Osh road. Another hostelry is at 2/3 **Pyervaya Maya** (take the road immediately before the Chebez Hotel, cross the railway lines and take the first left). A comfortable large house with Uzbek-style verandah in a pretty garden, it is generally open only to guests from known organisations but the hostess might relent if you're stuck. If you bring your own food, she will cook for your for a small fee.

Problematically, there are two bus stations, one on Lenina opposite the bazaar, serving the local villages, and one on the main Bishkek to Osh road but the latter is often closed due to landslides in which case buses are diverted to the 'local' bus station. Buses run north and south, the last one for Jalal-Abad leaving early afternoon. It is a good 11-hour trip to Bishkek and five hours to the Chychkan Guesthouse. For Sary Chelek, catch a bus to Kara Jygach (2.5 hours), departing at 10am and 1.30pm. From there a daily bus runs to Arkyt via Kyzyl Tuu. Buses to Kerben (often known by its Russian name, Caravan), on the edge of the Fergana valley, depart at 10am and 2.30pm.

Sary Chelek Biosphere Reserve

The literal meaning of Sary Chelek is 'yellow bucket', though it is usually more eloquently translated as 'golden hollow'. A visit to the Sary Chelek Reserve and surrounding buffer zone is likely to be one of the highlights of your visit to Kyrgyzstan. Covering the southern side of the Chatkal mountain range, Sary Chelek is deemed a charmed land and it is the dream of many Kyrgyz people to go there. It owes its popularity to its lofty beauty—turbulent rivers rush from glaciers and snow fields; its seven high altitude lakes, each a vibrant hue of blue, have a serene beauty; and jagged mountain ridges give way to hillsides clothed in ancient fruit and nut forests and rare alpine flowers.

Lake Sary Chelek itself, known as the 'jewel' of Kyrgyzstan, stretches for 7.5 kilometres into the mountains at an altitude of 1,940 metres, a long blue-green sliver that is 1.5 kilometres at its widest point. Surrounded by towering yellow boulders, with

THE KYRGYZ HORSE

If you're given only one day's life, spend half of it in the saddle.   Kyrgyz saying

For centuries the horse has personified the nomadic way of life. As well as providing *koumys* (made from fermented mare's milk) and horsemeat, it was a valued helpmate, carrying yurts and personal belongings as well as people. It was the horse that gave the nomads supremacy over sedentary societies in Central Asia for more than 2,500 years.

Over the centuries, quite a cult built up around the sturdy little Kyrgyz horse. Legends and tales feature horses almost as prominently as people and the animal dominates Kyrgyz sayings and adages (for example: 'Only a horse and an agreeable conversation can shorten a long journey'). The Kyrgyz language abounds with words for horses of all ages and coats: warriors invariably went to war on 'flat-hoofed, bronze-legged steeds' while heroes of folk songs gallop on 'mounts that feed on cornflowers'.

According to legend, the Kyrgyz horse has: 'eyes as big as bowls. Its muscles ripple as the waves of a great mountain river. Its eyes are keener than a raven's. Its lips are like a ladle. A fist can be passed into its nostrils. Each hoof is as big as a camp-fire that has burned out.'

Today the car is challenging the horse's centuries-old supremacy, although many people have returned to the saddle as a result of the economic collapse, which has halted vital road maintenance programmes and put petrol beyond many people's means. Since 2005, an initiative to revive the original Kyrgyz horse breed, which was cross-bred or killed almost out of existence during the Soviet era, has ignited passionate support among the Kyrgyz (see page 7).

In the past nothing was revered more than skill with horses, and equestrian games and races were performed at every festival and celebration. These include *alaman-baige*, a race involving boy jockeys over a 15–20 kilometre course, and *tiyin-enmei*, in which riders must pick up a coin from the ground at full gallop. *Korush* or *Oodarysh* is a wrestling match on horseback; the idea is to drag your opponent to the

Milking mares for koumys

Summer camp at Tash Rabat

ground or, better still, onto your own horse. Competitors are often stripped to the waist and their bodies smeared in sheep fat.

Ulak-tartysh or *Kok-boru* is a rough game played by two mounted teams and involving a goat carcass. Considered the king of traditional games, it dates from ancient times and is the supreme contest of horse riding ability. The aim is to carry or throw the carcass into the opposing goal (*moroo*).

The battle of the sexes is played out in the *Kyz-kuumai*, or 'chasing the girl', in which a man races across a meadow pursuing a girl on horseback, and tries to kiss her at full gallop. According to the rules, she does all she can to escape, fiercely whipping the unsuccessful man in scorn. If he succeeds, however, according to tradition, she cannot resist falling in love with him.

Equestrian races and games are still performed on special occasions such as Independence Day on 31 August and Nooruz, the spring festival, but the main horse festival is the three-day At Chabysh. Set up to revive horse traditions in 2005, it is held on the south shore of Lake Issyk Kul in late October or early November each year (see page 2).

In 2007 a sister festival was organised in Naryn the week before, and in the summer months CBT organises cultural festivals for tourists, including horse games, in several areas including Lake Song Kul, Tash Rabat, Lake Issyk Kul and Sarala Saz *jailoo* 65 kilometre north-west of Kochkor. For a list of events visit www.cbtkyrgyzstan.kg. Other events are often organised at short notice, so it's worth asking around.

spruce and firs clinging to its steep slopes, its trees support cormorant and merganser nests. A closer look will reveal orchids and ferns. To the south-east lie a further six smaller lakes: Kyla Kul, Bakaly Kul, Iyri Kul, Tuuk Kul, Choichok Kul and Aram Kul.

Sary Chelek Reserve, founded in 1959, provides habitats for more than a third of Kyrgyzstan's species of flora and fauna and many of the world's rare and endangered animal and plants. Snow leopards lurk in the higher reaches of the mountains but are rarely seen. Turkestan lynx, brown bear, deer and boar are occasionally spotted, as are the short-toed eagle and greater horseshoe bat.

Since 1978 it has been under the auspices of the United Nations. Largely, though, attempts to protect its complex biodiversity have met with minimal success. The damage to the Reserve through poaching, deforestation and over-harvesting of nuts, berries, fruit and honey has been especially acute during the economically difficult years since independence, when the local population came to rely too heavily on its produce. Poaching has been a big problem, with the penalty set at just a quarter of an animal's market value.

However, the future looks brighter. New initiatives to protect the Reserve include, since 2001, the West Tien Shan Inter-State Biodiversity Project, led by TACIS (a development arm of the European Union), which also covers Besh Aral, the Chatkal Reserve in Uzbekistan and an area of Kazakhstan. The comprehensive programme aims to reduce local reliance on the Reserve areas through training and grants for people to develop alternative livelihoods. In the Sary Chelek area it also addresses the contentious issue in nearby Kyzyl Tuu and Jylgyn of summer *jailoo* (high altitude pastures), as villagers have been prohibited from using their traditional grazing grounds in order to protect the Reserve. Homestays have been set up in the area and Reserve authorities are considering how best to organise tourism in order to maximise revenue and provide employment for the local communities while preventing further damage to the ecology.

SIGHTS

You don't have to be a weathered trekker to enjoy the Reserve, although for those who enjoy walking there is an extensive network of paths throughout the park. You can reach Lake Sary Chelek by car, where the Reserve administration runs a basic hostel (book through the office in Arkyt). To admire the area's wild spectacular beauty or stupendous mountain views, though, requires a good level of fitness. Trekking on horseback in these mountains (other than the trip from Arkyt to Lake Sary Chelek) is not for beginners as paths are often strewn with boulders or scree, which is difficult for even the extraordinarily sure-footed Kyrgyz horse.

An easy but fabulous five-hour walk starts at Lake Sary Chelek (which you can reach by car) and takes you into the hills and past four of the lesser lakes. A tremendously rewarding, though fairly demanding, trek climbs east from Lake Sary Chelek past the smaller lakes and over Kumurmo pass to the Kara Suu lake (see below). From here you can go down to Kyzyl Kul or you can trek north over the Mokmal pass to the northern end of Sary Chelek lake.

A three-day hike on foot or horseback from Arkyt to Aflatun valley to the west takes you through upper Karangitun, over the Kyz-Korgon pass, along the Aflatun river and over the Kuldambes pass to the Ak Donkoch gorge before crossing the Ashuu pass and descending to Arkyt. Arguably the most beautiful and dramatic trek is to cross the jagged Chatkal range to the Chatkal valley (see page 271).

To make the most of your time in Sary Chelek, it is worth planning it with some care. Regulations to protect the Biosphere prohibit visitors from wandering freely into the mountains and there is a daily charge (for details, see Arkyt, page 266). If you want to walk for a couple of days or visit Lake Sary Chelek by car, this can easily be arranged on arrival. In future the Reserve staff or Arkyt villagers may be able to offer horses, guides and provisions for treks but at present your options are to book through a number of Bishkek-based companies (costs may be high) or to arrange activities through CBT Bishkek office or on arrival with the Kara Suu CBT co-ordinator (see Kara Suu, page 267).

THE ROUTE TO SARY CHELEK

There are two roads to Sary Chelek, one from Tash Kumyr (70 kilometres away on the Bishkek to Osh road) and the other from Kerben (Caravan) on the edge of the Fergana valley (33 kilometres). The roads meet at the village of Kara Jygach (literally, 'black wood'), where there is an excellent market on Thursdays. A few kilometres north, the road forks at Kyzyl Tuu: the easterly fork follows the Kara Suu river for 21 kilometres of appalling road to the village of Kyzyl Kul in the buffer zone; the westerly fork heads up to the village of Arkyt (18 kilometres) and the Sary Chelek Biosphere Reserve.

Locals will tell you that the easiest way to get to Sary Chelek is from Kerben as there are direct daily buses to Arkyt and to Kyzyl Kul, but unless you are coming from the west this is a rather circuitous route. **Buses** depart Kerben at 4pm for Arkyt and 6.30pm for Kyzyl Kul. Buses from Tash Kumyr depart at 10am and 1.30pm for Kara Jygach where you change to the bus from Kerben.

A taxi from Kerben to Kyzyl Kul costs around US$25 and from Tash Kumyr US$30 or arrange a car through CBT for about the same.

Probably the most comfortable accommodation in the Sary Chelek area is **Ulan Ostanbaev's Guesthouse** in Kyzyl Tuu. If possible, book in advance through family in Bishkek, tel. (0312) 625802, 626885, mob. (0772) 388889. The new two-storey brick house stands in a large garden, accessed through a wooden archway and entry gates. Ulan and his wife are very welcoming and the guesthouse is equipped in international style, offering bedspace for three people and thick traditional mattresses on the floor for a further seven. The long-drop toilet is clean and there is a hot water shower. Bed and breakfast and an excellent dinner costs US$15 and the sauna can be heated up for US$2 per person.

It is located on the road which runs parallel to the Arkyt road, on the other side of the river. The guesthouse is signposted from the nearby bridge. Ulan and his wife, Cholpon, can arrange horses and a guide for day trips. If you don't want to use the more basic village accommodation in Arkyt, the Lake Sary Chelek can be visited as a day trip by car from here.

Another accommodation option is the Soviet-era *Turbaza* **Sary Chelek** (open from the end of May to September) in the buffer zone village of Jylgyn, eight kilometres north of Kyzyl Tuu. It offers a cluster of four-bedded wooden chalets on the hillside with great views over the valley. Prices are not yet fixed but expect to pay around US$9 per person.

ARKYT

The attractive little village of Arkyt lies within the Reserve itself, ten kilometres beyond Jylgyn and about two kilometres beyond the park gates. With its abundance of fruit trees in the gardens, fresh mountain honey for sale and farm animals wandering the dusty streets, it appears in many ways to be the archetypal Kyrgyz village. The organisational hub of the Sary Chelek Reserve and the only village within its boundaries, life for the 1,000 inhabitants here has been dominated by the Reserve for decades—the regulations around grazing and use of the forest fruits, the employment it offers, restrictions on hunting and the problems of poaching. In Soviet times several unsuccessful attempts were made to move the village wholesale elsewhere.

It was subsequently divided into two zones with all economic activity banned within one zone, even though this contained fields and houses. The last couple of years, however, have seen more sustainable and thoughtful attempts to marry the economic needs of the villagers with protection of the rare and precious biodiversity of the area.

Sary Chelek Lake is 16 kilometres (two to three hours by horse) from Arkyt. Camping within the Reserve is forbidden but in summer the Reserve runs **cottage-style accommodation** and some yurts at the lake, which may be booked at the Administration office.

PRACTICAL INFORMATION
Arkyt is developing a warm welcome for visitors. Located two kilometres inside the Reserve gates, it contains two museums (both next to the administration building), which display a topographical model of the Reserve, stuffed animals, insects and birds, and examples of the trees and plants found there. Exhibits are in Russian.

The pristine waters of Sary Chelek lake

Thanks to a recent TACIS project, the village now boasts four comfortable but simple **homestays** in clean village houses, all with long-drop toilet and most with a sauna. Bed and breakfast costs US$5. Dinner is an extra US$3 but you will need to give the family a few hours' notice. To find them, just ask for the householder by name: Sultan Chukutaev, Respek Urmanaliev, Atakov Umumbekov and Mamunali Duanaev.

Alternatively, the **Reserve Hotel** is next door to the admininstration building, accessed via the stairs at the back, and offers basic but comfortable rooms with an outside toilet. There are a number of workshops in the village producing **handicrafts** of felt, leather, silver and wood—ask in the Reserve office for details.

Arkyt's one **café**, signposted 'Café' on one side of a red triangular flag, sells good food at reasonable prices but out of the season you will need to give them warning if you want a proper meal. Eggs, bread, honey and homemade jam are always available.

To enter the Reserve currently costs US$10 per person per day, plus an overall fee of US$4 per car. The Reserve gates should be manned 24 hours a day but if you cannot get in, Ulan Ostanbaev offers summer yurt accommodation just outside. You must report to the administration office upon arrival; it is the long white building signposted ATC just inside the village (tel. (03742) 22284, not operational in spring 2003). If you plan to enter the Reserve from the mountains, you should get your US$10 daily permit in advance through a tour operator, otherwise you run the risk of a hefty fine.

Regulations and logistics surrounding access to the park are currently being redefined to be more efficient and visitor-friendly.

THE KARA SUU GORGE

KYZYL KUL

Several villages unwind along the banks of the Kara Suu river, merging into each other for some ten kilometres. The most northerly is **Kyzyl Kul**, home of the **CBT**

co-ordinator, Bezarkul Joosh-baev (see page 268). This is a tranquil, exceptionally pretty and very rural valley. Other than animal husbandry, livelihoods principally involve harvesting walnuts and honey. Indeed, in summer the valley is rich with wild strawberry and raspberry bushes, walnut forests and beehives.

Even in late spring, snow blankets the Kara Suu gorge

PRACTICAL INFORMATION

To get to Kyzyl Kul, you take the right fork at Kyzyl Tuu (see The Route to Sary Chelek, page 265) or a daily bus leaves Kerben at 6.30pm. If you are coming from Tash Kumyr, change at Kara Jygach, where the bus from Kerben stops around 7.15pm. The statue and small memorial museum shortly after the turn-off is to the *akyn* (poet-songwriter) Zhenizhok (1840–1918) who lived and worked in the valley. About 12 kilometres from here, **CBT co-ordinator** Bezarkul Jooshbaev's house is almost the last one in the village proper, just before the valley narrows to a steep-sided gorge. Tel: (0502) 501527, (03742) 22541; email: cbt_sary-chelek@rambler.ru. Little English is spoken so it might be easier to book through the Bishkek office.

Accommodation in the valley is comfortable and warm in village homes offering beds or the traditional mattresses, with long-drop toilet and sauna but no other dedicated washing space. Prices (printed on the CBT leaflet: please ask) are approximately US$10 B&B plus US$6 for lunch and dinner. Work out a deal for your trip before you start.

TREKKING

Bezarkul Jooshbaev can arrange trekking on horseback or on foot up the Kara Suu valley and beyond to Sary Chelek and the other lakes, including guide. As Kara Suu is in the buffer zone rather than the Reserve proper, there are fewer restrictions on camping. If you want to avoid the expense of the Reserve, Bezarkul can take you on a route which skirts it but enjoys excellent views of the lakes.

He also organises a spectacular eight-day trek over the mountains to the Talas valley, crossing passes of around 3,600 metres. A fairly easy four-day trek gives you aerial views of Sary Chelek's satellite lakes, while a tougher six-day trek takes you over the Makmal pass and down to the shores of Lake Sary Chelek itself.

An accessible and extremely beautiful two-day trip on foot or horseback (you'll need some previous experience of horseriding) is up the gorge to the **Kara Suu Lake**. From June to September, shepherds set up yurt camps on the *jailoo* around the lake. Some offer accommodation, or there is space to put a tent. It's a full day up to the lake.

From Bezarkul's house the valley narrows and you criss-cross the vast gushing river for an hour to the last house in the village. Despite the lack of electricity here, some of the younger generation prefer the isolation high up the valley to the bustle of village life.

After the last house, the V-shaped valley closes in dramatically before opening out where the river spills into numerous streams through a wood of pine trees, silver birch and juniper. Now you begin to climb steeply on sometimes alarmingly narrow paths through a variety of geological formations. One moment you're deafened by a huge waterfall roaring over boulders, the next you're scrambling over a tumble of giant rocks and jewel-like stones in pinks, oranges and duck-egg blues, past a white wall of marble.

Later, the path skirts a vivid blue lake, created by an earthquake some 50 years ago. Finally, after an hour's steep climb, you arrive at the stunningly turquoise Kara Suu lake, which curves around the valley between the dark granite walls of the surrounding mountains. From here you could return to Kyzyl Kul or cross the 2,440-metre Kumurmo Pass to Sary Chelek and the six other highland lakes.

Chatkal Valley and Besh Aral

In the far west of Kyrgyzstan, the Chatkal valley is one of the most remote and isolated parts of the country and offers an exciting potential route between Uzbekistan and Talas valley. At its western end is the ecological treasure house of the **Besh Aral Biosphere Reserve**, a miniature jumble of stark gorges, steep forested valleys cut deep by the rushing Chatkal river, mountain steppes and meadows.

The flat-bottomed Chatkal valley runs south-west to north-east for about 150 kilometres, in places up to 50 kilometres wide; in summer, it provides a transit route north to Talas valley via the 3302-metre Kara Buka pass, which is open only from late June/July until October, depending on the weather. The Chatkal is one of the top rafting rivers in Kyrgyzstan. Most people travelling to the Chatkal valley enter from the south via Kerben, as Chatkal's northern end is blocked by snow for much of the year.

THE ROUTE TO CHATKAL AND BESH ARAL

The 160-kilometre route from Kerben to Dzhaniy Bazaar in the Chatkal valley is bedevilled by the long-running border dispute with Uzbekistan. To avoid bullying and routine extortion by Uzbek police and border guards, most Kyrgyz drivers choose the circuitous and pot-holed route around the border, trippling travel times, rather than transit Uzbek territory. Certainly, foreigners should be wary of entering Uzbekistan by mistake as the Kyrgyz road sometimes swerves just a couple of metres round the Uzbek border post. Another potential danger is landmines laid by the Uzbek Government along parts of the Fergana border.

KERBEN

Often referred to by its Russian name of Caravan, Kerben has a prosperous and lively feel; it is very much a border town and an intersection between the Sary Chelek area and Uzbekistan as well as the Chatkal valley. Kerben's proximity to Uzbekistan has left the town with a distinctively Uzbek feel, in terms of faces, food and architecture.

The action takes place around the town's central crossroads of Karl Marx and Frunze, with its pretty paved square, yurt café and Uzbek *chaikhana*. This is where you will find, within a mere two-minute walk, Kyrgyz Telecom/Post Office (on Frunze), the ZUM department store (now metamorphosed into a more traditional marketplace filled with bazaar-style stalls), the taxi rank and exchange booth (all on Karl Marx), and the covered bazaar on the corner of Lenina/Karl Marx.

While you're here, a beautiful day-trip is to **Padysha-Ata mazar** (burial mound), in the valley of the same name. Follow the river upstream as it roars through a gorge of 400 metre-high walls, in places lined with thick groves of birch and Tien Shan fir; you climb to a flood plain in beautiful meadows at 2,000 metres. CBT (see page 270) can organise the trip.

ACCOMMODATION

CBT have recently opened an office here: Mirzakim Mirzarakhimov, 31 Niyazali; tel: (03742) 22745; mob: (0503) 449940; mirza-aka@rambler.ru; kerben-cbt@rambler.ru, offers homestays, transport and guides locally. Other good homestays include **Dilbar Sulaimankulova** at 5 Jany-Turmush, Plodopitomnik, tel. (03742) 22577, said to be extremely comfortable. Book in advance if possible—the rooms are quickly taken. **Tatyana Bozhoko** offers comfortable homestays in her Soviet apartment with outside toilet for US$4. It is the third two-storey building on the right several blocks from the post office (Appt 1, 115 Umetalieva—Umetalieva is an extension of Frunze), walking away from the centre of town **Sadermet Kulubaev** may be able to offer homestay at 70 Ulitsa Lenina, tel. (03742) 22275 in a beautifully decorated but somewhat rundown Uzbek house. If you are desperate, you could try the chilly scruffy rooms (for under US$1) of the old **Intourist Hotel** on Lenina/Karl Marx opposite the Tsum building. The entrance is up the stairs on the outside of the building on Lenina.

Probably the best place to eat during the day is the Uzbek *chaikhana*, **Amanbay Ata**, on the square next to Tsum. Old men sip tea on traditional charpoys in the shade and good typical Uzbek fare, shashlik and plov, are served. **Dyor**, the middle of three restaurants on Frunze, is open in the evening and serves reasonable food.

The **bus station** is on Karl Marx, opposite the big mosque on the outskirts of town towards Chatkal. Buses for Jalal-Abad (5.5 hours) depart at 7.30am, 9am and 11am; for Arkyt (2.5 hours) at 4pm; frequently for Kara Jygach; for Kyzyl Tuu at 10.10am and 1.30pm; Kyzyl Kul at 6.30pm and for Ala Buka (two hours, change here for Chatkal) at 8.30am, 11am, 1.30pm and 3.30pm.

SAFET BULAN MAUSOLEUM

A worthwhile detour on the road to Chatkal is this exquisitely carved mausoleum, located in the village of Safet Bulan, about eight kilometres from Ala Buka and so close to the Uzbek border that both currencies are accepted in the shop. Locals are delighted by visitors but the mausoleum is still a sacred place so please respect local mores and cover arms and legs; women should wear a headscarf.

The mausoleum contains the graves of two people—Shah Fazil, said to be related to the Prophet Mohammed, and Safet Bulan. The story goes that Shah Fazil's father, Shah Jarir, came to Kyrgyzstan in the eighth century as part of the Arab invasion to spread Islam, and was killed in battle. Safet Bulan was a local woman who washed hundreds of skulls of the dead in her search for Shah Jarir's remains. She achieved lasting fame and the title of Safet ('white') from this act of purification; even the village is named after her.

The two graves lie at opposite ends of the tranquil inner courtyard. Shah Fazil's mausoleum, deceptively plain on the outside, is beautifully decorated internally, with fine symmetrical patterns in typical Islamic style etched on the clay walls. The clay grave, covered with a green velvet cloth, is surrounded by sacred stones etched with Arabic inscriptions; devotees walk clockwise around the grave, clasping each stone with both hands, and praying. In the building opposite are two rooms; one apparently contains the skulls washed by Safet Bulan and in the other, decorously placed behind a colourful sequinned curtain, lies the pink satin-covered grave of Safet Bulan. Access is reserved for women only. The courtyard contains a standing stone, six metres of which is buried below the ground, said to bring luck to those who touch it.

ALA BUKA

About 50 kilometres west of Kerben is the bustling small town of **Ala Buka**, where a daily bus leaves at 8.45am for its six-hour journey to Dzhaniy Bazaar. The hotel on the main street is reputed to be operational year-round. The road from Ala Buka to Chatkal takes you through some exceptionally pretty scenery, winding through narrow canyons next to a fast-flowing river bordered by silver birch and blue poplar trees. About 32 kilometres from Ala Buka, you enter the village of **Buzuk** whose inhabitants are said to live entirely from the proceeds of illegal gold, filtered painstakingly from the river and sold in Uzbekistan. TACIS has set up homestay facilities in **Terek Say**, a satellite of Buzuk. Here the road swings over the river and climbs to the 2,841-metre Chapchama Pass, where you are rewarded with a stupendous view of the Chatkal mountain range. From here it is a 37-kilometre run to Dzhaniy Bazaar, the main village of the Chatkal valley.

THE CHATKAL VALLEY

Flanked to the west by the Chandalash range and to the east by the Chatkal mountains, with peaks of up to 4,400 metres, the Chatkal valley offers spectacular day walks or, for the hardy, a trek over the passes to Sary Chelek (see below) or possibly into Uzbekistan.

Located close to the great cultural centres of Uzbekistan, the valley has a rich settled and nomadic history; excavations of barrows from the early iron age were undertaken in Soviet times. Locals report petroglyphs in the hills but, to date, information is scant although scholars are beginning to research the mythology and history of the area. During the zenith of the Silk Road, Chatkal was well populated and a minor tributary of the Silk Road is believed to have carried silver from mines in the north of the valley and in the Talas river basin. Chatkal was once occupied by two small kingdoms; the remains of the Kurbes Khan settlement were discovered near the mines in the Kuru Tegerek gorge in the north of the valley, while Changar Khan appears to have had a stronghold just south-west of modern-day Dzhaniy Bazaar. After the onslaughts of Jenghis Khan, settled culture started to decline.

Today, the valley's 22,000 inhabitants lead a largely self-sufficient life, growing vegetables and animal fodder during the short summer. For most of the year, the only gateway out is south to Ala Buka and Kerben, as the road to Talas is blocked by snow. The valley's southern end, where green was just beginning to creep into the trees in late April, is considered balmy compared to its northern end where spring arrives 20 days later. Chatkal and Besh Aral are part of biodiversity projects by the World Bank and European Union development organisation TACIS, which aim to reduce local reliance on rare and endangered animal and plant species.

DZHANIY BAZAAR

A tranquil, straggling village burnished in summer by the hot sun and frozen in winter by fierce cold, Dzhaniy Bazaar sprawls on the valley floor alongside the fast-flowing Chatkal River. It is proud home to the **mausoleum** of Idris Paygambar which perches on a hill a ten-minute walk away, with rewarding views of the valley. Locals say Idris Paygambar was a prophet who came from Damascus seeking knowledge and wisdom either, depending on your source, around the 18th or 19th centuries or several centuries before Christ and Mohammed. Idrys Paygambar is said to have prayed and meditated upon the hill until Allah granted him enlightenment. The mausoleum is now a place of pilgrimage and people come here for solace and guidance. In the cemetery at this atmospheric site, tall posts marking the graves are carved with the names and the lifespan of the dead; life is hard here and few seem to have lived beyond their fifties.

TREKKING

The side valleys into the Chatkal range offer beautiful day walks. Longer trekking routes, including some to Sary Chelek, are rough and remote, crossing passes of 3,500-4,000 metres on trails that are often not discernible, so it would be unwise to attempt them unsupported. There are also said to be petroglyphs near the stunning high altitude Kara Tokoi lakes at the far northern end of the valley but the precise location is unclear.

The villagers can help with day walks but are not yet in a position to support longer treks. CBT co-ordinator, Bezarkul Jooshbaev at Kyzyl Kul (Kara Suu), Bishkek companies or Tashkent-based Asia Travel (tel. (071) 1735107, 1732655; fax. 1731544; email: at@ars-inform.uz; web: asia-travel.uz) can organise treks on the most accessible route, five days from the Aflatun river to Kyzyl Kul village in Kara Suu valley (see page 267).

It begins at the far northern end of the Chatkal valley, where the Aflatun valley climbs through verdant meadows and woods past two lakes to a canyon with 1000-metre walls. The Ashu Pass (3,368 metres) gives a bird's eye view of the mountain ranges descending to the Fergana valley. Snow leopards patrol these heights though, sadly, you are unlikely to see one. The route down the Uyalma river takes you through woods of Tien Shan firs and past shepherds' summer camps. Crossing the Kuldambes pass, you climb to the Ashu Tor pass and are rewarded with a stunning view of the emerald Sary Chelek lake. The descent to the lake shore takes you through woods bursting with currant and raspberry bushes. From here it is a day's hike over the Kur Airyk pass (where you have unrivalled views of Chatkal Peak at 4,503 metres) to Kara Suu lake and then down the gorge to Kyzyl Kul.

PRACTICAL INFORMATION

Tourism is very much in its infancy in Chatkal. In Dzhaniy Bazaar the **Baishan guesthouse**, used primarily by pilgrims to the Idris Paygambar mausoleum, has rooms for US$3 per person, but bring your own food for the hostess to cook. The guesthouse is the large white house set back from the road at the northern end of the village, just past the park with the war memoria, tel. Dzhaniy Bazaar 216 or 318 (ask the operator for Chatkal and then Dzhaniy Bazaar). Some of the proceeds from the guesthouse are donated to poor families in the village. There is no café but a few shops sell basics. The Besh Aral Reserve office is on the main street in the village, just south of the park. Kapalbek Sultanbaev, former Deputy Director, will also act as a guide.

The daily **bus** leaves Dzhaniy Bazaar for Ala Buka (see page 271) at 8.30am, arriving around 2.45pm. Public transport does not continue to the villages at the northern end of the valley, which are more spartan with no formal accommodation and few provisions, so if you plan to travel that way, take food and gifts of bread, tea or dried fruit if you hope to find accommodation.

BESH ARAL BIOSPHERE RESERVE

At the south-western end of the valley, the Besh Aral (meaning 'Five Isles') Bioshphere Reserve is bisected by the Chatkal river gorge, which offers a backdoor route (three days trekking) to Uzbekistan where the Chatkal river finally empties into the Charvak Reservoir. *Zapovednik* (reserve) staff claim to be able to provide a border permit for the crossing to Uzbekistan for those with an Uzbek visa; however, this is unlikely to be possible for the foreseeable future.

Besh Aral Biosphere Reserve opened in 1979 and has the same protection status as Sary Chelek due to the huge variety of endangered plant and animal species which depend on its delicately balanced ecology. In the Soviet period, and particularly in the lean years since its demise, the pastures were overgrazed and the forest denuded of its fruits, threatening the dwindling numbers of rare mammals and plants.

Since 2001, however, the West Tien Shan Inter-State Biodiversity Project, led by TACIS and encompassing Besh Aral, Sary Chelek, the Chatkal Reserve in Uzbekistan and part of Kazakhstan, has worked to ensure the conservation of this globally unique area, through education, training and funding of alternative livelihoods, and policing the sustainable farming of the forests and meadows. The future of both nature and villagers therefore look a bit brighter.

Delights of the park include the giant Menzbier's marmot, unique to the Tien Shan and whose population is now recovering; the elusive snow leopard, the brown bear and the Turkestan lynx. The skies and mountain tops belong to the black stork, short-toed eagle and bearded vulture. Reserves of wild apple, walnut, cherry, vine, apricot, blackberry and fig (said to be the ancestors of the cultivated trees of today) grace the slopes; poplar, birch and willow grow along the river banks, sheltering buckthorn, honeysuckle and dog rose, while Tien Shan spruce and juniper march across the uplands. Greig and Kauffman tulips are making a comeback. The area is also rich in medicinal herbs.

The Reserve is easily accessible on day walks, but the best it has to offer can be enjoyed on a light, four-day trek (on foot or horseback): make the easy ascent of the 3,890-metre Besh Aral mountain, cross alpine and steppe meadows adorned with rare tulips and other flowering shrubs from May to July. Two other seven-day routes, which are more difficult and require reasonable fitness, can be arranged by the *Zapovednik* staff. All tourists should be accompanied by a guide from the Reserve—call at the office in Dzhaniy Bazaar or ask for ex-Deputy Director, Kapalbek Sultanbaev, who is knowledgeable and makes an excellent guide. The Reserve can also hire out tents, sleeping mats and sleeping bags.

The Kyrgyz Pamir

Security Warning—This area, at the junction of Kyrgyzstan, Uzbekistan and Tajikistan in the Pamir Alay, is inevitably vulnerable to destabilisation by drug trafficking, and fundamentalist Islamic activity has spilled over from Uzbekistan, Tajikistan and Afghanistan, adding to tensions in the region. The British Government has frequently advised travellers to avoid the area entirely. At the time of writing, the warning has been lifted, but it is advisable to check.

The Pamir Alay

The magnificent melée of snow-bound peaks, known cumulatively as the Pamir, lies mainly in Tajikistan and China, with fringe ranges in Kyrgyzstan and Afghanistan. Kyrgyzstan claims the major part of their lesser cousin, the Pamir Alay, a series of ranges stretching approximately 800 kilometres from Samarkand (Uzbekistan) in the west to China's Xinjiang Province in the east, where they plunge to the second lowest depression on earth, the Tarim Basin. Forming the southern wall of the Fergana valley, the various ranges of the Pamir Alay merge at the Matcha mountain knot on the Kyrgyz-Tajik border. Few travellers make it to the rugged southern edge of Kyrgyzstan. But those with a taste for adventure, mountaineering or serious trekking will not be disappointed.

For all its remoteness and harshness of climate, the far south has attracted intrepid travellers for centuries. Two of Central Asia's earliest and busiest Silk Route branches passed this way. The valley formed the southern frontier of the Kokand khanate of the 18th and 19th centuries. The ruins of an Uzbek fort can still be seen at Daraut-Korgon, the local administrative centre.

Before Russia gained firm control of the area in the late 19th century, the Alay was a playground for Russian (and very occasionally British) explorers, adventurers and Great Game spies as they filled in the blanks in the maps between Russia, China and India. In the 19th century Alexei Fedchenko discovered one of the longest glaciers in the world: the 77-kilometre-long Fedchenko glacier, which lies in the Tajik Pamir.

The Pamir Alay, characterised by deep gorges, turbulent rivers and high glacial ridges, is popular with trekkers and mountaineers. The area was off-limits in Soviet times so now boasts scores of unclimbed peaks, many of which do not require technical skills or immense experience. The population of the valley, around 17,000, is almost entirely Kyrgyz, with a couple of Tajik hamlets on the border. Little grows here and people are very poor, relying almost exclusively on animal husbandry.

The **Alay valley** is a gateway to the mountains, to Tajikistan over the Kyzyl Art pass and China over the Irkeshtam pass. The Kyzyl Suu ('Red Waters') river winds its way through the 150- by 60-kilometre valley, framed by a phalanx of some of the ex-Soviet Union's highest peaks. At 7,495 metres, Kuh-i-Samani, formerly Peak Communism, was the highest of the former Soviet Union's mountains and lies in Tajikistan. Peak Lenin has been renamed as Kuh-i-Garmo ('warm mountain'), which has a more suitably local flavour. It stands at 7,134 metres and straddles the Kyrgyz/Tajik border.

TREKKING AND MOUNTAINEERING

For travel within 50 kilometres of the Tajik border, including the Pamir Alay mountains, a Border Zone permit is required available from tour operators; it takes four weeks to organise.

Kuh-i-Garmo is one of the most popular and accessible 7,000-metre peaks in the world. There are a number of routes to the summit, but the most popular go through the Lipkin Rocks, named after the pilot who crashed here at 5,200 metres and strolled down the mountainside along what is now the standard (*Razdelnaya*) route to the mountain. The basecamp for the Kuh-i-Garmo ascent is in the Achikh Tash valley, carved out by glaciers eons ago. The terminal moraine below the basecamp is now lush pastureland used by local herders. Something of an oasis amid the rubble and ice of the surrounding peaks, the camp also holds many reminders of climbers killed on the mountain. The most significant of these was in 1991 when an earthquake sparked off an avalanche that wiped out Camp II on the *Razdelnaya* route, killing 43 climbers in the worst accident in mountaineering history.

Expeditions to this and other peaks in the area can be organised, among others, by ITMC, Tien Shan Travel, Dostuck Trekking and Ak Sai Travel (see page 82) and Kyrgyz Nur in Osh.

For a less extreme experience, **Shepherds Way Trekking** run a 13-day horse trek from Chong Karakol on the northern flanks of the Alay valley, which are lush with juniper forests, lakes and rivers. They cross the Alay valley and climb to the basecamp via Tolpar lake and, for those who wish to, continue on foot up to Camp Two of the Kuh-i-Garmo ascent. CBT also offer a trek through the green gorges on the north side of the Alay valley and on to basecamp. Temperatures are low and warm clothing needed.

PRACTICAL INFORMATION

It is best to go between July and early September but the exposed Alay valley has an unpredictable micro-climate, staging violent storms which sometimes leave Achikh Tash knee-deep in snow in the height of summer. The area is particularly prone to avalanches, especially in the afternoon; October is safer in this regard.

A number of **mountaineering agencies** operate summer basecamps at Achikh Tash meadows (30 kilometres south of Sary Moghol). These include ITMC Tien Shan, Dostuck Trekking and Ak Sai Travel from Bishkek, Kyrgyz Nur from Osh, Asia Travel from Tashkent (Uzbekistan) and Kan Tengri from Almaty (Kazakhstan). If you plan to trek independently around the basecamps you will need to bring provisions from Osh's abundant market.

CBT have new co-ordinators in **Sary Tash**—contact Mirbek Akraev or Nargiya on (03234) 41153; in **Sary Mogul**—contact Umar Tashbekov at the *Ail Okmotu* (local administration building), tel. (03237) 23293, 23194 or Osh (03222) 20196; email: cbt_sarymogol@mail.ru; and at Gulcha (90 kilometres south of Osh)—contact Talantbek Toksonbaev or Aziz Alymkulov at 19 Lenina, tel. (03234) 22764, 21961, mob. (0503) 310326; email: cbtgulcho@mail.r; talant_85@yahoo.com. All can also be contacted through CBT Bishkek.

In the Central Tien Shan frequent avalanches leave mountain faces bare, exposing their geological make-up.

Apparently, there is a homestay shortly before the Tajik border but no buses ply this route. A daily **bus** leaves Osh's old bus station for Daraut-Korgon at 6am (ten hours); from here, hire a taxi to Achikh Tash. From Daraut-Korgon, two buses per day leave for Osh, at 5am and 8am, calling at Kashka Suu en route.

You need a **border zone permit** to go within 50 kilometres of the Chinese border. The permit should clearly mention the Chon-Alay and Alay regions of Osh *oblast*. If you plan to trek around Kuh-i-Garmo you also need a permit from the Ministry of Sport and Tourism, which can be arranged by the same trekking agencies for about US$40.

Irkeshtam Pass

Finally, after years of rumours, the Kyrgyz-Chinese border at the Irkeshtam pass has opened to international traffic. This modern Silk Road makes an ideal route to China and opens up the possibility of a three-day Kashgar excursion using the Irkeshtam and Torugart passes. The border is 238 kilometres from Osh and 250 kilometres from Kashgar. It is advisable to overnight at Sary Tash en route as the road between here and the border is very difficult and is infamous for accidents.

The border is closed on Saturdays and Sundays. Normal formalities apply and no special permits are required as long as you are transiting. However, there is a six-mile stretch of no man's land between the Kyrgyz and Chinese border posts, which you cannot cross on foot, but have to hitch across with a passing truck—this can be problematic. There is a small hotel and café at the border.

There is reputedly a bus between Osh and Kashgar, taking 24 hours and costing about USD60. A better option is to arrange a shared taxi—see page 240 for details.

BOURGEOIS JEALOUSY

While a room was being prepared for me I went out on to the stairs, from which post of vantage I was witness of a curious incident. A woman neither very young nor very beautiful but quite well dressed for that time, in white, was nervously walking to and fro by the staircase, evidently waiting for someone. Then she picked up a good-sized cobble-stone out of the street and held it in her hand. A few minutes later there came out of the door of the inn a young girl, poorly dressed and of homely appearance. Like a tiger the woman in white flung herself upon the girl, hitting her on the head with the stone. Blood streamed from the poor girl's head, and both women screamed and yelled like mad things. I was just going to intervene when both combatants, pulling each other's hair, screamed out something and went out into the street. People came running up from all sides, the militioner, the equivalent of the policeman, all out of breath, and I thought it wiser to slip off to my room. Even then it was fate to witness the finale of this extraordinary scene. After tea I went out into the corridor of the inn and I saw the two women sitting side by side. Before them, in the position of an orator haranguing a meeting, with two pistols in his belt, fully dressed in the black leather of his kidney, stood the commissar, who turned out to be the husband of the lady in white. Striking an imposing attitude, he held forth to the two women upon the Communist system of ethics, eloquently describing how by their unseemly behaviour they had lowered his dignity and prestige as commissar, Communist and commandant of the local militia. He explained how, in a society of collectivised Communists, there was not and never could be a place for so vulgar a feeling as jealousy. Jealousy! What a bourgeois thing! Dreadful! The proper punishment for having created such an unseemly scene was to shoot them both, but he, in the great mercy of his heart, as a true son of the proletariat, would magnanimously pardon them.

P S Nazaroff, Hunted Through Central Asia, 1932

Batken and the Turkestan Range

Batken is Kyrgyzstan's remotest oblast and has been troubled by some terrorist activity. However, the dramatic swathe of mountains that make up the Turkestan range offer some of the most superb trekking in the former Soviet Union. For the sheer beauty of its mountain landscapes, this area is hard to beat. Its appeal lies in its variety and drama. Glaciers spill from finely tapered peaks into lush, high pasturelands, strewn with wild flowers and peopled by Kyrgyz herders. Spectacular granite rock faces appear unexpectedly, wooded slopes drop to robust glacial rivers and, in the foothills, apple, nut and apricot orchards make excellent campsites.

Batken *oblast* is Kyrgyzstan's tail, its south-west corner bordered by the Turkestan Range. Formed late in 1999, Batken is bedevilled by its seven enclaves which belong to Uzbekistan and Tajikistan. The main ones are Shah-i-Mardan, Sokh and Vorukh.

Mountaineers cannot resist the Ak Suu (formerly Pyramidalniy) peak which rises in a perfect snowy pyramid to 5,509 metres. Its sheer two-kilometre high wall makes it one of Central Asia's best climbing destinations. Hire a four-wheel drive in Isfana for the 45-kilometre journey to Kara Suu or Katran where treks begin.

Batken is one of the few places in the world where the beautiful and rare aigul flower can be found.

BATKEN PRACTICAL INFORMATION

Batken town, a windy town of 11,000 people (its name is Tajik and means 'source of the wind'), is of little interest beyond a change of buses en route to Leilek (meaning 'stork') or Tajikistan. Batken is a lot more welcoming with the arrival of **CBT**. Contact co-ordinators, Sabir Shaimardankilov and Minovar Karimova, 9 Sabyrova, tel. (03622) 23280, mob: (0502) 667298 and (0502) 948616; email: cbt_batken@mail.ru. The Intourist Hotel is unappealing.

Buses for Batken (six hours) leave the Hotel Alay in Osh twice daily, around 7am and 11am. Shared taxis depart from behind the hotel and cost US$5 per person. In Batken, transport for the villages and Isfana leaves in the early morning from the bus station (*avtobeket*) near the bazaar while shared taxis leave from the post office. Bizarrely, the bus for Osh leaves from the Municipal hotel. Depending on the season and the weather, there is a weekly flight between Bishkek and Batken.

It is advisable to hire a guide for this region, either through a tour operator or, less reliably, on arrival at the camp in Aksu. You need a **border zone permit** for this area. These can be arranged by trekking agencies but you need to contact them at least four weeks in advance.

Warning—The Uzbek Government and, to a much lesser extent, the Kyrgyz army, laid landmines on some of the high mountain passes in this region following incursions by Islamic fundamentalist guerillas in 1999 and 2000.

TOP TREKS ON FOOT OR HORSEBACK

LAKES ISSYK KUL TO SONG KUL—14 DAYS

From the south shore you climb high into the Terskey Ala Too for a bird's eye view of Lake Issyk Kul; descend to broad fertile valleys before taking on narrow rocky gorges and finally steep slopes leading to a series of *jailoo* where you stay in working shepherds' yurts.

TALAS TO SARY CHELEK—8 DAYS

Starting in lush Urmaral gorge, head into the wilderness over stony, steep passes of around 3,600 metres, through woods high above rock-strewn rivers, past shepherds' yurts, ending up with spectacular views of Lake Sary Chelek and its satellites.

KARAKOL VALLEY TO ALTYN ARASHAN VALLEY VIA LAKE ALA KUL—4 DAYS

Kyrgyzstan's most popular route, it passes through stunning alpine scenery, with velveteen valleys, Tien Shan fir woods, harsh rocky passes and the turquoise Lake Ala Kul down to hot water springs in Altyn Arashan valley. Add a day for a detour towards Karakol peak.

TASH RABAT TO BARSKOON—30 DAYS

Not for the faint-hearted, this magnificent trek explores the vivid variety of Kyrgyzstan's scenery—soft green hills, boulder-strewn mountain passes, syrt (high altitude arid plateau), deserted river valleys, *jailoo*, snow-capped giants, narrow rocky gorges, and wide lush valleys full of grazing livestock.

ALAY VALLEY—14 DAYS

Climbing through valleys forested with fir and juniper, you pass mountains lakes, cross the Alay valley—a plateau at 2,800 metres—always in view of Peak Lenin and other giants of the Alay range. Visit Peak Lenin basecamp and walk to Camp Two if you choose.

THE EVER-USEFUL KYRGYZ SHEEP

Kyrgyzstan and sheep go together like valleys and mountains. The large fatty-rumped sheep seen grazing everywhere have played a crucial role in Kyrgyz society for centuries. Not only do they provide mutton, fat and milk, but their wool supplies the felt used to make yurts and *shyrdaks*. The *kalpak*, the white felt shepherd's hat worn by Kyrgyz men, could date back well over 2,000 years; the Greek writer Herodotus describes how the nomadic Saka living in the Tien Shan mountains wore 'stiff pointed hats made of close-woven felt'.

Managing flocks of sheep is a fine skill, as the 1930s Soviet writer Victor Vitkovich observed. He wrote:

It is a real art to make a flock of sheep ford a stream ... The senior shepherd, after sounding the depth of the water and choosing the ford, rides into the frothing stream on a horse, dragging a leader goat after him with a rope. Following the goat, the sheep throw themselves into the water in a bunch. The idea is to have them cross the stream in a broad column with 15 to 20 abreast, otherwise the swift-running waters will sweep them off their feet.

The shepherds have a golden rule: before the sun grows bright in the morning graze the sheep eastward, then gradually turn them to the south and, finally, back; in the daytime, have the sheep facing their shadow so that the noonday sun does not beat in their eyes. But ... in hot weather lead the sheep in the direction of the wind in the morning so that on its way back to the camp during the intense noonday heat, the flock moves against the wind.

Sheep were the principal wealth of the nomads. A year-old ram was the standard value for clothes, harness and the *kalym* (bride price). Clan chiefs owned thousands of sheep, the poor man typically had one or two, while the labourer worked for the right to milk two or three of his master's sheep. Sheep were also used as punishment, with flocks being driven over a man lying face up.

Today sheep are still sometimes used as a measure of value (a driving licence is said to cost so many sheep). The Kyrgyz name for path, *koi jol*, means 'road of sheep', while many legends and sayings are associated with them: 'If you shout loud enough, even a stubborn sheep will allow itself to be tied' and 'Cheap mutton has little fat'.

A herd of sheep raises a cloud of dust [Saffia Farr]

TULIPS OR DAFFODILS?

*O*n the morning of Thursday 24th March thousands gathered in Ala Too Square: aksakal in ak-kalpaks, irate young men, peasant women with headscarves and smiles of gold teeth and enthusiastic students from the newly formed KelKel movement. The curious, the angry, the hungry; some with pink armbands, some with yellow; some holding daffodils as symbols of peace, some waving huge Kyrgyz flags or carrying banners saying 'Get Out Thieves'. All yelling and raising fists in response to the zealous rhetoric of Kurmanbek Bakiev magnified through a megaphone.

"The people of Kyrgyzstan will not let anybody torment them. We must show persistence and strength and we will win!"

In their minds flashed images of injustices: Akaev shopping for penthouses in Moscow, children studying without books; Mairam greeting orphans in furs and pearls, babushkas eating from bins; Bermet skiing in Europe, thousands dying of tuberculosis; Aidar cruising in one of his black Mercedes, eight families living in one room.

International news networks were blaming poverty and endemic corruption for the social explosion. Finally it had become apparent to the masses that Kyrgyzstan was not going to be the Switzerland of Central Asia and Akaev, once hailed as a liberal in a region of dictators, was becoming entrenched as head of a ruling family.

* * *

The protesters would probably have gone home quietly had someone not sent in the White Caps—Akaev supporters impatient for a fight. They charged into the defenceless crowd brandishing billy clubs and shields. There was chaos as babushkas fled over rose borders and students scattered across Ala Too Square. The White Caps pursued, beating bodies into submission with sticks, aiming for heads with thick army boots.

"We are all Kyrgyz, we shouldn't be fighting each other," one bloodied man generously said. But years of anger at poverty and increased oppression had been unleashed and aimed unstoppably at Akaev. The crowd turned and hurled bottles and stones at police who cowered under riot shields in the centre of the square like scared tortoises. Baying, the pack pressed forward, pushing police lines back towards the White House, only momentarily impeded by the cavalry sent in on horseback. A rider was dismounted, his horse captured by a protester who galloped down Chui as if playing Ulak, banner streaming behind. The frightened horse reared for television cameras, symbol of the nomadic revolution.

Inside the White House compound police surrounded the building. The swelling mob bombarded them with stones, rattling at the gates before lifting them off hinges, *pushing through towards the president's centre of power. Uninspired by their recent training and unwilling to risk their lives for meagre wages, the policemen fled.*

Outside the tall wooden doors, carved with swirling sheep horns, the crowd hesitated, expecting the Father of the Nation to come out and give them all detention. But no-one came: Akaev hadn't been seen in public since his address on Tuesday evening and no-one was prepared to defend his honour. The crowd edged forward, tentatively throwing stones at windows to see what would happen. No response, no attack, no landmines under doormats. Heartened by the ease of conquest they surged up the steps, smashing windows and bursting into the building. This is when I arrived.

History was being made in Ala Too Square and I wasn't content just to see it on CNN. Dema had been booked for shopping so I went to Narodny, grabbing things off shelves because it's always better to have extra loo roll in stock when there's rioting in the main square. The assistants were blithely handing out application forms for loyalty cards, unaware there'd soon be nothing left to be loyal to.

There was a surreal atmosphere in town, a city polarised by ignorance. While CNN was broadcasting images of young men being beaten, a woman was dancing in a Christmas cake hat on KTR. On Erkendik, two blocks from the revolution, children were swinging and licking ice-creams, unaware that the helicopter roaring over them probably carried their fleeing president.

As we walked into Ala Too Square, Dema, my self-appointed bodyguard, and I heard a roar. Spectators were on the museum steps looking towards the White House. Incredibly, two soldiers were still standing guard beside the flag pole, staring motionlessly ahead as if this were just an ordinary day in Bishkek. Peeping around a pillar I saw an incredible sight: men climbing the fence, swarming into the sacred White House, waving flags victoriously out of windows and tearing up pictures of an unsmiling Akaev.

"Plokha," Dema muttered, "it's bad. No tourists will come now." I thought I might cry. People power always makes me emotional. Whether it's a Countryside March or men in felt hats climbing presidential fences, the fact people care enough to get up and wave banners chokes me. I bit my lip, I couldn't cry in front of Dema.

Any tears were dried by fear. We heard screams from the heart of the crowd and saw people running towards us. Was that shooting, was it not yet over?

"We're going," Dema announced, dragging me back into the square, out of the path of a pack of angry young men marching and chanting. We later heard they'd stormed Zum and tried to loot it. Reluctantly I let Dema drive me home, crunching over broken glass and stopping to let students clutching bloody heads cross the road.

From Chapter 24—Revolution Baby: Motherhood and Anarchy in Kyrgyzstan
by Saffia Farr (2007)

The yaks' frilly petticoats of hair provide much-needed insulation at high altitude [Saffia Farr]

THE LOSS OF
CENTRAL ASIA'S GLACIERS

Mountains across the world, from the Alps to the Andes, are melting and Central Asia's mighty peaks are no exception. It's only in recent decades that the sensitivity of mountains to climate change has been recognised, but study after study has come to the same conclusion: Central Asia's glaciers, including those of Kyrgyzstan, are retreating, with huge implications for the region's ecosystem and peoples.

The first significant loss began in the 1930s but the pace of the melt sped up alarmingly in the second half of the 20th century and the acceleration continues in this century. Even Tajikistan's mighty Fedchenko Glacier—the biggest in the world outside polar regions—has suffered.

It covers more than 700 square kilometres and, at 6,200 metres above sea level, is sited in such an inhospitably cold part of the Pamirs that at times it is buried in ten metres of snow. Yet, the Fedchenko, whose glacial melt eventually empties into the Balandkiik River near the border with Kyrgyzstan, has lost one kilometre in length since 1933 and its thickness has dropped by 50 metres since 1980, according to the Tajik Agency on Hydrometeorology.

So serious is this glacial retreat that some scientists have predicted that many of the region's glaciers will disappear by the middle of this century. Not everyone takes such a gloomy view but there is no doubt that the loss of Central Asia's ice stores poses a serious challenge to countries such as Kyrgyzstan, which depend on the annual run-off from glaciers and snow melt to refill rivers each summer, power hydroelectric plants and supply much needed irrigation for agriculture, not to mention drinking water.

Together, the mighty Tien Shan, Pamirs, Karakorum, Himalayan and Tibetan ranges hold the largest volumes of ice outside the polar regions, which has led Dr Gregory Greenwood, director of the Switzerland-based Mountain Research Initiative, to call them "the third pole of the planet".

Kyrgyzstan is one of the highest countries in the world, with 94 per cent of its land perched more than 1,000m above sea level and 40 per cent over 3,000m. One third is permanently under snow and glaciers make up more than 8,000 square kilometres, or 4.2 per cent of the country. Yet, despite this vast volume of frozen water at its heights much of Kyrgyzstan is arid.

As the Bishkek-based Scientific Information Centre Aral evocatively put it in a 2003 report, the country is located in "a zone of insufficient moistening".

Kyrgyzstan relies on the annual summer melt from its 8,208 glaciers and blanket of snow to provide 60–80 per cent of its river run-off—and so do its neighbours; three quarters of this run-off ends up in countries downstream.

Disputes over water are already a cause of tension in the region and in June 2007 Kazakhstan, Uzbekistan and Tajikistan were further displeased to hear Kyrgyzstan's monopoly power station company, Elektricheski Stantsi, whose hydroelectric dams regulate the water flowing downstream, warn that it would not be able to guarantee that they would get the volumes of water they had requested for 2008.

At the same time, voices inside Kyrgyzstan argue that the nation should look after its own interests before supplying neighbouring countries with water. Unlike some of its neighbours, which have ample supplies of coal, gold, gas and oil, Kyrgyzstan's powerful rivers are its only real natural resource and the country hopes to capitalise with more hydroelectric production.

All of this makes the Scientific Information Centre Aral's prediction that Kyrgyzstan's glaciers may shrink by 30–40 per cent by 2025 highly alarming. This would result in 25–35 per cent less water run-off, with potentially catastrophic consequences for Kyrgyzstan's agriculture, ecosystem, economy and relations with its neighbours.

Dr Stephan Harrison, associate professor in quaternary science at Britain's University of Exeter, has studied the northern Tien Shan mountains, which stretch through Kazakhstan and Kyrgyzstan and into China, and has found a "consistent pattern of retreat".

The Tien Shan glaciers tend to be relatively small valley types (as the name indicates, these are alpine glaciers flowing into a valley) or cirque glaciers, formed in bowl-like depressions on the side of mountains. "They are often frozen to their bed. Their velocity is low, they don't move quickly and they don't accumulate much mass so they're fairly good indicators of temperature," says Dr Harrison.

The horse is still vital to the herder's work
[Saffia Farr]

*Ala Archa National Park—water is a defining feature of Kyrgyzstan,
freezing into snow in winter and melting into cascading rivers in summer [Saffia Farr]*

He examined just over 400 glaciers on the Kazakh side of the Tien Shan and says: "They're all in major recession. These are fairly high altitude glaciers, 3,000 metres plus, and it's clear that they are melting very rapidly, losing about 0.7 per cent of their mass per year between 1955 and 2000."

Studies in Kyrgyzstan echo his findings. TE Khromova of the Russian Academy of Sciences, who examined glaciers in Kyrgyzstan's Ak-Shirak range found that it experienced a slight loss between 1943 and 1977 and then an accelerated loss of 20 per cent of their remaining mass between 1977 and 2001.

A joint Kyrgyz/Swiss study, published in August 2007, found "a clear trend in glacier retreat" between 1963 and 2000 in the Sokoluk watershed, in the Kyrgyz Ala Too in the Northern Tien Shan. The glaciers had lost 28 per cent of their surface area in that time, with the loss accelerating from the 1980s. And a 2004 study of 293 Kyrgyz glaciers in the Tien Shan found a similar pattern of retreat.

Dr Harrison believes the issue has serious implications for the political stability of Central Asia as many of the rivers and glaciers cross state frontiers. He says: "Many of the rivers which supply the irrigation schemes essential to agriculture are fed by glaciers and permafrost so the livelihoods of millions of people will be affected."

Melting glaciers also produce some serious natural hazards for the people who live below them. Glaciers stockpile rocks and soil which create dams during the melting process. The resulting glacial lakes are often unstable and can burst, casting catastrophic floods and avalanches on to unsuspecting towns and villages in the narrow valleys below. The debris flows produced by melting glaciers can also change the dynamics of river basins below.

Dr Harrison says: "Globally we're committed to 30–40 years of climate change, whatever we do. Land-locked and arid regions of the world like Central Asia need to think about their water supply now and perhaps stop growing water-hungry crops like cotton.

Suggested Itineraries

Kyrgyzstan's beauty and hospitality rarely fail to delight, whether you are there for several weeks or simply transiting between tourism giants Uzbekistan and China. Here are some skeleton itineraries to give you an idea of what's possible.

AROUND BISHKEK

There are plenty of one or two day trips around Bishkek. Enjoy magnificent views in the valleys of the Kyrgyz Ala Too, including Ala Archa to walk or relax, with dinner at 12 Chimneys restaurant on the way back; Shamsi gorge by foot or horse; the rarely visited Kegeti canyon with its waterfall and alpine meadows, with the option of a two-day trek to Kul Tor lake; the stark red canyon walls of dry Konurchuk gorge.

A GENTLE ITINERARY – ISSYK KUL IN FIVE DAYS

Bishkek to Cholpon Ata (hotel): possible activities include a trip on the lake, visit to petroglyphs, beach. Next day, en route to Karakol, visit Semyenovka valley and *jailoo* for yurt camp and cultural activities. On to Karakol for two nights (hotel/yurt camp): city tour, then visit stunning Jeti-Oguz valley for walks/picnics. Then to Tamga Guesthouse: trip up Barskoon gorge, Buddhist inscriptions in Tamga gorge, Skazka valley or the beach. Return to Bishkek.

BISHKEK TO CHINA TRANSIT VIA JELU SUU

Bishkek to Kochkor for lunch: possible felt-making demonstration. On through broad valleys to Jelu Suu hot springs (camp): bathe in springs. Through narrow, rocky Eki-Naryn gorge to Naryn (hotel/yurt). On to exceptionally beautiful Tash Rabat valley with 15th century caravanserai (yurt): day trek in mountains to view Lake Chatyr Kul or straight on to the Torugart Pass.

BISHKEK TO CHINA TRANSIT VIA LAKE SONG KUL

Very different from the above, this route shows open moor-like *jailoo*. From Kochkor to Lake Song Kul (yurt). Dramatic hairpin descent to Naryn via Jangy Talap.

OSH–KASHGAR–TORUGURT

This round trip boasts some of the best and most varied mountain scenery in Kyrgyzstan. From Osh enjoy the intense, high drama of the Pamir Alay. One night at Sary Tash (home stay). Over the magnificent Irkeshtam Pass to Kashgar. Return via Torugart Pass to Naryn; possible stop at Tash Rabat (yurt); see above.

KYRGYZSTAN TOUR FOR THE ADVENTUROUS

In this two-week trip you explore cities, ancient forests, wilderness, petroglyphs, jagged mountains, *jailoo* and dramatic passes. From Osh to Jalal-Abad (homestay). Trip to Arslanbob: walnut forests and Uzbek culture. To Kazarman (homestay); three-day round trip (horse or foot) to Saimaly Tash to view 5,000-year-old petroglyphs (camp two nights). From here either to Tash Rabat (yurt) or Eki-Naryn (homestay/yurt). Through Eki-Naryn gorge to Jelu Suu hot springs (camp). To Song Kul via Kochkor—either by car (five hours) or on foot or horseback (two days)—yurt. By road via Chaek to Kyzil Oi in Suusamyr Valley (home stay). To Bishkek via Suusamyr and dramatic Tor Ashuu Pass.

COMMUNITY-BASED TOURISM—OFF THE BEATEN TRACK IN KYRGYZSTAN

This excellent organisation offers the easiest, cheapest and friendliest way to meet local people and experience the 'real Kyrgyzstan'. It began as Shepherd's Life in 1996 when local families, supported by Helvetas, the Swiss Association for International Co-operation, started offering tourists food and lodging in their homes or yurts. From this early start, the concept has evolved into a widespread enterprise known as Community-Based Tourism (CBT), of which Shepherd's Life is one arm.

It's been hugely successful, enabling local people to earn valuable extra income and giving tourists the opportunity to explore most corners of Kyrgyzstan in relative comfort and safety.

Each region has a co-ordinator who has details of all the services offered in their area. Accommodation options range from traditional homestays with families, yurt stays on the *jailoo* with working shepherds, and uninhabited flats in Soviet apartment blocks. Each venue is given an 'Edelweiss' (quality) rating, from one to three, depending on comfort, the quality of the food and the bathroom facilities—for example, whether the toilet is indoors or outside and if the family has a shower or sauna.

Over the last few years, the network has mushroomed and now, to the alarm of mainstream tour operators, most regions offer a whole battery of tourism services—transport, short trips to local *jailoo* or places of interest, guides and horses for longer treks; with some notice they can organise felt-making demonstrations and several

Inside a Kyrgyz shepherd's yurt, Kochkor

times each summer they hold cultural festivals with traditional horse games, eagle hunting and so on.

Regions operate independently but come together under the umbrella organisation, Kyrgyzstan Community-Based Tourism Association (KCBTA), based in Bishkek, (to which providers pay a tiny percentage of their earnings), which undertakes marketing, offers advice and training in business skills, guiding on mountains and to heritage sites, environmental protection, catering and pricing, to mention just a few. It is also possible to make bookings through them for areas where there is no email contact or no common language.

However, CBT doesn't claim to be a professional travel company, so it remains tourists' responsibility to ensure that travel plans are adequate and workable. Made up of housewives, farmers, village school teachers, they ask visitors to remember that they are beginners in tourism. What they have to offer is knowledge and insight gained by being immersed in an ancient lifestyle and culture. Many areas are remote and telephone contact is limited, so that late bookings may not always get through. However, this is a hospitable nation and if you turn up unexpected, accommodation can usually be found. CBT co-ordinators don't keep dedicated tourist horses or vehicles so if you arrive unannounced, it may be a day or two before they can be found for your trip.

The livestock bazaar at Osh

Also, rural Kyrgyz people have a much more relaxed perception of time than most Westerners. *Azyr*, the Kyrgyz word for 'now' is probably better translated as 'soon', so sometimes you just have to shrug your shoulders, relax into the slower pace of life here and enjoy the view. Having said that, most co-ordinators are very efficient and only rarely do tourists report problems with delays.

For those who aren't after the catered experience offered by the excellent tour operators based in Bishkek, CBT is a traveller's paradise. Very good value for money, it is ideal for a country low on tourist and transport infrastructure; it allows independent travel without the struggle; you can explore remote, beautiful areas without the need to carry camping equipment; most importantly, you are welcomed into people's homes with a genuine hospitality and invited to share their lifestyle—milking horses, making *koumys* and *kefir*—or just relax.

Some CBT homestays have expanded and become quite successful. This raises the inevitable question of how far such an enterprise is likely, in the long run, to benefit the community as a whole, as originally envisaged, rather than just a few individuals. Some regions allocate guests to homestay families on a rota basis, but this is difficult to operate; as families make money from tourism, they are able to improve their facilities or buy more yurts, etc, thereby offering a more attractive option to visitors than those who are less well off—as elsewhere, money attracts money.

Unless members give a percentage of their takings to a central charitable fund, community-based (as opposed to community-owned) tourism will inevitably exacerbate the inequalities within villages, allowing some to build empires while others remain stuck in poverty. That said, most CBT offices run community projects of some description.

Nevertheless, CBT has revolutionised both tourism and livelihoods all over Kyrgyzstan. Prices in late 2007 were as follows—expect an increase as fuel and food prices rise:

Home and yurt stays B&B were US$8–11 in Chong Kemin, Kyzil Oi Sokoluk Kara Suu (for Sary Chelek), Arslanbob, Kazarman, Gulcho (Alay) and Sary Mogol (Alay). You pay up to US$15 in Batken, Sary Tash (Alay), Kerben and Talas. In Osh B&B costs up to US$19.

Contact details for KCBTA: 58 Gorky, Bishkek, tel. (0312), 540069, tel/fax. 443331; emails: cbttours@mail.ru; asylbek75@yandex.ru; reservtion@cbtkyrgyzstan.kg; marketing@cbtkyrgyzstan.kg, web: www.cbtkyrgyzstan.kg; www.cbttours.kg

Language Guide

THE ALPHABET

CYRILLIC	APPROXIMATE PRONUNCIATION
Аа	ah
Бб	b
Вв	v (pronounced f when ending word)
Гг	g, as in *gull*
Дд	d (pronounced t when ending word)
Ее	yeh
Ёё	yo, as in *yacht*
Жж	zh (in Kyrgyz as in *jolt*, Russian as in *pleasure*)
Зз	z
Ии	ee, as in *week*
Йй	y, as in *yet*
Кк	k
Лл	l
Мм	m
Нн	n
Оо	o, as in *horse* when stressed or ah when unstressed
Пп	p
Рр	rolled r
Сс	s
Тт	t
Уу	oo, as in *boot*
Фф	f
Хх	kh, as in Scottish *loch*
Цц	ts
Чч	ch, as in *chin*
Шш	sh
Щщ	shch, as in *fresh cheese*
Ыы	iy
Ээ	e, as in *egg*
Юю	yoo, as in *use*
Яя	ya
Ьь	'soft sign'—softens the preceding letter

ADDITIONAL KYRGYZ LETTERS

Өө	Ö, as in church
Ңң	ng
Ʋʋ	say ' e ' and round your lips

ENGLISH	KYRGYZ	RUSSIAN	RUSSIAN CYRILLIC

Bold print indicates the stress in Russian words.

ENGLISH	KYRGYZ	RUSSIAN	RUSSIAN CYRILLIC
Hello	Salamatsyzby	**Zdras**tvwitye	Здравствуйте
Goodbye	Kosh bolunguz Jakshy kalynyz	Do svidanye	До свидания
Please	Kichi peildikke	Pa**zhow**lsta	Пожалуйста
Thank you	Yrakhmat	Spa**see**bo	Спасибо
Yes	Oba	Da	Да
No	Jok	Nyet	Нет
How are you?	Kandaisyng?	Kak **de**la?	Как дела?
(very) well/good	(Eng) jakshy	(**orchen**) kharasho	Очень хорошо
Bad	Jaman/nachar	**Plo**kha	Плохо
Do you speak English?	Anglische suilöisuzbu?	Viy gava**ree**te po an**glee**sky?	Вы говорите по Английски?
I don't speak ...	Men ... suiloboim	Ya nye gava**ryoo** ...	Я не говорю ...
I don't understand	Men tushunböim	Ya nye pani**ma**yoo	Я не понимаю
Please can you speak slowly	Jaiyraak suilöisuzbu	Gava**ree**te pom**yed**lenne Po**zhow**lsta	Говорите помедленнее пожалуйста
Please repeat it	Kaitalap koyoonguzchu	Yesh**chyo** raz pa**zhow**lsta	Ешё раз пожалуйста
Please write it down	Jazyp berinizchi	Za**pee**sheetye pa**zhow**lsta	Запишите пожалуйста
How much?	Kancha?	**Skol**ka **sto**yeet?	Сколько стоит?
Expensive	Kiymbat	Do**ra**ga	Дорого
Cheap	Arzan	**Dyo**sheva	Дёшево
Do you have ...?	Sizde ... Barby?	Oo vass **yeest** ...?	У вас есть ...?
I want ...	Men ... kaalaim	Ya kha**choo** ...	Я хочу ...
My name is	Menim atiym ...	Mee**nya** za**voot**	Меня зовут
What's your name?	Sizdin atiyngyz kim?	Kak vass za**voot**?	Как вас зовут?
Where are you from?	Siz kaidan kelgensiz?	Viy ot**koo**da?	Вы откуда?
I'm from	Men ... kelgem	Ya **eez** ...	Я из ...
Any children?	Baldariyngyz barby?	**Dye**te **yeest**?	Дети есть?
What is your job?	Kaida ishteisez?	Kto viy po pro**fye**ssy?	Кто вы по профессии?
Where's the ...?	... kaida/kai jakta?	**Gdye** ...?	Где ...?
Bus station	Vokzal/avtobus ayaldamasiy	**Afto**vokzal	Автовокзал
Train station	Temir jol stantsiasiy	Vokzal	Вокзал

(top) Families sell fruit at the roadside in August [Saffia Farr]
(bottom) The superbly portable yurt may be erected and dismantled swiftly [Saffia Farr]

I want a ticket to ...	Maga ... billet	Adin bilyet dah ...	Один билет до ...
Toilet	Daahrat kana/Tualet	Tooalyet	Туалет
Money exchange	Akcha almashtiyroo	Obmyen valyootiy?	Обмен валюты
Tea	Chai	Chai	Чай
Beer	Pivo	Peevo	Пиво
I'm vegetarian	Men vegetarianmyn	Ya vegetaryanyets	Я вегетарианец
I need a doctor	Maga doktur kerek	Mnye noozhen vrach	Мне нужен врач
When?	Kachan?	Kugda?	Когда
Today	Burgun	Syevodnya	Сегодня
Tomorrow	Erteng	Zaftra	Завтра
Yesterday	Keche koonu	Fchera	Вчера
Monday	Duishombu	Panidyelnik	Понедельник
Tuesday	Sheishembi	Ftornik	Вторник
Wednesday	Sharshembi	Sreda	Среда
Thursday	Beishembi	Chetvyerk	Четверг
Friday	Juma	Pyatnitsa	Пятница
Saturday	Ishembi	Soobota	Суббота
Sunday	Jekshembi	Vaskrisyeniye	Воскресенье
One	Bir	Adeen	Один
Two	Eki	Dva	Два
Three	Uch	Tree	Три
Four	Tört	Chetiyre	Четыре
Five	Besh	Pyat	Пять
Six	Alty	Shest	Шесть
Seven	Jeti	Syem	Семь
Eight	Segiz	Vosyem	Восемь
Nine	Toguz	Dyevet	Девять
Ten	On	Dyesyet	Десять
Eleven	On bir	Adeenatsat	Одиннадцать
Twelve	On eki	Dvenatsat	Двенадцать
Twenty	Jyiyrma	Dvatsat	Двадцать
Thirty	Otuz	Treetsat	Тридцать
Forty	Kiyrk	Sorok	Сорок
Fifty	Eloo	Peetdesyat	Пятьдесят
Sixty	Altiymiysh	Shestdesyat	Шестьдесят
Seventy	Jetimish	Syemdesyat	Семьдесят
Eighty	Seksen	Vosimdesyat	Восемьдесят
Ninety	Tokson	Devenosto	Девяносто
Hundred	Juz	Sto	Сто
Thousand	Ming	Tiysicha	Тысяча

Glossary

GENERAL

Ak-Kalpak	Man's felt conical hat
Aul	Village
Ail okmoto	Village administration
Akyn	Singer, storyteller, composer
Aksakal	Elder, adviser
Ala-kiyiz	Lit. black and white felt, pressed felt carpet
Babushka (Russian)	Grandmother, old woman
Baibiche	Mistress of the house, respected old woman
Bi	Tribe leader, arbiter
Chechek	White wrap-around turban worn by married women
Chiy	Reed, used to make mats
Dastorkan	Lit. tablecloth, food offered to guests
Djigit	Skilled, courageous young horseman
Eptchi shak	Woman's section of yurt
Er shak	Man's section of yurt
Jailoo	High summer pasture
Kalym	Bride price, paid by bride-groom
Kanat	Yurt frame of birch poles
Kiyiz	Felt
Shyrdak	Felt carpet with sewn-in pattern
Tunduk	Wooden frame round smoke-hole in top of yurt
Turbaza	Hostel, Soviet holiday camp
Tush-kiyiz	Cotton, embroidered wall-hanging
Tyor	Place at *dastorkan* for honoured guest

TRADITIONAL GAMES

Alaman baiga	15–20 kilometre race on horseback
Kyz-kuumai	Kiss-the-girl
Odarysh	Wrestling on horseback
Tyin Gumei	Picking a coin from the ground at full gallop
Ulak-tartys	Polo played with decapitated goat

TRADITIONAL FOOD AND DRINK

Besh bermak	Lit. five fingers, special dish for festivities
Borsook	Fried bread for special occasions
Kalama	Thin flat bread baked on top of iron stove
Kattama	For guests – thin bread oiled in cream
Konku	Standard flat round bread, patterned on top
Plov	*Ash*, in the south, a traditional Rice Pilaf that is eaten at ceremonies and on holidays

(top) Four Russian friends meet on a cloudy winter's day in Bishkek [Saffia Farr]
(bottom) Kyrgyz boys fishing

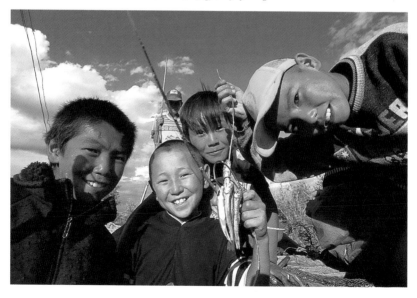

KURMANJAN DATKA —QUEEN OF THE ALAY

by Ian Claytor

Kurmanjan Datka was a hero and, reputedly, the only woman ruler of the Muslim world.

Born into a simple nomad family of the Mongush clan in the Pamir Alay mountains of south Kyrgyzstan, Kurmanjan showed her determined and independent nature from an early age; married at 18 to an older man whom she met only on her wedding day, she soon ran away from him, back to her father's yurt.

Three years later she married Alymbek Datka, feudal lord of the clans of the Pamir Alay, and became one of his closest advisers. In 1862, he was killed by troops of the Kokand Khanate and Kurmanjan took over as leader of the tribes. Gathering around

Woman wearing a traditional headdress [Saffia Farr]

her the loyal *batyrs*, heroes, it is said that she commanded an army of 10,000 *djigits*, brave young warriors.

Her popularity was widespread at home and, further afield, she was recognised by the khans of Bukhara and Kokand. In 1864, Kurmanjan Datka entered into rigorous negotiations with the Russian imperial troops then annexing central Asia, and accepted the Russian Empire's protectorate over her tribes. Officers in the region called her the Alay Queen and she was twice awarded the title of general (*Datka*).

Her star waned, however, when her favourite son was hanged in the square in Osh and two others sentenced to penal servitude in Siberia for 'contraband' and murdering customs officers. Shamed, she withdrew from society and died a hermit, aged 96.

The many colourful tales about her testify to the high regard in which she was held by all Kyrgyz, northerners and southerners alike, and today, she appears on the 50 som banknote.

Recommended Reading

TRAVEL LITERATURE

Akchurin, Murat. *Red Odyssey* (Secker & Warburg, 1992). An underground Soviet 'On the Road', tracing a Muscovite Tartar's tour of Central Asia, haunted by the ethnic violence of a crumbling union.

Bealby, Jonny. *Silk Dreams, Troubled Road* (Arrow, 2003). The stirring tale of a journey by horse from Kashgar to Turkmenistan. Jonny Bealby has visited more than 50 countries and is the director of UK tour operator Wild Frontiers.

Graham, Stephen. *Through Russian Central Asia* (Cassell & Co, 1916). Slightly pampered travels in pre-revolutionary Central Asia.

Krist, Gustav. *Alone Through the Forbidden Land* 1937 (Ian Faulkner Publishing, 1992). Gripping account of Krist's adventures throughout 1920s Central Asia.

Maillart, Ella. *Turkestan Solo* 1934 (GP Putnam's Sons, 1935). Spirited trek into Kyrgyzstan's most unforgiving mountain ranges.

Nazaroff, Pavel Stepanovich. *Hunted Through Central Asia* (WM Blackwood and Sons Ltd, 1932). An anti-Bolshevist, escaped from prison, dodges the authorities through Kyrgyzstan. His observations offer insight into a chaotic period.

Schuyler, Eugene. *Turkistan* 1876 (Routledge & Keegan Paul, 1966). Interesting and informtive account of travels through pre-revolutionary Central Asia. Only available in libraries or second hand bookshops.

Thubron, Colin. *The Lost Heart of Central Asia* (Heinneman, 1994). Reflections on post-Soviet Central Asia, punctuated by revealing conversations with local people.

Thubron, Colin. *Shadow of the Silk Road* (Vintage, 2007). Travels from China to the Mediterranean, with a few pages on his journey through Kyrgyzstan.

Tolstoy, Alexandra. *The Last Secrets of the Silk Road: Four Girls Follow Marco Polo Across 5,000 Miles* (Profile Books, 2004). A horse and camel trek across Central Asia, with some hardship and a personal touch.

Vitkovich, Victor. *Kirghizia Today* (Foreign Languages Publishing House, Moscow). Beautifully written account of a journey around Soviet Kirghizia of the 1950s; mix of delight in Soviet achievements and a fascination with Kyrgyz nomadic life.

Whitlock, Monica. *Beyond the Oxus: The Central Asians* (John Murray Publishers, 2002). A journalist's look at Central Asia, past and present, and its complexities.

HISTORY

Abazov, Rafis. *Historical Dictionary of Kyrgyzstan* (The Scarecrow Press, 2004). A highly respected dictionary of people, events, places and institutions, as well as political, economic and social issues.

Hambly, Gavin. *Central Asia* 1969. An excellent historical overview.

Hopkirk, Peter. *The Great Game* (Oxford University Press, 1990). A colourful resumé of the Great Game (Russian: 'Tournament of Shadows'), the glamorous and romantic period of high altitude espionage.

MODERN KYRGYZSTAN

Abazov, Rafis. *Culture and Customs of the Central Asian Republics* (Greenwood Press, 2006)

Anderson, John. *Kyrgyzstan: Central Asia's Island of Democracy (Post-communist States & Nations)* (Routledge, 1999). An analytical account of the struggles to develop a transparent and dynamic political system.

Ertürk, K. *Rethinking Central Asia* (Garnet Publishing Ltd, 1999.) A refreshing approach to Central Asian history, society and identity.

Farr, Saffia. *Revolution Baby: Motherhood and Anarchy in Kyrgyzstan* (Spire Publishing, 2007). An engaging, vivid and often hilarious account of ex-pat life in Bishkek—with a new baby and the 'Tulip Revolution' to contend with. Quirky and interesting observations about the country and its people. A great read.

King, David. *Kyrgyzstan* (Marshall Cavendish Benchmark, 2006). A profile of the history, geography, government, culture, people, and economy of Kyrgyzstan.

Kleveman, Lutz. *The New Great Game: Blood and Oil in Central Asia* (Atlantic Monthly Press, 2004). An incisive analysis of the international struggle to gain control over Central Asia's oil.

Marat, Erica. *The Tulip Revolution: Kyrgyzstan One Year After* (Publishers Graphics, 2006). A critical examination of the domestic and international influences that have shaped Kyrgyzstan and its neighbours. Analysis of developments since the 2005 revolution.

Rashid, Ahmed. *The Resurgence of Central Asia* (Oxford University Press, 1994). Excellent introduction to the region.

Smith, G, Law, V, Wilson, A, Bohr, A and Allworth, E. *Nation-building in the Post-Soviet Borderlands* (Cambridge University Press, 1998). An analysis of the emergence of new national identities in the republics of the former Soviet Union.

KYRGYZ LITERATURE

Aitmatov, Chinghis. *Tales of the Mountains and Steppes* (Progress Publishers, Moscow, 1969). Tenderly told stories about community and personal experiences of adjusting to the new Soviet order, offering a real insight into traditional life and values.

Manas: The Great Campaign (The Publishing House, 1999). Swashbuckling stories about the attempts of the Kyrgyz hero to secure a homeland for his people. Probably only available in Kyrgyzstan.

HANDICRAFTS AND ART

Antipina, Claudia. *Kyrgyzstan* (Skira, 2007). A lavishly illustrated volume of the costumes of the nomadic Kyrgyz. The author was a renowned Russian anthropologist.

Asankanov, A and Bekmuhamedova, N. *Akyns and Manaschis—Creators and Keepers of the Kyrgyz People's Spiritual Culture* (United Nations Development Programme, 1999). Brief description of the main *akyns*, *manaschis* and their themes. Probably only available in Kyrgyzstan.

Artists of Kyrgyzstan (United Nations Development Programme and Kyrgyz Qorku, 2000). **Dyadyuchenko, L,** Sorokin, E and Usubalieva, B. *Kyrgyz Pattern.* 1986. Information in Kyrgyz, Russian and English on Kyrgyz handicrafts—felt, silver and leather—illustrated with colourful photographs. Probably only available in libraries.

GUIDEBOOKS

Bloom, G., Noble, N., Mayhew, B. *Central Asia* (Lonely Planet, 5th edition, 2007).
Kadyrov, Victor. *Bishkek and Suburbs* (Raritet). A handy city guide available only in Kyrgyzstan.
Maier, Frith. *Trekking in Russia and Central Asia* (The Mountaineers, 1994).
Mitchell, L., *Kyrgyzstan* (Bradt, 2007).
Willis, G. and **Gamash,** M. *Kyrgyzstan: A Climber's Map and Guide.* (American Alpine Club, 2006). Climbing information for Ala Archa, Western Kokshaal Too and Karavshin.

USEFUL WEBSITES

amnesty.org—Amnesty International site
bbc.co.uk—News and analysis on Kyrgyzstan and the region from the BBC
bishkek-hotels.org—Online booking facility for hotels and apartments
catgen.com/cacsa/EN—Central Asian Crafts Support Association site listing artisans
cbtkyrgyzstan.kg—Community-based Tourism site
celestial.com.kg—Celestial Mountains (tour operator) site with extensive country information
cia.gov—Facts and figures on Kyrgyzstan from the CIA
eng.president.kg—Website of President Kurmanbek Bakiev
eurasianet.org—News and analysis on Central Asia including Kyrgyzstan
fco.gov.uk—Information and travel advice from the British Government
freenet.kg/kyrgyzstan—Kyrgyzstan Online site with information on the country and Manas
geohive.com—Geopolitical data, population and economic statistics hrw.org—Reports on Kyrgyzstan by Human Rights Watch
iwpr.net—Institute for War and Peace Reporting site
khazaria.com/turkic/kyrgyzstan—Web listings for Kyrgyz businesses, state institutions and more
kyrgyzbala.blogspot.com—Lively blog by a Bishkek student
neweurasia.net—Lively comment and debate from this Central Asian network of weblogs
stat.kg/English/index.html—Socio-economic data from Kyrgyzstan's National Statistics Committee
timesca-europe.com—Website of the Times of Central Asia newspaper
undp.kg—Development-focussed statistics and country information
yellow-pages.kz—Business telephone directory for Kyrgyzstan and its neighbours

Brightly painted traditional doors add a splash of colour to the yurt [Saffia Farr]

Index

Compiled by Don Brech,
Records Management
International Ltd.

(below and right) Sunday market, Karakol
(bottom) Participants wait to race or wrestle at the annual Chabysh
(bottom right) An eagle hunter shows off his bird at the festival

KYRGYZSTAN